To Ann & David
with bes wishes

Harry Westmith
Pesach 2009

The Exchanged Heir

BY

HENRY WERMUTH

authorHOUSE®

Henry Wermuth

AuthorHouse™ UK Ltd.
500 Avebury Boulevard
Central Milton Keynes, MK9 2BE
www.authorhouse.co.uk
Phone: 08001974150

First published by AuthorHouse   10/21/2008

ISBN: 978-1-4343-4716-9 (sc)
ISBN: 978-1-4343-4717-6 (hc)

Printed in the United States of America
Bloomington, Indiana

This book is printed on acid-free paper.

In memory of the nineteenth century writer Kark May.

Contents

Chapter 1

THE TWO ENGLISH TEACHERS

---

*T*HE year was 1820 in the Spanish town of Aragon, the time of the Carnival. It is a time when the Spaniard becomes a completely different person. He throws himself with almost wild desire into the stream of pleasure and joy seeking masses of mask wearing individuals. He becomes himself only after having enjoyed himself to the full.

One of the most splendid palaces in Aragon, built in almost entirety of marble, belonged to the Duke Enrico de Zaragoza. This Don was a member of the highest noblesse in the country and one of the richest property tycoons in town. He was only twenty-nine years old and a widower.

Don Enrico was a great patriot and aristocrat but many people maintained that he was not averse to the joys of life and secretly indulged in matters which he did not confess to his priest. Friends sought him out because of his position and influence; enemies envied him.

To his servants he maintained a distance in accordance with his social standing. There was one exception to this, the majordomo Pablo Carujo was his confidant and in the joys of life a like-minded character, although he was five years younger than the Duke.

The Duke trusted Carujo because of his tried and tested discretion. In the presence of others he treated him in accordance to his social standing. In private, however, all formalities were put aside and he associated with Carujo like a careless young nobleman with a partner in

1

crime or rather an associate in his not very noble pursuit – of a variety of young women.

Today he intended to indulge in his dubious pastime. "Carujo," he asked, "what about my costumes to compliment my masks?"

"They are ready, Don Enrico."

"So, what have you selected for me today?"

"A Persian costume."

"Very good; it allows me to wear my weapons and jewellery. But tell me, what are you going as?"

"I shall be a Mexican."

"All right, send me the valet and meet me in the plaza outside the bank house of Señor Caltiero."

Carujo went to the flat, where his beloved Rita Moreno waited longingly for herlover. She flew into his arms and gave him a passionate kiss. "Where are we going tonight darling?" she asked as he unpacked his Mexican costume.

"Unfortunately, we can't go out together, the Duke expects me in an hour."

"But later on tonight you will come to me?" she said, disappointed.

"Maybe" was his short reply. "It depends how long he keeps me" he then added,knowing he had other plans.

The Duke mingled with the crowd. He was very conspicuous, not only for his costume but because of giant size. As he strolled along, looking for his servant and friend of his indulgence, he gave a casual glance to the balcony of a building where he saw a beautiful young girl. In contrast to everyone around, she wore normal attire but her appearance surprised even the Duke who was used to beautiful women.

At this moment he heard the voice of Pablo Carujo calling out: "That girl is the most beautiful I have ever seen, you should try to get to know her, but I don't think you'll get far."

"I have to try, I don't give up so easily, I have to get her."

Don Enrico threw her a kiss. She noticed it and went red with embarrassment. His costume was worth thousands; he was no common person. Any girl would be moved by the admiration of such a distinguished man.

She took, almost unconsciously, a silken ribbon from her blouse and threw it to him. The piece of trimming fell in irregular circles but the Duke managed to catch it. He pressed a kiss on it and pinned it on his chest.

Ashamed of her own deed, the young lady withdrew from the balcony.

"Caramba, she's irresistible" said Don Enrico.

"Are you going upstairs?"

"Yes, I must."

"I as well?"

"No, she has to be treated with tenderness, you'd spoil everything. Walk up and down so I can find you when I come back."

He noticed the position of the window in order to find his way inside. Going upstairs he calculated which room must be hers. He knocked at the door. He heard a quiet, almost anxious "enter" and went inside. Shocked, she tried to flee to the adjoining room, but he stood next to her and held her hand. "Stop, don't try to escape, he said gently.

"Let go of me. It would be terrible if you were found here."

"What could anyone say? Today is carnival and freedom of the masks."

"But not for me!"

"For every woman"

"I'm a stranger, and in a subordinate position here" she replied anxiously.

He enjoyed the thought of her being in a subordinate position; he thought his game was won. He pulled her towards him and whispered:

"I love you, I am longing for you."

"Let me go or I'll call for help." She used all her strength to push him away.

He grabbed her tighter and kissed her. "Call out, my little one, masks can do what they like today."

Again he attempted to kiss her when she shouted. "Help, Mr. Stenton – help."

Frank Stenton was her neighbour and, like herself, was employed by the banker as a teacher for his son. She was the governess and teacher of the banker's little daughter.

It was as if he had waited for such a cry. The door opened and an average sized young man entered with a truncheon in his hand.

"Let go, leave the lady alone!" he shouted.

"Like hell," answered the masked Duke, "you'd better go before I throw you down stairs."

He'd hardly finished speaking when Stenton, a former fencing teacher, rained blows over the Duke's head and body and finally pushed him down the stairs before Duke Enrico de Zaragoza could raise his arms in defence.

Meanwhile, the Señorita had escaped into the adjoining room and bolted the door. She feared for her English compatriot. She feared that he could not withstand his giant opponent.

Timidly, she opened the door again when she heard Stenton's voice calling out for her, hardly believing that he was not even scratched.

"Are you hurt, Miss Hudson?" Stenton asked.

"Oh, Mr. Stenton, you saved me and I can't thank you enough. "Will he come back, did you see his face?"

"He's had enough He won't come back and I didn't bother to take his mask off, I'm not interested in the face of such a hooligan," replied Stenton.

"But if he seeks revenge? He seems to be a person of some standing!"

"Then I'll show him the door, just like today. I only hope the shock didn't do you any harm."

"Oh no, but I was so afraid. He was so strong!"

"I wish I could do more for you, if you get any more visits like that, please call me, and now, please take back your ribbon."

She hadn't noticed he held her ribbon. He passed it to her with an almost sad expression that made her turn red.

"You have seen …?"

" Yes, I stood on the other balcony. You didn't notice me. I saw the man enter the house and I was prepared. That was also the reason I could respond to you so fast , Miss Hudson." Stenton turned around and left the room. She didn't dare to say another word. For the man who would sacrifice his life for her, she didn't give him another glance, but to a mask she thrust her ribbon. She had tears of shame and regret in her eyes; how coolly he'd handled the intruder. What might he think of her? Maybe she could return his love, or be proud of him.

She closed the curtain. She didn't want to hear or see anymore of the carnival.---

Meanwhile Pablo Carujo waited for his master to return to tell him of a successful adventure. With secret pleasure he noticed the dishevelled costume. The Duke, although he told Carujo nothing of his defeat by Stenton, he did tell him of his amorous failure "I must have her," said the Duke. "Let's develop a plan. I'll give you the day off. Find out anything you can about her and her employer."

Carujo asked for 50 duros in advance for his expenses which was given to him by the Duke, who counted his fortune in millions. They had now gone for several hundred yards. Carujo turned around and planted himself near the banker's house.

Before long, he noticed a young man coming though the large entrance door of the observed house. He wore the suit of an employee and had some parcels in his hand.

Carujo approached him. "Excuse me Señor, are you working for Señor Caltiero?"

"Yes I am," replied the young man.

"What as?"

"I have only a minor position here. At this moment I am carrying these parcels to various addresses."

"Have you five minutes to spare?"

"For what purpose?"

"Perhaps we could drink a glass of wine together."

"With pleasure, Señor, I have to know the reason for this offer?"

"I just want to make an inquiry regarding the integrity of the bank, as I have an inheritance and I want to put my money where it is safest.

"I can accept your offer. The delivery of the parcels can wait a bit longer, especially as my principal gave me no time off for the carnival."

"In that case you can give yourself a quarter of an hour," laughed Carujo.

They went together to the next tavern, where Carujo ordered a bottle of wine. He poured the wine, took off his mask and said to the young man: "Your boss seems to be a real miser if he did not give you even an hour off today."

"That he is."

"Is he so poor that he cannot afford it?"

"On the contrary, he owns millions,"

"Is he a married man?" Carujo continued.

"No, he is a widower. He had two young children. a boy of eight and a little girl of seven. Unfortunately, the little girl died a short while ago."

"I'm sure there are more staff in that household,"

"Oh yes, there are two servants and two English teachers; Señor Stenton for the boy and Señorita Hudson for the late little girl. But it is quite probable that Señorita Hudson will have to leave. He wouldn't pay for somebody who is now superfluous."

"Have you heard whether she has applied for a new job?"

"Not that I know of. There was no talk about her going just yet, but this miser wouldn't pay someone he doesn't need."

Carujo thanked the young man and left him to finish the rest of the bottle. He then went straight to the Duke and told him he had good news, and a plan of how to entice Señorita Hudson. The Duke called him into his vestibule where they would be safe from unwelcome listeners. "Shoot," said the eager Don Enrico. "What is new and what is your plan – I hope it's a good one."

"Her name is Señorita Hudson and she'll soon be looking for a new job. The little girl she was helping to bring up died recently."

"I can't see any good news in that," the Duke said impatiently, "now let's hear your ingenious plan."

"Very simple. We put into three major newspapers that an aristocratic household is looking for a lady to bring up a five year old daughter; English preferred. That would do for the little princess. And we will put 'well-paid position' into it too," he added as an after thought.

"Ingenious! Waste no time and let's hope that your plan works. Of course, you would do the hiring. She might recognise me."

"If you haven't taken off your mask, she might not recognise you. Trim your beard a little and you should be all right."

Miss Ella Hudson was excited when the following morning she read the advertisement to prove so disastrous for her later. She answered immediately, hoping to be able to send some money to her poor mother and sister back home whom she was hitherto unable to help. She met Stenton and told him the "good" news. To her surprise he didn't seem to share her enthusiasm. "What kind of a face are you making? Aren't you pleased for me? Besides, I haven't received a reply yet."

"There are two reasons that may have no bearing on the situation," said Stenton with a worried expression.

"May I know what they are?" enquired Miss Hudson.

"As I said, I have a peculiar feeling about this. Firstly, it probably takes you away away from my protection and secondly … " he paused for a few moments, "and secondly" he continued, "it is not the usual way aristocrats acquire servants."

Next morning a splendid carriage arrived. A man in liveried uniform approached her and asked whether she would like to introduce herself for the new position. Indeed she would. It took her only minutes to get ready. She felt in turn elated and slightly worried. They stopped in front of an imposing building where Pablo Carujo seemed to expect them. With his most polite and softest voice he explained that the Duke, being temporarily away, had left him to do the hiring. Miss Hudson produced her papers and Carujo pretended to study them. He nodded and declared them as satisfactory.

"Let's go and see the princess now", suggested Carujo, and with this, he led Miss Hudson into the rooms that were arranged for the young daughter of the house. A nursemaid was in attendance; anyone could read in her eyes an instant dislike for the newcomer.

The little princess was a dear child but she greeted the newcomer in a most unfriendly way: "Are you my new Governess?" she asked and it was obvious that she wasn't pleased.

"Yes, my dear little Donna Elena" answered Miss Hudson.

"I don't like my governesses", the little girl ventured.

"Be quiet," thundered the nursemaid.

"And I don't like my nursemaid either", added the little one.

"Why not?" asked the new Governess.

"Because they don't love me."

On hearing this *cri de coeur* the Governess crouched down, took her hands and asked: "Would you dislike me as well Donna Elena?"

"You?" the child seemed to be thinking about it, "maybe I could like you."

"And why is that?"

"Because you look at me with love in your eyes."

"I would like to stay with you, my dear Elena", said the governess and drew the little girl into her arms. The little princess put her arms around her neck and asked: "And could we sometimes laugh together?" "Oh often, I like laughing very much."

"I do too, but I wasn't allowed," rejoiced the little girl. "Stay with me and I shall tell papa that I want you."

The nursemaid stood by with a grim face, but didn't dare to intervene. Carujo led Miss Hudson into the three rooms that would be her new home. She had an unpleasant feeling as she noticed the luxurious furnishings and asked if these were the rooms of her predecessor. "No, these were the rooms of the late duchess", he answered.

"Then I must insist on living near my ward, in the room or rooms of the previous governess," Miss Hudson ventured bravely.

This was not the Duke or Carujo's plan, but he agreed to let her have her way.

"We have finished our rounds and will come to a final decision"; Carujo pulled out some papers that she thought would be a contract. "I am at your disposal", she said while pulling a chair to be seated.

"From what I have seen, so far, I must say that you are very suitable," the hypocritical Carujo told Miss Hudson. He offered her three times the amount she had hitherto earned and added that he would pay her for three months in advance plus 300 duros moving expenses. She was overwhelmed and overjoyed; now she could send her Mother an undreamt-of amount. She could start the next day, she was told. She agreed and had no presentiment of the dangers lying in store for her.---

"Well done", said the Duke who had observed part of the procedure through a secret hole in the tapestry. "Now get me a duplicate key to her room and arrange that I should be able to open the bolt from the outside."

Carujo did as he was told and handed a duplicate key of the new governess's room to his boss.

Before starting her new job, Miss Hudson sent most of her money to her mother. On entering the palace, she found herself in the company of the unfriendly nursemaid.

Asking her about her obvious aversion to herself, Miss Hudson learned to her horror that her predecessor has not been dismissed but had been given a paid holiday so that she could be engaged as a governess. The Duke was not away as she had been told, but in an adjoining room; he had probably witnessed everything through a cleverly disguised hole in the design of the tapestry. On learning that the new governess was apparently innocent of all these doings, the nursemaid, Señorita Voltera's attitude changed and she became almost friendly to the newcomer. Miss Hudson felt like packing her belongings and leaving at once but then she remembered having accepted and sent away most of the money she had received. She consoled herself with the thought that during the day she would be with the little princess and at night she would close her door with the key and bolt it tight.

The Duke had other things in mind. When he was told that the new governess drank a glass of milk every night, his plan was ready. He would put a large dose of sleeping powder into her drink. Meanwhile, the little princess, really took to her new governess who had already taught her the beginnings of the Spanish alphabet. The Duke summoned her and told her of his satisfaction. Although he had trimmed his beard, Miss Hudson recognised her carnival attacker at once by his giant stature and his voice. She managed to control her immense shock and decided that she would inform her compatriot Frank Stenton as soon as she was given a day off.

"I am doing my best." She managed to keep her voice steady, although she found it hard to disguise the trembling.

That evening she locked and bolted the door as usual and unsuspectingly drank her glass of milk, heavily laced with sleeping powder. She tasted a slight difference but did not want to complain.

Carujo visited the nursemaid, whose room adjoined the quarters of the new governess. Señorita Voltera received him with open arms; this was not the first time he'd visited her. They were together for two hours, when the Duke, who knew where to find his majordomo, knocked at the door and before somebody could call "come in," had entered the door. He was pale and stuttered: "Blood, blood everywhere blood, come on quickly, she has killed herself."

"Let's call the doctor immediately" said Carujo, "maybe there is still hope of her being alive."

"I don't think so," continued the Duke, "when she noticed what had happened she took a knife and plunged it into her body." Carujo had already rushed out to call on the doctor who lived nearby. He knew that he could rely on the doctor's discretion. The doctor said that the girl would live; the knife she had used was only a penknife and the wound was not deep enough to be deadly. The loss of blood though, was very serious and it would take quite a few weeks before she could leave her bed. The Duke told him to call it a haemorrhage and asked Señorita Voltera to attend to Miss Hudson's needs.

Frank Stenton, became increasingly concerned that no word from Miss Hudson came through to him. He was convinced that she would let have him know about her well-being and her progress in her new job. After about five weeks he simply went to the palace where he knew Miss Hudson was employed.

Carujo received him and asked him whether he was a relation of Miss Hudson. He said he was only a colleague and compatriot of hers. He was told that Miss Hudson had had a haemorrhage and could not receive anybody at the moment.

Stenton, was not so easily put off and a debacle started between the two. The Duke, who heard the noise in the vestibule where Carujo had brought Stenton went down to investigate. Stenton mastered his shock when he realised that the Duke was the very person he had thrown out of Miss Hudson's room. He decided to leave and investigate secretly.

The next day he went over the wall into the garden of the palace. He stood behind some bushes and to his joy he saw a pale Miss Hudson enter the garden and walked to a bench near his hiding place. As he saw no one else with her, he called her name softly. She reacted with a jerk of her head. "Mr. Stenton" she said, "what are you doing here? You put yourself in great danger."

"I was worried about you, danger would not prevent me from seeing you, especially as I was told by the Duke that you've had a haemorrhage."

"Is this what they told you? I think you'd better come inside the house There's no-one there at the moment to disturb us." He followed her, glad that she had the confidence for that invitation. Inside the room she sobbed and told him that he was right when he warned her. She had been given a sleeping powder in her nightly glass of milk and had been subsequently raped. She also told him that she had tried to kill herself and that she still wanted to die. "Now I have told you everything, you'd better leave me and never come again"

"Why should I do that – do you hate me so much?"

"Hate? Oh no, but I am so worthless, you shouldn't be with me."

"Why?"

"You were right in everything you have warned me of before."

He stepped towards her. "Yes, I was right with everything but also that love never ends. I feel it now." He bent down, put his arms around her and kissed her. She let him. Then she broke loose and said: "This was our good bye, good bye forever. Farewell."

"So you don't love me? Please, please tell me." There was a gleam in her eyes when she said: "I love you, yes, I love you but I recognized that fact too late, oh God, too late."

"No," he said, "it is never too late to be happy." He pulled her up gently and held both her hands. "Tell me, Miss Hudson, would you like to be my wife and accompany me back to England?"

"Oh yes, so much, so very much if it were possible, but you do not know everything."

"I do, and I shall prove that I mean what I say, I'll give you the holy assurance that I shall bring up the child you expect as my own." She did not answer, she sighed deeply, full of pain. She lay in his arms without moving, with eyes closed for shame.

A few minutes passed while he held her close to his heart, then she opened her eyes. " Is it true, is it possible?" she asked, in a halting voice.

"Yes, because I love you just as before."

"And you will never reproach me for what has happened against my will?"

"Never!"

"And not hate my … my child because of its father?"

"No, I shall be the father, it shall be as if you had never entered this ill-fated house. Do you want to marry me with these conditions?"

"Yes" she rejoiced. The last bitter thoughts left his heart as he saw the happiness in the eyes of his beloved.

"Will you leave this house with me at once?" he asked.

"At once" she answered.

"And allow me to work out this situation with the Duke of Zaragoza?"

With tears of joy she nodded. So ended a tragic episode of her life. They returned to England where she brought a little boy into the world, and a little girl a year later. Frank Stenton kept his promise and brought up the little lad as his own. This little boy was named Charles and grew up never knowing about his real father only wondering where he got his giant body. Learning many a skill from Stenton and thorough schooling, he became a well-known physician, an eye specialist, and a very respected person. He succeeded becoming a champion in every sport he undertook. It will be many years before we meet him again in this story.

Chapter 2

TWO COUNTS OF MANRESA

SOME miles from Aragon, the town of our previous story, stood the vast estate of the Count Miguel de Manresa. He was a man in his forties with a very refined and aristocratic face and demeanour. He had a daughter of eighteen, who was of rare beauty, and Aurelio, a sixteen-year-old son. This son was brought to Mexico where the Count's brother Manuel had bought a large piece of land. Here he had built a magnificent palace. It was a suggestion of this brother who, at the time had no heir to his fortune and also thought that it was easier for his wife to bring up the lad, than for his brother in Spain who had to look after Rosetta who at the time of this change was only six old.

Count Miguel de Manresa had a butler, Emilio Carujo, who was employed in his present position for many years and was, contrary to his son Pablo, who was the majordomo of the Duke of Zaragoza, an utterly upright and decent character. This butler who suddenly took very ill and died at the time when Aurelio de Manresa was barely four years old. Pablo Carujo, who had, for some reason, fallen out with his master, applied for his father's position. Don Miguel was only too glad to have another Carujo in his employ, thinking, that the son might have the same qualities as his father. Although Pablo Corujo did his job perfectly well, there were evil and criminal plans in his head.

Rita Moreno, who had born him a son at about the same time as the Countess bore her son Aurelio, urged her lover to keep his promise to marry her. Pablo divulged his plan, to take possession of the palace of Manresa through the babies he would exchange. He would marry her and have her employed at the palace at a slightly later date.

Rita was glad to give her son this chance, especially that, as an unmarried mother, she had been the outcast of any society in her surroundings. When a new nursemaid was taken on and only a short while later ordered to take Aurelio to Mexico, Carujo executed his vile plan. ------

Ricardo Ramon, an unassuming and quiet citizen in Aragon, showed quite a different face to his imminent friends, a bunch of robbers and highwaymen who accepted him as their ruthless Captain. There was an inclement weather when Pablo Carujo, who has had several profitable dealings with him, paid him a visit. Señor Ricardo observed him sharply under his gold-rimmed glasses. "I assume that your visit is not a social one" he began the conversation.

"Indeed it is not," replied his visitor, "it will be quite a profitable business for you if you accept a different challenge."

"What is the challenge? There is nothing too difficult for an adequate reward," replied the Captain.

"You will be well rewarded; what I need are two skilled and silent burglars to do the job."

"Let me know the precise nature of the job and we'll get down to a price," said the captain of the robbers now.

"It is the exchange of two babies."

"That doesn't seem too difficult," replied Ricardo Ramon, "but I feel that there is more to this job than you're telling me."

"Yes there is; you first break into the baby's room which may also be occupied by the nursemaid. You then lift the baby very gently from his cradle and replace it with the one I shall give you."

"And what shall we do if either of the two wake up?" asked the robber. "If you have two careful men, the nursemaid should not wake up. If the baby stirs then you have to put something over his mouth immediately." Carujo had it all planned.

"But if the baby suffocates?" ventured the Captain.

"I don't care what happens to that baby, as long as no harm befalls to the one that I shall give you."

"That will be five thousand duros," said Ricardo Ramon unashamedly.

"You are mad; but I shall not bargain over this. Two thousand duros now and the rest after a successfully completed job." The Captain agreed and Carujo gave him the down-payment.

"One more thing; what will happen to the baby we snatched?" The robber seemed more concerned than his customer.

"Do as you like, I don't want to see it any more." With this decision he left Ricardo Ramon. ---

The only thing the new and slightly confused nursemaid, Clarissa Moyes, noticed in the morning was that the baby's garments, although of first class quality, had no name attached to them. Since she found no answer to that question, she thought that this must have been her own fault. Also the baby looked slightly different. but again she had no explanation. She decided to ignore it and went on her prescribed route to Count Manuel de Manresa in Mexico.

Count Manuel and Countess Teresa de Manresa, who were still childless, welcomed the nephew warmly. They had no inkling that this baby would grow up to plot against them. They gave him the best schooling a child could have, but the growing boy turned into a worthless gambler.

It was at the early age of sixteen that these unsavoury traits appeared. Aurelio de Manresa had visited Spain several times, where his real father, Pablo Carujo had explained the real situation to him. Aurelio soon saw himself as the owner of the two palaces of Manresa and agreed to Carujo's evil plans. Carujo, meanwhile had married his partner in crime, Rita Moreno, and managed to have her employed at the palace of Manresa.---

It was in the palace of Manresa in Mexico, where José Carujo, the brother of Pablo, held the same position as Pablo in Spain and he had similar criminal plans, especially after Don Manuel's wife Teresa had died after only a short illness. He was for years the major-domo of Manuel de Manresa, married to Maria with a daughter just a little younger than her cousin, the present heir to the fortune of their employers, the Count and Countess. This daughter was their only child, whose every wish her parents tried to please. When she was seventeen years old she had barely learned the secrets of her family, when she, unashamedly, approached her cousin Aurelio to marry her. She saw herself as Countess of Manresa and although Aurelio laughed her off initially, he signed an agreement that he would marry her as soon as he became the official owner of the palace of Manresa and held the title that went with it. He did this only after she threatened to disclose that he was not the real son of Miguel de Manresa.

José Carujo thought it was time to execute his plans. He asked the servant who looked after the horses to put a saddle on a lively black stallion and rode into town. There he went to a small house and knocked at the door. A puny man without a single hair on his head looked out of the window. "Ah, Señor Carujo, I shall open at once," he shouted.

Carujo entered a dimly lit room where his host asked him to sit down and state his wishes. "I will come straight to the point. I know that you are able to supply what I want; a liquid that could make a man appear dead for about thirty hours."

"That's an unusual order. If I could supply this liquid - and I am not sure that I can - who gives me the guarantee that there would be no comeback for me?"

"Firstly I shall give you what you ask in money beforehand, and secondly, we have done business together before."

"That is true," said the humble looking man, "but your orders have not been of this kind before. In any case, it will cost you one thousand pesetas and would take about a week to prepare: the money, as you said, to be paid beforehand."

Without further ado, Carujo paid him three hundred pesetas. "The rest when I collect the medicine."

The unassuming little bald man took the money and put it into his large trouser pocket while a little grin appeared on his wrinkly face. "In one week from now," he said and with a grandiose gesture that looked rather odd on such a little man, he beckoned Carujo to the door.

Three days later a man appeared and asked to see Aurelio. He was told that Aurelio had left Mexico and would not be back for a while. "This dishonourable coward not only owes four thousand pesetas to my master but also an apology." The Count, who passed by and heard these loudly spoken accusations, called the man inside and demanded an explanation.

He learned that his nephew had lost the four thousand pesetas in a card game and when asked to pay up, insulted his master, a well-known young nobleman. When challenged to a duel, he promised to be at an arranged spot in the morning. Instead he had left the Country altogether; hence the expression coward.

The enraged Count Manuel handed the man four thousand pesetas and offered to accept the duel on his nephew's behalf. The next day the same man came back and, while accepting the gambling debt, he said that his master had no quarrels with the Count and offered to wait until Aurelio would return. Don Manuel would not hear of it and asked to be told the time and the place where this duel would take place. The day after he received notice that the duel would take place at 7 o'clock the following morning. The weapons would be swords and the fight would be until the first blood was spilled.

The first thing Don Manuel did after the man had left was order José Carujo to bring a pen, ink and paper as the Count wished to change his will. Carujo paled, but brought his master what he required. In the case of his death he gave over the estate to his brother Miguel in Spain and the Hacienda del Alina to his tenant Martin Wilson who had arrived from England fifteen years ago, leased the ground from Count Manuel and built a thriving business with it. Aurelio was completely disinherited.

Carujo, who had to witness Don Manuel's signature, watched carefully as he placed the new will into a special drawer in his writing desk. He heard that his master would engage in a duel and hoped that he might not need the small apothecary's liquid.

The next morning, the sixth day after he had ordered that fateful medicine, Carujo had to accompany his master to the venue where the duel would take place. After a brief introduction took place, the fight began. The challenger declared himself satisfied after the Count fell with a superficial flesh wound on his thigh. Don Manuel was taken to his palace where the physician put on a bandage and prescribed a medicine. The Count had lost a lot of blood and lay unconscious on his bed. Carujo rode into town to collect the prescribed medicine and the little bottle of liquid that he had ordered. For another three hundred pesetas, the apothecary gave him a lotion to produce brown marks. This would dupe the doctor into thinking the patient had died.

Carujo gave his master a drink wherein he had put five drops, as advised by the provider. More would be deadly, he was told and so far he shied away from outright murder; at least by his own hand. He knew that the infamous pirate Ramirez Danlola was in town and went to find him. Danlola greeted his old friend and invited him to have some wine. Carujo agreed and the two brothers in crime were soon engaged in a lively conversation. Finally Captain Danlola asked Carujo if he had any business in mind. Jose Carujo had waited for this moment and asked Danlola what he would charge to make a person disappear. That person would be delivered to him unconscious in a basket; the rest would be up to him.

"Two thousand American dollars would not be unreasonable," mused the pirate.

"Yes, I will do it for this price," he added.

Carujo agreed and they arranged when and where this transaction would take place. The next morning, to his great surprise, the doctor found his patient dead. Already some brown marks showed up on the body and he signed the death certificate without delay. In his mind Count Manuel de Manresa had died of the wounds inflicted on him by the duel. A family tomb had already been built when the Countess Teresa de Manresa had died and the major-domo had no difficulties in arranging the burial with some pomp. The empty coffin would be placed next to the Count's wife, and in no time ceremony was over.

The basket containing the still-unconscious Count was delivered to Captain Danlola, who quickly transferred it onto his pirate ship.

Carujo's next move was to remove the new will from its place. He stored it carefully in his own hiding place, to be used only if Aurelio would not agree to his demands.

The first part of the unholy brothers' plans had been successfully implemented.

Chapter 3

DOCTOR STENTON

SIX months had passed since the last-described events, when a rider on an extra-ordinarily strong mule rode towards the castle of Manresa. The reason for this extra strong mule was the rider's unusually tall, strong stature. Experience teaches that such powerful individuals possess a peaceful character, so one could read in the open and trust inspiring face that he would never misuse his strength.

His dark blond hair and his features would entitle one to the assumption that he was not of southern extraction. The sun had tanned his face; the eyes had the embracing and penetrating looks that one can usually find only by men of the sea, hunters of the prairie and well-travelled people.

He was about thirty years old but his whole being breathed the calm, experience and certainty that make men appear older than they are. His suit was of the finest material, cut according to French fashion. From time to time he made sure that the bag behind him was still in place. The bag seemed to contain things that were of great value to him. He reached into his inside pocket and took out a paper that he unfolded perhaps for the hundredth time. It read:

"Dear Friend!
When we met last we said good-bye for life but events here make me wish to see you here urgently. You should save the life of the Count of Manresa. Come quicklyplease and bring your instruments with you. Go into the last

house of the village to a Señor Dinrallo and ask for me. I implore you to be here as soon as you possibly can.

Yours, Rosetta."

He folded the piece of paper and put it back into his pocket. He did not see the beautiful landscape he was riding through. He thought of when he met the writer of this letter for the first time. It was in St. James' Park in London as he had just turned into a pathway. There he saw her sitting on a bench. Astonished by the loveliness of the young lady, he stepped back. She also arose from the bench and he saw himself opposite a beauty of a perfection he had never seen before. He, the experienced doctor, felt his pulse standing still. That hour decided his fate – but also hers. They loved one another but this love was far from perfect. He was only allowed to meet her on that bench. She was, so she told him, the Lady-in-Waiting to the Condesa de Manresa who lived with her blind father in Spain. She had reasons, which she would not divulge to him, to stay unmarried. He felt very happy that she loved him but was equally pained by her unshakeable decision which he could not understand. Then she departed and made him promise never to try to find her. Ever since then, he had had to suffer unbearable pain.

Then, suddenly, he received Rosetta's letter, and his whole body trembled. Without hesitation he packed his bags and followed her call. As the sun dipped behind the western mountains, he reached the village of Manresa and soon found the house of Señor Dinrallo. The family were sitting at a table, having a simple evening meal. "Does Señor Dinrallo live here?"

"Yes señor, I am he." Dinrallo's open face was his best recommendation.

"Do you know the lady in waiting of the Condesa de Manresa?"

"What is her name?" Dinrallo wanted to know.

"Rosetta"

"Holy Madonna of Cordoba, you must be Dr. Stenton from London whom the Condesa ... I mean the lady in waiting so eagerly expects?"

"Was the Count operated on today?" Stenton asked because the letter mentioned his instruments.

"No, not yet. The Condesa has implored to have the operation postponed but tomorrow it will take place. The Condesa was convinced that you would come."

"So she knows of the letter that the lady in waiting has written to me?"

"Yes, hm, I am sure she knows it," said Dinrallo, slightly embarrassed. We've prepared a small room for you, and a modest meal that you can eat while I call the señorita."

With this he disappeared. Dr. Charles Stenton had time to refresh himself before sitting down to the provided meal. His mule was also provided for.

He then went to his room. The day slowly disappeared, dusk settled over the palace and the village. Stenton put on the light and examined his instruments, when he heard a soft creak of the stairs leading to his room. He answered a knock at the door and there she stood in full light, she, after whom he had yearned with all his heart.

"Rosetta," that one word was all he could say.

"Carlos," her voice trembled as she asked, "you haven't forgotten me?"

"Forgotten? You know that I could never forget you."

"Yet it has to be. But now we can be together and I want to thank you for coming here. Let's discuss right away why I've asked you to come and help."

"Your letter was indecisive, but let me suspect that the Count is in some kind of danger. I take it that doctor's say he needs an operation?"

" Certainly but there are other reasons that make me worry, reasons I can only mention to you because of my infinite trust in you. I don't really know it for sure but I suspect that there are other dangers for the Count. Now you are here, I feel calm."

His eyes lit up at this disclosure, he held his hands towards her. "Such is your trust, so I'm sure you still love me."

"Yes, I love you and I shall carry on loving you. I must have been a puzzle to you, but tomorrow you will learn that our only fate is separation."

"Why tomorrow, why not now?"

"Because it is too difficult for me to say the word. Let's be happy for the moment and in the knowledge that our hearts beat for each other. Let's talk about the cause that brought us together now."

Stenton had to overcome his emotions and led her to a chair.

"You should hear what I wish from you. You know that the Count is blind beyond healing. In addition to this complaint there is a new and very painful one, he suffers from an illness that seems to be progressive – stones in his bladder. All doctors we've asked agree that only an operation could save his life. The Count has agreed to it. The Condesa loves her father and is in terrible fear that the doctors have taken the wrong decision. She prays day and night for him to be saved. The major-domo Carujo and his wife are like demons who long for the blood of their master. They are constantly with him and Count Aurelio – the son … oh, how unhappy is the Condesa."

Rosetta put her hands over her pale face and cried. He pulled her hands away from her eyes and asked: "Tell me everything."

"I will do that," she replied drying her tears. "The Condesa was a small child when they sent away her younger brother to Mexico. Although he came back several times as a young boy, she was overjoyed when he was again expected several months ago.

He came, and she hurried towards him, but only one step. Then she stood still, she could not, as she intended, take him in her arms. She didn't know why, those were not the eyes or the voice of a brother. His face was hard and his words sounded heartless. His looks to his father said: 'I only lay in wait for your death.' She became scared and suspected some secret and in her need she wrote – she asked me to write and to ask you for your help."

"What I can do I shall do," he assured her. "The operation will take place tomorrow?"

"Yes, in no circumstances would they wait any longer. The operation should take place at 11 o'clock."

"Will I be able to see and speak to the Count before that?"

"Yes, when I report you to the Condesa. Come tomorrow at 9 o'clock. Have you done such an operation before?"

Stenton smiled a little. "Quite often, señorita. I believe that I have achieved some successes in this field of work."

"Is the operation dangerous?" Her voice betrayed great anxiety.

"To decide on that, I must examine the patient first. Let's wait until I have seen him."

"Yes, let's wait. I have complete trust in you and I am sure that you will bring help, if it is possible."

With this she arose.

"You want to leave, señorita?"

"Yes, they would miss me otherwise. Will you be there tomorrow at 9 o'clock?"

"Of course. Can I accompany you, señorita?"

"It's dark, no-one will see us Yes, come with me to the palace gate."

They left the house and he offered her his arm. As they stood in front of the gate, he took her hand to his lips.

"Good night, Carlos," Rosetta said warmly. "Have a good rest from your long journey."

"Good night señorita," he answered.

He turned around and wanted to go as she grabbed him by his sleeve. She stepped near to him and he heard her whisper: "My beloved Carlos, forgive me and don't be unhappy." Then she slipped into the park that surrounded the palace. ---

Meanwhile another conversation took place in the assigned room of one of the physicians who, with the participation of a doctor from Manresa would try to remove the stones from Count Miguel. It was Carujo who asked him: "So in your opinion the operation is definitely deadly?"

"Without doubt."

"So it remains as discussed, the cut will take place at eight o'clock without the Condesa knowing it. You will collect your fee afterwards in my flat."

The two men shook hands as if each one regarded the other as a gentleman, then they parted. Carujo hurried to his wife Rita who received him with the words: "Would you let me know the results of your conversation with the doctor? It took you ages."

"But the result couldn't be better. We have reached our aim, our long scheming will be crowned, the fortune of the Count will be ours tomorrow and our son will be the rightful heir." ---

Stenton could not sleep, he paced his room till the day broke, then he went out, settled his mule and went for a ride. It was about 7 o'clock when he stopped before a venta, a place where he could order a cup of coffee. In front of that building he noticed a horse and inside he saw another guest; probably its owner, he thought. The landlord brought him the coffee and then continued a conversation he had with the other guest.

"Are you one of the three doctors who are going to operate on the Count today? I heard the operation will take place at 11 o'clock, will everything be all right?" The landlord seemed really interested.

"There's always a danger with these operations, but the cut should start at 8 o'clock. They don't want the Condesa to know that because she seems upset at the idea of an operation."

Stenton, who had heard about this betrayal, quickly finished his coffee, paid and rushed to the palace. The first person he encountered was Rosetta, a servant who just left her with the words: "Yes Condesa, it will be done."

"Condesa?" A sudden realization shot through his brain.

"Rosetta" he called out.

She turned around. "Carlos, what are you doing so early in the park?"

"Oh my God, am I dreaming? You are the Condesa, you are not the lady in waiting?"

"Yes I am the Condesa." She stretched out her hands. "Can you forgive me Carlos?"

"Forgive? My God, how sad all this is; now I know why we have to part. Why have you done this to me?"

She looked away and confessed with a trembling voice:

"Because I loved you and wanted to be happy at least for a few moments, but that is finished now and the punishment is the harder. My father --- but I can see your instruments, you are coming so early, is there any reason for it?"

"A reason?" Stenton asked, still as if in a dream. "Oh yes, I nearly forgot the most important thing – your father is in great danger."

On her lovely face appeared a deep shock. "My father"? she hardly breathed. "Why?"

He pulled out his pocked-watch, glanced at it and replied. "My God, it's high time, the operation is imminent."

"Now? But the operation was to begin at 11 o'clock."

"No, someone has deceived you. The operation will start any moment now, I heard it from one of the doctors without letting anybody know who I am."

"Holy Madonna, they have wicked intentions, otherwise they would not deceive me. Come quickly señor, we have to prevent an evil deed."

She hurried to the palace, followed by Dr. Stenton. As they reached the entrance, they could see the local doctor's horse.

"Quickly," reminded Dr. Stenton, "they've all gathered and can start any minute."

They hurried along a hall that was covered with an expensive carpet. In front of a door stood a servant.

"Is the Count awake?" enquired the Condesa.

When she learned that he was, she asked: "Is he alone?" "No" was the answer, "there are three physicians with him."

"For how long?"

"About ten minutes."

"Good, so we are probably not too late, let's go inside."

They intended to enter, when the servant, politely but resolute, stopped them from doing so. "Forgive me, Condesa, I have strict instructions not to let anyone in."

"Including me?"

"Especially you," replied the servant.

She grew angry. "Who gave this order?" she demanded to know.

"Count Aurelio, who is also present."

"Ah, him – make room," she commanded.

"I mustn't, because …" The man could not say any more. Stenton had pulled him aside and, without further ado, opened the door to the Count's reception room. The door to the room where the operation was to take place was locked. The Condesa knocked. It was Aurelio's voice asking: "Who is there?"

"I am."

"You, Rosetta?" he sounded cross and surprised. "Didn't Juan tell you … "?

"Yes, he did, but now open quickly," she demanded.

"Go back to your room, this is not for a lady's eyes and the physicians wouldn't like it. Go away. Your knocking here doesn't help anyone."

"Open up, or I shall open it myself."

"You can try, but it won't help you." Aurelio laughed..

They listened; they could hear counting, … five, six, seven, eight, nine … "What is this?" Rosetta asked.

"They are starting to anaesthetize the Count with chloroform."

"Does that mean that they are going to operate?"

"Yes."

"Señor help me," she cried, desparately fearful.

"Have I your permission to use force?"

"Yes, but act quickly."

Stenton went to the door and lifted his leg. A loud crash was heard; the door flew open. The strong man had cracked the lock with a single kick of the foot and they went inside.

The Count, against their belief, was to be operated on in the next room. Aurelio and one of the doctors came from this room. "What is this? You dared to use force?" shouted the young Count who, in his anger, overlooked the fact that she was not alone.

"Dared you say? I believe that the Countess de Manresa has the right at any time to see her father. It is not I who dared, I want to know by what right you undertake to allow such a dangerous operation without my inclusion."

"It has been decided. Now, remove yourself."

"Not before I have spoken to my father, where is he?"

"In the next room. Your interference can cost his life. Ah, who is this stranger?"

"This is Dr. Stenton who came here from London to examine our father, I expect his presence is equally welcome by you."

The physician, who had also entered, looked contemptuous but Aurelio flared up. "From London? Who gave you permission? I expect you to leave now and dismiss that unwanted stranger."

At this insulting behaviour her person seemed to grow. "The only person who can decide that is our father Count Miguel de Manresa y Cordoba."

Aurelio turned to Stenton. "Away, or should I let the servants chase you out of here?"

Stenton answered with a slight smile. "I came here on the call of the Countess Rosetta de Manresa, to see the Count Miguel de Manresa and I shall do so in spite of any suspect objection from anybody. Condesa, please introduce me to these gentlemen who are probably colleagues of mine."

The other doctors had entered the room where this quarrel took place. "This is Doctor Stenton, consultant at the Broomfield Clinic in London – Doctor Rancas from Madrid, Doctor Dilanos from Toledo and Doctor Micelli from Manresa."

The three doctors bowed coolly and Doctor Rancas even blushed. He was probably the one who knew the reputation of that clinic. He declared: "I don't know this gentleman, our preparations are completed and we don't need anyone's help."

The Condesa wanted to answer but Stenton waved to her and then started himself: "Please, honourable Condesa, allow me a word. It is my presence that the quarrel is about. I am a doctor and your guest, the Condesa, who would expect politeness from her brother and simple comradeship from the others, but this is not forthcoming. So I stand here as the instructed and fully authorized medical agent of the Countess Rosetta de Manresa y Cordoba and say the following: As this highly dangerous operation was undertaken in such suspicious circumstances, I have convincing reason to believe that there are intentions involved that shy away from daylight and honest eyes.

I, therefore, declare that anybody who does this operation to be either careless or intentional murderous and if you want to remove me, I shall ask for police assistance and I am sure this would go with the Countess's wishes."

Before anybody could answer, the Count, whose chloroforming had not fully put him to sleep, appeared from the adjoining room. "What is going on here?" he wanted to know. "Why don't they start with the operation?

Rosetta hurried to him and embraced him affectionately. "Father, my dear father, thanks be to the holy virgin that they haven't started yet, they mustn't kill you."

"Kill me, who wanted to do that?"

"Oh, you would have died, I know it, I feel it."

"Your words are daughterly love and fear, you shouldn't have disturbed us."

"Just so, father," said the false Count, "she has interrupted us. She even had the door smashed in a manner not suitable for a Condesa"

"Have you really done that my dear child?" asked Count Miguel with an unbelieving smile.

"Yes, I have done that papa," she answered, "your condition requires the highest attention and your life is much too important to me, to allow the slightest neglect. Only someone who has my full trust must treat you. Therefore I asked Doctor Stenton from the Broomfield Clinic in London, whom I trust and who has arrived today. They did not even let him in; is it a wonder that I forced my entry?"

"Where is this doctor now?" asked the Count.

"Right here in this room, it is Dr. Carlos Stenton from London."

"Here in this room?"

"Yes," answered Stenton himself, "I ask your Highness's forgiveness that I have followed the call of your child. If the life of a human being is at stake, the highest caution is justified."

Stenton had talked with a strong voice, the sound of which seemed to please the Count.

"Did you attend similar operations before?" the Count seemed interested.

"Yes." That was a simple word but the Count lifted his head and said:

"Señor, you only said one word but the sound of your voice is significant. I feel that you have attended many such operations, perhaps even supervised?"

"Your Highness has heard right, I am the consultant in the Broomfield Clinic."

"Ah, I should trust you and one should not have rejected you. I thank you that you have come. Would you please examine my condition?"

"I am pleased to have your permission, Highness."

"Stop!" called Aurelio. "Father, I must tell you that I have shown this man the door, will you countermand my order?"

"My son, you have insulted this señor, I owe him satisfaction."

Aurelio had to stay back. He turned to his sister and whispered viciously: "I will not forget that."

Stenton stepped into the room behind the Count. There were all the instruments prepared for the operation. The Count turned to Stenton: "Señor, since the loss of my eyesight, I am used to judging people by their voice. Yours creates trust – please examine me."

The English doctor had treated many patients but never with such emotion. This man was the father of his hopelessly beloved; his feelings turned into a deep breath. The Count, who had heard that, asked: "Are you worried, señor?"

"No, Highness, what you have heard was not a sigh of weakness but a prayer to God that I may succeed and fulfil the expectations of Condesa Rosetta."

The Count stretched his hands out towards Dr. Stenton and said: "Señor, I thank you, your words have appealed to me and heightened my trust. A man, who in spite of his skills, appeals to God for His help, will achieve what is humanly possible. You may begin!"

Dr. Stenton inquired in detail about the Count's condition. He had many questions.

The Count had to lie down and the thorough examination proved to the three Spanish doctors that they had a superior spirit in front of them. Finally, the Count could get up. He enquired the result of the examination.

Instead of answering that question, Dr. Stenton asked whether he could examine the Count's eyes. The doctor then brought forth various instruments, threw light on the patient's eyes and examined these thoroughly. When he finally finished, he turned to his colleagues:

"Señores, Doctor Rancas from Madrid has declared that he doesn't want any interference, so I have to forego any consultation. But I am forced to speak without consideration: "Highness, in what way was it planned to remove the stone?"

"Through an operative cut in the abdomen." Stenton got a shock. "That is impossible, Highness" he called out. "Either someone has tried to deceive you or you have misheard; but I cannot see a reason for a deception."

"It is as I say," declared the Count, "ask these señores!"

Stenton looked at the doctors but only Racas made a defiant reply: "We think that success is only possible our way."

"But señores," said an excited Stenton, "do you know the size and the situation of the stone? My God, I do not comprehend this, here every cut is deadly. Señores, I declare anybody who uses a knife in this case to be an outright murderer."

"Señor," Racas called out threateningly."

"Señor," called Stenton with a sharp voice, "the Count is no physician; he couldn't know what had been decided. Every beginner would know that the Count could not survive such an operation; if I report you to the police you will be under suspicion for wilful murder."

"Ah," said Racas with undeniable scorn, "you, a stranger will threaten us; ridiculous, you want to become the personal physician of the Count. Our names are highly respected and without blemish. Let us hear how you would remove the stone."

"You should hear that" said Stenton calmly, "this stone can only be removed by Lithotripsie that is entirely without danger."

"Lithotripsie, what is that? What should that be?"

Stenton listened with astonishment. "Highness, did you hear to whom you have entrusted you life and the happiness of your daughter? This man has never heard of Lithotripsie, the crushing and removing of the stone with a catheter-drill."

A contemptuous laughter could be heard, coming from Rancas. "You are mistaken señor, the fairy tale of the catheter-forceps is long known to us, but it is just a fairy tale that only a beginner believes. But with somebody incompetent one does not quarrel. The Count will decide who has to leave the room at this moment – he or us."

"As long as I can treat this case, I shall only decide according to my conscience," said Stenton, " I have already said that his Highness is no physician. Maybe he will decide the way that will cost his life, but that I will not permit, even if I should put my own life at stake."

The Count stood up, stretched out his hands imperiously and said: "Señores, this is not the place for such quarrels. Would you please wait outside and I shall give you my decision later. I know your views but I wish to examine those of Dr. Stenton."

"That means we are discharged. Well, we shall go but this stranger will have to give us satisfaction and, Your Highness, we beg you to think everything over well before you make a decision."

They gathered their instruments and left; Rosetta immediately entered the room and put her arms around her father, then she rejoiced: "Saved. father I thank you."

"Not so fast," said the Count, "the decision has not been taken yet, let's first examine the views of Dr. Stenton."

"Oh, his views will be the only right ones," she called out looking at Stenton with such warmth and trust in her eyes that it penetrated into his heart.

"Highness, trust me, God knows how honestly I mean it, but please forgive me that I have spoken so harshly to these men. Had the operation taken place, I swear that you would no longer be alive."

The Count turned to his daughter. "This doctor has even examined my eyes."

Countess Rosetta glanced at Stenton with joyous surprise. "Really?" she asked, "are there any grounds for hope?"

"Certainly Condesa, I have treated many a blind person, practise has taught me to discern whether an eye has any hope or none at all."

"And what have you noticed?"

"That here the doctors were also wrong."

Rosetta jumped up and the Count lifted his head in surprise. Only Aurelio who had previously tried in vain to intervene on behalf of the doctors had a poisonous glance for Stenton.

"Highness," Stenton continued: "Have they told you that your blindness is total and without hope?"

"Yes, they called it Staphylom."

"Hm, as I said, it was wrong; what you have is the Grey Star in connection with a mother-of- pearl kind of gleaming, cloudy horn skin. We physicians call it 'Glaucoma'."

"Is this condition treatable?" the Count asked with bated breath.

Up to now this condition would be called hopeless, but I have had some successes with a few of my patients. We remove the Glaucoma by continual aspiration with a special needle, then we operate the Grey Star that one finds beneath it. Highness, trust me and I can give you with clear conscious the hope that you may recover some of your eyesight: not as clear as before but with the help of glasses you should be able to see."

The Count put his arms up high and called: "Oh my God, if that would be possible."

Crying with delight, Rosetta fell on her father's neck and with a sob she asked:

"Father, trust him, nobody else can help but he alone."

"Yes, I shall listen to your voice, I shall give Dr. Stenton all my trust. Here señor, take my hand, you have started with God and with God's help you will finish. Aurelio my son, will you not be happy with us?"

The false Count tried to restrain himself and answered: "I would be happy to have you healthy and with your eyesight intact, but is it not dangerous to awaken hopes? If they don't materialise, the ill person would be ten times worse off?"

"God will be merciful: how long will the treatment take, señor?"

"Because you have to get used to the drill, the stone cannot be removed in less than two weeks," answered Stenton. "Only after you have regained full strength shall I begin with your eyes. They will take longer."

"Can you stay that long, señor?"

"I will have to take a longer vacation, or possibly, have to give up my position."

"Give up your position, I beg you Dr. Stenton. You will find a new home here and ample compensation for everything you leave behind in London."

"My reward will be the knowledge that I have given back to you your health and your eyesight, Highness, I shall write to London today."

"Please do that. You will live with us now. Rosetta will show you your new home."

Stenton said good bye to the Count and went outside where he found the doctors.

They looked at him with eyes full of unadulterated hatred.

"Señor," said Dr. Rancas, "you have started the battle with us, but we will continue until you succumb."

"Pah," was his only answer. He opened the door and went for his belongings. On his return he found his rooms ready.---

A short while later there were four people gathered in another locked room. It was Carujo, his wife Rita, their son the false Count Aurelio and Dr. Racas. They discussed the extraordinary events of the last hour.

"Is it possible; we were so sure about the success of our plans and a stranger spoiled it all?"

"Spoiled?" asked Aurelio scornfully, "who talks of that? There is, at the most, only a small postponement."

"Will he succeed with the drill?" asked Carujo of the doctor.

"Quite surely," answered Dr. Racas. Even with the eyes he will probably have success if no inflammation occurs but we will gore this stranger himself and he will be squashed before he even thinks about it."

"In no case must the Count get his eyesight back. He might notice that our Aurelio has more similarity with my husband than with a Manresa."

"We have many possibilities but we have to be careful. It is best no-one sees us together. That English doctor has to die or, at least, he must disappear."

"But how?" asked Rita.

"Let me worry about that. I have in the mountains some acquaintances who by other people are called robbers; to me they are the most loyal and honest allies. They will help us to get rid of that stranger." ---

Meanwhile Dr. Stenton took a good rest to make up for the previous night, when he had not slept a wink. On his return to the palace, the first person he met was Rosetta. "Welcome señor," she greeted him, "may your entrance bring us blessings."

"It will bring us battle. That has been promised to me by Dr. Racas."

"Let it. The battle in which we are united will not only be a battle against falsity, lies and crime, it will also be a fight about our love. You will find in me a most loyal comrade".

Chapter 4

THE BEGGAR'S STORY

---

*H*IGH in the mountains in the West of Andora, mount 'Maladetta' the cursed, stretched its peaks into the clouds. A frail rambler crawled downhill on a wild path; no spring was in sight to refresh him, the sun shone with penetrating rays onto the naked rocks. He was badly in need of water and a cool place to hide from the consuming heat.

He was old. His hair was grey and his face drawn and weathered. His clothes were pieces of rags and his torn sandals made his feet almost touch the hot ground. He seemed very ill; a constant coughing came from his wheezing chest. His burning feet crawled on as if he were driven by a gruesome curse. Finally he stopped and looked around. "It should be near here," he mumbled. "This way I took the little boy. Here is where my anguish started and sucked the marrow out of my bones. Here is where I shall take a rest. He let himself down on that hot ground and his head dropped into his hands. Only the panting of his ill chest broke the silence.

"*O santa madre dolorosa,*" could at last be heared from him. "Where have I sinned and how was I punished? What did I have from my life of crime? Begging was my lot. Lord in heaven, let me find the one I seek that I may not end in hell."

Again he fell silent to ponder his crimes, constantly coughing. Then he started again. "Does he still live, that beautiful little boy who slept in my arms? I cannot take this uncertainty; I have to go left where the robbers had their hiding place. Nobody will recognise me They will take

34

me in, an ill and dying person and I'll find out what happened to him, the one I seek. Forward you tired legs, only one more walk should do, before resting forever." He lifted himself up and continued his arduous walk. He allowed himself no rest until he reached the position where he could see low undergrowth and bushes and finally densely placed trees. Between these bushes and trees, he climbed up until he saw a flat and surrounded by shrubs. He had hardly sat down when he felt a hand on his shoulder.

"What do you want here, old man?"

"I want to die here."

"You want to die here, why?" The questioner was a young strong man who, because of the weapons that he carried, could not be taken as a peace-loving citizen.

"Because I can't go on anymore, I'm seeking the root for my suffering but I can't find it."

"Have you any bread?" the young man continued.

No."

"Nothing at all? Holy mother of God, you will die of hunger before you die of anything else. Wait here, I am going to ask whether I can bring you some food."

The young man disappeared but returned shortly afterwards and said: "If you let me tie something around your eyes, I'll take you to a place where you can rest and look after yourself as long as you want."

"Something around my eyes, why?"

"We might be brigands but we have honour between us. Nobody must see the entrance."

"I am old and poor, I don't have to fear you; take me wherever you like."

The young man took his scarf from his neck and tied it around the old man's eyes; he then took him by the hand until they reached a passage where, after a few more steps he untied his scarf from the beggar's eyes. Twenty well armed fellows were sitting around, either drinking, smoking, playing cards or busying themselves with their guns. The leader of the brigands asked: "What is your name?"

"My name is Bernado, señor."

"I think I've seen you before."

"I don't know."

"Why are you not at home if you are so ill?"

"A gypsy woman told me about a plant root that would cure my illness."

"Have you no son who could search for you?"

"I have neither family nor a single friend on this earth."

"You can stay here and look after yourself: you won't carry on for long if you are a traitor. Take real care, as I don't make jokes with such people." The old fellow was shown a corner to sit down. He was given food and drink. After that, no one seemed to care about him anymore.

Shortly afterwards the watch came to the captain and told him of a masked man who wanted to see him. Ricardo Ramon, the captain, expected business and hurried to see that man. "Señor Carujo," he called out, "I haven't seen you for years I suppose you have new business?"

"Shush, no names please," said the gaunt man, "maybe I have business for you – if you are not too dear."

"Nobody can hear us here; what is this business?"

"Two people have to disappear."

"It all depends who they are."

"A Count and a doctor."

"Who is the Count?"

"The old Manuel de Manresa y Cordoba."

"Sorry, I can't touch the Count. He's under the protection of a friend and I cannot go against my own rules However, the doctor is different. Where does he live?"

"With the Count."

"That will not come cheap either. Should he die or just disappear?"

"The first is safer. How much do you want?"

"One thousand dublons."

"One thousand dublons? You are mad capitano!"

"Then we'll leave it."

"All right one thousand dublons, one half now and one half when it is done. Will it succeed?"

"It has to. How can we get to him?"

"That I can't tell you yet, you must send a few men to Manresa, I'll meet them in the park to give further instructions," said Carujo and gave five hundred dublons to the captain. "By the way, what happened to the little fellow, you know which one I mean?"

"He is a big fellow now."

"Why did he not die?"

"You asked me to exchange those little fellows. What happened afterwards, you left to me."

"Who does he think he is?"

"He thinks he was abandoned and that I just found him."

"I almost feel I want to see him."

"That you must forget. You paid me for my work, you are not a member and you will get no further than here."

"So I must be satisfied. When will your people be in the park of Manresa?"

"Tomorrow night. Adios señor."

"Adios." The men shook hands and parted.

They just negotiated about a human life as if it were something trivial. There is a question as to who is the bigger scoundrel, the captain of the robbers or the sly major-domo and notary who planned against his master. The next evening the captain sent five of his people to Manresa.---

That evening the beggar was asked by a young man, about twenty two years old, to come with him He was led through a dark gangway where he could see many cells hewn into the wall, seemingly used as sleeping rooms for the bandits. As he reached one, he said to the old man. "Here is your chamber, my good old man. Should I leave the lantern with you?"

"Yes, who knows whether I will ever leave this room?"

"Why?" asked the young man, whose refined features would not betray him as belonging to a gang of robbers, "God can heal the worst illness. Don't lose hope," the young man continued.

"Yes, He can take away the pains of my illness, He cannot undo what I have done in the past and the pains of the soul. Guard yourself from these; they are worse than any illness"

"You have a bad conscience? I wish I could help you," asked the sympathetic young man.

"You seem to have a sympathetic heart but only the capitano – or perhaps even you could help."

"I would like to if I can."

"Do you know whether there is a young man among you who knows nothing about his birth?"

The young man was suddenly alert. "How come you ask such a question?"

"Because I am looking for such a man."

"I have to tell you that I know of such a man but only of one."

With a joyous hope the old man looked up. "Who is he?"

"It is I myself."

"What is your name?"

"Rudolfo."

"How did you get to be among brigands?"

"The capitano found me in the mountains; all my searches for my parents have been, so far, in vain."

"How long have you been with the brigands?" the old man's eager questions continued.

"About eighteen years.

"Eighteen years," repeated the beggar thoughtfully, "that could be about right, have you no memories at all?"

"No, I don't remember anything although I dreamt quite a lot."

"What you dreamt may well be reality; what did you dream?"

"I dreamt of a little doll lying in a white little bed on the edge of which I saw a golden crown and the doll was alive."

"Do you perhaps know her name?"

"Yes," Rudolfo answered, "I know that I called her Rosetta or little Rose. I also dreamt of a tall man in a nice uniform who called me Aurelio. There was also a beautiful, proud lady who kissed Rosetta and myself quite often; I was only small but I recall that I called them papa and mama. I also was lying in a bed with a crown centrally placed at the head. Once a strange man came when I was asleep. I woke up and I had something over my mouth. I was scared of that man and I wanted to scream but when he tied the cloth over my mouth even tighter, I was full of fear and fell asleep again. When I woke up I was in a wood. That was all I dreamed."

"Nothing further? Nothing else? Maybe you know the name of the man in uniform?"

"Only that the servants called him Highness."

"Listen, my son, that was not a dream it was reality."

"Sometimes I have also thought that was not only a dream but the capitano always got angry and the crown I wasn't allowed to mention. I could describe it in detail. The captain threatened to hit me so I kept quiet about the crown."

"You are the person I am seeking."

Rudolfo was amazed. "You were looking for me? Why?"

"My son, if it is the will of God, you'll learn today what may eventually lead you to know who you are. Go now. If the capitano learns what I am going to tell you, he will have to kill you to preserve his secret. Come back when everybody is asleep. Bring paper and writing utensils and more light, it may take a long time."

Rudolfo went and left the old man alone.

"Have thanks, Madonna," the old man mumbled, "that you have given me the strength to reach this place. Maybe God will forgive the terrible crime I have committed in my careless youth." A new coughing fit nearly took his breath away.

Soon the robbers withdrew into their chambers. When Rudolfo left his small cell, he could hardly master his excitement The veil that covered his past would finally be lifted and his dreams would not be illusions but reality. As he crept through the passage to the old man, he felt the pounding of his heart. When Rudolfo entered the beggar's cell, he put the light on the floor and let himself down. The beggar sat up. The sick man had difficulty in breathing. "Rudolfo," he started his confession, "my name is Juan Marino. A great crime has been committed against you and I – I have helped. I don't yet ask you for your forgiveness. Listen to how I have sinned against you. You should know, Rudolfo, that I once was a member of the brigands."

"You, a member of these brigands here?"

"Yes, the capitano was my leader; my illness has changed me so much that he doesn't recognise me. I was a poor sailor and from time to time I smuggled a few yards of silk over the French border. Once they caught me, they confiscated my goods and my boat and put me into prison. I escaped and as I was safe nowhere. I joined the brigands.

The first deed I had to do was the exchange of two little boys. A little smuggling did nothing to my conscience but this deed scared me. I couldn't sleep at night and when the capitano then asked me to kill a man, I broke the oath to him and left."

"Tell me about the exchange of the two little boys?" Rudolfo asked.

"To be sure that everything went all right, the capitano came with us. In short, we exchanged the little boys and brought you into the den where you have been well looked after. You always talked about your papa, mama and Rosetta until the capitano forbade this. You were quiet after that and have probably forgotten all about it."

"No, I have not forgotten, but tell me, did you hear the name of the man who brought the other boy?"

"Yes, I heard that name mentioned, although I was not meant to hear it. The capitano called him once señor Carujo." An awful coughing hit the beggar's body. Rudolfo paced the small room. That old man had sinned against him but he was ordered by somebody else to do it. Should he be angry with this man whose body and soul seem to be shaken by remorse and who might not live to see another day? He stepped towards the old man and said. "Juan Marino, I forgive you, I can see your great crime but I am also a sinner and may God forgive me as I have forgiven you." The beggar's head dropped, his eyes closed and his features showed an expression of deep peace.

"Oh, how good I feel," he whispered. "My God, how much I thank you, now I can die in peace." The beggar wrote down the whole story and signed it.

"I shall take great care with this written confession," said Rudolfo, "I thank you for this information, it has lifted a great burden from me, I have forgiven you, and may God have mercy on you." With these words he turned and left for his own abode. What he had learned kept him awake. Hitherto he had thought of the capitano as his benefactor, now he knew that he was the originator of the crime that took him away from distinguished parents and had brought him to a band of contemptible people. He decided to find out more about his origin. He had to find out about this Carujo, the only name he really had.

The capitano also could not rest. This Carujo is a great rogue, worse than any brigand. Why would he want to kill the doctor? I get paid and I shouldn't really ask. He pays well and only a blockhead would not squeeze a lemon to the last drop. Rudolfo lives and I have the old scoundrel in my hand; his purse will have to bleed.

Pity only that I never could find out where the two little boys actually came from. Carujo is the manager and secretary of Count Miguel de Manresa y Cordoba. I shall investigate the family circumstances but by whom? Rudolfo, whom I have sent to the best schools and given the best education, who can speak French fluently and English like an English gentleman; he would be the only one who could move in these circles. He can ride, knows how to fence, swim, shoot, and is strong and true besides being clever. Yes, I will do it. *Per dios,* that is an adventure, a prank for which I deserve the greatest honour. The brigand laughed to himself.

One of the brigands came to the captain during the early morning hours. He reported that the beggar had just died. "Good, so we are rid of him. Bury him and don't burden me with this anymore," said the captain indifferently. "Ask Rudolfo to come to me."

After a short while, Rudolfo entered the chamber of the captain. He greeted the captain in a friendly manner and did not show his changed feelings for the man in front of him. The captain offered him a seat and asked: "How is your black stallion?"

"It will be hard to control. It is now more than a month it hasn't been taken out of the stables and it will be hard to restrain."

"So take good care that there should not be a mishap because I have a task for you that needs a clever man."

"Where should I go and what do you want me to do?"

"I want you to go to Manresa and possibly the palace of Manresa."

"That's far away," answered Rudolfo but he was actually glad to be far away from the capitano and his band.

"Is your stock of clothing in order?"

"Completely."

"Also the uniforms?"

"Should I dress up as an officer?"

"As a French officer, I shall give you a holiday pass with the name of Lucien de Moraeu. You must somehow try to get an invitation to the palace. I'm especially interested in someone there with the name of

Carujo and his relationship to the Count. Also about a son by the name of Aurelio who came back from Mexico recently. You have to appear as a rich, refined and independent fellow. I'll give you sufficient means to do that. After you have gathered sufficient information, I'll ask you to report it back to me."---

Chapter 5

A FAILED ATTACK

_I_N the palace of Manresa one could hear a pin drop. Dr. Stenton had given the order of silence. The three doctors hurried to see the Count. They brushed past the servant, who got in the way to stop them. "Highness," Doctor Racas began, "we've heard that you're not well and it's the duty of a doctor to see to that patient.

"You are mistaken, señores," said the Count, "I'm quite well actually; it was Dr. Stenton who asked for silence and he asked me to take a few hours complete rest."

"Ah, this English doctor, we have warned your highness of his methods which would, inevitably lead to your Highness's death."

"Dr. Racas," the Count said, smiling slightly, "please open the little box in front of you."

Doctor Racas reached for the box and opened it. Contemptuously he said: "If Your Highness thinks that he can cure you with this powder, he'd better go back to school. It is only our method that can free you from that stone."

The Count corrected him with a smile. "This powder is not to go inside my body, it is the stone that Dr. Stenton has removed." The Count could feel the embarrassment he had caused the doctors. "Please go and see señor Carujo, who will pay you for your services and accept my heartiest thanks you," the Count continued.

"Thanks we have already received," said Dr. Racas. As you don't seem to need us any more, we might as well go home where we get the respect of our patients." The three doctors went to their respective rooms.

Three people were waiting in Dr. Racas' room. Aurelio, Pablo Carujo and Rita received him with the question: "Successful?"

"Yes"-answered Racas.

"Thank God,"

"Save your thanks for later. It was successful, not for us but for Dr. Stenton."

"Really?" Carujo flared up, "the devil will take care of this foreign intruder."

"It had better be soon," said Dr. Racas wryly, "otherwise I'll be gone."

"Stay one more night and the Count will be glad that you are still here – I have got plans," countered Carujo.

"All right, one more night! If the Count doesn't call me tomorrow, I'll be gone."

"Don't worry, leave it to me. I have to go now," said Carujo. He left the room and the palace and walked towards the park, where he expected to find the people sent by the captain of the robbers. He whistled and a man stepped out of the bushes.

"Do you have an order for us? It's rather boring to wait around here."

"Yes, this man is in the habit of going for a walk before going to sleep. It's then you can catch him; I hope you'll be able to finish him."

"Don't worry señor, our bullets will hit him for sure."

"No bullets. It has to be with the knife. A shot would raise an alarm. If you put the knife into his hands afterwards, it will look like suicide."

"I have to obey you, but a shot would be far safer and we'd find no resistance."

"Are you afraid?" asked Carujo mockingly.

"Of course not. Your order will be executed, but what about the money? The capitano has asked us to collect."

"Come back here at midnight and I'll pay you the money. I can see that you are hooded, why?"

"What do you take us for? Beginners? It's always safe not to be recognised."

"I would have thought that a dead man couldn't recognise anyone, but have it your way, as long as you don't mess it up. Don't be afraid, there are five of us, and we cannot fail." Carujo went back to the palace where he stood in front of a window to observe Dr. Stenton leaving for his evening stroll. It was almost dark when he saw Dr. Stenton leave the palace. The direction he took was towards those who were planning to kill him. "Goodbye Dr. Stenton," he mumbled, "it does not pay to put your nose into other people's business." With this he went to Rita and told her that the last hour of the interfering stranger had come.

Stenton meanwhile met Rosetta who knew of his evening habit and also went for a walk. "May I accompany you?" she asked blushing slightly.

"I couldn't wish for better company," he answered and offered her his arm.

"Do you really believe that my father will see again?"

"Trust in God. He will guide me to find the right way."

"He will guide … oh my God what's that?"

These words were called out by the condesa, in the greatest shock. The bushes near them parted and a hooded head appeared. Happily, it wasn't for the first time the doctor found himself in such a situation. During his years in America's west, he had earned the name of Doc Ironfist by fighting with the Red Indians. With the Bedouins of the Arabian Desert, he had acquired a presence of mind that knows no shock.

"Hey, that's meant for me," he shouted, as the five hooded men raced towards him with raised knives. As the first nearly reached him, he gave him a kick in the stomach that threw him back into the knife of the man that followed him. They both fell to the ground. The next raised his arm for a deadly hit, Stenton gripped his arm with his right hand, lifted him up with the help of his other hand and threw him as if he had only a light weight against the last two who had raced against him. This did not happen without shouts. All five men lay on the ground now. Stenton turned to the one who managed to get up first and hit him on the head with his large fist, that he fell to the ground unconscious. The other three didn't quite manage to get up when Stenton's fist made short shrift of them. He then tore strips off their hooded garments and first tied their hands and then their feet together.

Rosetta leaned on a tree with her eyes closed, until Stenton's voice brought her back to life. The sudden change from deep shock to utter delight, when she saw Stenton alive was so extreme that she threw her arms around him. "How is this possible?" she rejoiced, you are not even wounded." He could no longer restrain himself and kissed her for a long time.

They heard steps and he released her. Two gardeners had heard the shouts and the commotion and asked Dr. Stenton the reason. It was, by now, too dark to see the black-clad brigands lying on the ground.

"Dr. Stenton has been attacked," said Rosetta "but thank God he is unhurt."

The two fellows who now saw the five robbers on the ground looked at each other. They obviously did not understand that one man, even a giant, could overcome such superiority.

"Have you a safe confinement for these people here?" asked Stenton of the two gardeners.

"Yes," they answered.

"May I ask you to put these fellows into this place?"

The gardeners agreed and lifted the first one onto their shoulders. It was then thatthey noticed that the man was dead. It was the one who received the kick into his stomach and fell onto the knife of the one behind him. Stenton asked them to leave this one behind until the local authorities took control.

Rosetta said. "I'd better inform my father before he hears it from anybody else." On her way she met Carujo who noticed she was still in shock.

"What happened to you gracious Condesa?" He asked faking anxiety.

"Nothing happened to me. Dr. Stenton has been attacked by five robbers with knives."

"Five men with knives? He is dead then? I offer my heartfelt sympathy," said the hypocritical Carujo with inner jubilation.

"No, he is not dead. This invincible man killed one of the attackers and took the other four prisoners."

"That is ... impossible Condesa. You must be mistaken," stuttered a disturbed Carujo.

"Not at all, the prisoners are now being taken to a safe place where the authorities can question them tomorrow," the condesa went on. Carujo went to see Rita.

"Well?" she asked, "is it over now? Did we get rid of this intruder?"

"If I don't free the prisoners, it may well be the end for us," he answered gloomily

"Holy Madonna, what happened," Rita trembled with fear.

Carujo told her what he had learned from the Condesa. Then he was on his way to find the prisoners. ---

Chapter 6

LUCIEN DE MOREAU

THERE was a fair on in Aragon. The Spaniard is a serious man but if there is fun and entertainment on offer, he indulges whole heartedly.

Two men approached the town from the east. They kept away from the usual roads; they wanted to avoid recognition. They had split up from the four whom Carujo helped to escape and discussed their future plans. "As we have decided not to return to the capitano, we have also to decide what we are going to do for a living,"

"You are the more experienced, I shall let you decide. I would suggest holding up one of the many carriages coming to this town today."

"Yes, that seems to be a good idea, good job we've hidden our rifles at a different spot. This señor Carujo told us not to use them, only our knives. Had he not given this stupid order, we would have finished the job. Our pistols are gone, but with our rifles we can order people to hand over their valuables. Let's start right now, Pedro. You go to the main road and select one of the carriages going into town. We'll take them in the evening when they are going back."

Pedro went on his way. Soon he saw a carriage showing a Count's crown, drawn by two horses. Inside was Condesa Rosetta who was going to Aragon to meet a friend she had met in Madrid. Lady Margaret Castlepool had written to her, that her father, Lord Castlepool of Nottingham had to go on a diplomatic mission to Mexico. His daughter, who wanted to visit Rosetta first, would accompany him.

Pedro went back to his comrade and told them about this find. "If there won't be enough money, there should at least be some valuable jewellery." The decision was unanimous to attack this carriage on the way back.

Condesa Rosetta went to the best hotel in town and asked the coachman to see when the post chaise would arrive, and to bring Lady Margaret to her. Before long the visitor arrived and was taken to Condesa Rosetta. By their hugging, anyone could see that their friendship was deep and joyous.

The greeting was over and the usual first questions and answers had been exchanged. Now the two ladies stood at the window observing the festive atmosphere of the big plaza in front of the hotel when Lady Margaret lifted her finger and pointed to a rider on a magnificent horse.

"Look, Rosetta, who can that be?"

"I don't know. He looks like a French officer."

It was Rudolfo who, on his way to Manresa, came through Aragon. Seeing him in his elegant uniform and confident seat on his horse, no one would know that he was brought up amongst robbers. Roberto, who was to accompany him, was dressed as a servant and rode behind him. Rudolfo rode toward the hotel, to have rest for his horse and himself. Across his way stood a tall barrow from which all sorts of fruit were being sold. Instead of riding around this barrier, Rudolfo pulled his stallion upwards and jumped over the barrow as if it were only a minor obstacle.

"Splendid," called Rosetta and clapped her hands.

"What a rider," said Margaret, her eyes resting admiringly on the youth.

He inspected the hotel and his glances went to the window. The girls noticed a joyous start; he even wanted to pull his reins but quickly rallied. He threw a second glance to the window and dismounted.

"Have you seen," said Margaret, "how he looked at you?"

"Oh no," said Rosetta, "his eyes went to you, I observed it."

"That's impossible," smiled the English lady. "You're so beautiful that every eye must fall on you."

"I think we should start on our way home. Father is so looking forward to greeting you." Rosetta gave the order to the coachman to harness the horses and left the room to board their vehicle.

Rudolfo entered the hotel and asked for a glass of wine but he didn't drink it. He thought about the blue eyes that had glowed at him in such admiration. Now he heard the sound of hoofs and looked outside. He saw the carriage where the coachman harnessed the horses. In two steps he stood at the window. His dream, the crown and the two letters, M and C, the exact embodiment of his dream. He felt upsurge of blood, but he rallied fast and waved to the waiter to join him at the window. "To whom does this carriage belong?

"To the Count of Manresa," was the answer.

"Manresa" Rudolfo said quietly to himself. And what is the meaning of that C?"

"The Count's name is Miguel de Manresa y Cordoba. The lady who is just entering the vehicle is his daughter, Condesa Rosetta."

"And the other?"

"She is from England for a visit to the Condesa. That's what I have heard."

The waiter moved away. Rudolfo did not know where to place his glances, the now unveiled face of the English lady or the crown, the exact replica of his dreams. The ladies had entered the coach and the vehicle drove off, but not before Lady Margaret glanced back once more and saw the admiring gaze of Rudolfo, still at the window. She felt her pulse quickening. Rudolfo threw a coin on the table and hurried outside.

"Let's go," he said to his servant as he swung himself onto his horse.

"Already?" asked Roberto who could not understand this haste.

He received no reply but had to hurry to catch up with the lieutenant who was almost out of his sight. The latter only slowed down when he saw the carriage at some distance in front of him. He had calmed down and thought: "Was this meaningful coincidence, could there not be other families with a crest like this? And why do I chase after this carriage now? My aim is Manresa and I probably will meet the ladies again."

Rudolfo slowed down a bit more. He could see the carriage disappear around the next bend. The next moment he listened, shocked. A shot had rung out and another one. Were those shots aimed at the ladies? In less than one minute he reached the scene and saw for himself. Two hooded men had killed the horses and one of these men threatened the ladies to hand him their money and their jewellery or they would lose their lives. When they heard the loud noise of hoofs, one of the men lifted his rifle and aimed it at the galloping rider. Rudolfo's brain raced. He knew the rifles of the brigands had only one shot but he had heard two. That meant that the rifle was not loaded unless the brigands had loaded it again immediately. In any case he ignored the threat, swung his sabre and split the robber's head open. Then he drew a pistol and shot the other who had reloaded his rifle and had aimed it at him. Both shots rang out, almost simultaneously. All in less than two seconds. Both robbers were dead.

"So, they have their reward," said the young lieutenant with a polite bow to the ladies, "are you injured señoritas?"

He stood there, with his pistol still in his hand. Lady Margaret was quiet, but her face reddened. Rosetta, who had rallied faster, replied: "No, you come at the right time. Please accept our heartfelt thanks, señor. I am the Condesa de Manresa and this lady is a friend of mine, Margaret Castlepool."

"I am Lieutenant Lucien de Mareau, señoritas, and I would be happy if I could be of further service to you."

"It appears, unfortunately, that we have to depend on your further help. My coachman has disappeared and we have no horses."

Rudolfo laughed. "There's a man hiding at the other side of the coach. You can show your face again, it's all over," he called to the coachman.

A visibly embarrassed man appeared from the other side of the vehicle. "I was afraid the robbers might shoot me and I had no weapons to defend myself."

He went to the men to take of their hoods. The face of the man who was felled by the sabre was not recognisable but when he lifted the hood of the second bandit he called out. "*Santa Laureta,* this is one of the escaped prisoners. Do you recognise him, Dona Rosetta?"

"Indeed I do," said the Countess. "Punishment has caught up with him fast."

"My servant will stay here and report this assault to the authorities; he can follow with a hired coach after he has left his horse. Together with mine, we'll use it to get you home. Your coachman could, perhaps, stay as well," ventured the lieutenant.

"Your suggestion is probably the best, señor Teniente," said Rosetta and asked her coachman to help remove the dead horses and harness those offered by Lucien to the carriage.

A short time later the coach was ready to go. Lucien swung himself onto the coachman's seat and the carriage rolled towards Manresa. Rosetta thought of who were the instigators of this assault, whereas Margaret's eyes were constantly on the young man in front of her. So they went on quietly, only interrupted now and again by Rosetta, giving the direction, until they reached the palace gates. A tall gaunt man looked wonderingly at the Count's carriage with strange horses and a strange coachman.

"Who is that man?" asked Margaret.

"That is Pablo Carujo, our major-domo," explained Rosetta.

Lucien remembered that name from the beggar. Carujo was the man on whose orders he had been exchanged. It was as if all his dreams had their roots in that magnificent building in front of him. He jumped off the coach with a feeling that his life from now on would take a different turn.

The eyes of the notary rested on the young man, darkly astonished. "Who is that?" he mumbled, "who is this fellow? What a similarity. That is Count Miguel as he looked 20 or 30 years ago. Is that coincidence or is it something else?"

By now the ladies had also alighted. Carujo bowed with a friendly smile towards the ladies. "May I please ask, Condesa, for you to introduce me to the lady and the gentleman?"

There was visible reassurance on Carujo's face when he heard the name Lucien de Moreau. This officer was French. The similarity must be coincidence. The arrival of the carriage had now been observed in the palace. Dr. Stenton, Aurelio and señora Rita came out to greet the guests. Aurelio wanted to know the cause why these strange horses were in front of the carriage?

"Señor de Moreau was so kind as to lend me his when ours were shot dead."

"Shot dead?" asked the advocate, "by whom?"

"By two of the men who escaped from us yesterday! Rosetta told the whole story and how the lieutenant had saved them. The young officer received everybody's thanks; even Carujo offered him his hand.

The latter told those present that the examining judge of the committee of enquiry was with the Count. These señores only wanted to speak to Condesa Rosetta to complete their enquiry. They went to the Count who welcomed Rosetta's friend and thanked the lieutenant warmly for the rescue of the ladies.

"Oh please," said the young man with a dismissive gesture, "if I saved something, then it was only the purse, not the life of the ladies."

"No, it is really our life that we have to thank you for. Be our guest; we can't let you leave Manresa so soon."

"I did my duty to bring you back to Manresa; I don't wish to misuse your kindness."

"It is no misuse," said the Count quickly. You will oblige us to even greater gratitude if you accept our invitation. You must take a rest from your travels. Rosetta will immediately show you to your rooms."

It was Dr. Stenton who asked those present for a moment's attention as he wished to make an announcement: "Tomorrow morning," he started, "about eighteen hours from now, I shall take off the Count's bandages and with God's help his eyes will see again." Rosetta uttered a cry of delight, the Count said: "With God's help;"

Aurelio and Carujo said nothing. A servant took the visitors to their respective rooms.

There was a meeting in Rita's room. Rita, Carujo and Aurelio discussed the imminent and final operation on Count Miguel's eyes. "We are in great danger," said Carujo, "there is no time to stop this Dr. Stenton, but I have new plans to do away with all our adversaries finally."

"I hope to God, you're right" said a sanctimonious Rita, "we have planned for so many years and were it not for this devil, Doctor Stenton, we would be in possession of the palace of Manresa now and our Aurelio would own it all."

"Don't worry, it won't take very long now," Carujo comforted his family. ---

The Count had been freed from his stone some time ago and felt well enough for his next surgery. Dr. Stenton was now ready for the final stage of the eye operation. He arranged for Rosetta, the lieutenant and Lady Margaret to sit opposite the Count. Aurelio stood near the window and Carujo next to the door. There was great expectation in the room, although the feelings of the participants were different. Doctor Stenton went to the Count and slowly removed the bandages. The room was kept in semi darkness so as not to hurt the Count's eyes during those first moments. The Count turned towards his visitors with eyes still closed until Dr. Stenton told him:"Your Highness, you can open your eyes now."

A breathless moment then Count Miguel almost shouted: "I can see you." He steered towards the lieutenant with open arms, "come and rejoice with me my son … "

"Stop Father, you are making a mistake, I am your son, "called Aurelio from the window. The Count dropped his arms. Visibly confused, he sat down again.

Again there was an urgent meeting of the three conspirators. "The Count was going to embrace the lieutenant – he called him my son," said an angry Aurelio, "I think this Dr. Stenton had placed him on purpose in front of the Count, I shouldn't be surprised if he knows or suspects the truth. It is high time we disposed of all our enemies."

"I've received a message from my friend and business partner Ramirez Danlola. He wants to meet me in Barcelona. He's the best person to help." An hour later Carujo was on his way to meet the pirate and business partner Ramirez Danlola. They greeted each other like old friends.

"My last trip brought us 60,000 Duros profit. Will you take your share or do you want to leave it in the business?" asked Danlola.

"I'll leave it in the business but I have another request." Carujo answered. "How much will you charge for letting a man disappear?"

"That depends who he is and how difficult it is to get him on to my ship."

"The man is a French officer; he is staying at the moment in the palace of Manresa. He's in a room to which I can lead you at midnight, without anybody seeing you."

"A little poison would help," suggested the pirate. "Would it be possible for you to put a few drops into his drink?"

"I hate poison, it's unreliable and treacherous," answered Carujo.

"Unreliable and treacherous?" laughed Danlola, "I have the stuff where two drops makes a person insane, five drops would kill him. The antidote to this poison is only known to some Asian peoples."

"Can you let me have a few drops?" asked Carujo.

"For one hundred duros I can let you have ten drops – and that's cheap." Danlola offered to his partner in crime.

Carujo gave him one hundred duros and Danlola Counted ten drops into a small bottle.

Danlola thought for a minute and then suggested five hundred duros would be a fair price for collecting the French officer. Carujo agreed and asked his partner in crime to write this amount over to his own account as well. At midnight he led two men to Lucien de Moreau's room. They knocked him unconscious, bundled him into a carpet and left the palace into a nearby waiting conveyance where they drove all night. Once on board the ship he was put into a secure cell and the carpet was removed from him.

"Where am I and what do you want?" he asked the two heavily armed men. Lucien received no answer. The door was locked and a bolt outside kept him imprisoned.---

Carujo rode home with a bottle of poison in his pocket and new plans on his mind. As he entered the vast grounds of the Count of Manresa's estate , he saw groups of Gypsies around several fires. He approached the one burning in front of the biggest tent. A middle aged woman arose. "Señor Carujo, I haven't seen you for a long time, do you bring us any business?" she asked bluntly.

"Yes and no. It depends whether you can handle it," was Carujo's answer.

"There isn't much we can't handle. We have the right man for every request you could make," boasted the queen of the Gypsies.

"Can you collect an insane man and throw him into an abyss?"

"Who is this man and where do we collect? I have to know before we can negotiate a price."

"The man is a Count and you have to collect him from his bedroom in the palace. If you call at midnight it might not be very difficult, especially as I will lead you into the side entrance of the palace."

"A Count will put up the price but we'll do it for two thousand duros – no less," emphasised the queen. "I will personally collect the money at the little park house after we've completed the job – and you'd better be there," the Gypsy queen stressed the last part of her sentence.

"All right," said Carujo "It will happen tomorrow night or a day later." With this he turned his horse and made his way home. ---

Chapter 7

FURTHER ATTACKS

$\mathcal{J}$T was a sunny morning in the beautiful park belonging to the Duke Enrico de Zaragoza but open to the public, Princess Elena liked to sit on the bench at the pond, feeding the ducks and swans, which seemed to know her. Today there was a young man sitting there who, twice before, when he saw her drawing near, had vacated the place for her. "You don't have to leave because of me. There's plenty of room on the bench and the park is for everybody to enjoy."

He thanked her and stayed. He watched her as she fed the birds. There was no conversation for twenty minutes. Then she turned towards him and said: "You're not from here. I could hear that from the few words you were saying"

"You're right," he answered, "I'm from England, and I'm here on vacation for only a few weeks."

She was strangely drawn to this young man, more than she'd ever been to anyone. She asked: "Why do you always come alone? Have you no family?"

"I have only a father who has rejected me," answered the young man sadly.

"Your father rejected you? That sounds terrible. There must be a special reason. You don't look like a person who would offend anyone."

"My father is a Colonel, now retired, who wanted me to pursue a military career. For a time I did as I was told. But it was against my nature, and I felt that I had other talents. Then, one day, I left the army. When my father heard about that he asked me to leave his house and never enter it again."

"How terrible, how sad. Did you pursue your other talents?"

"Yes, and I was successful with it. My paintings were exhibited in famous galleries and my clients were people of high standing. If you wish, I'll bring you a few of my paintings when I meet you here again."

"I'd like to see some of your work. Bring it here tomorrow." Princess Elena nodded and withdrew to look after an ailing father. The Duke had not felt well for some months now, and his doctors did not give him much hope. The foibles of his younger years were a memory. He looked thinner by the day.

"I shall not live very long; I feel my life draining away because no physician gives me hope. My only wish is for you to find the right mate for life, but you've rejected all your suitors."

Elena went to her father and put her arms around him. "Let's not despair; God will not take you from me at your age. He will send you help at the right time."

"God bless you, my child, but if He does not send me help soon I'm afraid it might be too late."

The next day the young artist brought some of his paintings to show to Elena. She looked at them with astonishment. "You are indeed a great artist; I am particularly drawn to the face of the man who looked like my father twenty or thirty years ago and whose name you have put at the bottom. It cannot be your name as is usual with artists."

"Oh, I forgot to mention yesterday that beside my father I have a very close friend and cousin, a schoolmate who is now very busy because he has reached some fame in his profession. He has been called recently to Manresa and has freed the Count Miguel de Manresa from a large stone inside his body. He also operated successfully on his eyes and restored his sight. He is a man of exceptional talents."

"Manresa? That's not very far from here and the daughter of the Count is a close friend of mine. My very ill father comes to my mind. Maybe your friend could help."

"I could send a telegram to him. He will, if he can, follow my plea for help." answered the young artist. "His name is Charles Stenton. I have not introduced myself. My name is Maximilian Masterson; friends call me Max."

"I am Elena; will you allow me to call you Max?"

Max felt a strange sensation when he heard his name from her lips. "Señorita Elena, you could offer me no greater pleasure than to call me by my first name. Let me hurry to send a telegram and hope my friend will be able to help your father."

"Yes, hurry. There's no time to waste ."

Max left after they'd arranged to meet the next day. Princess Elena looked forward to meeting the young artist again. He was eager to send the telegram and perhaps help the girl of his dream.

They met the next day. She was feeding the ducks and swans; he was looking at her angelic face. "I received a telegram from my friend," he began the conversation. "He let me know he's coming as soon as possible, maybe this afternoon."

"What did you write to make him come so soon?" she inquired.

"I told him the father of a girl that I very much admire needs his help," was his reply.

She blushed and was obviously pleased with his answer. The weather suddenly changed and raindrops started to fall. A thunderstorm seemed to follow a very hot week. They took shelter in a small park house that was only fifteen meters away. Lightning was followed by a mighty thunder in short succession. She was frightened and a maiden's instinct made her lean against him. He put his arm around her reassuringly. "What makes you admire me?" Elena wanted to know, I feel a way I've never felt before," he said, pressing his arm tighter around her.

She let it happen and confessed that she too felt something she'd never felt before. He was encouraged. Seeing her face so close to his, he pressed his lips on hers. She responded and asked him whether he would visit her ailing father one day.

"I accept with thanks but for the moment I am concerned not to miss Dr. Stenton. He'll will come to my hotel and, if it's convenient, he will see you this evening. That brings me to the question, where do you live?"

She pointed at the palace but as it could only be seen between the trees, he couldn't recognise it as an extraordinary building. He nodded and returned to his hotel.

Late in the afternoon Charles Stenton reached the hotel and greeted his friend. "It seems to me that it's not only for medical reasons you called me. There's more. Have you lost your heart old chap?" Max admitted that he was, for the first time in his life, in love. He took Dr. Stenton to the bench where he used to meet Elena, pointed at the house between the trees and asked his friend to go there alone and ask for señorita Elena. Stenton went and saw to his astonishment that this house turned out to be a palace. A servant in livery opened the large gate and asked whom he wished to see.

"I'm a doctor and wish to visit the patient, I'm asking to see señorita Elena."

"Princess Elena is expecting you. Would you please follow me." Dr. Stenton had a shock when he realised his friend was unaware of his beloved's title.

Princess Elena greeted the doctor with visible joy. "I've heard so much about you that I see my last hope for my father in your visit."

"That's very flattering and I hope I will not have to disappoint you." He followed her to her father's bedroom. The Duke gave the impression of a dying man. Dr.Stenton introduced himself. The Duke looked at him with astonishment. The similarity of this man to himself in his younger years was striking.

"You've been highly recommended but after the verdicts of my doctors, I fear that help is – doubtful."

Stenton did some preliminary examination. Then he said: "It seems to me that you have had some other illness in your younger years, such as scabies for instance. This has not been properly treated and bit by bit infected inner organs. Luckily, I have in my possession the right medicine; ten drops twice a day should make an improvement. I also recommend a change of air."

"What are you saying doctor? This illness is not fatal and my death is not imminent?" the Duke asked breathlessly.

"Who told you such a thing? Yes, if this illness of yours goes on untreated, the worst could happen, but your Highness's daughter and my friend have called me at the right time and you should be your old self in a few weeks."

Princess Elena waited in the next room when her father was examined. Stenton called her to her father's bedside. She was anxiously awaiting the doctor's verdict. When she learned that her father was not to die, she threw herself with a shout of joy into her father's arms. "I knew it; God would not take you from me so soon." Then she turned to Stenton. "There are no words to express my thanks … "

Dr. Stenton waved his hand, "let us pray and thank God for summoning me here at the right time. If your father takes the drops regularly and you manage to go on vacation for a few weeks, your father will be well in a short period."

"Where would you advise us to go?" intervened the Duke.

Stenton thought for a minute then suggested: "maybe your Highness would go to a friend and relation of mine? I could give you a letter to reserve you a place of peace and quiet. The place is Bradford on Avon and this relation is the forester in the area. My mother, who is a widow, is his housekeeper." "If for no other reason, I would like to get to know your mother. Would you be so kind as to write the letter but please do me a favour and let me go there with the name Baron Embarez. Oh, you may not know your patient: I am the Duke Enrico de Zaragoza."

"Although I do not understand your reasons, Your Highness, I shall write the letter with the name you wish to assume." Stenton sat down and wrote to his relations. He wrote two letters, one addressed to Colonel Masterson and one to his mother, Mrs. Stenton. "And now," he said, "I have to return to my other patient, whom I would not be leaving, were it not for the call of my friend Maximilian Masterson. I shall take a few hours rest and then return to Manresa."

"We are, of course, very beholden to your friend whom we wish to see as soon as possible. My daughter has already invited him to call on us and I would kindly ask you to add my invitation to hers. Now allow me to write you a note for saving my life; my banker will hand you this sum." When Stenton saw the amount he refused to take the note but when the Duke said that it might help his people at home, he accepted.

When Stenton had left, Elena turned to her father and remarked about the uncanny resemblance of the doctor with the portrait in the dining room. "I feel that life is already returning after his visit and I admit that I was attracted to this man the moment I saw him."

Stenton told his friend a surprise was waiting for him, but he did not disclose what it could be. Then he went to his room to take a few hours rest. He had no presentiment of what awaited him in the palace of Manresa.

Maximilian was already nervous before being told of the surprise that awaited him, and it was almost morning before he fell asleep. He put on his best suit and was in time for the midday meal. His first surprise was when he saw the palace. When he saw a servant in livery opening the gate he was astounded and were it not for the girl he loved, he would have left the place immediately. He was, however, soon put at ease by the joyous face of Elena who appeared in a plain white dress. "My friend," she said, "we can't thank you enough. My father feels like a new person, and I'm so glad you can visit him to receive his thanks personally. Let me take you to the dining room."

As he entered the room he saw a dazzling splendour. Elena showed him his place and asked him to sit down. He was not sure if he was dreaming. As he sat down he noticed the plates and the silver utensils showing a crown. He found his first words to her: "Why didn't you tell me?"

She laughed, "I didn't think that it is important. Besides I want you to feel at home: my father will be here in a minute."

"Won't it be too strenuous for him? After what you have told me, about him being a patient constantly in bed?"

"Not after Dr. Stenton's assurance that he would live and, of course, after taking the medicine that he has been given. But here comes my father."

Maximilian rose from his chair. He had no idea how to address the man but was soon put at ease by the friendly smile and outstretched hand. "You are Maximilian Masterson. My daughter told me and I have to thank you for introducing Dr. Stenton who saved my life."

Maximilian realized that he stood before a nobleman. "Your Highness, from what I have heard from your daughter, I have no greater pleasure than seeing you able to leave your bed; the fact that I played a minor role in this is of no consequence."

"Without you I would be a dying man. Now let us sit down and enjoy the meal."

Everything seemed so natural that young Maximilian soon overcame his shyness and was engaged in a lively conversation with the Duke;

until Elena reminded the men that she was also at the table. "Father, have you mentioned that we might be going to England?"

"No, perhaps you will tell señor Maximilian; maybe he will accept an invitation to join us. Señor," he turned to his guest, "will you please read this letter from Dr. Stenton to his mother and uncle in Bradford on Avon?"

When Max heard the familiar name, his interest was aroused. When he saw the name of the addressee his face changed into a grimace. "This is my father!" he almost shouted. "It will be impossible for me to join you."

"I have not told you, father, that our friend has been forbidden to enter his father's house because he did not want the military career as his father would have wanted for him."

"Tell me more, señor Maximilian. What were your other plans?" the Duke was obviously interested.

"That brings me to a little present I have for your Highness." Max produced a picture of Princess Elena that made the Duke gasp.

"I've never seen a portrait of such likeness before. It seems impossible. "Young man," he said excitedly, "you have a talent greater than I have ever seen. When I've recovered, I hope I can engage you to paint a portrait of myself. I understand why you declined a military career to dedicate yourself to your art. Have you a picture of your father? I'm asking with a plan in mind; provided, of course, that you want to be reunited."

"It's one of my greatest wishes that my father accepts me as I am, Your Highness."

"Well, you have a reason to join us. I shall do all I can to arrange a reunion. Tell me señor Maximilian: do you know something about Dr. Stenton's family?"

"Only that he has a mother who is the housekeeper of my father, Colonel Masterson and a sister."

"Is that all?" enquired the Duke, "I'm sure that as a friend and relation you know more."

"Well what can I tell you. Her maiden name is Hudson and she worked before her marriage for a Spanish aristocrat."

The Duke grew pale and jumped to his feet; Elena, shocked, asked him if he felt unwell.

Enrico de Zaragoza remembered his years as a lady's man but did not reveal the fact that Dr. Stenton, by all his reckoning, could be his longed for son. He rallied fast, sat down and continued the conversation as if nothing had happened.

"I accept your invitation with pleasure," said Maximilian, "may I bid you good bye now and may I, Princess Elena, have the pleasure of joining you tomorrow when you are feeding the ducks again?"

"I am looking forward to that, but please, just call me Elena." She accompanied him to the door and he thanked her for a lovely meal. "We're in your debt and shall remain so forever. There is no reward large enough for what you've done for us."

"My reward will be to see you again tomorrow," he said gallantly and with this he was on his way.

The Duke summoned his daughter and began with the question. "Elena my darling, what would you say if I told you that you are not my only heir? I think that I have a son."

"Father, what brought that up? I'd be delighted to have a brother," she replied.

"You're still the heiress of your mother's millions, but the title might be lost to you."

"I still say that I would be pleased for you, and to have a brother. Besides it's on the cards I might marry a commoner. Can you tell me who this son or brother could be?" she asked.

"Dr. Stenton!"

"I could see the similarity of face and of size but is that enough proof?" she questioned.

"No, I've other reasons to assume I am right but let me go to bed. I am in need of some rest now." ---

When Carujo returned home, he learned that Dr. Stenton had received a telegram and had left Manresa but had let it be known that it was only for a short time. That evening he managed to put two drops of Danlola's poison into the cup of milk that was presented to Count Miguel every night. Porido, a loyal servant for many years came to the Count to clear the table of the cup and other utensils, he noticed strange behaviour in his beloved master. He called on Rosetta who sat in the next room with Lady Margaret. Rosetta hurried to her father and saw him cringing when she approached him. "I mean no harm, I am the loyal Porido." The Count said in constant repetition.

"No, father, you are Count Miguel de Manresa y Cordoba, not our servant Porido," said Rosetta in despair.

"I mean no harm, I am the loyal Porido," was the Count's answer.

"Oh God, if only Dr. Stenton could be here! My father is out of his mind!" she almost shouted.

Carujo, who had been told by Porido about the Count's condition, made his way to the patient's bedroom. With Porido's help he put the weak Count into bed. All the while the Count whimpered the same words: "I mean no harm, I am the loyal Porido."

He wanted to call the local doctor but Rosetta insisted on waiting for Dr. Stenton's return. It was next day when Stenton rode into the gates of the palace. He was greeted by a despairing Rosetta and told of the Count's condition. Stenton told a servant to look after his horse and hurried to the Count. He was greeted by the same words: "I mean no harm, I am the loyal Porido."

"Induced insanity," was Stenton's verdict, "I have to find out which poison has been administered before I decide on a cure."

Anxiously Rosetta asked how serious it was, could it be cured? Was it deadly?

"It is not deadly but I cannot tell you much more until I have made a thorough examination. I have to do some bloodletting. Please ask the servants to catch a few flies."

Rosetta did not understand this request, but ordered two servants to do so. Stenton took the maximum of blood the Count's condition allowed. He put the flies into a glass containing some of the blood. He then asked the ladies to observe the flies. One could see them nibbling the blood. They started to tremble, then they died.

"It's a rare poison inducing that kind of insanity. It's called Pohon Upas. Fortunately I know about it and the antidote but it's hard to find the necessary ingredients. We can't use the antidote I learned in Java."

"What do you mean by that?"

"The magicians and medicine men of Java maintain that the antidote can only be obtained from the saliva of a man who has been tickled until he foams."

"And you believe that?" interjected Lady Margaret. "Should such a pain inducing process really produce a counter poison?"

"Who can say whether that is true? This gruesome process is forbidden in Europe, although the rascal who administered the poison would deserve it. It's entirely possible that such a process would produce an antidote. We need only think of rabies transferred to humans if they are bitten by a dog. Also the infamous Aqua Tofana of the Borgias is reckoned by some to come from the same source."

"All right but what are you proposing to do?"

"For me, the main thing is I have recognised the poison Pohon Upas. This contains mainly alkaloids, strychnine and brucin. Against these I have to fight. I think a carefully prepared mixture of coffee powder, tealeaves, katechu with capsicum, opium and iodine may be the answer. I have to stress that I can't treat the patient today or even tomorrow. First he has to recover from the severe bloodletting." ---

Meanwhile Carujo went to the gypsy camp and informed them that the deed, to collect the Count and throw him into the nearby abyss, should be performed that night. At midnight he met three men at the side entrance to the palace and showed them the Count's bedroom. He then withdrew to his own rooms. It was easy to chloroform the weak patient and load him onto the shoulders of the strongest of the three. Once they were well away with their burden, they began to talk. They all agreed that the Count had been good to them in the past. Instead, they decided they would throw into the abyss a person who had recently died. They went into the nearby cemetery and dug up a baker who had only been buried that day, dressed him in the Count's attire and threw him down the deep cliff.

The next morning Rosetta entered her father's bedroom. Her shock could not have been greater when she discovered that the Count was missing. She ordered the immediate search of the palace and its surroundings for his whereabouts. The news of the Count's disappearance spread fast. The search had not quite finished, when a Gypsy called on the palace and showed a bit of torn clothing he claimed that he had found on some thorns at the nearby gorge. Everybody ran to the ravine where they saw other clues of a person's fall into the abyss. There was blood on the protruding rocks.

Now Rosetta and her friend Margaret blamed themselves for letting this happen but Dr. Stenton said that the Count was much too weak to have left his room alone. The authorities were informed and made an appearance in a very short time. The previous house doctor of Manresa, Dr. Micelli, was also present. Carujo insisted that they should write out the death certificate for the Count. "We have to see the corpse first," said Stenton. The Gypsy said that he knew a way down and they all proceeded to descend the deep cliffs. Porido knew a quicker way and together with Stenton reached the spot where the others surrounded a smashed up corpse. Porido broke out in tears."Oh our dear Count," he cried. The corpse was unrecognisable. Dr. Micelli started to write out the death certificate, when Dr. Stenton intervened. "Stop señores, you're making a mistake; this corpse is not the Count." An angry Carujo pointed out: "We all recognise the Count's clothing. How can you still take such irresponsible attitude?"

"And I recognise the Count Miguel's ring," interjected Aurelio.

Stenton turned to Porido and asked him to fetch a pair of Count Miguel's shoes from the palace. "Here is a foot that is still completely recognisable. It is not my patient's foot, and the hair is of slightly different colour too. Please see this little indent in the ground where this stone comes from. The stone has been used to make the face unrecognisable. Now señores, follow me to the top."

Carujo protested and called the doctor's findings as pure fantasy. "Carry on, complete the death certificate of the Count and then let us take the corpse to the palace," he demanded.

"You will do no such thing. This corpse does not belong to the castle. It will stay here until you have disproved my reasons Then you can do what you want," Stenton insisted.

"Ah," said Carujo, "do you believe that you have a word in this? With what reason? And in what capacity?"

"Because I am the Count's phisician."

"No longer!"

"All right then, as a man who must be heard. In a case like this, the representatives of the law have the duty to listen to anyone who has to make a significant contribution."

"Agreed, señor, but your remarks don't seem significant. They sound ridiculous. Why should this corpse not belong to the palace?"

All eyes rested on Stenton. Carujo had spoken disparagingly and Dr. Micelli tried to put a scornful smile on his face. The young Count shook his head mockingly. The others were well disposed towards Dr. Stenton and waited tensely on his explanation.

He said quietly: "Because this is a stranger and not the Count."

While the others exclaimed in astonishment, Stenton's opponents burst into taunting laughter. "Ah, this is precious," said Carujo. "This corpse is not Don Miguel's. I think the doctor suffers the same illness that killed our master. Take the corpse and let's go."

"Stop," Countered Stenton. "This corpse stays until what I have to say is written down. Then you can do what you like."

"We don't need your reasons. Let's get on with it, and remove the body."

"Pardon me, señor," ordered the official, "I am the law here and I know that this señor must receive attention. This corpse should not be removed until the Corregidor is present. Just as it was with the robber whom señor Stenton had killed. But I thought that one could make an exception here because this seemed to be a straightforward accident and because this corpse was recognised as the Count's. As the situation is different now, no-one but I can make a decision, speak up señor Stenton."

Stenton nodded with satisfaction and he started: "I ask you, how long is it that Don Miguel has been missing?"

"Since yesterday morning," replied the official.

"How long has this corpse been dead?"

"Not much longer than a day."

"Please look at the corpse. The decay shows that this man had died at least four days ago. There is no need to be a physician. It is very cold down here where no ray of the sun ever penetrates and it would take at least fourteen days for a corps here to be in such condition ... "

"Stop," the major-domo broke into Stenton's speech, "I demand that this person be silenced."

"Señor Carujo, I shall listen to what this man has to say and then I shall make up my own mind." He turned to Stenton and asked him to carry on.

"What about the Count's attire?" intervened the major-domo.

"They have been put on him to make it look as if the corpse was the Count and that also goes for the ring," Countered Stenton.

"Ah, you suspect a crime?"

"Certainly, look at this man's foot, I have been the physician of the Count and I can assure you that the Count had no such calluses on either of his feet; also you can see that this foot is too large to fit the Count's shoes which señor Porido has brought us."

"Really, this seems to be true," called the amazed court official.

"Impossible, it's all fantasy," ventured Aurelio

"Follow me to the top señores," Stenton invited all at the bottom of this ravine. "I'll show you further proof." He climbed uphill, the others followed automatically.

He turned to the gypsy and asked: "Now show us the bushes or thorns where you found the piece of cloth you brought us."

The gypsy paled and looked around. No bushes or thorns could be seen where the corpse had fallen or been thrown down. "Look here, señores," continued Stenton, "the grass here shows the shape of a person lying down and it's surrounded by traces of men's shoes. I would say three men were involved. The corpse was lying here and then thrown into the gorge. It happened last night. You can see it by the partly erected grass."

"What observation," said the official.

"Damned fellow," mumbled Carujo.

Stenton turned to the official and said: "Now let's see whether you also can deduce. Can you guess through whom we can find out who was here last night?"

The man questioned thought for a while, then answered in the negative.

"So I will tell you." He stepped to the gypsy and said: "This is the one." He took the man by the arm and said: "Come with me. He found the corpse and will give us the information." With this he led the man to where the tracks could be found. He pointed to a footprint in the clay, then pointed to the man's sandals where one could still see traces of this clay.

"Indeed," said the official.

"And his foot fits exactly into this track?"

"That also is true. Now, guano, speak up if you can say anything in your defence."

Quickly composed, the gypsy answered: "Yes, I have been here with two other men. We were looking for herbs; the impression in the ground is from me."

"Ah, you are clever. And you found the piece of cloth on the thorns?"

"Yes," answered the gypsy, embarrassed.

"Please show us these thorns," insisted Stenton.

The man pretended to look round. "I cant' find them."

"I expect that, when a piece of cloth is torn by thorns, it is torn to pieces. This piece of cloth has a clean edge and has been torn by hand."

"That's true," confirmed the official.

"I therefore declare that we have not found the corpse of the Count Miguel in the abyss, and that a crime has been committed. Will you take this down? I ask that the traces remain untouched and the corpse stays where it is until the Corregidor comes to examine this case. This Gitano should be arrested."

The official agreed. Aurelio stepped forward; he had been told by Carujo of the danger to their plans if the gypsy were be questioned. "I will not tolerate a stranger interfering in this matter. I am the Count de Manresa, and after the death of my father I am in charge."

"You first have to prove that you are the Count's son. The real Count Aurelio has been kidnapped and is now at sea with Captain Danlola." Stenton only uttered an assumption but his words made a tremendous impression.

"Ah, listen to that," the surrounding people said to each other.

"Slanderer," Aurelio shouted and jumped at Stenton. "I'll strangle you."

Stenton grasped the swindler by the hips, stepped to the edge of the cliff and held him over the abyss. A cry of shock went around.

"You want to strangle me, little boy? Stenton laughed. "Should I throw you to the spot of your deceptions? No, it is no honour to claim victory over such an unworthy rogue. Suffocate in the mud of your wretchedness." With this he stepped back and pushed Aurelio away. He then turned to the official and said: "I trust that you will do your duty, otherwise it would be dangerous for you. Come on señor Porido, accompany me to the palace."

Aurelio stood up. He was extremely angry and roared at the official:" That was your fault entirely. I shall not forget you."

"I only did my duty," answered the court official, almost apologetically. He was the subject of the Count. He acted according to the law as long as he was under the influence of Stenton's personality. The doctor had gone and now he lost his courage against the young Count; especially as Carujo backed him up.

"Señor, tell me whether you know who I am?"

"The administrator of His Highness the Count."

"And what has an administrator to do?"

"You have to represent him in all matter-of-fact and legal matters."

"Very good but in no matter have I completed my mission. What I do is exactly as if the Count himself was doing it. Will you really arrest this innocent Gitano?"

The official found himself in difficulty and kept silent. Carujo turned towards the gypsy and said: "We don't need you anymore. You can go and I shall see if anyone tries to stop you."

The gitano's eyes lit up. He bowed to Carujo and said: "Thank you very much, I am really innocent." He went off without anybody daring too stop him.

To those men who carried the stretcher, Carujo ordered: You go down and bring the poor Count to the palace. If anyone refuses, he will be sacked." Nobody resisted.

They feared the strict Carujo too much. The Englishman's arguments were unsuccessful. The court official stayed silent and the group soon moved to the palace.

Carujo and Aurelio walked behind so that no one could hear them.

"Stenton will call the Corregidor," said Carujo's son.

"I shall not bend, besides the Corregidor is in my pocket"

"How can he say I am not the Count's son?"

"The devil's grandmother knows that answer. He is our biggest enemy now and we have to defeat him. I have just the plan. This morning I received post that will hang Stenton."

"How?"

"Stenton has paid a money order to the banker to be sent to his mother. You will ask how that can help us. Look at the amount.

Aurelio looked, he gasped. "That's a fortune but how will that help us?"

"I'll say the Count asked me to make out this money order for two thousand silver pieces and Stenton forged it to twenty-five-thousand."

"Ah, that might work."

"Ride immediately to Manresa to make a report about this to the police. The Corregidor will do the rest." ---

Stenton went immediately to Rosetta and told her that her father should still be alive and that the man in the ravine was a stranger. "We now need a man to observe the gypsies."

"I will send Dinrallo," said Rosetta, "he is loyal and clever."

A short time later she accompanied her friend Margaret to Pons.

Stenton went to Dinrallo and asked him whether he was prepared to follow the gypsies to find out what they have done with Count Miguel. Dinrallo agreed and received 50 duros for expenses.

A man came in the afternoon in a horse drawn carriage and asked for Dr. Stenton. When Stenton asked him, the man simply told him the Corregidor wished to speak to him. Stenton stepped into the carriage. When he asked why the driver went past Manresa he was told that they were going to Barcelona.

"Señor, who are you?"

"I am the Corregidor of Manresa and have to bring you to the Juez de lo criminalo. He wants to talk to you."

"What does he want to talk about?"

"I don't know, you'll find out."

"You have lied to me, señor."

"Only a little ruse to avoid lengthy explanations."

"And if I refuse to follow?"

"That wouldn't help you. Look through the back window, there are four policemen on horses following us and they carry loaded guns."

"That looks as if you're transporting a criminal."

"Oh no, that's only a matter of routine, you'll return today but as a foreigner I have to bring you in this company."

"I don't fear these fellows but my conscience is clear and I'll go with you."

"That's best, I'd be glad of your company on the way back."

They stopped before a building whose few front windows were barred with thick iron rods. "Let's go in here," said the official. Stenton noticed the four policemen following them into the building. They went through a gloomy floor and up a narrow spiral staircase.

"Wait here señor," said the Corregidor.

He left but came back shortly. "Enter here," he said harshly and pointed to one of the many doors. Behind Stenton he locked the door. Stenton now found himself in a room whose two windows were also barred. On three walls there were shelves and filing cabinets. Below one of the windows he saw a very large writing desk with a dried out little man sitting behind it. He took a sheet of paper and a pen and asked: "What is your name?"

"Charles Stenton."

"From?"

"Reading."

"Where is that?"

"In England."

"So you are an Englishman. What is your profession?"

"I am a physician. May I also ask you a question? Who are you and why am I here?"

"I am Juez de lo criminalo and the reason you are here, you will find out in the course of the interrogation."

"That sounds as if I am under investigation?"

"That doesn't only sound like it but it is so," replied the little man with a gloating look in his eyes. "Besides, don't think you're here to put questions to me, it is I who ask the questions. How old are you?"

"Thirty."

"Previously convicted?"

"No."

"Are you rich?"

"No."

"Really not?" asked the judge like someone who was lying in wait.

"No."

"How much cash do you have with you?"

"About thirty duros."

"Give it to me."

Stenton handed his purse to the judge who Counted the contents. The official then wrote down the exact sum as he did with all the answers Stenton gave him. "Where have you been last?"

"In the palace of the Count of Manresa where I was called to treat an illness."

"Did you assist in treating someone?"

"Yes."

"Did you have permission?"

"Who should have anything against that?"

"I," said the little man with pronounced emphasis. "Did you have official permission to do so?"

"No."

"Have you passed a Spanish examination or any tests?

"No."

"Have you paid any income tax in Spain?"

"No."

"Ah, the first crime has been proven during the first session, you are dismissed for now."

"You speak of a first session, will there be more?"

"Naturally, many more."

"And I? Where shall I stay in the meanwhile?"

"Where? Stupid question. With me, naturally. Second floor in cell number four."

"Should that mean that I am a prisoner?"

"Certainly," blinked the judge.

"What is the reason?" asked Stenton who was really aroused by now.

"You'll find out later."

"On whose report or accusation?"

"That too you will find out later."

"Señor, I have the right to demand an answer," Stenton flared up.

The little man beamed with pleasure. "You do have that right; I, on the other hand, have the right to refuse an answer."

"You have heard and written down that I am an Englishman. I ask to speak to the British Consul."

"Good. I shall see to it."

"At once, please."

"Good, all right." The official looked at his prisoner with undisguised pleasure.

He rang a bell and an guard entered the room. "This señor wants to speak to the British Consul," said the judge. "Lead him to the Consul, quickly."

The man smirked like a walrus and said: "Forward march."

Stenton turned to the judge. "May I have my purse please, señor?"

"You may ask, but you will not get it. Here nobody is allowed to carry a purse. We are not in a market, Go to your Consul."

It was clear, the man was making fun of Stenton. He was a prisoner, but that could not be for long. He followed, therefore, without further ado, one floor higher into a gloomy gangway and then into a room marked number four. The door was locked behind him. The cell was dark; it received its light from a tiny, barred window. It was six steps in length and four steps wide. Two small mattresses were spread on the floor, emitting a bad odour. One was empty; on the other was a human shape that rose from its lying position as the doctor entered.

"Ah, a new addition," a weak voice said. "Good evening."

"Good evening," answered Stenton.

"Why are you here?"

"I don't really know."

"Well, everybody says that, sit down on the mattress. What is your profession?"

"I'm a physician."

"Who interrogated you?"

"The Juez de lo criminalo."

"A damned fellow; do you know when you'll have the next interrogation?"

"Well?"

"In two or three months."

"That would be terrible."

"The guard brought in a double portion, so I gathered I would have company."

"What kind of meal is it?"

"Some plain bread and some unclean water."

"How long have you been here?"

"Nearly one year."

"With such meagre food?"

"Yes, this food will cost my life. I am deadly ill. I am so glad you are a doctor. You will be unable to help me, but you can tell me how long I still have to live. I hope to God that I'll soon be dying.

Stenton was convinced that the man in front of him was not a bad character. In the darkness he couldn't see the man's face. He felt sorry for this inmate and asked:

"How much time have you still to do?"

"Two years yet."

"May I ask why you got this punishment?"

"Why not? I've beaten a man up."

"Dead?"

"Unfortunately not, there would be one less rogue."

"What illness are you suffering from?"

"Now it's my spinal cord Before it was my longing for the open sea."

"Such contrast, the open sea and this devilish hole."

"Yes, señor, I have cried and sighed, I have raged and beaten my head against the wall but nothing helped. When I lost my strength, I became quite ill and daily more so until they bury me. I have to thank an advocate for all this."

"Then we are co-sufferers. I still don't know what I'm accused of but if I am not mistaken, there's also an advocate involved."

"Where were you before you came here?"

"In Manresa."

"Heavens, my troubles started there as well. I have to thank a Pablo Carujo for being and most likely dying here."

"Tell me more," Stenton asked.

"Not now, I am now too tired to speak." With this he turned around and closed his eyes. This man must be very weak. In spite of the joy of having company after a long solitude he could not continue the conversation. Stenton decided to overcome his nausea and ate the frugal meal provided. Then he stretched out on the mattress. The next morning with light coming from the window, Stenton could see his cellmate who sat upright. "When will the door be opened?" asked Stenton.

"Midday."

"Then one can tell the man what one wants?"

"You can tell or ask but you will not get a reply. No coaxing or force will help you."

"I'm a foreigner and a Consul will come for me."

"You will never see a Consul. Believe me; Carujo brought you here. The judge and Carujo are friends, and they are the biggest scoundrels on earth."

"You are frightening me."

"I'm speaking the truth. I was a strong man full of life and health. Look at me now. What am I? Those two rogues have done it." He leant against the wall. He was emaciated to a skeleton and Stenton had no need to examine him to know that he wouldn't live for many weeks. At midday a small opening in the door was opened and two dishes were put inside on a shelf. Stenton said to the guard if he would be so kind and … the opening was shut and Stenton didn't need to continue. In the evening they received plain bread and water. Two weeks passed with no changes. Stenton had lost his calm. How was it in Manresa? How was Rosetta? These questions were gnawing at him and he could neither eat nor sleep. Escaping was unthinkable. The guards didn't listen to questions, the walls were too thick and the window too high and too small.

A month passed. Sadness and melancholy took hold of the two wretches. "If I had this Carujo here and if I had my former fists, I would crash him," said Stenton's companion.

"Maybe he will get between mine."

"No hope that this will ever happen, although I would not begrudge it. You are a true Goliath who would easily take on twenty Niggers or Englishmen."

"How did you get to Negroes or Englishmen now?"

"You really want to know that, señor? You will think badly of me but I deserve it."

"You can tell me in confidence. Everybody makes mistakes."

"But not such mistakes. Do you know what I have been? At first a decent sailor but then a pirate."

"I'm amazed."

"Yes, it's true. I had decent parents and have been called a valiant sailor. I stayed that way until I went to another ship and into bad hands. I had no idea that the captain was a pirate and a dealer in slaves. Danlola was an American and a devil and he managed to make me a devil too. I have seen many a Nigger jump overboard out of desperation or homesickness. I had to hit some of the poor devils; but my punishment has come. You see me lying here." He went silent for a while to gather strength and continued. "The captain did business with Carujo. When we anchored in Barcelona, Carujo came on board. He seemed to have lots of money." continued the sick sailor.

After a pause he told of a prisoner who was brought on board in Vera Cruz. He was taken straight into the captain's cabin so that no one could see him."

"You also did not see him?"

"Oh yes. He had noble features and the captain once called him Manuel. The captain sold him to the sultan of Harare."

"That's terrible."

"Not any more terrible than when you sell a black. By the way, I could do nothing about it. When we returned to Barcelona I had to go to Carujo to report that this Mexican was seen to and sold to Harare. He'd wanted him dead and let go at me with reproaches. I answered as well as I could and he hit me. I returned it with a good sailor's fist. He sank to the ground like an empty sack and I left. The next day he came aboard and the matter seemed forgotten. Then I was given a letter to be delivered to the Juez de lo criminalo. He received me in a friendly way and then handed me to the guard who locked me into this cell where I am today. This, señor, is my fate."

He became silent and lay down. Stenton had no presentiment that this story was connected with the plan of the Carujo brothers. ---

Chapter 8

BRADFORD ON AVON

IN the rustic surrounding, two miles from Bradford on Avon, surrounded by woodland, stands the large Estate of the Forrester Colonel Terence Masterson. The man himself could be described as "grumpy but fair and good-hearted." His staff occupied a nearby smaller building. Mrs. Stenton, whose husband died years ago, took up the invitation of her relative to be his general housekeeper. There was a Mrs. Brooks who did the cooking for them all. Whereas Mrs Stenton had a daughter, Mrs. Brooks had an eight-year-old son, the darling of them all. Eric Freeman was serving under the colonel before his retirement and stayed on to be his valet. Although the colonel's whims affected all his staff, the main recipient of his moods was Eric. The colonel suffered from gout in both legs, which made him even more unbearable but also worthy of pity.

Mrs. Brooks met Mrs. Stenton. "Still no news from your son? she asked.

"No, I'm getting worried. I'm not used to such a long silence from him. The last time he wrote he told me of a conspiracy surrounding his patient the Count of Manresa."

"Letters sometimes are delayed. I received one today from my husband dated two and a half months ago. But he is sailing to Brasil in south America that is, of course, much further than Spain. He hopes to be home for Christmas."

Robert Brooks, her young son, appeared at the door. He was dressed in a green hunting outfit and he shouldered a small rifle given to him by the colonel for Christmas. "I'm going with Eric to hunt the fox. It's been stealing our chickens lately."

"All right, Robbie," said his mother, "take great care with your gun."

"Don't worry Mum, Uncle Masterson has taught me how to handle it. He said I have no more to learn now." He went across the yard and joined Eric and four dogs for the hunt.

They went through the wood for ten minutes when the dogs started chasing an animal who disappeared into a hole under a tree. "A foxhole," said Eric, while the dogs scraped the soil surrounding the hole. The fox may have two entries to his lair, thought young Robbie and watched out for the possibility. No sooner had this thought occurred to him the fox came out of a second hole. Two shots were heard almost simultaneously. Eric's shot had hit Woodlana, the colonel's favourite dog. Robbie's shot, however, killed the fox. Eric, said: "How can I tell this to the colonel? He'll probably dismiss me. Let's pick up the animal and go back."

As he wanted to pick up the fox, Robbie protested. "I've shot it and I'll carry it home. You can bury Woodlana in the meantime." He shouldered the dead fox and went his way.

Robbie put the fox into the stables and went to the colonel. He knocked at the door and after he heard a grumpy "come in," entered the room and stood erect as a soldier before the colonel. "What's up," said the old man laying down the papers he was holding. "I want to report that we've got it," said Robbie confidently.

"You've got what?" the old man inquired further.

"The fox."

"And you want me to believe you shot it?"

"Ask Eric, he was with me. I've put the fox in the stables."

"I think I've become proud of you. Tell me a wish and I'll grant it – if possible, he added."

"I have a wish, Uncle Masterson, don't be too harsh with Eric when he comes home."

"Why should I be harsh with him? That he didn't get the fox but an eight year old did is enough for him."

"So I have your word?" little Robbie made sure.

"Of course. I've given you my word, haven't I?"

"Yes, uncle you did. May I go now?"

"Yes, and tell your mother I don't want any chicken today."

Robbie had hardly gone when another knock elicited another grumpy "come in."

This time Eric entered and stood erect, as did Robbie before him. "Colonel I have to report … "

"No need," interrupted the colonel his former sergeant. "Robbie's done it already: this rascal made me promise not to treat you harshly and I told him you must feel ashamed that the youngster shot the fox."

"He's told you no more?"

"No, is there any more?"

"Yes," Eric's voice trembled slightly. I also shot, but unfortunately, I killed another animal."

"Why unfortunately?" went the questioning.

"It was, it hit, it killed …."

"What was, what hit, what killed – come out with it," stormed Masterson already annoyed by Eric's slow reporting.

"It was – I hit, I beg the colonel's pardon – Woodlana."

The colonel raged and shouted at the unfortunate Eric, when the door opened. Robbie, who had expected this scene, put in his head and called out, "Uncle, you promised."

The colonel turned towards the door. "Away, you rascal, away with both of you. And you can thank this little boy for not being dismissed. Now, get out of here – both of you."

Eric left the colonel. In the hallway he spoke to Robbie. "You've put a word in for me; you're the only one he would listen too. How can I thank you?"

"By not mentioning it any more, by taking me with you when you go hunting again and by not shooting another dog."

"You're a man, I'm proud of you. You can make me even more proud if you let me be your friend,"

"I thought we were friends already. Ah, here comes the postman, I hope he brings news from Uncle Stenton. I know his mother is worried."

Robbie took a letter from the postman. "It's from Uncle Stenton to Uncle Masterson," he exclaimed and ran back to the colonel's room.

He forgot to knock and entered breathlessly. "A letter," he shouted. "A letter from Uncle Stenton." The colonel wanted to flare up against the youngster for not knocking before entering his room but changed his mind after he heard a letter from one of his favourite relatives had arrived. He opened it and found one letter addressed to him and another to Stenton's mother. He read his letter first before handing the other to the boy.

"Tell Mrs. Stenton to let me know the news." His letter was a recommendation and by asking him to do Stenton a favour in giving a patient and his daughter, lodging for a few weeks. The patient being a Baron was enough for the colonel to write back his agreement.

Mrs. Stenton's letter was written before her son's imprisonment, repeating his story about the conspiracy around Count Miguel, the successful operations and about his falling in love with Rosetta, the Count's daughter. About his well-being but not about the attack on him. Mrs. Stenton was happy to have news after such a long time. ---

When Rosetta returned, her first request was to see Dr. Stenton. Nobody knew or pretended to know anything about his whereabouts. She only knew from Porido that he was collected by the Corregidor of Manresa whom Porido had seen before. Rosetta went to see this man and was told that he had to deliver Stenton to the Juez de lo criminalo in Barcelona. He had no further news. Rosetta decided that she would visit this Juez de lo criminalo the next day. Aurelio heard when she ordered Porido to prepare her coach for early next morning and asked him to accompany her to the Juez de lo criminalo. He immediately told his father, Carujo, of these plans, as they could interfere with their own intentions. Carujo managed to put two drops of poison into Rosetta's evening cup of chocolate. The next morning Rosetta's maid found her kneeling in prayer and not reacting to anything the maid said. Doctor Cielli was called and confirmed it was the same illness the Count had suffered from before his death. Carujo and Aurelio had her taken into a suitable institute where they would be looking after her.

Porido said to his wife Maria, Count Miguel's cook. "Maria," he said, "we have been here for twenty-five years. Count Miguel was kind to us, so was his daughter. I don't like it here anymore and I think we should retire. I have a brother we could live with and we've saved five thousand duros. Enough for retirement. Besides, we could possibly find employment elsewhere. Maria agreed and Porido told Aurelio they would like to retire now. Aurelio was secretly pleased to be rid of the pair he knew were loyal to the Count.

The three conspirators sat together. "We have finally won the big game," said the former Rita Moreno, now Rita Carujo. "Our son is now the official Count of Manresa with two palaces and no more worries."

"Unless Dr. Stenton manages to escape," Aurelio reminded the pair.

"No chance, I've put other people into that prison and so far no one has managed to escape. Stenton will die there and will regret ever coming to Manresa," answered Carujo. ---

Dinrallo, whom Stenton had asked to follow the Gypsies visited Porido and his wife in their new abode. He was also looking for Dr. Stenton: he had news for him. Porido told him all he knew and that the condesa Rosetta asked to be driven to Barcelona to see the Juez de lo criminalo. He and his wife loved Stenton and would give their savings to bring him back. Dinrallo asked them for a loan of fifty duros and said he'd try to find out what had happened to Dr. Stenton. Porido gave him two hundred duros and wished him good luck. Dinrallo went to Barcelona in search of Dr. Stenton. ---

Time passed and winter approached. Stenton was still with his cellmate who by now was too weak to get up in the morning. Stenton asked the guard repeatedly for medical help without receiving an answer.

One day, to their surprise, the keys turned in the lock at an unusual time and the guard entered the room followed by a physician. The guard pointed at the door and said to Stenton: "forward march."

The other prisoner asked for Stenton to stay. "He is my only consolation," he pleaded.

The guard looked at the doctor, who nodded agreement. The guard left the cell and locked the door. The doctor sat on the rim of the mattress, then, unnoticed by anybody, he threw something onto Stenton's lap. Stenton felt the item. It was a large key, surely a key for the main gate. A feeling of great joy shot through his body but he managed to control himself because a glance at the doctor told him that they were being observed.

The doctor spoke a few comforting words to the sick prisoner, who felt that the end was near. A deep calm spread over his emaciated face. I have less than an hour to live, thank God. Stay with me, señor medico and let my friend stay too.

"We shall remain," assured the court doctor. He leant over the ill person and pushed something to Stenton in a way, that could not be seen from the door.

Stenton felt a full wallet. He hid it carefully and slowly on his person. He thought he saw the door slightly ajar. Obviously the guard had observed the sad group in their dim cell.

After a while the features of the dying man began to change. He passed Stenton his hand and said: "Farewell – I thank you – be free and happy." These were his last words. A convulsive jerking of the body, a quiet sighing sounded through the cell and it was over.

The court doctor moved away silently. Soon the keys were heard again and the guard stepped inside. When he saw the corps he said: "Away with him, pick him up."

"If you want me to," said Stenton sounding indifferent although his pulses hammered. Stenton put the corpse over his shoulders and followed the guard who slowly went forward. Their steps echoed in the dim building. The officials who worked there, were by now at home with their families. Their way led them over several stairs into a smaller yard. This one ran into a dark floor through which Stenton had come two months ago into this prison. The guard opened a door. "Mortuary – put corps on table," he commanded in his staccato way. Stenton put the corpse on the table. The keys were still hanging in the door lock. The guard stepped to the table to straighten the corpse then turned to Stenton. "Forward march," he commanded.

"No – backwards march," answered Stenton and his fist fell like lightning on to the guard's temple. The man sank immediately to the ground.

"Thank God, the old strength is still there," rejoiced the prisoner. He left the guard next to the lamp, locked the door, harried through the floor and reached the gate. He pulled out the key which had reached him so mysteriously: trembling with anxiety whether it would fit. It did. Stenton opened the gate and stood on the street. He was free. Both prisoners found their redemption that day, one by death and one by freedom.

In the distance he saw a man with two horses rushing in his direction. He recognised the court doctor and hurried towards him. "Get on that horse quickly and let's get away from here."

Stenton swung himself on the horse and took the road to Manresa. The court doctor was galloping next to him. Ten minutes passed before Stenton turned toward his companion. "We are far enough from any danger now. Let me first say that a simple thank you is not enough for what you have done, but tell me now: who are you?"

The court doctor took off his false beard and his wig. "Do you know me now?" asked a smiling Dinrallo, "I've lots of news for you – good as well as bad."

"Tell me both and start with the good news."

"The good news is quickly told. Count Miguel is alive and has been put in care of a lighthouse keeper."

"This is good news indeed Countess Rosetta will enjoy it too," said Stenton.

"I am afraid that is a part of my bad news. Condesa Rosetta will not be able to enjoy this news … " Stenton reined in his horse. "What happened?" he asked breathlessly.

"Dona Rosetta suffers from the same illness as her father but I know where she is accommodated now. Not as you might think, in a hospital, but an institution for people who can't look after themselves and have relations to pay for their keep."

A man of quick decision, Stenton suggested going at once to the institution but Dinrallo suggested visiting Porido and his wife first. He told Stenton that this couple had left their job at the palace and that part of their money was used to get the forged papers of a court doctor. When they finally reached the abode of Porido and Maria, they found them overjoyed at seeing Dr. Stenton free. "Now everything will be all right," they rejoiced. Stenton warned them that the police might soon make enquiries about him.

"Save our Condesa Rosetta," they pleaded, "and we will go with you wherever you take us. We have enough money to take us abroad."

"Your money will be repaid as soon as we reach England. But for now, can you organize a coach in which at least five people can travel?"

That shouldn't be a big problem. When do you want it?"

"I am, unfortunately, unable to give you a time, but would advise you to be ready to travel as soon as possible." Dinrallo took Stenton to the institution. Looking over the fence, he saw a graveyard and a woman kneeling down and saying prayers. It was Rosetta. Stenton did not recognise her at once as she was facing away from him.

He jumped over the hedge and, as he drew nearer, Rosetta heard him but did not react. She was inadequately dressed for the cool time of year. Stenton saw who it was and threw his cloak around her. He lifted her and passed her over the fence to Dinrallo, who took the now lightweight Condesa into the coach. As they passed near the palace, Stenton asked Dinrallo to stop for a few minutes. He wanted to collect his medical instruments and the rest of his belongings. He would not be deterred by Dinrallo's warning and entered the palace though the main entrance. A servant who had not seen him for some time bade him a friendly good day.

Stenton reciprocated and went to his room. In less than five minutes he had all he wanted, went to Rosetta's room, took many items he thought would be needed and made his way back. As he reached the door to leave the palace, he saw Aurelio talking to the servant. "Impossible," he heard him say, "you must be mistaken, he is in prison for fraud."

"No, he's not mistaken and the fraud is your invention," said Stenton and felled him with a single blow to his head. Then Stenton turned to the servant who had watched the scene with astonishment and told him: "He will wake up shortly. Tell him his fraud has been uncovered and that he will receive his deserts very soon."

Unfortunately, Stenton did not anticipate that it would still take a long time before the Carujo brothers and Aurelio would get their deserts. Porido and his wife were already packed and waiting. They entered the coach and the two horses were driven hard towards the border with France, where according to Dinrallo who, for most of the time, was the driving coachman, Count Miguel was to be found in a lighthouse.

"It is a longer but safer way," remarked Dinrallo. "I had to go this way before, when I followed the Gypsies and when I was a smuggler."

"Porido will take over every two hours," suggested Stenton.

"It will take several days but the Juez de lo criminal will probably not search in that direction. Stenton had no doubt that a thorough hunt would take place. They travelled all night. In the morning they reached an inn where they could rest for several hours. The tired horses needed a rest and had to be seen to. The day passed without any incident. Maria knew Rosetta's favourite foods and the patient, although still apathetic, seemed to react by eating, even gaining some weight as well as improving her colour.

In the late afternoon, when they were near the French border they reached another inn. Stenton decided to take a rest before crossing over on to French soil. Inside the inn he noticed a man with a large dog which could easily handle three men. The man was also heavily armed. When he saw Dinrallo he made a sign of recognition and received from him a sign to come out of the inn.

They obviously knew each other. "How is it," asked the armed man, "that you are in such distinguished company?"

"The lady patient is Condesa de Manresa. The tall gentleman is her physician … the story is too long to tell but they are under my protection."

"All right, as long as they do no harm to our business."

"Harm? How is that possible?"

"We expect goods from the other side and we have thirty people in this inn, they could betray us."

"Don't worry. They won't notice anything and within an hour we'll be gone."

This assurance was enough for the smuggler. He went back to the guest room and sat down in the corner. He accepted with thanks a glass of wine that Porido brought over to him.

In less than half an hour the noise of many hoofs could be heard. Maria went to the window and turned pale.

"Santa Madonna – police."

Porido also went to the window. "The Corregidor of Manresa is there too."

"Well, I'm in the right mood for him," said Stenton.

"Oh, señor, defence is impossible. There are about twenty people."

"I'll fight them just the same."

At this, the man in the corner stood up and said: "Don't worry, señor, you are under my protection."

"Stenton looked at the speaker with amazement and asked: "Who are you?"

"Your friend. Didn't you notice that Dinrallo has disappeared? He is going for help."

Stenton sat down, calmly waiting for development of the situation. The door opened and four armed police with the Corregidor at the head entered the room. "Ah, señor Stenton we meet again," he said mockingly.

"That's right," answered Stenton composed.

"It seems you didn't like it in Barcelona. You escaped, señor, and that's bad for you. Besides you've committed several crimes since."

"What crimes?"

"Kidnapping, and a murderous attack against the young Count of Manresa."

"That really sounds dangerous," smiled Stenton.

"That is so. Can you see these handcuffs? I have to put these irons on to you and bring you back."

"Try it," Countered Stenton and rose from his seat.

The Corregidor carefully stepped back. "I'm warning you, señor. There is no use defending yourself. You can see four armed police in this room and there are fifteen more outside. Resistance is useless."

"I don't think so." The man in the corner spoke these words.

The Corregidor looked at him with astonishment. "Who are you?"

"A friend of these ladies and gentlemen," answered the smuggler with equanimity.

"Ah, so you have helped these people?"

"No, but I am going to help them now."

"So I'll have to take you prisoner as well."

"Or I'll take you," smiled the stranger.

"Me?" The Corregidor flared up, "don't you dare to make fun of me."

"Look around you."

The Corregidor looked around. There were ten rifles pointing at him and his companions. "And there are twenty more holding your policemen outside in check. How do you like it, my heroic señor Corregidor? Let me tell you I don't need all this weaponry. I only have to give this dog a sign and he'll tear all your throats. We in the mountains know how to handle people of your calibre."

"My God, we're lost," stammered the Corregidor.

"Yes, you're lost. How much do you like your life? Will you obey or not?"

"What do you want me to do?" he asked.

"Order your people to give up their weapons and leave your horses."

"I can't do that," groaned the Corregidor.

"You can, my people can hear every word. I'm Counting to three. If you are not by the window, thirty men will shoot their rifles at you, nobody will escape. One – two – thr … "The smuggler had not finished the last word, when the Corregidor jumped towards the window, opened it and shouted: "Put down your guns." The policemen heard the order of their leader and looked towards the inn, astonished.

"For God's sake put your arms into that wagon."

"Why?" asked one of the men outside.

"Because we are prisoners here. The house is full of smugglers and they'll shoot all of us." He had not finished his sentence when the door opened and twenty men came out and aimed their rifles at those outside.

"Surrender, surrender," shouted the anxious Corregidor.

"Are we free to withdraw? asked one of the policemen.

"Yes, after you leave your horses as well," answered the stranger.

The police laid down their weapons, got off their horses and left. The Corregidor wanted to leave as well but was held back by the smuggler.

"Stop, my friend. I have to discuss something else with you."

"What else?"

"You'll hear that in a minute." He turned to Stenton and asked: "It seems you are not happy with this man?"

"Indeed not," confirmed Stenton. "First he lured me under false pretences to Barcelona, and then I was incarcerated for several months, when I was totally innocent."

"He will pay for that. Take him out and give him fifty lashes on his back," ordered the smuggler. Soon came the cries of the official, who expected to take a prisoner, but received fifty lashes instead.

Only now did Dinrallo enter the room. He hid himself carefully, fearing he would be recognised by the Corregidor of Manresa. Stenton wanted to show his thanks to the smugglers but they would not hear of it. ---

In the year 1850, one of the boldly-built lighthouses stood near the height of the bay of Mont St. Michel. It served the ships at the dangerous coast of Normandy. The attendant of this lighthouse only seldom associated with other people and was considered an eccentric. At the nearby station a train arrived from Paris. A very tall man met a man dressed in the Spanish style.

"May I ask about the health of the Condesa?" asked the man in Spanish attire.

"Considering the whole situation, I'm satisfied. She has recovered well physically."

"And her mental well being? Did she recognise you?"

A shadow flew over the features of the tall man. "No, I did not dare to use the medicine until she is strong enough. I'll have to wait until we're back at home. Now to our other task. I've asked you here to find out whether the Count is still in the lighthouse.

"Sure, I haven't seen him but from the fact that the lighthouse keeper still refuses to let strangers visit the place as he did before, I think the Count must still be there."

"Now I know what I have to do, let us go to the mayor."

"And then?"

"With the mayor's help we shall bring the Count to his daughter."

They found the mayor in his workroom and were warmly received. They introduced themselves and took a seat.

"How can I serve you gentlemen?" asked the official.

"With a little information, monsieur," said Stenton. "Who has forbidden strangers to visit the lighthouse?"

"Nobody, as far as I know," was the answer.

"As far as you know? I think, monsieur le maire, you should be the best to know.

"Who has spoken of such prohibition?"

"The lighthouse keeper," interjected Dinrallo.

"Ah, Gaston. He is a misanthrope; he likes to be left alone, monsieur."

"There is an old man in that tower whose mind is disturbed Who is this man?"

"A relation of Gaston."

"What is his name and where does he come from?"

The official was visibly embarrassed. "Gaston has registered him but had nothing in writing."

"I thought that with every registration there are certain documents necessary?"

"Hm, yes, actually that is true. I'll have to catch up with this situation."

"We did not only come for this information This matter has a more serious face. We ask your help in criminal matters."

"Criminal? asked the mayor. There is a crime involved?"

Now Stenton told him the case of the Count's illness and abduction.

"What you tell me is a detective story but what has a crime committed in Spain to do with me?"

"Because the abducted Count in my story is now in your district."

"In this case I have to act immediately – where is the Count?"

"In the lighthouse."

The mayor stood up. "Impossible."

"No, it's true, this can really embarrass you. You have acknowledged a relative of this Gaston, who holds the abducted Count, without asking for any documents."

Sweat run down the mayor's face. "I have to have a word with the lighthouse keeper but can you prove to me that this old man is the Count?"

"Yes, the last thing the Count saw before he lost his mind was his loyal servant Porido. Now the only words he will utter are 'I am the loyal Porido'. You will agree that these words are not likely to be uttered by anyone else."

Stenton showed him papers that proved him to be the Count of Manresa's physician.

"Gentlemen, I'm at your service, but I hope you treat this matter in such a way, that no unpleasantness will ensue because of my little slip."

"We shall do our utmost. Let's take along the necessary help and go at once to the lighthouse Everything will depend on the result."

The Mayor, Stenton, Dinrallo and three policemen went to the lighthouse. Stenton suggested they go there as casual strollers. The rest would come automatically."

They parted. Stenton, Dinrallo and one of the policemen went separately to the tower. When they reached the entrance, it was closed. Dinrallo noticed a bell. He rang and the door was opened after a short wait. Gaston looked at Dinrallo and seemed annoyed: "You again? Go to the devil." He was going to close the door but Dinrallo held it open.

"Leave it open I want to visit the lighthouse."

"I told you that it's forbidden – are you deaf?"

The policeman who up to now stood out of sight came forward. "What is the matter Gaston. Who gave you orders to turn away visitors?"

The guard stepped back when he saw the official. "Should I let in every vagabond to disturb my peace?"

"Does this man look like a vagabond, you ruffian? I have to inform you on behalf of the mayor, that the visits to this lighthouse are not forbidden."

Stenton and Dinrallo entered the lighthouse. The guard hurried up the stairs. The two men followed slowly. Two staircases up they saw an old woman who looked at the men like a malicious crocodile. They took no notice and went up higher. On top of the tower were two little rooms. One was open, the other one locked. From the locked room they heard the lamenting words: "I am the loyal Porido."

"Why do you shut in that ill person?" asked Stenton.

"That's none of your business," Countered the Frenchman.

"Maybe you have no clear conscience regarding this patient."

"Monsieur, what is your business with my family? I was forced to let you in but if you insult me, I shall throw you down stairs."

"You, me?" asked Stenton disparagingly, "if I were not nauseated by you, you would be lying downstairs now." Then he took out a handkerchief and waved at the window.

Soon they could hear steps and the mayor appeared. "Where is the patient?" he asked.

"In there," said Gaston and pointed at the closed door. He was not worried as he thought that he had only to deal with the mayor.

"He's a relation of yours, what's his name?"

"Anselmo Marciello."

"Where does he come from?"

"From Navia."

"Have you got his papers?"

"My cousin promised to bring them but, unfortunately, he has died since."

"Open the door."

The guard obeyed. As the insane Count saw the people, he wailed: "I am the loyal Porido."

"Did you hear that?" asked Stenton; this is Count Miguel de Manresa.

"Monsieur is mistaken, this is Anselmo Marciello, I know him.

"Silence, deceiver. Monsieur le Maire I ask you to arrest this man."

"Arrest, me? asked Gaston. "See whether you can." He pushed the mayor aside and intended to run down stairs, but he run into the arm of three police instead.

"Nom d'un chien," Gaston called out, startled.

"Hold him fast," the mayor said. "This escape confirms his guilt."

He allowed Stenton to get hold of Count Miguel who led him to a carriage and then to the station. They took the next train to Paris. There was no joyous reunion between father and daughter – they did not recognise each other. Stenton sent a telegram to Colonel Masterson and his mother, advising them of his imminent arrival. Porido's wife, Maria, knew the Count's favourite meal and prepared it for him. Stenton noticed with satisfaction the Count's eating with apparent appetite.---

In the best hotel in Bradford five people signed the visitor's book. The oldest seemed to have been very ill but walked upright and had a distinguished imperious appearance. The younger man in his company could be taken for an artist and the lady obviously moved in exclusive circles. Another man and his wife were servants.

They were the Duke of Zaragoza, his daughter princess Elena and Max Masterson, by now engaged to the princess. Maximilian was especially moved by his love for his native surroundings. He was not prepared to wait and endure uncertainty and after they made themselves comfortable the Duke dictated to his daughter a letter to Mrs. Stenton.

"To Mrs. Ella Stenton at the Estate of Colonel Masterson.

Dear Mrs. Stenton, we would like to inform you of our arrival. As we do not yet know whether our visit is acceptable to Colonel Masterson, we request confirmation. We should be very pleased if you would call on us in preparation of our visit.

With our highest regards,

Baron Embarez"

A servant was to be sent off to deliver this letter and possibly collect an answer. Mrs. Stenton could not keep the letter a secret and spread great joy. "Thank God they have finally arrived. Of course they are welcome and if you wish, you could call on them and bring them here. Mrs. Stenton knew that this Baron, being her son's patient was only too willing to collect them.

When she arrived at the hotel, the princess Elena, whom she did not recognise, received her. Too many years had passed since those dreadful events in her father's home. She asked Mrs. Stenton to sit down and discussed her father's fateful illness and miraculous cure by Dr. Stenton. Mrs. Stenton listened with beaming eyes and red cheeks. Anyone could see how proud she was of her son's achievements. The princess then told of her engagement to Maximilian, the rejected son of the Colonel and that her father would try to reunite them. "And speaking of my father, I have to make a confession, please don't be shocked." Princess Elena did not know the entire truth of her father's rape. She did not question her father when he told her that he had a serious apology to make.

Mrs. Stenton did not expect any unpleasant surprises from these noble people and assured the princess she was prepared to listen. "I speak on behalf of my father when I offer his sincerest apology for something that happened in his younger years."

It dawned on Mrs. Stenton that the young lady, who introduced herself as Elena, was the child of the Duke who had raped her and Baron Embarez was really the Duke Enrico de Zaragoza. She paled but when princess Elena took her hands and said: "You did not recognise me; I am your little Elena who cried for you many nights. Please, please forgive my father." Mrs. Stenton quickly composed herself and the two women embraced each other. Yet when the door opened and the Duke came into the room, her body stiffened and she grew cold.

"My daughter's apology is not enough, it is I who must humble myself. I am not the same person you knew. Our son gave me back my life. It would have been lost without him. Please, please find it in your heart to forgive my dreadful error in my youth. I would like him to be my heir and accept my title as well."

Mrs. Stenton's face relaxed a little and she managed to reply without showing her trembling. "We'd better forget the past or this visit. As far as your offer is concerned, I can answer for my son. There is no chance that he would accept. Now let's set off and continue our journey to the Estate of colonel Masterson."

In the home of Colonel Masterson there was hectic refurbishing and cleaning. They were preparing for the visit of Baron Embarez and his daughter. When the visitors arrived, they found the colonel waiting at the entrance to his estate. He welcomed the Duke and his entourage; they hardly sat down, when the Colonel asked about their involvement with Stenton. He was told about a nearly-dying Baron and Dr. Stenton's miraculous help. "I feel great," continued the patient "and every day seems to bring improvement." The Colonel was delighted to have such noble guests and the conversation flowed fluently until Mrs. Brooks announced dinner was being served. The Duke, who had still not divulged his real identity, praised the food and was told that it was the combined effort of Mrs. Stenton and Mrs. Brooks. Mrs. Stenton, he was told, would not attend dinner because she was feeling slightly unwell.

Colonel Masterson called the visit delightful and successful. He became very friendly with the 'Baron'. They had so much to talk about the next morning that the Duke thought the right time had come to speak about the Colonel's son. He started. "Colonel Masterson, I have to make a confession. I also have to ask you to be my daughter's father in law." The astonished colonel found no words to reply and the Duke continued. "I like to travel incognito and my confession is that I am not Baron Embarez but the Duke of Zaragoza …"

"A Duke?" the colonel stood open mouthed, he then rallied, "and what did you say about me as a father in law – I have no son."

"But we know that you have. He is now engaged to my daughter Elena."

Elena, who heard these words, took the Colonels hands into her own and pleaded.

"Surely the time has come when a father's heart takes over? Do I have to ask for your blessing in vain?"

Masterson didn't know what had hit him. A princess asking him to be her father in law? Maybe his son was not the nobody he'd thought when he gave up his military career.

"But … "he stammered, "my son is not here." Maximilian had stood near the open door. When he heard his father's last words, he entered the room and embraced his bride, who was still holding his father's hands. At the same time, put his arms around his perplexed father, who did not resist.

Max kissed his bride and then his father who was still shocked and felt as if in a dream. He eventually rallied and put his arms around the two lovers. "How can I withhold my blessing from a son I have misjudged, and an angelic face that would melt an iceberg? Be happy the two of you, with my wholehearted blessing.

Two weeks had passed since the happy reunion and the Duke felt his old strength coming back. Mrs. Stenton, who avoided contact with the Duke, had not told anybody about her ordeal when she was employed by him, neither did her late husband. Happiness ruled all around while Dr. Charles Stenton was still in prison in Barcelona.

Plans were made for a wedding at Christmas and everybody hoped for the doctor to come back. The Duke spoke to his new friend, the colonel, about the cost of his family and servants during this vacation during this vacation. He asked that he be allowed to contribute. The colonel, however, refuted the idea. "You are my guests and practically my relations. Please stay as long as you wish, I won't accept."

Christmas was just over three weeks away, when Stenton's telegram from Paris reached the Colonel and Mrs. Stenton. The joy this news caused was indescribable.

The day came when Stenton, the ill Count, Condesa Rosetta, who suffered the same illness, Porido and Maria arrived. There was room for all on the estate. Stenton refused to stay in his mother's home; he preferred to stay near his patients and was given a room near Count Miguel and Rosetta, who also had their separate rooms.

The meeting with the Duke was cut short by Stenton's determination to start treating his patients. The Duke, who did not mention his relationship with Stenton, understood but expressed his hope that the doctor would stay for the wedding. "I have two patients to look after and I also have the urgent task of freeing a certain Lucien de Monreau who is the brother of Condesa Rosetta and a prisoner in a pirate ship.

He told the Duke the circumstances and went to his patients. He administered the prepared medicine that he hoped would cure them of the rare poison in their blood. Here he noticed progress.

A week after he had started treatment he set at Rosetta's bed. Besides him only his mother was in the room, doing some work behind heavy curtains. Rosetta had slept for an unusually long time. Not even the twitch of an eyelid. There she lay like a beautiful picture in marble.

"Mother" it sounded very quietly in the room.

"Yes, my son?" came the equally quiet question.

"Come here, please." Mrs. Stenton rose and slowly went to her son. She looked anxiously into her son's eyes where she could detect a slight glimmer of hope.

"Feel her hand," he asked. She took the white hand of the sleeping girl into her own and nodded joyfully to her son. "Can you feel her pulse, mother? Look at her lips - they are reddening. Also the pale shine of death has left her cheeks. Go to the colonel and tell him hat the Condesa will be awake in an hour.

"Charles, is it true?"

"Yes."

She pulled his head to her heart, stroked his cheek and ask: "Will it be for good?"

"That is up to God, I am praying ardently, as I never prayed in my life."

"God, the Lord, will listen to your prayer – you deserve it, my child."

She left the room but came back soon afterwards. She prayed with the heart of a mother that God be merciful and that the next hour should bring salvation.

Half an hour passed and they could hear the slight breathing of the patient. Then her cheeks began to redden and her eyelids to twitch. Stenton's heart was nearly bursting. "Heaven help – the time of decision has come," implored Stenton quietly.

Rosetta's eyes had the dreamlike expression peculiar to awakening. Adjusted finally to full consciousness, she observed her surroundings.

"Complete recovery," rejoiced the soul of the physician.

Rosetta's glances went from item to item; they could see a slight disturbance in her features. Then she was suddenly aware that her hands were held. She recognised Stenton.

"Carlos, is it you? Where am I? Did I sleep long?

"Relax, you are with me."

"Yes, I am with you," Rosetta said happily. But I must have slept quite long?"

"Very long. You were ill."

"Ill? she asked thoughtfully, "how? It was only yesterday I accompanied my friend Margaret on her travels to her father and then – ah you were not there. Later I felt unwell and wanted to sleep and I fell asleep while I was praying. Where have you been, my Carlos?"

"I was in Barcelona."

"Without telling me anything? She heard a soft and suppressed sobbing from behind the curtains. "Who is crying? Who is there? Is it the good Maria?"

"No, my heart, it is a lovely lady who very much wants to meet you."

"Oh, a stranger in this room?" she asked with a slight shock. Who is she?"

"My – mother."

She looked at him and at first she did not understand, then she called joyously: "Mother? oh what a surprise, please call her here, quickly, quickly.

"But you have to talk to her in English, she doesn't understand Spanish." He turned to his mother, "please come, Rosetta wants to see you."

"My son, I do not understand what you were saying, except that Rosetta regained consciousness and you seemed very happy. Is that so?"

"Yes, God has listened to our prayers."

Stenton's mother drew nearer slowly. Rosetta stretched her hands towards her and said: "You are the mother of my Carlos. Oh, now I have a mother too. May I be your daughter?"

Mrs. Stenton put her hands on Rosetta's head and spoke with a trembling voice: "My child, I implore God's blessing upon you. I would give my life to see you happy."

They embraced each other. Then Rosetta stretched her hands towards her beloved:

"My Carlos. I thank you for giving me a mother. Oh, I love her already, but is it true that I was ill for such a long time?"

"Yes, my heart, nearly three months."

"For nearly three months? So I was unconscious for that long and you have cured me?"

"God helped me to find the right medicine."

"And where are Aurelio, Carujo, Porido and Maria?"

"Porido and Maria are here. Everything else you'll learn later. You mustn't talk very much, you must look after yourself."

"I shall listen to you. Only tell me where I am?"

"With a good friend of ours."

"Not in Manresa?"

"No, but you'll learn that later."

"And" … she paused for a moment. "My father, is it true that he was killed by falling into that ravine?"

"No, he's alive. Now be quiet, my heart, otherwise you might fall ill again."

"I've one more plea but I don't like to say it."

"Speak with confidence."

"I'll say it not to my beloved but to the physician" said Rosetta blushing. "If I was ill for that long did I eat very little?"

Stenton uttered a little cry of delight. "You can tell that to your lover as well, because that makes him very happy. That you are asking for food makes me sure that you'll be cured very soon; mother will bring what I prescribe. Or should Maria bring that food?"

"I would very much like to see Maria but mama should also come."

Stenton wrote something on a piece of paper which his mother took to the kitchen.

It didn't take long for the food to be prepared. Maria took it into the patient's room. The Countess sat upright and Stenton sat next to her. "Welcome Maria, I couldn't speak to you for a long time."

Tears ran down Maria's cheeks. "Oh, my dear Condesa, the holy Madonna be thanked that you know me again. We have suffered during your illness."

"I am all right again and you can be happy."

Rosetta ate her light meal. Her cheeks glowed even more and Stenton's conviction that she would recover grew. Soon they would be able to speak about the sad events in Spain.

After the food, the patient fell asleep again. Mrs. Stenton and Maria stayed with her while the doctor went to see the Count. The doctor knew that he had to wait longer for the Count to wake up, on account of his patient's age. When after an hour he went back to Rosetta, he found her and Maria in tears. Mrs. Stenton was again behind her curtains. "Good that you have come, Charles. I do understand Spanish, something unpleasant must have happened."

Her voice was moving when Rosetta begged Stenton not to be angry with Maria. "I asked and she told me everything."

"But it could have done you great harm," he sighed.

"No, certainty does no harm to me. I feel strong enough to take it but please, take me to my father."

Stenton had objections but these were refuted by Rosetta and he permitted her the visit when he saw that she was strong enough to see her ill father. He prepared a soft armchair next to the bed of the Count and carried her on his strong arms into the other room. The sight of her father, from whom she had been parted under such circumstances, released another stream of tears. She took his hands and covered it with kisses. Then she discovered Porido, whose eyes rested with touching joy on his mistress. She dried her tears and passed her hands toward the loyal servant who put them to his lips.

"Oh, my dear gracious Condesa, how I thank God you are saved."

"I thank God no less that I am able to speak to all of you again."

"It's all due to Dr. Stenton. Only he could have made you healthy again."

"I know," said Rosetta, "but I also know what you and Maria have done for me."

"That's nothing," Porido assured her,"we would have followed you to the end of the earth."

"I'll think about how I can make up for your sacrifices. Only wait until my father has recovered."

On the next day it would be decided whether Stenton's magic would have the same results with the Count as with his daughter. Rosetta sat by her father and didn't take her eyes off him. He'd slept for three days and could wake up any moment now. Stenton entered the room. He seized her hand.

"Rosetta."

"Carlos, will my father recover?"

"I hope so – it won't take long."

He released her hand and took the patient's, which he held in his for a while. Then he suddenly stepped to the end of the bed. The Count moved slightly. He opened his eyes and let them skim around the room, like someone who has just woken up. Now his eyes met Rosetta's. He looked at her for a long time and said quietly: "My God, where am I, what did I dream? Rosetta, my dear child, where is señor Stenton who has saved me?"

Rosetta sat stiffly She was pale but she rose with a cry: "Father, dear, dear father, do you recognise me? do you really recognise me?"

There was a happy smile on his face: "Yes, I know you. You are Rosetta, my daughter. Don't let Carujo, Rita and Aurelio come in here. Let Stenton guard me. I'm tired, give me a good night kiss and be with me in the morning."

Rosetta couldn't hold back her emotions. A groan came out of her mouth and tears streamed from her eyes. Again and again she pressed her lips onto her father's, until she noticed he was asleep again. Her eyes met Stenton's and, sobbingly, she threw her arms around him.

A week had passed, Don Miguel had completely recovered. With a joyful heart he agreed to the marriage of his daughter to Dr. Stenton. The only thing that grieved him was the fate of his son. He had not decided what steps to take for his rescue.

A diligent and happy activity took place in Colonel Masterson's estate. Two weddings were being prepared. Rosetta's wish was that there should be a minimal amount of people and all agreed. The next day saw the arrival of the long expected helmsman, George Brooks. It was a great joy for his family. After the meal, where they all sat together, he withdrew with his wife and child into his rooms and was informed of all that happened here and in Spain. George Brooks listened with great interest. After his wife had told him all she knew, he told her that he had to speak to Dr. Stenton.

"You seem in a rush. Is it that important?"

"For Dr. Stenton it is."

He met Stenton outside, preparing for a stroll in the woods. "Have you a little time for an information that may be of importance to you?"

"Yes, of course, let's sit down on this bench, I'm listening."

"I know from my wife you are interested in a French officer named Lucien de Mareau."

Stenton became attentive. "Yes, indeed I am, what can you tell me about him?"

"The story begins in Nantes, France. There I saw a ship the captain of which is called Ramirez Danlola. He wanted to hire me but I changed my mind after listening to two sailors in a bar. From their talk I gathered that this Danlola is rather a pirate than a trader. My interest in their conversation grew when they talked of a prisoner they had on board. They said it's likely the captain would sell him to the ruler of a place they called Harare. A place in which they sold someone else before. Only this man came from Mexico."

"Did you hear any names?"

"Oh yes, I heard this man being a Count Manuel and I heard a name involved in that deal, a señor Carujo."

With lightning speed it became clear to Stenton who knew that Count Miguel had a brother named Manuel in Mexico who employed a Carujo, a brother of the major-domo in Manresa. This brother of Count Miguel had been reported as having died. Stenton was sure now, that this other Carujo had arranged with this captain Danlola to have him disappear. Thus, with the removal of Count Miguel and Condesa Rosetta, the Carujo brothers would be heirs to the fortunes and the two palaces through Pablo Carujo's son Aurelio.

"And what about the name Lucien de Mareau?"

"Well, that was the name of the prisoner they had on board. This man had promised one of them that a señor Stenton in the palace of Manresa would give one hundred duros for information about himself. He actually did go to Manresa but had been informed that señor Stenton had left. Nobody knew where he had gone."

"So I just need to know the name of the ship?"

"Oh yes, the name was Penrosa." ---

As weddings go, this was a small but very happy double event. A happy and proud Colonel Masterson who hosted it all. A happy Ella Stenton who saw her son's culmination of his many travels. A happy Duke Enrico de Zaragoza. Happiest of all were the two couples involved.

Stenton, immediately after the wedding, made known his plans to buy a ship and to hunt down the pirate Danlola. When the Duke heard these plans, he offered to carry the costs of this expedition. He was told it would take a lot of money for just the ship without any equipment. "That will be my wedding present to the man who saved my life."

Stenton asked the helmsman George Brooks whether he would join him.

"Yes, I wouldn't mind making a hunt for the pirate."

"Do you trust yourself to lead a ship, maybe a little steamship or yacht?" asked Stenton"

"Yes, if I get a reliable machinist. I've the captain's licence for a long ride."

"Would we be able to take on a ship like the Penrosa?"

"That's not an easy question. We should at least have a few cannons and a few heroic men."

"So you think it's possible?"

"With the given conditions, yes."

"Where would we get the ship we need?"

"I say we should try the shipyards in Greenock."

"I don't understand very much about these things. Would you accompany me?"

"With all my heart, Dr. Stenton."

"The Count has to oust his false son, Aurelio, and bring the Carujo clan to justice. To do this he needs to find Lucien de Mareau, his real son. He also needs a certified witness's statement from the nursemaid who would have noticed something when the babies were being exchanged."

Stenton allowed himself just four weeks of the joys of a newly-married couple.

"Would you mind if I gave you a suitable advance to make yourself independent? And when we get our yacht you will, of course, be its captain?" he asked George Brooks.

"All right," nodded the helmsman.

"If we reach our goal, I'll help you further; now I'll have a stroll in the woods, I've a lot of thinking to do and tomorrow we'll leave. Good night."

"Good night, doctor." They shook hands and parted.

There were tears when Charles Stenton and George Brooks bade their families and friends goodbye. Rosetta didn't want them to go. Within nine months she bore a baby daughter who wouldn't see her father for many years. ---

Chapter 9

HUNTING THE PIRATE

---

*T*HROUGH their inquiries with various consuls, they learned that the Penrosa was sighted in St. Helena and left for Capetown thereafter. "At least we know where to start our search," said Stenton.

They rented a room in one of the most popular hotels in Greenock at the Clyde, where they also learned of a steam yacht belonging to a lord Castlepool who was on a government mission to Mexico. That lord turned out to be lady Margaret's father. The yacht was forty metres long, six metres wide, ten metres deep and was fast. George assessed this little yacht as suitable for their purpose and the agent let them have it for a reasonable price.

The ship had two masts and sails to use the power of the wind in support of the steam. It would be hard for any ship to outrun this boat. They hired ten sailors, several machinists and two stokers. George was the captain and Stenton was the owner. The yacht was named 'Rosetta'.

The agent was helpful in their purchases of ammunition and weapons. As it was meant to hunt down a pirate, two ninety degrees swivel cannons, were added plus a quantity of comestibles.

The 'Rosetta' sailed down the Clyde towards the ocean. Nobody knew the exact direction, only that they were searching the west coast of Africa for captain Danlola.

They had come happily over the dangerous bay of Biscay, whose name was also 'the sailor's cemetery' and made inquiries, but without any success. Now they went to St. Helena to restock their supply of coals, when they found their first clues. The 'Penrosa' had taken fresh water there and had sailed south. It could be expected to learn more in Capetown. Stenton, for that reason, decided to sail toward the 'Cape of good Hope'.

It was early morning when Captain Brooks entered Stenton's cabin and reported he had sighted a three-mast ship, but it wasn't clear yet what kind it was. "I intend going toward him."

They stepped unto the deck and took their telescopes in hand. After a few minutes they noticed the ship had a southward course, the same as they had. Their yacht hat a better wind and, therefore, was faster, especially as the speed was supported by steam power. The man who sat high up in the mast for observation shouted he had discovered another ship. "What is it?" asked Stenton.

"I can't see it very well because it has black sails." answered the sailor.

"Black sails?" asked Brooks quickly. "That can only be the pirate ship 'Penrosa'."

He pointed the telescope west, the direction of the outstretched arm of the sailor who had discovered the ship. He now saw the second ship sailing with full wind toward the first. "It must be captain Danlola," said Brooks.

"Are you sure,? ventured Stenton.

"No but this Danlola is a clever boy. He has white sails entering any port, but at sea he puts on black ones. It seems he's taking course toward the trading ship."

"We'll help that ship. I have got him, let's hope he won't escape."

"We shouldn't forget we can damage that far bigger ship, but to get the pirate into our hands this way is practically impossible," replied Brooks. He then asked for the sails to be taken down: that would help to get nearer without being seen.

The pieces of artillery were loaded. They were heading for a probable fight. After a while the pirate was near enough to the trader. He showed the red pirate flag and fired one of his cannons as a sign for the other ship to give in if they didn't want to be shot to pieces. The trader seemed to see the danger. They could see that he put on more sails and tried to escape. A rush turn by the trader got him out of reach of the pirate's bullets. The pirate, however, made the same manoeuvre and quickly regained the original distance. A second shot rang out and the bullet tore large chunks out of the trader's woodwork. A loud cry of jubilation came from the pirate's ship. Sounds of anger and shock were heard from the damaged ship which suddenly dropped all its sails. The pirate shot passed. At that moment the trader answered with two shots and seemed to have created havoc on the robber. Both shots were hits.

"Very good," praised Brook. "The trader is English and has cannons on board. He seems determined to defend himself. Her boys are good shots and we shall take the robber from the other side.

The pirate seemed to dislike a long exchange of cannon bullets and tried to get near the trader in order to board it. "Now I will make steam. In five minutes we shall be in a position to have a serious word with them," said the helmsman, George Brooks. The yacht had avoided showing steam and, so far, had not been noticed by the others. Now a dark stripe appeared from their chimneys and one could hear loud jubilation from the English ship. The pirate too saw the new opponent but didn't think this nutshell was to be taken seriously and carried on with his attack.

The yacht passed the English ship whose captain stood on board and shouted: "Yacht ahoy, are you help or not?"

"We shall help, don't give in," answered Stenton.

"We don't dream of giving in."

"The English captain supported his words by firing a new salvo that, judging by the cries and cursing of the robbers, was well aimed.

An angry voice called out: "Engage the rudders, get at him, we'll board him."

"That was Danlola's voice," said Brooks. "We'll stop him.

The yacht turned in a circle and stopped at the backboard of the pirate. They could not be hit by its cannons. "Fire," ordered Brooks.

All the cannons crashed into the pirate ship, which visibly shook, for all the bullets, had hit its hull. The cannons were loaded again immediately.

"Now the rifles," ordered Brooks again. While the cannons tried hard to hit the enemy below water level, the rifles did their damage on deck. The pirate saw that the little David was a noteworthy opponent and directed his attention to it but his cannons were unable to hit the much lower yacht which was too near for such an exercise. Brooks had protected the sides with mats against rifle bullets.

Danlola knew that his position between the opponents was precarious. He called out to his men: "Board that nutshell." Two boats were lowered to attack the yacht. "Let them drink water," laughed Brooks. He ordered reversal of the yacht for a better aim, stood at one of the cannons, aimed carefully and fired. The bullet went through the whole length of the boat and out at the other end. Many of the rowers were hit and the boat sank. Those in the other boat wanted to save the men in the water, but were themselves hit by a second salvo. The pirates still alive tried to swim back, but were all hit by rifle bullets.

Danlola shook with anger. He ordered hand grenades to be thrown. "Let's tear this dwarf to pieces," he shouted.

Stenton stepped away from his protective mats and shouted: "Danlola, I have greetings from Carujo in Manresa."

Danlola paled. He saw he was unmasked. He roared: "Grenades, quickly, quickly, this scoundrel mustn't escape." Brooks had his steamer controlled, he withdrew sufficiently. No grenades could reach it. But now they were threatened by the pirate's cannons. Brooks steered the yacht toward the helm of the pirate ship where there were no cannons. Danlola saw there was no victory to be had. He raised the sails and ran.

There was jubilation on board the English ship. They greeted Stenton with joyous thanks. Stenton went with Brooks on to the saved vessel. "That was help at the right time, Sir," called the captain as he shook the hands of the two. "Your yacht is a real hero."

"You are not a coward yourself," countered Stenton.

"I did my duty, but I'm curious whether this pirate will attack me again."

"He'll leave you alone now, because I'll be with you."

"That sounds as if you're going to accompany us."

"I'll not accompany you but the robber. I've been seeking for this rascal for weeks now, and I won't let him out of my reach."

"That sounds as if you've something to settle with this pirate."

"Yes, well. Would you do me a favour?"

"Of course."

"Report at every port you reach that you've fought with Danlola and his ship the 'Penrosa'. I'll go in your wake to Capetown to make him feel sure I'm no longer after him."

They returned to their yacht and followed the bigger ship south, while the pirate went southwest. As soon as they where out of sight of even the strongest telescope, they changed to same direction as the robber.

Danlola could 't imagine who sent him greetings from Manresa, but it must have been an enemy in the know. The yacht would go to Capetown to report the encounter. He had to go to Capetown to receive messages not yet received the last time he was at the port. He couldn't be seen now at this haven because the yacht would be there before him.

When they were near Capetown, it was night and he could go closer to the coast. There he found a lonely bay where he dropped anchor, unseen. Then he sent two men with a letter to atrusted agent One of them stayed in the boat, the other went to deliver the letter and to receive messages. The agent told him they were reported and that after today, it would not be safe to pass on any letters or messages.

On his way back Brooks spotted the man. George Brooks, who'd once served with him on another boat believed he'd seen him on Danlola's pirate ship. The man had been ordered to inform himself about the yacht. When he'd noticed he was followed, he went around a few corners and managed to disappear.

Brooks hurried back to the yacht where he told Stenton to observe the dinghy that he believed belonged to the 'Penrosa'. "I think we traced them." Stenton ordered four sailors to take a boat and follow the dinghy without going near enough to be seen.

The waves were high and the boat that, unlike the dinghy, had no sails, was hard to see from a distance. The two pirates reached the 'Penrosa' where one of them handed Danlola the coded letters he had received. One of the letters read: "Doctor Stenton, whom we imprisoned in Barcelona, is after you. He knows everything. Carujo."

The major-domo had his spies in Bradford-on-Avon and had sent this message to several places, to be sure it reached Danlola. He went to his first officer and told him to lift the anchor.

"Now?" asked the astonished officer. "Isn't it dangerous to leave here by daylight?"

"Yes, it is, but it's even more dangerous to stay. We shall go to the West Indies."

When the 'Penrosa' left the bay, Stenton's yacht was barely half a mile away at the shore from where it could hardly have been distinguished. The four men looked after the Penrosa until she was out of sight and went back to report to Stenton. The 'Rosetta' was prepared to go to sea but Stenton asked Brooks for the most likely place Danlola would head. Brooks deliberated and said: "No one can be a hundred percent sure, but I think Danlola knows his ship's name and description is betrayed and that he can make no alterations in a known shipyard, he'll have to go to the West Indies to one of hundreds of small isles. I think my supposition is probably right."

"We have to follow at once then."

"That would be difficult. He'll avoid the usual routes and would be hard to find. The equatorial route he cannot avoid and if we steam ahead of him, we're most likely to find him."

"I don't understand this."

"Dr. Stenton, you're no sailor. For us there are streets as there are for a carter on land. Leave it to me, we'll find him. To reassure you, we'll go west at first and then cruise between north and south, where we will surely find him and we see which route he's going to take."

"We attack him at once?"

"No, that won't work. We can only wound him while he could kill us. He has boats to save himself. Should he manage to hit us, our boats wouldn't take half of our men. They were built for short stretches, not to go over the ocean."

Stenton had to agree with the captain.

The 'Rosetta' left Cape Town shortly afterwards. ---

Lady Margaret lay in her hammock when her father Lord Castlepool approached her. "I would not disturb you," he began, but I may have to ask you to do me a big favour."

"Ask me, Pa, you know I won't refuse."

"You like travelling, don't you?"

Lady Margaret was interested. "You know that, Pa. Have you somewhere special in mind?"

"I have to hand over some important documents to the governor of Jamaica and they can't be trusted to strangers. There's a military ship in the port of Vera Cruz that should take them, but I mustn't give them to the captain. He's no diplomat. I know of no other way but to send you. A lady isn't usually allowed on a ship like this, but if it's my wish for you to go on this mission, the captain will permit it."

Lady Margaret jumped up. "Father, you can trust me, I'm ready to travel."

"I'll accompany you to Vera Cruz. The governor's a friend of mine and he'll welcome you."

A troupe of twenty riders accompanied the carriage taking Lord Castlepool and his daughter to Vera Cruz. They were welcomed and the captain offered Lady Margaret his own cabin. Lord Castlepool handed the documents to his daughter and left.

The weather was favourable and the military ship made good speed. To reach their destination, they had to pass the Pedro Bank whose coral reefs were a danger to many ships.

It was morning. The sun was not low in the sky. Suddenly the man at the lookout reported a small steam yacht that was supported by sails. The captain stood next to lady Margaret on deck.

"A devilish little vehicle," said the captain, "a speed I never thought possible from such a small ship, can you see it, Lady Margaret?"

She stepped to the rails to see the ship well. A cannon set off as a sign for the yacht to heave to.

"What kind of a ship are you? called the officer on guard.

"Private yacht 'Rosetta', came the reply.

"Belonging to whom?"

"Charles Stenton from England."

There was a cry of surprise from Lady Margaret. She looked more sharply and saw the tall figure of Stenton at the helm.

"Do you know this man? asked the captain who had heard her call.

"Yes, he's one of my best friends May he please come on board?"

The captain put his hands to his mouth and asked: "Is Mr. Stenton on board?"

"Yes," came the reply.

"Come over here."

Stenton knew he had to follow that call if a warship ordered him, but he answered "I have no time."

"Lady Margaret Castlepool is here," explained the captain.

"Ah, yes I'm coming over."

Margaret shook his hands joyfully. "I thought you were in England, trying to heal Count Miguel and Condesa Rosetta?"

"I'm pleased to report a complete cure for both of them and, that I've married the Condesa Rosetta since."

Another cry of delight from Lady Margaret. She offered her congratulations.

"And I am now chasing the pirate Danlola. I hope to free Lucien de Mareau, who I have reason to believe is held prisoner on his ship."

"The pirate?" exclaimed the captain excitedly. "Do you know where he is now?"

"He's about half an hour away from here, behind the Pedro Bank. Perhaps you could help me to catch captain Danlola?"

"At once, at once, this is a piece of luck I can't miss."

"We'll approach him from both sides so as to get him between us."

"But for heaven's sake, how do you get to follow Danlola in a nutshell?"

"There is no time to explain now, sir. We have to hurry to catch him behind the Pedro Bank. Lady Margaret will explain it to you."

Stenton returned to his yacht and charged full steam ahead. After half an hour they saw the 'Penrosa'. "Don't shoot below the waterline, the prisoner will be there."

When they came near enough they fired salvos aimed to disable the ship from manoeuvring. They must have hit a bull's eye because all the men on the 'Penrosa' came from below on to the deck. "That's the same scoundrel," shouted Danlola, "give it to him!" But the 'Penrosa' was not prepared. Here, with so many ports nearby, they had masked the hatches and hidden the artillery. The few rifles they brought did not reach the yacht. There, Stenton stood on deck. "Greetings from Manresa, he called and lifted his double barrelled, very far reaching rifle, on to his cheek. The shot rung out and hit captain Danlola. "He's been hit in the shoulder and it's shattered his bones; that's good, we need him to talk," said Brooks. Stenton fired the second shot and the first officer distinguishable by his hat, fell dead. Stenton ordered the engines to stop, so that the yacht had a very slight shake.

He loaded his gun again. His next shot hit the helmsman and then another officer.

At that moment the warship turned up. "Hello," called the captain, "you've paralysed him. Great going." Then he fired a shot above the pirate's deck as a sign for them to show a flag.

The pirate showed the Spanish flag.

"What kind of ship?" asked the Englishman.

"'Penrosa', Captain Danlola.

"How many men on board?"

"Twenty-four," came the answer.

"Damned liar, get across to my ship," came the order.

The 'Penrosa' was lost. For the crew there was no other way to escape. They pretended they would follow that command,. They let down their boats but they rowed with all their might towards Jamaica. They had no time to take anything; they saved nothing but their lives. Stenton was immediately behind them with his yacht, but when he noticed they had no prisoner on their boat, he turned towards the pirate's ship.

The wounded captain was missing; his men had taken him into their boat. The search of the pirate ship revealed many a proof it had at times been used as a slave ship. Stenton took a lantern and went down to the keel room.

To have a sailing boat go deep enough into the water, stones and sand are used as ballast in the lowest part of the ship. With the 'Penrosa' it was all sand. The fact that, in those days, every ship let through a small amount of water, made the sand very damp. A pit had been dug into the sand and laid out with planks. In this polluted environment there was a living skeleton in chains. Stenton stepped nearer.

"Friends are here, Lieutenant."

The prisoner pulled himself up laboriously and stared at the speaker. "That voice, is it true or am I mistaken?" Stenton held the lamp so that its shine illuminated his face. "Oh my God," the prisoner called out, "Señor Stenton." He could not say more. Joy overcame him and he fainted.

Stenton examined his chains and found they could be undone with pliers. As he looked around to find a suitable tool, a sailor came down and handed him a key he had found in the Captain's cabin. He freed the lieutenant and carried him, still unconscious, upstairs into a cabin. Lucien de Mareau's eyes could be harmed by direct daylight. Then he sent a boat to collect Lady Margaret.

Meanwhile, the lieutenant, or Rudolfo, as he was called among the mountain robbers came to again. "Señor Stenton, heaven's angel, is it true or is it a dream?"

"It is true," Countered the doctor. "You will learn everything later. Your clothing is rotten, you cannot remain in that condition. Captain Danlola will surely have something that will fit you. Let's find some clothes. You'll have a visitor soon."

"Who is the visitor?"

"A lady More I can't tell you; here are your trousers and there's water for you to wash too. Knock when you've finished." Stenton left the cabin and Rudolfo changed and washed himself. He was very weak, but he managed. He looked into a mirror, He was clean again. He opened the cabin door and a lady fell into his weakened arms.

Their lips found each other again and again; then his eyes closed and he staggered. "Lucien," called Margaret anxiously, what's the matter?"

"This happiness is too much for me," he sighed. He was too weak to stand and she helped him to an armchair.

It took a while until Rudolfo felt stronger. He opened his eyes and looked into hers. Margaret stroked his gaunt cheeks with tenderness. "You will be strong as when you were in Spain, I'll look after you until all traces of your suffering have vanished. And then … " she blushed and did not finish the started sentence.

"And then …? he asked and put his arms around her again.

"And then …" she continued quietly, "then we shall be united for life."

She snuggled against him, but he shook his head. "That will not be possible."

"Why not?" she asked perplexed.

"You don't know me and the little you know – is not the truth." It was difficult for him to say this.

She looked shocked and gazed searchingly into his eyes. "Has your suffering so disheartened you? Your courage will return, my beloved.

Yes, I know little about you but I know you love me and that's enough for me. Nothing else matters.

"You should know. Listen to me, I'm not what I seem to be …"

Margaret put her hand over his mouth and interrupted him. "Not now, Lucien. You are clean and noble; I don't have to learn more now. Let's thank God your troubles are over and you are given back to me."

A happy smile spread over his face. He held her hands and looked at her beautiful features. They only thought of each other and didn't notice the noise from above, as weapons and other items were loaded on to the warship.

Finally, a knock at the door and at Margaret's invitation Stenton came in.

"Sorry to disturb you, but I'm worried about my friend. I've come as a physician and I'm asking the lieutenant to come on deck with me. A man who was imprisoned for months in such conditions must no longer neglect his health."

They followed him upstairs. In broad daylight, one could see the results of Rudolfo's imprisonment. His face had a greenish appearance, his eyes were sunken in their sockets and his skin was stretched over his cheekbones. "Thank God we have reached you today; a few weeks more would have been too late," said Dr. Stenton. He continued: "Lady Margaret, may I suggest that I take you to the governor of Jamaica and then back to Vera Cruz. We have to speak to a woman, Clarissa Moyes, who was Count Aurelio's nursemaid. She lives in a hacienda belonging to Count Miguel de Manresa's late brother. So we have to go to Mexico anyway. It's no detour for us."

Lady Margaret agreed and her luggage was brought over onto Stenton's yacht. ---

Chapter 10

BUFF-HE

$\mathcal{T}$HE journey to Vera Cruz passed happily and quickly. Stenton and Brooks decided to accompany the two lovers to Mexico City; the yacht was left in the care of the sailors.

It was impossible for Rudolfo to ride a horse, he was still too weak. They used the post-coach, travelling regularly between Mexico City and the port. All three took their weapons and provisions. In those days there were no inns on that stretch of road where they could eat decently.

In the evening they reached a place in which they thought that they could stay the night. The building belonged to the postmaster, but was terribly dirty. Margaret preferred to sleep in the coach. A resting place was prepared for her. Later she walked arm in arm with her beloved. Their hearts were full and yet they found no words.

Finally her quiet voice mentioned the time between Manresa and now. "Yes, it was terrible for me."

"And for me it was a time of great anxiety, my dear Lucien."

He stopped walking. "Don't call me Lucien. My name is Rudolfo."

"Rudolfo?"

"Yes, Lucien was an assumed name, but that was only part of it. Let's sit down. I have to be truthful with you."

"Can't we give that a little time? Can't it keep until later?"

"No, it rests heavily on my soul. I want to tell you about it."

"But you're ill and you'll excite yourself."

"Don't worry about that, Margaret To be dishonest with you hurts me more than the memory of a time I wish had never been.

They sat down on a rock. Rudolfo said: "You've learned from Dr. Stenton about my presumed descent?

"Yes, in Manresa and later in letters."

"I'm the victim of a crime. I've been robbed from my parents and I grew up in a thieves' den."

Margaret uttered a cry of surprise. "In a robber's den?

Margaret hadn't expected this. She breathed in deeply but couldn't speak for a while.

He noticed, and it hurt him terribly. He moved away from her and said:

"You are silent, you despise me. I was afraid of this."

She took his hand. "It wasn't your fault tat you came to this horrific place."

"No, I was a small child, almost a baby. I lived among these brigands but was not brought up as such. I never had to do anything unlawful."

"Thank God. But how could you become the man you are, among robbers?"

"The captain of the robbers had higher plans. I was brought up in the class to which I actually belong. The only wrong I have committed was to come to Manresa with a false name."

"You couldn't do otherwise, my Rudolfo." It was the first time she'd called him by that name. He pressed her hand and replied: "I thank you. Now I have the courage to tell you what has troubled me for so long."

He moved closed to her and began to tell. He told her of his memories of the early days of his childhood, life among the brigands and everything that happened later. It took a long time but when he'd finished and told her of Dr. Stenton's conclusions. She wound her arms around him and said: "Thank you for your candour. Now everything will be all right. You are worthy to be mine. God will guide us."

"But your father …" he asked.

"Don't worry about him. He loves me with all his heart, he will do what fatherly love demands."

After a short time they returned to the others. Margaret slept inside the carriage. The others wrapped themselves in their blankets and slept next to it.

Margaret intended to bring her three companions to her father right away but Stenton refused. "Do you want to take our friend Rudolfo to your father and tell him he is your fiancé without proper introduction?"

She blushed and answered: "You may be right. "But you must promise that if my father wishes you to stay at his palace you will accept."

"I promise. I've come to Mexico to get to know José Carujo and that may be easier when I stay with your father. Perhaps we'll find the key here to solve our riddle."

Lord Castlepool was surprised at his daughter's speedy return. "Margaret, is it possible that you are back already?"

"Oh Pa," she laughed, "I'm for real, I hope you don't think it is my ghost."

"But you couldn't have been in Jamaica."

She passed him the governor's answer. "Here is the proof."

"But how is that possible?"

"We have to thank the people who accompanied me, especially Dr. Stenton."

"You don't mean that doctor from Manresa?"

"Exactly."

"He brought you to Mexico?"

"First to Jamaica then to Mexico. He's in the company of two men. I'll explain that to you, but first read the governor's answers. I'll put away my clothes.

Soon she was at her father's side and told him everything. He listened and what he heard was like a book. He had plans for his daughter. Now she told him she's in love – with a Spanish robber.

She finished and waited in vain for an answer. Then he said mildly: "Margaret, my child, up to now you've been pure joy. For the first time I am grieved."

She threw her arms around him. "Forgive me father, I don't want to grieve you but I'm in love, there is nothing I can do."

Castlepool pushed her away gently. "And you believe everything you've told me about this Rudolfo?"

"Yes, I believe it positively."

"You really believe this man who was brought up by a captain of robbers?"

"I love him and I shall never be happy without him."

"And you don't think about your father?"

"Yes Pa, I do think about you."

"And yet you speak of this – adventurous love."

She stood in front of him and asked: "Father don't you want me to be happy?"

"Certainly, but because I do want you to be happy, it hurts me to find you in these chains."

"Test Rudolfo, Pa, test him. And should you say he is unworthy, I'll listen to you and never see him again."

There was a great childish trust in these words. He felt this and his features cleared. "Thank you for what you've said, Margaret, you won't be disappointed in me. Have a rest, and I'll think seriously and I'll do my best to see you happy." He kissed his daughter and turned to his work – but only while she was in the room. The moment she'd left, he rose from his chair and walked restlessly to and fro. Finally, he came to a conclusion. He would ask this Dr. Stenton. He had learned enough about this man to trust him completely.

Lord Castlepool went to the guesthouse where Stenton and his companions were staying. He asked for Dr. Stenton. "He's in his room," was the reply.

"Who, should we say wants him?" "Tell him a man wants to see him privately."

Stenton wondered who that might be and asked for this man to be sent to his room.

He saw at once that the stranger was not a common individual. The Lord's eyes rested with admiration on the giant's open face.

"You wished to see me?" Stenton asked in Spanish.

"We can speak English, maybe that's easier?"

"Ah, you are English?"

"Yes, my name is Castlepool."

"Castlepool? Perhaps you are the father of …?"

"Yes, I am, sir."

"Please take a seat, milord. I had no presentiment that such an unexpected visitor would call on me."

"Unexpected perhaps but you might guess the reason for my call."

"Perhaps," said Stenton seriously.

"Let me first thank you for taking my daughter to Jamaica and for bringing her here."

"Oh please, I did only what any gentleman would have done."

"Then please allow me to address you on a more serious matter."

"You mean my friend who is with me?"

"Yes, I mean the relationship of this man to my daughter."

"Please ask the questions and I shall answer."

"Tell me what you know about Rudolfo. My daughter's story was inconclusive."

Stenton told him all he knew. That it was he who first was suspicious, then about the dying beggar's confession. He told Castlepool why he thought that Rudolfo was Count Miguel's exchanged son. His deliberations and conclusion were clear to the lord. He asked Stenton what he intended to do and how it would be possible to and help Rudolfo to regain his true position.

"I would like to speak to a certain José Carujo," said Stenton I have a suspicion that Count Miguel's brother Manuel has not died, but was sold by Danlola somewhere in Africa. There is also the nursemaid, Clarissa Moyes, who probably could shed some light on this matter.

"I think I can help you to meet this Carujo, I move in circles where he also sometimes appears. He wanted to sell a hacienda to me. I found out it belonged to a Mr. Martin Wilson, who inherited it after Manuel de Manresa was proclaimed dead. In other words, he tried to cheat me. But why do you go to so much trouble and put yourself into such danger?"

"Remember that Rosetta de Manresa is my wife and, therefore, Rudolfo is my brother-in-law. By the way, is it possible to find out where the grave of Manuel de Manresa is located?"

"I'll make enquiries about that. My question will not stir anyone's curiosity."

"Thank you milord, I have to ask you to expedite matters because ..."

He was interrupted, the door opened and Rudolfo entered. When he saw the stranger, he wanted to withdraw, but Stenton waved to him to come in.

He turned to the lord and said in Spanish: "This is señor Rudolfo." Then he turned to Rudolfo, and said: "This is Lord Castlepool, the father of the lady we had the honour to accompany."

When Rudolfo heard the name of the father of his beloved, he blushed slightly but quickly overcame his embarrassment and bowed in the proper manner. "We have just talked about you," said Lord Castlepool frankly. "I wished to see you. You have been one of my daughter's protectors and I wish to thank you for that."

He held his hand toward the young man. Rudolfo took his hand and replied: "Oh Milord, my protection would not have saved the lady Margaret from any danger, I am ill and could, therefore, not be as chivalrous as I would have wished."

The lord felt sympathy for the poor fellow and said: "You need nursing and recuperation. Will you find them in these strange surroundings?"

"I hope so, Milord."

"Your hope to be cured in a Mexican guesthouse, is unlikely. That is why I beg you to stay in my abode."Milord, I am a poor and homeless man and would not dare to make use of your kind offer."

"You may accept my offer just the same; Dr. Stenton has told me about your cruel fate. That makes it even more important for me to prove to you that you may be poor but you are not homeless. Will you accept?"

Rudolfo, considering the lord's invitation looked at Stenton and said: "I would not like to be parted from my friend, milord."

The lord answered with a smile: "Dr. Stenton and helmsman Brooks are naturally invited too."

Stenton held his hand out to the lord: "That is more than hospitality; God will repay you for this. We shall come."

"As soon as possible, gentlemen, I'm leaving now to send you a carriage. Good bye." Stenton accompanied the lord to the door. When he returned he saw Rudolfo on the sofa with tears in his eyes.

"Anything the matter?" asked Stenton worried.

"Nothing, my friend, they are tears of happiness, I was afraid Margaret's father would not accept my story."

"Now you can see, he's not angry with you."

"And I think I have to thank you for that, I'm sure he came to you to find out about me. I'm delighted of the way this man talked to me."

The carriage arrived and took the three men to one of the most splendid Palaces of the town, where they were given rooms fit for a prince.

Rudolfo was too ill to ride. Brooks had sat on a horse less than ten times in his life, so it was Stenton who rode down the Alameda, the main street in Mexico City, where his tall figure created a sensation. --- Josefa, daughter of José Carujo, lay on her hammock and smoked a cigarette. She had a book in her hand but didn't look at it. She thought about her beloved cousin Aurelio who had promised to marry her when he had the inheritance and title of Count. Admittedly, he did so only after she had threatened to divulge his true identity. She had told him she had the latest will of Manuel de Manresa in which he was completely disinherited. She thought of the beautiful Spanish ladies and was afraid that one might captivate him.

Her father entered her room, his forehead wrinkled and a letter in his hand. He told her about his brother and Dr. Stenton, their most dangerous enemy.

Josefa pulled a contemptuous face. "Pah, a doctor, who would be frightened of him," she said. "We have to fear him, he saw through our plans almost the day he came to Manresa. He's amazingly astute and has the devil's own luck. Please read the letter. Josefa opened the letter and read:

Dear brother

I have things of importance to tell you. As you know, Stenton has escaped and has married Condesa Rosetta. He is now after Danlola to rescue this Lucien de Mareau. I have immediately sent letters to all the ports that Danlola could possibly call at. We can only hope that he will not succeed, as this could end all our plans. Now some good news: Our son Aurelio is now head of Manresa and I think that I have found a suitable match for him to marry, she is of old Spanish nobility and would take the name of Manresa to even higher honours. I shall write to you of any progress.

Your brother Pablo.

When Josefa read the second part of the letter she paled. She threw the crumpled letter to the ground and clenched her fists. "If Aurelio doesn't keep his word to me I shall crush him."

Her father put his hand on her shoulder. "Be calm, it hasn't happened yet."

"No, it hasn't happened yet but the mere thought is agony to me."

"My brother probably knows nothing of Aurelio's promise."

"The more his disloyalty. I shall not give him up, he is my own and no other woman shall have him. I want to be Countess of Manresa and what I want, I'll get, no matter how." She stood like a fury before her father but he replied calmly:

"I shall write to my brother."

"Yes, write to him and demand an immediate answer."

"And if he says no?"

"Then he is lost, I swear that to you."

"Josefa, he is my brother."

"Just because of that he should heed our will. If he doesn't, I still have the Count Manuel's last will."

"You won't use that against him."

Josefa stood with a mocking smile and went boldly to her father: "What are you? Your brother has a son and you have a daughter. We are all thieves and cheats, we even became murderers to get Manresa. Should his son get all and your daughter to go away empty? No, it belongs to him and to me. If he'll be Count then I'll be Countess. That's the right way and I shan't give in, never."

Carujo told her she was right, but there are bigger things to worry about.

"There is this Dr. Stenton"

"Do you think this Dr. Stenton who stays with Lord Castlepool is the same as our enemy? He might not be the same Stenton."

"I think it most probable, he is"

"I'll get us an invitation!" Josefa seemed even more determined than her father.

Stenton was prepared that such a meeting would sooner or later take place, but he would not allow himself to be interrogated.

About a week after Stenton's arrival, Lord Castlepool invited him for a ride. When they reached a wall, the lord pointed at a large tomb on the other side of the wall and explained: "You asked me to find where the grave of don Manuel is, it's the one with the Corinthian columns."

"May we enter?"

"Why not? The cemetery gate is open all day."

They dismounted and strolled as if by chance to the vault. " Here's the name. The gate to the tomb is not very high, I can climb over it, I'll pay it a visit tonight. Will you come with me?"

"I'm afraid I can't accompany you, I'm the representative of a nation and have to be careful."

Stenton and his two companions were at the cemetery shortly before midnight. Rudolfo had sufficiently recovered during the last eight days to take part in the adventure. They climbed over the wall. Stenton asked them to wait until he'd searched the surroundings. "Now come behind me but quietly". Stenton swung himself over the gate, the others followed. They had to step down a few narrow stairs. Stenton had prepared himself with tools. Brooks had a lantern but made sure that no light went to the top. There were two coffins made of metal. The one nearest to the entrance bore the name of Manuel de Manresa in golden letters. Stenton examined the screws securing the lid and began to work with them.

"What are we going to find?" mused Rudolfo.

"Either the remains of your uncle or, more likely, an empty coffin," was the reply.

"I'm dreading this. Think of my situation; the kidnapped nephew stands before the grave of his uncle."

"Take hold of yourself, we're not robbing a grave. We're representing the law and for what we do, we can answer to God with a clear conscience. Now let's open the coffin." Stenton took hold of the lid but it slipped from his hands and fell down. It made a hollow sound in the deep vault.

"It's as if the dead defends himself against the disturbance of his rest," whispered Rudolfo.

"He won't be angry if we want to make sure no crime has been committed against him," replied Stenton. He lifted the lid again, this time with more care. It came off and was put on the ground. Brooks made his lantern shine into – an empty coffin.

As if on command, the three looked into each other's face.

"It's empty," said Rudolfo.

"Just as I thought," remarked Stenton.

Brooks reminded Stenton of the man who was put on board in Vera Cruz and then sold to Harare.

"I'm convinced of that. Let's close the coffin and leave no trace we've been here and know the truth."

Lord Castlepool waited tensely for the result of the investigation. He'd told Stenton and Rudolfo to call on him as soon as they knew the result.

"This is an enormity. What a crime! I wouldn't believe it, we should make a report,"

"That would lead to nothing. I've no trust in Mexican justice."

"We can force them to do their duty."

"Who will force them, Milord?" asked Stenton

"I will" replied the lord resolutely.

"It would be in vain."

"I'll prove it to you."

"All you'll prove is there is a corpse missing. Where it went, whether it was buried in the first place, dead or alive, who were the criminals would be left undiscovered. We'd make the enemies aware of us by a report and also they'd realise the danger they are in."

"But should such a crime go without punishment?"

"No, they or he will be punished, but we have to find Manuel de Manresa first. Then we'll lead the perpetrator to the cemetery and ask for the corpse. Not sooner."

"So you are going to Harare?"

"Certainly, but first we have to go to the hacienda Del Alina to speak to the nursemaid Clarissa Moyes. Rudolfo needs another week at least to get in shape. Señor Brooks has to improve his riding skills."

" You'll go through Red Indian territory."

"We have to. But I'm no stranger to the Indians. I've spent three years in the West, and I gained a lot of skills that might come in useful."

Two days after they had found the empty grave, Lord Castlepool and Stenton were invited to a party which, they had learned, Carujo and his daughter would attend. They went early to be there before Carujo. The feast was given by a well-to-do Mexican family and several rooms were at the disposal of the guests. After he had greeted the lady of the house, Stenton told the lord that he would take a stroll in the garden, Would someone please call him when Carujo had arrived.

"Would you introduce me, Milord?"

"As you wish. They are here now, come with me."

They saw Carujo and his daughter talking to some of the guests. "The gaunt one is Carujo and the lady next to him is his daughter," explained the lord."

"He looks a bit like his brother," remarked Stenton.

The lord went toward the group. Carujo had his back turned but when he noticed Lord Castlepool, he addressed him immediately, "Ah, Milord, what joy to meet you here, have you thought over the proposal?"

"Which one?"

"About the purchase of the Hacienda del Alina."

"I have to know whether it really belongs to Don Manuel de Manresa."

"Of course, it does."

"Rumour has it that it belongs to a Mr. Martin Wilson, who inherited it after the death of Don Manuel."

"That is a lie, Milord, empty talk."

"Well, I shall soon know the truth through a friend who intends to visit the hacienda."

"Who is that?"

The lord turned around and called Stenton. "This is my friend Dr. Carlos Stenton."

Carujo and daughter turned quickly to be introduced. "A great honour to get to know you, Dr. Stenton, you are English I've heard?"

"Yes."

"I love England. Allow me to introduce my daughter Josefa."

Stenton exchanged a bow with Carujo's daughter, then he was taken to a bench where Carujo immediately questioned him. "I've heard you want to go to the Hacienda del Alina?"

"Maybe," was Stenton's short answer. He was annoyed the lord had betrayed his intentions.

"May I ask to what purpose?"

Stenton noticed he was being interrogated. "I would like to know about Mexico and its inhabitants. When the lord realised that, he asked me to go to the hacienda because he intends buying it."

"Ah, that's it," said Carujo satisfied. "I have a wilful tenant there who maintains that he is the owner. Ridiculous. It seems that you travel a lot?"

"I do."

"A man who's the master of his time is enviable. Which continents have you visited already, señor Stenton?" Josefa seemed very interested.

"America, Africa and part of Asia."

"And Europe?"

"That's where I was born," Stenton smiled.

"Have you been to Spain?" The questions went on.

"Yes, I have been there."

Josefa exchanged glances with her father; "Spain is our motherland. May I ask what town or provinces?"

Stenton answered indifferently: "I've been in that beautiful Country only a short time. I received a call as a physician to a Count de Manresa, to relieve him from some evil."

"Did you know that this Count had a brother with very substantial property here in Mexico?"

"Yes."

"And that my father is its administrator?"

Stenton pretended astonishment. "Really?" Then, as if a thought had occurred to him, "there was a señor Carujo, are you perhaps related to him?"

"He is my brother."

"I'm very pleased about that. I met señor Pablo Carujo on many occasions."

"He's not very sociable."

"I didn't notice that. On the contrary, we came to know each other very well."

Josefa angrily bit her lip. She understood the double meaning but she said with the friendliest voice: "If only you could have saved the good Count Miguel."

"Yes, I would have given a lot to do that, señorita."

"I believe he died in an unhappy fall."

"Yes, the fall was an unlucky one." These words also had a double meaning, well understood by Carujo and his daughter.

"You knew Countess Rosetta as well?" Josefa continued searching.

"Indeed. She is my wife. We were married in England."

Stenton was convinced these facts were known to them, although they appeared surprised."

"And Count Aurelio did not mind?"

"He hasn't hindered us. Would you please excuse me? Lord Castlepool waved to me, he probably wants to introduce me to someone."

"It was lovely to meet a señor who knows Manresa," said Carujo."Would you like to visit us?"

"I am at your disposal."

"Or we might pay you a visit, I'm very good friends with lady Margaret," lied Josefa.

"By all means."

Stenton bowed slightly and went to Castlepool. José Carujo and daughter waited until he had gone. Josefa showed her rage: "It was him. We have to find out what he wants here in Mexico. In any case, although he's a man women could fall easily for, he has to be destroyed for our safety." ---

"What do you make of these two?" Castlepool enquired.

"Hawk and owl, only the owl has more courage and energy than the hawk.

The next morning a servant reported the visit of señor Carujo and señorita Josefa. They entered the next moment. "Forgive us, señor Stenton, for looking you up so soon. Josefa longed to hear more of her home town. We've had no news for such a long time, so we've decided to make use of your friendly invitation."

Stenton welcomed them with the uttermost politeness. The moment they were sitting down the expected investigation began: "You've landed in Vera Cruz?" asked Carujo."

"Yes, señor."

"I take it you were recommended to Lord Castlepool?"

"I came to know Lady Margaret in Manresa."

"Were there a lot of visitors in Manresa?

"Not really."

"But we have heard of a French officer?"

Stenton knew they would question him about Rudolfo.

"He left soon after arriving in Manresa."

"He went back to France?"

"He left without telling us his plans."

At this moment Brooks entered the room and gave Stenton the opportunity to leave. He went to Lord Castlepool who asked him about the rush when he came in.

"Carujo and daughter are here I'd be so grateful if you'd invite them for breakfast."

"Why? I hate that kind of vermin."

"I must know what impression the appearance of Rudolfo will make."

"Ah, that's different. But why don't you take Rudolfo to him now?"

"I want you two to be witnesses."

"That's different, I'll invite them," said Lord Castlepool.

Stenton returned to his visitors. but because of Brooks's presence was spared any more uncomfortable questions. Lord Castlepool entered after a while and pretended he thought Stenton to be alone. He greeted the others with extreme friendliness and invited them all for breakfast. All were present except Rudolfo. Conversation started about Mexican food when Rudolfo entered. Carujo and daughter sat with their back toward him. As soon as Carujo saw Rudolfo he jumped up and called out: – "Count Miguel!"

Carujo's face grew pale and his eyes stared at Rudolfo. There was a picture in the palace of Count Miguel in his youth. The painting's similarity to this young man was such that Josefa's owl's eyes widened with shock.

"You're mistaken," said Stenton, "This man is not Count Miguel de Manresa but the lieutenant Lucien de Mareau after whom you asked yesterday."

Slowly the two recovered. "Pardon me," said Carujo, "a slight similarity led to this mistake. I had completely forgotten that many years have passed since the Count was similar to this young man."

"I too was shocked," apologised Josefa.

"Really remarkable," said Lord Castlepool. Soon the conversation became more general. ---

When Carujo entered his home he asked Josefa: "Do you know now where you stand?"

"Yes, this lieutenant is the genuine Count Aurelio. In three days Stenton will go to the hacienda. Will you let him get away with it?"

"I wouldn't think of it, we won't let him go further." Carujo brooded most of the night. Then he made his decision. He went to his stable where he asked for a horse to be saddled. When his daughter arose, she was told he had gone away. ---

Stenton and his two companions said their good byes. He asked the lord: "One never knows what can happen in this Country. Would you be so kind as to look after the yacht and the men?"

Margaret didn't want to leave her beloved Rudolfo and in spite of the lord's warnings about the Red Indian territory they had to cross, she insisted on riding with them. The four took the same way that Carujo has taken two days before. ---

Stenton had a map of Mexico and they followed it without losing their way. About a day's ride from the hacienda, Stenton suddenly told his comrades to stop for a while. He, who observed every stone pushed out of its place, every broken twig and every track on the ground, told them there was a man lying in wait about eighty metres away, hidden behind bushes and trees. Brooks and the others said they didn't see anything. It takes practice and experience to notice such things. "Take up your arms but don't shoot until I do." They rode on until they were almost next to the suspected trees, when Stenton suddenly aimed at the bushes; the two men with him did the same.

"Hallo, señor, what are you seeking in there?"

A short laughter sounded from the undergrowth. "What business is that of yours?"

"It's very much my business," answered Stenton, "please show yourself."

"Well, I'll do you that favour." The bushes parted and a man, dressed in buffalo skin, stepped out. His face showed traces of Red

Indian descent. He glanced at the men and said: "That was not done badly, señores. This is not the first time you've been on the prairie."

Stenton understood at once but Rudolfo asked: "Why."

"Because you seemed as if you had noticed nothing and then, suddenly, aimed your rifles at me."

"We thought it suspicious to see a man hidden here," said Stenton. "What did you do in that bush?"

"I waited for someone."

"For whom?"

"Who knows, maybe for you."

Stenton raised his eyebrows and warned: "Don't make stupid jokes and declare yourself."

"That I can do, but first tell me where you are going to?"

"To the Hacienda del Alina."

"Good, you are the people I waited for."

"That sounds as if they knew of our coming and have sent you to meet us"

"It was nothing like that. I was hunting buffalo and found some tracks of people. I eavesdropped on them. They talked of attacking some men on their way to the hacienda. If you are these people, all right If not I shall wait again." Stenton held out his hand to the stranger and said: "You are a good man and I thank you. We are probably the people they expect. How many of them were they?"

"Twelve."

"I feel like having a word with them. If it were up to me, I'd have a look at these people. Having a lady with us, I think it is safer to avoid trouble."

"I think so too," nodded the stranger.

"Where are you going now? asked Stenton.

"To the hacienda. Should I lead you there?"

"If you like, yes."

"Let's go!" The stranger mounted his horse and went to the front of the little group. He leant forward on his horse in Red Indian fashion, in order to see any tracks immediately. Stenton recognised that this man knew the ways of the West, that one could rely on him.

When, in the evening, they were on the lookout for a suitable place to lie down and rest for the night, the leader seemed to be the apt person to do so. He ate with the four and accepted a cigarette but declined the offer of rum. On his advice no fire was lit. It was safer and more secure, having the war and roaming tramps in mind.

"Do you know the people on the hacienda? Stenton asked their leader.

"Yes, there is Señor Wilson, the owner, his daughter Alva, then there is Señora Moyes and a hunter whose head has been badly injured. There are also forty vaqueros and Kaya, the girl I was brought up with and who is friends with Miss Alva.

"And you?"

"No, I am a free Mixteka."

"Then you must know Mokashi-tayis, the chief of this almost vanished tribe?"

"I know him," answered the Indian calmly.

"His name Buff-he, as the hunters call him here, is known even over the big ocean."

"He will enjoy that, if he hears about this. The white hunters called him Buffalo-head at first and then Buff-he, for short. How should I call you?"

"This is lady Margaret, this señor is called Brooks, the other is señor Rudolfo and my name is Stenton. How do we call you?"

"I am a Mixteka – call me that."

With this, the conversation ended. Then they went to sleep. The four men took turns with the night watch. Early next morning they were on their way again. At midday they saw the hacienda from the distance.

Buff-he pointed his finger toward the hacienda and said: "This is your aim. You don't need me anymore."

"Aren't you coming with us?" asked Stenton.

"No, my home is in the woods." The Mixteka gave his horse the heel and soon disappeared in the distance. ---

Chapter 11

ON THE HACIENDA

$\mathcal{T}$HE four went toward the walls and stopped before the gate. A Vaquero asked for their desire.

"Is señor Wilson at home?"

"Yes."

"Tell him that there are guests from Mexico who want to speak to him."

"Are you alone or will there be more?"

"We are alone."

"So I will trust you." The Vaquero opened the gate and the riders entered. They jumped off their horses, they were taken by the Vaquero who led them to water.

The haciendero walked toward them. He looked at his visitors. When he saw Rudolfo he uttered a cry of amazement:

"What is that, Count Miguel? but no, it can't be, the Count is much older.

He hen looked at Brooks and put his hand on his forehead. Am I bewitched? he called out.

"What is it, father? asked a clear girl's voice behind him.

"Come here my child; is that not a miracle? First there is a man who looks like Count Miguel in his younger years. Then there is another that is the image of your ill fiancé.

Alva stepped nearer.

"It's true, this man looks just like my poor Antonio."

"This miracle will soon clear up. Welcome señores, step into my house." He led the guests into the dining room, where they were offered refreshments. Brooks had lifted his glass to have a drink but put it down again. He saw a pale man entering the room, who glanced at the visitors with an empty look in his eyes. Brooks made a few steps toward the person. "Is it possible," he called out, "Anthony, Anthony! Oh my God!"

Antonio looked at him, shook his head and whimpered, "I am dead, I have been killed."

Brooks dropped his arms and asked: "Mr. Wilson, who is this man?"

"He is, like you, a Country man of mine and the fiancé of my daughter; his name is Anthony Brooks."

"So it's my brother, oh my brother." With this cry he embraced the strange person and pressed him to his chest. The brother, indifferent, repeated: "I am dead, I have been killed."

"What is the matter with him? What's wrong with him?" Brooks asked the haciendero.

"It's a short sad story. Aurelio, the son of Count Miguel de Manresa, whose brother was the owner of this hacienda, came here for a visit. Our daughter's friend Kaya, who was brought up with the chief of the Mixtekas, fell in love with him. He cajoled her with false promises of marriage to betray the whereabouts of the secret hiding place of the treasure of the almost extinguished tribe of the Mixtekas. It was only known to her and, of course, the chief himself.

At the same time Buff-he, the chief of the Mixtekas, wanted to make a present to his friend here, Anthony Brooks, also known among other hunters as Old Surehand, who had become engaged to my daughter. The treasure was hidden in a cave, the entrance of which was only one hour's ride away from here and, of course, disguised.

Antonio saw a treasure of many, many millions in gold and precious objects, several rooms full of them. He was allowed to take what one packhorse could carry, only a tiny part of the whole treasure. As he sorted these items, Aurelio, who knew the secret from Kaya, crept behind him. He saw no one else because Buff-he had gone to the back of the cave. He took a heavy item and smashed Antonio over the head.

At that moment Buff-he returned and grabbed Aurelio, who made no resistance. The shock of seeing the Indian had paralysed him.

In short, Aurelio was being hanged under his arms, on a tree, whose trunk was bent over a lake containing crocodiles. Just high enough to be caught by these beasts, unless, of course, he lifted his legs in time. He would tire and then be torn to pieces, so Buff-he thought. A group of tramps found him hanging there and, because Buff-he had not taken his wallet, he promised them money and they took him off the tree.

Buff-he at first thought that his friend was dead, but when he discovered that he was still breathing, he tied him onto a horse and brought him back here. Doctors were called but none gave any hope of recovery. My daughter, of course, is devastated by this assault.

That is the sad part of the story but for Mr. Brooks, there is also some good news. One half of that treasure was destined by Antonio, before he went to see the treasure, of course, to his brother and his family, for good schools for his nephew Robbie. But I'm sure he didn't expect to become a millionaire and to be able to dish out millions for his brother's family as well."

George Brooks wiped his tears away. Stenton asked whether he could examine the patient. They both went to another room where Stenton had a good look at the wound. He came to the conclusion that Anthony Brooks was not beyond help. He went back to Wilson and his guests and announced: "The doctor you had was a quack.

George, your brother is not mad. His spirit is disturbed – help is still possible."

A loud cry of jubilation could be heard. Alva flew toward Stenton. "Are you telling us the truth, are you a physician?"

"I am a physician and hope for the best."

"Will you treat him now? asked Alva impatiently.

"Slowly, such examination takes time and I've come here for a purpose."

"I'm sure of that" said the haciendero, "what is it you have come for?"

"First, I must explain we are sure that Aurelio is not the real son of Count Miguel de Manresa." Stenton explained. "My researches have found that an exchange of two children has taken place, while in the care of the nursemaid Clarissa Moyes. She herself had no part in this exchange, but I would like to speak to her."

"Amazing," said Wilson, I shall call for her immediately."

Kaya, the Red Indian girl had entered the room and was introduced to the visitors. She was asked by the haciendero, to look for Clarissa Moyes and bring her to the dining room.

When Clarissa entered the room, Stenton asked Rudolfo to stand aside until he called him. Now it was her turn to be introduced. She remembered Lady Margaret who, with her father Lord Henry Castlepool, had visited Manresa as a child. Then Stenton called Rudolfo. A cry of astonishment "Count Miguel," she shouted, but soon it dawned on her that this was impossible and she looked at the young man in bewilderment.

"This is not Count Miguel but the exchanged child you had in your care when you travelled to Mexico," Stenton explained to the nonplussed former nursemaid. He then continued. "You must have noticed something, even if you dismissed it at the time. Please take your mind back and let me know."

Clarissa's mind went blank at first, then she started to remember: "That is the answer to a riddle that has plagued me for many years. There were many changes I'd noticed in the morning but could find no explanation and put them down to my inadequacy of memory. There was slightly different hair, some garments that did not have the usual label with a crown and an M y C insignia. His crying had a different sound and, of course, his face was not the same. But, as I said, I had no explanation and an exchange would have never occurred to me. Even had I remembered the tiny birthmark just under his left arm, I would have put it down to my own inadequate memory."

Rudolfo bared his left arm and everybody saw the birthmark." That is exactly why we came here. You will, of course, put all this in writing, to be signed by you and witnessed by us. And now give me some time to make a proper examination of the patient. I have the instruments with me. Is the patient obedient?

"Yes, fully submissive," answered the haciendero.

Stenton took the patient once more to another room and began a thorough check up. Except for the vaqueros, all were assembled in the reception room to expect the outcome of Dr. Stenton's examination. It took quite a while but when he eventually joined them, he had a smile on his face. "I have good news for you, I shall be able to fully restore señor Brooks.

There were shouts of delight when Stenton continued. "There was a strong blow on the head but the skull has not been broken. Beneath the skull, a blood vessel has poured its content over the organ of his memory. That's why the patient has forgotten everything except that he had received a blow on the head meant to kill him. Help is only possible if I operate to remove the blood. The pressure will be taken away and the brain will resume its function. His memory will return."

"Is this operation life threatening? Alva asked anxiously.

"Painful but not life threatening," explained Stenton. "If the relatives of the patient give me the authority, then I shall start tomorrow."

They all gave their consent. "You don't have to worry about compensation," smiled the haciendero, "the patient has just received a king's ransom to pay for this operation."

"Let's hope for the best," replied Stenton and left to look after his instruments.

After their evening meal they convened a meeting to discuss in detail the actual purpose of their visit. What Clarissa Moyes had told them, confirmed Stenton's supposition. Martin Wilson immediately offered Rudolfo the hacienda. There was no- one who doubted that Rudolfo was the proper heir.

The next day, when the operation was to take place, Stenton asked Brooks, Rudolfo and Wilson to stand by when he needed help. He rejected any other offers and asked for absolute quiet. The four men went to the patients room; the floor was locked for everybody.

Now and then one could hear painful whimpering or a loud shrill sound though the house. Then it was quiet again. Finally, after a long time, Wilson came down and joined the others. He looked pale and exhausted.

"How did it go?" asked Alva.

"Señor Stenton thinks the operation will be a success. He asked you to come and stay with the patient."

"Only me?"

"No, I shall be with you. When Antonio wakes up, he should see only familiar faces."

She followed her father. As they entered the room, they saw Stenton feeling the pulse of the patient and Counting his breaths. "Señorita, would you please sit so that he will see you when he wakes up; I myself will wait behind the curtain," whispered Stenton.

"How long will it take for him to wake up?" asked Alva.

"Ten minutes at most, let us wait and pray."

Stenton went behind the curtain and Alva sat near the bed while Wilson also took his place nearby. Minutes seemed eternities. Finally the sufferer started moving his hands. "Don't get a shock if he utters a loud cry," said Stenton quietly, "by my reckoning he will utter a death cry, because he thinks that he received a deadly blow."

The physician was not wrong. The patient moved his whole body and then lay stiff for a few seconds. Those were the moments when his memory returned. Now he uttered a horrific cry. Wilson trembled and Alva had to stop herself from fainting. Then followed a deep sigh and then – then, the patient opened his eyes. In these eyes there had been no normal consciousness for days. Now he looked as if he had wakened from a sleep. His eyes went to the left then to the right and as their glance sharpened he noticed his fiancé. He opened his lips:

"Alva! Oh God, I dreamed that Aurelio wanted to kill me. It was in the cave of the Mixteka treasure. Is it true that I'm with you?"

"Yes, you are with me, my Antonio." She took his hands into her own.

Suddenly his hands touched his bandaged head. "That's where he hit me. My head hurts; why am I bandaged, Alva?"

"You've been injured," she answered.

"Yes, I feel it. You'll tell me everything but now I'm tired, I want to sleep." He closed his eyes and soon was breathing calmly asleep.

Stenton stepped forward from behind the curtain and, beaming with delight, he declared: "We have won. When the traumatic fever passes, he should be completely cured. Go and tell the good news to the others who, I am sure, are waiting for it. Señorita Alva and I will keep watch here."

The good haciendero hurried and brought the joyous news to the resident people of the house who were all delighted. Two days passed, the patient improved daily. Then the morning of the third day brought disquiet, not about the patient but about Buff-he. He appeared and delivered news that made the haciendero and Alva anxious. The anxiety was not for themselves but for the patient. ---

The band of tramps hired by Carujo to assassinate Stenton and his friends were in vain waiting for their prey. They wanted to be paid. Carujo refused but then made them a bigger offer. They should attack and rob anything they wanted from 'his' Hacienda del Alina, provided they killed Stenton and Lucien. He gave them a full description.

"The others you want us to keep alive?" asked the one in command.

"Not at all," replied Carujo, "I don't mind if you kill all of them."

"When should the attack take place?"

"Tomorrow night. There are forty vacueros who sleep in a nearby building. By the time they are on the scene, it will be all over. Remember, to get your reward you must eliminate the two people I have named. Now I'll give you the plans of the building and the guest rooms where they will probably sleep."

Neither the tramps nor Carujo were aware that an eavesdropper overheard their plans. Baff-he withdrew from behind the bushes where he had listened to the whole conversation. ---

"I have to tell señor Stenton," said the haciendero.

"Señor Stenton? The tall man whom I brought to you?" asked the Mixteka, "how can he help?"

"By giving advice."

The Red Indian's expression showed disdain. "Who is this man?"

"A physician."

"A physician of the pale faces! How can he advise Buff-he?"

"He should advise me. We should discuss our plans together."

"Is he a chief or an adviser in the fight against an enemy?"

"He is a clever man. He has operated on Old Surehand and given him back his memory."

The Indian was amazed. "My friend Old Surehand can speak like a sensible man again?"

"Yes. He will be a healthy person in a few days."

"So this señor Stenton is a clever medicine man. A warrior he is not. Have you seen his weapons?"

"Yes."

"Did you see him ride?"

"Yes, I saw him arrive from the distance."

"Well, he is sitting on a horse like a pale-face and his weapons are shining like silver. That is never the case with a great warrior."

"So you don't want any discussions with him?"

"I am a friend of the hacienda. Let him come but he won't be of any use."

The haciendero told Stenton about the chief's comments. Stenton greeted the Mixteka with a smile and inquired: "I'm told you are Baff-he, the chief of the Mixteras?"

"Yes I am."

"What message do you have for us?"

"The twelve pale-faces who wanted to attack and to kill you want to do it again. Only there are twice as many now and their attack is the hacienda."

"Did you eavesdrop on them?"

"Yes."

"When do they want to attack?"

"Tomorrow night. They are now in the 'valley of the tiger'."

"Is that far from here?"

"By the measurement of the pale-faces it is a ride of one hour or two hours' walk."

"Do they have any guards?"

"I've seen two, one at the entrance and one at the exit of the gorge."

"Would you take me there?"

The chief looked at the questioner with obvious amazement. "What do you want there?"

"I'd like to take a look at these pale-faces."

"What for? I've looked already at them. Who wants to see them has to crawl through the woods and moss. That would dirty your Mexican attire," said by Baff-he with an almost insulting smile they will kill whoever eavesdrops on them."

"Are you afraid to accompany me?"

The Mixteka looked contemptuously into Stenton's face. "Baff-he knows no fear. He will take you, but cannot help you when more than twenty pale-faces attack and kill you.

"Wait a little." With these words Stenton went to prepare himself for the way.

"This doctor will die," was the Indian's dry remark.

"So you will protect him," said Wilson seriously.

"He has a big mouth He speaks a lot but he will bring no results." With this he went to the window and looked outside, as if this matter did not concern him.

Stenton returned after a short while. "We can go now," he said.

The Mixteka turned around. When he saw Stenton, he looked amazed. Stenton wore a pair of elk-leather trousers, a strong hunting shirt made of leather, a wide- brimmed hat and very high boots. This hunter's outfit he had bought in Mexico City. Over his shoulders one could see a double-barrelled rifle. In his belt he carried two revolvers, one Bowie knife and a tomahawk. His outward appearance was so warrior like and imperious that even the Mixteka was influenced.

The Indian walked past him and just said: "Come on." He mounted his horse.

Stenton asked: "Do you want to ride to the 'valley of the Tiger'?

"Yes."

"Leave your horse here, we'll walk. A man can hide better without a horse and I don't want to make horse tracks."

The Mixteka's face lit up; he saw that Stenton was right. He dismounted and went ahead without looking back. Once he looked back when the ground became sandy and looked at his tracks. These were the tracks of a single man because Stenton went in the footprints of his leader. "Uff," said Baff-he and nodded approvingly.

The way led over sandy ground and, finally, through a wood whose trees were wide enough for a man to hide behind. About two hours had gone, when Stenton noticed that the Indian became more careful. Baff-he suddenly stood still and whispered to Stenton: "They are not far now. Be absolutely quiet."

Stenton did not answer at all to this warning. Finally, the Indian lay down on the ground and waved to Stenton to do the same. They crawled forward until they heard loud voices. They reached the edge of a deep gorge whose walls were so steep they were impossible to climb. The valley was about eight hundred steps long and about three hundred steps wide. A little stream wound along the ground. On its banks were ten armed figures. A guard on either side of the entrance of the valley.

Stenton turned to the Indian and whispered: "You've seen twice as many as we see here?"

"Yes, the others probably went away spying."

"Or robbing, more likely."

Stenton listened. They talked loudly so he could understand every word. These people must feel secure.

"How much would we get if we kill them?" asked one of them.

"Twenty pesos for each of them. That's enough for one English and two Spanish people. They're not worth any more."

"We would have killed them yesterday and earned our money, if they hadn't taken a different route. To hell with them," said a second person.

"Why are you cursing? It was a good thing we have missed them. We'll get the loot of the whole hacienda now."

"Have we got enough people? This haciendero has forty vaqueros"

"Don't be stupid, we'll surprise them."

Stenton knew enough now. He was not the man to kill unnecessarily but here it meant saving themselves from a band of robbers and murderers. He grasped his rifle.

"What are you doing?" asked the Indian.

"I want to overpower them."

On the face of the Indian one could see that he thought his companion was mad. He wanted to withdraw but Stenton demanded: "Stay here, or are you afraid? You've heard of me, I'm known in the prairie as Doctor Ironfist."

When the Mixteka heard the name of the most famous hunter in the West, his expression changed to one of respect.

"You take the guards. None should be able to escape." With these words Stenton lowered the barrel but he changed his mind.

"You should see how Doctor Ironfist defeats his enemies. Shoot the bandits in the arms or the legs." With these words he got up that he could be seen by the people on the ground and uttered a loud cry. All eyes looked up at him.

"I'm Stenton," he called down.

His voice echoed from the walls and, at the same time, his rifle sounded for the first time. The bandits jumped up and grasped their rifles. Stenton lay on the ground again and both sent down shot after shot. Before the desperadoes came to their senses, five were hit, the others were shooting in vain and then fled. They were shot down. There were two left. One was shot by Baff-he in the thigh. The other Stenton wanted to save.

"Lie down and don't move," Stenton called down. The man obeyed immediately.

"Go down to him while I guard the situation," Stenton told the Mixteka.

Buff-he rushed to the edge of the gorge until he reached the bottom and the man who still did not move. Stenton hurried after the Indian and told the man to get up. The man trembled as he rose.

"How many men are you?"

"Twenty four."

"Where are they?"

The man hesitated.

"Speak or you are dead."

"They went to the hacienda Candora."

"What are they doing there?"

"They're visiting the friend of the man who asked us to attack the hacienda del Alina."

"What's his name?"

"I never heard it."

"All right, I know who it is. How far is the hacienda Candora?"

"Three hours' ride."

"When are they coming back?"

"We don't expect them back before tomorrow noon."

Stenton took three of their best horses. One for himself, one for Baff-he and one to carry all their weapons. They then bound the prisoner lightly, so he could soon free himself and help the others. The residents of the hacienda were amazed when they saw the riders, who had left their horses behind, returning on horseback. Stenton, who had had to leave his patient, immediately went to see him. The Mixteka, in the meantime, told the astonished listeners what happened.

"This physician is famous in the prairie," he told them, "he is Doctor Ironfist."

They had all heard of Doc Ironfist but none had connected this doctor with that famous name.

Stenton found his patient asleep with Alva at his bedside. When he retuned, he met the haciendero who held out his hand to Dr. Stenton and said: "You have saved us from a terrible enemy. We are twice indebted to you. Stenton waved his hand, "you don't owe me anything but tell me, is the haciendero of the Candora a friend of yours?"

"Rather an enemy," replied Wilson.

" We have to go there to catch José Carujo. Give me twenty vaqueros and let's ride as soon as possible."

They had almost reached the hacienda Candora when they met a rider coming from there. Stenton asked him whether he belonged to the hacienda. The rider said, "Yes."

Were there any visitors? "There were a dozen of them but when a colleague of theirs arrived and told them of a shooting in the Valley of the Tiger, they left a short while later."

Stenton turned his horse and took the group in the direction of the Valley of the Tiger. After ten minutes they saw the track of about a dozen horses, which they then followed. As expected the valley was cleared of any enemies. Carujo knew that his intention to attack the hacienda in the near future was not possible, as they would be on their guard now. He decided to postpone these plans and went to the nearest town, where he would rest in a guesthouse overnight.

The glimmer of the first house of Santa Rosa was seen when a gruff voice called out: Who is there?"

"What is that?"

"What is that? I want an answer!"

"Who are you?"

"Caramba, don't you see? I am a guard." The man blew a whistle immediately answered by another. In a few seconds four armed men appeared and asked: "What's the matter?"

"These men want to enter the town but haven't give me their name."

"Come along, this town is under siege by Benito Juarez," said the leader of the four.

"Benito Juarez? That's different. My name is Josè Carujo. I am from the capital. Now I'm returning and want to stay in Santa Rosa over night."

"The others, do they belong to you?"

"Yes."

"Who are you?"

"I am administrator of the estate of Manresa."

"A distinguished bloodsucker, follow me."

"I think I would rather ride back." Carujo felt that this situation could not bring him any advantage.

"This is not possible now. You reached our sentry and you have to come along."

It would have been easy to turn the horse and disappear in the dark, but Carujo was no hero and followed.—

Benito Juarez was, at this time, the leader of a party, but was famous enough to be feared. People knew he was daring, bold astute and cold-blooded. But he possessed an unshakeable character, enough to bring clarity and strength to the chaos of his Country. A famous historian said: Benito Juarez is one of the most important figures of the Red Indian race.

He had his quarters in the best house of that little town to which they brought Carujo and his people. Four guards stood at the entrance with drawn sabres. Inside, at the top end of the table was Juarez. He wore simple attire, simpler than all the others present.

"Whom do you bring?" was his question when he saw people entering the dining hall.

"These people were stopped by the guard," reported the NCO.

The Indian's eye was on Carujo. "Who are you?"

My name is Josè Carujo. I am the administrator of the Estate of Manresa and I live in Mexico.

Juarez thought for a moment. "The rich Spaniard who owns the hacienda del Alina?"

"Yes."

"Where do you want to go?"

"Home to Mexico."

"Where do you come from?"

"From the hacienda Candora."

"What did you do there?"

"I visited the haciendero."

"To what purpose?"

"Just friendship."

Juarez's eyebrows pulled together darkly. "You are a friend of his?"

"Yes," said Carujo ,oblivious of his danger in answering.

"So you are not my friend. This person is a supporter of the president."

Carujo paled with shock. The president at the time, Herrera, went around the Country to gather supporters. He destroyed everything and everybody who did not support him.

"I did not ask him about his political views."

He hoped to defend himself but he did not improve his position. "Don't tell me that. When two people meet in this Country, they talk about politics. I believe that you are a supporter of Harrera."

That sounded even more dangerous than before. "That must be an error, señor, I have always kept away from politics," answered Carojo.

"So you are neither warm nor cold. That is even worse. I have to treat you as a spy until I am convinced of the opposite."

"Señor, I am no spy," Carujo said anxiously.

"That will transpire in time. You appear suspicious to me. No one makes a visit out of friendship from Mexico to the hacienda Candora."

"But señor, I did not even know that you are in Santa Rosa."

"So you wanted to learn it. Is Santa Rosa on the way to Mexico? Why did you ride in the opposite direction?"

Carujo could not hide his embarrassment. He couldn't tell Juarez that he wanted to mislead any pursuer.

"You have no answer Well, I shall incarcerate you and tomorrow we shall find an answer."

"I am innocent," protested Carujo.

"That will be good for you but for now, away with you."

At this moment, one of the members at the table was heard to say: "Señor Juarez, with permission. Do you think of me as a true friend?" The speaker was a tall and uncommonly strongly built Mexican. He was conspicuous as the Mexicans were, on average, not very tall.

"What a question, señor Dojerva," answered Juarez, "would I have made you a captain of the guard if I didn't trust you? What do you want with this question?"

"I would ask you to believe this señor Carujo," retorted the large fellow.

Carujo recognized the voice of he speaker. He was the owner of a neighbouring farm and after a piece of land belonging to his master in which there were disused mercury mines. Dojerva was after these mines but Don Manuel did not want to sell.

"How is that. Do you know him?" asked Juarez.

"Yes," was the answer.

"You don't think that he's dangerous?"

"No, on the contrary, he is your friend. I vouch for him."

Juarez looked again at Carujo. "When you vouch for him, he may go but you are responsible for everything."

"Gladly, señor."

Juarez turned again to Carujo: "Who are the men with you?"

"They are my companions, decent people who do no harm to anybody."

"They are dismissed and can search for a place to rest for the night. You can eat with us. I am handing you to señor Dojerva, you have heard he is responsible for you and I hope you do not bring him any danger." With this, the matter that looked ugly at first turned out to be for the best. They made room for Carujo at the table next to Dojerva and he ate with the man, who was destined to become president of Mexico and tear the crown from an emperor's head.

At the end, they were all more or less drunk, except Juarez who, as the Red Indians usually were, was moderate. When he rose, it was the sign for departure.

Dojerva and Carujo left the house. Now they could talk to each other. "You have to sleep in my quarters. I hope this is not inconvenient for you."

"On the contrary," said Carujo, "I am very happy about it. By the way, please accept my thanks for your intervention, señor Dojerva. Without you my night might not have been very comfortable."

"Very likely. I was amazed that you have been on the hacienda Candora. In confidence, this hacienda is our next visit."

"Is that possible?" Carujo had a subsequent shock. He knew the reputation of the Indian and that his life had been in real danger.

"What did you have to do on that hacienda? I thought you are enemies?"

"Not any more, señor Dojerva. He is no longer my neighbour. The tenant, a Mr. Wilson inherited the Hacienda del Alina."

"He wouldn't sell a little piece of land to me and here he gives a present of twenty square miles."

Dojerva had the best room in the house He offered his guest a hammock to sleep in. "From what I have heard, Count Aurelio is in Spain now, Dojerva began."

"For one year."

"So you have the administration of all his estate in Mexico? Well, I don't begrudge you this," said Dojerva with a smile. "You're sitting pretty and can feather your nest. Couldn't there be something in it for me, my dear José Carujo?"

"You mean the mercury mines? Well, we can talk about that now. But tell me, what does Juarez want on the hacienda Candera?"

"I shouldn't tell you this, but Candera has betrayed Juarez at some point. He will be dead at this time tomorrow. I shall be on the Hacienda del Alina as well. Juarez will make his quarters there."

Carujo was silent for a moment.

"What are you thinking about? asked Dojerva.

"About the piece of land you want," smiled Carujo.

"Do you want to sell it?" asked Dojerva quickly.

"How much are you offering?"

"It can't be much. It has no pasture and that's what I need at the moment."

"Don't behave like a dealer who denigrates the item he wants to buy. We've known each other for a long time. We can speak openly."

"It has, as I said, no pasture. It consists of deep plantless gorges but it is in my neighbourhood and for this reason I offer ten thousand pesos."

Carujo laughed: "You are ten thousand times wrong."

"Why is that?"

"The land has been bought by don Manuel for one hundred thousand pesos, and at present has a value of four times that amount."

"This is only a matter of opinion."

"There are grounds to assume that, next to mercury, there are other precious metals to be found; in which case a million would not be enough."

"You're dreaming."

"Suppose I gave you this as a present?"

Dojerva jumped off his bed. "What do you say? Since when are you so generous?"

"You heard, I am giving this land to you as a present."

Dojerva sat down again and replied coolly. "Nonsense, that sounds monstrous."

"That may seem so but I know what I am saying."

Dojerva became impatient. "Talk seriously and don't make such silly jokes. No sane person would give this land as a present."

"Not without other purpose or condition."

"Now comes the explanation. You have a calculation in all this. What is it?"

"It is a small service I require of you."

"Well talk, I'm eager to know why I should get such a reward."

"Hm, one has to be a little cautious We know each other and can trust each other. I know that you are very strong …"

"That's correct but what has this to do with the matter in hand?"

"You are good at fencing and skilful with a gun …"

"Certainly. I also know how to handle a dagger."

"That's exactly what I need, I take it you are in good condition …"

"Naturally," the captain laughed. Quite a few who started with me, had to bite the dust."

"So is the matter is in good hands .There are a few people who are in my way."

"Ah," cried Dojerva, "You want to hire me as an assassin?"

"No, I merely want to turn your attention to people with whom you can easily get into an argument. I know that in this case you could help yourself."

"I think so. If these people would try something with me and thereby collect a bullet or a dagger, so – hm?"

"So you would get the mercury land as a present."

"*Caramba*, is that true?" asked Dojerva enthusiastically. "But the land belongs to the Count Aurelio."

"He would agree with that action."

"And he would sign a document regarding this present?"

"Yes, exactly this. There's nothing else I want to say, señor Dojerva."

"Now I'm longing to see these people."

"Nothing easier. You'll meet them on the Hacienda del Alina."

"Caramba, you don't mean the old señor Wilson?"

"No, but some of his guests. There is an English physician with the name of Dr. Stenton, then a Spaniard with the French name of Lucien de Mareau and another Englishman named Brooks. The first two are the most important people. Without their elimination our contract is not valid."

"Why don't you do this job yourself?"

"Wilson and I are enemies now and I cannot go to the hacienda. I have hired a group of people, but unfortunately without success. They have shot a number of these, the rest and I just managed to escape."

"Escape? Because of three men?" Dojerva laughed.

"Yes, you can laugh. These fellows have ninety nine devils in them."

"That makes thirty three devils each." The mocking laughter did not stop. The people who were with you seem no great heroes but they have an easy-going conscience. Could you leave them to me?"

These people were a millstone around his neck now, because he had promised them revenge. He therefore gladly agreed.

"Good, I'll talk to them tomorrow morning. Are you going back to Mexico?"

"Yes."

"I will let you know as soon as I have succeeded."

"The necessary document will go to Spain for Count Aurelio's signature."

Carujo smiled to himself. He could go back to Mexico, having left the assassination of his enemies in the best hands. He knew Dojerva as a man without much conscience who would take on even twenty murders for the mercury land. Besides, what could Dojerva do if he went back on his word? Nothing. He couldn't claim a price for a crime he himself had perpetrated.

Dojerva had his own thoughts: This Carujo is astute He wouldn't give away one million's worth of land if he wouldn't benefit much more. What if I do his dirty work and he behaves as if he knew nothing about it? The land would go to the devil but Carujo would as well. Well, I'll think about that tomorrow.

Next morning, he called Carujo's companions. "Who are you?" he asked.

"Did señor Carujo not tell you? We're poor devils who earn our bread in many different ways."

"You mean to say you don't care much which way? Would you want to earn your bread with me?"

"We cannot do that, we are engaged by señor Carujo."

"He handed you over to me."

"He can't do that. He promised us that we'll be able to revenge our comrades."

"Who comes with me, will accompany me to the Hacienda del Alina."

"With the military?"

"No, you follow us. Has the hacienda a fence?"

"Yes, a strong one."

"All right, one of you will call at the southern point, where I shall tell him his orders."

"And the price?"

"The same as with señor Carujo."

"So we are satisfied. Can we ride off now?"

"Not yet, Juarez hasn't given orders yet."

Juarez called for Carujo. "I can't let you go because people will learn through you that I'm here."

"Señor, I shall be silent."

"A pale face cannot be silent," said Juarez disparagingly, "perhaps I can let you go if you swear to tell no-one."

"So I will swear."

Carujo lifted his hand and swore not to divulge the facts of Juarez' whereabouts.

"You can go and take your people with you. But remember that you are responsible for them as well."

Carujo was on his horse a few minutes later and took the guerrillas with him. Nobody would know that they had any connection with Dojerva.

There were bad times for Mexico. It did not have the strength to be an independent state. One president pushed another. The finances were in a bad state. Every general wanted to be president. Whoever came to power drained finances dry because he knew he wouldn't be president long.

Juarez appeared in the midst of this chaos and soon obtained great influence, He made contracts with America, although he was not yet president. Soon he was here and there to reward or to punish people, but also to win new recruits. It was a great shock to Candora when Juarez with his armed men arrived.

"Do you know me? asked the Indian severely.

"No," replied the haciendero.

"I am Juarez."

The man paled and called out. "Oh holy Madonna."

"The Madonna will not help you. You are exchanging letters with the supporters of the president Herrera."

"No." The man trembled.

"Don't lie, I shall investigate myself. – Search!" he commanded his men.

After a short while, one of the officers brought a bundle of letters in his hand.

Juarez read these and the haciendero looked fearfully on Juarez's face.

"You are a member of a conspiracy against the freedom of Mexicans. Here is your reward." With these words he drew a pistol and shot the haciendero in the forehead. Many voices uttered a cry of horror. Juarez turned to the haciendero's family with unshakeable calm.

"Be silent. You are also guilty but you will not die. I confiscate the hacienda for the ownership of the state. You will leave here in one hour. You can take your money and horses. Now away with you."

"Can we take the dead?" wailed the wife.

"Yes, but be gone now."

Juarez called Dojerva. "That's how they end who sinned against the fatherland. Dojerva, are you loyal?" he asked while looking at him like a tiger.

"Yes, señor you know that," answered Dojerva calmly.

"Good, you will receive an order now. Do you know the province Chihuahua?"

"I was born at its borders and I still have possessions there."

"Good, you will go to its capital of the same name to represent me there. You will take a company of thirty men, but first you come with me to the hacienda del Alina."

Minutes later they were on their way with only eight men. One of the vaqueros had to lead them. At the hacienda they found the door locked. Juarez himself knocked.

"Who is there? asked Wilson from inside.

"Soldiers, open up."

"What do you want?"

"*Caramba,* are you going to open or not?"

Stenton, Brooks and Rudolfo stood next to him. He asked them quietly whether he should open.

"Yes," answered Stenton , "there are only a few of them."

When the gate opened and Juarez and Dojerva had entered, he examined them, his eyes glittering with anger. "Why did you not obey?" he thundered.

"We don't know you." said Wilson, "are you someone who has to be obeyed, señor?"

"I am Juarez. Do you know my name?"

Wilson bowed slightly without embarrassment. "Pardon me, señor, that I did not open immediately, step into my house. You are welcome."

He accompanied the two into the guest room where they sat down before being offered a meal. In spite of the friendly reception, Juarez still had a dark expression in his face. "Did you see us arrive?"

"Yes señor."

"And you saw that we were soldiers?"

"Yes."

"And you did not open instantly. That deserves punishment."

"Oh, señor, the president also has soldiers. They would not be welcome. We didn't know that it was yourself."

Juarez's features brightened a bit. "So I am welcome to you?"

"With all my heart. You have a strong hand, that's what's missing in this land."

"Yes, this hand has been felt already by some people. Tell me, do you know the hacienda Candora?"

"Of course, he's my neighbour."

"How much rent would it be worth?"

"The hacienda is in private ownership."

"Answer my question," ordered Juarez impatiently.

"In better hands, about ten thousand pesos."

"Good, you shall have it for seven thousand pesos rent."

Wilson looked astonished at the Indian. "Señor, I do not understand you."

"You heard me distinctly. Candora was a traitor and died of my bullet The family left the hacienda which now belongs to the state. Decide quickly."

If that is the case, then I say yes. But..."

"No but. Bring pen and paper and we'll regulate this at once."

Like everything Juarez did, it was done in haste but also in perfect order. Then he said: "This señor is Captain Dojerva. He and thirty soldiers will stay here for a few days, on the hacienda. Can you cater for them?"

"Yes," said Wilson, although he rather would have said no.

"The men will be here by tonight, look after them and present señor Dojerva with the bill. Farewell."

Juarez left with his people and the inhabitants of the hacienda in amazement at his resolute handling of life and death matters. This man was Juarez, the feared Indian, loved and hated by many.

It was evening when thundering hoofs announced the arrival of Dojerva and his men. Only the officers were meant to sleep in the house. The others had to sleep outside under the sky. Alva stood in the room prepared for Dojerva. She heard his steps but it was too late to withdraw. Prior to her fiancè's illness she had been a beautiful girl. Her grief for her beloved hadn't spoiled any of her charm. The sun had sunk below the horizon, but her last beams surrounded her figure in a golden light.

Dojerva was surprised. He was deeply moved but not with the clean, holy sentiment which appreciates beauty and honours it: rather the sudden passionate feeling of a brutal man.

"Step in, señor, you are in your own room."

Dojerva obeyed and greeted her with the decency of a gentleman. "I am delighted to see my room dedicated by such beauty."

After American custom she wanted to offer her hand of welcome, but pulled it back. There was something in his nature and his words that touched her as unpleasant.

"Oh, please, the whole dedication was to make sure that everything is comfortable."

"Ah, so you are probably ..."

"The haciendero is my father." Alva cut him short.

"I thank you, señorita. My name is Dojerva, I am captain of this outfit and at this moment infinitely happy to kiss your delightful hand," Dojerva wanted to reach out for her hand but she managed, somehow, to retreat through the door.

"Stop, I will not let you go," he called out but, quicker than his arm, she closed the door. He just stood and stared at the door for a while. "*Caramba*, what a beauty! If I had the talent for marriage, I think that I would do it now."

Alva was happy to have escaped. The desire she saw in his eyes gave her a shock, and she decided to avoid him. She went to her fiancé, where she found Stenton and Brooks. The condition of the patient was very satisfying. The operation was a complete success. When he saw Alva, his face was joyful. "Come here, Alva. This doctor told me he knows my hometown." Alva pretended this was news to her.

"By a happy coincidence. He also knows my brother, he has seen him before leaving England." This brother was sitting behind the curtains. That he was here, the patient should not know in order to avoid any harmful excitement. He hardly had said this when he fell asleep again.

Could there be any complications?" Alva whispered to the doctor.

"No, his physical and mental condition will, through this rest and this healthy sleep, only improve."

At the meal, Wilson introduced his guest to each other. Dojerva looked for Alva but to his disappointment, could not see her. The

Mexican officers' behaviour was polite but withdrawn. Such fine caballeros had no need to carry favour with Englishmen. Dojerva observed Stenton, Brooks and Rudolfo whose death would bring him land valued hundreds of thousands pesos but his eyes remained on Stenton, who was much taller and stronger than him.

Then Wilson made a remark that was taken up by Dojerva immediately. "It is not only a joy that you are present here but also a reassurance," said the haciendero. Only yesterday we were under great threat."

"A great threat? asked Dojerva with apparent impartiality.

"We were going to be attacked by more then twenty Bandits."

"Was this an attack against the hacienda or persons?"

"The latter, but since these were guests on the hacienda everybody was threatened."

"*Demonio,* may I ask which persons were meant?"

"Certainly, they are the señores Stenton, Brooks and Rudolfo."

"How did you defend yourselves against these rogues?"

"Our señor Stenton rendered half of them incapable."

"That sounds incredible. Ten men made incapable by one man without Counterattack?"

"It's true," said the haciendero enthusiastically, "there were actually two men, but let me tell you the story."

Stenton threw a serious glance at Wilson. "Please leave the subject. What we did was no heroism."

"It is a heroic deed to make ten men incapable without being wounded," answered the captain, "and I hope you don't mind us learning this interesting story?"

Stenton shrugged his shoulders and yielded to the inevitable. Wilson then reported that the officers hung on to the last words of his mouth.

"Is this valley of the tiger far from here?" asked Dojerva.

"You can reach it in one hour," explained Stenton.

"I am eager to visit this place. Would you lead me there, señor Stenton?"

"I am at your disposal."

The officers withdrew into their rooms. A young lieutenant looked out of the window to enjoy the scene from the campfire area. At the other end of the garden he saw a lady's white dress in the dark bushes.

The Mexican is used to flirt with every young woman. He's seldom rebuffed and lieutenant Randero had no scruples in seeking a little entertainment. The soldiers did not go into the flower garden and Kaya was alone. She was thinking about her former beloved Aurelio. How could she have been so stupid to believe this pale face and tell him the whereabouts of the Mixteka treasure as well as betray her half-brother Buff-he. The love of the white men is like a comet, it appears in one moment and disappears as fast.

The lieutenant who tried to put his arms around her disturbed her. It was as if her figure gained in strength. Her eyes glowed like those of a panther. She twisted her body out of his arms. "Who gave you the right to touch me?"

"My love gave it to me."

He tried again; the Indian girl bent her head back and tried to get away from him. She hit him with her fist under his chin and slipped out of his grip.

"Wait you little devil, you shall pay for this."

Kaya run toward the house, the lieutenant ran after her. The captain had his window open to let the smoke escape. When he looked into the garden he also noticed the white dress. He also saw a manly figure with her. "Is that the daughter of the haciendero? He rushed downstairs, opened the door and Kaya flew into his arms. When her pursuer saw this he stopped. Dojerva, however, held her tight. She pushed her fist into his throat with all her strength. With a cry of pain he let her go, she quickly disappeared. "*Caramba*, who is this she cat?" At this moment he saw lieutenant Randero, who wanted to pass him. "What's the hurry? he laughed. At this, Randero stood still.

"Ah captain, did you meet that little witch?"

"I not only met her, I also felt her."

"You felt her?" the lieutenant was amazed.

"Yes," was his answer, "her fist collided with my throat."

"So you did no better than me. Did you also look out of the window and see the white dress?"

"Twice right."

"You thought to collect a kiss or something similar?"

"Correct."

"So we had the same intentions with the same success."

"I am actually after señorita Alva, the daughter of the haciendero," said Dojerva.

"Is she beautiful?

"Even more beautiful than this little Indian girl who, I believe, is a friend or companion to her. May I make a suggestion? Do you want this Red Indian girl?"

"For any price. And you want the señorita Alva?"

"Also at any price. Let's help each other."

"No question. Here is my hand."

"But we have to find out first if their hearts are already given."

"Perhaps this Dr. Stenton has staked his claim before us?"

"I don't think so," said Dojerva, "rather Rudolfo who is treated with a certain reverence by the haciendero and who seems to be the highest of these three.

"Until tomorrow then Good night captain."

Dojerva bade his lieutenant good night but as it was close to midnight he went to the southern point of the hacienda for the arranged meeting with the guerrilla. The man was already waiting and whispered from behind some bushes: "Señor, I am here."

"Good. Where are the others?"

"Not very far from here; what are your orders?"

"Do you know this Dr. Stenton?"

"No, none of us knows him."

"That's unfortunate. He's coming with me to the gorge of the tiger tomorrow."

"And we should expect him there?"

"Expect and shoot him down."

"That we shall do. He has killed many of our comrades. He will die – he and the others."

"But you don't know him and I don't know who is coming with me. He is taller than I am and has a blond beard."

"All.right, that is enough. Keep, if possible, always at his right side. And what is it with the other two?"

"I shall tell you tomorrow, here at the same spot."

Dojerva turned back. He slept very soundly. The arranged assassination made no difference to his conscience.

The captain decided the morning would be best for his plans. He made that suggestion at the breakfast table and Stenton agreed to lead him. Two lieutenants asked if they could come along. Their wish was granted. Nobody else asked. They didn't like these officers. Dojerva was happy. Stenton would be the only civilian and a mistake was therefore unlikely.

When they were near the gorge, Stenton asked them to dismount and leave the horses to graze. They went on foot now without their horse. Stenton had his rifle with him and a knife in his belt. As they reached the entrance of the gorge he suddenly stood still and bent down to observe the grass.

"What are you searching for?" asked the captain.

"Hm, let's go on." The Englishman said nothing further, but his eyes clung to the ground. The captain was constantly on his right side as arranged. His eyes were seeking the walls and the borders of the gorge. Any moment he expected the deadly shot. "It happened here?" asked Dojerva.

"Yes," declared Stenton simply.

They observed the tracks and did not notice that Stenton bent further down and that he was carefully seeking cover behind their bodies. They also did not notice that he observed the surroundings sharply.

"You are a good marksman, señor."

Stenton shrugged his shoulder disparagingly. "There is nothing in hitting ten visible enemies. They are easier to hit than one invisible foe." He still managed to stand so that their bodies covered him from a possible assassin.

"It would be impossible to shoot an invisible enemy," remarked Randero.

"A good marksman will kill them as well," smiled Stenton still taking cover behind the officers.

"That is impossible," Countered the captain.

"Should I prove it to you?"

"Please do ," said one of the lieutenants curiously.

"I am asking you whether you believe that there could be an enemy round here?"

"Who should that be and where would he hide?"

Stenton smiled. "Somebody lies in wait for me in order to kill me." With these words he took his rifle off his shoulders and kept it in his arms. The captain got a shock. From whom did he know that his life was threatened?

"You are just joking," said the officer.

"I'll prove to you I am serious." With these words he pulled his rifle up, aimed and shot twice. Cries from several throats were heard. Stenton jumped to the side and rushed toward the exit of the gorge. After that he disappeared.

It was less than a minute from his first shot until now, when Randero asked: "What was that?"

"He's killed someone," answered another officer.

"We're in danger, let's withdraw," called Randero. They hurried to the entrance and waited there. Two more shots were heard and then it was quiet. About a quarter of an hour later they heard a rustling in the bushes and they grasped their weapons. "Don't fear, señores, it's only me." It was Stenton who stepped out.

"Señor, what have you done? asked lieutenant Randero.

"I was shooting," laughed Stenton.

"We know that – but why?"

"Self-defence. It was me whom they meant to shoot."

"Impossible. Who should that be and how do you know?"

"My eyes told me."

"And we didn't notice anything?"

"I don't blame you for that. You are not men who know the Wild West and the prairie." He pointed to the ground. The officers tried hard but could not see anything.

"Well, it takes a trained eye. Let's go on. Those imprints lead to the top. I searched at the borders and saw two heads behind some bushes. They couldn't see I saw them because my hat shadowed my eyes.

"How did you know they were enemies? asked Dojerva.

"Because I saw clearly two rifles sticking out of the thicket. They were trained at us."

"*Caramba,* that could have been us they threatened instead of you, said Lieutenant Rodero."

"No, it was meant for me. I was constantly hiding behind Captain Dojerva and it was noticeable how these men observed the shield he made." This remark made Dojerva think that maybe, Stenton knew something about the plot. The Englishman continued: "It was made easy for me. The captain was keeping on my right side." The captain grew pale. No doubt that Stenton suspected who was the guilty one in this attack. He carried on: "I saw two guns and knew where to shoot. I aimed and hit the shoulders of the perpetrators but at this moment, there came two more rifles forward and I jumped to the side for cover and hurried to the exit. I tried to get at the back of these two but they had escaped. I heard the rustling of broken twigs and sent some shots after them.

"Señor, you dared a lot when you saw the rifles aimed at you and you still came with us."

"I dared very little but these people dared a lot when they let me see their rifles. An experienced man of the West would never do that. If I am not mistaken these people were with señor Carujo in Santa Rosa where you also come from.

Stenton talked very indifferently but the captain noticed a trace of accusation.

"Yes, a certain José Carujo came to Juarez yesterday," explained the second lieutenant, unprejudiced and unsuspecting.

Dojerva threw him a furious glance that went unnoticed. "Were there people with him?" asked Stenton.

"Yes, about ten, our captain can tell you more about that. He housed señor Carujo."

A second furious glance hit the speaker but went also unnoticed. Only Stenton caught it, but did not react and said calmly, "I don't think that señor Dojerva will give me any information. In any case, the matter is done with." Stenton and Dojerva were silent on their way back to the hacienda. Only the two lieutenants spoke about the courage they just seen. About Stenton's presence of mind and skills, they spoke in admiration. Within an hour of their return, everyone on the hacienda heard about this adventure. Some thought that their safety was now endangered, others were amazed that Stenton only wounded the highwaymen.

The second evening went like the first, only Kaya kept away from the garden. Stenton said his good night and pretended to go to his room. But soon he crept downstairs into a room where he could observe the entrance. His reasoning was that Dojerva could only contact his accomplices at night. The back door was locked, so Dojerva, if he had any intention to see someone, had to use the front door. He opened the window to hear better.

Midnight was near when he heard footsteps. A glance through the window showed him the figure of the captain. Stenton jumped out of the window and crept after the officer. When he looked back, he saw Alva walking to and fro on the roof of the building. He had recommended fresh air and, as her fiancé was asleep, she went for a walk on the roof to avoid any meeting with the military. The captain walked to the southern point of the hacienda. What was his business there? Stenton asked himself, why did he not walk upright like a person who went for a walk? He followed him with silent steps. At the furthest corner of the garden he heard two people talking to each other. As he came closer he heard a voice say:

"You yourself were in our sight. We would have hit you."

"Who would have thought he is that astute? It almost seems he is omniscient. For the moment I have no new plans. It's possible that this señor Stenton is observing me.

"We can't meet here again."

"Where else?"

"Have you pen and paper?"

"No."

"But you can read and write?"

"Yes."

"Here, take both. When you reach the first trees on your way to the gorge of the tiger, you will see a large stone. I shall go there in the morning and leave my orders under that stone. You can leave your answers there as well."

"All right, but tell me, who is that figure walking on the roof?"

"The captain turned around. "Ah, that's Alva, the daughter of the haciendero. I shall pay her a visit. Any more questions?"

"No."

"You can go now but if you behave as clumsily as this morning, our business is finished. I can't use blockheads. Good night."

When Stenton heard these last two words, he slipped back to the house and entered it again via the window. He'd heard enough. His suspicion was correct, Dojerva was his enemy. When the captain entered the house, he took the stairs to his room but there he went on to the roof where he saw Alva. Stenton crept silently after him. When he came to the top and put his head above the stairs to see the roof, he saw Alva desperately looking around for help.

"You really want to escape, señorita?" asked Dojerva.

"I must go." She made a move towards the trap door.

Stenton saw that the captain gripped Alva's hand and held it tight.

"No, you shall stay here, señorita," said the officer. "You will stay and hear what I have to tell you from my full heart and my undying love. Come Alva, it would be futile to resist.

"I pray you, señor, let me go." She begged anxiously.

Dojerva tried to pull her close. She defended herself and murmured: "Should I call for help?" In a moment Stenton stood next to her.

"No, señorita, you don't need that. Help is here. If señor Dojerva will not take his hands off you at once, he flies down into the yard."

"Ah, señor Stenton," stammered the girl relieved, "please help me."

"Stenton." The officer exclaimed angrily.

"Yes, I am Stenton. Let go of the lady."

The captain put his arms around her and hissed: "What do you want here? Who are you to give me orders? Be off, you impudent rascal.

Hardly had he spoken these words when Stentons iron fist hit Dojerva's head. He fell down like an empty sack. Then he turned to the girl who was almost down with the officer. " Come, Señorita, I shall accompany you."

"Oh, my God," wailed Alva, her body still trembling. "I've done nothing to encourage this attack."

"I know. People like him don't need encouragement."

He accompanied her to the patient's room, went to his own and left the door slightly ajar. The captain, when he regained consciousness, would have to pass here.

After a while Stenton heard him coming down from the roof. Only then did Stenton rest.

The next morning, when Stenton returned from riding, lieutenant Randero at the gate accosted him. "Señor Stenton, I have to speak to you," His approach was impolite.

"What about?" was Stenton's short answer.

"I must speak to you."

"You must? Does that mean that I am forced to listen?"

"Certainly," there was more than a trace of mockery in his voice.

"Ah well, an educated person does not refuse to listen to anybody, provided that the necessary politeness is not neglected. At the gate I shall not speak to you. You may come into my room."

The lieutenant changed colour and stepped back. "You speak haughtily. Do you think yourself that important?"

"You will agree that we are in respect of civility, mentality and morality not equal, but I still agreed to listen to you." He intended to walk away but the lieutenant grabbed his arm and asked threateningly:

"Do you mean that I am morally beneath you?"

"When I say something I mean it. Take your hands off me." Stenton shook off the Mexican's hand.

The lieutenant was intimidated by the Englishman's tone and expression of his eyes. He took his hand away and mumbled with eyes flaming with hatred:

"You will pay for that. These English are like mules. They carry patiently and without any feeling of honour. Sometimes they are stubborn and only tamed with a good beating. I wonder whether he will be so proud when I tell him the reason I am calling." After a while he went to Stenton's room. "You see, señor, I do come," the Mexican said mockingly." Stenton nodded but said nothing. "I trust you will listen to me now."

"Yes, if you behave decently."

The lieutenant flared up. "Did you ever see me misbehaving?"

"Let's hear what you have to say," replied Stenton coolly.

"Good but I am not used to discuss matters while standing."

"We are not speaking of a discussion, only about a hearing. The one received has to deliver his petition while standing. If that is not to your taste our meeting can be considered as closed." Randero's face flamed with anger, his voice trembled when he said:

"Señor, I am no longer able to regard you as a caballero."

"That is a matter of indifference to me. Please get on with the matter in hand, I'm not willing to be kept with empty talk."

Randero wanted to flare up but when he saw Stenton reaching for his hat he overcame his anger and said with all the composure he could summon:

"I am here regarding my superior, Captain Dojerva." When Stenton kept quiet, Randero continued: "You admit that you have insulted him?"

"I have hit him. Is that an insult in your view?"

"Yes," said the lieutenant, "it certainly is. The Captain asks for satisfaction."

"Ah," said Stenton with well-played amazement. "Satisfaction? And he asked you to be the carrier of the cartel? Are you acquainted with the rules of a duel?"

"Do you doubt that?"

"I doubt your knowledge of the laws of duelling because you represent a dishonourable affair. Did the captain tell you why I have hit him?"

"Completely;" the lieutenant answered with rage in his voice.

"So I despise you too. I knocked the captain down because he insulted a lady who is the daughter of your host. Whoever is the middleman in such a case is, in my eyes, a moral zero."

The Mexican grasped his sword, pulled the blade half out and cried: "What did you say? How dare you? …"

"You will do nothing," said Stenton calmly but his calm was like that before a storm. In his eyes was a lightning that would have intimidated a more valiant person than the lieutenant. "Take your hand off the sword or I shall break it in front of your eyes. No wonder you are the messenger of the captain: you are the same kind of rascal he is. You have …"

"Stop," cried the lieutenant whose rage had overcome his reason. "Say another word and I put this through you. You will apologise at once or …"

Randero had pulled out his sword completely and swung his arms back in order to hit out. But at the same moment the sword was in the Englishman's hand; Randero did not even know how it happened. It was broken in two pieces and Stenton said: "Here, take this apple peeler. You have insulted Kaya just as your superior insulted señorita Alva. You are as big a rogue as the other. If you don't leave my room at once I shall throw you out of he window.

Stenton stretched his arm threateningly toward his enemy. It was deftly avoided and Randero jumped to the door. There he turned around and, with clenched fist he called to the Englishman: "You will do penance for this, soon. You will have a duel with both of us and one of us will surely kill you."

Randero had gone and Stenton lit himself a cigarette. It was less than a quarter of an hour after when the expected knock at the door came. "Come in," he called. Another lieutenant entered He bowed politely and said: "Pardon me, señor Stenton, that I disturb you. Could you give me five minutes of your time?"

"With pleasure, señor. Please take a seat and take a cigarette."

The officer was surprised by his friendliness. This was not the way he was described by Randero.

"To tell you the truth," the lieutenant began, "I do not like to come to you on a matter of such hostility."

"Speak confidently, señor, I am well prepared for what you are going to tell me."

"Well, I am coming from the señores Dojerva and Randero, who believe that you have insulted them."

Stenton nodded lightly, "They have found in me an avenger. You have used the right expression. The señores believe that I have insulted them but on the contrary, they have insulted two ladies who were without defence. You are bringing me a demand for a double duel?"

"Yes, señor Stenton."

"I'm sorry for you. You are a messenger of two men that I cannot respect. I don't actually accept your demand because I only accept such a thing from men with honour but you have been polite to me and I don't want to hurt you. Did the challengers make any demands?"

"Yes, the captain wishes to use the swords and the lieutenant the pistols."

"I shall accept these wishes but have two conditions of my own."

"I want to hear them, señor."

"I shall fight with the captain until one is forced to drop the sword. And with the lieutenant there should only three steps between us."

"That will probably be all right but in this case you go to your certain death. If you escape the captains onslaught, Randero is the best shot I know."

"Maybe there is even a better one than he is," laughed Stenton. Have no worry that I fear this lieutenant Randero. The rest please arrange with señor Rudolfo who will be so kind as to be my second."

"Do we want impartial witnesses?"

"No, neither do we need a doctor. I am a physician myself."

The officer went. Stenton went to instruct Rudolfo. Stenton had the right to bring his own pistols and, as he felt sure about them. He was sure of his success. From this moment he did not leave his window. He knew what was going to happen and kept an eye on the exit of the hacienda. It was about noontime when the captain rode off. Stenton assumed he would leave a letter under the stone and went to saddle his horse himself. The captain went north and Stenton went south. Both intended to mislead others. The stone was to the west and as soon as he was outside the sight of the hacienda, Stenton galloped to the west.

When he was near, he dismounted and tightened his horse to a tree. He went on foot and in a wide circle around the rock to make sure no other person was there. Then he looked for a suitable hiding place. Ten metres from the rock stood a cedar whose densely hung branches were easily reached. Stenton swung himself up and succeeded in hiding himself so it was impossible to see him. Hardly had this happened when he heard the sound of a horse approaching. A man jumped off his saddle and placed a folded piece of paper under the stone, went back to his horse and rode off. Not a moment later Stenton lifted the stone and read the paper:

"Today at midnight at this place. It is absolutely necessary. Tomorrow we will reach our goal."

There was no signature. Stenton folded the paper and placed it again under the stone. He then destroyed his own tracks, went back to his horse and rode to the hacienda. Dojerva returned later, not suspecting that his secret was discovered. Stenton mentioned nothing to anyone and sat with the patient, who had made astounding progress and was almost back to normal. He enjoyed meeting his brother.

His memory had returned fully and he related the story that made a poor hunter become a millionaire. ---

Chapter 12

DOUBLE CHALLENGE

---

*W*HEN George Brooks heard that his brother wanted to share his fortune with him, he absolutely refused. "You have suffered for it and if not for our Dr. Stenton, you may never have enjoyed it." Alva told him that he should take everything, as she would own the hacienda and that would suffice. Stenton advised to share and give halve of the fortune to Robby, who was a promising lad. George finally accepted this.

The officers did not appear for dinner. They, understandably, preferred to eat in their respective rooms. Stenton said after dinner that he had work to do and also withdrew to his room. When midnight drew nearer, he put his revolver in his belt and also took some strings. He locked the room from the inside, left the light on and left the room through the window. He left the hacienda unnoticed and went in the direction of the midnight meeting of the criminals. His eyes were experienced and he was not afraid to go in the right direction.

Suddenly he stopped and sniffed the air. There was the smell of fire mixed with the smell of roasting meat. Are these bandits as stupid to make a fire? He crept nearer and saw a man who ate his roasted hare with such a hunger that there was soon nothing left of it. He was strongly built but Stenton thought that it would not be very difficult to overcome this man. He sought to hide opposite the way to the hacienda, as not to have to worry about the person who would come that way. The bushes parted on the other side and the captain appeared.

"Are you mad?"

"Why," asked the Mexican?

"That you have such large fire."

"Oh, there is nobody nearby and I was hungry."

"But I could smell the smoke at a hundred steps."

"But a hundred steps would only come the one that has business here. We are safe here, come closer."

"I must make it short, where are your people?"

"Behind the mountain in the woods."

"Do they know where you are?"

"No."

"I like that, I want as few as possible to know my plans. Can you get rid of them?"

"Yes, but can I do what you want by myself?"

"I hope so. I shall give you the whole sum that I would give to the others. What I need now, you can do by yourself. I can see a double-barrelled rifle. How good a shot are you?"

"I never miss."

"Good, you should do two shots, one for this Stenton the other for the Spaniard."

"Alright, they will get their bullets but when and where?"

"Do you know the quarry behind that mountain?"

"Very well, I have been there already."

"Tomorrow morning I have got a duel there at 5 o'clock."

"*Caramba,* do you want to be killed?"

"Without your help, that may be quite possible. The lieutenant and I have challenged the Englishman to a duel. Stenton has to fight two but he is a devil and one has to take care. He must be eliminated before the duel and that is where you come in."

"With pleasure, señor, the two will taste my lead."

"Before five o'clock you must hide there. There are enough trees and shrubs nearby.

"I understand, you will arrive a little later and when you come, those two will lie there with bullets in their skulls?"

"No, not like that. I must be there; I must see the rascals die. When I shall stand opposite Stenton, you will shot him and then, immediately the Spaniard."

"This plan is not bad but the reward?"

"You will get that tomorrow here at midnight."

"Good, I am satisfied."

"I hope that I can rely on you. Good night for now."

"Good night, señor, be assured that my bullets will hit their target."

The captain went. The Mexican scraped some more off the rabbit's bones. He then shouldered his rifle and climbed up. Stenton stood at the bushes where the man had to come out from. He took the man who did not expect an attack by the throat. When he lost consciousness, he was gagged and tied up with the prepared string. He carried the man and his rifle to the hacienda where everybody seems to be asleep. He was careful not to meet Dojerva who must have returned minutes earlier. The light was still burning in his room. The search of the prisoner's pockets revealed the crumpled up piece of paper collected from under the stone. Stenton put it back.

"I don't need it just yet," he said to the prisoner who had come to and looked at Stenton with horror. "I let you think over night whether you want to give a full confession." The prisoner was then checked whether he was bound tightly enough to make an escape impossible. He was then tied to two legs of the bed, after which Stenton lay down for a few hours rest. Rudolfo waked him up. He found it not necessary to leave a last will, checked the prisoner once more, locked the door to his room and went downstairs. They rode off. Rudolfo looked at Dojerva's window and saw him standing there. Stenton didn't look back and asked Rudolfo to guess what Dojerva was thinking.

"If you will not fall at the first duel, you will fall at the second. The lieutenant is a very good shot."

"No, I tell you what he is thinking: That we are both dead before the duel has even started."

"I do not understand."

"You soon will, listen." Stenton told his friend how he observed the captain and about the prisoner in his room. Rudolfo was in great shock about all this.

Shortly after their arrival at the quarry, the three officers appeared. After formal but cool greetings, Stenton and Rudolfo noticed with satisfaction, the roving eyes of the captain who searched the bushes around the area. A sword was handed to Stanton because he had none of his own. At the usual questions about reconciliation, the captain proudly refused. "Not another word," he said, "my opponent has made the condition that satisfaction only takes place, when one of the combatants will be disabled and drop the sword. I accepted this condition and have no desire to change that."

As the two opponents stood at opposite sides, Stenton asked whether it was allowed to say a few words.

"Speak."

"My challenger expects that two shots will fall before the duel has even started. The payoff would take place at midnight tonight at the quarry."

The impartial officer stepped back and said angrily. "Señor, that is unworthy, this is a disgraceful insult."

"It is the truth," said Stenton coolly, "look at your captain, this caballero, does he not look pale as a corpse with shock? Don't you see the blade shaking in his hand? Do you not see his lips trembling? Is that the sight of innocence?"

The officer looked at his superior and said while he paled himself: "*Oh Dios,* it is true, you are shaking."

"He lies," stammered Dojerva.

"And listen how even his voice trembles?" asked Stenton. "It is fear, let's start the comedy."

The captain pulled himself together. "Yes let's start," he said and began attacking at the same time.

"Stop," ordered Stenton and, with a mighty whirl, he wrenched the sword off his opponent's hand. If you can't wait for the sign, if you can't fight with the proper rules, I shall throw away the sword and take a cane to whip you into shape. The sword was taken up again; the opponents stood face to face and waited for the proper signal.

The fight started. The captain threw himself with wild courage onto Stenton. The latter stood there, proud and calm and he met every lunge with ease. Until, suddenly, his eyes lit up. A tremendous blow put the arm of the opponent to the side. The blade hit with lightening speed at the hand – shriek of the captain and his sword fell down to the ground.

"My hand, my hand he roared."

The sword lay on the ground and four fingers next to it, while the wounded dug his bleeding stump into the lap of his tunic.

Stenton turned to the others and declared: "This man will never again touch a lady against her will."

The captain lifted the bleeding stump and said: "You are a devil but I shall still tame you." His team tried to still his bleeding with emergency dressing. Then he turned to Randero and whispered: "If you kill him, I shall release you from all your gaming debts." Randero nodded but it was an automatic and soulless nodding. He looked just as pale as the captain.

The two double pistols were carefully examined and loaded, they stood opposite. The lieutenant lifted his hand and Counted: "One." The adversaries lifted the pistols in line with their opponent's chest. "Two." Randero's hand trembled, his teeth bit together but he overcame this trembling and kept his eyes on Stenton's heart. With only three steps between them, he could not fail. This conviction gave him back his self-confidence. Stenton stood proudly in front of him. On his lips was a smile of superiority.

"Three!"

That was the word of death. In lightening speed, Stenton changed his gun from Randero's chest to his weapon. Both shots rung out, Randero's hand including his pistol was thrown back. His second shot that followed with equal speed a moment later and hit Randero's hand. A loud shriek "my hand," followed this second shot.

Two fingers were lost.

"Who has the courage to insult ladies, must have the courage to take the result. I have the habit to take the right hand off these people. Good day, señores. Stenton took the two pistols to his horse and rode off. Rudolfo followed him. Randero stood with a maimed hand and sent curses behind them. The two rode to the quarry to follow the tracks of the bandits' leader to their camp. They took a number of vaqueros off the field. The tracks were still clearly seen and led them to a gorge behind the mountain. After overpowering the guard, they succeeded to arrest the sleep drunk bandits, without shedding any blood. They were tied to their horses, then they all galloped to the hacienda. The vaqueros were sent back to the herds. Unseen by anybody, they reached the hacienda and managed to put the prisoners into the cellars.

The two friends went to the dining room to have their breakfast. Wilson, Brooks, Alva and Kaya who had left the patient for a short while, were told about the latest adventures. They expressed fear about the captain and his soldier's revenge but Stenton did not agree with them. "Juarez likes you and the soldiers don't seem to like Dojerva very much, besides I have some prove of these rogues being in connection with bandits and the next in rank are decent soldiers. He collected the prisoner in his room who was still tied as before. When he saw the people in the dining room, he asked, "what should I do here?"

"To answer my questions, nothing else."

"I protest against such treatment," said the Mexican.

"You are being interrogated and your life depends on your confession. I have heard every word of your discussion yesterday, I also know that you wanted to murder me in the gorge of the tiger. You have the damming piece of paper still on you and I will hang you in ten minutes if you don't tell the truth."

These severe words by Stenton made an impression, the bandit noticed with a shock that everything was betrayed. He looked gloomily to the ground.

"If you do that, my comrades will take revenge. You can be sure of that." The Mexican still showed a trace of spite.

"You told the captain where they are last night. We went there and took them prisoner. You will see them soon."

The bandit grew pale. "I don't believe you, you are telling me that to soften me up."

"You are not the man for whom I would tell an untruth. Look through the window, their horses are still there, including your own that you have left in your camp."

The man looked through the window and knew that Stenton had told the truth. But he tried once more. "The captain will revenge me."

Stenton had stepped to the window as well and saw in the distance three more riders approaching. "Look further and you will see three riders. Two, with their hands bandaged. I punished them this morning. They will be unable to help you."

The prisoner got another shock. The others stepped to the window and observed their arrival. Soon, they heard the steps of the officers going into their rooms.

"Now, do you still expect help from the captain?"

The bandit kept silent, he did not want to show that his resistance was broken.

"Answer me now," said Stenton, "admit that you were hired by the captain to kill me?"

"Yes, I admit that."

"And you have shot at me in the gorge of the tiger?"

"Not I but the two that you wounded."

"You are their leader and equally guilty, you agreed to kill señor Rudolfo and me before the duel had started?

"Yes."

Stenton asked Rudolfo to bring up the other prisoners. They were shocked when they saw their leader.

"You are murderers and I shall not hesitate to hang you all if you don't agree to one condition."

"What condition?"

"That you admit in the presence of the captain that you were hired by him to kill three people. Myself, señor Rudolfo and señor Brooks? Your leader has already confessed.

They looked at each other until one of them said: "For the captain we are not prepared to hang, if there is no other way, we will confess in his presence."

They were led back into the cellars. ---

Chapter 13

A COURT OF HONOUR

THE three officers had to stay longer at the quarry. Randero's hand was quickly bandaged but Dojerva's bleeding was hard to stop. This Stenton is a fighter the like of which I have never seen before. Who would have thought It," Randero pronounced bitterly.

"That is correct," said the other lieutenant. "He accused you, captain, that you have hired a murderer."

"Despicable behaviour."

In spite of these words a suspicious redness showed on his very pale face. The lieutenant had a sharp eye. He was a man of honour and had no idea about the intentions of his superior. He was convinced that the accusation was true and he asked: "What could be the reason for the Englishman's accusation?"

"His evil mind," said the captain.

"You are mistaken I know señor Stenton. He is not the man to utter such malice."

"So it was theatre."

"I don't believe that either. A Doc Ironfist is no actor."

Dojerva stamped his foot angrily. "Silence, or will you tell me you believe what this man said?"

"He has made an accusation that you did not refute," answered the lieutenant calmly, "I shall not make a judgement until it is proven that the accuser was wrong."

"That I would strongly advise you to do."

The young man who was busy with the bandage, looked up, pulled his brows together and asked: Is that a threat, captain?"

"Yes," was the angry answer.

The lieutenant let go of the bandage and stepped back. "I will not tolerate that," he said seriously, "you are my superior in rank but in the matter of honour we are equals. Your behaviour toward me is intolerable and I tell you that, on our return, I shall speak to señor Stenton. He accused you of hiring a murderer. Should he not be able to substantiate that, he has to retract and give satisfaction. If he was right, I shall give up military service."

"I forbid you to talk to this man." snorted the captain.

"You can only order me in military matters. You know my intentions, if you want me to continue with your bandage, I must ask you to drop the subject."

Dojerva kept silent. His anger prevented the bleeding from stopping, and that prolonged the time until they could return.

On the hacienda he saw the messenger from Juarez. He brought the order to set off immediately for Monclave. There was an upheaval and he was told to give assistance to the Monclavians against the government troops.

The lieutenant who assisted Dojerva went to Stenton and asked him to substantiate his accusation. Stenton refused to give an explanation at the moment but the lieutenant insisted. "If you are right, I cannot serve under Dojerva any longer."

Stenton asked him to keep a horse ready, secretly. He expected the captain would go to the stone and leave another message, and the lieutenant could see for himself.

Not much later Dojerva asked Randero to accompany him, as he had to talk to him. They went together to the north to mislead any observer and the west, toward the stone under which he intended to leave another message. Stenton and the other lieutenant left five minutes later.

"Why are we going tomorrow to Monclave? Our order is to go immediately" asked Rodero.

"You and I have to do something today, or would you leave Stenton unpunished?"

"Ah, if I could get him," Rodero looked into the distance with an angry expression in his eyes.

"We'll do that, let's be allies," Dojerva passed his left hand which was taken by Randero's left. I have an order from influential people to eliminate Stenton and his companion." Dojerva intentionally lied to give the impression he was only an authorised agent and, therefore, not responsible. He also spoke of a reward that really influenced Randero, who was poor and driven by his passions.

"Shall I be rewarded as well?"

"Sure, there will be a promotional and financial reward. I have to be sure that you can keep a secret."

"Completely, captain. I am at your disposal."

"If my contacts had obeyed my orders, we would still be in possession of our two hands. I have to find out why they did not appear this morning."

"Will we meet them now?"

"No, we'll give them a sign to meet me tonight, firstly in order to learn what had kept them, secondly to discuss new plans. That's the reason we don't go to Monclave today." Randero had to be satisfied with these explanations.

Stenton and the lieutenant left their horses and went the last stretch on foot. The lieutenant climbed up the cedar and Stenton hid behind some bushes. As they had gone to the stone without detour, they arrived before Dorjerva and Randero. It took quite a while until the expected pair arrived. The captain lifted the stone put a piece of paper beneath it and left. Now the two came from their hiding places and Stenton lifted the stone.

"Randero was here as well. He is, therefore, an accomplice?"

"Not originally but now he is," answered Stenton.

"May I see that piece of paper?"

Stenton had read the contents and passed the paper to the lieutenant. It read:

"Stay near to this place. At midnight we shall meet at the stone. You'll have to justify yourself."

One could see that the note was written with the left hand. The lieutenant asked Stenton: "This note is for the person who was going to kill you and señor Rudolfo?"

"Yes."

"Do you intend to be here at midnight to eavesdrop on them?"

"No, that is not possible because the man in question will not appear. He is already my prisoner on the hacienda. Now you have observed the two murderers, I shall tell you the rest on our way home."

"What do you intend to do?"

"I shall unmask them."

"That is the correct way. Can I be present?"

"Certainly. I shall even ask you to be my witness."

"And what will you do with the prisoners?"

"I promised them their lives if they testify against the captain. I have to keep my word."

"That is not wise," said the lieutenant. "These people deserve to be hanged. Their freedom will endanger your life."

"I know that, but I have never broken my word. Perhaps my leniency will make an impression."

"I don't think so. Leniency makes no impression on these people; humanity is seen as a weakness."

They reached the hacienda later than Dorjerva and Randero. The captain saw the arrival of Stenton in the company of the lieutenant. He frowned and asked:

"Lieutenant, where have you been?"

"For a stroll."

"Did you have my permission?"

"Do I need it?"

"I think so. We are not stationary, but on the march."

"And I think we are in a field camp, captain."

"These differences are not for discussion. You have to ask for permission if you remove yourself from the unit."

The young officer flushed angrily, because the soldiers stood around and heard every word. "I have to do that only if I intended to travel or if I had otherwise official business. At the time I rode out like you and lieutenant Randero."

"Señor, do you know the meaning of refusing to comply with an order?" the captain said.

"I know that as well as you, señor. There is no question of obedience. There are simple differences of opinion that can be handled in a decent manner. It is understandable that an officer does not allow himself to be rebuked in front of soldiers."

The eyes of the captain were alight with anger. He stepped nearer and demanded:

"Hand in your sword, at once!"

The lieutenant was young but a courageous man. He knew how to restrain himself and he answered smilingly: "My sword? You cannot demand that."

"I am your superior."

"You have been. You are a rogue. It would be a shame if you would touch my honest sword."

These words were spoken with a loud voice and all the soldiers heard it. When they heard the tremendous accusation, they put a circle around the officers and Stenton. The accusation was such that Dojerva, at first, found no words. Then he threw himself against the lieutenant and with a trembling voice he called: "Retract what you just said – at once!"

"Retract? No I repeat what I said," was the fearless answer. Dojerva became violent but Stenton hit him so hard that he collapsed.

"What are you doing? How dare you?" said Randero.

"Nothing," said Stenton, "the most I dare is to dirty my hand."

"Yes," called the lieutenant to his comrade. "I declare you also to be a rogue whose touch would make me dirty."

Randero blushed with fright and anger. "You are dreaming," he called out.

"I am in possession of my senses, unlike you."

"You are the younger officer and I am your superior."

"You are no longer my superior. I do not serve under you at this moment. Either I leave or you will."

"You forget that it is not easy to leave," said Randero with a mocking smile. "For the moment I arrest you for disobedience and señor Stenton for grievous bodily harm."

"You think so? You, worm, would have the skill to make me prisoner" said Stenton, "come here."

Stenton grabbed the lieutenant by his collar and threw him forcefully to the ground where he stayed put. The next in line of command stepped forward and asked: "Señor lieutenant, may we know what this is all about?"

The lieutenant gave him a friendly nod and countered: "Landero, tell me honestly, who is the officer you most like?"

"You, señor lieutenant, you know that. We would not have looked on so calmly when you insulted señores Dojerva and Randero, and certainly not when they were insulted by a civilian if that were not be the case."

"Well, Landero, I will tell you. These señores are planning with bandits to murder decent people and have insulted ladies. They had a duel this morning and lost their right hand. They are not worthy to command decent Mexican soldiers. I do not serve any more under them."

"Señor, I withdraw as well."

"That is not necessary. We shall examine the case and then decide who has to go, they or I."

"That is true señor lieutenant," said Landero. If you go, I will go and I think the whole company will dissolve. If these two, whom no-one likes, go to the devil, then you will be our captain."

"And you will become lieutenant."

"Should we make a court of war?"

"No, their crime is not a military one. We shall arrange a court of honour."

"Do we take their weapons and tie them?"

"Yes, we shall take their weapons but we shall not bind them. For the moment we'll take them to their rooms and put a watch outside their door. The court will then convene in the yard to allow all soldiers to be present."

Table, benches and chairs were put into the yard and everything was to be prepared for a court of justice. The main people took their place. At one table sat the lieutenant and Landero and two other sub officers. They were the justices. Stenton and Rudolfo were the accusers and were sitting on the other side. Opposite them were Brooks, Wilson and the two ladies who were witnesses. At a slight distance were the vaqueros and the soldiers.

Now the two defendants were brought down. Their condition was indescribable. The had thought such a case and such a humiliation impossible. They foamed with anger and if they could have used both hands, the four vaqueros would have had a difficult job to handle them.

"What is this" shouted Dojerva. "Why do you stand around here? Away with you, you dogs."

"Restrain yourself. You are here as a defendant, and it is up to you how we shall treat you."

"As a defendant? Who accuses me?"

"That you shall hear in a moment."

"And who are the judges?"

"We who are sitting here."

Dojerva broke into resounding laughter. "Am I among the insane here, that my soldiers want to judge me? Rascals all of you, go to your quarters or I shall shoot you all."

He lifted his left fist and went toward Landero but the vaqueros held him back.

"I propose having the two accused bound if they don't calm down right away," said Stenton.

"Proposal accepted," answered the lieutenant.

"You dare," shouted the captain, "I shall flatten the whole hacienda. How dare you hold a court of war on your superior."

"This is no court of war but a court of honour," countered the lieutenant. "And it will be decided whether men of honour can still serve under you."

Dojerva wanted to continue his threats but Randero put his left hand on his shoulder and whispered: "For God's sake, be quiet, or we won't get through."

The captain quietened down. "Well, start your farce, I'll deal with you later."

"Señor Stenton, speak"

Stenton stood up. "In the name of the two señoritas I accuse these two men of dishonourable behaviour against unprotected young ladies. I further accuse the same two men of attempted murder against me and señores Brooks and Rudolfo."

"Can you prove these accusations?"

"Yes."

The lieutenant turned to the accused. "What have you to say about these accusations?"

"They lack any basis and are not worth a reply," declared Dojerva, Randero agreed.

"The accused offered no defence and that simplifies matters. We shall take the first accusation as proved. The second accusation requires more detailed evidence."

Stenton brought his accusation in detail, without letting the accused suspect that he had the bandits as evidence. He told the court about the events in the gorge of the tiger, what he had overheard and Dojerva's last ride that was probably for the same purpose, the killing of the three of us."

When he finished, Dojerva, although he had said that he would answer no more, spoke: "It appears that that we are dealing with madmen. This man has uttered empty assumptions and upon two caballeros and officers of the glorious republic contrive a so-called court of honour. This is a disgrace that I shall punish, as this comedy is at an end."

"Such a punishment I do not have to fear," answered Stenton. "I shall give proof to my assumptions. When the two went for a ride this morning, I suspected the purpose of this excursion. I took the lieutenant with me to discover the plans of the two. Dojerva has a secret way to pass a message to the bandits. I found a piece of paper under a stone, the contents of which are: Stay near to this place. At midnight we shall meet at the stone. You'll have to justify yourself. "I don't think that señor Dojerva will deny this."

When Stenton produced the paper, the accused paled. Both kept silent while all eyes were on them. Stenton continued: "I must also remark, that I have listened to them and acted accordingly. I shall bring witnesses to what I have said." He asked for the prisoners to be brought to the court. When Dojerva saw them, he visibly recoiled with shock. The prisoners gave their statements with signs of embarrassment but truthfully and detailed. There could be no more doubts.

The accused hid behind wordless spite and refused any admission.

"The guilt of the accused is proved beyond doubt," said the chairman of the court.

"After the law of the Country Dojerva deserves the death penalty. We shall not go into the entire participation of Randero. We are only a court of honour. We do not punish but decide whether we want to serve under such leadership. As far as I am concerned I relinquish my position forthwith."

"I refuse your discharge," called Dojerva.

"You will be unable to hold me or others. I am convinced that by my example others will follow."

"They wouldn't dare," Dojerva flared up.

Landero stood up. "I also declare that I am not willing to serve under such rascals and hope that all the comrades will do the same."

Dojerva lifted his voice to reject what Landero proposed, but all the ranks and the entire team of soldiers drowned his voice. They declared that they don't wish to serve under Dojerva and Randero any longer but that the lieutenant should lead the company in future.

After they had calmed down, the lieutenant said: "I shall accept the leadership and the officers will advance according to their ranks. I shall make a report to Juarez and he will decide whether this stopgap is valid. The court of honour has done its duty.

The accused we will give into the hands of those against whom these attacks have been made. We shall leave here within a quarter of an hour to go to Monclova."

This order was accepted with general jubilation. The prisoners were put back into the cellars and the lieutenant went back to his room to make his report as soon as possible. They then said good bye to the inhabitants of the hacienda and rode off. ---

Chapter 14

THE PYRAMID OF THE SUNGOD

DOJERVA'S condition after he had been locked in his room, was indescribable, but he did not show it to Randero. "Señor Dojerva, can you explain your behaviour?"

"What do you mean?"

"I begin to doubt the truth of your assertion that you have been empowered by a higher authority. You spoke of protection and reward …?"

"Randero, should I call you an imbecile? Can't you see that the whole matter is only a passing embarrassment? I have an order to eliminate certain people in all circumstances, and that will happen. As we have suffered the present inconvenience, the reward will be higher."

"Are you sure? We should kill people in whose hands we are. They can kill us."

Dojerva had the same fears but could not let him see them. He was at such pains to calm down Randero that he finally conceded. From Juarez he had nothing to hope for; other parties would view him with suspicion. He decided to give up any military career and devote himself to two aims: The acquisition of the land promised by Carujo and Alva, whose possession would be a revenge on his opponents. He needed an accomplice, so he had to say: "I am actually quite satisfied with all that has happened to me. Service was a deterrent to my plans. Do you know how much your gambling debts are?"

"Probably several thousand silverpiaster."

"Which you could, in your present situation, never repay. If you help me, then I shall tear up your promissory notes and give you a financial reward on top. The best price, however, is Kaya, the beautiful Indian girl."

"*Caramba,* if you keep those promises, I am yours."

"Your fear that they will kill us is groundless. We shall be freed and we shall act."

"Today's shame needs punishment; what will you do?"

"Exactly what they have done with us. Take them prisoner. I shall take them to a place where they will enjoy all the fun of custody to its bitter end. Not far from my hacienda, there is a place where the old Mexicans made their sacrifices. There are many long caves with separate compartments. It is a secret that was passed on from my ancestors to me. There we shall bring the two señoritas."

"You are a devil," laughed Randero cynically.

"Yes, we shall be two devils, but it's not revenge alone that drives me. I'm after a big reward that was promised to me if I eliminate the three people. But I shall be careful. If I kill them, I cannot enforce my reward. By keeping them alive in the caves from which there is no escape, I can ensure payment."

"If we're followed?"

"We're riding through the Mapimi desert where nobody sane will follow us."

"Through the Mapimi? Said Randero shuddering. We may die there."

"Don't worry. I know this desert like my own pocket.

While these two made plans for further attacks, they themselves were under discussion by the inhabitants of the hacienda. The decision was that they had planned murder but did not succeed. They had lost their right hand and it was decided to take their weapons and let them go after two days, so that they should not reach Juarez before the messenger. As for the others, Stenton wanted to keep his promise. Their knives and lassoes were given to them. Then they were freed one at a time with the threat, that if they showed up near the hacienda, they would be shot. Dojerva and Randero were freed on the third day. They left without a word in the direction of the town of Saltillo. ---

After all these excitements there were a few weeks of quiet life on the hacienda. The patient had recuperated enough to ride out for a while. Stenton did not want to leave before Antonio was completely physically and mentally cured. He wrote a letter to his wife, asking her to send her replies, as previously, to Mexico, to Lord Castlepool. A weighty letter arrived from Bradford on Avon. It contained a long letter from Rosetta, two pages from Mrs. Brooks and one page from George's son Robbie. On the whole, everything was all right over there. Rosetta was pregnant and expected to give birth in four months. Robbie did very well at school. It was decided that Stenton, Rudolfo, Brooks and Margaret were going to leave in one week. These weeks were a time of great happiness for Alva and her beloved Antonio, and they were very grateful to Stenton.

Buff-he had come for a visit and was told of all that what happened. He talked to Stenton, for whom he showed great respect. Stenton learned that Kaya, whom he had named as Buff-he's sister or half-sister, was of entirely different parentage. His parents had taken her in after she was orphaned at a very young age.

The haciendero needed to visit the hacienda given to him by Juarez. He didn't want to miss seeing his future son in law, so he asked Stenton whether Antonio was strong enough to ride with him. Stenton agreed and the two went off for a matter of two days. Alva wanted to join but they thought the hacienda would as yet not be sufficiently comfortable for a lady.

Stenton stood at the window when he saw a rider approach. He recognised the uniform of a soldier. The man was led into the dining room where the inhabitants of the hacienda were gathered. He asked whether this was the hacienda del Alina and the owner a señor Wilson? "Yes," said Alva, I am his daughter.

"I am a messenger from señor Juarez. My destination is Monclava and I was told that I would be permitted to stay here over night if I could not reach my destination before nightfall."

"That is quite all right, you can have dinner with us and then we shall show you your room."

His behaviour was that of a nobleman, although he did not speak very much during dinner. When asked by Stenton where Juarez was, he answered that diplomatic reasons forbade him to divulge the whereabouts of Juarez. The soldier asked for the room as soon as the meal had ended. He needed the rest, as he would be off early in the morning. Clarissa Moyes led him to his room. He did not undress and smoked cigarettes until near midnight when the inhabitants of the hacienda were asleep. Now he stepped to the window and made a circle with the oil lamp. Minutes later, little sand corns were thrown at his window.

Stenton felt anxious about this soldier. The uniform did not really fit. It was as if it had been made for a different person. There was something about this stranger that worried Stenton, but he could not discover anything really suspicious. He slipped onto the floor where the stranger had his room but it was all quiet. He then went into the yard, into the garden and then walked around the house.

Dojerva was already under the window of the visitor who heard him approach. He put his finger to his mouth as a sign to Randero to be quiet. It was new moon and very dark. Stenton passed them without noticing anything. Dojerva crept behind him and, although his steps could hardly be heard on the grass, Stenton's sharp ears perceived them. He turned round but too late. The butt of Dojerva's rifle hit him over the head and he sunk unconscious to the ground. Randero had the material to tie and gag him. Stenton, when he woke up, would not be able to shout or even move.

With the help of a rope ladder, the two criminals and several of the bandits then climbed into the stranger's room. Next they went to Rudolfo's room where they knocked at the door.

"Who is there?

"I, Stenton,." replied Dojerva whispering but loud enough to be heard inside.

"Ah, you? What's the matter?"

"Open quickly. I have to tell you something important."

"All right." Rudolfo could be head getting out of bed.

"You don't have to put any light on," whispered Dojerva carefully.

Rudolfo put on some necessary clothing and unlocked the door. Several hands grabbed him and before he could utter a word or cry out, he was gagged and tied.. Now to Brooks ordered Dojerva. With the same method they overpowered Brooks. Now to señorita Alva. "Who is there? She asked answering a knock at her door.

"It is I, Kaya," whispered Dojerva softly.

Alva opened the door. Dojerva seized her throat with his left hand. Alva fainted with shock. The same happened with Kaya, except that she had better nerves than the Mexican girl. They were all gagged and tied without any disturbance and taken out of the hacienda and on to prepared horses. There were only a few vaqueros present. The others had accompanied Wilson.

Dojerva took any items out of the ladies' rooms he deemed necessary for them and off they went. They made groups of three men who took one male prisoner with them riding in different directions to mislead any pursuers. They arranged to meet in two days when they would all ride to Dojerva's hacienda. The meeting point was the border of the Mapimi where Dojerva awaited the other groups. Half an hour later, the first of them arrived. The gags were removed to enable their prisoners to breathe properly but the straps were tied in an inhuman way. None of the eventual arriving groups reported any pursuers and Dojerva thought that they were secure from now on.

They made a fire and prepared an evening meal. Up to now the prisoners had not spoken a word. They were hand fed, as they could not move a limb. Then the bandits laid in a circle around the prisoners and went to sleep. Dojerva had the first watch. He could not refrain from tormenting his prisoners and stepped first to Rudolfo. "How do you like the stroll? I should give you greetings from someone who has great interest in you."

"From whom?"

"From a certain señor Carujo."

"In Mexico?"

"Yes, he seems a great friend of yours."

Dojerva told him an unnecessary secret. He wanted to find out why Carujo wished to have these men dead.

"The devil will take care of him and you too," answered Rudolfo.

"Silence, rascal, I will show you soon whom you have as your master." He kicked Rudolfo and turned to Brooks. "You can see now what happens if you keep the company of rascals? You go together, you will hang together. Do you know señor Carujo?"

Brooks did not answer. "Ah, I see that I have to make you more submissive. You will learn to talk." He kicked him and turned to Stenton, who was tied so that he could not move his arms or his legs. The knees he could pull to his body. "Now to you, you dog," said Dojerva. "You have disabled our hands and you will get double punishment. How was it when you got the knock on your head?"

Stenton did not answer and did not move. "You also will not answer? Wait I'll make you answer." Dojerva stepped nearer to kick him. Stenton, with lightning speed drew his legs under his body, stretched them immediately and kicked the Mexican with such force in the stomach that he fell backward with his head into the brightly blazing fire. He got up immediately but his painful outcry showed he was wounded.

"My eye, my eye," he shouted.

The sleepers got up and examined him. It turned out that a little burning twig had stuck in his eye. It was broken off, but the end remained inside the wound. "The eye is lost because there is no doctor," said a Mexican.

"There is only one person who can help to take out the splinter in your eye, Stenton," said Randero.

"Stenton? The dog I have to thank for this misfortune? I shall beat him to death," called the wounded man furiously.

"He is a doctor and the only one who can help."

"He can do that, yes, he can do that and afterwards I'll tie him crookedly on his horse."

Randero stepped to Stenton. "Are you an eye doctor?"

Stenton said "yes." He would not have answered if he hadn't thought of a possibility to escape.

"Will you be able to remove that splinter?"

"I don't know without examining the eye."

"Well, I'll loosen your bonds enough that you can get up." Randero loosened Stenton's bonds and led him to the fire, where Dojerva was whimpering.

"Examine him," ordered Randero.

Dojerva took the hand from his wounded eye, stared at him furiously with the other one and said: "Rascal, if you don't heal that eye, I shall tear you apart with red-hot pincers."

Randero held a burning piece of wood to light Dojerva's face. Stenton knew that Brooks spoke enough German to understand him. He said in German as he observed the wounded eye: "Mut ich werde euch befreien." In English it meant 'courage, I shall free you'.

"What are you talking about?" roared Dojerva.

"We physicians have a Latin name for any medical condition," replied Stenton.

"Is the splinter removable?"

"Yes."

"Do it, at once."

"My hands are bound."

"Untie him."

"But if he escapes?"

"Are you stupid? We are thirteen men, how would he escape? Make a circle around him."

This was done. When Stenton spoke those German words, Brooks coughed as a sign that he had understood. Now was the time to act. " I can't remove it with my fingers. Give me a knife." He was given a knife. He was free of all fetters and had a knife. Now he only needed a rifle and ammunition. The rifles were stuck in pyramid fashion and Dojerva had a broad belt holding ammunition and money round his waist. Stanton only took a second to make up his mind. The knife was sharp and pointed. He stepped toward Dojerva and asked him to put his hands above his head. All eyes were upon them. "Open the affected eye and close the healthy one," ordered Stenton. He intended Dojerva to see nothing.

Suddenly his hand went down and cut the belt that he put between his teeth to have his hands free. He grabbed Dojerva ant threw him with Herculean strength towards some Mexicans. Three or four were knocked down by the body. He then jumped into the opened breach took one of the guns, swung himself onto a horse and galloped away. The whole action took seconds and the Mexicans were too shocked and surprised to do anything. When the cry of fifteen voices was heard it was too late. Some shot their guns after him but none hit him.

"After him, we must have him," roared Dojerva.

A few of the Mexicans jumped on their horses and went after him. Stenton thought they would do that. He examined his rifle. It was double barrelled and loaded, enough to keep in check several pursuers, who followed in a very broad line.They didn't expect Stenton to stop. It was dark, they could hear but not see each other. Stenton stopped after half a kilometre. He dismounted quickly and made his horse lie down.

The Mexicans rode past him, one on the left and one on the right. A minute afterwards he was between them. Each one of them thought he was a comrade. Stenton rode to the right of a Mexican who shouted: "Go further left." Stenton's rifle shaft hit him on the head. The valiant Englishman grabbed the reins of the other horse and stopped it. In two minutes he cleared the pockets of the Mexican of anything useful, took his rifle and ammunition and chased after the next pursuer. When he had almost reached him, he heard him shout: "To me you called to go further left and now you are going in the wrong direction." Before he could suspect anything, he suffered the same fate as his predecessor. Again his pockets were cleared and his rifle and ammunition ended in Stenton's possession.

He heard only two more were on his right side, he called out loudly: "Come here, I've got him." The two came closer and shouted:

"Where are you?"

Stenton shouted back: "Here, here, he took a dive, his horse must have thrown him."

They came, one after the other. Stenton took his double barrel rifle and killed them both. He listened but there were no others. He now had five rifles and plenty of ammunition. His main worry was to escape further pursuers. He knew that the wounded and the dead were going to be found in the morning, so he took the other horses by the reins and rode into the unknown desert. He also knew, that there would be people coming from the hacienda. He therefore tried to keep Dojerva and his team at the same spot as long as possible. He decided to ride in a large circle.

At dawn he reached a place, about two hours to the east, where they had last camped. Here he gave the horses some rest and smoked some of the cigarettes he had taken from the robbers. There was even water for the horses and they could do some grazing.

It was about four hours after daybreak that he rode on and reached the place where he had killed the two Mexicans. He examined the tracks and came to the conviction that the bandits had followed his trail with their prisoners but without the wounded. He had to laugh. They thought they had him before them, while he was behind them. He rode immediately behind them. The disadvantages were the extra horses he took with him. On the other hand, he could change horses to enhance his speed.

After Stenton had ridden for two hours, he found they had stopped for a while, obviously to discuss the turning to the south Stenton had made previously. When they reached the place where he had turned east, they had stopped again but rode on into the Mapimi desert. Whereas Red Indians and Prairie-men ride in single column, the Mexicans rode as a troop, next to each other. Stenton could Count the tracks. There were thirteen horses, Dojerva, Randero, four prisoners and seven Mexicans. Stenton hoped to reach them that night and possibly eliminate some more.—

The night before, when four of the Mexicans followed Stenton, those that were left listened for hours. Even Dojerva forgot the pain in his eye. For a long time everything was quiet until two shots were heard, hardly perceptible.

"They've got him," said Randero.

"Yes, but not alive," said Dojerva angrily. "They have killed him,. How can I take revenge now? Who's looking after my eyes?"

"Maybe he's only wounded," said one of the Mexicans. "This giant seems to be tough."

"Then they'll bring him, they'll be back in less than half an hour."

The time passed and Dojerva became anxious. "What makes them so slow? I'll punish them for that.

Another half hour passed then another hour with no-one coming back. Dojerva's eye was really painful and he had to tie a wet cloth over it. He couldn't sleep and walked the whole night up and down, uttering curses. As daylight broke, he sent two Mexicans to search for their comrades.

They saddled their horses and galloped off. After a short while they found one of their companions still half-stunned on the ground. His horse grazed in the distance. They went for his horse and, on their way, found their other comrade still on the ground. Both were helped to mount their horses. As they looked around, they found their dead comrades whose horses Stenton took with him. They made their way back. As they were in sight, the ones who stayed back jumped up expectantly.

"Where is Stenton?" asked Dojerva.

"We have found our comrades All four were robbed."

When the prisoners heard this, their eyes lit up. Alva uttered a cry of joy.

"Quiet," shouted Dojerva, you are rejoicing too early, he hasn't escaped yet. Forward, after him, I have to know which direction he took."

The prisoners were tied to their horses and they went to the place where the battle took place. But they could not find out how Stenton could overpower four men. One of the Mexicans crossed himself and said: "He certainly has the devil in him, how could he overpower four men otherwise?"

"Be quiet, idiot. This Stenton is an astute man, nothing else. He has taken the two horses of the wounded, here is his track, we must go after him."

"He's going back to the hacienda," said Randero.

"No, the hacienda is not in that direction. I don't know what his plans are but he has five rifles now, enough to wipe us all out. He is the famous 'Doctor Ironfist' and needs no help from the hacienda who, even if they were quick, could not be here before three days. By then our tracks would have disappeared. No, this Ironfist wants to handle us himself, but we'll show him we're not without brains ourselves."

Anyone could see from his distorted face that Dojerva was in terrible pains. He foamed with fury but for now it was important to reach the pyramid with its secret passages. Revenge could wait for later. The whole day they went west, over stony lowlands, barren stretches of land and bare rocks, until they reached the beginning of a wood. Here, the tired horses were rested for half an hour. Then they went on.

While those areas were hot during the day, they were very cold at night. This was an advantage for the horses as they would tire less. The stamina of Mexican horses is unbelievable..The next morning they had reached a longed for pond where they rested. The saddles were taken off the animals and they could drink and graze. The people enjoyed the food and the prisoners were also fed. When the horses began to play one with another it was time to continue the ride in the direction as before. Again they went the whole day then, after crossing through a large wood they reached the border of the Mapimi desert. They had a short rest and continued. In an overgrown gorge Dojerva left three men to hide and lie in wait for Stenton, who would be stopping to read the tracks of the place where they had rested.

The next day they reached Dojerva's destination, the pyramid. He put his finger in his mouth and whistled loudly. The bushes parted and a man stepped out. "Did my messenger reach you?" asked Dojerva.

"Yes, he came to your hacienda. Everything is prepared, light as well."

Dojerva took Alva off her horse and tied her hands at the back. Her eyes were blindfolded; he then put Alva over his shoulder and carried her away. She submitted because resistance could not improve her position. Soon she heard the dull tone of his steps and she knew that they were in an underground vault. The further they went, the worse the air. Finally a door opened and he put her to the ground. When he took her blindfold off, she saw she was in a chamber hewn into the rock about two and a half metres long, one and three quarter metres wide and two metres high. There was only a bed of straw, a piece of dry bread and two candles.

"Now we are at the place I wanted. You will never be able to escape from here and I'll, take off your bonds."

"What have I done to you," asked the unhappy girl, "that you have robbed me and brought me to such a place?"

"You have robbed my heart," he answered" and you will learn to reciprocate my love."

"Never, you rascal," said Alva and withdrew to the furthest corner.

"Oh yes." He stretched out his hand to pull her toward himself. She grabbed his knife from his belt, held it against him.

"Stand back or I shall defend myself.

The Mexican got a shock and stepped back. He then uttered a mocking laugh and said: "A knife in this hand is no more dangerous to me than a needle. Give it to me!"

She held the knife to her chest, "if you come closer, I'll kill myself."

The expression of her face made him believe her threat. That, however, was not his intention. "All right, I'm sure of you. Hunger is a hard guest, it will break your will. You'll get no more to eat until you are obedient." He took the lantern off the floor and went back to the others. The girl, used to freedom, fresh air and plenty to eat and drink, had none of these now. A narrow rock chamber, dirty water and a piece of dry bread, was her lot now. Kaya advised her on the way to get a weapon. She still held the knife in her hand and had learned how useful it was. She was determined to defend herself. Now, she was exhausted from the long ride and sank to her bed of straw where her tears flowed freely. There was only one hope: Stenton would not give up finding them.

The pyramid was an old Mexican art of building places where noblemen or priests kept their secrets and served their sungod. Below were numerous chambers connected by passages. Time and weather has taken off the top and it looked like an overgrown hill now. But the inside was not affected and kept in good condition. The entrance was a secret that was only passed down to the descendants of the family.

After Dojerva came back, the Indian girl was untied from her horse. Randero's eyes were also blindfolded and was taken off inside the pyramid. They took Kaya by the hand and led her to a cell next to Alva. Dojerva said that he would leave Randero now. When he finished he would only have to shout and he would come for him.

Randero took Kaya's blindfold off and untied her.

"No man can take you from me, he said.

Kaya's eyes sparkled with pride and anger. She, brought up by an Indian chief and with the famous Buff-he, did not fear Randero.

"Coward," she said disparagingly.

"Coward?" he laughed, "have we not conquered you and taken you prisoners?"

"Taken us prisoners when we slept. A real man does not fight with women. Has not Stenton escaped? He is a man and you could not hold him. You are like wolves that only go in packs for any loot. When you hear a shot, you cry with fear. I am a girl and fear you less than an insect I squash between my fingers."

"Be silent, you are in my hands and it depends on you whether I shall crush you or improve your condition."

"Crush me? laughed Kaya, you are not the man who would manage to crush me. You are lost as soon as you touch me. "She stood there with her arm lifted. He stepped nearer and stretched his unhurt left toward her. It was her aim to get a weapon and took a step forward. She then grabbed his knife and revolver with both hands before he could stop it.. At the same time she gave him a hearty push and he fell against the door. "Beast. I shall tame you," shouted Randero and drew against her. Her knife sank with terrible speed one, two, three times into his chest.

"*Oh Dios*," he groaned as he staggered.

"Go to hell, she answered and her knife went the fourth time between his ribs. This time she hit his heart and Randero fell backward onto the straw bed. The valiant girl pulled from him his second gun, his ammunition, his watch and his bag of provisions, when she heard a loud knock. "Who is there? she asked.

"It is I, Alva." Her voice sounded hollow.

Kaya rejoiced, grabbed the lantern and stood before Alva's cell, where it took all her strength to shift the rusty bolts. Alva flew toward her, "You have weapons, you are free," shouted the white girl.

"I have weapons, I killed Randero, but I am not free yet," answered Kaya

"My God, that is terrible."

"Terrible? Oh no. It was self-defence and he has his reward. We have to make use of our time. Under no circumstances will I let them lock us up any longer Here, take a revolver. Whoever wants to touch us will be killed. Come, let's examine the passage."

It turned out there were several passages. Suddenly Kaya stood still and uttered a little cry of joy. "Look here, several lanterns and food. We have light and needn't be hungry."

"What luck!" said Alva, I thought I had to die of hunger here."

They heard voices and went back into the cell, where they bolted the door. People passed their cell and soon stopped. "Here," said Dojerva to his servant, "put them into these two chambers and put them into chains." The servant did as he was told. He chained the prisoners' legs first, untied and spread their arms to the left and the right. Then he put them into chains that had bolts instead of keys. Dojerva knocked at Kaya's door and called Randero's name. When he got no reply he laughed. "He's still busy."

"We have to wait now," grumbled the servant.

"He doesn't want to be disturbed and we're not prepared to wait. Let's go home to the hacienda," suggested Dojerva.

"He can't leave without us," warned the messenger servant.

"So he has to wait until I come back in an hour," the ex-captain didn't worry.

They went and the girls breathed easier. They listened until the sound of steps was no longer heard. "What now?" asked Alva.

"We are going to free our friends. Then there'll be four of us and we have nothing to fear," answered Kaya.

The Indian girl knocked at one of the next doors. There was no answer. She pushed the bolt back and entered. Someone lay there in two chains. When she put the light on herself Brooks said in amazement: "Señorita Kaya, how is this possible?"

"I have killed Randero and I took his weapons."

"And señorita Alva?"

"I'm here too, let's free you now. Dojerva will be back in an hour", said Alva.

She started to undo the bolts with which the chains were fastened, while Kaya did the same next door to a surprised Rudolfo. Minutes later the two señores stood upright and stretched their limbs to get their blood into proper circulation. *"Ascuas,* what luck within our bad luck." Rudolfo suggested that the girls should keep the knives and the men should have the revolvers. This was arranged and they decided that they should stick together and not leave the girls separate. In any case, they divided the provisions into four parts. "One can never be sure," said Brooks.

They searched the exit but whichever passage they went, it ended with a closed door they were unable to open. They returned to their original place and decided to wait for Dojerva. They would capture him and force him to show the entrance. Rudolfo suggested trying finding the secrets of the doors but it was no use. They failed to shift the door even an inch. More than an hour had passed when they heard a distant sound of someone approaching. Rudolfo turned the light off. Steps came nearer. It was the messenger who knocked at the door where he thought Randero to be. Rudolfo stood nearby and said in a disguised voice: "Captain, is it you?"

There was no need to disguise his voice as Dojerva's servant did not know Randero's voice, neither did he recognise Rudolfo in the half-dark passage and he replied: "No, señor Dojerva went to his hacienda, I was told to bring you."

"And the others?"

"They went to catch Stenton and bring him here, dead or alive."

Brooks noticed Rudolfo wanted to find out as much as possible and crept quietly behind the messenger. "And the other three prisoners?" asked Rudolfo.

"They are safely chained in other cells."

"Are they?" Rudolfo stepped forward. Brooks took the servant from behind by his neck. He dropped down immediately. Whether it was from shock or Brook's powerful hands was not clear.

"It is all right," said the sailor, "he's fainted." Rudolfo put a light on the stiff person on the ground. The eyes were open and the face was grey-blue.

"He has not fainted, he is dead," said Rudolfo.

"Impossible, I only squeezed a little," replied Brooks.

"Look at him, it's not the face of someone who's fainted. He probably died of shock."

"The stupidity of this man, now he can't show us the entrance.

"That's right, but we only have to go back to where he came from

"That sounds simple but the passages are like a maze and closed with doors we can't open. Let's look to see whether this man is really dead. Here's his knife and a pistol." Rudolfo handed the pistol to Brooks and kept the knife.

They worked ten minutes with the corpse until they decided that he was really dead. "Who can understand this?" grumbled Brooks. "This man creeps about in these passages and at the slightest unexpected touch, he breaks down with a stroke."

They went though various passages but only found them closed by a door whose secret they could not discover. "We have to wait until Dojerva arrives," said Rudolfo resignedly."

"That will probably not be until the morning. Let's have a rest," suggested Brooks.

They put the messenger into the cell with Randero and went to two other chambers. One shared by Alva and Kaya, the other by the señores.

"I hope that señor Brooks will not kill Dojerva as well." Alva voiced her fear.

"Not at all," answered the sailor, "the two of us are strong enough to hold him while the ladies bind him."

"Remember it may be our only chance," said Alva, still fearful.

"I have great hopes for Dr. Stenton," replied Brooks.

It was decided that Dojerva would not come before the next morning, when he had missed his servant. He will then think the man might have had an accident. The señoritas should have some sleep and the men would take their turn keeping watch.---

Dojerva had a distant relative looking after the hacienda. She had a surprise as well as a shock when he arrived. A speech of sympathy was cut short by his order for a meal, and one prepared for a señor Randero who would turn up later. After the meal he felt tired and went to bed.

The next morning he was brought a cup of chocolate. He asked whether señor Randero was up. The señora had not seen him. "Where is Gasparino whom I've sent to fetch him?" It turned out he did not come back either. Dojerva asked to have his horse saddled. Ten minutes later he left for the pyramid. He left his horse to graze and went to some of the rare bushes that surrounded the pyramid. Behind them were some shattered rocks. Where the rock rested on the ground a few cracks were seen. Dojerva kneeled down and put his shoulder against the rock part of which gave in. The rock seemed to slide inward. A big hole was visible, the circumference of which would let a man in a bowed position go through. Dojerva stepped inside and pushed the rock back to its former position. There were a few steps down where he found some lanterns. He lit one and went in a passage going downhill.

Then, after a while, there were some steps going up, then straight on and then a slight bend. He opened some doors and locked them again with only a slight pressure of his hand. One could hear the sound of metal. The way now went uphill and he opened and closed some more of the secret locks. Finally he went through the door left open by his servant. He first stopped at the cell where he had left Alva. His light fell on Rudolfo. Just as he recognised him, Brooks grabbed him from the back.

"I've got him."

"Not yet," roared Dojerva, tore himself lose, kicked Rudolfo in the stomach so that he fell down, then ran into the passage. He still held the lantern in his hand. He guessed that his servant and Randero were killed. Otherwise the prisoners could not have been freed. He decided not to continue the fight but to flee and make sure that they could not escape.

"After him," shouted Brooks. Rudolfo, who had stood up asked: "Without the señoritas?"

"Yes," shouted Brooks rashly.

"But if we lose them? I'll call them."

"I'll go first." Brooks run after the escapee, while Rudolfo went for the girls.

It was not necessary, they stood behind him with lanterns in their hands. Kaya took the precaution to grab a bottle of oil.

"Come on, quickly," called Rudolfo and hurried after Brooks who nearly caught up with Dojerva. The Mexican opened another door and reached a room in which there was a large hole spanned by a board. Dojerva stepped on it as Brooks reached the door. He rushed over the board. There were two steps before the other side of the large gullet, when the board snapped and he fell with an outcry: *Oh Dios*!" into the yawning depth. They heard the impact of his body.

"My God," called Brooks, as he stopped at the door, "Dojerva has crashed to his death"

"Where, how?" asked Rudolfo who had just arrived behind him.

"Down here."

The girls came running and Alva stepped toward the large hole and almost let the door close. Rudolfo just reached it at the right time. "For heaven sake, señorita, we mustn't let this door close, we cannot open it again."

They could hear dull sounds from the debth. Brooks kneeled down and called:

"Dojerva."

A horrible whimpering answered.

"Can we help? asked Brooks again.

From the groaning that followed they could make nothing. "He is lost. The well is at least twenty metres deep," ventured Rudolfo.

"Dojerva has his punishment," said Kaya, "but what's going to happen to us?"

"The door is open," remarked Alva, "maybe we could discover its secret device?" To their amazement, the doorframe was part of the door. At the top and the bottom they noticed bolts and the holes to go with them but how to open the bolts on the other sides, they were unable to discover. There was no possibility of bridging the hole to reach the other side. The groaning of the wounded man was becoming more horrible. They returned to the passage where they had been before. The door leading to the room with the well they kept open by putting straw from their beds between it and its frame.

Now they looked at each other. "Maybe Dojerva left the door open when he came to us," ventured Rudolfo. "We'd better look for it." They all rushed through the passage but found the door locked.

"We are locked in and damned to die of hunger," sighed Alva.

"Not yet. God will not let us die here," said Rudolfo.

"Let's think and try everything to get us out of here," said Brooks.

"We'll discover nothing Help can only come from señor Stenton," Kaya put in.

"But if he doesn't come? If they catch him and kill him?" lamented the distressed Alva.

"A Doc Ironfist is not easily caught. He knows Dojerva will set traps for him and a man like him can foresee where they are likely to be," Kaya consoled her.

"And we have our knives," added Brooks.

"Ah really," called Alva, "we should cut the doors out.

The helmsman, in spite of the serious position they were in, couldn't suppress a laugh. "No, that's not what I meant, señorita. The wooden surround of these doors is hard as iron It would take months to get through only one door. After which we find other doors. We have to remove the part of the wall where the mechanism is hidden.

"There is perhaps a quicker way," remarked Kaya, "we take the leather straps with which we were tied up, maybe some clothes of the two dead men, even some of our own and go down to Dojerva. He must tell us the secret."

"Good idea," said Rudolfo, "let's do it." They made a rope but had to cut some of he blankets that were prepared for the ladies. Rudolfo, as the lighter of the two men. volunteered to be let down to ask Dojerva about the secrets of the mechanism to open the doors. Brooks was strong and could hold the rope by himself when Rudolfo climbed down.

The two women saw the light of the brave young man's lantern going down. Eventually the rope slackened, Rudolfo had reached the ground. He saw Dojerva lying there, bent like a dog. His wailing sounded even worse than above. His lips showed bloody foam; the healthy eye expressed that he was fully conscious.

"Don't groan but answer, I have come to help you."

Dojerva's whimpering stopped for some seconds and he looked at his saviour with a devilish hate. "Where is Randero?" "Dead," replied Rudolfo. "The servant?" "Also dead."

"The girls?" "They are above, with us."

"Murderers!"

"Be quiet, it is all your fault In spite of it all, we are going to save you."

"You? How?"

"We'll pull you up and take you to your hacienda."

The pain distorted face lit up for a short moment. Then it darkened again and he asked: "How will you get out?"

"You will tell us how to open the doors and which passages to take."

"Ah, you don't know that?" Schadenfreude – joy of other's misfortune, distorted his face even more than his pain. Then he added: "You will die of hunger and thirst." The obvious satisfaction even anaesthetized the pain.

"We will not die of hunger, because you want to be free and healthy. That you can only achieve through us."

"Free – healthy, ah, groaned Dojerva. Never. Arms and legs are broken, spine is broken, and I have to die."

"You will not die, trust us."

"Never, never, you all will die too."

"You are doing your own destruction."

"I want it - and you will rot in hell."

"Is that your last word?"

The human wreck showed his teeth. "My last, last, last."

"All right, love ends and severity begins. We don't intend to die because of your depravity. He knelt next to Dojerva, grabbed his arms where they were broken and pressed them with all his strength. It elicited the roar of a tiger but an answer was not forthcoming. Rudolfo then grabbed his legs, but Dojerva had no feelings there because of his broken spine. A mocking laughter was his answer. Rudolfo then grabbed his hands with a most powerful jerk that he thought to pull the arms out of their sockets. Dojerva again uttered a terrible cry but did not answer.

"You are even too bad for the devil," shouted Rudolfo, "Die if you want to. God will help us." He took everything of any value and shook the line as a sign that he wanted to climb up.

"Robber," Dojerva spat at him.

"We can use these things but not you, rascal." Once again he tested the line and climbed up.

When he told his comrades the result and the torture he had tried, Brooks remarked that now the knives would have to be tried.—

Martin Wilson and Antonio Brooks returned home after spending one night on the neighbouring hacienda. Clarissa Moyes told them that she at first thought that the guest had gone for an early outing. But when Margaret appeared for breakfast and knew nothing about such an outing, they feared something had gone wrong. The haciendero and Antonio were shocked when they heard the news. While Wilson was rushing through the rooms, wringing his hands, Antonio was no longer the helpless patient but the former knowledgeable man of the west. In less than a quarter of an hour he saw from the tracks, half the happenings. The other half he guessed.

He was after all the famous prairie hunter Old Surehand who could read tracks like a book. His horse was still saddled but he asked the haciendero for his best stallion. He was following the now barely visible tracks of the robbers and their prisoners. Margaret would not take no for an answer when she saw his intention to follow them.

She was determined to play her part in the freeing of her beloved Rudolfo. She had the best horse and Antonio or Old Surehand had to make do with the second best. The haciendero wanted to be with them too: his daughter Alva was one of the prisoners, but he was persuaded he was more important at the hacienda and would not be of much help to his son in law.

The two rode fast, the horses were fresh and they reached the place where the Mexicans made their first camp. With amazement Margaret saw how for Old Surehand every foot print, every bent or broken blade of grass was like an open book.

"Ah, what is that? A battle took place here. We can see somebody's heels were deeply dug into the soft earth. Another man's feet left the ground. It seems that one man was lifted and hurled into others to make a path for himself.

Old Surehand went around the place where the fire was and continued his search. Here stood the rifles. One of them was torn away by the fleeing person – probably Stenton. Now he and Margaret rode after the tracks of the escapee and his followers.

He read exactly the events of the previous night. "Stenton " he said "has three horses now, he has gone in a circle and is behind the enemies now." Suddenly he jumped a few steps to the left where he saw a heap of sand that could only been put there by hand. He searched inside the heap and found a piece of paper with writing on it. He unfolded it and read: *"I escaped. The others are still prisoners but OK. Have horses and enough ammunition. Don't worry the prisoners will be freed. Follow me as quick as you can. I shall leave a visible track.*

5. September 1851 8 o'clock in the morning. Stenton.

They were both extremely happy about this note and rode their horses at full gallop. Because Stenton went as fast as he could, he couldn't be caught up quickly. The morning went and also a large part of the afternoon when Old Surehand noticed three little points in the distance. "That's him and two free horses," rejoiced Antonio. We have to try and catch up with him before night." They spurted their horses and flew over the ground with a furious speed. Another half-hour passed and the three points were larger now. They could recognise a rider with three horses. The rider held his rifle horizontally above his head, lifted himself up and whirled it in circles.

"He has turned around and seen us," remarked Old Surehand.

He thinks we're enemies," said Margaret, "he would have stopped otherwise."

"Margaret, you're a clever girl but not a man of the prairie. If Stenton had waited for us, he would have lost time and space. Here, every minute counts. We can't follow their tracks at night, while they can use the night to get further away.

We're getting nearer," said Margaret.

"That's understandable," declared Old Surehand. "He had to take the horses as they came, while we have taken the best horses on the hacienda. His horses were not fresh, while ours came fresh from grazing. Also, he's much heavier than we are. See, he's changing horses now without even stopping." Soon they were in earshot and Brooks shouted in English: "Hello Dr. Stenton."

"Mr. Brooks, I've recognised you long ago."

"How is that possible?"

"Only a man of the west rides like that and there was only one at the hacienda. But let's make headway." Soon they were at Stenton's side. He greeted them heartily but did not diminish his speed.

Night stopped them from going further. Luckily there was some grass for the horses, but no wood to make a fire. Stenton explained what had happened on the hacienda. He gently chided Lady Margaret for joining such a dangerous adventure, but soon saw her determination to be with Rudolfo.

"The bandits will ride the whole night."

"That's for sure," agreed Stenton, "they will take a rest in the morning that we must use to our advantage. After only a few hours' rest the riders and the horses were refreshed and the first light saw them galloping full speed ahead. About midday Stenton reined in his horse and observed the valley in front of him, the surrounding hills and the many rocks of various sizes. "A dangerous hole," he said, "if Dojerva hasn't arranged an ambush here, he deserves a hiding. We'll go forward slowly and behave as if we were unconcerned, while I'll observe."

"Here they've rested," said Old Surehand. Stenton looked around and said hastily: "Off your horses quickly, as if we're preparing to rest here and keep on the right side of your horses." Old Surehand followed Stenton's glance. "You are right, don't let them suspect we know where they are. Let's take refuge behind the big rock to the right."

They followed Old Surehand's advice and were out of sight of the prospective assassins. "How many do you think they are?" asked Margaret, quite calm about the situation.

"Two or three maximum. The others he needs to guard the prisoners." Stenton replied.

Then he asked Old Surehand to put his hat on the rifle and slowly lift it over he rock.

Stenton then put himself into a position to shoot. When the hat became visible a bandit's rifle showed and Stenton had a target. His shot rang out before the bandit's.

A loud cry told him that he had hit somebody. While he was shooting he saw two Red Indians not far behind the robbers. They were standing up only for a moment for him to see them. He recognised Buff-he and a stranger. He could not speak the language of the Mixtekas but knew that Buff-he could understand Apache of which he knew sufficient to shout: "How many are they?"

Buff-he lifted two arms and put them down immediately. The two Indians could no longer be seen. Stenton shouted again in the Apache language: "Do not kill them, I need them alive."

"What's he shouting about?" asked one of the bandits. "Is he making fun of us? There's a stalemate We have to wait until darkness to escape."

Stenton noticed the Indians creeping nearer and decided to engage the robber's attention. He stood up full length and lifted his rifle as if to shoot.

"He wants to shoot," laughed the Mexican and looked carefully from behind the rock. "I'll give him a bullet." But it was different from what he'd expected. He reached for his gun and aimed but he sunk down with shock when he felt a pair of hands around his throat. Both were overpowered and bound with their own lassoes. Buff-he waved to Stenton to come over.

They ran across the valley and shook hands with the Indians. "Buff-he saved my life for the second time," was Stenton's greeting to his friend.

"This is Flying Horse, the Chief of the Apaches." Buff-he introduced the other Indian. They sat down but not in earshot of the Mexicans and told their story. When Buff-he heard that Kaya was among the prisoners he urged Stenton to start after them immediately. They went to the prisoners and Stenton asked:

"Do you belong to Dojerva's group?" There was no reply.

"I saw you with him. Your denial or your silence won't help you. You will only worsen your fate if you play hard. Why did you stay back?"

"We had to take you prisoner or kill you."

"Did you three really think you could catch me, kill me from behind, perhaps?"

"We expected you tomorrow and then we will be joined by others."

"Where did Dojerva take his prisoners?"

"We don't know that."

"The people who come here tomorrow will know. Where were you going to meet them?"

"Here, in the valley."

Buff-h suggested to have the prisoners killed, but Stenton succeeded in saving the bandits' life. Their weapons were destroyed and their horses confiscated. They were put far from the group. During the night there was nothing to interrupt the loneliness of the valley. It was late in the morning when they heard horses. Stenton ordered only the horses to be shot but not the riders. Four shots killed the four horses. The riders were entangled with their falling horses and before they could free themselves from the chaos, four rifle butts hit their heads. They were bound before they realised what happened.

The leader of the four was the same man who had pretended to be a messenger on the hacienda. "Now we meet again and you won't play a messenger any more."

The man looked at Stenton with hatred in his eyes. "I am a free Mexican and no foreigner gives me an order."

"A free Mexican? I didn't know a bound man is free. Where did you take the prisoners?"

"That is nobody's business."

"I repeat my question only once more. Where are the prisoners?"

"I won't tell you."

Buff-he drew his knife, held it against the prisoner and said: "Where is Kaya?"

The man obviously did not know the way of the Indians and was spitefully silent.

The chief of the Mixtekas said calmly: "Answer!"

"I won't tell you."

"You don't need to live. The dead are silent and who is silent, is dead." With these words he plunged his knife into the chest of the prisoner who died immediately."That is their lot if they don't talk, he said." He put the knife against the next bandit's chest.

"Will you be silent too or will you tell me where they are?" The man thought only a minute, He wanted to save his life but not betray his comrades. This minute was too long for the Indian; he sunk his knife into the Mexican and went to the third man:

"Speak, you dog. Where are the prisoners?"

"I'm going to tell you," he answered hurriedly. "They are inside a pyramid near Dojerva's hacienda."

"Describe it to me."

"It is a pyramid of the sungod in the north of the hacienda surrounded by bushes."

"Where is its entrance?"

"I don't know that. We arrived at night and were left outside."

"On what side is the entrance?"

"Unknown to me."

"You must know which direction he went."

"He went to the bushes at the corner of the pyramid and then disappeared at the south."

"The entrance must be there; how long did it take you to come here?"

"Two hours before midnight until now."

"You will lead us. The slightest suspicion and you're dead. That's enough, we don't need the last man." He went to the fourth bandit and plunged his knife into his chest.

"Buff-he is gruesome," scolded Old Surehand. "These scalps are easily obtained."

The reprimanded answered proudly: "The chief of the Mixtekas only takes scalps of those he has battled with. These are dogs whose skin I don't want. They've died like jackals you kill with a stick."

The Flying Horse was on his way to Juarez to offer his tribe's help. He cut the lassos used to tie up the prisoners of the previous night and left. The others had quick breakfast, then took the horses of the prisoners and sped toward their aim, the outlines of which they saw at nightfall.

It was dark when they reached the pyramids. "For every sigh from Kaya I shall kill an enemy," said Buff-he.

"I hope we can find the entrance in the dark," said Lady Margaret who could not wait to see her beloved Rudolfo free again.

"I'm no less eager to see my Alva," chipped in Old Surehand.

"Patience," comforted Stenton, "We'll have our friends free in no time."

It wasn't going to be as easy as he thought. He turned to the Mexican still bound.

"Where did you stop?"

"Come along," said the Mexican, rode a short stretch on and then stopped. "Here it was."

"And where did Dojerva disappear?"

"Here's the bush where he went into the thicket and there's the corner I saw Dojerva's lamp lighting up."

"Good, if everything turns out as you said, you'll get your life as a present." Stenton called Buff-he, Old Surehand and Margaret and went in the direction indicated by the Mexican. Although they had lights and scrutinised a large area, they did not find the entrance. "We must look for any tracks made by Dojerva, and we can only do that by daylight," said Stenton resigned. Lady Margaret didn't want to give up the search but Stenton advised her she might only delete Dojerva's tracks, if we haven't done so already.

"Why wait till tomorrow," said Anthony Brooks impatiently. "We should ride to the hacienda and force Dojerva to tell us where the entrance is. Alva and my brother should not have to stay imprisoned for a second longer than necessary" At the hacienda they learned that Dojerva had left the morning before and had not returned.

"If he has done anything to Alva I'll make him regret it," Antonio vowed.

"Or if anything has happened to Kaya," echoed Buff-he.

Stenton searched the house and found Dojerva's writing desk. He broke it open and discovered plans of the inside passages its chambers and the square well in the middle of the pyramid but not its entrance. They took crowbars, other tools and ammunition from the hacienda and in less than half an hour they were on their way to the pyramid.

Again they spent their time in vain. After two hours, Stenton thought of measuring the exact middle of the side where Dojerva, according to the Mexican, disappeared. He noticed a rock with peculiar crevices. He put his shoulder to one and it gave way. "I've got it," he shouted. Here is the entrance, I felt it. The part of the rock I pushed slides inward," said Stenton still pushing. He glanced at the opening; "there is a lantern here."

"Let's light this quickly and go inside," said Old Surehand and picked up a bottle with oil. He rushed forward without looking whether anybody followed. They all did, Stenton, Buff-he and Lady Margaret. A long passage ended with a door. Stenton held the light to the plan and studied it. "Doors are not shown here. Is there a lock?"

"No," answered Old Surehand "but it's closed tightly."

"There are either bolts at the other side or there's a secret way to open it. We have no time to find it but enough powder to blast it open. Let's use our knives to make holes for the powder. They started to work at once and when Stenton came back after collecting sufficient explosives, they were ready. They had made holes between the brick wall and the doorframe and Stenton filled them. He made a fuse with threads, rubbed it in with powder, lit it and they all ran back to the entrance. Four explosions were heard in succession and they all ran back. They had to wait until the dust settled before they could crawl through the opening. Stenton examined the door completely torn from the wall. He discovered a metal protrusion at the bottom and one in the ceiling but could not discover how to move them.

"We have enough explosives to use on all the doors. There's no alternative," said Stenton. Soon they reached another door and used the same method. Again they had to shift rubble before they could crawl through into another long passage.—

The prisoners, in the meantime, were in different moods. Whereas Kaya was taciturn, Alva, on the other side, expressed her fear: "I've given up hope now. We're here two days and two nights, our food ration won't last long and we're almost out of water. Stenton doesn't now where we are. The only people who could tell us how to get out of here are dead. Dojerva won't talk."

"I still have hopes," replied Rudolfo. Stenton is not the man to leave his friends in the lurch."

"But Dojerva has sent men to kill him," Alva said.

"That's my last worry," said Rudolfo, "you don't know the instinct and skill of a man like Doc Ironfist. His brain is trained to foresee danger and he's certainly aware that Dojerva will do anything to ambush him. I would bet that he is near already -"listen." A sound like thunder was heard.

"What was that?" Alva asked, "it seemed to me like distant thunder."

"Impossible," said Rudolfo, "no sound gets through to this depth."

Depression silenced them. Then they heard the thunder but louder and nearer. "That was no thunder, that was a rifle shot," said Brooks.

"It's impossible to hear a shot down here," said Alva.

"But if this shot came from down here?"

"Who would shoot?"

"What we heard was not a shot but an explosion," ventured Rudolfo.

"Almighty God! You believe …?"

Brooks nodded. "Yes. I believe Stenton is here and it's the explosions to break through the doors."

"You give me hope," said Alva, "I will see my father and my Antonio again." She broke down in tears.

A mighty bang shook the walls and when after the bang the sound of cracking debris was heard, Brooks shouted: "Hurrah, Stenton is here, he's really here. We're saved."

Alva tried to stand but was too weak. "Is it possible?" she whispered.

"I believe señor Brooks is right. What do you think señorita Kaya?" asked Rudolfo.

The Indian girl opened her eyes slowly. "It is Stenton. I knew he would come."

Alva embraced Kaya and rejoiced: "God, I thank you. I'll never forget your love. You have not forgotten us."

Some time elapsed while they all listened. Then they heard voices. " This door now, it leads to the well. We have enough powder." It was as if they had had an electric shock. They couldn't speak and held each others hands. "Stenton," whispered the helmsman finally. "He even knows about the well in here."

They listened. Then a voice said: "This will take a lot of powder, it's a door with a double bolt." Alva jumped up with a cry: "My God! Antonio, Antonio!"

There was silence. Then Antonio called: "Alva, my Alva is it you?"

"Yes my beloved, it's me."

"Thank God. Are you alone?"

"No, we're all here, the four of us."

Now there was a new voice: "All four? Kaya, you as well?"

This voice flushed the brown cheeks of the Indian girl with delight. "Yes," she called, "your sister is here."

Stenton's voice asked in English: "How is my captain?"

"Thank you, Dr. Stenton, open the waterway soon, so we can sail out of here."

"Go as far back as you can, we'll burst the door open."

A few minutes later another explosion and the last connection was cleared. Before the dust had settled four lovers embraced each other. Alva and Antonio, Rudolfo and Lady Margaret who had kept in the background. There were tears of joy, even some of the men had moist eyes. Stenton shook hands with all the freed people and then talking began. "Old Surehand asked Alva: You really took Randero's knife and threatened him?"

"Yes I would have killed him or myself, rather than be touched by him," she answered.

He embraced her and said: "My heroic girl."

Buff-he: "The daughter of the Mixtekas has killed Randero and freed others from their chains. She is a heroine too and worthy to be the squaw of a chief."

He did not know it was fated that Kaya, the daughter of different parents and brought up with him by his own parents would soon be his squaw, his wife. ---

Chapter 15

LOST

THE port of Manzanillo was visited by ships of considerable tonnage. One of these was now in the port. Two men observed it. "Quite new and good to look at," remarked the older of the two, "It was built in an American shipyard." He was tall and thin.

"We can see it at first glance," said the other, a strongly built figure. He could be taken for a sailor, but his clothes were odd: old evening shoes and old leather gloves.

"Could one build a secret cannon hole there?" asked the older man.

"Don't ask me, captain, you understand these things better than me," answered the other.

"Do you mean that? Ha ha ha, don't call me captain. I am director Guzman of an actor's group. You are my stage producer. Understood?"

"Yes señor," replied the other with an unconvincing bow.

The director asked: "Where do you think she'll go?"

"Who knows? There's a boy coming along who probably belongs to the ship's crew. We can ask him."

When he came close they asked him: "Señor, do you belong to that ship?"

The boy had never been called señor before. He had a good impression of these two, who treated him so politely. "Yes," he answered

"Has it a Captain?"

"Yes, Captain Wilcox."

"What do you carry?"

"Various, plus a nice cargo for Guaymas."

"Guaymas? We intend to go there. Maybe we could go with you. Where's the captain?"

"He's on land but will return soon. Ah, here he comes."

"Which one? The short one?"

"The one with his hands in his pockets."

The two went to the shore and glanced at the man coming nearer. He was short and lean with red cheeks and a staggering walk. From his watery eyes it seemed he had had one drink too many. "Good morning, Captain," greeted the one who looked like a sailor assuming a humble posture.

The captain smiled. "You are land rats?"

"Pardon me Capitano. I am the director of a theatre, my name is Guzman."

"Actors? Good-natured, funny people. What do you want from me?"

We've heard you're sailing to Guaymas. I and my company of four ladies and eight men, all young and lively, would like to come with you."

"That will be fun but can you pay?"

"Yes, if the price is not too high."

"That would be seventy dollars for the ride. Everything else is your own affair."

"Can you do it for sixty dollars, senior capitano?"

"Actually no but you are actors and have ladies with you, all right. Payment as soon as you come on board. Otherwise I'll all throw you into the water. We are sailing tonight at eleven o'clock, punctually. *A Dios señores.*"

The two artists went through the town until they reached a public house. They went inside where a group of men were sitting at a broken table, sipping the local brew.

"Any news, director?"

"Yes tonight, four of you be ready, dressed as women. I'll collect you here at nine o'clock."

"Ha ha ha, that'll be fun."

Evening came and the ship hoisted the sails. The guests arrived, all fourteen. The captain stood on the steps of the ship, waiting for the money. The director paid and a crew member showed them to their cabins. Ladies separately, of course. There was no question of a pass or identification. The helmsman at the back looked at the stars and the captain was in his cabin to sleeping it off.

The actors seemed asleep. As a matter of fact, the whole crew except the man at the wheel seemed asleep. Two hours past midnight the director moved. "It's time," he whispered. I'll count to ten then every one of you takes his man. The knives into their hearts and leave it there: no blood will show then." He started counting and when he called out ten, fourteen shadows glided noiseless across the ship. The director himself went to the helmsman. He was looking at a cloud when he felt something cool and hard penetrating his heart. He wanted to shout but couldn't. He sank to the floor and the director took the wheel. A whistle brought the stage director to him. "Everything all right? Asked the director.

"Everything in order," was the reply.

"Here, take the wheel. I still have to deal with the captain."

"What will you do with the boy. He sleeps below?"

"We have no use for him."

Thus were the decisions made about two more lives. The corpses of the killed were brought on deck. Heavy stones were found in the ballast room and tied to the corpses they were all thrown into the sea. The director went into the captain's cabin and studied the books and all the papers that were lying about.

The next morning the new captain or former director spoke to his crew. "The fun has worked out, boys. Now will start a life for which kings will envy you. For the next few days, however, we must be careful. We have freight for Guaymas. The ship is not known there neither are the names of the crew. We shall take the names of our predecessors. I am Captain Wilcox."

He gave everyone a name as shown in the books and told them their roles. Then he gave the order to dock in Guaymas, a little town belonging to the Mexican state of Sonora. Captain Wilcox dealt with the port authorities and with the business men impudently, as if he were the rightful owner of this name and the ship.

Captain Wilcox and his helmsman hired some mules and went for an outing. They rode into the mountains. In the evening they spent a few hours in a bar before making their way to the ship. A figure went by. The light of an open window lit up his face for a moment. "*Demonio,* was that a spirit?" asked the helmsman.

"Yes. I also think it was our former prisoner. Let's go after him."

It was Rudolfo they followed. He rang the bell of a house standing in the middle of a garden. A woman answered the door. They could hear her voice when she said:

"Ah, señor Rudolfo, señor Stenton is waiting for you."

"The devil, it's him," said the captain, and do you know who lives here? It's that Stenton who shot my officers and wounded me. You have saved me and that's why I made you my helmsman."

"*Caramba,* couldn't we take a little revenge? I'd be delighted if we could."

"For me it's not only delight, it's a question of life and death to get these rascals into my hands. Listen, they're coming to the garden veranda. Maybe we can hear something. Quickly over the fence."

The pirates swung themselves over the fence and hid behind some bushes. The inhabitants of the house came on to the veranda. Two tables were put together and covered with a white tablecloth. Some fruits were passed around and a lively conversation began. At the tables were Stenton, Rudolfo, Buff-he, Anthony and George Brooks, Lady Margaret, Alva and Kaya. They had only arrived yesterday and, as they could not find a ship they could use, they decided to find refuge until they found a suitable one. The conversation then took a more interesting turn. Alva asked: "And when you've reached Mexico, señor Stenton, will you return home?"

"I would have loved to but I have to go to Africa first to search for the Count Manuel de Manresa."

"Do you believe he's still alive?"

"I know he hasn't died in Mexico. Have you heard about that scoundrel Ramirez Danlola?"

"The pirate whose ship you have sunk in Jamaica?"

"Yes, he has shipped the count to Africa. At the east coast of this continent is Harare where I hope to find him if he is still alive."

"And then you'll be able to pull the sling around the Carujos?"

"Yes, but let's leave these nasty thoughts. I've written a letter to my wife and I don't want those shadows to spoil my image of her."

The conversation changed and was of no interest to the secret listeners.

"This rascal, this Stenton," growled the captain, who was Danlola himself.

"Should we take him?" asked the helmsman.

"I will, if it costs my neck. But how?"

"We'll find a way, but you can't be seen."

"I have my disguise."

"With these people you can't rely on that. I'll do the necessary. I'll spy on them tomorrow and I'll find a way."

"I hope so but now let us get out of here. We must follow this Rudolfo. I have to know where he lives." They waited until Rudolfo passed them and followed him separately as disinterested strollers. They observed him until he'd entered a house, his apparent abode.

"Now we know where he and Stenton live, it depends on knowing what they intend to do."

"I'll find out," said the helmsman. "Neither Stenton nor any of the other people know me."

They went to their ship and the next morning the helmsman intended to make the necessary enquiries. He had hardly stepped off the landing plank connecting the ship with the shore when he was accosted by Stenton and Rudolfo asking for the captain. "May I ask what you wish from the captain?" asked the helmsman, "do you want to go with this ship or have you any freight for it?" The helmsman had a sudden idea how he could help his boss.

"The former," answered Stenton. "We intend to go to Acapulco or any southern port, I have some comrades with me."

"That could be done, we intend to go to Acapulco."

"Ah, you are the Captain then?"

"That's about right."

"When do you heave anchor?"

"Early tomorrow morning. Any guests have to board tonight. Do you want to view the ship?"

"Maybe in an hour. We can talk about your conditions." Stenton intended to bring George Brooks along who knew more about ships than he did.

The helmsman went back on board where he hurried to Captain Danlola. "Captain, I have better news than we could hope for. Our enemies intend to come aboard as passengers to Acapulco."

Danlola heard this report joyfully. "That's far better than expected, we'll take them prisoner as soon as possible."

"Should we leave them alive?"

"Yes, it's better for me if they stay alive."

"It'll be a terrible fight. Every one of these men will take several of us."

"Don't be stupid, we'll take them singly It won't be too difficult. Stenton is the most dangerous, we'll take him first. They have to disappear without trace. I know of a lonely island in the west not yet charted. No ship comes there. They have water and plenty of fruit. Every attempt to escape will be in vain. They'll be our prisoners for life if there's no reason for their release."

"Why keep them alive at all?"

They'll be a permanent source of income if a certain client of mine refuses to pay up. If we kill them, I have no trump card to play."

"Where is this island?"

"It's far from every course of a ship. It's a better prison than one with solid walls. It has no name yet, and is surrounded by corals. The trees there are too small to build a ship and if they could build one it would be smashed to pieces on the corral reefs by the wild surf surrounding the island."

"But we shall have witnesses. Every one of the crew could one day spill the beans."

The captain threw a sympathetic glance at his helmsman and said slowly: "We'll have no witnesses. We'll be the only ones leaving the ship on its return."

That was clearly expressed. The helmsman shuddered. Suppose the captain wanted no witness at all? He decided to be careful.

Buff-he and Kaya wanted to make their way to the hacienda on horseback. That was more strenuous but faster. The haciendero would be pleased to hear the good news but they decided to be with their friends on board that night. Toward evening the passengers arrived. They were received with great politeness by the crew and received an ample evening meal in the captain's cabin. Danlola meanwhile asked three of the strongest men to stand by. One man went down to the captain's cabin where the helmsman received him brusquely: "What do you want here?"

"Pardon me, señor Captain," the man apologised. "A messenger has arrived who wants to speak to señor Stenton."

"With me? What does he want?"

"He said he was the landlord where you lived and that he had important private information for you."

"All right, I am coming."

Stenton got up and followed the sailor on deck. It was dark. He felt two fists around his neck. At the same time he was hit by a rifle-butt on his head. He fell down without uttering a sound.

"He's done for," laughed the Captain. "Tie him up and put him in the ballast room.

Now call the Indian. He seems to be the next strongest. After a while the sailor went into the Captain's cabin again and asked for Buff-he to come to señor Stenton. Buff-he followed the sailor unsuspectingly and was clubbed and bound.

Rudolfo stood up and said: "That has to be important news we're not supposed to know about. I'll go and find out. The brothers George and Anthony Brooks were alone now with Lady Margaret, Alva, Kaya and the alleged Captain.

They waited in vain for a report and then they also left the table, telling the three ladies they would return shortly and report to them. After a while Danlola came into the cabin. The ladies eyed him with anxious astonishment. He bowed politely and asked them to follow him and join the men. He led them on to the dark deck where they were each grabbed by two men. When they shrieked, he ordered them to be quiet.

"Silence. Listen to what I have to say. You and the men with you have treated me and my friends with hostility. You are my prisoners now."

"By what right?" asked Kaya who had calmed down first.

"By the right of the stronger," he laughed. "I don't know whether you know me, I am Danlola."

"Danlola, the pirate," whispered Alva shocked.

"Yes, the pirate," he repeated proudly. "Resistance is useless and dangerous for you all. Nothing will happen to you and you will be free here on deck. But if you try in the slightest to act against my orders, I shall kill the señores. They are tied below and I shall tell them that if they try the slightest resistance, I shall kill the señoritas."

"And what will be our fate? asked Kaya, composed.

"I'll put you on an uninhabited island. Nothing will happen to you on the way if you follow orders. None of my people will touch you. Now come, I'll show you the room where you'll stay.

When he had locked them in a dark room they fell into each other's arms. One moment had pushed them from the height of happiness into the abyss of misery.

The pirate now went to his other prisoners. They were in a place below water level. They were lying in chains on the damp sand that almost filled the room. They were placed far enough apart as not to be able to help each other. They were also bound hand and foot so that they lost the use of their limbs. When Danlola went into the room with his lantern, all the prisoners had regained their consciousness.

"Señor Stenton, do you recognise me?" he said mockingly.

Stenton took no notice of Danlola's presence.

"Ah, you are playing the proud one?" laughed Danlola. "Let me introduce myself to the others. I am Ramirez Danlola. I'm sure you've heard about me."

Nobody said a word. "Well, I'm sure you're listening. I have rendered you harmless. You are finally in my hands and I could kill you easily. I've decided not to do that. Not out of pity, that would be a weakness unknown to me. Alive, you are my insurance that I get paid. When I get my reward, you'll be lost forever. If not, you will have to pay me for your freedom."

There was still no reaction, so he said finally: "I am the man who punishes disobedience with death. The ladies will not be harmed unless you try to escape. Good night."

After he left, there were minutes of silence, then the voice of Buff-he was heard.

"Uff!"

Again there was silence until Rudolfo asked Stenton. "What do you say, Carlos?"

"Nothing, or is it possible for you to free yourself from your chains tonight?"

"Impossible! They're too strong and we're tied down hand and foot."

"Well, we have to adapt ourselves."

They were all men who had looked danger and death in the face on more that one occasion. They were not used to wailing. They knew only a clear spirit would make it possible for them to save themselves. But still it boiled inside everyone, although they wouldn't show it.

"How did they get you?" Stenton asked Anthony Brooks.

"They choked me."

"You were lucky. A blow on your head would have killed you."

Through the darkness of the room one could hear the turning and twisting of the chains. To no avail. "Nothing doing," said Rudolfo, "we have to wait for a bit of luck."

"That will hardly come in time. Danlola will go to see during the night and we'll have to await his whim: whether he wants to kill us or set us on an uninhabited island. There's no use trying to free ourselves of our chains, we have to keep our courage and our health and hope to God that our freedom and retaliation will come soon." Stenton said resignedly.

These words raised the downtrodden spirits of the others. A soundless calm was in the room. Soon was heard the regular breathing of sleeping people. They only awoke when water rushed on the planks, only to prove that the ship was under sails and heading ... who knew where.

Why describe the anguish of the days and weeks that passed. The girls, although they enjoyed fresh air and light, suffered more, because they had not the consciousness of the men, who knew their worth in spite of their chains and were convinced that the day of reckoning would come. Only a few minor storms were experienced. The ship never stopped. The waves finally hit the planks quieter and slower. One could hear the anchor being lowered. A deep calm descended. Steps of men coming down the stairs.

"Now is decision time," said Stenton. "The worst fate is better than this uncertainty."

The hatch was opened. Danlola and several men stepped in. "Loosen the chains," he ordered "but make sure they are tied securely, that they cannot stand up or move their arms."

Now the prisoners were carried on deck and put down like wooden blocks. For the first time after being locked up in the dark, they saw light and breathed fresh air but how did they look? They had not suffered from hunger or thirst but their clothing was half rotten and torn to pieces by rats. Neither could they care or look after themselves. The girls nearby were also bound; otherwise they would have thrown themselves on to their loved ones.

To the left they could see an island surrounded by corals where the surf foamed high. Within this ring of surf there was one opening, but even that one was negotiable only by a strong boat. Danlola turned to his prisoners: "Señores and señoritas, we are at our destination. This island will be your home. You will never know its name or where it is situated. No man will give you that information because this island is uncharted. There is drinking water, birds and fish aplenty, also eatable mussels. You will not get your weapons except for two knives. You will probably make bows and arrows; there are masses of hares for meat and clothing. You will free yourselves on some sharp stones after we have left. Farewell, señores and señoritas.

The sailors put the prisoners into two boats. They managed, with difficulties, to get through the surf and laid the prisoners on the ground. Stenton and Buff-he rolled themselves to a sharp edge. They freed their hands in no time. Then they took the sharp edge and freed their legs. The ship was pulling away swiftly. There was no chance to reach it any longer.

Stenton and Buff-he untied the others without cutting their straps.

Danlola observed the landed group for a while and said: "They are looked after."

"For sure?" asked the helmsman, "what about these?" He pointed to the sailors.

"They will be taken care of," he assured the helmsman, "I intend to go to the island of Pitcairn."

"Hm," growled the helmsman. He thought he understood his astute master.

The reached Pitcairn and the Captain went alone on land. "There is a meaning to this," thought the helmsman, "I will have to be careful. None of the sailors really knows the island where the prisoners were left. I'm the only one who knows to find it. I think I have to be very careful."

When Danlola returned he had a dissatisfied expression on his face. "Nothing doing," he said, "it's much too slow to get a new crew together."

"Maybe I should try?" suggested the helmsman.

"Yes, you do that," agreed the Captain, "and take a weapon with you. The natives can be dangerous."

The helmsman was just putting on his jacket with its shiny buttons, when the Captain came into his cabin. A pistol lay on the table. The captain took it in hand and asked: "Is it loaded?"

The suspicious helmsman tried to grab it. "This thing is not for fun."

"I don't want it for fun." The Captain lifted the pistol and shot the helmsman through the eye.

As he fell dead on the floor, Danlola run on deck and shouted: "Come down quickly, the helmsman was not careful with his pistol and wounded himself."

Sailors ran to help. The helmsman was, of course, dead. The men were without feeling. All it meant for them was, that there would be advancement between the rest of the crew. The corpse was put into a sack and thrown overboard into the sea. The only witness capable of finding the island was dead. Danlola told his men that the fun had only just started For many years the oceans were insecure, until he had enough for his retirement.---

Chapter 16

IN HARARE

---

*H*OW often has the human mind experienced the force of unforeseen events? How often has the unexpected turned up and given life a new meaning so that loss of faith in an almighty plan is realised and reinstated?

In Bradford on Avon, they had no news about their beloved husbands or fathers; years had elapsed since the last letter forced them, after a long time of hoping, to resign themselves to the fact that their loved ones must have perished. Lamenting gave way to silent memories and no one admitted that their hopes had not completely disappeared.

Many years went by before past events had their continuation. ---

It was now 1864. On the west coast of Aden, where the Red Sea connects with the Indian Ocean, was a land the boldest travellers tried in vain to explore. A British officer, Richard Burton reached this land cut off from outsiders and brought information. Some Europeans reached Harare but never returned. They ended up as slaves.

Lord Wilberforce had reached agreement with other Countries that slave trading was illegal. Warships of all Countries had the right to intercept slave ships, free the prisoners and hang the crew from the captain to the youngest sailor. These rules had little effect for more than a decade. In the middle of the nineteenth century one could find houses in Constantinople where slaves of all colours could be bought.

Especially profitable were the hunting for slaves around the Nile, at the Red Sea and areas at the east coast of Africa. Harare was one of these.

Harare is not near the coast. The land of the Somali tribe had to be penetrated. These tribal people are the handsomest of the black race. They were warriors forever at war with their neighbours. To travel through this land was dangerous and that was also the reason why a flight from Harare was never successful. ---

A caravan with heavily loaded camels went toward Harare. Brown and black men All well armed with rifles, clubs, bows and arrows and carrying long sharp knives in their belts. The camels were tied by their tails to one another, except for two at the front. One of these carried a howdah its sides closed by thin curtains to allowing air to flow through. There was probably a female inside not to be seen by anyone. Next to this camel rode the leader of the team who ordered one of his men to him. "Abdul, do you see that gorge in front?"

"I see it, master."

"That's where we'll stay for the night. Do you know the way to Harare: you have been there a few times?"

"Very well, master."

"From this gorge you have only one hour's ride to the seat of Sultan Achmed. Tell him to expect me tomorrow morning."

Abdul asked his master whether he should mention the slave they had with them.

"Tell him we have shawls, silk cloth, knives, powder, sugar and paper. We want to exchange it for tobacco, ivory, and butter. About the girl slave say nothing."

"Should I take any gifts?"

"No, this sultan is never satisfied. If you give him presents now, he will only want more tomorrow."

Abdul went and the caravan reached the gorge just when the sun was at the horizon, at six o'clock in the afternoon: the time to say the evening prayers prescribed by Prophet Mohammed. Although the Bedouins at those times, were mostly robbers, they were religious and thought it a great sin to miss these prayers. They had no water to wash, they used sand instead. Only when they had finished praying did they look after the camels. The emir took some dates and a leather tumbler filled with water and asked the inhabitant of the howdah whether she wanted to eat. A hand took the fruits and the water but said nothing. "Allah is great and I am forgetful," he mumbled. "I never think that she doesn't speak our language." Two men kept watch for enemies and to make sure the slave would not escape. The others slept.

Abdul had reached Harare after sundown. The gates of the town were closed and no one could leave or enter without the sultan's permission. He knocked repeatedly before a guard appeared. "Who's there?"

"A messenger for the sultan."

"Which tribe are you from?"

"I am a free Somali."

The inhabitants of Harare looked down on the Somalis with contempt but without real reason. "I cannot allow a Somali to enter and I would be punished if I disturb the sultan because of a Somali."

"Yes, you would be punished but only because you let a messenger of Emir Arafat wait."

The guard knew the sultan made good business with Arafat and said: "All right I shall dare to ask." The guard made his way to the palace. The palace was actually more like a barn than a 'palace'. This famous capital was notorious. It is surrounded by a wall, has a length which would take half an hour to walk and a width a quarter of an hour. The houses are like sheds build of stone. Near the palace is a stone building where one can hear the prisoners' chains clanking day and night. It was the state prison with deep underground cellars where daylight never penetrates. Woe to the prisoner who had to stay there. The sultan never fed them, and when a friend brought them daily water and customary cold pulp of millet, in time they would rot in their own filth.

The throne of the ruler who was master over the life and death of his subjects was a simple wooden bench the like of which you could find in the poorest English family. There he was sitting in the oriental way; legs crossed and giving his orders. Everybody trembled if they came near him. His bad mood meant blood would be spilt. Today, Achmed sat as usual on his bench; behind him on the wall were old rifles, sabres and iron fetters for hands and feet, a sign of his absolute powers. Before him sat a Mohammedan scholar. In the background were slaves and prisoners in chains. The sultan loved to decorate the place with these unhappy people. Another sign of his power and glory.

On his side was one of these lamentable men chained hand and foot. He was tall and lean, bowed more from grief than age. His lifeless eyes and his inward fallen cheeks were the result of hunger and deep sorrow. He wore nothing but a torn shirt. He must have spoken, for all eyes rested on him. Also those of the sultan; dark and threatening like a torturing hangman.

"Son of a bitch," he said to the old man. "You are lying. How can a Christian ruler be bigger and mightier than a supporter of the prophet Mohammed? What are all your kings to compare with Achmed the sultan of Harare?"

There was lightning in the slave's eyes. "I was not a king. I was only a subject but one of the noblest of the land, a thousand times richer and happier than you."

The king stretched out his fingers and someone from the corner of the room appeared, lifted a heavy bamboo stick and gave the slave ten beatings. The slave did not move or react. He seemed used to this treatment. The beatings no longer hurt.

"Will you retract?" asked the sultan.

"No."

The ruler ordered fifteen more strokes. After that he said: "I shall prove my might. I have ordered you to worship the prophet. You haven't done so. I shall ask you today for the last time; will you obey?"

"Never!" answered the old man firmly. "You have taken my freedom: you can take my life, but my faith – never. You want to prove your might? Here it ends."

The sultan clenched his fist and shouted furiously: "I shall throw you into the deepest hole in my cellar."

"Do so," said the slave. "I want to die, I'm longing for death. Then my suffering will end and I shall find peace and tranquillity."

"Put him in the worst dungeon we have."

Two prison guards led him to the prison. An indescribable stink and the clanking of chains received them. It was dark and the prisoner couldn't see where he was led. At the other end outside the jail, the two guards lifted a stone and pushed the prisoner into a hole.

"Down with you, Christian dog, in two days you will be eaten by rats." The heavy stone was put back in its position. Hungry rats immediately attacked the prisoner. The hole was about one metre square and two metres deep. The unhappy man tore the rats off and stamped them with his feet. He managed to choke some in his hands but there were too many and he suffered many painful bites until he crawled up the wall like a chimney sweep. That couldn't last very long.

My God, should this be my end? What have I done to deserve it? He groped in the dark and found a protruding stone. Grasping it with his hand, it fell and killed several rats. "Thank God, at least a weapon," he called out with joy. He climbed down again, grabbed the stone and hit the ground around himself. Judging by the many squeaks, he seemed successful. He stood in the dark and lifted his fists. "Cursed be Carujo, cursed be Danlola," he shouted in anger and misery.

He got a mighty shock when he heard a voice. "Carujo? Danlola? Yes, they should be cursed and damned to eternity." The voice sounded furious. The old slave asked:

"Who is there?" he asked. "Who are you who speaks Spanish, the language of my homeland, in this place?"

"Say first who are you?" The answer came from up high. You who have made a hole in this wall of my prison."

"I am a Spaniard from Mexico," answered the slave. "My name is Manuel de Manresa."

"*Santa Madonna,*" sounded the voice. "Don Manuel the brother of Count Miguel de Manresa?"

"*Valgame Dios!* You are talking about my brother – do you know him?"

"Do I know him? I'm – but no, it's not possible, Count Manuel died many years ago."

"I tell you he is not dead; he was declared dead. He was in reality sold by Danlola to a slave merchant who sold me to Harare."

"Señor, what you tell me sounds like a fairy tale but when I think what happened to Don Miguel – but that later, I shall come down to you, Don Manuel. Maybe, with your help, we can shift another stone."

"With pleasure, I'm coming at once."

They succeeded in moving a second and even a third stone. The opening was now big enough to let the other prisoner through. They had to stand chest by chest but that did not disturb them. It was bliss for the Count to be with someone whom he could expect to be a friend. The newcomer took the Count's hands and said: "Oh, Don Manuel, let me touch your hand. I am so happy to have found a fellow Countryman. I was born in Manresa."

"Manresa? So near to my family? asked a surprised Don Manuel."

"Yes. I'm an ordinary citizen. My name is Dinrallo. Oh, sir, I have lots to tell you. When did you leave Mexico?"

"A long, long time ago. It is not possible to be sure but it must be at least fourteen years since I languished here as a slave."

"*Dios,* so you don't know that your brother Don Miguel was declared dead?"

"No, when did this happen?"

"About thirteen years ago."

"You said my brother was declared dead. Then he did not die in reality?"

"He is alive and lives with his daughter in England; Condesa Rosetta has married a Dr. Stenton. Aurelio has inherited both, the fortunes of your brother and yours Don Manuel."

"Ah," answered Don Manuel, amazed." He thought about the second will that was hidden and entrusted to Clarissa Moyes, when he had disinherited Aurelio. Had it not been found or was it embezzled? Aurelio? How does he rule his subjects?"

"Oh, like a tyrant. Everybody hates him. And señor Stenton thinks he is not the real son of Count Miguel."

"How did he come to think at such things?"

Dinrallo told the Count all he knew. About the miraculous operations about Count Miguel's and Condesa Rosetta's induced madness and his involvement in their rescue.

The princely reward Dinrallo had received for his part in that rescue. The Carujos and Aurelio through their spies must have learned of his involvement and had him kidnapped and, through the pirate Danlola, sent into slavery. He went from one owner to another each one more cruel than his predecessor, until he ended here six days ago.

Shortly after his arrival here, he was ordered to become a Mohammedan, which he refused.

Count Miguel wanted to make his claim after Dr. Stenton had found the real Aurelio. "Before they kidnapped me, I heard that Stenton had found the real Aurelio who was a prisoner of Danlola's pirate ship.

But Stenton and the newly found son had disappeared again. Much more, unfortunately, I cannot tell you.

Dinrallo expected an answer. The old man was quiet. Finally he had received the key to a riddle that had plagued him all these years. He sunk to his knees and prayed. Dinrallo did not see it but he felt it. After a long pause he said: "We have to do our utmost to save ourselves. God is love, and He will help us but only through our own doing."

"Yes, you are right," answered the Count as he got up from the floor, "let's discuss calmly how we can escape."

They discussed every aspect of such an undertaking and agreed it was only possible to escape from Dinrallo's prison.

"Should we start at once?" ventured Dinrallo.

"Oh, I would like that. Unfortunately, it's too late for today. They'd discover our escape too soon and we'd probably be lost."

"You're right but one thing we can try now. Can we shift the stone above my hole."

"All right, if we manage that we could leave our prison at any time."

The Spaniard crawled into his hole and the Count followed. Dinrallo's hole was not as deep as the Count's. He could reach the stone above with outstretched hands but was not strong enough to shift it. The combined effort, although not at the first try, shifted the stone a little.

"Thank God," whispered the Count, "now we have fresh air. Can you read the time according to the stars?"

"Yes, it's past midnight."

"Too late for us to escape now. Harare is in deep calm. Over there I can see sacks of dates that were received by Davud al Gossara today. He is the head of the sultan's stable. I haven't eaten all day. It is a bit careless to grab some of these but we need all our strength tomorrow. I also know that under his roof there is a hose full of water. My thirst is even greater than my hunger. Should we dare?"

"Why not, who would see us? I am the younger and perhaps more agile of the two of us. I shall nip over," said an eager Dinrallo.

They managed to shift the stone far enough to crawl out. They both crawled over. The hose was there and the Count wanted to drink but Dinrallo suggested taking the hose. "We need it more than this Davud al Gossara." With this he put a sack over his shoulder and Don Manuel took the hose. As they went back to Dinrallo's hole he suggested staying there, as he had fewer rats and he had already stapled their carcasses to the side of the wall. They managed to sit down and were having a feast of water and dates. When they'd ended, Dinrallo asked: "Are we staying together?"

"No," said Don Manuel, "that would be too dangerous and might put our escape in jeopardy. It's possible that someone may wish to see one of us. Let's put the stones in their original position. The sack and the hose they won't see, it's too dark in here."

They departed and were both happier than before. ---

The guard entered the palace just as Don Manuel was taken away. The sultan was still angry about the slave's refusal to obey his command to worship the Prophet Mohammed. He looked at the guard with angry eyes. "What do you want so late?"

The guard threw himself to the ground and answered: "There is a messenger from Arafat at the gate."

"Arafat? Finally he has come; he will feel the force of my anger. What messenger did he send?"

"A Somali."

"A Somali? And you son of a dog dare to disturb me so late? Take ten lashes and tell the messenger, whom Allah may send to hell, I expect his master to be here two hours after daybreak. The guard received his ten lashes, went back to the gate and told the messenger that the Sultan will not see a Somali.

"Allah is great, why not?"

"Because the Sultan despises the Somali."

"We are a free people but you are the slaves of a tyrant who could take your life as he pleases. We despise you: farewell you slave of your hangman."

The messenger rode off before he had been told when the Sultan would receive Arafat. Two hours after daybreak the sultan sent somebody to the gate. "Has the caravan arrived?"

"Not yet," the man was told. He went to the Sultan to report this fact. The guard who saw him the previous night was ordered to appear before the Sultan. The poor man trembled. Nothing good could be expected from this meeting. He threw himself to the ground and waited to be addressed.

"Has the Emir arrived with his presents?"

"Not yet, Your Majesty."

"Why does this dog hesitate; have you not told the Somali that I expect him two hours after daybreak?"

"There was no time, he rode off too quickly."

"So I have to wait because of you? Allah is great and just, I have to be just too." The ruler waved and the guard was taken into the yard where one could hear his cries as he received a beating. The Sultan has said that he despised the Somali but his avarice made him impatient.

The whole morning passed before the Emir Arafat was reported to have arrived. The Sultan initially intended to make him wait outside the gate but he changed his mind and ordered that he should be brought at once.

The five men with Arafat were told to put down their weapons and take off their shoes before appearing in the throne hall.

"Why don't you kneel?" called the Sultan.

"We are free men and we only kneel before Allah," said the Emir proudly.

"Why were you so late?"

"Because I liked it that way."

"Your language is very daring. Have I insulted you?"

"Who insults a messenger insults the one who has sent him. Tell me whether you want to receive my presents and carry on dealing with me, otherwise I shall move on."

"What do you bring this time?"

"Silken cloths and scarves, brass, copper and iron, powder, paper and sugar."

"And what do you want in exchange for that?"

"Ivory, tobacco and coffee."

"I shall see. Spread out your presents."

Arafat spread out the presents. They were powder, nice cloth and ironware, all made in England. The Sultan's glances fell especially on the revolvers that were also included.

"These weapons are very useful," said Achmed. "I know how to handle them but once the bullets have been shot the revolvers are useless without a further supply."

"I have many bullets. You can buy them all."

"Buy them? The bullets belong to the weapon."

"They are a separate item; I've paid a lot for them. I also have other bullets for two beautiful rifles for sale. These rifles have never yet been seen. They have two barrels and are made in America."

"Bring them," ordered the Sultan.

"I'll bring all my goods after you've declared that you are satisfied with the presents and we can start trading."

"I am the mightiest ruler far and wide. Those presents aren't worthy for a big sultan but Allah is merciful and I also want to be merciful. Bring what you have, I shall choose first and after me, my subjects."

"I am going, first I must tell you I have something that no other Sultan has."

"What is that?"

"A female slave."

"I don't need her. All women are mine in Harare and I can choose whomever I want."

"You are right but a girl like this slave you cannot find in Harare. She is white."

The Sultan's expression changed to one of joyful surprise. "Is she a Turk?"

"No, one from Turkistan would only cost five hundred Maria Theresiantaler. this one is worth several thousand."

"She is a white Christian, a disbeliever?"

A European slave girl was very high priced in those areas. "Yes," declared Arafat, "she is a Christian slave."

"Is she very white?"

"Like ivory bleached in the sun."

"Beautiful?"

"There is no haura in Paradise that can match her."

Achmed's lust for her was rising. "Describe her to me, how are her hands?"

"Small and soft, like a child's."

"Her mouth?"

"Her lips are curving, soft and pink, her teeth are like pearls. Whoever kisses her is indanger of forgetting the world and himself."

"Allah, you have kissed her?" The Sultan seemed jealous as if she belonged to him.

Arafat could hardly suppress a smile of satisfaction. He knew he would be able to get a high price for her. "You are mistaken; no man ever has touched the lips of this girl."

"How do you know that?"

"I know that. Who wants to kiss her as she can't speak to anybody?"

"Allah, is she deaf and dumb?"

"No, her speech sounds like the song of a nightingale, but she speaks in a language that nobody here understands."

"Where did you get her?"

"I met a Chinese slave trader in Ceylon and I bought her for a high price to bring her to you."

"Bring her in with your other goods."

It didn't take long. Arafat spread his goods on prepared carpets. The Sultan was alone. Nobody was allowed to see what he bought. "Where is the slave?" was his first question.

"There inside the howdah."

"I want to see her."

"First the dead goods and afterwards the living."

Achmed made an angry face. "Here in Harare I am the ruler. I want to see her."

"Over my things I am the ruler. Who shall buy a lot from me, may see her."

"And when I force you?"

Arafat drew a pistol. "As soon as you open the curtain of the howdah, I shall shoot her in the head."

"All right but I warn you, don't try me again or you'll regret it. Show me your goods."

Achmed thought too much about the girl to give attention to what he bought. He bought quickly without the customary haggling. Only when he saw the double barrelled rifles did he forget the slave girl for a short time. He bought them for a high price including all the bullets available.

The trader was satisfied. He'd earned more than he expected. Achmed could see the girl now but not here. The Sultan could see her inside the palace. People were ordered to remove what he had bought and four men had to carry the howdah and put it down before his throne. Everybody except Arafat had to leave the room. "Open the howdah now." The Sultan saw a face with tear-filled eyes, the like of which he had never seen in his life. He was determined she would be his. "Let her step out, I have to see her figure." Arafat gave her a sign to step outside. She seemed not to understand or she didn't want to. He took her by the hand and pulled her out. There she stood, tall, slim, trembling with shame and yet proud as a princess. The Sultan bought the beautiful slave without haggling for five thousand Ashrafi.

The deal was done and Arafat left. Achmed took her by the hand into his treasure room. He wanted to show her that he was the Sultan. He waved her to sit on rich upholstery and opened many of the baskets in the room. She saw he must be one of the richest men in his Country. He spoke to her in all the languages he knew but soon realised she did not understand.

"I know a way," he thought. The slave I have asked to be put in a hole yesterday is a Christian. He could not understand me at first but soon learned our language. He can be my interpreter. He ordered the Christian slave be brought to him.

Don Manuel thought about the planned escape when the stone above him was removed. "The Sultan wants to speak to you," he was informed. "Have the rats not done too much damage and can you still walk?"

"I shall try," said the Spaniard carefully.

"Then come up, I'll let the ladder down to you."

The ladder was a branch of a tree with cuts to be used as steps. At daylight he saw the many wounds the rats had made. His shirt was in pieces. He was curious to know what the Sultan wanted after telling him that last night was the last time he would ask him to worship Mohammed. The Sultan's question was intriguing. "Do you know many languages of the infidel?"

"There are many," Don Manuel answered.

"Do you understand them?"

"The most important ones."

"Listen to what I have to tell you. I have a slave. She speaks a language nobody here understands. I shall lead you to her. You must not see her face but if you can teach her our language you don't have to die in prison and you will enjoy my mercy. One bad word about me will bring you a thousandfold deaths.

"I am your slave and will obey," answered the old man. As he bowed down, several thoughts struck him. He would be parted from Dinrallo. Wouldn't it be better if he could not understand her? Perhaps he could do a good deed.

"Come along," the Sultan interrupted his thoughts. Outside the room he ordered the old man to wait. He went inside and arranged her veil so that her face could not be seen. Don Manuel entered the room and saw that this must be the treasure place of the sultan's fortunes. The slave girl looked at the Count as he entered. A movement of surprise made her sit erect. "Speak to her," ordered the sultan Achmed. "Find out whether you understand her language."

Don Manuel came a few steps closer. The light of the small window was on his face. The slave moved in surprise again. The Sultan saw it and thought she was surprised that he allowed another man to enter.

"*Quelle est la langue, parlez vous Francē mademoiselle?* The Count asked her whether she spoke French.

At the sound of his voice she straightened even more but hesitated to answer.

The Count repeated his question in English. "Do you speak English Miss?"

"*Bendito sea Dios!* answered the girl finally, "I understand French and English but let us speak Spanish."

Now it was Don Manuel's turn to be surprised, but his situation made him careful. He controlled himself and asked with forced indifference, "*Dios,* you are Spanish? Please be calm, do't look surprised, We've to be careful in our situation."

"I'll remember your warning but I find it difficult," she answered. "Heavens, is it possible or are my eyes deceiving me? What joy, if I am not mistaken."

"What do you mean, señorita?"

"I am Mexican," she declared.

"A Mexican? Señorita, I must not look surprised. We're observed by the sharp eyes of a tyrant. I'm also from Mexico."

"*Santa Madonna,* it's true my eyes did not deceive me. You are our dear Don Manuel de Manresa."

It was almost beyond him to restrain himself but he succeeded somehow. "You know me, señorita? Who are you?"

"I am Alva Wilson, the daughter of your tenant Martin Wilson."

There was a pause while a storm of feeling went through the hearts of both. By the sound of her voice, Don Manuel knew she was crying. He suppressed his own tears when the Sultan demanded: "You know her language, which one is it?"

"It's from a Country that nobody here knows."

"What's its name?"

"Mexico," said the Count purposely not mentioning Spain. Dinrallo might be known as a Spaniard and for this the Sultan might still want to kill him.

"I don't know this name, it's probably a wretched little Country."

"On the contrary, it is very large."

Achmed made a doubtful face. "What did she say?"

"She is glad to have been bought by you."

The Sultan's face brightened up and he asked further: "Who is her father?"

"Her father is one of the most distinguished men in the land."

"I knew that," said the Sultan, "she's very beautiful. More beautiful than a flower and brighter than the sun. How did she get into the hands of the Emir?"

"We haven't talked about that yet, Should I ask her?"

"Ask her, let her tell you and repeat it to me."

The old man turned to Alva: So you are dear Alva. Oh God what a meeting. But we must stay with the presence. The sultan wishes to know how you got here. I have to answer him."

"Here? I don't even know the name of this Country."

"This land is called Harare and so is this town. The man in whose hands we are is the gruesome Achmed ben Sultan Abubekr. But answer my question."

"I was brought by a Chinese pirate to Ceylon. There I was sold to the man who brought me here."

"And how did you get into the hands of that Chinese?"

"I drifted on a raft for days until a Dutch ship picked me up. That again fell near Java into the hands of Chinese pirates."

"On a raft? I'm amazed. How did you get on a raft?"

"We've all been on an uninhabited island."

"All? Who do you mean, dear Alva?"

"Ah, the joy to see you again made me forget that you probably don't know them. They were my fiancé Antonio, señores Stenton, Rudolfo, a Red Indian Buff-he, my fiancé's brother George Brooks, Lady Margaret, Kaya and myself."

"These are all riddles for me but I know the name of Stenton. I have very recently heard from another slave about whom I'll tell you, hopefully, another time."

"Oh, this señor Stenton is an amazing man. He performed two miraculous operations on Don Miguel and he went out to find the real son and brother of Condesa Rosetta, whom he married in England. He also tried to find you. He freed the real Aurelio from Danlola's pirate ship. We were later kidnapped by this pirate and put on this island."

"How long is it that you have left your homeland?

"About thirteen or fourteen years," she sighed.

Fourteen years are a long time, but the beautiful daughter of the haciendero had changed very little. In Harare, where men and especially women age quickly, Alva could easily be taken for twenty.

"My God, I'm perpetually amazed."

The Sultan interrupted. "Don't forget that I am waiting for an answer. What did she tell you?"

"She was on a sea shore when the Chinese grabbed her. Then she was sold to Arafat."

"Arafat has told me the truth. Is she a woman or a girl?"

"A girl."

"I'm satisfied. Has she spoken about me?"

The Count bowed down deeply. "I am your obedient slave and think first of you, oh Sultan. I have asked her what her heart says when she sees you."

The ruler's face showed satisfaction. He stroked his beard and was obviously in a good mood: "What did she answer?"

"She said you are a man who has made her heart speak to her."

"Why?"

"Because your Countenance shows sovereignty, your eyes are full of power and your walk is exalted."

"I am very satisfied with you, slave, and with her too. You think her heart will be mine without ordering her to give it?"

"A man should never force a woman's love. His eyes should look upon her mildly and then love will spring up like a flower brought to life by sunshine."

"You are right, I shall show this slave all my clemency."

"Do you know that love speaks first in words before it proves in deed? The slave girl is longing to speak to you in your language, so that she can say with her own mouth what her soul feels."

"This wish will be granted. You shall be her teacher. How long will it take before she can speak to me?"

"That depends when the instructions start and how many hours daily she will study."

"This girl has taken my whole heart. I can hardly wait until she says that she wants to be my wife. The lessons should start today. Are three hours a day enough, slave?"

"If I can teach her for three hours every day, then within one week she will be able to tell you that you will be happy. But the daughters in her Country are not used to seeing a man almost unclothed."

"You will be given different clothes. You will no longer stay in prison. You'll have as much meat, rice and water as you want. You'll look much better for it."

"I thank you. When should the lessons start?"

"At once, after you have changed clothes. I have no time to be with you, I shall order a eunuch to watch you. Now come!"

"May I first tell her you've granted her request to learn your language?"

"Yes, tell her."

Manuel was glad to have achieved that much and turned to Alva: "I'm sorry to leave now, but I'll return soon. Then you can tell me everything."

He followed the Sultan, who ordered a chamberlain to take the chains off the girl's feet and bring good clothes and food to the now-favoured slave. He had changed his clothes and had hardly finished an ample meal, when he was ordered to appear before the Sultan. He took the Count into the treasure room again, where Alva was still heavily veiled. Opposite her was a black eunuch who knew the white man was a slave. "You are the teacher?"

"Yes," was the Count's short answer.

"She has to stay veiled."

"Naturally,"

"You must not touch her."

"I have no intention to do so."

"You must not say anything bad about us, or I will tell the Sultan."

"How will you know whether I have said something good or bad, as you don't understand the language?"

"I can read it from your expression." The eunuch was not as stupid as one would assume from his looks.

"How long will the instruction last?"

"Three hours."

"And how will you measure the time?"

The eunuch took a sand clock from his belt and told the Count where to sit. Don Manuel began: "Now, dear Alva, we have three hours to talk. We have to pretend that this is a lesson in their language and I shall from time to time say a few words which you will repeat. We don't have to be as careful as in the presence of the Sultan. Now tell me your story."

"The island was almost a waste and it took us a long time to grow trees in order to get enough wood for a raft that could take us all."

"Tell me, tell me, I want to know what happened during my absence."

Alva began with the requested report. Her tale intrigued the Count. Now many mysteries were clarified. He recognised José Carujo was a criminal and a traitor. He immediately agreed to Rudolfo being the genuine son of his brother Don Miguel. He almost forgot he was here as a teacher. He taught Alva a few words of the Country: "You are a mighty ruler." "You are the joy of all women." Your presence refreshes my soul." "Be merciful and my heart will love you."

"Do you have no idea where this island could be found?" continued the teacher.

"We had no idea until Dr. Stenton, after the lapse of several years, has calculated by the stars and other conditions, about which I know nothing, that we were about forty degrees southern latitude and about ninety degrees longitude on the west of Ferro. He also said that we were thirteen degrees south of the Easter islands and we could reach them on a raft if we had enough wood to build one."

"What a calamity. So near to freedom and yet so far. You had no trees at all?"

"No, we had no tools either. Slowly we managed to create from the coral reefs. We robbed the shrubs of their lowest twigs and forced them to become trees."

"How did you live?"

"First from roots, fruits and eggs. We also found mussels and we ate them like oysters. Later we made nets and fishing rods and we ate fish. Then Buff-he made bows and arrows and we had birds to eat. There was an abundance of rabbits. We also bred them and we had meat."

"How did you make fire to cook or fry that meat?"

"Oh, we soon had fire. Stenton had been in many Countries where they used two pieces of wood to make fire. We had to be thrifty; we had to save our supply."

"How did you get clothes?"

"We learned how to make them from rabbits' skins. Our dwellings were simple earthen huts with holes as windows. The singles ate with the married couples and had their own hut."

"With the married couples?" asked the Count. Ah, I understand, Buff-he took the girl he was brought up with as his wife. The Indians don't have the same ceremonies. But how was it with the others?"

For a while she was silent and if he could have seen her, he would have noticed her blushing. Then, hesitatingly, she started again: "Oh, dear Sir, think of our situation. We had little hope of being saved. We loved each other and intended to get married officially, should we ever be freed I'm speaking for the other couples too; they were in the same position. Shall I see my friends ever again? They must have been so shocked when I drifted away."

"How did you drift away?"

"That was so sad and terrible I can't describe it."

"Tell me, Alva, even if it is difficult. What I have experienced is just as terrible."

"We finally managed to grow strong trees and could think of how to make a raft. With a lot of trouble we built one. It was large enough for us all and for our supply. There was a mast, a helm or rudder and a sail made of rabbit skins. It was now ready to sail and we were prepared to get through the high surf that was always there A storm broke out at night and woke me up. I thought of our supply on the raft we wanted to use the next day. I wanted to see if everything was securely fastened. The others had worked hard that day and I didn't want to trouble anybody. The raft was swung high and low by the waves. It was only tied with rope made of rabbit skins, which weren't strong enough. On the raft was a similar rope and I jumped on it to double the tie. I was hardly on board when a high wave tore it loose. At the next moment the raft flew into the sea. I lost consciousness with the shock."

"Go on," urged the Count.

"What came next I don't know, neither can I tell you how the raft got over the cliffs."

"The explanation is easy," ventured Don Manuel, "the sea was so high, that the cliffs were no hindrance."

"When I came to the sun was shining and the sea was calm. The island was out of sight. I cried and prayed the whole day and night. Then exhausted I fell into a deep sleep. When I woke up, I'd lost all sense of time because I didn't know how long I'd slept. Now I was thinking what I should have thought of before."

"About the rudder and sail?"

"True. It seemed to me that I was drifting east but the opposite was true. For fifteen days and nights I used the sail, steering the raft by day and tying down the sail by night. What I went through during that time I can't describe."

"I believe you, dear Alva. It's a miracle that you didn't lose your mind. Now let's repeat one of the sentences again. It's important the Sultan hears something in his own language,"

They did that a few times until she had a good grasp. She then continued: "On the sixteenth day I saw a ship. It was Dutch and sailing to Batavia, it rescued me. The captain asked the ship's tailor to make me a suit and consoled me with the hope that I would find help in Batavia.

When we were later attacked by a Chinese pirate, I was taken prisoner and the whole crew of the ship was killed. I was sold in Ceylon to the man who brought me here."

"Child," said the Count sympathetically, "there is a good God who turns everything that appears as bad luck into happiness at the end. It's a great question whether the lot of you would have found somewhere to land. It was God's will that you've found me and from that I draw the conviction, that our plan to escape will succeed."

"Oh, if it comes true. I tell you I'd rather die than be the wife of this man."

"You'll neither die nor belong to him. Tonight we'll escape. I would have liked to tell you more but the eunuch gives me the sign that our lessons are nearing the end. There are a few minutes left; let's repeat the sentences. If nothing comes in between, I'll see you tonight."

The Count went though the sentences with Alva and the eunuch nodded approvingly.

"Your time is up," said the eunuch imperiously.

At this moment the Sultan entered the room. "Allah, you are punctual." He seemed pleased, then he turned to the eunuch; "did you hear everything?"

"Everything, my sultan," the black said with a high pitched voice of the eunuch.

"Did he speak good or bad things?"

"Only good things."

"Are you sure?"

"Very sure, I have heard everything."

The Sultan smiled with satisfaction then he turned to the Count. "Did she learn anything?"

"Yes," he answered with confidence.

"Can I hear it?"

"Yes, if that is your order. Ask her what she thinks of you.

The Sultan was curious and asked Alva what she thought of him. The Count waved to Alva and she replied, "You are a mighty ruler." A friendly smile showed on the Sultan's face.

"Does she know more?"

"Ask her whether she thinks you are kind."

"Do you believe that a woman could hate me?"

"You are the joy of all women."

"You are the best teacher. This slave will be my wife today and you will be rewarded."

"Don't hurry like that, oh Sultan. Think that her heart is still with her own people. Have patience for only a few days. The kinder you are, the faster you conquer her heart. Ask her yourself."

"Is it true you wish that from me?"

"Be merciful and my heart will love you," was the last learned sentence.

"She wants to love me," called the Sultan with delight. "I shall do as she wishes.

"You," he turned to the teacher, "you shall have a room in my second palace that you must not leave. You must be there when I need you."

The Sultan gave orders for Manuel's changed quarters. This second palace was not a beautiful building. It was only a side building of the other hut and contained nothing but a rug for sitting and sleeping. That the sultan thought differently about the slave he had condemned yesterday was seen in the slave receiving a small pipe and a little tobacco. A pleasure that was denied him for many years.

Meanwhile, Dinrallo waited lonely in his hole. He was longing for evening to come. When, according to his calculation, the time had come, he climbed like a chimney sweep up on two walls and listened for any sound, trying to work out whether Harare had gone to sleep. Eventually he took out the stone that connected him to Don Manuel's prison hole. He called but received no answer. "My God, if anything has happened to him?" he mumbled to himself. Eventually he took out the second stone to enable him to climb into the other hole. Except for the many dead rats, he found it empty. He felt a great disquiet as he climbed back into his own prison hole. An anxious time passed. He had almost lost hope when he heard somebody trying to remove his stone. Who was it? The executioner or the Count? A voice called his name.

"Yes, Don Manuel."

"Push from the inside, I am too weak." Dinrallo pressed the stone with all the strength he could muster. The stone moved and he stepped out into the dark.

"*Dios,* I was afraid; where have you been?"

"I've been called to the Sultan, my dear Dinrallo; I have much to tell you but not now." They put the stone carefully back in its place and moved toward the palace. It was very dark. Thy could not see more than three steps and they managed to crawl toward the guard. The old man stood up and grabbed the guard by the throat and pressed it with all his strength until the man lost his breath and opened his mouth. A piece of cloth was pushed into it at once, and then he was bound so that he could not move. He was carried into the stables where Don Manuel had saddled the best camels already.

Now the way into the palace was open. The Sultan was not in his bed. They went to the treasure room where he sat with Alva. Don Manuel had taken a knife from the wall. He knew that the door opened without a sound. He pushed it slightly open and put his finger over his mouth. Alva had expected him and showed no surprise. The Sultan was sitting with his back to the door. Two steps and the Count had the Sultan by his throat and Dinrallo pushed a corner of the ruler's own attire into his mouth. They had found plenty of ropes in the stable to tie the Sultan with. He was then thrown onto the bed from which Alva had risen.

The Sultan was conscious and enraged but could not move himself or shout because his gag had been tied around his mouth too. Don Manuel bowed down to him and whispered: "If you make the slightest sound, I'll put this knife into your black heart." Then he took a spanner to undo his friend's chains. He said to Alva: "For you we have a howdah but you have to wear men's clothing to deceive possible pursuers. We also have to put on better clothes to look like important travellers. There are plenty of them here for me to choose."

To impress the Somali people, through whose territory they had to flee, he took some richly ornate mantles. Next he took the new rifles and revolvers and the necessary bullets. There were three sabres with inlaid handles that seemed very valuable.

"We'll need money, let's open the baskets," said Don Manuel advisedly.

"I know where the money and gold is," said Alva, "he has shown it to me."

"It's possible we must hire or even buy a ship to reach our friends' island," added the Count. They found gold, silver and gems worth millions and packed it all into carpets. As well as pipes and good tobacco, they carried it all to the stables while Alva guarded the sultan.

"What thoughts may the sultan have now? We're lost if he catches up with us."

"Do you believe he could?" asked Alva anxiously.

"There's almost no chance. We have taken the best camels but I've an idea to prevent the Somalis from handing us back, should we fall into their hands. We provide ourselves with protectors," answered Don Manuel.

"Where will you get those?" asked Dinrallo.

"Right here in prison," answered the Count. "Come with me. The señorita shall wait here and guard the Sultan."

At the prison, leaning in a corner, stood a guard who seemed deep in thought. "Let's tie and gag him like the other," whispered Dinrallo.

"We haven't any ropes," came the answer.

"But knives; we cut his clothing and use that."

"All right let's do it."

A few steps took them to the man. Before he could say a word he felt his throat tightly gripped and a few moments later he was gagged and bound. Dinrallo had to stay at the door to keep watch for any surprises. Don Manuel went inside, where a terrible smell almost drove him back. By the sound of chains he noticed that the prisoners were awake. Somebody calling at this time could mean death to any prisoner called out. That's why there was no answer when the Count asked for any Somali. Only when he called: "Are there any free Somalis here? No harm will come to them because I am a freed slave myself.

"There are two of us, father and son answered a voice."

"Come with me and be very quiet. If you are obedient you will be free." Manuel took the spanner from his belt and opened their chains. He then asked them to follow him. The guard was put inside the prison and Manuel pushed the bolts across the door. The Somalis were taken a few steps away and asked how they got into the Sultan's hands. They were warned to speak very quietly so that only Manuel could hear them. They obliged and whispered:

"We are peace-loving people. One of our tribe stole a horse from the Sultan and he grabbed the next best Somali."

"How long have you been imprisoned?"

"Three years."

"That is cruel; do you want to be free?"

"We are longing to be with our family again. Who are you, so secretive and asking these questions?"

"You are free, Somali. We have been slaves ourselves and have outwitted the Sultan. We intend to escape and reach the coast as fast as possible. We need somebody who knows the way and will serve as our protector. Answer quickly, we have no time."

"Take us with you," asked the Somali.

"Do you swear to protect us from your people or any other enemy?"

"Yes, by Allah and the prophet we swear."

No religious Mohammedan will break this oath. Don Manuel took them to the stables where he left them with Dinrallo. Alva was pleased and calmed when she saw the Count again. She had put up her hair and Manuel tied an East Indian veil around her head to make people think she was a young boy. He took two more rifles and clothes for the Somalis. Now he had to find the right keys for the gate.

In the stables the Somalis had waited impatiently. "Here you have rifles, ammunition and clothses. Put them on quickly, take two good camels. Hurry we're in a rush."

"Sir," answered the older Somali, "we don't know you but our lives are yours. We know all the roads and will bring you to the ocean with no need to fear pursuit. You don't have to pay us. Our freedom is more to us than gold or silver."

"Your speech is that of a grateful man. I won't pay you but you'll receive a present befitting your loyalty. We have six camels. My young friend here is a woman and since we have a howdah, she might as well use it. These animals and the howdah will be yours at the end of our journey. You will both act as our servants until we are outside the gate. I shall act as the Sultan, here are the keys. You unlock the gate and lock it behind us again. That's all – now forward."

At the gate they found the guard asleep. the sound of the gate opening woke him up. He came running, but since he had no time to put a light on, he couldn't recognise anyone. "Who are you?" he asked. "Without permission of the Sultan, nobody must leave. I forbid you to open the gate."

"How dare you, son of a dog," called Don Manuel imitating the voice of the Sultan. "Don't you know I am to visit my wife's father? Don't you know your master? Tomorrow you will crawl in the dust, you son of a jackal!"

The man threw himself on the earth and did not dare to say another word. The escapees rushed through the gate which was locked again by the Somali. ---

Chapter 17

CAPTAIN THOMAS WRIGHT

A WEEK later, a ship sailed through the straights of Bab-el-Mandeb. It flew an English flag and anyone could see it was a trading and not a warship. Although it had four cannons on board, they were for the security of the ship. Their destination was not the safest of areas. The captain went to the helmsman who wanted to rise from his sitting position but the captain waved to him to stay seated.

"Terribly hot today, I prefer the north don't you?"

"I do indeed," answered the helmsman.

"I'd be able to do good business if only I could speak Arabic and not have to rely on the interpreter. I can see something in the distance that might be another ship. Hand me the telescope."

The helmsman looked through it first before handing it to the captain. "I've never seen a ship like this in my life," he said.

The captain looked through the telescope and smilingly said: "That must be an Arabian vehicle. We'll reach it in an hour."

The sailors also saw the foreign ship; it only had one mast and two unusually shaped sails. When the other ship was near enough they could see a number of men in turbans. These turbaned men were themselves observing the trader.

"Should I load the cannons?" asked one of the crew.

"Yes, send me the interpreter," answered the captain.

The interpreter who only spoke broken English, asked the captain: "Do you want speak with him?"

"Yes."

"What would you like know?"

"For the moment, what kind of a ship it is."

"I can tell. It is guardship of governor of Seïla."

"It is a warship then?"

"Yes, everybody is armed."

"What are they usually doing?"

"Usually they do trade, only sometimes they have warriors. It must be something special happen in Seïla."

"We must learn what happened there as we want to trade in Seïla."

Now the ships were near enough to recognise each others features. The helmsman wanted to shoot a cannon as a sign that the other ship should heave to, when there was a shot from the much smaller ship to do the same. The captain laughed It amused him that the nutshell wanted to appear like a warship.

"Did you hear that, Jenson? This dwarf gave us an order. We shall obey; I'm curious to know what he wants.

The ordered manoeuvre was obeyed. The ships lay next to each other when the Arab captain called:

"What is the name of your ship?

"Mermaid," the interpreter translated the captain's answer.

"Where is it from?"

"Southampton."

"Where is that?"

"England."

"What do you carry?"

"Trading goods."

"No people?

"No."

"I shall come over to you to see whether you are speaking the truth."

That was too much for Captain Wright. Via the interpreter he asked: "Who are you?"

"I am a captain of the Sultan of Seïla."

"There is a governor at Seïla but there is no Sultan. I do not have to listen to him nor his servants."

"Do you refuse to allow us to investigate your ship?"

"Yes, you have no right to enter my ship."

"I shall force you to let me and my people on board to search your ship."

"Why, am I suspected?"

"We are looking for slaves escaped from Harare. You refuse to have your ship searched; therefore, you have the slaves on board."

"They are not with me. They cannot be with me because I am coming from the north and have not yet landed at the coast here."

"That is what you say but I don't believe you. I shall put a rope to your ship and shall take you to Seïla. There the governor shall examine it."

That was a ridiculous threat therefore Captain Wright answered: "I think you're out of your mind. How can you force me to take your rope on board?"

"I order you to let three of my people take the rope on board."

The captain thought it over. He, like any good English sailor, was fond of a bit of fun. Here was a good opportunity. He said: "All right send your people. You may take me in tow."

Three men were ordered to take the rope on the ship, fasten it to the bow and then give a sign that the journey should begin.

"Ridiculous," laughed the helmsman, "that rope not strong enough."

"But it's strong enough for us to pull them," smiled the captain.

The Arab raised its sail and the rope was pulled tight. It would have torn but that was not Captain Wright's intention. "All men to the sails," he ordered, "we must help them."

A few minutes later the ship was at full speed; the captain turned to the three Arabs.

"Ask your people to go faster, otherwise we'll run them into the ground."

The three shook their heads. They didn't dare give their leader an order but he noticed the danger and shouted: "Go slower. Don't you see that we'll crash?"

"Sail faster, you fool, and don't take a superior ship in tow."

In a few moments a crash would have taken place, but the captain himself took the rudder to change course a little. "I don't want to run them over but I'll give them a lesson."

Now they were side by side and had overtaken the smaller vessel; a cry of rage on the other side. The rope tightened again and as it was fastened to the stern of the Arab ship, it made it turn around. From the deck of the English ship came loud laughter. The little ship was taking some water and ready to capsize. Their leader cursed and thundered. The crew roared instead of cutting the rope. They used their rifles without hitting anything. One of the three asked the interpreter to order the captain to stop and repair their damaged ship.

This was an absurd presumption. "You cannot order me," said the captain. The man pulled a knife from his belt and threatened:

"If you don't listen at once I shall chastise you. You have to obey me, you son of a dog."

"Ah, you said son of a dog? Here is the answer." Wright lifted his hand and, without the interpreter, gave the man such a slap in the face that he stumbled and rolled over. Now the other two pulled their knives but they had chosen the wrong man. The captain had a sailor's fist a hand as hard as steel. With two fast blows they were disabled. "Boys, tie these rascals to the mast," ordered the captain. "We want to teach them a lesson for calling an Englishman a son of a dog."

The situation of the other ship had worsened. "Stop, you rascals: don't you see that we will drown if you don't obey orders?"

"It's all the same to me whether you drown or not," said the Englishman. "Why don't you cut the rope if you want to save yourselves?"

"I must not damage it; it belongs to the governor."

"Well, drink seawater until you burst."

"Maybe we should cut the rope," ventured the helmsman.

"Not yet," decided Captain Wright, "I've never been in this part of world but I have heard a lot about the presumptions of these people. They are slaves and bootlickers of some unknown rulers. Everyone who does not share their believes is an infidel, an untouchable dog. I don't know their customs but I'll show them mine."

"But we are going to Seïla and will probably be in touch with the governor. He'll revenge himself," said the helmsman.

"He may try."

The Arabian vessel leant so far to the side that it seemed about to sink. It took so much water it could hardly right itself.

"Are you so stupid? Cut the rope," the captain called though the interpreter.

They were so confused they did not listen. The captain finally cut the rope, untied the three prisoners and threw them near their ship into the water.

The Mermaid sailed on and reached its destination in the evening. Seïla had no port only a protected anchorage. The entrance was difficult and the Mermaid had to cruise nearby all night. Seïla had about four thousand inhabitants, half a dozen houses and several hundred huts. It made no favourable impression, yet it was the collective point of people in caravans from the surrounding towns selling their wares here.

From the deck of the ship one could see people, camels and horses. Many caravans must have arrived and the captain hoped to do profitable business. A boat came toward the ship and an Arab stepped on board. It was the port master, who assumed a dignified posture. He asked for the ship's papers to put them before the governor whose decision it would be whether the ship received permission to trade here. He returned after several hours and reported that they would receive permission, provided they paid the usual fees and gave a good present to the governor.

"The Wali ," he continued, "will send you a few soldiers. They will protect you from every danger. You have to pay for the soldiers and their food."

"We don't need these soldiers," said the captain. "They would not be able to protect us should we be in danger."

"Oh, they are very brave," said the official.

"I don't believe that, I have witnessed the opposite.

"How can you say that, since you maintain you have never been here?"

"That you will soon learn. I shall only speak to the governor or Wali as you may call him and prove to him that I know how to defend myself."

The port master received a good meal and a present that seemed to satisfy him. Then he returned to the Wali to report what he had been told.

It took a long time until the captain saw a group of armed soldiers in whose midst a howdah was carried. A richly-dressed man alighted from it and stepped into a boat with some of his men. They rowed toward the Mermaid until the voice of the governor could be heard on the ship. He stood up and called: "Why do you want to speak to me? I have to put soldiers on your ship to guard it."

"Who are you to ask obedience from us?"

"I am Hadji Abbul Abbas, the ruler of this town. Everybody here has to obey me."

"If you are the Wali, come up to me so that I can talk to you."

"You come down to me, I am more important than you!"

"If you don't come there will be no trading."

The Arabian official was displeased. He would miss out on the usual port fee and his expected present. He talked to his people and said: "You are acting suspiciously. I can't trust you."

"I give you my word nothing will happen to you."

"And I can leave your ship any time I want?"

"Yes,"

"I shall think about it."

"All right, think. I give you two minutes, then we sail away."

The official talked again to his people. After two minutes the anchor was heaved. That sound decided his attitude. The governor knew this stranger meant what he said. He came on board. With dark glances he observed the crew of fourteen people. Without greeting he asked: "Are these all your people or are there any more?"

"Everybody is on deck," was the captain's answer.

"You dare to resist me with only fourteen people?"

"You have seen and experienced I can dare that. We are English and one of us would take on twenty of your people." This was indeed a proud claim but it did not miss an effect. The governor sat down on a prepared carpet with the captain opposite. On his right the helmsman and on his left the interpreter. The two observed each other. The conversation started: "I've come to call you to account for disallowing my soldiers to enter your ship. This deserves punishment."

"You are mistaken," answered the Englishman. You followed my will to come on board. Had I allowed your soldiers it would be acknowledging that you are my master. Don't you know it is a shame to have one's ship occupied by strangers?"

"We only wanted to ascertain whether you have escaped slaves on board."

"Were your slaves very valuable?

"They belong to the sultan Achmed of Harare."

"They are probably valueless people," said the captain disparagingly.

"No. There were two white Christians and a beautiful Christian girl."

Hadji Abbul Abbas was very imprudent with these descriptions. The captain became attentive. White Christians? In other words Europeans. There was probably something very illegal about that and it was up to him to help? He asked:" Do you know where they are coming from?"

"Yes, the land of the men is called Isbânje."

Spain. The captain found his assumption was true.

"And the girl?"

"The Sultan doesn't know that but she speaks the same language as one of the slaves. They have tied up the Sultan and robbed him of his treasure. They took his best camels and escaped with two Somalis. The Sultan has sent many warriors to follow them. The most likely place they would go was the coast. He himself came to me. He is mighty and if one does not do as he says he would revenge himself on us."

"Was the treasure big?"

"Gold and precious stones worth millions. One could buy a whole Country with it."

"They did get away then?"

"They have taken the fastest camels and have reached the coast sooner than their pursuers but we know so far there were no ships to pick them up."

Captain Wright thought it was his duty to help the Christian slaves. Who knows how they got into the hands of this infamous Sultan? He asked: "You did not find any trace of them?"

The face of the Wali assumed a malicious expression. "Not a trace but something better."

"What?"

"Tell me first that you haven't any of these slaves on your ship?"

"No, until now, I did not even know about them."

"The younger of the Somalis, who must have served them as a guide, fell into our hands. I have sent my soldiers to the coast. They surprised him at a spring. He defended himself and wounded a few of my people but we caught him, nevertheless.

So far, he did not tell us anything but tomorrow he will be tortured until he talks."

"You will not catch them because your ships are no good."

"Do you want to insult me?"

"No. How will you catch them if they find a ship like mine? Have you such cannons or any ship that is as fast as mine?"

The Wali looked thoughtfully to the floor. "Yes, I agree, if we had a ship like yours, then they would have no chance."

"But you haven't got one. I bet that I would catch them if I wanted to."

"The Sultan has put a big price on their capture. As much coffee as can be carried by twenty camels."

"Heavens, that is real wealth."

Over the face of the Wali went an expression of real avarice when he said: "How much do you want if you succeed in catching them?"

The Englishman laughed. "I am richer than you, I don't want a reward. I would try to catch them for the fun of it."

"Do it, do it," said the governor with excitement, as he thought to get the whole reward.

"Unfortunately, that's impossible," said the captain regretfully. "I have to stay here to sell my goods."

"Oh, these you will have sold within a few hours if I decide you should."

"How will you do that?"

"There are four large caravans in town. I myself need a lot and the inhabitants of Seïla too. The Sultan himself would buy a lot in order that you could sail soon."

"I thought he is poor now without his treasure?"

"Sultan Achmed has a lot of silver with him that the slaves haven't taken."

"And how do the caravans pay?"

"With ivory and butter. In Seïla we pay with pearls that were fished at our coast. If I order that today they can only buy from you, then by tonight you will have sold out."

The captain was pleased. It was of great advantage to sell in one day instead of weeks or sailing from one port to another. Also the exchange items were of great interest to him. Ivory and pearls were cheap here. In England, they would fetch a high price.

"Will the Sultan agree?"

"At once, you only have to speak to him yourself. I'll recommend you."

Now the governor had an idea that he should have had before. "But you are also a Christian like those Spaniards. Do you live in one Country?"

"No, there is a big Country between ours and his."

"But you have one religion?"

"No, we are Protestants and they are Catholic."

"What does that mean?"

The captain had a splendid idea. He declared: "That is like with you. You have Sunnis and Shiites."

"Ah, I don't have to worry then," said the Wâli now reassured. "We Sunnis hate the Shiites more than the infidels. You also hate each other and we can be sure. Now I shall speak with the Sultan and order the sale to start."

"And I repeat that you can keep the twenty camel loads of coffee when we have captured the slaves. You can see that I mean well with you and I hope you will not disappoint me."

The hope of the big reward, encouraged the governor to call: "I am your friend, what is your name?"

"My name is Wright."

"That name is too difficult to pronounce but that does not disturb our friendship. Won't you come to Seïla?" You can speak to the sultan about Harare."

"Shall I be able to return unmolested?"

"I swear by Allah and by the beard of the prophet that you will be able to return a free man. You can also bring your goods ashore; I shall punish anyone who insults you."

"No, I shall not do that. Not all buyers are as honest as you are," answered the captain. "Only ten men at a time may step on board. I shall not sell the goods retail but only wholesale. I shall prepare myself to come with you."

The captain gave the helmsman the necessary orders and went to his cabin. There he did two things. Firstly, he put on ceremonial dress and all sorts of weaponry. He intended to make an impression. Secondly, he took his Arabic dictionary to supervise his interpreter somehow and write down a few words. What is the word for I? Ah, there: I is "ana". Now the word for am. I cannot find it, never mind; the word for also is "ayda" and Christ is "nassrani". Together "ana ayda nassrani" means I also Christian. The imprisoned Somali will understand that I shall free him. He will than have hope. Ah what is the word for hope? Here it is "amel". When I free him, it can only be at night. Here it is: "nossf el lel" is midnight. My difficulty is imitating those Arabic letters. He wrote from right to left: "ana ayda nassrani – amel nossf el lel." Freely translated it means: "I am also a Christian, have hope, I will come at midnight." If I succeed in getting the paper to the Somali somehow, he will understand.

If my wife knew I dare to involve myself in an adventure to free a beautiful slave girl! Well, one has a heart; one has a tolerable head and capable fists; that is the main thing.

The helmsman, who was more friend than subordinate to the captain, warned: "You are exposing yourself to great danger. What if they take you prisoner?"

"They surely won't do that. The governor has sworn by Allah. Mohammedans usually don't break such an oath."

"Very well. I think one and a half hour is sufficient for this visit. If you are not back after two hours I shall shoot at the town."

"I actually wanted to tell you that."

After giving some further orders, he went with the interpreter and the Wâli ashore. They then went to a building that belonged to the governor. Inside a room was a big carpet and something that could be taken for a chair. The Arab asked the Englishman to sit down. On his orders servants brought pipes and coffee. The Wâli intended to relish these fineries but the captain warned him and asked: "When can I speak to the Sultan?"

"After we have rested and when he finds it convenient."

"Ah, when he finds it convenient. I hope it will be soon, otherwise you might regret it."

"Why?"

"Because my people will shoot at the town if I don't return soon."

That worked. The governor jumped up from the carpet and groaned: "There must be determined men in your Country. Have a little patience, I'll hurry to the Sultan and tell him about you." Soon after he had gone they were called to a bigger room where the Sultan awaited them. He threw a searching glance to the captain then he turned to the interpreter: "kneel down, slave, when I'm talking to you."

The interpreter did as he was told. Wright did not understand what was said but he understood that obedience was asked for. He asked the interpreter: "Why do you kneel?"

"The sultan ordered me to."

"Ah, who do you have to listen to?"

"To you."

"I order you to rise."

"The sultan would kill me."

"Pah. I'll put a bullet into his head if he does so. Get up; you will stand while we are sitting, that is honour enough."

The interpreter got up made a few steps backward to be out of reach of the Sultan's knife. The Sultan looked at him with flaming eyes. "Son of a dog, why did you get up? Kneel down at once otherwise you'll have my knife in your heart." The interpreter was trembling and whispered to the Englishman: "He wants to stab me to death if I don't kneel."

"Tell him my bullet will hit him sooner than his knife will find you." The tyrant's face assumed an indescribable expression. No one had ever dared to talk to him like that. The Englishman's posture was determined enough for the Sultan to take his hand off the knife.

"Why do you tell him not to kneel in front of me?"

"Because he is my servant and not yours."

"Do you know who I am?"

"Yes, I was told that I would meet the Sultan of Harare."

"Well, look at me, I am he."

These words were spoken as if the Sultan would now expect the Englishman fall to his knees but Wright calmly Countered: "Do you know who I am?"

Achmed looked at the captain with amazement. "You are a sailor but I am the Sultan of a large state."

"Your state is not very big," Countered the Englishman with equanimity. You are the master of slaves. It is much more praiseworthy to be a ruler of free men. I forbid my servant to kneel in front of you. This order you must note, otherwise I shall force respect."

Captain Wright sat himself next to the Sultan and put his two revolvers in front of him. The governor, up to now, would never have dared to sit down without being ordered to do so. Now he sat down without such an order, although at a respectful distance. The Sultan found no words; he did not know how to react. The two revolvers, especially, made an impression on him. He made an involuntary movement away from the Englishman and said: "If you had been in Harare, I would have killed you."

"And if you had been in our realm, your head would have been lost a long time ago. In our Country we knock off the Sultan's head if the people don't like him," Countered Wright.

Achmed had his mouth wide open, also his eyes widened as if he was on the scaffold. "Were you at such an execution?" he asked involuntarily.

"No, I'm no hangman. I see you are smoking and I'm not used to denying myself that pleasure. Order a pipe for me too."

Never in his life was the interpreter an intermediary to such a conversation but the fearlessness of the Englishman gave him encouragement and he interpreted the speeches word by word, although he could have given a more polite version. The governor clapped his hand and ordered pipes. After Wright had a few puffs he said to the Sultan: "Now you can start. We want to talk about our affairs."

He sounded the highest and most distinguished of the three, as he decided the subject of discussion. His personality was so overpowering that Achmed couldn't find words for a reprimand. So he said: "Hadji Abdul Abbas has told me about your plea."

"About my plea? I have never uttered a plea. I thought to hear your wishes," countered the captain.

This was not expected by the Sultan. He told himself that this man would be very suitable for his purpose, so his answer was unusually mild: "Yes, I have a wish but I don't know whether you are the man to fulfil it."

"Try," said the captain simply.

The Sultan followed this invitation and gave a report about everything that happened without putting himself into a bad light. Woe to the people if they were caught.

Than he asked: "Do you think it possible to reach the escapees?"

"Yes."

"How? Do you mean through the Somali prisoner?"

"No, this Somali is a valiant man and would rather die than betray his father. There is a better way to catch them."

"How?"

"These people want to find a ship and if I were you, I would let them find one."

Achmed looked at the captain with amazement. "Are you mad? I myself should help them to escape?"

"Who says that? smiled the Englishman. "I myself would have hidden on this ship and if they are on board with all the treasure, I would have taken them prisoner."

The Sultan jumped up and called: "Allah, Allah. You are right, you are cleverer than us."

The Wali also nodded in agreement. "Where were our senses that we did not think of such a simple solution? You are not only fearless and valiant, you are also clever."

"Let's do that right now," said the sultan.

"Not so quick, you have to think it over first."

"Why not? We're sure to find them this way."

"Do they know your ships?" asked the captain.

"Yes, the Somalis do."

"You're right again," exclaimed the Sultan. "Give us advice and I shall give you thirty camel loads of coffee."

"I'll give you my advice: The ship must be a foreign one. If possible a European vessel. The Spaniards will trust a European ship."

"Your advice is good. But where would I find a ship like this other than yours?"

"He will help you," smiled the governor.

"Will you really help?" asked the Sultan.

"I will, but I have my conditions. As we can't lose any time, my goods must be sold by tonight."

"I'll see to that," declared the Wali. "I've promised you and I'll keep my word."

"I myself will buy from you as much as I have gold and silver with me," called the Sultan of Harare who wanted to get his slaves and his treasure back as soon as possible. "What kind of goods have you?"

Wright named everything he had for sale.

"That is all right, I'll buy, the Wali will buy and the caravans will buy too. Have you any other conditions?"

"Yes, I don't want any rewards but Hadji Abul Abbas is my friend. He'll receive everything. You give it to me in writing, that I shall give him as soon as I have caught them."

The official nearly embraced his generous friend. The Sultan did not understand such unselfishness. "Did I hear right, you want nothing?"

"Nothing. Some people like hunting, some like sports but my passion is catching escapees. I have enough reward with the joy in the catch. But may I make one more condition?"

"Say it."

"I must see the Somali you have caught. The two Spaniards shall send the father of this Somali to find a ship. If he is similar to his son I'll recognise him."

"Allah is great and your wisdom enormous," called the Sultan. "Indeed they look similar. I myself will show you the prisoner."

"Not at once. First you shall give me your written promise."

The Sultan ordered parchment, ink, wax and a feather. Then he asked the captain to tell him what to write.

The following was then written down:

"I, Achmed Ben Abubekr, Emir and Sultan of Harare, promise by Allah and theprophet: I shall give Hadji Abul Abbas Ben Saleh, the Wali of the town of Seïla, one month after Captain Wright has caught the slaves who run away from me, thirty loads of coffee with the camels that carried the load, as a present."

He then signed it pressed his signet ring on the wax and asked: "Are you satisfied now?"

"Yes," said Wright, turned to the governor and added: "I've promised you will be handed this document later but in so that you see that I'm speaking the truth, I shall give it to you now."

The Wali grasped the document with two hands and called enthusiastically: "Yes, you've proved that you are a good friend; the benefactor of all benefactors. What can I do for you?"

"I ask nothing, only that you keep your promise."

"I'll give orders that people can buy of you only until evening."

The Sultan lay down his pipe and asked the captain to follow him to the captured slave. They entered a yard about eight metres square. He asked the captain to lift a basket standing in the middle of the yard. Wright did as he was told and to his horror he saw a man buried to his neck. The Somali looked with hatred at the Sultan and with angry curiosity at the Englishman. The latter pulled the piece of paper out of his pocket. "Don't you want to see whether you can make him talk? asked Wright.

"No, it's useless. You'll catch his father and the others without him saying anything. Then he will receive his punishment."

"Can't he get out? When he turns the earth will be loose."

"No, he can't, he is tied to a stake."

"Really? It seems to me he's tried it." With this he bowed down and pretended with the left hand to test the earth, while he held the paper, unseen by the others, in his right palm in front of the Somali's eyes.

"Don't worry, the earth is firm," said the Sultan.

"But how can you let him be without a guard?"

"There is no need during daytime. At night there's a soldier here. He has no possibility of escape."

"That's enough now. We can go." These words were spoken by the Captain with great satisfaction because he saw from the glance that the native gave him that he had read and understood. His purpose was fulfilled. For now, he had given the poor devil consolation and much needed hope. Back in the room they found the Wali who told Wright that he had given the necessary orders. Both the Sultan and the governor wanted to be the first to buy and take the best for themselves.

"Hurry then, it's high time," warned the captain looking at his watch. He had hardly spoken when a cannon shot was heard.

"Allah, Allah, why do they shoot?" inquired the Sultan, shocked.

"Because my time is up and my helmsman thinks that my reception here was not friendly. I have to hurry and tell him he's mistaken."

"Yes, hurry, we'll come soon after you," called the Sultan.

The captain left the house with the interpreter. A loud hurrah greeted them on board. "How did it go?" asked the helmsman in the presence of the crew.

"All went well," answered Wright. "We'll have a decent bit of work to do, tonight and probably longer. If all goes well, I shall give you all a full month's salary."---

Chapter 18

THE CHEATED SULTAN

"YOU'VE shot ten minutes too soon," The captain opened a conversation with Paul Jason, the helmsman.

"That's no mistake. I thought you were lost and if you were in danger these ten minutes could possibly help you."

"You meant well and I thank you. Everything went as planned, but I shall have to tell you later. Customers will be here any minute."

"Look around you," said Jason with pride. The deck was laid out with opened boxes and bales.

"You've been diligent," nodded the captain. See to it that the men have a strong drink. By tonight we may have sold everything."

"Really?" doubted the helmsman.

"Yes, look, the governor's coming with the Sultan. They 'll take the best for themselves. We'll add twenty percent to our prices and sell only whole bales."

When they arrived, the captain wanted to take the two into his cabin to first entertain them with a good meal but they declined because that meant wasting time to hunt the slaves. The sultan brought a whole sack of Maria-Theresia-Talers as well as a box of golden arm-and-foot bangles, pearl necklaces and other gems he had taken from his subjects. They asked to see the best and bought without wasting time bargaining. The goods were then taken into their boat until it was dangerously overloaded. In any case it went to and fro several times.

"You see I have kept my word?" said the official pointed to the people on land who were queuing up to come on board as soon as permitted.

"When will we be able to sail?" enquired the eager Sultan.

"I can't tell you the exact time it depends on many things and the wind. I'll send you a messenger when we have a favourable breeze."

"Send him, I'll be awake and will order the guard to let him in."

Achmed and the governor left the ship. Now the other buyers rushed in. It was as expected. By evening they had sold out. Everybody, including the interpreter worked hard and they were all hoarse. Paul Jason went on deck to get some fresh air. He met the captain who had come for the same purpose.

"That was an afternoon like no other," said the helmsman.

"And it will be a night for us like no other," declared Captain Wright. "Did you ever read a novel?"

"Which one? asked the embarrassed helmsman.

"Any one."

"Just this one I haven't read."

"Did you hear what the governor told us this morning?"

"About the escaped slaves and the one they have caught?"

"Yes, I want to save them. Listen to what I have to tell you."

The captain now reported what he had learned and about the buried prisoner. He also told him his intention to free the captured slave. Jason listened attentively and banged his fist on the rudder: "The devil take these rascals, the Sultan and the governor. The Spaniards must be capable men. It would be a shame if their pursuers caught them. I'll help you to free the Somali."

"Not possible: one of us has to stay on board."

"That's true. You must go because you know where that prisoner is. I have to stay here."

"Yes. I'll take four of our boys. We'll land north of the town and one will stay with the boat."

"Will you take hoes and shovels?"

"No, only spades. We want to avoid noise," said the Captain. "Get everything ready to sail while we're away. Everything else will be played by ear."---

Sometime after ten o'clock, when everything in town was quiet, a boat left the ship. The oars were covered and no-one could hear them touching the water. The captain sat at the rudder with four of the crew with him. Without exchanging a word, they reached the shore in half an hour. It was a lonely spot and in complete darkness.

The captain and three men reached the wall built around the town. They searched and found a place where part of it had collapsed. They climbed cautiously over the rubble. For a while, they listened, but could not hear the slightest sound. Now they took off their boots and shoes and crept toward the governor's building. Their steps were silent. Here they doubled the caution, because the sultan had said he wouldn't sleep. If he was awake, the servants, of course, must not sleep either.

The four crept around the building and reached the yard's wall. One of them acted as a ladder upon which the others climbed. He was then pulled up too. Up to now everything had gone well. Now one of the sailors jumped down and touched the wall with his spade there was a light sound. "Hurry everybody down and lie flat on the earth," whispered the captain.

This order was obeyed but steps were heard coming close. It was the guard whose post was the small entrance to the yard. He saw nothing and wished to leave. The captain erected himself behind him and gave him such a knock in the neck that he fell. "This one has had it," he whispered, "now let's go on." They reached the middle of the yard where the prisoner still was under a basket. Suddenly he heard a low voice saying in English: "Are you here Captain?" Who was that speaking English and addressing him as Captain? But before he could answer the voice spoke again: "You can trust me; I'm a friend of the prisoner."

Now the Captain dared to ask: "Who are you?"

"I am soldier of the governor. I am from Abyssinia and have learned to speak English in Aden. If you hadn't come tonight, I would have escaped with the prisoner."

"So I can trust you: now, quickly, let us dig him out." It was difficult to work without noise but it was successful. The Somali had no feeling in his legs and lay flat on the ground. "You are coming along? asked the captain.

"Yes, if you'll take me" answered the soldier.

"All right, forward."

It wasn't difficult for the sailors to take the freed Somali over the wall, since they didn't have to fear any guards. Two of them put him on their shoulders. Only after they had the town's wall behind them did they feel safe and the captain asked the soldier why he wanted to free the Somali. "Because I do not like it here and because I felt pity for this young man."

"Did you guard the Somali before?"

"Yes, and he told me about your coming so I waited for you. As the Somali can't walk it might not have succeeded if I had freed him on my own."

"Ah, that's the explanation, you can speak to him?"

"Yes. He speaks Somali as well as the Arabic language."

"Splendid, I have to talk to him and don't want to use my interpreter. Now let us rush to come on board. They walked quickly to the boat where it turned out that the Somali could now stand up. The shaking movement of his bearers had contributed to his better blood circulation. Four sailors brought the boat to the ship in less than half an hour. The helmsman had waited for them. "Is the interpreter asleep?" asked the captain.

"Yes, he didn't notice anything."

"That's good. Send a messenger to our guests and tell them we're sailing as soon as possible.

"You have the Somali. Should we not leave our guests in Seïla?"

"No," said the captain, "they have to be punished." The Somali and the Abyssinian were taken to the captain's cabin adjacent to a little chamber where they could be hidden. Then he ordered a meal. The Somali had not been given any food at all. After he had eaten he told his story. He was sent out to look for a ship and was seized at a well.

"Oh how my father and the others will thank you for freeing me, they must have felt great anxiety."

"Where are they now?"

"In the Elmes Mountains."

"As you have been caught there, searches will take place in every cranny of the mountain. They might be discovered by now."

"They're still secure. There's a hiding place only known to our tribe. In ancient times there was a lot of enmity with our neighbours. There was a deep cleft in the mountain that our ancestors managed to close, except for a small hole on the top, for air and an overgrown entrance at the bottom where they could hide their belongings and, should the need arise, themselves."

"And the Spaniards are waiting there for you?"

"Yes, my imprisonment must have been noticed but we arranged to wait five days until they had given up on me."

"Have they enough food?"

"Yes, we've bought lots of dates during our journey and water they can obtain at night. The well where I was caught is quite near."

While they were talking one could hear the rhythm of oars in the water. "The Sultan and the governor," said the captain.

"For God's sake, we are lost," wailed the Abyssinian.

"Don't worry," consoled Wright, "they won't come in here and when they sleep, you can go on deck for fresh air."

"They're coming with us?" asked the soldier even more anxiously.

"Yes, sultan Achmed and Hadji Abdul Abbas want to be there when I catch the escapees. I have taken them on board to see the former slaves but they will not be handed over and that's their punishment."

The captain went on deck. There he found his two guests and a few servants. The Sultan recognised him in the light of the lantern; he was excited and talked to him.

The interpreter was called and Wright was told the prisoner had escaped. That he had nearly killed one guard and that another had run away because he feared punishment. The captain feigned astonishment and was visibly unpleasantly surprised. "What did you do to catch him again?"

"We didn't want to miss the departure of your ship but have sent pursuers along the coast and to the south where the other escapees will be."

"That's the best you could do. I've erected a tent for you from where you can overlook the coast as soon as daylight breaks. The interpreter should look after you regarding to food. I myself have to take command when we go to sea."

"Will you get through the cliffs at night?"

"I hope so. We'll take your boat in tow."

The tent was big enough for two. They could hear the captain's voice giving the necessary commands. The small sails were hoisted and the ship went slowly through the cliffs. Once outside they hoisted the big sails and the beautiful ship flew proudly into the sea.---

Count Manuel with his companions had reached Mount Elmes. From the top of this not very high mountain one could see the sea. The Somali had shown him this hiding place and they decided to wait there for a ship. A full day passed without them seeing one. The younger Somali was going to the next town beyond Seïla to Tadshura which the Sultan's men had probably not yet reached and look for a suitable ship. At night they took their camels to the nearby well. Dinrallo found a broken bow and a piece of string with something round attached to it. When the older Somali looked at it he jumped up with great shock. "This is my son's talisman. It was hanging round his neck. He has been attacked."

"You are probably mistaken. He may have just lost it."

"That is not possible. The string is too strong for the talisman to fall off easily and the bow is of a type the governor's soldiers use." The father's fury was indescribable. A gloomy day passed. From time to time one of the men dared to go on top of the low mountain and saw in the distance the governor's ships cruising.

"You can see we're betrayed," lamented the older Somali. The day passed. It was the day when Captain Wright sailed into Seïla. The night came and disappeared without incident. To wait another three days as he'd arranged with his son was too much for the father of the caught Somali. This worry consumed him. ---

The Sultan and the governor were taken aback by the captain's brusque behaviour towards them since they came aboard. For them the captain was too slow. "If you carry on like that, how will you keep your word?" said the Sultan grumpily.

"Be quiet," answered the Englishman, "you are not in Harare where your tyranny counts. I have given you my word that I shall catch the escapees and I shall keep it."

"How dare you talk to me like that?" the Sultan raged.

The captain shrugged his shoulders contemptuously and turned to the chef to whom he gave a small paper bag containing sleeping powder. Put this into the coffee of our unwanted guest. They and their servants should be anaesthetised for a while. After an hour the guests were asleep.

Wright went into the cabin assigned to the Abyssinian and the Somali. "The time has come; we are getting near the mountain. We'll see it in a quarter of an hour through the night telescope. Get ready."

"Allah, that will be a joy for my father," beamed the Somali.

The captain observed the coast for a while. Then he turned to the helmsman. "Stop here; put down the anchor, we are at our destination." A boat was lowered. Only Wright, the Abyssinian and the Somali entered it. At the mountain the Somali put his hand into the grass and pulled slightly at some hidden device. A small sheen of light was seen. The captain looked though the small opening and saw Count Manuel and Alva Wilson talking. He knew enough Spanish to understand simple conversation and he heard them talk.

"Only to see my country and face the enemy, then death may come," sighed Manuel.

"You will conquer your enemies and carry on living for a long time," said Alva encouragingly. "I hope to God that a saviour will appear soon."

A powerful voice was heard from the entrance: "The saviour is here already."

They jumped up, astonished and shocked. The entrance widened and Wright stepped in and the light of the candle lit up the younger Somali. "My son," called the older Somali, putting his arms around him.

"My God, who are you?" asked the Count with a trembling voice.

"I am Captain Wright from England," came the answer. "I have come to take you wherever you want to go."

"Lord in heaven, at last, at last."

Don Manuel sank to his knees. Alva bent down to support him. She leaned her head against his and their tears of joy united. Dinrallo was leaning at the wall with tears in his eyes. The father still had his arms around his son. It was a scene that brought tears to the eyes of the seaman. The Count found his words again. He stepped toward the captain and said: "You are an Englishman? No, you are an angel of light, a messenger from God, sent to us to save us. How did you know about us?"

"This one over there has told us about you," declared Wright and pointed toward the young Somali who noticed that it was about him. "He has freed me from imprisonment at danger to his own life," he rejoiced in Arabic. He spites the Sultan, he is a hero, Allah bless him although he is an unbeliever."

Now the telling began in Arabic and in the Spanish language until hearts quieted down. Wright was shocked when he learned the identity of this slave of many years. He opened a bag with bottles of wine and comestibles. After this it was time to go back to the ship. The Abyssinian and the Somalis received a present taken from the sultan's treasure. It was arranged to take the Count, Dinrallo and Alva to Calcutta, the Somalis and the Abyssinian to Aden, well out of reach of the tyrant. At this opportunity, the Count asked the captain whether he should return the treasure. "I leave that to you," was the answer.

"Perhaps you might think that is theft. I shall keep it for the years of slave service."

"I don't doubt that I'd do the same."

"Achmed deserves this; besides, I'll need a large sum for a purpose I'll tell you later. Now, the time is too short. I think you'll approve."

On board the guests were still fast asleep. The chef had the captain's cabin arranged for Alva and a tent for the Count was erected as well. Now everybody could sleep. They woke up very early. Excitement ruled that a long rest was impossible. After a short breakfast, the main persons went into hiding and the guests were woken up. They tore themselves yawning out of their narcotic sleep and asked for coffee. The Captain went as if by chance near the sultan's tent. "Are we sailing again as slow as yesterday? called the tyrant.

"Possibly."

"So we will never catch the fugitives. We have made a mistake with you."

"You are right but in a different way. While you were asleep I've worked. I've caught them all tonight."

"Allah, Allah, last night?"

"Yes, none of them is missing. Even the escaped Somali and the Abyssinian guard is there."

"By Allah, they will suffer for it. I have to see them at once, do you hear, at once. Where are they? Where?"

"At the shore. I'll let a boat down; yours is still hanging behind the ship. Take all your servants with you."

The Sultan's boat was already pulled to the side of the ship. On the other side they pretended to let the boat down for the Captain, but it was only half way down when the Sultan, the Wali and all their servants had entered their own. The sails were hoisted and filled up. The ship was ready to sail. Now he looked over the parapet into the governor's boat and said to the Sultan: "Now you can see that I have kept my word and that I have the escapees in my hands. Which one is the most important to you?"

"The white slave girl," answered Achmed, "but why don't you come?"

"Because I can show her to you without coming with you – look here."

At this moment, Alva stepped to the parapet and showed herself without veil to the men below her in their boat.

The Sultan looked up in amazement and called: "Allah, Allah, there she is. I must get on board again."

A sailor cut the rope that had tied the boat to the ship and threw it into their vessel.

"Stop, what is that? Why do you untie us? I have to come up, I have to have my slave, she is mine. Where are the others?"

"Here," he pointed at Manuel and Dinrallo who had stepped to the parapet to be seen. The interpreter, who was present during these exchanges whispered to the captain: "What have you done? It will be your and my ruin. The Sultan and the governor will take a terrible revenge."

"I do not fear them."

"You probably not but I have to go to Seïla quite often."

"Don't go there again."

"That means great financial loss to me."

"We'll repay and replace the damage."

"But I can no longer be an interpreter in this matter."

"There is no need for you to do that, I'll speak from now on," said Count Manuel.

"By Allah, there they are. I order you to take me aboard again." The Sultan was furious.

"We wouldn't dream of it," laughed Manuel.

"Come down. I order you to."

"Are you mad? What can you command now, we are free men."

"You are villains Where is my treasure?"

"Here on board."

"Give it back."

"That's ridiculous. A nobleman of the Christians was forced to be your slave for many years. He is forcing you now to pay him a princely salary. Don't forget. Your slaves are human beings."

The boat drifted away from the ship. The Sultan's fury stopped him from uttering a word. The governor, however, commanded: "I order you to take us up again. Should I use force?"

"You can try," laughed Manuel de Manresa.

"The Sultan has given me a promissory note that I should get the price for the slaves' capture."

"Let him pay you. The conditions of the document are fulfilled. The captain has us in his hands. The camel loads must be paid."

"Son of a dog, you have cheated us."

"But you didn't cheat us. You are too stupid for that. You believe in your kismet, it had been predestined that we should not return to slavery."

The wind filled the sails and the ship won the open sea in no time. ---

Chapter 19

THE ISLAND OF THE LOST

---

*T*HE plan was to sail to Aden where they would say good bye to the two Somalis and the Abyssinian. The former were well rewarded, the latter satisfied. The next aim was Calcutta. The heat in those latitudes was so great that almost everybody slept during the day. It was evening when they came together and the captain learned from Don Manuel the story of the brothers of Manresa and the crimes committed against them. Wright listened without interruption, on only the angry spitting of his chewing tobacco betrayed his emotions. Then he walked a few times across the deck and said:

"Outrageous, abominable, appalling. Does your whole heart demand revenge?"

"Naturally, we'll take revenge if these rascals are still alive."

"Still alive? I would take a bet that such scoundrels are not in hell yet. What do you intend to do?"

"That we intend to go to Calcutta you know …"

"To hire a ship?" interrupted Wright.

"Or to buy one," Countered Don Manuel. "For this purpose I have taken the sultan's treasure. Are you able to handle a steamship, Mr. Wright?"

"Of course! The main thing is to get a good engineer. A captain has little to do with the engine. Why do you ask?"

"Because I trust you. I wish you could help us find that island."

"I? With all my heart," laughed Wright. "If you intend trying it with me, I hope to God that you'll be satisfied. We've done good business in Seïla, I have to take a load in Calcutta. My helmsman will bring it home and excuse me with the ship-owner."

"Splendid, we have a deal then. O.K.?"

"O.K. Let's shake hands."

With a good wind they reached Calcutta in three weeks. Captain Wright found a suitable load and while the crew was busy stowing the goods, he was on the lookout for a steamship. Unfortunately, there was none available for sale. Those that were there were owned by some governments or organisations whose staff were not empowered to sell. Just as Wright began to doubt he could serve any purpose here, an Englishman came on his own steamer and, as he wanted to stay as an officer, he offered the ship for sale.

Wright examined the vessel and found it in perfect condition. He acquired it for a reasonable price and kept the whole crew as well. The steamship was paid in full on the spot and was loaded with coal and food. Alva received lady's outfits again. The count and loyal Dinrallo did not deny themselves little comforts they had been forced to forego for a long time.

Count Manuel told no-one his intentions, except to the Spanish consul who gave necessary documents. Finally the anchor was hoisted and the steamship began the journey and search for the unknown island.

To know the position of the lonely island was now the main thing. Alva had given the latitudes and longitudes that Stenton had calculated, but he had had no instruments and took his whereabouts mainly from the stars. His calculations were, therefore, defective. There was no alternative but to search the given area until the island was found.

With a favourable wind and sails, the journey went fast. On their way they took on coal in Colombo, Singapore and Brisbane and finally they reached Ducie, south-east of the Paumotu- Islands.

Here, according to Stenton's calculation should be the island. Captain Wright began to cruise for several days without success. It would have been easy to hit some coral reefs, so they let the boat drift at night without steam. This had the merit of not running against reefs or sandbanks and the saving of coal for which the ship had only limited space.

Wright stood on the bridge with Don Manuel. It was night and he observed the shining stars. Suddenly he asked Manuel to hand him the night telescope.

"Did you see something?"

"Hm! In the very back and low in the ocean I noticed a star whose light appeared unusual to me. I would nearly bet that it is below the horizon."

"Then it can't be a star."

"No but an artificial light – a flame."

Wright took the telescope and looked for a long time through it. When he finally put it down, he declared: "No, it's definitely not a star."

"Maybe it's the lantern of a ship heading toward us?"

"No, it's the flame of a fire on land."

"We are near an island then?"

"That in any case, my telescope has never yet failed me. I know exactly where we are and there is no island around here on the map. We can only conclude that we have found a so far unmarked island."

"God, if it's the island we're looking for, should I wake señora Alva?"

"Not yet. Look, the fire seems to be going out now."

Manuel also noticed that the flame went lower and lower. "Maybe it is a meteor and no artificial fire," he said with anxious doubt.

"Oh no, it was a fire made by human hands, look it has gone out completely while it had high flames two minutes ago. What can you deduce from these circumstances, Don Manuel?"

"That the material was a light one."

"Right. That is natural to the island we are looking for. A fire of hard wood does not go out so fast and señora Alva has told us that wood is a rarity on this island."

"You maintain there are people on this island. Wouldn't they see our light as well?"

"No, the flame flared up high while our lantern gives a small, quiet light that from their distance will look no different from a small star – if seen at all. In any case, I'll give a sign."

Wright ordered a few rockets to be sent up. No success. We'll have to wait until tomorrow," he suggested.

"How can we wait all this time?" called Don Manuel impatiently; can't we use steam to get nearer?"

"No, Alva has told us that the island is surrounded by cliffs and we have to beware of them. We have a slight breeze from west to east and by morning we'll see what lies in front of us."

"Perhaps we could shoot a cannon, captain?"

"I would advise against that," Countered Wright. If the island is not the one we think, the people on it will hide in fear. If we reach them by day, it maybe possible to make useful enquiries."

"But if it is the right one?"

"We would achieve nothing further than to disturb the peace of these poor people."

Wright ordered a man to be on the lookout and warn for possible surf. A quarter of an hour passed. The captain asked the Count to have a rest but Don Manuel could not decide to do so. Anxiously he wandered to and fro. After a long night came the dawn. The captain saw the one gap through which it would be possible to sail nearer. The sea was calm, so it would not be too difficult to sail through this entrance today. The Count went on the bridge and asked: "Now captain, what do you think?" His voice trembled with emotion he could not master.

Wright looked at him with seriousness and damp eyes. "We have reached our destination, Don Manuel."

"Really? Are you sure?" rejoiced the Count.

"Pst, you are going to wake up the señora."

"Why should I not wake Alva?"

"Because I wish to surprise her. She should find her friends on board when she awakes."

"What reason do you have to believe that this island is the right one? I can see no people and no dwellings."

"To start with, I really respect this Dr. Stenton. He has calculated almost correctly the position of this island without the help of the necessary instruments."

Secondly, the description that señora Alva has given us. The people are still asleep and the dwellings are beyond those hedges where the wind will not bother them. Let's throw anchor here and get a boat ready. The inhabitants of that little island will still be deeply asleep."

The captain, Don Manuel and four sailors went into the boat. They managed to negotiate the cliffs and fastened it ashore. The oarsmen waited while Wright and Don Manuel stepped slowly and carefully on the land. They went around some hills and noticed a row of small huts, erected with earth and small twigs. Just before them, dressed in trousers and a jacket made of rabbit furs, stood a tall, broad shouldered figure. His features were tanned by weather but noble, his large open eyes had an expression of devotion as he looked towards the rising sun; it also showed strength of spirit. It was Stenton. What did this man think about, what feelings were there in his broad chest? There, in the east, where the red of the new day began to glow, was America, and further still the homeland with all his loved ones. Were they still alive or had they died with grief and heartache? Here, on this spot, he had stood for many years and prayed. He knelt now.

Stenton had not noticed the two men who stood sideways at some bushes. He could not see the ship either because of the hills in between. Manuel wanted to step forward but was held back by the captain. Stenton prayed:

"Lord, father of all your children, you console the sad, you help the harassed, I am yours, on you I depend. Here, in this desolate spot of the oceans, my voice is calling you, a cry of deepest need, a call for mercy and pity. My heart will break and my life is dissolving in sorrow. Save us, O ruler of the world. Lead us away from here, where the floods of misery are threatening to drown us. Send your angel and redeem us from languishing in the depth of despair. If it is your will that we stay here until our death: have mercy on those who are praying at home for our salvation. Give them a strong heart to bear what you have decided for us. Give consolation and peace to their souls and dry their tears. Amen."

The giant now rose and tears ran down his cheeks but his trust in God lightened his features. Suddenly a great shock went though his body as if he had had a stroke. A heavy hand was put on his shoulder and a voice spoke in English: Your prayers have been answered. The saviour who will redeem you is here."

Stenton turned around and saw the captain and the Count. He staggered back and fell to his knees again. His eyes were wide open, his lips moved, he wanted to speak but could not utter a word. He almost gave the impression of an impaired spirit. The terrible shock paralysed him for the moment. Wright realised his mistake. He had forgotten that sudden overwhelming joy could kill a man. He had been careless. "My God, what have I done?" He was shocked at himself. "Take hold of yourself, take hold of yourself."

There, finally came slowly from his mouth: "Oh – oh – ah! God O God! Is it possible? Who are you?"

"I am an English captain, who will take you away from here. My ship is anchored behind these hills."

Wright expected that Stenton would get up now, but not so. The strong man sank further down, his arms dropped, his head leaned over and his giant body stretched out in the grass. The two men saw him trembling and they heard a heartbreaking sobbing but they did not disturb him. The captain suspected that in this flood of tears the effect of his careless doings would resolve itself. He was right. Stenton, after a while, stood up slowly and looked at those two. Still with an expression of doubt, he asked: "Is it really true? There are people here? A ship has come? God o God what joy. I thank you for it but it nearly killed me."

The captain begged his pardon. "I was careless, but you were described to me as a man who could stand the shock of seeing me suddenly."

"I? Being described to you? Impossible."

"Yet it is so. I must be very mistaken, if I do not recognise you by your figure as Dr. Stenton."

"True, you know me. What a puzzle. Who has told you about me? Where do you come from?"

"This gentleman has told me about you."

Wright pointed at the Count. Stenton looked at him. His cheeks reddened and his eyes lit up.

"You are saying 'this gentleman' instead 'this señor'? He asked.

The captain astonished said yes. Stenton took a deep breath as he called: "I have asked you where you come from but ..."

"We come from ..." the captain wanted to answer.

"… from Harare." Stenton finished his sentence.

"Yes from Harare," Countered Wright, even more astonished than before.

"And this señor is Don Manuel de Manresa y Cordoba? continued Stenton.

"Yes, I am the one," said the Count for the first time – in Spanish.

"Oh my God, I went out to save you and now you have come to save me. I recognise your features. You look very similar to your brother Don Miguel."

Stenton opened his arms and the two so sternly tested by fate, who had never seen each other, stood clasped in each others arms as if they had been friends from childhood.

"Uff!" called somebody from one of the huts and after a pause of mighty astonishment another: "Uff! Uff! Uff!"

Buff-he, the chief of the Mixtekas had woken up. He had heard voices and had uttered this Red Indian word in his mighty surprise. The furry doors opened at once, Rudolfo and then the others appeared. All in good health, all in similar outfits. Antonio and his brother George, Kaya and Lady Margaret. All stood there wide-eyed but without words. Buff-he had not seen the Count because he was covered by Stenton. Now he saw him. "Uff! Don Manuel." The Count recognised him too. "Buff-he," he called out while his arms released Stenton and in the next moment the chief lay on his chest. A Spanish Count and a half savage Indian. Joy made equals of them all.

Loud rejoicing followed and hundred of questions flew about. It was impossible to answer them fast enough. Embracing followed. One flew into the arms of another and then into a third and fourth. They hurried onto the hill to see the ship and they could hardly contain themselves with joy. Only one of them, although also participating in the rejoicing, was more reserved. The captain saw it and stepped toward him.

"Aren't you as glad as the others to be freed?"

"Oh yes, I am glad but it would have been greater if ---"

"If ---? Please continue.

"If I could have shared this joy with someone else"

"May I ask who that might be?"

Anthon Brooks, also named Antonio or Old Surehand, shook his head sadly and turned away. Wright did not find time for further questions because Stenton asked him whether they could come on board.

"Sure." The captain smiled with pleasure.

A true race started. Stenton was the first to reach it. Even the serious Indian ran like a schoolboy. The boat took them all. When they came around the cliffs a cannon shot greeted them. All the ship's flags were hoisted.

Alva woke up and asked anxiously the reason for the shooting. She went on deck and saw the island. Wild looking figures came on board. One of them stood there and looked at her in astonishment, it was Anthony Brooks, then he rushed over. "Alva," he cried with delight.

"Antonio," she rejoiced.

They lay in each other's arms. They laughed and they cried. They caressed and kissed like children who could not contain their joy. The captain who stood next to them delighted in their happiness. "Is your joy complete now," he asked Antonio.

"Oh, it is immeasurable," was the answer. "But tell me how did Alva come to your ship? We believed her dead."

"That we shall discuss later, for now, please come down all of you, breakfast is being served. As they were sitting around a long table, Stenton looked at someone he had not expected to see on this ship. After a brief hesitation he went over with open arms. Dinrallo, my dear Dinrallo! I am not mistaken, you must be he. The Spaniard had tears in his eyes as he returned the joyful greeting.

"Yes, I am he, señor, and I can't tell you how glad I am to see you again.

"How did you get on this ship into the south sea?"

Dinrallo described his experience in a few words. Stenton listened with the highest concentration. When Dinrallo finished he said: "Poor Dinrallo, I am the one who's guilt it is that you have experienced such terrible things. And how you have become grey in these years! As far as I am concerned, I'll do everything I can to make you forget them. The family of Manresa will appreciate your services.

Shortly after this exchange there was merriment in the cabin and it was decided to have one more meal on the island and then go to sea.

"But where to?" asked Stenton.

"To Mexico, to my father," said Alva.

"To Mexico, to Carujo the cheat," said Don Manuel.

"To Mexico, to the Mixtekas," said Buff-he.

"Very well, we'll go to Mexico. We all will go there," said Stenton.

"And where shall we land?" enquired the captain.

"Where we went to sea or rather to our misfortune."

"Guaymas, then?"

"Yes, there we'll think what to do next."

Breakfast passed with laughter and tears. Later they returned for the last time to the island, their unwanted home for more than thirteen years. The captain brought the British flag and allowed most of his crew to come on the island.

The midday meal consisted of the best foods and wines that the captain could find in Calcutta. The people, all clad like Robinsons Crusoe, ate like princes. Before the champagne was opened, the captain asked his guest to follow him. He went on the highest hill, where the sailors had prepared a table with glasses of the finest wine. There he planted the flag in the ground and proclaimed:

"Ladies and gentlemen, we have to fulfil a holy duty. This island is not marked on any maps and has no name. I take this little but worthless island in the name of our Queen Victoria and give it the name of the tested family 'Manresa'. Take up your glasses and drink with me to this new name.

A loud hurrah followed this proclamation from the involuntary inhabitants and their liberators and the cannons sounded their contribution.

"Now let's open the champagne. I don't love the French but I love drinking their wine."

Many things were taken off the island. Worthless, but as mementoes, invaluable.

It was early afternoon when the ship hoisted anchor and left the island of their exile. The happy guests went to a new life. ---

Chapter 20

SEÑORITA RESEDA

ABOUT 120 English miles above where the Rio Pecos flows into the Rio Grande del Norte, at the Mexican side of the tremendous river was the village Ford Guadalupe. The richest man in this village was Señor Rodrigo. He had the biggest shop in the neighbourhood. His wife, who was the sister of Martin Wilson, the haciendero of the Hacienda del Alina, has died years ago. Rodrigo mourned for a while but his cheerful nature was not made to grief for too long. She left him with a daughter who grew up a beautiful girl. She was thirty now but looked much younger, not like Mexican girls who are withered at that age. She did not want any of the suitors who tried to court her. She joked and laughed with them but favoured none. This left Rodrigo rather indifferent at first but when age crept up on him, he wished for a capable successor and at the same time he wanted to see his daughter well looked after.

Today was a summer's day. A sharp wind blew across the river. A wind that was disliked by hunters and shepherds. The lower part of his house was used as a tavern. There was also a kitchen. Señor Rodrigo sat at the window of his tavern while Reseda, his daughter, sat at the other end busying herself with sewing a present for one of the female servants. Her father drummed with his fingers at the window. He was in a bad mood and this was a sign that Reseda would hear the well known reproaches that didn't worry her very much. On the contrary, she found the way he approached the subject funny.

"Terrible wind," he growled peevishly.

Reseda did not answer, therefore he continued. "Almost a storm."

She again did not answer. He asked the question directly. "Isn't it so, Reseda?"

"Yes," Her answer was monosyllabic.

"Yes? What? asked her father, irritated by her short answer.

"All right, terrible storm."

"Good! And a terrible dust, as well."

Reseda kept silent again. He turned toward her and said: "If you can't make better conversation, how will it work once you find a husband?"

"A silent wife is better than a chatterbox."

Rodrigo coughed a little. He felt beaten and was embarrassed about continuing the conversation. After a short while he started again: "Extraordinary wind, terrible storm." Reseda didn't think it worth while to answer such an intelligent question. He shook his head, drummed at the window and growled: "And not a single guest in sight."

When Reseda did not answer again, he turned to her. "Am I right? Or do you see a guest in the room? No guest, none at all. That's bad for a girl who is looking for a man. Or have you perhaps ..."

"No," she said, "I don't want anyone."

"Not anyone! Hm, nonsense! A man is for a girl, what a sole is for a shoe."

"One has to step on it; true? She laughed.

"Nonsense, I mean that one cannot walk without one." In spite of his justification he felt the put down he had received. It nettled him and he thought how he could get to his aim as a tile fell off the roof. "Did you see that?"

"Yes," answered Reseda again monosyllabically.

"Now we have a hole in the roof, who will repair it, I myself naturally?"

"Who else? You don't expect me to do it?"

"You? Nonsense. The son-in-law. It would be his duty to keep everything in order. Where there is no son-in-law, there is no order. Understood?"

The good señor Rodrigo was thrifty. The small damage made him angry and double talkative. He continued: "But an orderly son-in-law it must be. Not like a ragged long bloke who comes here from time to time with his clothes torn.

His daughter blushed a little but Rodrigo did not notice. This 'ragged bloke' was apparently not quite indifferent to her.

"Do you know who I mean?" asked the father.

"Yes," replied Reseda.

"Well, not that one. I am ambitious. I have got that from my dear parents. Do you know what my father's profession was?"

"Yes, a chimneysweep."

"Very good. These are people who were aiming high. And my grandfather?"

"He was a trader in horseradish."

"Very good. You can see they were enterprising and, because of them, I became a rich man. One cannot remind a daughter enough about such an origin." Rodrigo would have continued, if the sound of hoofs had not been heard. A man who instead of getting off his horse outside the fence, made his horse jump over it and dismounted on the gable side of the house before entering the tavern. Rodrigo had noticed the arrival of the new guest. He muttered angrily: "There he is the no-good. Such guests I can do without. Such a person should never tell me, that he wants to be my son-in-law.

Reseda bent down a little more to hide her blushes. The guest entered the room. He greeted politely, sat down at a table and asked for a glass of julep; a cooling drink, drunk in the southern United States and the bordering area. The guest was tall and strongly built and his face was framed in a dark beard. He was probably in his early thirties. He wore a threadbare pair of Mexican trousers and a woollen blouse open in front, exposing his chest. Around his hips was a leather belt with two revolvers and a knife. The rifle seemed not worth a cent, as the whole person made a neglected impression. But anyone who looked in his strong and melancholic features and his big dark eyes, would not have judged him by his appearance.

"What kind of julep do you want, mint or caraway seed?"

"Please give me mint," was the answer.

The drink was brought and Rodrigo sat down again at the window. The guest also looked through the window, but an attentive observer would have noticed that his glance went over to Reseda from time to time who, blushingly, dropped her eyelids. The old man found the silence too depressing and said for the third time:

"Terrible wind."

The stranger took no notice and after a pause he asked again: "Isn't it true?"

"Not very bad," was the indifferent answer.

"But a terrible dust."

"Pah."

"Pah? What do you mean, that this is no dust?"

"It is dust, so what?"

"So what? What a question," called Rodrigo annoyed. "The dust flies in your eyes so …"

"So you close them," interrupted the stranger.

The intelligent landlord felt beaten again but added: "But the clothing, the clothing is suffering."

"So you put on bad ones."

"Yours are bad enough, haven't you got any other?"

"No."

That word was spoken with such indifference that the old fellow became indignant.

The Mexican man makes much of his appearance. He dresses in colourful attire, likes to carry shiny weapons and decorates the harness of his horse with golden adornments. On his boots he carries large wheels.

"Why not?" asked the landlord.

"They are too expensive."

"Ah, so you are a poor have-not?"

"Yes," answered the stranger with utter indifference but he noticed that the daughter blushed and threw him a glance like asking him to excuse her father.

Rodrigo took no notice of this and continued: "What is your profession?"

"Hunter."

"A hunter? And you make a living from that?"

"I sure do."

The old fellow looked at him contemptuously and said proudly: "I feel sorry for you. Yes, a few years ago there were men one had to respect. Did you ever hear of Buff-he?"

"Yes, he was the chief of the Mixtekas."

"Or about Old Surehand?"

"Yes, he was an Englishman."

"My compatriot, like the most famous of them all, do you know whom I mean?"

"The most famous was Doc Ironfist, they have all gone."

"Now there is Black Gerard who has acquired a name for great deeds. Do you know of him?"

"Yes, what about him?"

"That must be a devil of a fellow. He seems to be in this area lately. This westman with the name of Gerard has a black beard, hence the name Black Gerard. He doesn't fear the devil. His shot never misses and his knife always finds the right spot. In former times he wiped out the robbing bands of the Llano Estacado. Since he came down from the north, the ways are free from rabble. I have much to thank him for. Prior to his appearance on the scene, they robbed my goods ten times before I received them once. Such a man should become my son-in ..." he stopped and thought it over. He could not continue with his favoured litany in the presence of this guest. Nevertheless, he continued. "I would like to know where he comes from. Perhaps from England or even from Shropshire, that's where I come from. People there are enormously valiant. Where, actually, do you come from?"

"From France," answered the hunter.

"Oh, Hm, then you are French?"

"Certainly."

"Hm, that's good."

Rodrigo turned away and discontinued the discussion. After a while he left the room but gave Reseda a wink to follow him. He went to the store room.

"Did you hear who he is?"

"Yes, he is French," answered Reseda.

"I have to warn you, then. You know that Napoleon has brought over the Austrian Duke Maximilian who should become Emperor of Mexico."

"Certainly, everywhere one hears about that."

"Now I have to tell you that I have nothing against the Austrians and this Prince Max is a good person, but the Mexicans don't like him having been brought in by the French. They say that this Napoleon lll is a liar and won't keep his promises. Also that he would let down this Prince Max in the end. They don't want an Emperor, they want a President and that should be Juarez."

"The one who is now in Paso del Norte?"

"Yes, the Frenchmen would like to catch him. They have occupied the whole country and nearly caught him in Chihuahua. One hears that the French are to send a troop of men to get hold of him. We must be careful and beware of every Frenchman."

"But not you, surely, what have you to do with Juarez?"

"Oh, very much," he countered, looking important. "I, so far, have never told you that I have an extraordinary gift for politics ..."

"You?" interrupted his daughter in great amazement.

"Yes I. Where I come from, everybody is big in politics. Max is good but he cannot possibly stay on for long after Napoleon leaves. Juarez has asked America for a loan and as they don't want an Emperor in Mexico, they agreed to send us thirty million dollars. A few million are on the way already; they should be transported over land. Somehow the French got to know about it and it is probable that they want to intercept that consignment. It is quite possible that it will come to Ford Guadelupe and be hidden in our house. Juarez, therefore, is going to send a strong occupation here. We have to fear the French. They are going to send spies to listen to us. The man who sits in there, is a spy. He speaks little and always looks through the window to see what's happening outside. He's not even looking at you."

Reseda knew better but took care not to let on. "I don't believe that he has the eyes of a spy."

"Not the eyes of a spy? You are wrong. You should know that one can see at once that I am a diplomat and it is better that the French don't see me. He could read in my face that I belong to a higher class of diplomacy and become suspicious. You shall serve him by yourself but for heaven's sake don't let on that I am a supporter of Juarez."

Reseda suppressed a little smile and answered: "Don't worry. I've inherited the diplomatic genius from you. He won't catch me out."

"Yes, it is the heirloom from father to daughter. Go inside, I know that one can mislead an enemy with a little smile."

Reseda returned to her former place, where the guest during this long and strange discussion was sitting quite alone. The long silence that followed was oppressive and she decided to come straight to the point. "Are you really French, señor?"

"Yes," he replied, "do I look like a man who could lie to you, señorita?"

"Honestly, no. I thought it was said in fun, because the French are not liked in this area."

"I don't like them either."

"Ah!" she said, astonished, "but you are French yourself?"

"Yes, I was born in France but I shall never return to my fatherland.

"Were you forced to leave it?"

"No, I went voluntarily but I no longer have anything to do with my fatherland.

"That must be sad."

"Not as sad as her disloyalty and betraying me."

"Did you suffer from this?"

"Unfortunately."

At this, a melancholy expression was seen on his features but his answer only excited the interest of this beautiful girl even more. She asked: "Was it a sweetheart's disloyalty?"

"Unfortunately, yes"

"She must have been a heartless girl, señor."

"She has ill-treated me and darkened my life."

"You loved her very much?"

"Very much," he answered, simply. Just that attracted the tender-hearted girl. Someone else might have been discreet opposite a lady. Anyhow, she thought so.

"You should try to forget her, señor."

"It doesn't work. I don't love her anymore but she's made me so unhappy I can't possibly forget."

"I don't understand this, señor. How can you be unhappy when you don't love her anymore?"

"Because my misfortune is not a question of her disloyalty but her betrayal."

"Ah, she told lies about you?"

"No, señorita, it was the truth."

Reseda felt strange at these words. She could not account for her behaviour but continued asking: "It isn't true, is it? You were only speaking lightly?"

"Why should I speak lightly to you, señorita? No, no, I'm telling you the truth."

She lowered her head; there was disappointment in her face. Her voice sounded cooler than before when she said: "Please excuse my pestering you with my questions. But whenever you came to us, you were always still and sad. It was almost as if there were tears coming from your eyes."

"Yes, there are people who carry a flood of tears inside but are too proud to let anyone notice."

"Oh, I have noticed. I thought you would enjoy a friendly word. There are people who never feel like strangers to you. Have you ever felt this?"

"Yes, but only with you, señorita."

The girl blushed. He said apologetically: "You should not be offended by my words. If I have hurt you, then I shall go and never return."

"No, you must not do that," she replied quickly. "Only it would please me to see you a little less sad. If you don't want to tell me more, let me at least know your name."

"You can call me Mason, señorita."

"Mason? Yes, that is a French name. And your first name?"

"My first name is Gerard."

"Gerard? Just like the Black Gerard about which my father was talking. You have a black beard like the one he is supposed to have. Can you tell me the meaning of that name?"

"It means: the powerful or the defender, that's what my teacher has told me."

"The powerful? Yes, that fits you, and someone who is powerful can be a defender."

"Unfortunately, I was not – exactly the opposite is true."

"What do you mean?"

Gerard looked sadly into the distance and replied: "I was a garrotteur."

"A garrotteur? I do not understand. What is the meaning of that?"

"To your innocent mind, this word is unknown. Please know, señorita, that in the big towns there are thousands who do not know in the evening where to get a piece of bread the next morning. Worse still, those who said in the evening: If you don't steal then you will have to be hungry tomorrow. They are the slaves of crime. Many of them are not guilty. The father brings up the son and the mother brings up the daughter to crime. They don't develop a feeling for right or wrong. They are the predators of mankind."

"My God, that is indeed sad."

"Sadder than you think."

"And you, señor? You wanted to speak about yourself?"

"Certainly, I myself was such a predator."

"Impossible!" Reseda jumped up with shock.

"It is true, I do not accuse anyone but I listened to my father. We were poor and learned to despise work. My father was weak and stole for the family to live. Originally I was a blacksmith. I was strong and garrotted, that means that I went out at night and pulled a rope around people's necks so that I could empty their pockets."

"Oh, my God, how terrible," stammered Reseda, trembling. She was pale as death itself. There was the man, the only one she was prepared to love and he tells her he has been a criminal. Why this awful frankness? All her limbs shuddered.

"Yes, it is terrible," continued Gerard Mason, "but it became worse, I loved a girl, we both loved each other and I gave her everything I robbed, but she became disloyal. She met a refined man whom she preferred. Together they squandered everything I had robbed. When I threatened her, she told me she would tell the police about me."

"Did you kill her?"

"No," he countered contemptuously. I went away and worked. I suffered and I fought. I was the worst opponent of myself, but I decided to become an honest person. And I remained like that. When I aspire seriously I see it through. But in the presence of good people I became aware of my misdeeds and my conscience drove me away from home. Now all I want is to atone for my sins and die."

A noiseless silence followed. In the eyes of the girl a tear welled up. Was it a tear of pain or was it the reflection of the bible word from the repenting sinner, about whom there is more satisfaction or joy in heaven than for ninety-nine just ones. She took a deep breath, looked at him seriously and asked: "But señor, why are you telling me that?"

"I will tell you," he answered. When I thought that I loved Mignon and was disappointed, I went to America and wandered many years in mountains, deserts and prairies. I became a hunter and a scout with a good name. There in the solitude I learned to know my heart. And when I saw you, I knew what true love is and I couldn't be without seeing you. It was pulling me toward you. But now when I see your eyes full of sympathy, it awakens the consciousness of my duty. You must not give your heart to an unworthy person. Señorita, I've told you what I have been, so you should learn to detest me. Besides, I feel as if I had spoken to God himself. He who acknowledges his sins and repents, he'll be forgiven. I shall go now and I shall never return. You will be saved from pollution by a damned soul. But I ask you not to tell anybody. It would harm many people to whom I am useful and I would have to leave this area."

Gerard took his rifle and prepared to leave. Reseda also stood up and blocked his exit. Her face grew paler than before. "Señor," she said, "you have been honest, be honest again and tell me whether you are a French spy?"

"No, I am not a French spy."

"And you are not supporting the French?"

"No, I hate Napoleon who rules by blood and lies, who is about to lead to ruin an honest prince. But his time will come. I support the Mexicans and I love Juarez. Is that enough for you, señorita?"

"Yes, I'm satisfied, and unhappy."

"I'm sorry. Farewell then."

"Do you really want to go."

"Yes, for ever, from you but not from Guadelupe."

He looked deep into her eyes, both of them had tears in their eyes. He felt he could pull her into his arms without her resisting but he controlled himself. He must not chain her fate to his. He went.

When he had left, Reseda stayed on the same spot and broke into sobs. Her whole body trembled. "Yes, he is powerful," she cried, "he conquered himself. How difficult it must have been for him. How difficult it will be for me – perhaps impossible now, all the more impossible now."

Gerard still heard her sobbing before he mounted his horse, pulled it up and jumped over the fence toward the water.---

Chapter 21

CHIHUAHUA

GERARD wanted to atone for his sins not with sack cloth and ashes but with the gun in his fists which enabled him to eradicate the criminals of the prairie. He preferred not to disclose to Reseda that he himself was Black Gerard. In the middle of the prairie he met Flying Horse, the Red Indian Chief.

"I come from Paso del Norte from the chief of the Mexicans, Juarez, to whom I have reported that I shall bring five hundred Apache warriors to regain Chihuahua. I shall meet you in one week from now at the big oak tree on the Tamis Mountains." "Good. I shall visit señorita Emilia in Chihuahua to bring her some money from Juarez; she is doing a valuable job."

"May the Great Spirit protect my white brother. Howgh!" With this Red Indian expression to end a speech or sentence, meaning 'that's that', he went on his way.

Gerard continued on his way to the occupied town of Chihuahua which he reached when darkness of night had already settled. It takes a man like Gerard to go unseen through the chain of posts surrounding the town. Soon he was at a garden that seemed familiar to him. He swung himself over the fence, ducked down and uttered the call of the black headed vulture three times. A dark female figure came nearer. "Who is there?"

"Mexico," he whispered.

"And who is coming?"

"Juarez."

"Wait a little." After these words the figure removed herself for about a quarter of an hour. When she returned, she came over to Gerard and handed him a monk's cowl which he put on. Then she said: "Today you'll have to be more careful because the major is visiting her."

"Is he there already?"

"No, he'll be there in two hours."

"Good; here's my rifle, take good care of it."

"When are you coming back?"

"I don't know that yet. I'll wake you when I come back." Gerard wrapped himself in the cowl and stepped to the left, where there was a small open door in the wall. Then over a yard where there was an entrance between columns. He went up the steps and stopped before a door, having passed other doors before. He knocked and heard a loud: "Come in."

The door opened. A brilliant light flooded toward him and in its midst stood a lady of extraordinary beauty. The fur hunter, who had taken off his cowl, stepped toward her.

"At long last you are here again, dear Gerard," she called out. Emilia pulled him to the divan and sat down next to him. He in his dirty blouse, she in a lovely silk dress.

"You intended to go out," he began the conversation.

"Yes, to a party in two hours and I'm expecting the major, but I forego this pleasure gladly."

"Which pleasure do you want to forego, the party or the major," he asked smilingly.

"The former The visit of the major is no pleasure."

"There seem to be important things in preparation. I hope to find the key to them here in Chihuahua."

"What's the situation with Juarez?"

"Up to now, not very good. So far he was forced to a defence situation, but he's waiting for a favourable moment to advance. That will happen when the promised and expected money from America arrives."

"Money? I wish it would arrive soon. Juarez, you should know, owes me three months wages. I have to lead a prosperous life in order to serve him. I owe money already and it won't take long before I am unable to work here."

"Yes, Juarez is without finances now. The fact that he is sending you money shows he appreciates the value of your services."

"He has sent money?" she asked excitedly.

"Yes, through me. I have carried it with me for two weeks but you must excuse me, I couldn't come sooner."

"You are excused, dear Gerard, I know that you do your best for me. How much is it?"

"Half a year's wages. Will that help?"

"Very much. Is it in paper money?"

"Yes, I couldn't carry that much in coins."

"I hope the money isn't North American. That could betray me."

"No, they are good English pounds."

"That's splendid and shows great care."

"Here, take it." Gerard pulled a parcel from his boots and handed it to her. She then offered him a hearty meal that he accepted with thanks, declaring that he was very hungry. While he was eating she talked about casual things. After he'd finished she seated him next to her on the divan.

"Let's talk about our business. Do you know there's someone new who aspires to become president?"

"Yes, I have heard of this Carujo whose daughter seems very active on his behalf. She must think of herself as beautiful because she distributes thousands of her pictures to recruit supporters," said Gerard.

"I don't think he can harm our case very much. He seems to have money and Mexicans are partial to that."

"Have you got a picture of her?"

"Yes," she said and handed him one."

He looked at it and laughed out loud. "This could serve as a study in ugliness. I don't understand how she can be so smug about it."

"Have you other news? she asked.

"Napoleon is finally talking to America about the fate of Mexico."

"That means the Archduke Max is at the end of his career as an Emperor. The United States can't tolerate an Emperor of Mexico."

"The big question is whether Maximillian will leave Mexico as well or whether he does that in time?" he mused.

"You must hide now, the major is punctual. He'll be here in two minutes. How long will it take you to copy the documents?"

"I don't know, give me an hour."

"Good, in one hour I'll claim I have a head-ache."

Gerard left through a side-door into a small room soon he heard the major's voice. He then left the room and went through a long corridor into the major's apartment. Emilia had given him the main key that opened all the doors of the house she had rented. He locked the door from the inside, and went though a couple of chambers into a room with the major's writing desk. There he made copies of various important documents. After forty-five minutes he had finished and returned to the small room adjacent to Emilia's reception area. He heard the major wishing Emilia speedy recovery of her head-ache and asking her to inform him when she felt better. Then he said good bye and left. Gerard did not immediately enter her room. The major might have forgotten something. Emilia herself opened his door. "Are you there?"

"Yes, did he tell you something?"

"No."

"What a pity. Just when I have come to find out about any important plans. Never mind, the documents I've copied will be of great importance to Juarez."

"Did you discover something?"

"Yes, something important."

Emilia looked at him, expecting him to tell her about his discoveries. He said there was no time because what he'd learned need quick actions. I can only tell you that Bazaine has ordered that in the next few days three companies will go from here to take possession of Ford Guadelupe.

"That's bad."

"Pah, I'll be able to see them off. I've not told you that I shall have five hundred Apaches at my disposal that my friend Flying Horse will bring to me. Now I must leave."

He left to exchange the cowl for his rifle from the gardener lady he had met before. He did not anticipate the danger awaiting him. ---

When Gerard crept between the French posts, he passed a soldier who thought he had heard something. "It was almost as if somebody passed by. It was probably an animal," he mumbled to himself. After a while he felt like smoking a cigarette. By the flame of his lighter he saw some tracks. They looked quite fresh. He used up a few more matches and saw the direction of the man who made the tracks. "This rascal went between us and into town. He probably had bad intentions. I must report that," he whispered to himself.

He went to his officer and told him about his discovery. The officer went to the commander who took this matter seriously. He went to the soldier and looked at the tracks until they disappeared on firm ground where he could no longer follow them.

"He went into town but not out yet," said the commandant. "Where he got through he will try to come out again. A dozen of you lie down on the ground and wait. You should catch him." With this order he went back to the party that was still in swing.

Hour after hour they waited. He must have come through somewhere else, thought the lieutenant, when a slight sound of moving feet was just about audible. Soon they saw a figure who wanted to get by quietly and carefully. At this moment, more than twenty fists held him down. "*Nom d'un chien!*" said the man.

"We want you," countered the sergeant.

Gerard made tremendous efforts to free himself but there were too many of them to hold him down. He didn't want to use weapons. They might make his position worse.

"You can let go, people, I don't want to escape. I have no reason to hide from you."

The lieutenant put a light on him. "Ah, he is armed. Take his weapons and bind him."

They used his belt to tie his arms against his body but every experienced westman knows how to hold his arms so as to make a very close fit impossible. When Gerard got up from the ground, he noticed it would be possible with a jerk to withdraw his right hand. The left would follow easily.

"Who are you?" began the sergeant.

"A vaquero," maintained Mason.

"You don't look like one. Where are you coming from?"

"From Aldama."

Aldama was only a few hours ride from Chihuahua.

"What did you want in this town?"

"To visit my bride."

Why did you not come the correct way?"

"Did you never go secretly to your girl?"

"You speak French perfectly, how come?"

"Very simple, I am from Paris."

"A Parisian and a vaquero in Aldama? That's suspicious. Let's see what the commander will make of you."

The walk was in the dark and if he could get his arm out of the belt, he could flee. But that would be without his weapons. His rifle was close to his heart. It had accompanied him for many years, it fed and guarded him. Should he abandon it? Never. A prairie man looks after his rifle like himself. For that reason, Gerard went along without trying to escape. He hoped there would be another way.

The headquarters were in a building that we would call a town hall. The commander lived here and the party was there too. On the ground floor were a number of guards with a bottle and a few non-commissioned officers; among them a woman who was past her youth but still good looking. The entertainment was noisy.

"Yes, Juarez is finished," proclaimed a sergeant."

"Pah, who cares about him," said another. "The whole campaign was child's play. It was like swatting flies with a handkerchief. I wouldn't do any more for this Austrian Archduke."

"For him? Nothing was done for him. He's only a dummy to make other people think that it's not a French conquest. He'll probably leave soon and Bazaine will be president of Mexico. He'll create frictions and Napoleon will be forced to step in and then declare the land as a French possession."

"And the other powers?"

"The matter will be concluded by then and nobody can change it. Many will feel the knife, including Black Gerard, that rascal."

"Yes, he's a rascal. Our army has to fear him more than ten other spies. He's more notorious than ... hallo who are they bringing here?"

Gerard was being pushed through the door. His glance fell on the non-commissioned officer and then to the woman. Shocked he realised it was Mignon, his former beloved. That's what had become of her.

"Who is this man?" asked the non-commissioned officer.

"A vaquero from Aldama, that's what he said. I think somebody else is in this blouse."

The woman arose, looked at the prisoner and called: "A vaquero? Don't let him fool you. He is Gerard Mason, a blacksmith from Paris."

"Mason, from Paris?"

"Yes, he was a garrotteur."

"That he's from Paris, he has admitted. This mademoiselle has told us you were a garrotteur. Is it true?"

"Do you take notice of what a broad tells you?"

"A broad?" called Mignon. Rascal I'll scratch your eyes out." She was going to attack Gerard but the sergeant intervened.

"Stop it," he said. Who insults you, insults us all but first I have to report it to the commander."

He was going when a lieutenant appeared at the door: "What's this noise and who's that prisoner?"

The soldiers greeted him and the sergeant reported: "We have the man who went into town thee hours ago and then tried to creep out again. He told us that he is a vaquero from Aldama, but we know now that he is Gerard Mason from Paris,"

The officer was taken aback and called out: "Gerard? Soldiers, do you know whom you have caught? This man is probably Black Gerard who did enormous damage to us.

"Black Gerard!" they called.

"The officer waved to them to be quiet and asked the prisoner: "Was my supposition right?"

Pride stirred in Gerard. Should he lie and deny his name? No, but an admission would worsen his situation. That also wouldn't do. He wanted to know how the commander would receive him. He shrugged his shoulders and countered: "Investigate, Lieutenant."

"You address me lieutenant Sir. Understood?" bawled the officer. "It doesn't matter whether you admit it or not. I shall soon know. It is known that the butt of Black Gerard's rifle is made of solid gold. Have you taken his weapon?"

"Here it is," reported the sergeant.

"Take a knife: lead is soft, see whether there is gold beneath."

Gerard saw himself betrayed. What people said about his rifle was true. This rifle butt served not only as a weapon, it was, when needed, his purse too. Sometimes he had to cut off a bit for payment. That made it famous.

"Ah, *Diable,* that is why the rifle is so heavy, "said the sergeant. He made a slight cut into the outer shell of the butt. "Gold pure gold," he called out in astonishment.

"It is Black Gerard," said the lieutenant proudly. I shall report this important event to the commander myself. He went and those staying behind looked at the prisoner with timorous awe. There was complete silence. Even Mignon kept quiet. Her former beloved was a famous and feared man. The lieutenant went upstairs where the commander, officers and many Mexican men and ladies were enjoying themselves at a party. When the lieutenant appeared, all eyes were directed towards him. One could see that he was the bearer of important news.

"So excited, Lieutenant? What's happened?" questioned the commander.

The lieutenant took an official posture. "I have the honour to report to Monsieur Colonel that we have caught Black Gerard."

"Black Gerard, is it possible?"

There was general excitement. The French were delighted to get their hands on a dangerous enemy, while the news had the opposite effect on the Mexicans. Had they really caught the famous party member? If so, Juarez had received a great loss and the fatherland a great setback. But all were united in wanting to see the feared man. When the commander asked the lieutenant to bring Gerard into his office, he was approached by one of the ladies.

"Monsieur, surely you will not do this to us? You will not be so unchivalrous as to deny the ladies sight of this man?"

The commander thought for a moment. He would enjoy showing the prisoner to the party and he ordered the lieutenant to bring the prisoner and his famous rifle before him.

The lieutenant went and, after a while of silent anticipation, returned with Gerard, accompanied by a group of armed soldiers.

"Step here," ordered the commander.

Gerard made no move to follow this command.

"Step forward, I said!"

The colonel pointed with his finger where he wanted the prisoner to go to. Gerard did not follow this order either, so the lieutenant gave him a push. Like lightning, Gerard turned around, lifted his leg and gave him such a powerful kick in the stomach that the lieutenant staggered back and fell to the floor, dropping his weapons in the process.

"I will teach you not to push Black Gerard around."

This incident and the words of the prisoner caused great excitement. The French saw one of their comrades insulted and the Mexicans were convinced that the daring man was lost. The ladies were enraptured by the audacity of a man tied up and behaving so bravely in the midst of his enemies. The officer wanted to throw himself against Gerard but was ordered by the commander to be calm.

"Let's forget for a moment this defiant act. The punishment will soon follow. I promise you he will be whipped until blood spurts from his wounds. Turning to Gerard he asked: Why didn't you obey?"

The prisoner looked at him calmly and replied: "I am not in your pay but a man of the free prairie to whom respect is due and I will not answer until I'm addressed politely."

The commander smiled in a superior manner. "I'm not accustomed to speak politely to people who kick my officers."

"That makes no difference to me. A capable and experienced prairie man with dexterity and skills stands no lower than an officer. It is my duty to teach the lieutenant to behave properly in the company of ladies."

"I shall address you politely because the ladies want to hear you speak. You are Black Gerard?"

"Yes."

"What did you do in town?"

"I paid someone a visit."

"Who is this someone?"

"That is my secret."

"To what purpose?"

"To chase out the enemy?"

"Ah, who do you regard as the enemy?"

"The French."

"I must say that you are very honest or should I call it impudent. You are calling the French enemies, while you are French yourself."

"I was French, but never a tool of the imperial thirst for blood. I love Mexico and its inhabitants, and I gladly risk my life to free them from the present illegal government."

The commander was amazed at Gerard's apparent contempt for death. Then he said: "You will not be able to do much for this so-called liberation. What you have said so far is enough to condemn you. You will leave this hall only to be shot. Before that you will be whipped until your flesh falls off your bones. That is an additional punishment for the kick. Have you anything to say concerning your last will?"

"Not now. I ask you to leave it to me to make my last will. A prairie man is in this case independent."

"You are insane. Where do you come from?"

"From Paris, like so many insanities."

"Don't mock, your judgement could be even harder. Have you many connections in town?"

"So many you'd be frightened if you knew."

"It's known you are friends with Juarez. Do you know his plans?"

"His and yours."

"Don't show off. What would you know about our plans?"

"Everything. The future will prove that."

"I've had enough about your big mouth. Let's talk about something else. Those weapons are yours?"

"Yes."

"Show them to me, Lieutenant."

The rifle, the two revolvers and the knife were laid out before the commandant. He lifted the rifle and examined the butt. "This is gold. Where does it come from?"

"I've discovered a gold vein in the mountains."

"Would you sell your knowledge of it?"

"Why? I thought you intend to kill me?"

"Certainly. But you may have relatives."

"I wouldn't tell the location of this place even if you offered me the full price. No decent Mexican would do that."

"You are malicious. Have you killed Frenchmen with this rifle?"

"Yes."

"How many?"

"I only count game, never Frenchmen."

"*Morbleu!*" The commander flared up. "Think before whom you stand."

"Before a man I do not fear."

"Well, I see for some reason you seek death. You will have it but not as soon as you think. We can find out a lot from you but as I know from your present behaviour, you are not willing to part with any information. So I order torture for you."

"What do you want to know?"

"Before anything: who are your acquaintances?"

"That, of course, you will never know."

"We'll see about that," laughed the officer mockingly. "Next, you will be good enough to tell us the plans of your friend Juarez."

"There's no need, you'll find out yourself once they are carried out."

The Mexicans listened with bated breath to every word, while the French ground their teeth with fury and shame that their colonel had let himself fall into such an outrageous conversation. The officer himself felt furious. He jumped up and called: "My patience is at an end. I only talked to you to show you to these ladies and gentlemen. Now I'll show you how I tame a fellow like yourself. You will receive fifty lashes and then you will be brought before me again."

Gerard shook his head, his eyes sparkled. "I have proved to you that I do not tolerate being pushed or lashed, because I would be dishonoured."

"What do I care about your honour? Take him away."

"And I don't care about your honour either," called Gerard. "I'll show you who gets the beating and the dishonour."

The next moment he pulled his arm from under the belt, tore the straps from the commander's shoulders and gave him such a blow with his fist that he fell to the ground. He then grasped his weapons. "Here, taste my gold," he called and threw himself against the soldiers. With a single blow of his rifle butt he drove them apart and made toward the open window. "Good night, señoritas," he called out laughingly, before disappearing through the window into the dark night.

All this happened faster than could be described. The soldiers were still rolling on the floor. The officers and all the others present were paralyzed for a few moments then one of them shouted: "After him, quickly."

With this call the officers ran down but no-one dared to jump through the window. Only the Mexicans remained and went to the commander. "That was a blow," someone said. "I believe he is dead."

"No," said another, "he's only stunned."

A few ladies had fainted; others stood by and exchanged admiring remarks about Gerard, others hurried to the window to see whether he had escaped. They did not need to worry. Gerard had reached the ground unharmed, jumped on the nearest horse and reached the next corner before his pursuers reached the street. Their shots in the dark did no harm but alerted the soldiers who guarded the town. Soon the outposts called: "Stop, who's there?" The next second he'd passed them, but he felt that one of their shots had hit the horse. With his spurs he made the animal storm on further into the field, before it broke down possibly preventing an unhappy fall. He had now gone far enough to make his way on foot. He knew the area and soon reached the spot where he'd left his own horse. He now made his way over Guadelupe to El Paso del Norte. ---

Chapter 22

THE RIFLE BUTT

---

*I*T was a Sunday afternoon. Old Rodrigo, as usual, sat at the window and began a conversation with his daughter the usual way.

"Terrible rain."

As usual, his daughter gave no answer. He continued. "Just enough to drown." Again no answer. He turned to her and asked angrily: "Did you say something? Am I not right?"

"Oh yes," was Reseda's short answer."

"If I drowned outside you wouldn't mind?"

"But father," she called out.

"Why? Isn't such thing possible? Take the case that I drowned. What would you do? How would you be able to keep the house and the business? Without a man? Impossible."

Her father's train of thought was amusing. Reseda had to laugh and joked: "You are not going out to drown, just to prove that I need a man?"

"Why not? A good father must do everything to bring his child to reason. But – ah who is coming there?"

There was the sound of hoofs outside. The rider stopped in front of the door. "Ah the ragged fellow, the spy. I'm not going out for him."

The new arrival was Gerard. Reseda blushed when he came in. Old Rodrigo barely answered his greeting but Reseda gave him a friendly nod. He asked for a julep which Reseda brought to him. Silence ensued, then the old fellow started again: "Terrible rain."

"Yes," said Gerard lost in thought.

"Enough to drown you."

"Not that bad."

"What do you say? You have a different opinion?" Rodrigo turned to look at the guest angrily. He'd forgotten the diplomatic smile. The trapper's clothing dripped water on the floor. "We couldn't drown, you say? Look at this puddle. If two more like that came in, we'd surely drown."

Gerard noticed the puddle on the floor and apologised. "Excuse me, señor Rodrigo, you wouldn't want me stay outside?"

"No, but you could have put on dry clothes. Haven't you got a wife who looks after such things?"

"No."

"You have no wife? Well that says it all. You make other people's floor wet. A man should marry. Am I right or not?"

"I heartily agree with that."

"I can see you have brains, although you're not as good a hunter as Black Gerard. I'd like to meet him."

The trapper smiled. "You should have been in Chihuahua. He's been there."

"Don't tell me fibs. The French are there."

"He was there because of them. I've heard about it."

"What did he want of them?"

"To discover their plans."

"To spy on them? Nonsense! I'd rather believe they send their spies here."

"He was there and they've caught him."

"*Caramba*! Is that true?"

"Yes," declared Gerard, smiling a bit. He was pleased Rodrigo cared about him.

The old fellow noticed his smile and asked angrily: "You're pleased he's caught because you're also French?"

"Yes, I'm French, although I don't approve Napoleon sending his army to Mexico."

Rodrigo forgot his political talent and walked over to the guest. "You think I believe that? I believe that you yourself are a French spy.

You pretend not to like your emperor but I am not so stupid to believe that. You've betrayed yourself."

Reseda paled, she was frightened but Gerard asked calmly: "How did I betray myself?"

"Because you enjoyed his capture."

"He enjoyed it himself it gave him the chance to rub their faces in the mud before he escaped."

"Ah, really? Please tell us."

Gerard now told them his adventure without mentioning Emilia or that he himself was the hero of this story. Rodrigo listened to him intently.

"Yes," he called at the end. "This Black Gerard is a devil of a boy; they wouldn't be able to keep him. But how is it you enjoyed the fact of his escape. Aren't you a Frenchman yourself?"

"Certainly, I am born in France but I love Mexico and I'll stay here and do my utmost to drive the French out again."

"You?" asked the old man, "you'd better leave these things to a man like Black Gerard. I have a lot to thank him for. He's cleared the roads of various unwanted people, mainly rabble. Do you know whether he is married?"

"As much as I know, he's single."

"Hm, that's a good move that I approve, but it must change. A man like him must have a wife who brings him property. Then he has a home. Do you know where he likes to hunt?"

"Wherever there's game. I've learned he'll come to this area."

"Does he perhaps drink julep?"

"The most, one little glass full."

"Whether much or little; who drinks julep in Ford Guadelupe, must come to this tavern."

"I am convinced that he'll come to you."

"Really? Are you listening Reseda?"

Rodrigo's daughter did not answer. The way her father talked about marriage was embarrassing. "Well, didn't you hear it?" he muttered angrily.

"Yes," she replied.

"Good. And the best of it is, I'll recognise him at his rifle. The butt is pure gold and he cuts a piece off whenever he wants to pay for something. It's quite a different thing from your shooting-stick. Where do you actually live?"

"Everywhere and nowhere."

"Where will you sleep tonight in this weather?"

"Here."

The old one pulled a long face. "Here with me? Have you any money? You are drinking only one glass of julep and that's no sign of riches."

"Father!" The daughter reproached her progenitor.

"What is it?" he answered. "Yes, you have a sympathetic heart but I want to make sure. If this señor pays for it in advance, he can stay here."

"I shall pay beforehand. How much is it?"

"One quartillo."

"Only one quartillo? The Trapper asked in amazement.

"Yes, because you will sleep on straw."

"Why? I can pay for a bed.

"That's not on, look at yourself."

Reseda blushed, but did not dare to make a remark.

"Good," said Gerard. "Here is a quartillo for the straw and a tlaco for the julep. Are you happy now?"

"Yes."

One tlaco is half of a quartillo.

"As everything seems to be in order, may I go to sleep now?"

"Already? During daylight? What's the matter with you?"

"I'm tired. You'll agree that this can happen to a hunter?"

"To a good hunter. What did you shoot today?"

"Nothing yet."

"There you are. But I won't keep you; sleep as long as you want. Reseda, take the señor to the vaqueros."

Reseda got up and waited at the door. "Good night, señor Rodrigo," said Gerard as he took hold of his rifle.

"Good night señor," answered the oldy. He sat again at the window and continued his boring weather observations.

"Excuse my father," said Reseda, "he is sometimes a bit odd but he is a good person."

"There's nothing to apologise for, señorita, he can direct his guests where he wants. I'll sleep well on straw because I haven't slept for six days."

"Oh, it is a miracle you don't fall over, come quickly."

"Stay indoors, señorita. You'll get wet. I'll find my way to the vaqueros."

"Do you really believe that I'll let you sleep on straw? No, come with me."

The girl went upstairs and Gerard followed. Upstairs she unlocked a door and let him enter. The room looked almost too good for a guest. "That's no bedroom for strangers," he said astonished.

"Actually not," she smiled. Only relations of ours sleep here when they come for a visit. Sit down for a moment; are you hungry?"

"No, but very tired."

Reseda went out for short while and he sat in an upholstered chair. In his wet clothes he didn't fit in to this pretty room. Tiredness closed his eyes. When Reseda returned with a candlestick and water for the washbasin, he was fast asleep. She looked at Gerard sympathetically. "Poor fellow," she was sorry for the hunter. "How tired he must have been to fall asleep so fast. Here's his rifle, I have to convince myself.

Quietly she took his rifle. It was very heavy. She looked at the butt and saw the place were the French sergeant had cut into the lead.

"Gold, really gold," she whispered. "My presentiment didn't deceive me. I'm so glad. But he doesn't want to talk about it, so I'll be quiet too." She put the rifle down and touched the sleeper to wake him up.

"Reseda," he whispered without waking up.

She blushed, but touched him again. "Ah, I fell asleep. Excuse me, señorita."

"There's nothing to apologise for. I wish you a long rest and a good night, señor Mason."

"Good night, señorita."

Reseda went down where her father still sat at the window. She thought about the sleeper and the discovery of his identity. Her pondering was interrupted by her father's voice. "Damn weather."

"Yes, dear father."

"Outside is bad and inside even worse."

"How is that?"

"How? What can I see here? The same bottles the same glasses, the same furniture and you, nothing else."

"What else do you want to see?" Her question was rush. Her father lay in wait for this question.

"What do I want to see? A son-in-law, what else. I need a son-in-law. Can't you see?

"Is he so important for you?"

"Not to me but to you."

"To me?" she laughed. "What would I do with a son-in-law, I haven't got a daughter."

"Nonsense, with a son-in-law one can talk or even let him feel when you are angry."

"If he will stand for it."

"Why not? If you don't take one soon, I'll get you one. Guess who that might be?"

"Who can guess? Tell me."

"Who other than Black Gerard."

"Black – Gerard? She asked slowly and with a peculiar emphasis.

"Yes, he. He's a capable man, just as my son-in-law should be."

"But if he should look like the hunter whom I just led to his sleeping quarters?

"Girl, don't make silly jokes. Black Gerard looks different. Don't talk about this one. When did he shoot anything? What can he drink? What can he pay? Now he lies on straw and sleeps the day away. Oh no, Black Gerard is definitely different.

Gerard was the first to come down in the morning. Reseda heard him and came to wish him a good morning. "Did you sleep well, señor?" she asked.

"Very well, thank you, señorita," he replied leaning his rifle on the table.

"You haven't eaten for a long time, shall I bring you a cup of chocolate?"

"Yes, please and a hearty breakfast."

Reseda went into the kitchen and her father appeared. He was sullen in the morning. "Good morning," he greeted sour faced.

"Good morning," answered Gerard.

"Do you sleep that long in the prairie?" Rodrigo enquired."

"Perhaps."

"No wonder I've never seen a piece of game in your hand. A good diplomat can see at first glance that you are not a good westman but a marmot."

Gerard took this outburst with equanimity. Rodrigo sat down at the window. Before long he started again: "Miserable weather."

Gerard did not answer. After a while Rodrigo continued: "Almost like yesterday, I don't believe he will come."

"Who?"

"Black Gerard, who else? You said yourself he is coming to this area."

"Oh, the weather wouldn't bother him, if he wants to come."

"Well, perhaps. You're coming here lately quite regularly; you haven't got your eye on my daughter, have you?"

"Both of them," declared Gerard calmly.

"Take your shooting-stick and get out. Don't ever come back or I'll scalp you."

"Good, I shall obey, señor Rodrigo but as I am now, you will not chase me away, will you?"

"How do you mean?"

"I mean in this weather it doesn't matter how I look. People don't look at that but if the weather improves, this bad clothing is noted. Haven't you got something better for me in your store?"

"The old man frowned. "You're not going to beg from me, are you?"

"No, I've saved enough for a suit."

"You may have enough for a cotton pair of trousers and a cotton jacket, but for your size I have only one outfit and you can't possibly afford it."

"What's it made of?"

"Trousers, hunting shirt and hunting jacket made of stag leather, a hat of short cut beaver fur, a belt and all that goes with it."

"Hm, you make my mouth water."

"Let it water, you won't get the suit."

"But you don't mind me having a look?"

"Well, I suppose that will do no harm. Maybe you'll meet someone who can afford it, then you can send him to me."

"All right, let's go to your shop."

"Oh no, a man who drinks one julep and has his eyes on my daughter can't go to my shop. I'll bring everything. Wait here before I ask you to go."

He soon brought the outfit and put it on the table. Gerard looked at it and found it suitable. "May I ask the price?"

"Why not? It is eighty dollars.

"All right, I'll buy it if you let me try it on."

"Not without money. You can't afford it."

"Who told you that? Please bring your gold scale."

"The scale is right here but where are your nuggets? he asked.

"I have no nuggets …"

"That's what I thought," said Rodrigo and began to gather the items on the table.

"Hold on for a minute, does it have to be nuggets I put on your scale?"

"What else?"

Reseda, who could hear the conversation, came out of the kitchen. She expected what was coming now and wanted to see her father's face.

Gerard took a knife, chopped off a piece of his rifle butt and put it on the scale. Rodrigo's eyes nearly popped out. He took Gerard's arm. "Señor, he asked. "Who are you?"

"The buyer of this suit," Gerard laughed.

Rodrigo stood there, open mouthed and rigid.

"Now, señor," Gerard smiled benignly, "is it such a bad rifle?"

"Then you must be --- must be …"

"Black Gerard" said Gerard Mason laughingly.

"But, why didn't you tell me sooner?"

"I had my fun."

"Oh what an ass I am." The old man hit his head with his fist. Reseda beamed.

"I thought you were a big diplomat," Gerard smiled.

"A big ass, but not a diplomat," admitted the old man "but I'll make it up to you, at once." He went to Reseda and pulled her toward Gerard. Here she is, you shall be my son-in-law. Reseda's face was deepest red. Gerard noticed it and shook his head.

314

"Señor Rodrigo, don't make a second mistake. The señorita has the right to choose a man she likes."

"But señor, why didn't you tell me who you are?" asked the embarrassed old man.

"Diplomacy, I didn't want people to know my whereabouts.

"You have disclosed it now, has anything changed?"

"Indeed it has," nodded Black Gerard. "Tell me señor Rodrigo, do you have a mayor in this town?"

"Yes, we do have a head of the town."

"Would you ask one of your vaqueros to ask him to come to you? It is of the greatest importance."

The mayor, a bald and unimposing man, came at once. "Hallo señor Rodrigo, what is so important that I have to come to you, instead of you calling on me?"

Rodrigo pointed at Gerard who had changed into the new suit and made an imposing impression. "This is señor Gerard Mason, also known as Black Gerard, who wishes to speak to you."

"It is an honour to meet you, I've heard a lot about you and how can I be of service?"

"How many men with rifles can you muster in case this town is attacked?"

"Heavens, is there such a possibility?"

"Unfortunately, yes. The French are sending three companies any day now to take Ford Guadelupe in order to be here before Juarez."

"I can't tell you exactly but there won't be more than one hundred."

"That would be enough to hold them for a while. In confidence, I have been so fortunate as to arrange five hundred Apaches coming here to help us."

"Oh, señor, how can we thank you?"

"By not creating a panic and by bringing these men here when I call for them."

The mayor went and Gerard took his rifle to leave as well. Reseda asked him whether he could let her know where he was going? Gerard looked into her face and saw anxiety, it made him happy. "Why señorita?"

315

Once more she blushed but kept silent. He took her hands and said: "Reseda, I really thank you. I can see your concern and that gives me courage to hope that you have forgiven my past."

The girl looked at him and countered warmly: "Your confession was so sincere that it would be a sin to be angry with you. Gerard. I only see what you are now and not what you have been."

He pressed her hand against his lips. He wanted to reply but was overcome with emotion. Then he left. With a pounding heart she looked until horse and rider disappeared at a bend of the road.---

Chapter 23

DOC IRONFIST RETURNS

---

*J*OSEFA Carujo sat in her armchair and smoked a Mexican cigarette. A messenger had told her to expect her father tonight. She fondly played with the thought of her father becoming the president of Mexico.

It was late that evening when she sent her maid servant to open the door when her father arrived. Suddenly her door opened and a strange man stepped in. After her initial shock she asked: "Who are you and what do you want?"

"The stranger asked with a hollow voice: "Does señor Carujo live here?"

"Yes, did you want him?"

"No, I want to see you."

"What do you want of me and how did you get in here?"

"Over the back wall."

This answer gave her a renewed shock. Only a thief or someone equally suspect, would come over the back wall. "Why didn't you use the main entrance?"

"I didn't want anybody to see me," he explained. "But now I know that it wasn't necessary, as my own daughter doesn't recognise me." With these words he took off a wig and his beard. He took her into his arms and gave her a kiss. This tenderness between them was rare.

"It is you? I really didn't recognise you."

"What's new?" asked José Carujo.

"On the order of the Emperor, I have to leave the country," answered his daughter.

"Ah, really? asked Carujo, unsurprised. "That's because of my posters, but you only have to go out of reach of this Emperor Max and nothing will happen to you. In any case we're leaving town today."

"Today? Why?"

"You will accompany me to the Hacienda del Alina."

"Is that so? To old Martin Wilson? What do you want there? He is our enemy."

"That's why I want to visit him."

"I don't understand," admitted Josefa.

"I'll tell you: I have three hundred armed men waiting for me. I chose the hacienda because it's a good starting point for my campaign."

"But if he defends himself?"

"Then he gets a bullet. You have to leave town anyway. Do you know where Juarez is?" enquired Carujo.

"I hear that he is north in El Paso del Norte."

"Good, I must become friendly with him. Together we'll be able to throw out the French; Emperor Maximilian is no real obstacle. I've learned that he gets a shipload of weapons and millions of English pounds. I'll intercept this load and will be doubly welcome to him."

"But if he finds out these weapons were for him in the first place?"

"Who should tell him?"

"I thought you wanted to become president?"

"If the time comes, he will disappear," he said with a smile and a wave of his hand.

"Do you know who brings these weapons and the money?"

"Yes, our old friend Lord Castlepool with his own ship that will not belong to him much longer."

Josefa was enthusiastic. "You are riding with three hundred men; I shall need my servant with me."

"She'll have to stay here and you'll look after yourself."

"The daughter of a president without a servant?"

"I'm not president yet Afterward you can have as many servants as you like. By the way, the treasure of the Mixtekas is near the hacienda.

I'll capture a few of them and with a little torture they'll tell me its whereabouts. ---

After fourteen years in exile on the lonely island in the ocean, Stenton or Doc Ironfist, his widely known name in the West, and his companions landed in Guaymas. They intended to go to the Hacienda del Alina. Captain Wright received the order to take the ship to Vera Cruz where he would be given new orders. They had learned that the City of Mexico was occupied by the French and that there was a citizen's war. There was also the danger of running into marauding gangs. It was therefore important to acquire good weapons. At Stenton's suggestion they chose not to take the road over the Sierra de los Alamos, but to reach Chihuahua. They did not suspect that this town was already taken by the French army. When they learned this fact, Don Manuel said: "We have suffered too much to put ourselves into danger."

"I am convinced the French would not harm us, but there is danger from the guerrillas who surround the town."

Alva suggested: "I have relations with a guest house not far from here in Ford Guadelupe, may be we could make our way through this Ford?"

"Who are these people?" asked Stenton.

"It is a señor Rodrigo with his daughter Reseda. He had married the sister of my father's wife and he is English, though a bit peculiar."

"What is his peculiarity?"

"It was more than fourteen years ago that I visited him. He started every conversation with the weather and ended up with a wish for a son-in law. I wonder whether he has succeeded by now."

"I wouldn't mind sleeping in a proper bed after all these years," said Stenton.

The others, with the exception of Buff-he, agreed. "But I'll stay with you until we reach the Mixtekas," he said.

It was not until the next morning that they reached the Rio Grande where Ford Guadelupe was built. "It can't be far now," said Stenton, let's hurry. ---

It was a wonderful sunrise and Rodrigo woke up early. He strolled outside the gate of the town's surrounding wall. While he enjoyed the splendour of the morning, he saw a small point in the distance on the river becoming bigger as it came nearer. "Ah, a boat with only one man," he growled in wonderment over the speed it drew nearer. The rower must have inordinate strength to be able to row against the stream at such speed.

"Good morning," he greeted in English.

"*Buenas dias*," answered Rodrigo in Spanish.

"That is Ford Guadelupe, I reckon?"

"Yes."

"A small dump?"

"Not large."

"A lot of military here?"

"None at all."

"Is there a store or boarding house in this place?"

"Yes, into the gate and then the third house on the left," Rodrigo directed the stranger to his own place.

When he returned, he saw the man sitting there with a drink. There was deep silence in the room only interrupted by unrestrained and incessant tobacco spitting. This man was passionately chewing tobacco. A Yankee who did not care whether it disturbed others if he was spitting or just clearing his throat. Rodrigo was eager to know who this stranger was. He started the conversation: "Lovely weather."

The stranger answered with a grunt, the meaning of which was impossible to guess.

Rodrigo repeated after a while: "Incomparable weather."

"Hrrrmmmrrruhm," coughed the stranger.

Rodrigo turned around. "Did you say something?"

"No, but you did."

This answer made it difficult for Rodrigo to continue the questions but not for very long. "Today even nicer than yesterday."

"Pshtishshshsh!" The stranger spat again.

Rodrigo turned around again and said: "I didn't understand you, señor."

The stranger rolled the tobacco from the right side of his cheek into the left, pointed to his mouth and spat the brown tobacco broth across the table near Rodrigo's nose on to the window. The landlord, shocked, pulled his head back and called out: "Señor, the spittoon is next to the cupboard!"

"Don't need one."

"I believe that. Whoever spits at the window doesn't need a spittoon but this is not the custom here."

"Well, open the window." It sounded so indifferent that Rodrigo's blood began to boil. He controlled himself and asked: "Are you staying here?"

"Hardly, I calculate."

"I mean today?"

"Yes."

"Do you have any business here?"

"Pshtishshshsh," the man spat again exactly over Rodrigo's head on to an oil painting.

"What do you think señor? You spoiled my oil painting."

"Take it away."

"Is that a reasonable answer to my question?"

"Yes, whoever is so pushy with his questions will be spat at."

"Do you know that you are a ruffian?"

"No. Get me another drink."

Rodrigo poured him another drink. "Do you want to stay here tonight? May I ask that?"

"I will think about it. Is it secure here?"

"From whom?"

"Hm, from Red Indians, for instance."

"Completely."

"From the Mexicans?"

"Oh, from them certainly. They belong to us."

"From the French?"

"Ah, you are an opponent of them?"

"That is not your business. But tell me where is Juarez now?"

"In Paso del Norte, I believe."

"You believe, so you don't know for certain."

"For certain? No."

"How far is it from here to Paso del Norte?"

"Sixty hours to ride. Do you want to go there?"

"Possibly."

"Ah, señor, I assume that you have secret business with the president?"

"Pshtishshshsh" From the pointed mouth of the stranger spurted the brown juice so near Rodrigo that he was forced to jumped aside.

"Now I've had more than enough. I'm not used to such behaviour. Do you know where I come from?"

"Well?" asked the guest with indifference.

"From Letchworth."

"Don't know it. Is it behind the North Pole?"

"No, in England."

"That doesn't matter to me, but I shall stay here."

"Señor, that is not possible."

The stranger looked at the landlord, amazed.

"I don't like you," Rodrigo continued.

"But I like you, that balances things."

"I don't need such a spatter."

"Do you want a better one? I can be of service."

"No, no, I don't want you. Go somewhere else, where you can spit. Look at my window and my oil painting. I can't allow such venerable objects to be spat at. Do you understand?"

"A venerable window? No, I don't understand."

Rodrigo was furious; he stood in front of his guest with his fist clenched. It looked as if he wanted to hit him.

"Pshtishshshsh," the tobacco juice shot again toward Rodrigo, so that he had to jump aside.

"What? That as well?" he called. "Now push off, or I shall call my vaqueros."

"Pah," said the stranger calmly, "don't make such a noise or I'll spit at you that the juice will push you through the wall into the garden. Whether I stay or not is not up to you but up to me. I've rowed the whole night and I'm tired now. I shall sleep for one hour."

With these words he stretched himself on the bench against the wall and leaned his rifle next to him.'

"Stop, you can't sleep here," he ordered, "sleep where you want but not in my place. I won't touch you but I shall call my vaqueros who will show you who is the owner here."

The stranger pulled out his revolver and said: "Do what you like, but I'm telling you I'll shoot dead anyone who comes closer than I wish."

This made an impression on the landlord. He stood for a while then said: "You are a dangerous fellow. All right you can sleep for an hour, but I hope you don't spit in your sleep."

"No, only if I dream about your nosy questions." With the revolver in his hand, the stranger lay on his side and was soon asleep. The man must really have been tired.

Only a few minutes later, Rodrigo heard the sound of hooves. The rider jumped off his horse and came inside. He was not young but strong and sprightly. "Are you Señor Rodrigo?"

"Yes."

"Is Señorita Reseda still alive?"

"Certainly, do you know her?"

"No, but I have come here because of her. You know the Hacienda del Alina, don't you?"

"Naturally, Señor Wilson is my brother-in-law."

"Well, I am Juan Ernesto Vastorez. Don Martin Wilson, my master, has sent me to you with a message. Please call her, so that you can both hear it."

Rodrigo had forgotten his anger by now and brought Reseda from the kitchen. The girl shook hands with the guest and asked to be told the message.

"Well, you know that my master is old ..."

"Yes, older than I am," interrupted Rodrigo.

"He has no children. Señorita Alva is lost and will not come back. This ruined his life and made him look even older as he actually is. You know that the hacienda was a present from Count Manuel. He wants Señorita Reseda to be his heir."

"I hope he lives for a long time yet," said Rodrigo.

"At his age and in such times it's no wonder he thinks of death"

"Don't let's give up hope that we shall find Alva again."

"My master has given up all hope. Too many years have passed since he heard from her last and he asked me to tell you he wishes to see his heir once more before his end."

"That means he wants to see her as soon as possible but the war, the war intervenes."

Before the vaquero could answer another rider appeared. "Ah, Señor Gerard," called the old one. "Reseda and I were very worried."

"You too?" smiled Gerard, "How's that? I only drink one julep."

"Don't make silly jokes. I didn't know who you were, but now you are welcome even if you don't drink one julep. I'll call Reseda."

There was no need. Reseda had recognised his voice. She came rushing in and shook his hand. "Welcome," she greeted him. I was worried because you didn't tell me where you were going. Thank God you're back."

"Thank God, yes. But I hope I'll be able to say that tomorrow or the day after. I have to warn you, there is danger approaching: the French are on their way here."

Reseda paled; her father called: "My God, is that true? When are they coming?"

"I don't know yet."

"I'm going to pack everything on to horses and we'll leave for Paso del Norte," said Rodrigo. He intended lo leave the room but Gerard held him back.

"Hold on, wait a little," he urged him. "Even if the French would take the Ford, they won't touch privately owned things. They can't risk enraging the inhabitants against them. Besides, help is on the way. Juarez has five hundred Apaches beside his usual army and he is on the way here."

"Ah, so we are saved."

"Not yet, don't rejoice too early. Juarez doesn't know exactly which way the French are coming. It's possible he will miss them and not be here in time before they are. We have to hold the Ford until they arrive. Please send a vaquero to the mayor and tell him to have his one hundred men that he has promised, at the ready to come here when the French are getting near."

"You mean that the Ford should be defended? For heaven's sake we have no army."

"We'll do it and you as well Señor Rodrigo."

The face of the landlord grew twice as long. "I as well? I should shoot at people? O no, I won't do that. No I'm not going to shoot."

"So you'll be shot."

"Rodrigo paled. "But señor, I never even shot a rabbit."

"We don't need people like that." It came from the corner where the stranger had woken up."

Gerard turned around; he hadn't noticed the sleeping guest who'd listened to the conversation with equanimity. He stepped toward him and asked: "Pardon me, señor, may I ask you who you are?"

"Yes."

The guest only said the single word, then he reached into his pocked, pulled out a large ring of chewing tobacco and bit off a sizeable bit.

"Well, your name?" asked Gerard.

"Hm, you've asked me whether you could ask my name and I've permitted you to do that but I haven't promised to tell you."

"Good, keep your name but don't interfere in the conversation."

The stranger nodded thoughtfully, pushed the tobacco from one side to the other and said: "I calculate that you are not wrong. But I have my reasons not to tell you mine until I know yours. Did you say that Juarez has sent you?"

"Yes."

"Do you know where he is?"

"Yes."

"You are one of his and don't stick to the damned French?"

"Yes."

"Then be so good as to tell me your name?"

"They call me Black Gerard."

"Well, everything is all right then. Here's my hand, give me yours."

"You seem particular to start new acquaintances, so am I. You know my name, may I have yours now?"

"Ah, I nearly forgot that," laughed the other one. "My real name I have almost forgotten. The redskins gave me a name you have probably heard. It doesn't sound nice but I brought honour to it. Look at my face and you will probably guess it."

"What is noticeable in your face? It's the enormous nose, here is my hand señor Bighorn, your name is famous all over the west."

Bighorn was known as one of the best and most peculiar trappers in the west. Gerard felt sincere joy to meet him here. "What leads you to Ford Guadelupe?"

"About that we'll talk later. For now it must be enough that I am looking for Juarez. At this moment it's most important to consider the present situation. I'm in the Ford now and I feel it my duty to help in defending it. I take it that you have been entrusted with the defence?"

"Yes I have."

"Good, we have to obey you then." He turned to Rodrigo and asked: "You don't want to shoot at the French?"

"No, no. I can't do that," wailed the landlord.

"But you have the courage to throw out guests. Rest on your mattress; I'll step in for you."

Rodrigo grabbed his hand. Señor, I thank you. Do you really want to do battle in my stead?"

"Yes."

"Oh, I give you permission then, to spit as much as you like."

Reseda wanted to express her disquiet to Gerard when there was the sound of many hoofs and the windows darkened with many horses outside.

"What is that?" asked Rodrigo, shocked "Not the French, I hope?"

Gerard went to the window. "No, according to their clothes they are Mexicans."

"But so many. Reseda there's a lot of work to be done."

The door opened and the guests stepped in. It was Stenton and his companions. The eyes of those present looked admiringly at the giant figure. His dense beard had grown to below his chest. Behind him came the Count, also a striking figure. Then came the two ladies in veils and the others.

"Are you the landlord?" Stenton asked Rodrigo.

"Yes, señor."

"Have you room for us all?"

"Plenty of rooms."

"And the horses?"

"We have clean stables and good feeding," promised Rodrigo. "If you stay here, it is my duty to tell you that the French are on the march here to attack the Ford.

"How do you know that?"

"Juarez has sent us this señor to defend the Ford until he comes with five hundred Apaches."

"What is the name of this señor whom you just mentioned?"

"It is Black Gerard."

Stenton stepped towards the two sitting man and greeted them politely. "If I am not mistaken I see here men who do not fear the French and will help to defend the Ford."

"What do you infer that from?"

"I think that Bighorn will not show his back to the French."

"You know me, sir?" asked the astonished trapper.

"From a long time ago. A face like yours one cannot forget: but let's talk about the present situation. What have you done so far for the defence of the Ford?"

"Almost nothing."

"Speed is important now: or do you want to fight them outside the Ford?"

"No, we are too weak for that."

"Then behind field-or-earthen works?"

"Yes."

"Who are the people to defend the Ford?"

"About one hundred inhabitants, but I am going to send for the vaqueros in the area."

"You are doing the right thing, señor. By the way, you can count on us too."

"Ah, you want to fight as well?"

"Yes, if there is a need."

Gerard wanted to express his astonishment when, from the kitchen came a loud cry.

Reseda was curious to see the guest. Now she stood wide eyed and stared at the chief of the Mixtekas. Red Indians have hardly any beards. The chief, beardless, had changed little and was easily recognised by an old acquaintance.

"Buff-he!" called the vaquero.

The chief threw an enquiring glance at the vaquero. "Juan Ernesto," he called out.

"*Santa Madonna!* Are you really Buff-he? We were told you were dead." With this cry he ran to the chief and took both his hands.

"Yes, I am he," said the serious Mixteka.

"But the others, the others?"

"They are also alive," answered Buff-he calmly.

The vaquero's eyes now rested on Stenton. "Señor Stenton, oh Señor Stenton." With this he ran toward the giant. Stenton held his hand out: "You still recognise me, Ernesto ?"

"Who would not recognise you, the saviour of the Hacienda del Alina?

"Hallo, hallo, Stenton, Doc Ironfist," the voice came from the table. "That's why he recognised me."

These words were spoken by Bighorn. Then he jetted a large beam of tobacco juice across the tables and benches through the now open window.

"Doc Ironfist?" Gerard called this name now.

Reseda, who had taken Stenton's hands before, still held on. "Señor," she said with excitement, "as you reappeared, I believe that the others are still alive too. But where?" Tell me, for heaven's sake tell me quickly."

He pointed around: "Dear child, they are all here. Nobody is missing."

Alva lifted her veil. She had gained weight but aged little. Reseda at once recognised her. "Alva, my Alva!"

"My Reseda!"

Sobbing, they stood with their arms around each other until Alva asked: "Is my father still alive?"

"Yes, he's still alive," confirmed Reseda joyfully.

Alva dropped her arms and folded them in prayer: "Dear God, I thank you."

Everyone had tears in their eyes..

"We have a letter from uncle; you can read it later, dear Alva but please introduce me to the other señores."

"To whom do you want to be introduced first?"

"Your fiancē, of course"

Alva mischievously smiled beneath her tears and replied: "See whether you can find him."

Reseda looked at the gentlemen and pointed at Rudolfo. "This one?"

"Wrong, this one is Aurelio de Man – I wanted to say Monsieur de Mareau."

"De Mareau?" Asked a voice from the table behind. It was Bighorn.

"Yes," Answered Rudolfo or Lucien de Mareau. "Do you know my name?"

The Yankee came forward. "I know your name well, an Englishman told me about you."

"An Englishman?" asked Rudolfo. "What is his name?"

"Lord Castlepool."

Rudolfo grabbed Bighorn's arm and asked excitedly: "Where did you see him – in England?"

"No, not far from here in El Refugio?"

"That's at the outlet of the Rio Grande. When did you see him?"

"A few days ago."

"My God, he's in Mexico. What did he do in El Refugio?"

"That's a secret, but as things are here I think I can, no should, tell you."

"You can tell us in confidence, no harm will befall you," said Stenton.

"I have been recommended to Lord Castlepool as a scout," explained Bighorn. "He is an authorised agent of the English government and brings large supplies of weapons and money. All that should come up the Rio Grande ..."

"For whom?" interrupted Stenton.

"For Juarez," explained the American. I've been sent to report this arrival and to ask where Juarez wants to collect it."

"And Lord Castlepool will be there too?" asked Rudolfo.

"I can't tell you yet, it depends on Juarez."

Alva now introduced Reseda to her husband and explained that, they had been quietly married in Guaymas and then to her brother-in-law, helmsman George Brooks. Reseda passed her hand to each of them and expressed her good wishes. Then she pointed to Don Manuel and asked who he was.

"You will be surprised," answered Alva, you remember Don Manuel who suddenly died?"

"Yes."

"Well, this señor is Don Manuel."

Reseda's astonishment cannot be described. The old count smiled at her. "I'll tell you all about it," said Alva "and this last señor is Dinrallo who was imprisoned with the count."

At this moment Flying Horse came through the door. "I saw the tracks of the French, they will be here in an hour. "Are you prepared for them?"

"When you saw the tracks, did you notice any cannons?" asked Stenton.

"They have no shooting-carts with them."

"How far away are your five hundred Apaches?"

"They will be here in two hours."

Stenton waved at Gerard. "We, the señores Buff-he, Old Surehand and I'll take part in holding the Ford until the Apaches arrive. Señor Bighorn has offered his help. Don Manuel will stay here to guard the señoritas."

"Who will assume command?" asked Gerard.

"You. Juarez has given the command to you."

"O no, señor, don't expect that of me. Who am I if Doctor Ironfist is here and Old Surehand or Buff-he and trapper Bighorn? I ask you to take command."

"Then I would also bear the responsibility."

"I'm convinced you are not afraid of that."

"Well, don't let's lose time. I'll fulfil your wish and I want to look at the Ford now."

The two men went to study the defences. The Ford was small and stood on the bank of the river on a steep rocky hill. There was only one riding-path leading to a strong wooden gate. Except at the side of the river, it was surrounded by a fence made of sturdy wooden stakes. It was easy to defend unless there were cannons and no superior force to attack it. There were barely thirty inhabitants with rifles, but they should be able to hold the fort against three hundred French until the Indians arrived.

The excitement of the reunion had abated. Alva stood in the kitchen with Ernesto, the vaquero from her father's hacienda and could not hear enough about her father. She read his letter. Tears came to her eyes. "He absolutely believed in my death," she sighed.

To divert her mind, Reseda said: "Let me show you your room."---

Chapter 24

SABRE AND TOMAHAWK

AFTER Stenton had studied the Ford and its defence possibilities, he wanted to return but was stopped by Gerard. "Please wait for a moment; although I only got to know you today, I have unlimited trust in you and I am in a peculiarly soft mood. Please let me tell you about my past.

Gerard told him about his life as a garrotteur in Paris and his present task to free the Wild West from its bad elements. "I became famous but the remorse gnaws in me."

"Gerard, God is not angry forever," stressed Stenton seriously.

"But the people."

"What do you care about people?"

"Oh, very much. I got to know a clean, good girl. She reciprocates my love but I was honest and confessed my past in other words, a professional criminal."

"I don't want to judge here but was this confession necessary?"

"Yes, my conscience drove me to do that. I see that she fights in vain with her love, she will give her hand to the former garrotteur and she will perish internally."

Stenton admired this former man of violence, who showed so much tact but he said nothing.

"But she shall not suffer," Gerard continued. "I am a hunter and thousands of dangers are threatening my life. It could easily happen that

I die. She will be free then. Will you do me a favour for which I shall pray for you even in the life beyond?"

"Gladly, if I can."

"If you hear that I have died, tell her that she was my last thought and that, at the day of judgement, I find forgiveness because my love for the clean girl has made me clean too."

Stenton felt peculiar when he heard that plea. "You are thinking of death? I doubt if I shall be present when you die. I don't even know who the lady might be?"

"It is Reseda Rodrigo."

"Ah, I understand that you love her and I take it that your love is reciprocated?"

"I don't assume it, I know it."

"In your place I would let love prevail. If God has planted love into her heart, it is a sign that He has forgiven you."

"I have told that to myself but during the last hour I have changed my mind. Reseda is a cousin of Alva and acquainted with the Count and other honourable people. She should not step down to my level."

"You are wrong. This tactful feeling deceives you. If you are feeling a little intimidated now, you will soon overcome that."

"I doubt that. In any case, will you do me that favour?"

"Yes but you will not die."

"Who knows that? Are we not going toward a battle?"

"Let's go back now."

Gerard went to Reseda's room. He had no hopes anymore to overcome his inner battles and reproaches. That should take an end today. He found Reseda alone busying herself with some flower arrangement.

"Did you not enjoy the return of my lost cousin Alva? She received him."

"I enjoyed it with you."

"And think, just today I received a letter from her father making me his heiress. I should visit him."

"In this dangerous time?"

"I have hoped for your protection."

"I would give you that with all my heart."

"I know that, señor Gerard and I very much like you for that." Reseda looked at him with such friendliness that he dropped his eyes.

"Don't say that señorita; it must not be that you are so friendly disposed toward me."

"Tell me the reason."

"I felt it only today when I saw you among these other señores, that I must stay away from you for ever. Any step from you in my direction is downward and a humiliation."

Reseda suddenly paled. Gerard saw that she was shocked. "My God, who told you that, who gave you these thoughts?"

"They came by themselves," he admitted.

"Don't give them any room, Gerard. Don't you know that you professed and that I have forgiven you?"

"I remember you were so mild and good; I think you will be like that if I ask you for a favour."

"Favour granted – which one?"

"Close your eyes señorita."

"Ah," she smiled, "you want to surprise me like one does with little children?"

"Yes." But I think that you will not like this surprise."

"Well, let's try, my eyes are closed."

Gerard stepped to her and put his arms around her. She felt his lips pressing onto hers, once, twice, three and four times. Then he whispered into her ears: "I thank you dear, dear Reseda. Please think of me when you will be happy in future."

He let go of her, hurried down the stairs and grabbed his rifle, "What is it? Is the enemy coming?" enquired Bighorn.

"I don't know but it is better to be on guard."

"I am coming with you." The Yankee took his rifle and both went outside where one could overlook the area. That was unnecessary for, at this moment there were calls: "They are coming, they are coming!"

Everybody grabbed their weapons and hurried to the gate where all the defenders were gathered. Stenton sent some of the inhabitants to Rodrigo to bring some more ammunition. From the water there was no fear that the enemy would attack.

The French came on horses. They came in gallop and stopped near the Ford. Fifty of them continued toward the gate. They seemed to believe that the little Ford could be taken by surprise. They were twenty metres away from the gate when Stenton stepped towards them without anybody with him. A captain led the company. He involuntary reined his horse when he saw the tall figure in Mexican attire.

"What are your wishes, Messieurs? Asked Stenton politely but serious.

"We want to enter the Ford," declared the captain.

"Is your purpose peaceful?"

"Certainly."

"You may enter then but I must ask you to first lay down your weapons."

"*Morbleu,* who are you that you dare to speak to me like that?

"I am the commandant of the Ford."

The officer greeted with a cynical smile. "My great honour, Monsieur Comrade. How many men are under your command, five or six?"

"My six men are sufficient."

"And what rang do you have?"

"Find out with your sabre."

"Ah, good, I call upon you to hand over the Ford."

"And I call upon you to leave this place."

"I give you ten minutes to think about it."

"And I give you two Minutes to withdraw."

"*Parbleu,*" if you offer the smallest resistance, everybody will feel our blade."

"I am curios to get to know this awful blade."

"Here it is. Forward people, get inside."

The captain drew his sabre and made a start. The others began to follow him when Stenton pulled his revolver. The captain fell dead off his horse with the first shot. Stenton quickly jumped back. The gate was shut immediately behind him. At the same time it thundered through the crevices of the fence. There were all people who knew how to handle a rifle. The riders fell off their animals. The shocked horses without their riders reared up and somersaulted. There was complete chaos and the shooting never stopped. The few remaining Frenchmen took flight and reassembled with their compatriots out of reach of the deadly sharpshooters.

Gerard stood next to Stenton. "That was a lesson," he said. If they are clever they will not try again."

"Unfortunately, they will not be clever," answered Stenton. "You can see that their officers are together, they are consulting and we shall know soon what the result that will be.

"Yes, but out there at he border of the mountains something is happening." With these words Gerard pointed in an easterly direction. An attentive observer, if he had a sharp eye, could see a dark line moving slowly to the left.

"The Apaches," smiled Stenton.

"They will encircle the enemy."

"They will need at least a quarter of an hour if they will not make the French aware of their approach."

"Oh, the French will not notice anything, their position is too low," said Gerard. "It seems that they have come to a decision now."

"They intend to storm the Ford," maintained Rudolfo who stood nearby.

The French had dismounted and led their horse further back. They put their bayonets on to their rifles. They spread out to get the Ford near the river. Stenton sent some inhabitants to observe whether the enemy would approach from the waterside. One officer drew near with a white handkerchief at the point of his sabre but stopped just far enough that one could hear his voice. It was the commandant.

"Ah, the major in person," said Gerard when he saw him.

"Do you know him?" asked Stenton.

"Yes. Will you allow me to talk to him?"

"Of course."

"I shall go down to him."

"That is too dangerous."

"Not for me, I am under the protection of your rifles."

"Alright, go." Stenton asked for the gate to open. Gerard took his rifle and climbed calmly down the rock. Soon he stood next to the officer who was not a little amazed about this boldness. When he looked at the man he involuntarily pulled his reign. "By God, the Black Gerard," he called.

"Yes, the Black Gerard," encountered the hunter calmly. "My presence will tell you what to expect."

"What else as the possession of the Ford."

"Pah, don't even dream about that; the commandant has sent me to enquire what you want to tell us."

"As we have lost so many of our men we demand unconditional surrender."

"No more than that? You are extremely modest. Your losses are the fault of the captain because he drew his sabre against out commandant. To talk about surrender unconditionally is pure madness."

"*Monsigneur,* don't forget who you are talking to."

"Pah! A little major speaks with the famous Gerard. Nothing else. Don't behave so proudly, because your troupes will also be beaten."

"What are you chatting about? You are talking like a madman. Take my orders to your commandant."

"There is no need for that. You have the answer already."

"Is that final? Well, I tell you that we will show no mercy."

"This would be ridiculous; you will not get to that stage."

"So we shall start right away." The major held up his sabre without the handkerchief; the French started to move forward. That was, of course, the act of a rogue. It would allow Gerald, the negotiator, no time to withdraw. The major swung his sabre and attacked him.

"Here, you rascal, take your deserves for everything." With this he raised his arm for a fatal blow but he did not reckon with Gerard. He parried the blow with the barrel of his rifle and, with a forceful jerk he tore the rider off his horse and twisted his sabre away from him.

"Die on your treachery and nailed to the earth you will see how we shall defend our selves." With these words he threw the major down and pushed the sabre into his body that the blade went deep into the ground. He then climbed on to the nearby rock where, buzzed by French bullets, he took refuge behind a tree.

"Come through the gate, quickly," the call came from the other side.

"Too late," answered Gerard, "I am alright here.

Then he hid behind the only tree that stood near the fence, laid down and sent bullet after bullet into the fast nearing French.

"This man is seeking death," said Stenton.

"It almost seems like that, do you know the reason?" asked Rudolfo.

"Yes, come along, we must save him."

The garrison were only a few but men like Stenton, Gerard, Old Surehand, Bighorn and Buff-he counted for many. The enemy had not reached the foot of the rock when his dense line began to thin out. But he moved irresistibly forward. Near Gerard, the battle raged fiercest. One of the officers recognised him, now they wanted the feared opponent a prisoner and many climbed up the rock toward him but his rifle tore one after the other down. And if one would reach the top, he was hit with the heavy rifle butt. Stenton and Rudolfo stood behind the fence and not far away was Bighorn. These three gave themselves the task to hold the enemy off Gerard.

It was particularly exciting to observe the Yankee who, with miraculous speed loaded and shot, thereby speaking loudly as if the enemy would hear him.

"Ah, there is another who wants to give Gerard the bullet, his endeavour will be foiled. I calculate that my bullet will reach him first." He lifted his rifle and the aiming Frenchman sunk to the ground. "Another is creeping up there; he thinks that no-one sees him. I calculate that he will be faster down than at the top." With this he emptied his second barrel and the Frenchman slipped down again.

Gerard bled from several wounds: now he was hit by two bullets at the same time and the defenders saw that he sunk to his knees. Now one could hear Stenton's strong voice: "Attention everybody! Help is coming."

As yet, in spite of their superior numbers, no French soldier had reached the fence works when, in order for them to gather, the horn sounded. They had not noticed what happened behind them. When they turned around they were horrified to see a half-circle of riders galloping toward them. Many succeeded to form squares and that was lucky for them as otherwise they would have been overrun. From the safety of the fence and to their relief, the garrison observed the attack of the Apaches and the North American hunters.

"Should we make a sortie now?" asked Rudolfo.

"That would be best."

Rudolfo, Bighorn, Old Surehand and Buff-he run forward to finish off the attackers. Stenton, the commandant, staid behind and the inhabitants of Ford Guadelupe, who so far had very few casualties, did not want to risk their lives. The Apaches found resistance which threatened to bring their orderly line in disorder. Whereas in other places they were successful in mowing down the enemy, the squares, however, brought the battle to a standstill. It seemed that some of the French would be able to escape.

Behind the battle lines, amidst a group of riders, high on his horse was Juarez. With glowing eyes he observed the battle. With him were about sixty American hunters. They were powerful figures. They had not taken part in the fight yet as the Flying Horse has asked to leave the taking of scalps to the Apaches.

Juarez waved to the leader of the group and asked him: "Do you see that the battle comes to a standstill?"

"Unfortunately."

"Do you think that the Apaches will be victorious?"

"Certainly but they will not be able to stop a breach by the enemy. The intention of the French on the Ford has been frustrated but many of them will be able to escape."

Juarez nodded darkly. His lips pressed together. "That mustn't happen. What advice can you give me?"

"Let us advance," said the westman, "our bullets will soon tear apart these dangerous squares."

"Good, attack then!"

The hunters scattered as not to offer an easy aim for the enemy and, as westmen, they used every cover available. They attacked one of the bigger squares just as they had shot their bullets and while reloading. "Turn your rifles, use the butts," commanded the French leader.

Buff-he saw horses that were guarded by several chasseurs. He pointed at the big group of horses. "Take the horses and beat down the guards," he called to Flying Horse who acted immediately on this advice. He called a number of men and hurried with them to the horses. The chasseurs were beaten in no time.

The white hunters had meanwhile thinned the lines of the French. When Buff-he reached the second square it was so disheartened and exhausted that he had not much difficulty in almost wiping out the rest. The Apaches were enthusiastic about the reappearance of an old friend, the chief of the Mixtekas, that they wanted to celebrate his reappearance with the conquest of many scalps.

At the end of the right wing of the French assault that nearly reached the water, stood a sergeant who would have liked to play an officer. When the Apaches came to the help of the Ford, he anticipated what might result. "Follow me," he ordered to his people. "We are being surrounded but I know a way out."

"What way?" asked one of the men as he rubbed the sweat of his forehead.

"The Ford gets help; they are going to make a sortie, while we are going in from the side of the water and open the gate."

"By God, that's true. We shall follow you."

There were ten men who stepped into the water without being noticed. The guard that Stenton had sent to observe this point stood behind some trees that hindered him to do his job properly. The sergeant crept behind him and finished him with a blow of his rifle butt. As they went further they wondered that they could not see a single person. The inhabitants were at the fence; the women and children stayed indoors.

"The Ford is ours," rejoiced the sergeant, "do you hear them shout? The sortie has taken place just as I predicted. We are going to open the gate for our friends now."

"Do you think that they really need to withdraw?"

Who knows, there are many Indians."

"Indians? No French soldier will run away from an Indian."

"And," countered another, "what advantage have we if we open at once. We will have to share the loot with the others."

"You are right," said the sergeant, "we can take something beforehand. But none of us should betray our little trick."

They all agreed to keep quiet. "Where should we start? Most of these places have a store where most probably the money is."

"Here is a venta where there is booze and things for sale. Let's go in," suggested the sergeant.

The man saw the sign above the door of señor Rodrigo who let Bighorn fight for him. The house had an upper floor where Count Manuel could observe the battle. Reseda, Alva and Lady Margaret were with him. Kaya staid in her own room. Rodrigo sat, as usual, at the window and held his hands over his ears. The sound of every shot went though his soul. The old vaquero Juan Ernesto from the hacienda came in, still holding his rifle in his hand. He had stoutly participated in the first part of the battle. "Did you shoot any French soldiers?" asked Rodrigo.

"Yes, six or seven of them," replied Juan Ernesto.

"That is not excessive," said the valiant Rodrigo. "Do the French still defend themselves?"

"Yes but the Apaches and Juarez have arrived. The battle will soon come to an end."

"I have not seen him yet but I hope that he will come here for a glass of pulque or a julep. I am ... ah, ah!" Rodrigo stopped with a shock. The door had opened and the sergeant stepped in. He was followed by ten men. He stamped the butt on the ground and asked in broken Spanish:

"Here is a venta?"

"Yes," answered the paling landlord shaking with all his limbs.

"What is your name?"

"Rodrigo. But señor is the enemy already in the Ford?"

"You can see that."

"But I thought that we are winning?"

The sergeant laughed cynically. "The devil will give you victory. Who else is in this house?"

"I am."

"Go on."

"This señor."

"Who is he?"

"He is a vaquero."

"He should give us his rifle."

Juan made a gloomy face, he couldn't understand how it was possible for the halve conquered French to enter the Ford. He intended to defend himself but Rodrigo grabbed his rifle and handed it to the sergeant. "For God's sake," he whispered, "don't make any stupid moves, you endanger us all." He turned to the sergeant and said: "Here, señor, take the rifle as a sign that the Ford received you with joy."

"With joy?" asked the sergeant, "with bullets have you received us. Who else is in this house?"

"There are four señoritas –"

"Ah, were?"

"On the next floor, they have probably locked themselves in."

"They will have to open up. Who else?"

"The Count of Manresa."

"A Count? Olalla, is he rich?"

"Very."

"Good, we shall see what he possesses. Bind the vaquero."

The chasseurs went to the vaquero but he drew a knife. "I will not allow you to tie me up."

"Holy Madonna, what do you think," called Rodrigo. "One against ten!"

Juan saw the impossibility of the situation and held out his hands. "And now the landlord," ordered the sergeant.

"Me as well?" asked Rodrigo with a shock, "I am the most loyal subject of the emperor."

"The more reason to send you to hell, quick give us your hands."

The landlord was being bound as well without any resistance. "Now you will take us to the others," ordered the sergeant.

He left two of his men to guard Juan Ernesto, locked the entrance to the house and went upstairs where the three señoritas listened to the Counts commentary about the progress of the battle. "Now the French have no more chance; the Apaches with their tomahawks will finish them off." He had hardly spoken these words when the door was being pushed in and ten French soldiers entered. ---

The Black Gerard was on the ground bleeding from many wounds. He felt that life and strength was draining away but did nothing to stop the heavy bleeding. He thought that he was dying but wanted to see his beloved Reseda once more.

"Reseda, o Reseda."

That thought gave him the strength to get up. More staggering than walking he went the shortest way by the waterside into the Ford. When he saw the bloody guard on the ground he had dark foreboding. He managed to quicken his 'walk' slightly and soon looked through the window of the venta. Seeing the two French guards, loading his rifle and his revolvers, smashing the window and stepping into the room was a work of seconds.

"Stop," called one of the guards and lifted his rifle.

"Bastard." Only this one word he uttered and hit the man with his rifle butt. Before the other even grasped the situation, the butt split his head open.

"Untie me," asked Juan.

"Later." Gerard had no time. As long as his strength would last, he wanted to help his beloved. He dragged himself upstairs. ---

The sergeant and his men entered the room and heard the Count's last words: 'Now the French have no more chance; the Apaches with their tomahawks will finish them off.' "Oho, that is not quite true," he hissed. The four turned to the door and were deeply shocked when they saw the tied up landlord.

"Father, my father," called Reseda and hurried to him to hug him.

"Stop! Go back, ordered the sergeant," no scene here."

The Count stepped to the sergeant. "What do you want?"

"You do not have to ask me that. Who are you?"

"I am the Count de Manresa."

"That's the one we are looking for. You are my prisoner."

"You make a mistake. I am no enemy of the French."

"We shall find out. Tie him up."

The Count was tied up in spite his resistance.

"Now the women," ordered the sergeant.

Kaya, who had heard the commotion came in and saw with one glance the situation. Her eyes glistened as she pulled the sabre from the nearest soldier.

"Ah, another one, that makes exactly one for each two of us," called the sergeant'

"You just dare," Kaya called while lifting the blade.

"Parbleu, are these women here venomous," called the sergeant, "hit her on the head,"

The soldier who wanted to grab Kaya had his body pierced then she collapsed from a blow on her head from another soldier.

When Reseda wanted to defend herself she was warned by her father: "Give in; defence will only harm you."

She was tied up, so were Alva and Lady Margaret who both had fainted.

"Resistance against the victors," shouted the sergeant, "You will suffer for that." Then he turned to the Count he continued: I heard that you are rich; I am prepared to let you go for a ransom."

"How much do you want?"

"How much do you have with you?"

"You have heard my question, sergeant, answer!"

"Oho, that sounds as if you are the one who gives orders. Where are your properties?"

"In Mexico City."

"But travel money you have with you?"

"It will be enough for the ransom, if a son of the *Grande Nation* wants to play the robber."

"You better reign in you tongue. It is war and we are the masters. If you think that your cash would be enough, you must have a tidy sum with you and I would be a fool to name an exact sum. Where is you money?" With these words he stepped threateningly toward the Count. Don Manuel kept silent.

"Well, so I shall force you to give me an answer. Put him down and give it to him until he talks."

The old man was grabbed by the soldiers; one of them ventured: "Sergeant, I have a nice idea, why not hit the women. The old one will talk sooner then."

"Your idea is priceless; hit them one after the other. First this one. He pointed to Reseda.

"My God, this is impossible," called Reseda deeply shocked.

"Señor, be reasonable, be human," begged Rodrigo.

"Take her," ordered the sergeant as an answer.

Four of his people grabbed her. Reseda's hands were bound but she defended herself with all her might against this raw force. Her silk blouse was almost torn off.

"Stop that," called the Count, "I shall tell you were the money is."

The sergeant grinned and nodded. "You see how quickly you give in but I don't worry about your money anymore. I have granted my people a little entertainment and they should have it. Give this Mademoiselle ten lashes and the others as well."

Loud laughter resounded from the lips of the soldiers. The four who had let go while the Count made the offer, grabbed her again. Reseda defended herself desperately but without success.

"Devilish rascals," shouted the Count and, in spite of his age and tied hands, threw himself against the four soldiers until he received a blow on the head from the sergeant that stretched him unconscious to the floor.

"Forward, make and end," ordered the sergeant.

These people were so engrossed with their intentions that they did not give the out side a thought. One glance through the window would have taught them that their only way of escape was across the water. Reseda was finally torn to the ground. She uttered a cry for help.

"Now we have got her where we want; finally"

"Yes finally," it came from the door. At the same time a shot hit the soldier who just had rejoiced.

"What is that?" called the sergeant.

"It is the Black Gerard." The hunter who was half dead himself and hardly managed to stand up, shot the next three soldiers who held Reseda. Two more shots from his revolver stretched another to soldiers who fell to the ground with a bullet in each head. The sergeant with one more of his soldiers was in the first few seconds shocked. Now he roared: "The Black Gerard, get him." He swung his rifle to beat down his enemy but the ceiling was too low. Irritated he looked up. He fell over one of his shot comrades. This gave Gerard time to shoot the one remaining soldier. The sergeant who had got up managed to tear down the weakened man and aimed his rifle at his head. Reseda threw herself against him and the shot failed. The angry sergeant threw Reseda to the other end of the room. "Gerard, my Gerard," called Reseda who made renewed effort to ward off the enemy.

"Farewell, Reseda," breathed Gerard hardly audible and not being able to move a limb, as he looked at the rifle that was aimed against his forehead. Then he closed his eyes. ---

Buff-he, the chief of the Mixtekas, saw that he was no more needed at the battle. He threw his rifle over his shoulder and climbed up the hill to go to Kaya, the girl he grew up with and took as his squaw on the island where they lived for fourteen years.

When he found the door locked he swung himself through the smashed up window. He saw the French soldiers who Gerard had beaten down with his heavy rifle butt. He just started to free Juan, the vaquero of the hacienda del Alina, when he heard the shot that was diverted by Reseda. Immediately he stormed up the stairs. He reached the room just when the sergeant held his rifle to Gerard's forehead. "Dog!" With this word he rammed his rifle butt against the sergeant who flew several metres away. He went to Kaya and saw her unconscious on the floor. Her forehead was bloody. "Have the French done that?" He asked Reseda.

"Yes, she defended herself and stabbed her attacker to death."

"Ah, she is a Mixteka," he said proudly as he went to the sergeant who was doubled up in pain. "What did they want?"

"They demanded money from the Count and intended to give every woman ten lashes. I was already on the floor when Gerard came in and shot five of them."

"Buff-he ground his teeth. "Death was too good for them, that dog here should suffer." As he spoke he grabbed the sergeant by his long hair and drew his knife.

"Heavens, what are you going to do?" wailed the sergeant.

"You are not human but an animal; I shall scalp you before I shall kill you."

"God, o God not that," roared the Frenchman in desperation.

"Don't call for your God because you are the devil."

"Rather kill me."

"Don't do it," begged Reseda shuddering.

"He deserves even more," said the Indian coldly, Buff-he is no murderer but the daughter of the Mixtekas must be revenged."

The sergeant, condemned to this terrible punishment, implored for mercy with shrill cries. Rodrigo as well as his daughter begged the chief to refrain from this type of revenge. The angry chief gave in. "The scalp of a coward is not worth having," grumbled Buff-he as he pushed his knife into his heart.

Rodrigo stood with eyes closed at the wall. The Mixteka went to him and said: "My white brother can open his eyes now, it's all over. I shall cut your ties now as well as those of the others.

One could hear hurried steps now. Stenton, Old Surehand and Rudolfo came through the door. They all had their weapons in their hands.

"Ah, Buff-he has cleared the desk already," said Stenton relieved.

"The Black Gerard before me," declared Buff-he modestly.

Old Surehand, or let us call him by his other name, Antonio saw Alva on the floor. "O God, is she dead?"

Stenton kneeled next to her and examined her. "She only fainted," he said soothingly.

Rudolfo went to Lady Margaret who had recovered already and put his arms around her.

"And the daughter of the Mixtekas?" urged Buff-he.

"Stenton also examined Kaya. "A nasty bruise, no more," declared the doctor.

Then he stepped to the Count who slowly began to recover from the rifle blow but when he saw Gerard his face assumed a gloomy expression. "God, such a cut and shot person I never saw in my life. We have to bandage him immediately to stop his bleeding."

"He is not dead then?" asked Rudolfo.

"Not yet but I can only see later whether his wounds are deadly. Let us put him carefully onto the bed.

The dead soldiers were put into a mass-grave with the others after everything useful had been taken from them. ---

Chapter 25

THE CONQUEST OF CHIHUAHUA

$\mathcal{J}$T was the day after the battle when Doctor Stenton approached Reseda who was sitting on her usual place in the guest room. "Excuse me Señorita; I have come here with a plea."

She stood up and just looked at him questioningly.

"Have you got some linen for a bandage?"

"Yes, at once." With these words she went and fetched the wanted item. "Were they not all bandaged yet? Who requires these, señor?"

"Gerard."

She paled. "Is it really so bad?" she inquired with a trembling voice.

"Very bad," he regretfully told her.

"O God, is there no help possible?" These words she only breathed as her eyes filled with tears of anxiety.

"God is merciful. But here, help can come only from one physician."

"And who is he?"

"He is called love."

Reseda grew even paler than before. Then a dark red covered her face and a river of tears ran over her face.

Stenton took her hand and said: "Reseda, he wanted to die."

"Gerard?" She sobbingly asked.

"Yes. He went on purpose into death. Everybody fought from behind the fence, he staid outside."

348

"O God why?"

"I do not know that but you will probably know or at least suspect why. He practically offered himself to the bullets of the enemy. Why do you hate him?"

"Hate? I – Him?" With these words she put her face into her hands and her sobbing nearly choked her voice.

"Do you know him for very long?" Stenton continued his questioning.

"Only for a short time but long enough."

"Do you know his past?"

"Yes, he was frank and open. You know it too, don't you?"

"I know it too, señorita, why don't you forgive him?"

"Oh, I have forgiven him a long time ago."

"And yet, you avoid him when he needs your help."

"I must not go to him. I – must – I cannot tell you," she answered.

"I do not understand this. Before the battle he asked me to tell you that, should he die, you were his last thought. He is still alive but his words are from a dying person." With these words he turned around and walked to the door. Reseda hurried after him and said with a heart rending voice:

"Señor Stenton. I must not go to him; my misery would surely cost him the rest of his life."

"My child, you don't know yourself, a woman is strong in her grief. Come, you will not kill him but help him to return to life." He took her by her hand and they left the room. Weak-willed she followed him. Gerard laid there, covered in Bandages and cloths. Even his head was bandaged. Only his face was showing but it had the pallor of death. Reseda felt icy cold. Her body felt like ice and her feet seemed heavy as a ton. It was like an eternity until she reached the bed. Stenton renewed the bandage around his head and Reseda helped him. Her hands slightly touched his face. He whispered as if he had recognised the touch of his beloved.

"Reseda."

"Answer him," asked Stenton, "He has not opened his eyes as long as he lay here."

She bent down to his ear. "My dear, dear Gerard," she said softly.

His eyelids lifted slowly and his deadly weak glance fell on her. "Oh, now I am not going to die." The words were hardly audible.

Reseda did not care that Stenton was present. She put her mouth on Gerard's lips that were empty of blood and said: "No, you must not die my Gerard, because without you I couldn't live. You must recover and see that I love you more than anything on earth."

"O God, that is heaven." Whispered Gerard and closed his eyes.

This sudden happiness was too much for his weakened body, he fainted again.

"Señor, señor, he is dying," called Reseda full of fear.

"Don't get a shock, it will not harm him. On the contrary, he will get stronger. Stay here with him then I shall have the biggest hope that he will recover. ---

Bighorn has asked Juarez for an audience. "I am here as messenger from an English lord, who in turn is an envoy of the English government."

"I trust that you bring good news?"

"Very good, I calculate, a ship full of arms and ammunition and several barrels full of gold coins."

"Do you know the name of the lord?"

"Yes, it is Lord Castlepoole."

At this moment Stenton knocked at the door. "I have come to say good bye," he said.

"Where are you going to," asked Juarez.

"Ultimately, back to England but first to the Hacienda del Alina."

"Actually, I wanted you to come with me to Chihuahua. The detour is minimal and I would be much obliged."

Stenton thought for a moment. Juarez would probably regain his presidency and could help in matters of the Count de Manresa. The detour was not substantial and he wouldn't mind to have taught the French a lesson. "I am with you, señor," he said "but I hope that we shall make an early start."

"We can leave within the hour if you can leave your patient."

"He will recover from now on, Reseda is looking after him and there is no better person whom I would trust."

It was decided that the ladies would leave directly for the hacienda, guarded by Buff-he and thirty Apaches. The others, Stenton, Old Surehand, George Brooks and the Apaches were riding with Juarez toward Chihuahua.

Juarez, who rode next to Stenton asked him, whether he would go and warn the remaining French of his coming. If the French would go voluntarily there would be no bloodshed.

"Ah, you want to act the honest broker and a gentleman; yes I shall ride ahead."

Juarez told him to get in touch with Emilia and described the venta he should visit first. He then gave Stenton the best horse. Within minutes Stenton was out of sight.

He tied his horse to a tree outside the town and made his way on foot. He found the landlord of the venta who brought him to señorita Emilia. "You are coming from Juarez," she seemed very agitated.

"Yes, he is only a few hours behind and wants me to offer the French free withdrawal to avoid bloodshed."

"I am afraid they will imprison you and not believe you. But there is worse, they have taken sixty inhabitants who should be shot a two o'clock in the morning. A new officer, Colonel Laramel, has arrived and the commandant is giving a party in his honour. He has a cruel reputation and is responsible for the arrest of suspected citizen."

"But you can't shoot these people without a trial?"

"The French and especially this colonel do not go by international law. They are the supreme masters and above any law," sighed Emilia.

"Nevertheless, I have to speak to them."

"Alright, I shall ask the doorkeeper to help you. I shall ask my maid to call him." She clapped her hands and the maid came from an adjoining room. "Call your brother to me I have a task for him," Emilia ordered.

Within minutes the doorkeeper appeared. "Alfredo," she addressed him, this is Doctor Stenton. He wishes to speak to the commandant, will you take him please."

Alfredo waved Stenton to follow him. He gave him a key that would fit all doors of the building. It was a dark night; they went through several streets without being noticed. The doorkeeper opened a door and explained that it was the rear entrance were he would expect Stenton if he had to flee. They went upstairs where Alfredo led him through several empty rooms into a corridor. He pointed at the door across and told him that all the officers were gathered there to honour Colonel Laramel and to await the time for the mass execution.

Stenton went down again to the other side of the building and through the main entrance. When he passed the guard room, a sergeant came out and asked politely: "Pardon me Monsignor, where do you want to go?"

"Can I speak to the commandant?" asked Stenton.

"At such late hour?"

"That is not your business. I've asked whether the commandant is at home."

The young man seemed impressed by this coarseness and answered "*Oui Monsieur.* Who shall I say that you are?"

"Doctor Stenton."

"Very well, follow me."

The officers were sitting and drinking pineapple punch and talking about politic in the way of the French, easygoing and making fun about the enemy. The sergeant stepped in and reported: "There is a Doctor Stenton outside, who wishes to speak to the commandant."

"That late? He seems to be English and is probably the surgeon of the emperor's battalion. Let him come in."

All eyes turned to the door expecting a submissive little plaster man. Instead they saw a giant clad in a rich Mexican attire. "Good evening *Monsigneurs*," he greeted with a bow. Moved by the impression of his personality, the officers stood up and reciprocated that greeting. "I have been told to see the commandant of Chihuahua."

"I am he," said the one asked for. "Would you sit down? But let me first introduce you to my officers. Stenton nodded at each name but when colonel Laramel was named he examined his face more precisely. Then he sat down.

"What gives me the unexpected honour to see you here?" asked the commandant.

"I am coming from the south sea and I had family reasons to come to Mexico where I had the pleasure to get to know a man who is closely connected with the history Mexico's. You may know who I mean?"

"*Diable*, probably Juarez," called Colonel Laramel excitedly. "Did I guess correctly?"

"Yes *Monsigneur le Colonel.*"

"Splendid, finally one hears something more precisely; where is he?"

"I beg permission to continue with my introduction."

"That has time, answer first my question that is the main thing."

These words were totally inconsiderate but Stenton continued uninhibitedly: "Yes, it was Juarez whom I got to know during ..."

"I have asked where Juarez is," called the colonel imperiously.

Stenton turned to him with a smile. "*Monsigneur le* Colonel, you are not in front of a company for punishment but you re sitting with a man who is used to speak without interruptions. Besides, I came here to speak to the commandant."

That was a reprimand the like the colonel had never heard. He stood up grasped his sabre. "*Monsigneur,* do you want to insult me?"

"Not at all, I only had the intention to get the consideration due to a cultured man."

The commandant feared a serious scene mixed himself in. "Let it be. The doctor has declared that he meant no insult to Colonel Laramel and I ask you sincerely – let the doctor speak. Please continue."

The last words were directed to Doctor Stenton. As they were friendly the doctor bowed politely and continued: "I said that I got to know Benito Juarez and I don't believe that I commit a political crime when I confess that I felt him sympathetic and I had the good fortune to find this reciprocated."

"Do you want to tell us that you are a friend of his?" the commandant asked with a serious expression.

"Nothing else."

The commandant's forehead wrinkled. "You seem to have a great openness."

"I am used to regard openness as a virtue."

"This virtue, under certain circumstances, can be dangerous if it becomes careless."

"I hope that, up to now, I was not careless."

"O yes, you have confessed that you are a supporter of Juarez."

"It is easily possible to be a friend without to share ones politics. Let's go in piece over this point. I repeat that I had the luck to get to know Juarez. My presence here is the prove that I have his trust because I have come as an envoy of the Zapotec."

"Ah," said the commandant, "as an envoy perhaps even his authorized agent?"

"Yes, I have the authority to negotiate."

One could hear Colonel Laramel's derisory laughter. The commandant countered: "I am in full agreement with my comrade who proved by his laughter that your words are more than strange. Do you really think that Juarez is a man with whom a French officer would negotiate?"

"I believe so," said Stenton calmly.

"Then you are mistaken. No authority would even think to negotiate with a criminal and a traitor. Every educated man knows that."

"I agree with this view but would ask whether you mean Juarez when you say criminal and traitor?"

"Naturally," answered the commandant. He is a traitor and resists us with arms."

"Very peculiar," said Stenton as he shook his head. "Juarez is of the same opinion about you."

"Ah," called everybody.

"Yes," pronounced Stenton without fear. "Juarez maintained that he is the rightful president of Mexico and had not been deposed by his people and that the French have come by force to Mexico like a burglar who enters a house that is not enough guarded."

Colonel Laramel jumped up put his hand on his sabre and called to the commandant: "Do you want to allow this insult?"

The commandant also stood up and said to Stenton: "You have named us as common burglars."

"I don't think so," answered the Englishman. "You called Juarez with a name that he decisively rejects and I would say that is the way that I have expressed my opinion."

"We would forbid that. I am considering your visit a useless and dangerous one. Useless it is for Juarez because we will not negotiate with him and dangerous it is for you, *Monsieur.*"

"Dangerous for me?" Stenton looked at him disbelievingly.

"Because you are in danger to lose your freedom or even you're live. Juarez is fair game to us and I have received an order only yesterday, to treat every supporter as a bandit, that means to shoot him."

"High day," laughed Stenton, "so I shall have the pleasure to be regarded as a bandit?"

"You are very near to this danger. I am sorry to tell you that we do not accept an envoy of this former president and that you are my prisoner."

Stenton put one leg over the other and encountered calmly: "About your second point we will talk later. Regarding the first point, I shall, in spite of your refusal to listen, execute my order and I have to tell you …"

He was interrupted by Colonel Laramel who stepped one step nearer and called angrily: "Not another word. Every syllable would be an insult."

Stenton shrugged his shoulders: "I have already mentioned that I have come to speak to the commandant of Chihuahua but not with anybody else. If you don't want to listen to an envoy of Juarez, then there is no harm in listening to a man whose message can be of use."

"Your opinion cannot be of use to us," said the commandant seriously.

"You could prevent greater harm. If you will not recognize Juarez as the person to deal with, he shall by his power and facts procure recognition."

"What facts are they? Do you mean his escape, his powerlessness or his helplessness?"

"Escape? He has not escaped; he only withdrew for a short while: "Will you call a man powerless who frustrated your latest undertaking?"

"*Monsieur,*" take care of what you say." The commandant flared up. "I don't know what you mean. There are three companies on the way to wipe out any supporters."

"Do you believe that this undertaking will succeed?"

"Without question."

"Then I can tell you that you are mightily mistaken. Your undertaking has completely failed."

The officer received a real shock. "How is that? What do you know about this undertaking?"

"Oh, Juarez was for a long time aware and prepared his counteroffensive. Your attack on Ford Guadelupe has taken place but was completely defeated."

The officers who had been seated jumped up. "Impossible," called the colonel, "who has defeated the attack?"

"Juarez."

"Juarez was in Ford Guadelupe?"

"He went there as soon as he knew of your intention. I was with him."

"You were there when the attack took place?"

"Yes."

"Well, the success of the expresident will only be short. Our troops will take the Ford and take him prisoner."

"I am sorry to have to tell you that it cannot happen. You have no more troops for that."

The commandant paled. "What do you mean?"

"Your troops have been wiped out."

"*Monsieur,* do you put a trap my way?"

"No, I am saying the truth."

For a few moments there was silence then the Colonel Laramel shouted: "That is a cheeky lie."

Stenton did not look at him but said to the commandant: "Please stop these insults against me or I must help myself."

"A lie," repeated Laramel, "this man is a liar."

Hardly had these words been spoken when the speaker lay on the floor unable to move. Stenton had stood up with lightning speed and smashed his fist on Laramel's head, the man immediately broke down. The shock of this deed made everybody stiff for a moment, then the commandant called threateningly: "*Monsieur,* what do you dare? You have hit a commandant of a regiment. There is only one punishment. Death." With this he went to the door.

"Stop," ordered Stenton.

The officer stopped in his movement and stared at Stenton. "You are mad to speak to me in that tone." He drew his sabre and the others did likewise.

"Leave your weapons were they are," countered Stenton, I have come here to be heard. I do not fear your swords; my bullets are faster and

356

more dangerous in any case. With these words he drew two revolvers and directed them against the French. His mighty outward appearance, his lightening eyes and the imperious tone of his voice, made an irresistible impression. The commandant withdrew with a shock. "You are not going to shoot, are you?"

"Yes, I give you my word that I am going to give anybody who makes an unfriendly gesture a bullet. Your only weapon is the sabre, I am therefore superior. The men saw the truth of these words.

"Unheard-of," said the commandant, you are lost, nevertheless."

"Not yet. Rather you are lost in my opinion if you don't follow my order to sit down calmly."

Stenton looked threateningly and the officers sat down. He kept both revolvers in his hands. "You were talking of an order to shoot every supporter of Juarez. Will you obey this order?"

"Unconditional."

"Juarez is warning you. He is letting you know that he will treat every Frenchman who falls into his hands as a bandit. Furthermore, I have to call upon you to leave Chihuahua with all your troops forthwith."

The commandant, with a hoarse laughter called: "This sounds farcical."

"But it is meant seriously. Juarez will let you go quietly if you obey his order."

The commandant rose again. "Order? What expressions dare you use," he called. "I tell you that I shall obey my order to shoot Juarez's supporters in the strictest way."

"I am sorry but mostly about yourselves."

"I shall begin my duty tonight. Do you know who will be the first whom I shall let shoot as a bandit?"

"I suspect you mean me," said Stenton smilingly.

"Yes, you are my prisoner. Surrender voluntarily. Your first shot might kill one of us but then we shall have you before you shoot a second time."

"To prove that might be difficult for you but I do not like to spill human blood and will, therefore, put my weapons back." With these words Stenton put his revolvers back into his belt.

"Good, you are surrendering?"

"O no, I only wish to take my leave." He bowed down mockingly and, with three steps he reached the door. "Halt. Grab him," called the commandant and jumped to the door. But the door was locked. "He is escaping, after him." With these calls all officers rushed to the exit. Nobody thought to open a window and shout down some orders. After a long time the doorkeeper opened up. He made an astonished face.

"*Dios mio*, who has locked you in?"

"Where were you?" asked the commandant.

"Downstairs at the door, señor."

"Did you see anybody leaving?"

"Yes, señor, the stranger who entered previously."

"In what direction did he go?"

"He did not walk, he whistled and a man came with two horses, then they rode to the south," the doorman told them misleadingly.

"He will not escape. A few will follow them on good horses. Who of you will do that?"

Some of the younger officers offered to go. The commandant chose ten of them who rode with a lieutenant in the given direction. ---

Stenton went and left town. He found his horse were he had left it. He hurried to Juarez to tell him about the sixty supporters that were going to be shot at two o'clock in the morning. The Apaches and Juarez were approaching in good speed. They were one hundred of them with the best horses; the rest came at a slower pace. They calculated that they would be in Chihuahua shortly after midnight.

"We shall be in time to frustrate this mass execution," declared Juarez abruptly. "We shall surround them and, at the right moment, will shoot them down."

"If you want to save innocent people, I know a better and shorter way. We simply take all the officers who are presently with the commandant prisoners and force them to hand over Chihuahua without blood let."

"*Caramba,*" if that would be possible."

"It is not difficult. Fifty Apaches suffice. The doorman who helped me will let us in the back way."

"Will it be possible to speak to señorita Emilia without danger?"

"Yes, I shall take you to her and back if you trust me."

"Let's go," ordered the Zapotec.

Shortly before they had reached the town, the two men left the troop. They reached the house without being seen. The housemaster asked: "Who is there?"

"I am back again," said Stenton. "How was it with the commandant?"

"Very well, I told them that you had a horse waiting for you and have sent them in the wrong direction where eleven men have followed you."

"That was a good idea. Is señorita Emilia still awake?"

"She would not go to sleep as long there is a danger that sixty citizens will be shot. Should I give you the lantern?"

"No, I know the way."

When Emilia saw the president, she uttered a shout of joy and took his hand. "I welcome you in this town and I am proud to be the first one to do so. May your arrival bring the fruit that your land and its people expect."

"I thank you señorita," answered a serious Juarez. "You have a lot contributed that my coming here has been possible. Actually, I should let you rest now but I wish to send you to Mexico to the emperor."

Her cheeks reddened with delight.

"Señor Stenton will not wait for the hour of execution but to attack the officers inside the townhouse."

"We only need the housemaster to open the back entrance," ventured Stenton.

"Our one hundred Apaches will suffice for this action. The others will arrive soon to keep general order."

"You don't have to leave it to your Apaches only. I shall bring several hundred men who, when they hear the news that Juarez has arrived, will take to their weapons. I know them all and will bring the news, at least to the most important ones."

"Good, now señor Stenton bring fifty Apaches and the housemaster to me; unobserved naturally."

"Can you open the back door of the townhouse?" he asked the doorkeeper.

"Do you want to go to the officers? They will take you prisoner."

"I shall bring fifty Indians and I will take the officers as prisoners."

"Fifty Indians? That's enough and then the town belongs to you."

"And now call the landlord of the venta opposite to me."

The man came and was overjoyed that he was chosen to bring the news to all supporting citizens. That meant almost the whole town. Stenton returned and reported to have fifty Apaches in position. "We can start," ordered Juarez. "Señorita Emilia; for the sake of your future mission, I shall have to arrest you with the officers."

"Oh I am prepared for that. Call me when you need me, she answered joyously.

"You will go to the officers and tell them that your spies have told you that Juarez is close. You advise them to take precautions and I shall appear at the right moment."

When the three left the house a few moments later it was too dark to see the fifty Indians who were lying on the ground against the row of houses. They hurried with mooted steps to the rear of the townhouse where the doorkeeper already waited for them. "Everything alright?" asked Juarez.

"Yes, they are all up there," came the answer.

"The Apaches?" Juarez had turned to Stenton. He had, so far not seen any but he hardly uttered the question, when a dark figure rose next to him. It was Flying Horse who answered "here."

The same moment, the fifty Indians stood around him. The housemaster, who had a small lantern, led the whole group up the stairs. Behind the rear door of the large room, where the officers still stood around Colonel Laramel who still had not fully recovered from Stenton's mighty blow. "If I had that damn swine here," the colonel ranted, "I would whip him to death."

"We shall catch him," the commandant consoled him.

At this moment, there were hasty knocks at the door opposite the one where Juarez and his men waited. Emilia, rather breathless, stepped in.

"Señorita, you here, at that late hour?" questioned the commandant.

"It is not the customary hour for a visit but duty made me call on you."

"Duty? That sounds serious."

"It is serious, señores; I have to make an important report."

"Please take a seat, señorita Emilia," offered the commandant.

She refused. "Excuse me señores that I am not sitting down. I have come in a hurry to tell you that we are in great danger."

The politely smiling face turned worrying. "What could that be?" he enquired.

"Juarez is coming."

"Oh that, I thought that you have much worse news."

"I am surprised; did I not bring the worst news?"

"No, we had already been notified that Juarez had left El Paso del Norte to win back Chihuahua. This Indian imagines being president of Mexico but he is not dangerous, not for us."

"You make a mistake. I was told that he had beaten your troops."

"We were told that already but it is a lie to make us worry." The commandant did not actually believe it to be a lie but he did not want to show any fear to the señorita.

She continued, showing urgency: "I am convinced that it is the truth. The man who brought me the news is reliable.

"Where is this man?"

"He is a gold digger and is in my flat now."

"Could we speak to him?"

"Yes, I shall send him to you tomorrow if that isn't too late already."

"That sounds that there is no time to waste but gold diggers are not reliable. No Juarez with a few adventurers can take a town like Chihuahua."

"Who gives you the certainty that he and his Apaches are not already in town?"

Colonel Laramel took the word: "Your news in all honour, señorita. "If Juarez would be in town already; a few words to my men would suffice to clear the place."

"Maybe you should try that." These words came from the other door from a man in Mexican attire but his features could not deny Indian descent. His face looked serious despite a little smile.

"Ah, who dares to enter like that?"

"I am Juarez, the president of Mexico," he simply declared.

"*Diable.*" The colonel jumped up and drew his sabre. "Yes, we have our man. I have seen a picture. Take him prisoner." He stepped toward

Juarez who opened the door again and fifty Apaches streamed into the room. More than four to one they overwhelmed bound and gagged all officers in no time.

"Señor Stenton," called Juarez.

Stenton stepped forward. When Laramel saw him he reared; being gagged, pushed a sound of rage through his nose. "Leave ten men here and go with the others to arrest the guards." Then he turned with a serious expression to Emilia: "I have heard some of the words you have spoken. Who are you?"

Emilia kept silent in apparent embarrassment.

"Answer!"

"I am called Emilia," she Countered hoarsely as if in fear.

"Señorita Emilia? I have heard that name, you have caused me more harm than a whole brigade of French soldiers. I shall render you harmless. Stenton had returned. It caused no problem to overwhelm the surprised guards. He was given the order to take Emilia to her flat and have it searched. "If we find anything suspicious you will be hanged like a common spy."

Stenton took a lasso and tied her in a way that it looked that she was properly bound.

"Let's go!" he ordered roughly as he pushed her through the door. He waved to four Apaches to follow him. Outside he took off the lasso and apologised: "I am sorry, señorita that I have treated you a bit rough."

"I did not expect anything else; may I stay with you?" she asked Stenton.

"I would not advise this, one never knows if the rest of the soldiers will not fight. There is the doorman who will take you to a place where you can await further development."

Juarez, in the meantime, had started negotiation with the commandant whose gag was removed. He was allowed to sit on a chair whereas the others lay on the floor. "You are the commandant of Chihuahua?"

"Yes," confirmed the prisoner short.

"Good, let's talk to one another."

"Don't expect a word from me until I am being untied. It is barbaric to bind officers."

"You are right, answered Juarez calmly. "The French have tied down my officers and two of my generals and shot them without having the right to do so – in other words, they have murdered them. I, therefore, have reason to regard that nation barbaric. Any sensible person will understand this and not complain."

"The comparison is wrong. Those shot were rabble-rousers."

"Am I a rabble-rouser if I chase away someone who pushes his way into my house to rob me of my possessions? Don't make yourself ridiculous. I had the intention to go easy on you because I am not a French barbarian. But, if you spoil my intention, you have to take the consequences."

"I do not fear these consequences," muttered the other.

"This is an unfortunate delusion, Colonel. You seem to be unaware of my helpers and your present condition."

"I shall not answer that, my troops will do that."

"I have encircled Chihuahua. The guards and you are in my hands. The troops you have sent to Ford Guadelupe have been beaten. The inhabitants of this town, when they hear of my presents in their midst, will rise to a man. Your few soldiers will be crushed in five minutes. Do you want to talk to me?"

"I can, unfortunately, not negotiate with you."

The brows of the Zapotec pulled together darkly. "If I regard you as political equal, then it is I who lowers himself."

"You have to prove that."

"This proof is not difficult, you are dishonoured."

"*Marbleu!* Were I not bound, I would show you how a French officer punishes such an insult."

"Pah, there is no way to call this an insult. The Black Gerard has hit you with his fists and tore off your shoulder straps. There is no bigger disgrace for an officer and I bend down considerably if I honour you with a glance. The case of Colonel Laramel is similar; he also has been knocked down by a fist. I am in no way in a good company. I ask you again, are you going to speak to me?"

There was an uneasy silence from the officer.

"Your silence indicates that I am right. By the way, there is no question of who of us is capable to negotiate. The situation speaks for itself. You are in my hands. Has the order to shoot us down as bandits reached you already?"

The commandant saw that it was better to yield to the unavoidable and answered "Yes."

"Who brought it to you?"

"Colonel Laramel."

"And you were prepared to execute it?"

"To obey orders is the duty of a soldier."

"You have given the order to shoot my supporters tonight?"

"How do you know that?"

"That is my secret. I have sent you my envoy. You threatened his life. Did he tell you that I am going take retribution?"

"Yes."

"History will be your judge. Not the millennia, not the century but this year. Your disregard of all the laws and righteousness shall fall back on you. The Zapotec stands before the murderers of his people who devastated his land. If you want to listen to me – good. If not, my heavy hand will be on you. I am master of Chihuahua now. You have a choice! You will either sign a paper that you will never fight against me anymore; I then let you return to Bazaine, without your weapons, naturally. Or you will be shot and thrown into the waters the way you had planned to execute your prisoners. I shall not negotiate with you. I shall give you ten minutes to talk among yourselves. I expect a simple yes or no." He ordered to remove the gags off the officers and then left the room where he met Stenton sitting at a table in the guard room.

"Stenton rose when Juarez entered. "Did you finish with them?"

"Finish? O no," answered the Zapotec angrily. "I gave them ten minutes to make up their minds."

"You gave them a choice?"

"Yes, I don't want my name besmirched as the enemy have done with theirs."

"Señor, I have a wish."

"You know it will be granted if I can."

"It is not personal; I wish to free the sixty Mexican citizens who must be in a terrible situation."

"Where are these people?"

"I don't know but I shall ask the doorman."

"Do that. Nine and a half minutes have passed. I must go upstairs." Juarez went and Stenton looked for the doorman. He found him sitting with his wife and Emilia who quickly asked: "What is the situation, Señor Stenton?"

"Good, I hope. Where are the prisoners that were going to be shot? In prison?"

"No, they have been brought here into an underground vault in this building. They are tied to the wall. Five soldiers and three French priests are with them."

"French priests? What cruelty. The person to die wants to confess and ask forgiveness for his sins. Here they cannot understand each other. I shall bring a dozen Apaches, and then you will take me to the prisoners."

Only a short time later, Stenton appeared with the Apaches. They stepped down the stairs and reached an iron door. "There is light in the vault?" whispered Stenton.

"Yes, señor."

"Extinguish your light; it is better that the soldiers don't recognise the Indians before it is too late."

A short skirmish ensued, a few cries, the soldiers and the priests where lying tied up on the ground. The prisoners where much further back around a corner. They had heard goings on but did not see the encounter. When they saw Stenton coming toward them, they asked: "*Santa Madonna,* should we be led to the slaughter already?"

"No, you are free," answered Stenton.

"Free?" they rejoiced.

"Yes, free. Juarez came in time to rescue you from certain death."

"Juarez." Rejoiced sixty people and a hundred questions were buzzing in confusion.

"Silence now," pleaded Stenton, "The town is not in our hands yet. We have to be careful. Would you take arms and are you prepared to fight for the president?"

A generally happy "yes" answered.

"Good, off with the chains and those freed will help the others. We have the soldiers tied up upstairs. We shall bring them down and put them in your chains. Their weapons are yours. Let's hurry." ---

When the president entered the room, the officers were at the same position as before. "The time is over, señores. Are you going to surrender?"

"Your conditions are too hard. I hope ..."

"Yes or no," interrupted Juarez.

"Our death would be revenged immediately."

"I despise this threat. You reject my forbearance. We had enough of the French treatment. However, that you see that I am serious I shall give you a foretaste of your fate."

"*Sacre,* what are you going to do?" The commandant asked in fear.

"Colonel Laramel," answered the president abruptly, "is the murderer of hundreds of my compatriots. He gave mercy to no-one. He is guilty of tonight's intended execution. He behaved like a bandit and will be treated as such. I shall have him hanged on this hook on the ceiling."

"You will not dare," shouted the commandant, "a French colonel."

"A French colonel, under these circumstances, is like any other bandit."

In the language of the Apaches he told them: "Hang this man on this hook," he pointed at Colonel Laramel and then at the hook in the ceiling that was meant for a Chandelier. With an Indian dexterity, the Apache threw the middle of his lasso onto the hook then around the neck of the shocked Colonel Laramel – a quick jerk and the officer hang from the ceiling.

"Murder, murder," shouted the commandant and the other officers moved furiously in their fetters.

Stenton and some of the prisoners, already armed, came into the room. Seeing the president and the hanging officer provoked cries of joy mixed with horror. "Here, señores is the beginning of justice. The others will be drowned at the place were the prisoners were going to be shot."

"The commandant now asked: "Would you stand by your former conditions?"

"I have given you ten minutes to accept or refuse. You let this deadline pass without making use of it. The consequences will come over you,"

"And if I would plead for the innocent soldiers?"

Juarez hesitated and turned to Stenton. "What do you say, señor?"

"It is my opinion, that forgiveness is better than revenge."

"Alright, I shall yield to your opinion. Bring pen and paper," ordered Juarez. He then turned to the commandant. "You can thank this señor for my leniency. You, as well as the other officers here, shall sign to the fact that you will go straight back to Mexico and that you will never fight against me again. It goes without saying that all your weapons stay here. You can take your deluded female spy with you. I don't want to hear another word or I shall revert to my original order to drown you."

The officers signed without another word. The rest of the prisoners now came in. All were armed now. Hurrah Juarez, hurrah the republic went the shouting. Stenton made a stop to that and said: "Quiet now, we have to take the rest of the soldiers first."

Enough Apaches were sent to capture the handful soldiers who still guarded the town.

The walk of the Nemesis that is usually slow and lame, was to be a rush and fast one.

Juarez now thought of meeting Lord Castlepool. This was the beginning of his victorious fight to regain his Country. ---

Chapter 26

TAKING OF THE HACIENDA

$\mathcal{T}$HREE hundred men, mounted on fresh horses rode over the plain, north of Montclova. All were armed and rode gallop. At the head were three men or rather two men and one female dressed as a man. They were the leaders of the group, José Carujo and Josefa. The actual leader had a dark expression on his face. His piercing eyes observed the surrounding. Finally he uttered curses and added: "When does this journey come to an end?"

"Be patient for only a short while. We shall soon come to a wood where we can have a rest, water and food for the horses."

"But I cannot see the hacienda yet."

"Beyond that wood, only half an hour's ride is the hacienda."

"I have brought my people to you for the booty you've promised and not to drift about in woods."

"Who tells you to do that? It is only a short delay."

"This is unnecessary."

"Do you think so? What if the French are there?"

"*Demonio*, that is true. They are crawling around everywhere but I thought the hacienda is a lonely spot. What would the French want with it?"

"It is a lonely spot but north of Monclava. It is thinkable that the enemy might use it to put a commando there."

"Hm, you may be right. We have to send someone to make enquiries. Let's ride sharply to reach the wood."

The hacienda had not changed in years but presently there were at every corner dug-outs where a French sentry was standing guard. There were a number of soldiers in the yard under the order of a captain who presently talked to the haciendero and his old friend Clarissa Moyes. Martin Wilson lay in his hammock. He had aged consider-ably since he had lost his child. His hair was long and snowy white. The old Clarissa was also grey but much more vigorous and sprightly than her master. A sergeant came in and reported a man who wished to speak to the haciendero. "Bring him in," ordered the captain.

The man came in and while the captain gave some orders to the sergeant, gave the haciendero a wink. Although Wilson did not quite understand, he knew that there was something the French should not know.

"Who are you?" asked the captain.

"I am a poor vaquero who lost his job because part of my master's herd has run off and he doesn't need so many people anymore. Señor Wilson has a good name among hacienderos and I was going to ask whether he could employ me."

"Have you an identity card or any papers of your dismissal?"

The man smiled as he answered: "That, señor, may be customary in France, nobody here asks for such things."

"I can, unfortunately not go by your customs. I have to stick to my guidelines. We can only allow people who can identify themselves," concluded the captain.

The haciendero declared that he knew the man. "His brother had worked for me and I vouch for him."

"That's different Monsieur. Do you know his name?"

The haciendero mentioned the first name that came to his mind.

"Do you intend to give him a job Monsieur? Good, you have my permission to do so. I shall add his name to the house list, said the captain."

"Thank you, señor, I am begging you pardon for causing so much trouble."

"If that would be my only trouble," continued the Captain, "I just received news to return to the capital early tomorrow. We shall all have to leave you."

"I am sorry," the haciendero forced himself to say as the officer left the room.

Martin Wilson and Clarissa Moyes were alone now with the alleged vaquero.

"Now, my dear friend, I hope that you are satisfied with me," said the haciendero, "I have been untruthful, a thing I don't usually do. Tell me who are you and what do you want here?"

"My name is Alessandro and I am a messenger from General Diaz to Benito Juarez, I shall only be here for two nights and then be on my way."

"Alright, but as a vaquero, you must eat with them and either sleep in their hut or, like some of them, sleep under the sky."

"I thank you, señor; I shall probably sleep under the sky." Without another word he went to join the vaqueros.

"Do you know," started Clarissa, "that you have let yourself into a dangerous thing. What if the French discover that he is a messenger for Juarez?"

"That would be a pity but would do no harm to me."

"Did you have a good look at this fellow, how do you like him?"

"How I liked him? Oh, I am not a young lady, señorita, joked Wilson.

Clarissa smiled but continued: "Did you notice his restless eyes; I do not quite trust him."

"You may be right but he will leave soon, so it doesn't concern us."

Meanwhile the stranger joined the vaqueros. He received food and he could walk away without anybody taking notice of him. In the evening he joined those who slept outside in the field, covered himself with a blanket and pretended to sleep. It was about midnight when he stole himself away without being noticed. When he reached his group in the wood Carujo received him. "Finally, what is the situation?"

"Bad and good at the same time," declared the spy. The hacienda is occupied by French soldiers. That is the bad news. The good news is: They are leaving tomorrow."

"How many soldiers are there?"

"Only about fifty."

"That is not bad, we can handle them."

"If you attack the soldiers, there will be bloodshed on both sides and a possible come-back. If, however, we wait one day, I shall be able to let you in and you will take possession without any bloodshed. The vaqueros will be surprised but yield to the inevitable."

"When would that be?"

"Tomorrow at midnight."

"Your plan is good. Now go back before you are missed."

"Remember: Midnight at the entrance. I shall open the gate for you; the rest is up to you." The spy went back and covered himself again with his blanket.

The French captain and his men left the next morning. The day passed uneventful. This time he joined those vaqueros who slept in the yard. He placed himself near the entrance. All was quiet at midnight and it was not difficult to open the gate for his comrades. The three hundred men went inside without any vaqueros waking up. Carujo and his daughter went upstairs to waken the haciendero.

With considerable shock, Wilson recognised Carujo. "What do you want here?"

"Let's sit down and you will soon learn what we want," answered Carujo.

Clarissa Moyes came into the room. "My God, what's happening here?"

"We are holding court," came Josefa's voice from the door, "over you and this one," she pointed at Clarissa.

"You are not serious, señorita," said Wilson. "We have not done anything to you. Will you be so good and explain your presence on the hacienda?"

"I shall give you the explanation," answered Josefa, did you hear about us lately?"

"Yes, but I didn't believe it."

"We took the hacienda with three hundred men, I am the owner of del Alina, the place you have cheated us out of and you are in my hands," answered a proud Josefa.

"The hacienda is mine, I bought it."

"Prove it!"

"I have the necessary documents to prove it."

"These documents are a forgery," said an angry Josefa, "you received this hacienda as a present. The purchasing documents are a sham."

"Even if you were right, the hacienda would still be mine and if not mine, the brother in Spain would have the next right but not you."

"Pah, what belongs to the Count belongs to us. You don't, of course, understand that."

"Oh, I understand very well," Wilson reared up. He was gripped by anger and therefore more courageous.

"You understand? Really? Josefa said sardonically. "How extraordinarily clever of you."

"Yes, I can see through your whole swindle. Aurelio is a Carujo. Therefore, you believe what belongs to the Counts of Manresa, belongs to you. Do you want to deny that?"

Deny? To you? Your senses have left you. What a madman says has neither to be confirmed nor denied. Where are your documents?"

"They are in a safe place."

"I have come here to ask you for them."

"They are not in this house."

Josefa jumped off her chair, clenched her fist and hissed angrily: "I want to know where they are?"

"The document and my last will are in safe hands. Don't trouble yourself."

Josefa's anger grew. "You have made a will and have appointed an heir? Who is it?"

"One doesn't tell anybody the secrets of a will, señorita."

"I shall put you into the deepest cellar. I shall torture you and you will slowly starve to death."

"I do not fear death."

Josefa answered with a scornful laughter: "You are old and infirm and you do not know anymore what you are talking about. When your skin is torn to pieces by my whip you will talk. And now to the other one."

The old and decent Clarissa Moyes, shaking and trembling, had listened to these threats. She knew that Josefa would not shrink from any cruelty. Now it would be her turn.

"Did you know about that will?"

"Yes," answered Clarissa.

"Do you know who the heir is?"

Clarissa hesitated but Wilson told her to tell anything she knew and not suffer on his behalf. "Yes," she whispered, "to a relation."

"Who is this relation?"

"A merchant in Ford Guadelupe, his name is Rodrigo."

"That name I have to remember. He is the heir?"

"Not he but his daughter."

"Does she know that she will be his heir?"

"Yes, Señor Wilson has sent a messenger there recently."

"Is that man back already?"

"No."

"What message did he have for her?"

Clarissa hesitated again but the haciendero told her again that she could talk. "You heard it, speak," ordered Josefa.

"The vaquero should ask Señorita Reseda to come here."

Josefa gloated. "The heiress will get a worthy reception. Where you there when Wilson made his will?"

"Yes, it was in this room."

"Who else was with you?"

"Three señores, they stayed for two days."

"Who were they?"

"I don't know any names. One was called señor mandatario, the other was a señor advocatore and the third one was a señor secretario."

"Have they taken the will with them?"

"Yes, the señor mandatorio took it and said that it was safe with him."

Carujo who had listen to all the conversation now turned to Josefa. "Leave it. Wilson himself will have to speak. We shall put him into the cellar. Hunger and thirst will make him talk. He will give us a written certificate that the hacienda belongs to us."

Josefa went to the door and begged two guerrillas to enter. "These two will be taken into the cellars; tie them well."

The two men looked at each other then, one of them asked: "Good, señorita. You will agree that we are prepared to fight for you but we are not your servants."

"Will two pieces of gold do?" She asked.

"Yes but while we are standing at the door, the others are plundering and we are getting nothing of what they have taken."

"If you obey, you will not go short and you will be satisfied with me."

The two Mexicans agreed and tied Wilson's and Clarissa Moyes' hands and feet. They did not resist. Wilson had fainted. Following the excitement and unexpected change of circumstances, the old man had broken down. One of them took Martin Wilson; the other took Clarissa Moyes on their arms and moved, followed by Josefa, past the noisy rabble into the cellars. Josefa locked them in one of the darkest vaults and took the keys.

"I am curious how much Señorita Carujo will give to us?" asked one of the Mexicans.

The other one remained silent. The first, therefore, continued:"Why don't you answer?"

The other took a deep breath and countered: "I wished that I had nothing to do with this business."

"Why? This gold-piece was easily earned."

"I wished that I hadn't earned it."

"*Caramba*, I believe that you getting sentimental."

"Listen, you know me, I Have loaded many a thing onto my conscience. I have locked up this pair with the greatest of pleasures but letting them die of hunger – I must say that I feel sorry for them."

"Nonsense, nobody has to know about it."

"I won't tell anybody."

"That girl is a real she-devil, woe to all of Mexico if her father becomes president."

"President?" grumbled the other one, not in his life. We follow him because he pays us, but to be a servant for all his or her meanness or the ambitious of this ruthless pair? Not me."

They parted. One to see whether he could make some loot, the other stepped onto the yard and mumbled to himself: "I shall never forget this old man in my whole life."

As he walked along the back of the house, he noticed a small hole at the bottom of the wall. "This might be connected with the cellar," he mused. He bent down, put his mouth near the hole and called with subdued voice: "Is somebody there?" A muffled voice answered.

Although he could not understand the words, it was enough for him to know that he had found the right hole or connection. Without any hesitation he tied a small bread to a string and let it down through the opening. Then he went to find a bottle and filled it with clear water. "So," he talked to himself, "at least they won't die of hunger or thirst. I feel much better now already." ---

Chapter 27

A PECULIAR LORD

CARUJO left with two hundred men to intercept Lord Castlepool and his cargo of weapons and millions in money destined for Juarez. Josefa stayed behind to represent her father as well as she could. The group reached the Rio Grande in three days, when the leader turned to Carujo. "Are you sure that the lord and his ship haven't passed yet?"

"According to my reports, he should be here this afternoon at the earliest."

"We must find a way to stop him and come near to this side of the river. He certainly won't if he sees our group of two hundred men."

"You're right," said Carujo, what's your plan?"

"We leave one man at the bank pretending to be ill. When addressed he will tell them he has a message from Juarez for the lord. We force the lord to hand over the cargo."

"This plan should work, I'm sure glad that I have hired you. You have a good head on your shoulders."

"This head will demand the right price."

"Certainly, the weapons are for me, one third of the money and everything else on board is for you and your men. How you distribute it is your business." ---

Lord Castlepool meanwhile sat at his desk and studied some papers. A sailor entered the room and reported a man with a giant nose wished to come on board. "He is in all probability our scout and contact with

Juarez. Ask him whether his name is Bighorn. If he says yes, let him come aboard."

A few minutes later, Bighorn entered the room. He was joyfully greeted by the lord. "I can see in your face you have good news for me. Am I right?"

"Yes, I calculate that you're right, but you won't expect this momentous news."

"There's been no good news for me since my daughter disappeared nearly fifteen years ago."

"Well," began the trapper, "let me give you the greetings of Juarez, who is on his way to you with a few hundred Indians and some people you know who, of course, also send their greetings. Let me name them: "There is one Dr. Stenton and ..."

The lord jumped off his chair, he almost shouted: "Did you say Dr. Stenton? That seems not possible he disappeared at the same time as my daughter."

"With him, there's a young man called Rudolfo ..."

The lord interrupted him again: "For God's sake, don't play such cruel jokes."

Bighorn bit off a large piece of tobacco, leaned comfortably back in his chair and continued undeterred: "There's further a Señorita Alva and a Lady Margaret ..."

My daughter? Sir, you are going too far ..."

This time the trapper interrupted: "Further a Señor Antonio and somebody called George Brooks."

The lord listened with bated breath. "You couldn't know these names unless you'd met them. My daughter, she's coming here? Where from? Where were they all these years?"

The scout unfolded the story and the lord wiped away his tears. But they were tears of joy. "And they are all well?" he asked.

"Yes, with Dr. Stenton around, how could they not be. I forgot one more important name: Count Manuel de Manresa y Cordoba."

"I've just began to believe your story but Count Manuel is surely dead."

"He'll be there with all of them. He was the man who saved them all." Bighorn now told Lord Castlepool about the miraculous meeting of the Count with Alva, as well as their escape."

"Forgive me, I am speechless. Let's open a bottle of my best Champagne."

"Leave that for the big celebration when they come here. For me, a glass of julep or rum will be enough. More important, we should steam toward them, we could save a full day."

"Of course, you are right. I'll give orders." The lord went and soon after that the yacht steamed ahead. He returned shortly and asked Bighorn to tell him more. The battle of Guadelupe and the taking of Chihuahua were mentioned. The lord could not hear enough and Bighorn obliged. In the afternoon a sailor came to Lord Castlepool and reported a man at the river bank who seemed ill. Lord Castlepool went on deck and, with the help of a loudspeaker, asked the man whether he needed help.

The man shouted back that his horse had thrown him and that he had a message from Juarez to Lord Castlepool. The lord did not hear exactly what the man said, but the word message and Juarez made him ask the machinist to stop. He went back to Bighorn and told him about the stranger.

"A message from Juarez so soon after I left him sounds suspicious to me."

"He's wounded and we can't just pass by and leave him there," said Lord Castlepool.

"You're about the same size as me. You must have in your wardrobe something I could wear. Then I'll go and see for myself. It sounds suspicious to me and you're too important on board to take the risk."

A few minutes later a man with a grey checked suit, a grey checked umbrella, a grey high-hat, grey shoes and yellow gloves was rowed toward the bank. A wide cravat and a monocle completed the outfit. This unlikely figure had a large nose. He got out of the boat and asked the two sailors who came with him to move back a few yards and return to the boat if there was any trouble. He had told the lord that in case of trouble he would make his way to Juarez and utter twice the cry of the Mexican vulture when I jump on a horse and again when I am out of danger. Also load your cannons in case they try to attack the ship at night.

Bighorn made a rare figure here in the jungle. The Mexican with the apparent accident mumbled to himself: "He's on his way. These mad

378

Englishmen can't leave their caprices at home. *Carajo*. Has he got a long nose! Now I have to pretend that I have difficulties in getting up."

Bighorn came toward him. "Pain? Where?"

"Terrible, all over my body."

"Miserable, very miserable. What is your name?

"Frederico."

"Who are you?"

"Vaquero."

"Messenger from Juarez?"

"Yes."

"What message?"

The Mexican pulled a face and groaned as if in terrible pain. That gave Bighorn the time to observe the surrounding area. He could not detect any other footprints, the edge of the wood seemed clear as well. Finally the man answered.

"Are you Lord Castlepool?"

"I am Castlepool. What have you to say?"

"Juarez is on his way. He asks you to dock here and to expect him here."

"Ah, wonderful. Where is he?"

"In Paso del Norte two weeks ago. He's coming down the river."

"Good. I'll go on then; if he comes down the river I'll meet him. Good night."

Bighorn turned around and made his way back to the bank when the man suddenly embraced him from the back.

"Stay milord, if you value your life," called the Mexican.

Bighorn had enough strength to defend himself but he preferred different behaviour. He stood still as if shock had paralysed him. "What is that?"

"You are my prisoner," panted the man.

The 'Englishman' gasped. "Ah, deception. No pain?"

"No," laughed the Mexican.

"Rascal! Why?"

"To take you prisoner, milord." He threw a contemptuous glance at the 'Englishman' who seemed baffled and cowardly and did not even try to defend himself.

"Why prisoner?" asked Bighorn.

"Because of your cargo that you have on board."

"My people will free me," said the supposed lord.

"I don't believe that. See how your people are fleeing, Look around you."

The people in the boat had turned back as previously instructed, especially when they noticed that he voluntarily let the Mexican overpower him. A large group of riders came from the woods. In only a few seconds he was surrounded. He pretended to be astonished and fiddled with his umbrella, apparently embarrassed. The riders jumped off their horses. Carujo, looking disappointed. "Who are you?" he asked the 'Englishman.

Who are you?" growled the disguised Bighorn back.

"I'm asking who you are," ordered Carujo sharply.

"And I asked who you are," answered Bighorn. I am Englishman, highly educated, distinguished family. I'll answer after you."

"All right, my name is Carujo."

"Carujo? Ah, José?"

"That's my name," was the proud answer.

"The deuce! That's odd." This exclamation was sincere. Bighorn was surprised to see Carujo but at the same time delighted.

"Odd, isn't it." laughed Carujo. You didn't expect that. Now tell me who you are?"

"My name is Castlepool," answered Bighorn.

"Castlepool? That's a lie, I know Lord Castlepool. You are not him.

Bighorn was not the man to lose his composure. He spat a beam of tobacco juice past Carujo's nose and replied: "No, I am not him."

Carujo had quickly pulled his head back and said angrily: "Take care where you spit, señor."

"I do. I hit only when I want to."

"I hope it isn't me you want to hit."

"That depends on you."

"So you are not Lord Henry Castlepool?"

"No."

"Then why did you tell me you are a Castlepool?"

"Because I am."

Bighorn's calmness upset Carujo He asked angrily: "The devil, how should I understand that?"

"Been in Old England?"

"No."

"No wonder, lord only eldest son. Later son no lord."

"So you are a later son of a Castlepool?"

"Yes."

"What is your name then?"

"Sir Lionel Castlepool."

"Hm, you don't look like your brother."

Bighorn again spat near Carujo's face. "Nonsense."

"Do you deny that?"

"Yes, it is not that I am not similar to him; he is not similar to me."

Carujo could find no answer to this logic. Self-confidence and fearlessness made an impression. After a pause he said: "I expected your bother."

"Henry? Why expect him?"

"I heard he would accompany the cargo."

"Mistake, that. I'm doing it."

"Where is Sir Henry?"

"With Juarez."

"Ah, he has gone ahead. Where is Juarez now?"

"Only know El Paso del Norte."

"And how far should your cargo go?"

"To Ford Guadelupe."

Sure of victory, a cynical smile went over Carujo's face. "You don't have to go that far You must unload here and give everything to me."

The 'Englishman' scanned the surroundings. He looked indifferent, almost absent-minded, but this was a blind for his sharp inspection of the horses. He knew, at this moment, which animal he would take.

"Give everything to you? He asked. "Why you?"

"Because I need it."

"Need it? I am sorry but I can't sell it."

"Oh, señor, I don't wish to buy it I expect the whole cargo to be given as a present."

"Present? I don't give presents."

"O yes, I'll force you."

"Force me? The trapper laughed as if he had no idea what Carujo was up to. He pointed his mouth and sprayed his tobacco juice at Carujo's hat so that it fell down.

"*Caramba!*" Carujo shouted. Do you know that this is an insult?"

"Go away," said Bighorn calmly. Gentleman can spit where he wants to. Who doesn't want to be hit must get out of the way."

"Ah, we'll have to cure you of that type of fun. You must now declare that you hand the cargo over to me."

"I don't do that."

"I'll force you. You are my prisoner."

"Pshtishshshshsh!" The beam went near Carujo's nose. Bighorn fumbled with his umbrella. "Prisoner? How odd. How very odd. I always wanted to be a prisoner."

"Well, your wish has come true. Now tell your people that they should stay here."

"Good, shall do that."

The trapper said this in a voice as if he was completely in agreement with the Mexican. He put his umbrella under the arm, his hands to his mouth and shouted loudly. "Stop here, it is José Carujo."

"*Demonio*! Why did you shout my name?"

"Why did you give it to me?" asked the 'Englishman' with indifference.

"Not to be roared to everybody. By the way, I didn't just mean to stop here but to unload here."

Bighorn slowly shook his head and countered innocently: "They won't do that, I'm forbidding them to do it."

"How many people have you?"

"I don't know, I'm forgetful, sometimes, but it will come back to me later."

"We'll easily find out. Now, order your people to unload here."

"I won't do that."

Carujo put his hand on Bighorn's shoulder and hissed: "Sir Lionel, your boats must be at the river's bank before it gets dark. If you don't give the order, we'll force you."

"Force? How?"

Bighorn still held the umbrella under his arm and put both hands into his trouser pockets. He looked as if he had no idea of the danger of his situation.

"We'll whip you. I'll give you fifty strokes."

"Why only fifty?"

"Sir Lionel, you are mad."

"Well, you too."

"If fifty are too few for you then you will be whipped until you have enough."

Bighorn squared his shoulders and pulled a contemptuous face. "Beatings? Me, an Englishman?"

"Yes, you may be a thousand times an Englishman or ten times the brother of a lord, I shall still whip you if you don't obey at once."

"Try it."

Carujo did not see the glances that the supposed Englishman had for a magnificent black stallion whose rider had just moved away from it. He also didn't see the two revolvers that Bighorn drew halfway out of his pockets but threatened: "You will be whipped in front of my eyes, like a poor tramp, if you don't obey."

"We will see whether your eyes are really going to see that." Bighorn, at the same moment, took his umbrella between his teeth. He did not think to sacrifice the umbrella in spite of the danger of being surrounded by two hundred enemies. The next moment he drew both guns and with all the power he could muster pushed them into the eyes of Carujo. He then emptied all the chambers of his revolver. Every shot felled a man. Carujo was on the ground and could not see. He stamped about with his hands and feet, and roared like a lion. His men were speechless and paralysed for a moment.

Nobody could expect such a sudden attack from the apparently crazy 'Englishman'. But the short time was enough. When the last shot of his revolvers were spent, he uttered the shrill cry of a Mexican vulture and swung himself on the black stallion he had previously earmarked for his escape. He pushed his heels into its side and the horse flew toward the wood. He turned around and saw the Mexicans just recovering from their shock and he heard shouts to follow him. But it was too late and he uttered the second cry of the bird of prey, to indicate that he was on his way to Juarez.

Most of the Mexicans jumped on their horses while others stayed behind to help Carujo. "My eyes, oh my eyes. Take me to the water, I want cooling, cooling," he roared.

The people took him to the river and tried to soothe the terrible pain of the blinded man with cooling water. After a while the whimpering decreased and he could talk to his subordinates. The pursuers returned eventually and said they couldn't reach the escaped. The truth was that they were more interested in the rich cargo of the still stationary ship than the crazy Englishman.

Only the owner of the black stallion was annoyed about the loss of his horse. But there were replacements through the demise of twelve men who had been eliminated by Bighorn. They made a fire and sat down. After a while the leader of the group got up and left the camp. A few of his favourites followed him.

"What have you in mind?" asked one of his followers.

"I have a splendid idea but this Carujo needn't to know about it."

"Speak!"

"First I want to know what you think of Carujo."

They were silent, undecided whether to tell the truth. "Let us first hear what you think?"

"Well, I think he suffers delusions of grandeur or he is plain stupid."

"We never noticed you thought of him like that."

"It is just that I am not stupid. Did you ever think that he could be president?"

"Oh no."

"I think we can take the cargo of this boat for ourselves."

"Without Carujo? *Caramba,* that would be a good catch."

"Splendid."

"I'm not so sure. What will Carujo say to all this?"

"Not a word. We won't ask him. Do you think anybody would mind if he suddenly disappeared?"

"Yes, his supporters."

"We're his supporters."

"His daughter."

"What do we care about his daughter? A quick push with a knife and finish."

"A murder? Brrr!"

"Think what there is on the boat."

"A few thousand rifles. They bring a lot of money."

"I know of a few cannons. They bring even more."

"Carujo himself told me there's money there for Juarez – that's many millions."

"*Ascuas!*"

"Should we leave that money for Carujo to squander on his mad ideas?"

"We'd be fools to leave the money to him."

"But Carujo is our leader. Didn't he let us plunder the hacienda? I wouldn't want to have him killed. Why not put him on a raft on the river. There he could swim until somebody finds him."

"That would be a way out. What do you all think?" Everybody agreed. After a short discussion it was decided to put him on a raft. Then they returned, each to his group.

"What shall we do?" mused the blinded Carujo. "Await the return of the English? We could take the ship before that."

"But how? We have no boats, should we build rafts?"

Carujo thought a little. "That's not clever. Rafts are difficult to steer. Oh if I could see. The ship would be ours in no time."

"A little difficult, señor. We have no boats and we should not use rafts."

"Quite right but who would stop us swimming over?"

"That's true, but not everybody can swim."

"Isn't there enough wood around here to help them get across?"

"But the powder gets wet."

"No, the rifles stay here, we only use our knives. We'll be on the steamer before the crew realises what's happening. They'll be dead in minutes. Then we can bring the cargo ashore. If only I could be there."

"You can be there, señor. We'll build you a larger raft."

"But I couldn't steer it."

"There's no necessity. Two or three men will help you."

"That's possible. The pain has lessened somewhat and, maybe by tomorrow I shall be able to see in one eye."

"But we can't wait until tomorrow."

"All right, are there any lights on board?"

"Not one, señor."

"They're asleep. They think that the danger has gone."

"Where do you want us to take you?"

"I'll have to see what's going on."

The people exchanged significant glances and went to work. It was surely stupidity of Carujo to ask to be present on board, but he didn't trust his people and believed that his presence would ensure the loot was his. This way he actually helped the dark plans of his opponents. They built a raft for him.

"How big is the raft? Carujo enquired.

"Two and a half metres long and two metres wide."

"That's enough for one man. Those who steer it can swim."

"Yes," said the leader of the troop, "and it's not too big to be easily noticed and it'll be safer for you."

That sounded caring and satisfied Carujo. "I just want to repeat: the cargo is mine."

"Could we not claim part of it for us señor Carujo?"

"No, you know what it's for. You'll get your award. I'll give you one tenth of the value of its contents."

"Is that not too little?"

"Be silent. There are millions aboard this ship. You can calculate what that means per head."

"I never thought of it that way. I declare that we are satisfied."

"I should think so."

Carujo did not see the looks to each other of these guerrillas, otherwise he would have a different opinion. "Douse the fires, it's time to begin."

This order was obeyed. The Mexicans were convinced of the success of their plans and trembling with desire to lay their hands on those millions. They went into the water while Carujo was put on a raft that, in turn, was guided by two swimmers.

"Forward," he ordered.

The swimmers had reached about half the distance to the ship, when there were rockets shot into the sky. Everything was lit up. They had their first shock. Then the lord called "Fire!"

The cannons were loaded with spreading shell and caused terrible losses among the attackers. Quite a few heads disappeared below the water level, never to rise up again. One of the swimmers with Carujo called: *Santa Madonna,* I'm hit in the arm." He stopped holding on to the raft. Carujo asked: "What's going on?"

"They've noticed us and they are shooting at us."

"Did they hit us?"

"Yes, señor."

"Make them hurry to get on board."

"Nothing doing, the survivors are swimming back."

"Hell and damnation. Has our attack failed?"

"Completely, señor."

"Get me back to the bank."

"Sorry. It is forbidden to bring you back."

"Who has forbidden that?"

"The comrades," he said as he left the raft.

Carujo was overcome by a dreadful fear. Blind and helpless, he was drifting on the giant river. "Are you still here? I shall pay you double, no, treble. Just stay with me."

There was no reply. Alone, alone, drifting to certain death. What shall I do? How can I save myself? He still had enough energy not to give up. Somewhere, somehow, the raft will land ashore and someone will find me. I have enough money on me to pay someone to get me to the hacienda – to Josefa. He stretched himself out on the raft. A few hours later he even fell asleep. Finally he was woken by the jerk of the raft landing somewhere ashore. He felt cold and was riddled with fever. One of his eyes could see a little. At least I didn't drown, he thought. So far I've been lucky. Who knows, may be I'll be saved. Excitement, pain and fever made him to fall asleep again. ---

Where the Sabinas flowed together with the Rio Salado, Juarez and his men reached the spot where he hoped Lord Castlepool would turn off the Rio Grande and unload his cargo to help him arm and finance enough men to drive out the French. The Austrian Emperor Maximilian would then either flee or, if foolish enough, stay and be captured. In spite of the darkness they searched the river bank for miles but no trace of the expected could be found. They made camp. The hunters among them rose at the earliest to find food for everybody. They went on the nearby hill where Buff-he pointed at a distant rider who came across the plain at a furious gallop. It was the appearance of the rider which made everybody, except the serious Indians among them, smile. The man looked strange in these surroundings. As soon as he noticed the group he waved his grey high hat and his grey umbrella, but did not diminish his speed until he was with them.

"Bighorn," Stenton greeted him, "what on earth are you doing here and in this outfit?"

"Where is Juarez, I want to tell him the news then you can hear it," replied Bighorn.

"It must be urgent and important. Let's go," countered Stenton.

Juarez rose when he saw the group coming and greeted Bighorn with a smile. "I'm sure there are special reasons for you to come in such a rush and in this outfit."

Bighorn told him about the events of the previous day and urged Juarez to come at once to the Rio Grande where he might apprehend Carujo and his men and also take the cargo that was meant for him.

Juarez ordered everybody to mount and almost immediately, the whole camp rushed behind Bighorn, who had to change horses. The one he came with was left behind to graze and rest. It couldn't take any more. They had barely ridden four hours, when he saw a cloud of dust in the distance. Bighorn stopped and asked Stenton for his telescope.

It looked as if Carujo's men were coming. He asked Juarez to let him have the fun of greeting them and asked that everybody would hide behind nearby bushes. Juarez obliged and Bighorn sat down on the grass, opening his umbrella to give him shade from the burning sun. It took twenty minutes for the men to reach him. They were the same group, only fewer, he had escaped from yesterday. "Hallo, our Englishman, now we have won. He won't escape again." Thus Bighorn was greeted by the leader of the group.

They surrounded him and the leader addressed him again: "Hello, señor, is it you or is it your ghost?"

Bighorn turned slowly toward the speaker. "My ghost, of course, I have been shot yesterday as well as being beaten to death."

"Don't talk nonsense. But you have a different horse."

"That is the ghost of the other one."

"You shot twelve of our men yesterday. Your people have killed more than sixty in the water and you'll have to pay for that."

"Why did they go into the water?"

"Because you run away without giving orders to unload the cargo."

"I had to, otherwise Señor Carujo was going to beat me. By the way, where is Señor Carujo?"

"He was shot by your people as well."

"Why do you need the cargo?"

"It's the money we are after, the rest we'll sell."

"Is that all? Why didn't you tell me yesterday? I always wanted to get rid of these stupid millions but nobody wanted them."

Bighorn had risen from the ground and folded the umbrella. The speaker had drawn a gun and started to wave it in his direction. "You have played the fool long enough. You are our prisoner now and you will order your people to hand over the goods. Otherwise you will die."

Bighorn took the gun out of his hand. This happened with lightning speed and before he had finished the sentence. He calmly turned it round and emptied the double barrel into the leader's head. Before the others could move to revenge him, the war cry of the Apaches shook the air. The gang of a hundred and twenty men were surrounded by five hundred Indians, three hundred Mexicans and many more who had since joined the Juarez movement. The famous hunters like Doc Ironfist, Old Surehand, Buff-he and two dozen others kept behind with Juarez, Count Manuel, Rudolfo, Alva, Margaret and Kaya.

The leaderless group soon put down their arms. They were only tied by their hands. One of them stepped forward and asked to speak to Juarez. He gave his permission and asked the man whether he was the leader. "No," came the answer, "the leader has been killed by the 'Englishman'."

"All right, what do you have to tell me?" asked the Zapotec.

"I am a Mexican who wanted to fight for my country. I originally went out to join Senior Juarez. Carujo came and made the same promises, so I followed him. When I found that his methods where inhuman, it was too late."

Stenton had listened to this but Juarez continued the questions: "Are you speaking for yourself or the whole group?"

"I am speaking for myself, although, no doubt, there are a few who are of the same mind and were mislead by Carujo's promises."

Juarez turned to Stenton. "He may be right but how shall I find out?"

Stenton asked the man. "How will we find those who are possibly of a better character than the others?"

"My suggestion is to ask the men to return voluntarily what they have looted from the Hacienda del Alina."

Stenton exchanged glances with Juarez who, by nodding, asking Stenton to continue the questioning. "Tell me what happened to the hacienda?" The man told how they were promised that they could take from the hacienda whatever they could find.

"And what have you taken?"

"Nothing. I received a gold coin from Señorita Josefa, that's the daughter of this Carujo, for services I wished I didn't have to supply."

"What services were they?"

"To tie up the haciendero and an old woman and put them in a cellar, where they would be given no food or drink until they died. Señorita Josefa took the keys. "

"My God, did you have to do that?"

"I had to do what I was told but I found a hole that led into the cellars and I sent down some bread and water."

"How long ago was that?"

"Only two days ago but I have found somebody who, for the gold piece that I gave him, was prepared to supply the two old people with food and water daily."

"You have given us valuable information and, if I find it's true, you have saved the lives of two people who are dear to us. You will be rewarded." Stenton turned to Juarez. "I intended to go with you to Lord Castlepool but I must go to the Hacienda del Alina to help our friends." Turning again to the Mexican who gave him the disturbing news, he asked: "How many men did Carujo leave with his daughter?"

"About one hundred."

Juarez asked Stenton: "Will two hundred men be enough?"

Before Stenton could answer. Buff-he chipped in: "There is no need to slow us down with so many people. We shall be tonight at the mount

El Raparo, not far from the hacienda and I'll have between six hundred and one thousand men on our side in the morning."

"Buff-he's advice is good," said Juarez. "Take the best horses and send a few more men to me at intervals, to keep me informed."

It took less than five minutes for Stenton, Don Manuel, Old Surehand, Buff-he, George Brooks and two messengers to be on their way to the hacienda. Rudolfo did not want to leave Lady Margaret who was naturally desparate to see her father. Alva and Kaya followed the first group with ten white warriors to accompany and guard them. ---

Chapter 28

THE INTERCEPTED LETTER

---

*J*UAN Ernesto Vastorez, the old vaquero, was happy to bring the good news to his master Martin Wilson whom he had served for many years. Yet it was not before evening that he saw the hacienda in the distance. He spurred the tired horse to go faster. Finding the gate locked he knocked.

"Who is there?" asked a strange voice.

"Juan Vastorez."

"I don't know that name."

"You must be new here."

"Yes."

"Well, open up, I am a vaquero of Señor Wilson coming from Ford Guadelupe where we have beaten the French."

"From Ford Guadelupe? I think you're expected."

The guard opened the gate and lead the vaquero to Josefa. It was dark and the vaquero did not notice that the place was not quite the same. He didn't expect a lady and asked to be taken to Señor Wilson. Josefa decided to act in a friendly manner to put him at ease and tell her everything. "Come in and take a seat. Señor Wilson and Señora Moyes left for a short while on urgent business. He left me in charge until he comes back. He told me to expect you in the company of a lady and to send a message immediately on your arrival."

"I can see he took you into his confidence I was eager to bring him very good news."

"Good news is rare nowadays; tell it to me so that I may send a messenger to him immediately."

"It concerns his daughter whom he believed to be dead. She's alive and there is no need to look for another heir," the unsuspecting man told his shocked listener.

"Did she tell what happened to her and, I believe, to other people who were with her?" Josefa could hardly contain her excitement.

Juan Ernesto was eager to oblige. "Yes," he blurted out, "all those who had disappeared at that time were alive."

Josefa jumped up. It took all her strength to hide the impression that this news made on her. "Where are these people now?" she asked almost breathlessly.

"They accompany Juarez to El Refugio at the Rio Grande where they will meet a Lord Castlepool and then they, probably, will come straight here. Except Count Manuel who …"

"Count Manuel?" Josefa shrieked, "I attended his funeral, he is surely dead.

"It was he who freed the others," continued the vaquero and told Josefa all he knew.

He did not observe the feelings expressed on her face. Disbelief at first, then doubt, anxiety, conviction, shock and fury sped one after the other over her features. What she heard meant they were again at the beginning of their schemes. They would be lost if measures were not taken at once to Counteract. She decided to make a start with this simple fellow.

"Señor, what you've told me here, will you swear to?"

"Any oath you need."

"Well, if these people are unmasked now, they are stronger than before. Carujo has now a great party behind him and will be president of Mexico shortly."

"Oh, don't imagine that, señorita. Bazaine is still here."

"Bazaine. He'll be chased away."

"And Maximilian of Austria."

"That emperor in name, that mock-regent? He will escape by himself."

"But Juarez, the president?"

"The Indian of the tribe of the Zapotecs? He will be hanged and eaten by vultures."

Josefa's face had assumed a dark, almost devilish, expression. Juan Ernesto noticed that, he didn't know what to make of it.

"I don't believe that," he said, "I think that Carujo and his daughter deserve to be hanged."

"Have you ever seen her?"

"No, I have no desire to. She'd better watch out and not to be seen by me."

Josefa now dropped every reserve. She stepped to the vaquero and hissed at him: "You will see her sooner than you think. Albeit different to your liking." Her eyes sparkled, her self-control had gone.

"But señorita," Juan Ernesto said astounded, "I don't understand you."

"You will understand quite quickly. You indicated that you as well as your master are supporters of Juarez. If all supporters of his are as stupid as you, then there is no doubt he will hang in a short time. Do you know where Wilson is?"

"He has gone away for a short time. You said so yourself," said the embarrassed vaquero.

"And you believed that? You are more stupid than I thought.

"But you told me so."

"He has been imprisoned by me and you will join him."

"Don't play such gruesome jokes, señorita."

"If you knew who I am, you would not think that I am joking. I had to deceive you to find out what I wanted to know. I have succeeded brilliantly. Can you guess now who I'm?" With this challenge, her eyes rested on this simple but not stupid man.

"Heaven help," he called with a shock. "You are ... you are - Señorita Josefa."

"Yes," she pronounced, "I am Carujo's daughter.

"Oh, oh, what have I done?"

"I have learned everything, everything I should not know. Do you know what I shall do now? I shall send a message to my father and Lord Castlepool and all the others with him will be killed ... "

"I hope you won't succeed," groaned the vaquero, "it would be my fault."

"Yes, furthermore, we shall lie in wait for Juarez. They will all have to die." With this she called the guards that stood outside her door. "Tie this man up and put him into the cellars with the other two prisoners. Ask them whether they are ready to talk. Then bring back the keys I'm giving you now."

Juan Ernesto Vastorez was bound and taken to the cellars where he could barely stand up. He stepped on a body near the entrance. "Who are you," asked a female voice from the dark.

"Señora Moyes," he replied, "I recognised your voice. Is Señor Wilson in here?"

"Yes," answered Clarissa Moyes. He's very weak and faints time after time. But tell me who are you?"

"I am Juan Ernesto Valtores, the vaquero who has been sent to Ford Guadelupe."

"Did you bring Señorita Reseda with you?"

"Thank God I didn't, this female devil would have killed her."

"That's what she wants to do with us but I keep praying to God that he will send someone to save us."

While Clarissa was talking, a body nearby moved. "Who are you talking to Clarissa?"

"It's Juan Ernesto, the vaquero you have sent to Guadelupe."

"So he's imprisoned too. I had a vague hope that he might save us," sighed the haciendero.

"Rescue will come Señor Wilson; there are people on the way here, who are capable of saving you."

"Who could possibly do that? Carujo is a cunning devil and his daughter, if anything, is worse."

"Before I tell you, let's get rid of our fetters. They've tied my hands and forgot to search me. There's a penknife in my pocket. Maybe you could reach it?"

He knelt down and Clarissa took the penknife out of his pocket. With the help of his teeth, Ernesto managed to open it eventually. While he was trying, Clarissa Moyes told him that somebody had let down some bread and water but they were unable to make use of that kindness because they were bound hand and foot."

"You'd better eat something first. What I have to tell you may take some strength to bear."

"Is it that bad,? I thought nothing worse could happen to us," enquired the now fully awake haciendero.

"It's good news," ventured Ernesto. "In fact so good that I fear for your heart.

"Let's hear then but good news will not kill me." The haciendero's voice has strengthened somewhat, even before his first bite. Ernesto was quiet for a short while, then he could no longer contain himself.

"Among the people I'm hoping will save us was a Señor Stenton."

"Don't play such cruel jokes," said the haciendero, who had stopped chewing for a moment.

"It is no joke and there are others with him. A Mixteka called Buff-he."

The haciendero and Clarissa stopped eating. "For God's sake, you know something and want to give it to us slowly. Speak, speak quickly, who are the others, where have they been?"

"Señor Wilson, can you take the best news of your life? I say this because it will also provide you with a shock." Ernesto prepared the haciendero carefully.

"The best news of my life could only be the reappearance of my daughter – and she is surely dead."

"I have seen and spoken to your daughter."

There was silence. The haciendero breathed deeply. "I cannot see your face, your voice sounds true but why has she not written in all these years?"

"Señorita Alva couldn't write from where she was. She has been on an unknown island in the South Seas. She is also on the way here but on a slower track."

"Oh God, forgive me that I wanted to die but now I have the strength to live and take anything that may come." There were tears of joy in the father's eyes and Clarissa was crying loudly.

Upstairs, Josefa wrote a letter to her father. She sent it off with the instruction to tell him to hurry and to wish him luck. The messenger left early in the morning. ---

After six hours of fast galloping, Stenton suggested a short break, which seemed a more important rest for the sweating horses than for the men. A rider came near but after seeing the little group, he veered off. Stenton jumped on his horse and chased after the man. The other, seeing only one man, slowed down and asked him what he wanted.

"In the wild the person who obviously wants to avoid you, is always interesting" said Stenton in the friendliest manner.

"I'm in a hurry."

"Where do you come from?"

"From the Hacienda del Alina. I carry a message from a daughter to her father."

"That's interesting. We are going to the hacienda and we have a message from a father to his daughter."

"Would this lady's name be Josefa," asked the stranger now more interested.

"That's her name." Stenton was, of course, eager to find out more.

"I'm not expected to bring back an answer – are you?" asked the unsuspecting man.

"Why do you ask me that?" Stenton asked.

"We could exchange messages and return to our places of origin," ventured the messenger innocently.

"Good idea. My message is verbal, and yours?"

"I have a letter with no other instructions than to give it to Señor Carujo and wish him luck. It would save me searching for him if we could exchange messages."

"All right," said Stenton. "Come to our group there and I'll give you the message."

The man, pleased to have completed his task so quickly, followed Stenton to his comrades who were sitting on the grass, awaiting the outcome of their conversation. The newcomer did not find it unusual to see an Indian in the group. Stenton asked him to tell his name:" I am called Josemaria," answered the young fellow.

Stenton observed him sharply when he introduced himself and the others. There was no sign of recognition. The messenger, apparently, knew none of them and handed Josefa's letter to Stenton without suspicion. Stenton asked:

"Josemaria, do you know what a ruse of war is?"

The young man looked at him wonderingly. "Of course, doesn't everybody?"

"Carujo is a criminal. We have not come from him, we are after him and his daughter."

The young man could hardly understand. Old Surehand and Buff-he had their guns already in their hands. "Return the letter," he stammered, "I'll deliver it myself."

"That won't be possible, you are our prisoner." Stenton had drawn his gun as well and George Brooks had rope to bind the prisoner. Against three guns, he let his hands be tied without resistance, but speechless.

Stenton opened the letter from Josefa to her father. It read:

"Dear father,

The old vaquero whom Wilson had sent to Ford Guadelupe, has returned today.

I succeeded in eliciting from him the following:

Danlola has betrayed us. All our enemies are alive. Stenton, Rudolfo, the Brooks brothers, Buff-he, Alva Wilson, Kaya and Lady Margaret. Even Count Manuel is with them. He escaped from slavery. The haciendero and the old woman in the cellar are still alive but haven't talked yet.

You know yourself what to do. They must all die, otherwise we are lost. They are with Juarez (who has beaten three French companies), on the way to Lord Castlepool. They will meet, where the Sabinas flows into the Rio Grande.

Act quickly and return soon.

Your daughter Josefa.

Stenton turned again to Josemaria: "Did you know the contents of this letter?"

"Of course not."

"Do you know what happened to the haciendero?"

"We were told he'd run away." Stenton gave the letter to the others to read. He told the fellow: "Either you are a good liar or you are innocent. We were told that Carujo is dead. So you could not deliver the letter in any case."

"All I wanted was to free Mexico of its usurpers. That's what Carujo promised to do and that is why I joined him."

"If I send you to Juarez with my recommendation to take you on. will you join him and fight for him?"

"Gladly." The young man sounded honest.

"If I take off your fetters, will you escape?"

"Tell me first what crimes have been committed by Carujo and his daughter."

"That is too long a story but in your time they have been acting in an inhuman way with the haciendero. They put him into the cellars to let him die of hunger."

One could see genuine astonishment on the young man's face and it took a while before he said: "In that case, let me join you to free him."

"There's no need for that," said Stenton. "You will go with a messenger to Juarez with a recommendation from me. However, safety demands that you will be tied up until tomorrow night.

"I understand and will not resist. I am even happy, that things had turned out this way. I have always mistrusted Carujo and I hope that you will be able to free the haciendero."

They rode another three hours toward the hacienda, before the messenger with his prisoner, who was now tied on his horse, made a hundred and eighty degree turn and galloped to Juarez. Stenton had written to Juarez, telling him the exact story of his meeting with this former Carujo supporter. The letter was given to the messenger who, with his prisoner, was going to reach the Zapotec and his entourage during the night or early in the morning.

It was evening when Stenton and his little group reached mount El Rapero. Buff-he led them to an opening where he went straight to a large rock. The top of it was almost flat, eight foot square with a dip in the middle filled with many smaller stones not less than the size of a large fist. He removed most of these and revealed a large box made of hardened wood. The contents were a number of apple size coloured pieces made of something none of the onlookers could define. Buff-he then proceeded to make a fire with some dried twigs. Into this fire he threw two of the box's items which immediately made a fifteen foot flare and collapsed after only several seconds.

Buff-he sat calmly on the ground as if expecting something to happen. His comrades had too much trust in him to query his behaviour. Only three minutes later they had an answer. At a distance of several miles in a semi circle similar flares were to be seen, all of different colours. Buff-he explained that by morning many hundreds of Mixtekas would assemble at this spot and he suggested having a short nap. They made themselves comfortable after the night watches were chosen.

The Mixtekas started to arrive, eight hundred of them. Anyone could see their astonishment but with typical Indian stoicism nobody asked where their chief had been for the last fifteen years. Buff-he assembled the various chiefs around him and said they had to wait for an explanation. The task now was to take the Hacienda del Alina off the hands of its enemies. No questions were asked and within minutes, the Indians, none of whom had slept that night, were on their way to retake the hacienda from Carujo's people.

Before Stenton could ask that they should take them prisoner, they were all butchered and scalped. Señorita Josefa was still asleep when Stenton entered her room. Having just awoken and because of his long beard, she didn't recognise him immediately. "Who are you and what do you want?" she questioned.

"I'm here to take you captive and put you into the cellars where you have detained your prisoners." Stenton was prepared. With three steps he grabbed the revolver under her pillow before she could take it. "Your game is up señorita. You've been in possession of the de Manresa fortunes for too long. Your father is probably dead now and you may not meet a much better fate."

With his strength, her struggling meant nothing. She was bound hand and foot and carried by two Indians into the cellars where, at the same time Martin Wilson, Clarissa Moyes and Ernesto Vastorez were freed.

It was the haciendero who spoke first: "Dr. Stenton, what Ernesto, my vaquero told me, is really true. I cannot express my thanks and feelings, and because of your reappearance I must believe that my daughter and son-in-law are alive too."

"Don't thank me; thank God who makes sense where humans have doubts. Your son-in-law is already here; your daughter will follow by tomorrow, maybe even by tonight."

Clarissa kissed his hand and Ernesto wanted to pour out his thanks but Stenton warded them off. "Let's go upstairs to greet the others." Martin Wilson suddenly became younger. He climbed the stairs with energetic steps. There is no need to describe the great joy of his meeting Antonio and the others. He ordered the slaughter of two weighty cows and everything to provide a festive meal for over eight hundred rescuers. ---

Chapter 29

DOCTOR HIDALGO

CARUJO'S raft had drifted onto the left river bank. His joy was great when he noticed that one of his eyes could see a little light. He found himself surrounded by tall reeds that would cover him if he lay down. He found the piece of cloth formerly dipped in water to cool his great pain. Once more, he used it to cool his eyes, hurting less now. The sun was already warming his body and he bedded himself as well as he could on the ground to have a further rest and wait for something to happen. In less than an hour, he was just falling asleep again, when he heard the noise of a horse coming closer.

Carujo deliberated: "Most of the night I was drifting on the raft. It would be unlikely to be one of my men. A stranger, on the other hand, could be just as dangerous. However, not many people know my face yet." He decided to show himself. He stood up and waved both his arms. The rider, who was just passing by turned his horse slightly and rode toward the stranded Carujo.

"Hallo there," the stranger called out, "you look quite a mess. What happened to you?"

"I'm almost blind. The work of a bunch of Indians," Carujo lied.

"Who are you?" came the next question.

"Just a vaquero," Carujo lied again.

"I don't believe you but I don't care. You obviously need help. I live nearby and can give you some shelter."

"Can you tell me who you are?"

"I'm an American hunter. I am apolitical and have no-one to fear. My name is Peter Danlola."

"Danlola? A rare name. I've come across it only once."

The stranger became interested. "There is only one other Danlola that I know of and I've been after that owner for more than twenty years."

"That sounds unfriendly; do you have a grievance against this man?" Carujo enquired with certain expectations.

"More than just a grievance but tell me more about the person you know." The stranger seemed really interested.

"I have a business contact with this Ramirez Danlola and I expect to hear from him via an agent in Vera Cruz."

"Ramirez? It seems to be the same person that I am interested in. Who is this agent?"

"I will tell you after you've taken me to the Hacienda del Alina. I shall pay you for that." Carujo had new hopes.

"I know this hacienda; it's a good day's ride from here. I would first like to get you a horse."

"Do we have an agreement? You get me to the hacienda and I'll help you to find your brother. Can you tell me your grievance?" Carujo had no qualm of handing his associate to this stranger.

"To tell you only part of the whole story. He is only a stepbrother of mine. He beguiled the only girl I was ever in love with. When she became pregnant by him he murdered her and managed to put the blame on me. Somehow, my advocate convinced the court that it happened while I had diminished responsibility. I was given a twelve years' jail sentence. By the time I was released, our father had died and he cheated me of my inheritance which he subsequently squandered. Is that enough?"

"I believe you and will give you the address of the agent, after you have helped me to get to the hacienda."

The sound of an oncoming horse was heard. The stranger stood up, his rifle in hand, he challenged the rider to stop. The man obeyed and saw Carujo still sitting on the ground. "Hallo, señor Carujo," he shouted, I am on my way to you. You look terrible. What happened?"

Carujo stood up. "I'll tell you later. First tell me whether you are coming from the hacienda?"

"Yes, I'm. I'm one of very few who managed to escape. We've been ambushed by many hundreds of Indians who took possession of the hacienda."

"Do you know what happened to my daughter?"

"No. If they haven't killed her, they certainly took her captive."

Carujo stood silent for a minute. Danlola had been listening and drawn his conclusions: "I knew that you weren't a vaquero and, as I have said, I am not interested in politics. I suggest taking you to my home until your wounds have improved and you give me the address of that agent."

"I have another suggestion," said the newcomer. In one hour we could be in the small town of Santa Helena. I have an uncle there, Dr. Hidalgo; he is the head of a hospital. He will look after you and we could get a horse for you there."

"Maybe that's the best but I must free my daughter somehow."

"I'll take you on my horse," said Peter Danlola. "For a thousand American dollars and the address of the agent, I undertake to free your daughter."

"All right then, let's go to Santa Helena," Carujo consented. ---

Bighorn led Juarez and his men to the place where he had advised Lord Castlepool to wait. Who can describe the moment a father and his daughter, whom he thought had died, found each other again. They embraced for several minutes with tears of joy in their eyes, until Margaret loosened her grip and said: "Father dear, we are forgetting another member of our family. Here is my husband, your new son, who is just as eager to greet you."

They embraced joyfully until Margaret said: "Father, Rudolfo, we mustn't forget the president and all the others who have a right to be greeted by you."

"Oh, I'm happy to be a witness of your reunion," replied Juarez with a mild seriousness.

It was Count Manuel who, after a friendly but moving handshake, reminded everybody: "Time is master of us all. Did you know, milord, that Carujo was on the river bank?"

"Yes, Bighorn called his name aloud."

"Has he taken part in the fight?"

"It was dark; I don't know whether he took part personally,"

"Bighorn believes he has blinded Carujo."

"That's probable. I heard him roar with pain and I saw they cooled his face with water."

"In that case he has not taken part in the battle. It's important for us to know of his whereabouts."

"It's probable he was killed by his own men."

"That's unlikely," chipped in Bighorn. I noticed some trees have been felled. The stems are not here. It must be assumed a raft has been built. Where is it? Who was on it?"

"You're right. We must search for the place where this raft has landed. Most likely in the direction the water is flowing."

Juarez sent four groups of Indians to search the banks on both sides of the river. Up, as well as down. It was four hours later when the first group returned. They reported to have spotted the place where the raft had landed with one man gone from it. Two more tracks led to the spot. Someone had picked up the man and rode in the direction of Saint Helena. They had found a wet handkerchief bearing the initials J.C.

"That's proof enough for me. The wet handkerchief belonged to Carujo. Santa Helena is not a great detour from the direction to the Hacienda del Alina. They might even find a doctor there and acquire a horse." Bighorn showed his power of deduction. ---

Not far from the northern borders of the province of Zacategas is the little town of Santa Helena. There is nothing special about it except the ancient cloister that was built on top of a very high hill. The building, far from its original purpose, serves as a nursing hospital for mentally and physically ill patients. Dr. Hidalgo, the head of this establishment was, studying some ancient books about mysterious poisons, when there was a repeated knock on his window. He opened and looked out. A male figure stood in the dark. "Who's there?" he enquired.

"It is I, Alfredo," was the answer.

The old doctor recognised the voice of his nephew. He opened a side entrance to the former monastery. It seemed that he had visited his uncle in this way before. "I didn't expect you, do you have any news?" whispered the old man.

"Yes, it may be important."

"Come in and tell me about it. Where are you coming from?"

"Let me tell you from the beginning. I was recruited by Carujo …"

"Carujo, the madman who squanders riches and thinks he might become president?

"Yes, in short; we have taken the Hacienda del Alina and were in turn attacked by Indians. I was one of a few who managed to escape. They kept Señorita Josefa, Carujo's daughter, captive. Carujo himself was absent and I met him by chance. You are able to be of service to Carujo. Between us, only if it suits your plans. He is now an escapee – a refugee. He needs shelter; maybe a hiding place."

"Is he with you?"

"Yes, and an American hunter who plans to rescue his daughter."

"What a coincidence, I'll give him shelter. Bring them in."

Carujo stood at the door. He distrusted the old man. Dr. Hidalgo looked at him in the same light and asked: "Your name is Carujo, señor?"

"Yes," he confirmed.

"Are you José Carujo who was employed by the Count de Manresa?"

"I am."

"Welcome and sit down." The doctor himself kept standing and continued: "My nephew tells me that you are looking for a place of refuge?

"If you could offer that, but it must be safe from any treachery."

"Do you have to fear treachery?"

"Unfortunately. Are you familiar with my circumstances?"

"Only that you intended to be president."

"I am being expelled by Maximilian."

"You are safe here. This old monastery has enough secret corridors and caves to hide a thousand people."

"I like that and I will show my appreciation."

"About the reward. What have you in mind?" With these words Hidalgo's face assumed the expression of someone laying in wait.

"I am wealthy," answered Carujo.

"What does your wealth consist of?"

This question made Carujo uncomfortable. "Have you special reasons to know that?"

"Yes," said the old one calmly. "I have the right to ensure you are able to reward my protection. I shall refrain from any reward. I only wish to enquire about your conditions and the way how I can serve you best."

"Why are you so interested in me?"

"I'll tell you soon. Now tell me what your wealth consists of."

"I am the administrator of the properties of the Count of Manresa."

Around the lips of Doctor Hidalgo was an enigmatic smile. "In other words, you are able to exploit these properties for your own purpose."

It was obvious that these questions embarrassed Carujo. "I didn't want to imply that."

"What or how much you want to imply is irrelevant. I keep to the facts. By the way you are finished as far as this administration is concerned. You are being expelled from this Country."

"I have cash, señor," assured Carujo fearing the doctor would not give him shelter. "It's well hidden; I had to be prepared for any situation."

"You mean that you made the most of the riches of Manresa. These must be finished by now."

"How do you mean that?"

"Well, you must be thinking the Count will put a stop to that."

"Count Manuel is dead, long ago."

Dr. Hidago smiled. "From what my nephew has heard before he escaped from the hacienda, the Count is alive and well."

These words drove Carujo's blood to his head. "I don't understand you. Your nephew must have misheard."

"No, he has heard clearly that Count Manuel had been sold into slavery. He escaped and is now with a Lord Castlepool. He's expected on the hacienda soon."

"I insist that your nephew has misunderstood what he has heard,"

"Pah, don't trouble to deceive me. I know the situation very well. You have not been true to me and I cannot give you shelter."

"But why are you interested in the family de Manresa?"

"I've no interest, none at all, but I cannot hide a man who is wanted by such a group of pursuers."

"You don't have to fear them."

"You don't believe that yourself. My nephew hasn't told me a lot. He's heard many names but could only remember a few. There was a Dr. Stenton who is well known as Doc Ironfist and someone called Antonio Brooks who is known as Old Surehand. There are determined people on your heels. What have you to do with them? You can confide in me." These were names Carujo did not expect to hear. He nearly fainted. Sweat ran down his forehead. He looked silent and uncertain. His situation was thoroughly awkward. He had to disappear for a time and this doctor could help him. What harm could it do to tell this man his secrets? He could get rid of Hidalgo later. The method needn't worry him now. He lifted his head with a sudden movement and said: "All right, I have decided to let you know my secrets but can I be sure of your silence?"

Alfredo and Peter Danlola had left the room at the beginning of this conversation. Dr. Hidalgo was alone with Carujo. "I swear," said the doctor, "that I shall keep your secrets entirely to myself."

"I'll trust you but be assured that I'll kill you if you utter a single word to anybody else." And now Carujo did something he would have thought impossible before. He told this man about the secrets of the house of de Manresa, without implicating himself too much. But the old one learned enough to be astonished. "But señor is this possible? Haven't you told me just a novel?"

"Not at all. It was difficult enough to tell you my secrets."

"And you're convinced your pursuers will follow you?"

"If the people you've named are really alive, they will not rest until they find me."

"Well, we'll receive them but Señor Danlola, I cannot shelter."

"He does not need it but he will free my daughter and bring me news of his stepbrother who seems to have betrayed me."

"He's having a meal. I'll call him." He left Carujo and returned with Peter Danlola.

"I've spoken to Alfredo," said the hunter to Carujo. "He's willing to help me free your daughter. I would probably need another person. I've promised him two hundred dollars but he wants it at once."

Carujo understood and handed seven hundred dollars to Peter Danlola. "The other three hundred when you bring her," he added.

Peter Danlola agreed and asked Dr. Hidalgo for three horses. Within half an hour, he and Alfredo were on their way to the hacienda. It was the afternoon of the next day when they saw their destination. Peter motioned Alfredo to wait as he wanted to reconnoitre the situation. It was night when he returned. "There are only about fifty Mixtekas left on the hacienda," Peter reported. "We shall go there after midnight,"

The time came and both of them found a place where they could get over the fence into the hacienda yard. Peter had collected a few small pebbles. They were lucky. From the first hole into which Peter had thrown a couple of stones, he heard a female voice answering: "Who's there? Are you coming to free me?"

Peter spoke into the hole and asked quietly: "Señorita Josefa, is it you? Are there any guards?"

"The guards have gone, but I'm bound and the door's locked," the voice answered.

The opening was too small to enter. They both had sharp knives and managed to loosen a few more stones until the hole was big enough to admit someone. Josefa became excited when she noticed the debris falling down. Finally, Peter let himself down on a lasso and untied her. "Will you be able to heave yourself up?" he asked.

"I'll have to," she answered while massaging her stiff limbs. With him pushing and Alfredo pulling, she crawled out of the hole. The lasso was let down again and Peter pulled himself up. Only two minutes later three riders left the outskirts of the hacienda and rode the whole night through toward Santa Helena. About midday they greeted Dr. Hidalgo and a delighted José Carujo. He and Josefa exchanged stories of their misfortunes.

Hidalgo led them into a room well hidden in the cellars and corridors of the ancient building. There was light in the room and the air was breathable. A table with a bowl of fruit, two chairs and two camp beds were the sole furnishings of this apartment. Carujo did not complain but was worried about what would happen when the pursuers would show up. He was comforted by the doctor's assurance that he knew how to handle them. He did not anticipate Hidalgo's plans to make use of his secrets for his own benefit and Carujo's ruin.

Carujo gave Peter Danlola the address of the agent in Vera Cruise and the pair, Carujo and Josefa were left alone. Josefa asked her father whether he had received the letter in which she described that all the enemies they'd thought were dead were still alive. He said it hadn't reached him and would probably do no harm if it fell into the wrong hands. They decided it would be best to stay here for a while and resume planning for the future. ---

Naturally, Stenton and his companions were greatly disappointed and angry when they found the cellar empty and Josefa escaped. It presented no difficulty for men like Doc Ironfist and Old Surehand to detect the tracks and direction of the people who helped with Josefa's disappearance. But who had helped her? They were baffled. Some thought of Carujo but, beside of his blindness he was not the man to manage a hijack like this. The future would solve this puzzle.

They were all eager to recapture Josefa. Only Old Surehand, otherwise Anthony Brooks stayed with his father in law to help guard the hacienda and to welcome the imminent arrival of Alva. Buff-he, Stenton, the helmsman George Brooks, Rudolfo and Don Manuel took fresh horses and followed the easily-visible tracks leading toward Santa Helelena. They rode at a sharp gallop. Stenton observed that by nightfall the tracks were only two hours old. They gave themselves and their horse one hour's rest. The tracks had not varied all day long and the direction was still Santa Helena.

They rode through the town but stopped at the other end. "We have to wait for daybreak to see whether the tracks continue," suggested Stenton. They agreed and had a further rest. At early dawn they spread out and agreed to meet at the same spot in an hour. Stenton and George Brooks went to the left around the outskirts of the town. Buff-he and Rudolfo went to the right. When they met again, none of them was able to report having seen any trucks that looked the same as before. No threesome had left the town. Stenton thought Josefa was surely looking for her father. Carujo, on the other hand, had been terribly injured.

They would be looking for doctors, hospitals and guest houses. The four spread out again to return within an hour.

They'd found all available guest houses taken up by a French military company who came without weapons. "Obviously those from Chihuahua," observed Stenton.

There were only two doctors in this town. Both were reported to live and work at the only hospital on the mountain. The former monastery where a Doctor Hidalgo is in charge. "Let's go," said Stenton. ---

Alfredo hurried from his post to his uncle. "You're quite out of breath," the nephew was greeted.

"They're coming," he reported, "four men, one of them a giant."

"That must be Stenton. Go away; they should not see you or Señor Danlola. When I call you, you know what you have to do in the small corridor."

"Yes," nodded the nephew and left the room.

Dr. Hidalgo was apparently engrossed in a book and listened for any sound. But he was no hunter of the prairie. Stenton stood at the door without him hearing the slightest sound.

Stenton asked: "Are you Dr. Hidalgo?"

Hidalgo jumped up. After a short while he answered: "I am he. Who are you?"

"You will learn that later. First we have a few questions. Are you alone?"

"Yes, but señor, I don't know what to think. You didn't enter the usual way."

"This has its reasons. If our coming creates unrest, it is up to you to get rid of us as soon as you answer the following question: "We are looking for three riders. One of them a woman who arrived here during the night. Where are they?"

Stenton had knocked the nail on the head. He declared as a fact what was an assumption only. Hidalgo thought they had correct information and answered: "Yes, should I bring them to you? They are probably still asleep."

"No, you will take us to them," said Stenton firmly.

"Please allow me to call my nephew. He is next door and will provide us with light. The people you want to see are below ground, the only accommodation we have for guests. I'll just knock for him on the wall."

He did so and Alfredo appeared. "Get some light, these señores want to see our guests," Hidalgo told him.

When they went underground, Stenton asked Dr. Hidalgo to go in front and his nephew with the light behind them. That was actually what Hidalgo wanted. He also carried a lantern and led them through several doors into several corridors. They entered a shorter one and Hidalgo reached another door. He called out the name Alfredo. The nephew who seemed to have trained for this, jumped back through the door and bolted it. The four men turned their head towards Alfredo. Hidalgo opened the door in front, went outside and bolted it as well. Buff-he immediately shot at the door, without any success. Stenton had matches with him. He lit one but all they could see, was a vapour coming through the keyhole. With all their might they pressed against the iron door. It didn't help.

The old Hidalgo stood outside and listened. In his left hand he held a lantern, in his right an empty thin husk the contents of which he had blown through the keyhole. On his face could be seen the delight of success. "Victory," he rejoiced. "They're caught. In two minutes everything will be quiet." He was right. He only waited a few more seconds and opened the door. "Alfredo open your door," he shouted and jumped back to avoid the overpowering odour from the corridor. The poisonous gases escaped through the opened doors. The outwitted four lay unconscious on the ground. "Take everything they have and bind them," ordered Dr. Hidalgo. "Keep watch until I return. The Carujos will be happy to see these people. I'll enjoy their discomfort afterwards."

The old fellow went through various corridors to the cell where Carujo and his daughter were sitting on a mat. "What's new in the upper world? Are the French still there?" Carujo received him.

"The French will be gone soon. Why don't you ask me whether any of your pursuers have called?"

"Well, did they? Tell us what happened."

"They came and I managed to ward them off."

"But it was arranged that you should take them prisoner."

"How should I have done that?"

"You are asking that?" chipped in Josefa, "You're a coward."

"Do you really think so? Is that your thanks for my willingness to help you? Should I hand you to the French?"

"Nonsense, my daughter didn't mean it that way. We believed that you would take these scoundrels prisoner, now I'm forced to take things into my own hands. How did they behave?"

"I'll tell you later. Follow me now; I want to show you your new abode." Carujo and his daughter left their cell and followed Hidalgo through the corridors. When they saw the prisoners bound on the floor Carujo called: "*Demonio,* you have caught them!"

Josefa hurried closer. "Yes, Stenton, Rudolfo, Antonio and the helmsman. I thought you said they have got away?"

"I was only joking, No-one escapes me whom I wish to house," Hidalgo said proudly. The others had regained consciousness. Their eyes were open but they did not speak.

"I haven't had such a happy day for a long time," rejoiced Carujo. "What shall we do with them?"

"Lock them up, naturally," said Josefa. "In the worst holes possible. They should be beaten daily and fed only once a day."

"Couldn't you be a bit more lenient? You never know when you'll need a bit of leniency?" Josefa did not see how Hidalgo glanced at her and answered enthusiastically:

"No leniency, not a trace. All right father?"

Carujo nodded his head in agreement. "I've lost an eye: they took away my hacienda. There's no punishment too cruel for these people. Where are the holes for them?"

"One floor below, señor," said Hidalgo, "do you want to see them?"

"Yes, we want to see for ourselves what bliss is in store for these devils. Should we take them with us? We could release the fetters on their legs to enable them to walk."

"I wouldn't do that. I wouldn't give them the slightest opportunity to regain their freedom. We'll take them later one by one. They won't be able to defend themselves. Follow me downstairs now." Hidalgo went ahead to a lower floor and cells that were barely large enough for one person. Every one had a door with a round hole.

"Are these the dungeons? Show them to us," demanded Josefa.

Hidalgo opened the door and shone the light along the wall. "Two iron rings," observed Carujo, "what are they for?"

"To make sure of the prisoners."

"How do you do that?"

"It is actually a trick, señor. You are unfettered. Take a seat and I'll convince you that none of them will be able to escape."

"Very well, I'll try it. It will be a joy to know how secure we have these people."

"Yes father, I want to know too. Will you show it to me too, señor?" asked Josefa.

"With pleasure, señorita, I have here a double hole suitable for such a trial. I'll open it." Hidalgo pushed a bolt back and a hole two metres wide was visible. The ground was stone and the height just enough for a man to sit upright. At the back were two open iron rings.

"Will these rings be enough to hold the prisoners?" asked Josefa. "I don't see any locks"

"They have no visible locks. There's a secret mechanical device. Will you convince yourselves that an escape is impossible?"

"Yes, I'll try it out," replied Josefa. "I'll feel surer then."

"So will I," added Carujo.

"Come here and sit next to each other."

They obeyed and with two grips of his hands the rings closed around their bodies.

"Marvellous," rejoiced Josefa. "Whoever sits here is well looked after."

"Yes," laughed Carujo. "The prisoners will never escape from here. But now open the rings. We have had enough of the joys of this hole."

"But señor, you said you are satisfied with this new home; your daughter agreed."

"Yes, satisfied for our prisoners, you don't mean we have to stay here?"

"Yes, that's what I mean."

The shock brought a short pause. The terrible trap dawned on them.

"You are crazy," Carujo finally called out.

"I? Oh no, but you were crazy enough to give yourself into my hands. I tell you that you will never leave this hole again."

"Don't drive this joke too far, señor. We know now what it is to languish in these holes."

"No. you don't know that yet. It has to be serious before you really know."

Josefa shrieked as she realized what was in store for her. "Señor, you are a monster. You can't leave us here, I can't survive it."

"Quiet right," grinned Hidalgo, "Nobody could survive it."

"But we haven't done anything to you."

"No, but I want my reward for what I have done. I've rid you of your enemies."

"Make us free," implored Carujo, "I'll reward you richly."

"Wait a bit. You don't know what I'll ask you."

"Well, what?" asked Carujo and threw expectant glances at the doctor.

Hidalgo answered as if he asked for a trifle: "I'm asking you for the inheritance of the Count de Manresa."

"The … inheritance … of … Manresa? What do you mean? You are a thousand times mad."

"Not madder than you who imagined putting Manresa in your pocket."

"Señor, you are a mean scoundrel."

"I advise you to be more careful with your expressions. You yourself are the greatest scoundrel I've ever seen. I'm doing a good job in taking away your loot."

"You've betrayed us. I curse you, you devil."

"Don't get excited, it doesn't help. I'm thinking of making better use of the riches of Manresa than you, who imagined you could be president. You a president. I tell you I have certain plans for which the riches of the Manresas are opportune. You've finished your roles. My nephew Alfredo will be Count instead of your Aurelio. I'll skim the cream off the milk."

It sounded so incredible that both Carujos were struck dumb. Hidalgo didn't expect any reply. He picked up his lantern bolted the door and returned to Alfredo. After they had carried the other prisoners into nearby common cells they tied them to the wall, Hidalgo gave

414

orders to his nephew to supply them with bread and water. He went to his office where, to his surprise, his chair was taken by an uncomfortable visitor.

"Ah, Señor Arazzio, to what do I owe the honour of seeing you here?"

"A message from our brotherhood. You know that among the many parties who vie for the presidency we, after Benito Juarez and, perhaps, General Porfirio Diaz, are the most likely to proceed. It is your task to discredit Juarez with the other nations," said the stocky little man."

"And how am I supposed to do that. I have important obligations here and, for a while I would have difficulty in leaving Santa Helena."

"The stakes are too high to consider your private concerns. You know that disobedience means death. Your task is to let Maximilian know that a revolt has taken place in Santa Helena and that the Emperor's flag was hoisted here and in ten other places. The idea is to prevent him from fleeing the Country. When captured, Juarez would have no choice but to order his death. The nations will consider him a savage and it would not be too difficult to oust him as president. If Juarez will not order his death, his own party will revolt, considering Maximilian's decree to shoot all Mexicans supporters of Juarez. When can you leave?"

Hidalgo sweated, but he knew that disobedience would mean his destruction. If the brotherhood gained the government, he would have a high position. He could leave his nephew in charge for a few days but first he had to eliminate those who knew the Count de Manresa affair. Most of them were on the Hacienda del Alina. "I need two days, at most," he declared."

"We accept this as the latest date of your departure. We will, of course, facilitate your entrance to the Emperor. You'll be given exact instructions before you reach the capital." With this Señor Arazzio departed.

Hidalgo went back to the dungeons and opened the cell of the Carujos. "If you want a better place you must answer two questions," he began.

"If you bring us to a different place with decent food and you look after my eyes, we'll answer your questions."

"You are in no position to make conditions, but I am in a good mood and will oblige." Hidalgo loosened their fetters but only to enable them to walk constrainedly to a place which could almost be classed as a room. His nephew was ordered to bring wine and food. By the time Alfredo returned he had examined Carujo's eyes. There was only hope for improvement in one eye. He proceeded immediately with his questions. "How can I find the pirate Danlola?"

The helpless Carujo, seeing the improved quarters and the food, replied: "I wanted to get in touch with Danlola and I have written to my brother. The answer will come to my agent in Vera Cruz. Don Manuel is with Juarez and Lord Castlepool at the Rio Grande."

"Why Vera Cruz and not Mexico?"

"You've forgotten that I can't show my face in Mexico."

"What's the name of your agent and how could I reach him?"

"I'll give you that if you promise to show me my brother's letter."

"I promise," said Hidalgo.

"He is the fisherman Gonsalvo Verdillo," declared Carujo

"Will he hand the letter over to whomever we send?"

"I advise you to send Peter Danlola, who is also interested in the whereabouts of his stepbrother. He would be handed the letter if he produces an instruction from me."

"All right let's have this letter." Alfredo brought the necessary utensils and Carujo wrote the missive. Hidalgo checked it and put it in his pocket. He then confronted Peter Danlola whom he asked to collect the letter when it arrived. Danlola refused at first. "Why doesn't Carujo come to me in person?"

"He had to leave for General Diaz and said it would be in your interest to get the letter as it contained news about the whereabouts of your stepbrother."

Peter was satisfied. He asked where to bring it and was told to bring it here as Carujo would probably be back then. Both saddled their horses, Peter Danlola to ride to Vera Cruz and Doctor Hidalgo to ride on a deadly mission to the Hacienda del Alina. It was Old Surehand who noticed a person creeping behind the hacienda. When he called out from his window, the person ran away. As it was after midnight, he decided to make enquiries in the morning. He rose very early and went down where he had seen this stranger. There were footprints beneath the kitchen window. As it was unlikely that a vaquero had entered for a midnight feast, he went into the kitchen to investigate.

There was nothing unusual to be seen, except a little cork on the floor of an otherwise impeccably clean kitchen. He picked it up and asked Clarissa Moyes, who had just entered the kitchen whether there was a bottle to fit this cork. Clarissa denied ever to have seen a bottle to fit this tiny cork. Old Surehand, the experienced prairie man, was not satisfied and searched further. He noticed some fatty spots in the kitchen's water tank and asked Clarissa whether this was the water for the hacienda's cooking. She nodded yes to this question. He then asked whether he could have some animals that were of lesser use to the hacienda.

She brought him a deaf old bitch and two rabbits. Old Surehand, or Antonio as she called him, gave the dog and the two rabbits some of the water to drink. The dog died after ten minutes, the two rabbits died five minutes later. Somebody intended to poison the inhabitants of the hacienda – but who and why?

When there was no news of Stenton and his companions after a week, that it dawned on them that an enemy – Carujo? – had schemed their destruction. ---

Chapter 30

A WAGER

ONE Sunday a group of young army officers sat at breakfast, drinking wine in spite of the early hour. They were in an elegant officers' mess near Hyde Park in London, frequented by sons of the nobility and high ranking officials. There was much jollity and the cause of it was a bet.

They were all of an elite regiment favoured by Queen Victoria. Lieutenant Lord Edmonton, the son of the Duke of Edmonton was known to possess a large fortune and, being handsome, his luck with the ladies was proverbial. Quite naturally, he aroused great envy. There was Lieutenant Carrington of no less wealth and more angry than envious. Especially when, induced by wine, Lieutenant Edmonton boasted that no girl ever resisted him. He even went so far as to offer a bet on this delicate matter.

"Take care, my dear fellow," Carrington lifted his finger. "I might take you at your word."

"Do," called the slightly intoxicated Edmonton, "if you don't I declare that you are afraid to treat the company to another breakfast."

Carrington's eyes lit up and he asked: "Any bet?"

"Any," answered an overconfident Edmonton.

"Well then, I wager my Friesian against your Arab horse and I'll point out any girl who passes this house."

Loud laughter greeted this offer. One of the present ventured: "Bravo" Carrington wants to sacrifice his Friesian for Edmonton's doubtful fame to conquer a seamstress or chambermaid."

"Stop here," answered Edmonton. "I said any girl but please vary your choice to a girl that drives – not walks past."

"Agreed," said Carrington, I shall point to the next girl that passes in a cab."

"It is 10 am now, the bet ends at the same time next Sunday."

"Agreed again," said Carrington.

Edmonton stood up and put his sabre at his side. The spirits of wine were hardly noticeable. With his confident expression on his handsome face, few doubted the he would win the bet. Such a bet had never occurred before. Dashing, unbelievable, extraordinary and daring were the expressions heard. Another lieutenant who stood at the window called out: "Ah, a real beauty."

"Where?"

"There, at the corner, the cab with a team of beautiful horses." He pointed excitedly.

"Who would that be? Called a second."

The cab came along slowly. In the background was a middle aged lady. Next to her sat a beautiful young girl in her first bloom. Her face was slightly pink; her hair was full and parted. Two heavy plaits fell down her side. Her features were clean, childish and unspoiled. They all agreed they had never seen such a beautiful girl before.

Carrington pointed to the cab and called: "Edmonton. This one for the bet."

"Ah, agreed, positively agreed," rejoiced Edmonton. One look into the mirror and he hurried outside.

"A lucky fellow, on my honour," ventured one of the group. "I wonder how he'll start to met her."

"No doubt he has experience and to save his Arab, he'll expedite matters," answered another.

"I see he takes a cab. I'd like to be there."

Edmonton asked the coachman to follow the cab in front of them. The carts turned into St. James' Park and it was evident that the two ladies intended to have a drive round. The lieutenant ordered the coachman to overtake the one in front. He held some money in his hand to pay for his ride. As his cab went past the ladies he leaned out with a surprised expression. He greeted them as if they were old acquaintances. He asked the coachman to stop and jumped off his carriage. The other one had stopped. "Go on," ordered the lieutenant as he opened the door, and without fuss and beaming, he sat down. He pretended not to notice the incensed faces of the ladies. He then stretched out his hands to the young girl and said with well-played enthusiasm: "Sarah, is it possible? What a meeting. You are in London. Why didn't you write?"

"Sir, you seem to have misjudged us," said the older lady seriously.

Edmonton's face expressed surprise and the supposition that they were making a joke. "Pardon me, milady, it appears I did not have the honour of your acquaintance. Sarah will rectify this." He turned to the young lady. "Please, dear Sarah, be so kind as to introduce me to this lady."

From the serious face of the girl came a probing glance and she answered: "That is not possible. I don't know you. Who are you?"

He looked disturbed and said: "You want to deny me? How do I deserve that? Oh, I forgot, you always liked a little joke."

Again a probing glance but darker than before. "I never joke with people that I don't know or wish to know. I hope it is really a similarity which caused you to enter our carriage. Please introduce yourself."

He pretended great dismay and he replied hastily"

"Ah, really? My God, could I possibly be mistaken? The similarity is baffling. I never thought it possible." With a double bowing for the ladies he continued: "I am Lieutenant Lord Edmonton of the special cavalry to her Majesty."

"That confirms we don't know you. My name is Helen Stenton and this lady is my mother."

"Helen Stenton? he asked, apparently shocked. I'm really surprised. I'm the victim of an unbelievable similarity and I beg your pardon."

"If it's really such a similarity then we have to forgive you. May I ask who my double is?"

Now he really made a mistake. "Certainly, certainly. It is my cousin Mayfields"

"Sarah Mayfields?" Helen asked with a peculiar glance at her mother. Where is this lady now?"

The face of the lieutenant lightened up. He assumed that she was prepared to engage in a conversation. Her name was just Stenton – a commoner. He believed he'd have an easy conquest. What common girl would not be happy to know a lord and lieutenant of her Majesty's cavalry? "Yes, Sarah, the daughter of Lord Mayfields. She lives in Manchester. "I was surprised to find such a spitting image."

There was a smile of rejection about her small mouth when she answered: "I ask you to bother no further."

"May I ask why, dear lady?"

"Because I, myself will inform Sarah of this incident. She's a friend of mine."

"Ah." He sounded shocked.

"You are shocked," said Helen, proud and cool. I wasn't wrong when I assessed you. Sir, you may be a lord and an officer. A gentleman you are not."

"Young lady," he flared.

"Lieutenant," she replied with deep resentment.

"If you were a man I would ask you for immediate satisfaction. I can't be responsible for a similarity which is the only reason for my mistake."

"Be silent. If I were a man I would only give satisfaction to an honourable opponent. Whether you acted like a gentleman, you must ask your conscience. My similarity to Sarah is equal to you being a gentleman. You looked for a cheap adventure and I must request you to leave us now. "

It was a despatch he had never experienced before. He was not willing to accept defeat. Should he accept the loss of the bet right at the beginning? His horse was too costly for that. "Well, dear lady, you are partly right. I'm in a position where I have no choice. I'm forced to tell you the truth, even with the danger of increasing your anger."

"Anger?" Helen had a superior smile. "There is no anger. You have acquired my contempt. I forego any explanation and ask again that you leave our carriage."

"No, and no again. You must listen to my explanation."

"Must? We'll see if I must." Her eyes looked along the road while he went on.

"The truth is. I have followed you for weeks and …"

"You have followed me? Here in London?"

"Yes," he said dejectedly.

"Well, you've lied again. I arrived here yesterday and have never been here before. I'm sorry for the men who call you their comrade and I order you for the last time to leave our carriage."

"I shall not leave before you hear my explanation …"

"John stop here," she shouted when she saw a policeman.

The coachman obeyed. She waved to the policeman who stepped nearer. "This man has encroached upon us and will not leave. Please help us."

The lieutenant knew he could only avoid harsher treatment by leaving as fast as possible. He left the cab and said: "The lady is joking but I shall see to it that she will be more serious next time. He walked off throwing a threatening glance at her.

The lieutenant was humiliated as never before. He felt he had to find out where this teenager lived. He hailed an empty cab and asked the coachman to follow the barely visible carriage. It was not long before they stopped. The building was rented by Count Miguel for a vacation of the friendly families. Edmonton stopped his cab and went into a public house opposite. He did not have to wait for very long, when he saw a person crossing the road. It was Eric Freeman, Colonel Masterson's valet who had accompanied the group to rent separate accommodation for his master. Eric ordered a beer. He was in civilian clothing but it was clear that he had had military training. Edmonton turned to him and began a conversation: "I can see you have had military schooling?"

"You are right but I only got to a NCO before retiring."

"I've seen you coming from this building. To whom does it belong?"

"The building is only hired by Count de Manresa for a vacation."

"I saw two ladies entering it a few minutes ago. Are they family of the Count?"

Eric was simple in his way but not stupid. He noticed that the questioner was sounding him out. He had just heard from the coachman the ladies' experiences, and replied: No they are the wife and daughter of the coachmen. I've finished my beer and I'll go now. I'll call the coachman over to see whether you are the person who disturbed the ladies. He is very handy with his fists and will not take it very kindly if he recognises you. Good bye."

He had hardly gone when Edmonton left the public house too. He did not fancy a fight but did not suspect that Eric had misled him about the two women's identity. It was midday when the officer's mess filled up again. When Edmonton entered he was greeted with a hundred questions but tried to sidestep them when Captain Lord Winnington entered. He threw his hat on a chair. Obviously in a bad mood. He was immediately questioned about this and answered: "I've come from the Colonel whose opinion is there are no dashing officers in our regiment."

"No dashing officers? We can't let that rest."

"There's worse to come. We're getting a new officer from an ordinary family."

"Who is it?"

"Someone called Robert Brooks."

"Never heard of an aristocratic family called Brooks."

"That's it, just Brooks. The father is a helmsman."

Everybody jumped up. "A commoner?"

The captain nodded. "This regiment's going to pieces. I think that I'll ask for a release. He's recommended by a important patron and we have to take him and tolerate him."

"We have to take but not to tolerate him," called Lord Edmonton. "As far as I'm concerned, I will not suffer a peasant or son of a sailor next to me. The fellow must be kicked out of our regiment."

"Yes, he should be kicked out. We owe it to each other," agreed another and all stood by him.

It's hard to believe how developed this class spirit, especially of the cavalry guard, was. It was a condition of membership of this regiment to belong to the aristocracy. And it is, therefore, understandable that the admission of a commoner caused such general indignation.

"When will we see this fellow?" asked one of those present.

"Today," answered the captain. He will first go to the colonel, then I'll have the honour to introduce him to you; probably in the evening. I suggest we should all be here to show him, once and for all, that he doesn't belong."

This proposal was enthusiastically accepted by all. The newcomer had no idea what was in store for him. Robert Brooks was often sent on military missions. At present he stood in his room in the building hired by Count Miguel and put on his military uniform, it suited him excellently. The promising boy had become a splendid young man. His figure was not very tall or wide but one could see the powerful shape in which his muscles and nerves had had an extraordinary schooling. The lower part of his face was browned and his forehead was high. The serious expression on the face of this youthful officer was one to instil respect. Whoever looked in his eyes was convinced they were not looking at an average man. He knew of Helen's and Rosetta's adventure in the St. James' Park.

A carriage drew up and he went to the window. It was Helen. A happy smile went over his face. What a long time since he saw her last. She was at an age when great changes occur in a week "I have to go to her," he said to himself. He went down stairs into the reception room. "What an enchanting young lady she has become," he thought. He stood delighted at the door when she turned round.

"Ah, there is our Robbie, our good Robbie," she called out and hurried to him with outstretched hands. He tried to master the impression she had on his heart: he took her little hands to his lips but uttered no word. His trembling voice would have betrayed him. "So estranged, so formal. Does the Lieutenant not know me anymore?

"Not know you anymore?" he asked, pulling himself together. "I'd rather forget myself." He heard her silvery laugh when she said: "You remembered the circumstance that Mother was a Countess de Manresa?"

"That's right," he countered a little embarrassed.

"Robbie, I was little Helen and you were Robbie. That's how it was and that's how it should stay. Or have you become too proud since you've been placed, in the elite regiment?"

He looked at her more thoroughly. The mischievous smile had disappeared and a blush had taken its place. He had mastered his feelings, grasped her hands and said: "Thank you Helen. I am still the one who is prepared to go through a thousand fires or to fight an army for you."

"Yes, you always sacrificed yourself for that malicious and ungrateful little Helen. I shall not chase you through a thousand fires and I shall not ask you to fight a whole army, although I had reason today to put a sword into the hands of my loyal knight."

"Is it possible, Helen, that you have been insulted?" he asked with lightning eyes.

"A little," she answered.

Now Don Miguel, who was also present, took up the case: "You've been insulted?

By whom my child?

"By Lieutenant Edmonton who is with the regiment Robbie is to enter. By the way, I have successfully fought him off. Isn't that true, mother?"

"Yes, that's true," said Rosetta, who had also entered the reception room. "I'd never have thought this child could develop such quickness of repartee."

"I'm curious now, please tell us," said the old Count.

They were all sitting down and Rosetta told them the course of events. While the Count kept calm, Robert became excited. "By God, that's strong stuff; this man belongs before my sword."

"Don't be hasty," said the Count, or you'll make enemies of your fellow officers at the start of your new career."

"Regarding my fellow officers, I've had warnings that they'll be against me because I am not an aristocrat. A challenge would not make it worse."

"We can talk about that later. It reminds me you have to go to the colonel. You're in his good books for your past achievements and should get a friendly reception. I wish it would be the case with your comrades."

A coach with a single horse was prepared for him. The fact that he was ordered to appear before the Minister of War was a sign of preference, an honour not given to anybody. It was also an extraordinary sign of preference that he was called in despite the number of people in the waiting room.

"You're very young, Lieutenant, and you were recommended. I am inclined to consider these recommendations. You have, in spite of your youth, studied many foreign military services. I have read your excellent reports with approval. It is my opinion that your talents justify the hope of an extraordinary career. I enjoy witnessing your transfer to the Queen's special regiment, but I must not conceal the difficulties you will encounter. I ask that you ignore the difficulties as long as they do not touch your honour as an officer." He gave a sealed envelope for the Colonel. The beginning was encouraging; the continuation was unfortunately less enjoyable.

Robert drove to the barracks to introduce himself to the commander. Colonel Winslow was sitting at his desk, busy signing many letters brought to him by Captain Winnington. When he finished, he looked at the Lieutenant through a monocle. "It is unusual that an infantry man should be transferred to our regiment. We're very demanding here. You should have thought it over. Do you know any of the officers of this regiment?"

"No Sir."

"As you are a bachelor you will have to eat in the officer's mess. Captain Winslow will arrange that. He will also introduce you."

"I stay with acquaintances and ask permission to eat there," answered Robert.

"That is against regulations but we shall see. Anyhow, you will not experience much joy with us. Report tomorrow morning at nine o'clock for duty. You are dismissed."

Robert handed the letter to the Colonel. "Yes Sir, may I hand you this letter from the Minister of War."

Robert left but the Colonel still looked after him. "An unpleasant fellow," he uttered angrily. He opened the letter and read:

"Colonel, the bearer of this letter has been recommended by influential circles. I expect this will be considered by his comrades. I am prepared to consider his abilities after tests. It is my wish that his bourgeois descent will not be in the way of a friendly welcome."

The Colonel stood there, open mouthed. "The devil, this is a recommendation signed by the Minister himself but I wouldn't permit it to make a breach in our aristocratic circle. There ends even the power of a Minister."

Robert went to the officer's mess. He was under no illusion regarding the difficulties that awaited him. Only Lieutenant Pluton greeted him with open comradeship and won Robert's affection. He was rebuked for this friendliness but answered: "I shall never do anything that would affect my honour."

Robert's appearance and behaviour made a pleasant impression on him and he couldn't face him with enmity. The guard in every Country is the proudest corps and the cavalry is the privilege of the aristocracy. "I didn't push myself into these circles," thought Robert, "I came here by order and the officers would have to see that eventually."

He returned home and found a new guest had arrived. Lady Margaret visited her friend Rosetta. She was just telling the experience on the unknown isle. She told the astonished listeners about the rescue by Count Manuel.

"Count Manuel? My brother? He died before your disappearance …"

"I can assure you that it was your brother. He did not die but was sold into slavery. Please listen to the whole miraculous story." She continued and also told of the two brothers Brooks, one a famous prairie Hunter the other a helmsman.

"The helmsman is my father," Robert intervened.

Margaret told them a bout the treasure and the present of Buff-he. And the parcel that the haciendero had sent via Juarez to the helmsman's son to further his education.

"I have never received a parcel," said Robert.

"It must have been lost," Margaret continued "but it was insured so you will, in the end, not lose."

"I'm not after the money but it's my father's legacy and I'll make special enquiries," emphasised Robert.

"The last I know," Margaret continued, "was their ride from the Hacienda del Alina toward Santa Helena."

"And there was no more news from any of them after that?" asked Rosetta, shaken.

"There were a number of searches made by famous trackers. One with the prairie name of Black Gerard and another named Bighorn. They all agreed that the traces ended in Santa Helena."

Margaret's portrayal of these happenings became more gripping every minute. The listeners were riveted by Margaret's tale, while she glanced out of the window. Her sudden shriek brought them all to her side. "That man down there," she said breathlessly, "is the pirate Danlola."

"You must be mistaken," said the Count, "Mexico is far away and London is big. It's unlikely that this could be him."

"That face I could never forget. Besides, can't you see he's observing our building?"

The man entered the public house opposite from where he would have a good view of the place hired by Count Miguel. Margaret's words horrified all of them. "The man who ruined our lives is thinking of new plots," called Rosetta.

"He's going into the pub to inquire about us," said Robert. "He'll be served." With this he hurried to his room and exchanged his uniform for civilian clothing. He then hurried across into the public house. The only guest was Danlola who sat at the same table as Edmonton before him. When Robert sat down at another table, he said:

"Please, won't you sit at my table; it's lonely here and with a drink one prefers company."

"I think so too and accept your offer," answered Robert Brooks.

"You look disturbed; you came from that large house. Were you a petitioner?"

"Maybe. These aristocrats don't care if they cause us misery."

"Who actually lives there?"

"It is Count de Manresa."

"That is a Spanish name."

"Yes, he is from Spain."

"Rich?"

"Very."

"Do you know anything about his affairs?"

"He's a widower, otherwise he won't tell a petitioner anything."

"Who are you or what is your profession?"

"That doesn't matter. You seem to be a distinguished gentleman and it doesn't concern you who or what I am."

Danlola's eyes lit up with satisfaction. "I like that. You are secretive. I like such characters. One can rely on them. Have you often been in that villa?"

"No," answered Robert.

"Will you have to go there again?"

"Yes, I must."

Danlola moved nearer and asked with subdued voice: "Listen young man, I like you, are you rich?"

"No, I am poor."

"Would you like to earn some money?"

"Hm, how?"

"I wish to know more about the Count's circumstances. You are well placed to gather some details. If you want to tell me about them, I shall be grateful."

"I'll think about that," said Robert after a short reflection.

"That's enough for me. I want you to be careful and after you learn that I'm not mean, you'll tell me more. I'm a stranger here and I need a man I can trust."

"What should this man do?" asked Robert pretending to be pleased about the secretive offer.

Danlola looked sharply at the young blanc-faced man. He thought this young man, who seemed intelligent, could well be used for his purposes. "May I at least know who your father is?"

"My father is a sailor."

"Ah, you don't belong to these people. Are you looking for a position?"

"I was told of one, but they made difficulties."

"Let it go. I'll probably offer you a better reward if I see that you make yourself useful. However, you have to be astute."

Robert winked. "You'll soon see."

"But I must at least know your name."

"You'll learn that after I've proved to you that I'm useful. I have to tell you that I am not in some people's good books. So I've to be careful."

Danlola nodded pleased. He thought this man was in conflict with the existing order and would make a useful tool. "That's enough for the moment. I'll give you an advance for your services." He pulled out his purse and put ten shillings on the table.

Robert pushed the money back. "I'm not broke and I need no advance. First the service and then the reward. Tell me what to do?"

Danlola looked satisfied. "It will not be to your disadvantage. I have the same principles. Firstly I want to know about the Count and his family. Then about a family called Stenton and another family called Brooks."

"That won't be difficult. Do you work for the police?"

"Maybe," answered Danlola seriously, "but I also dabble a bit in politics. I would like to entrust you with something but I'm not sure whether I can do that without danger."

"Tell me about it without the danger," Robert laughed.

"I notice you are not stupid. That's in your favour. Napoleon has made the Archduke of Austria an Emperor of Mexico. This friendship will not last. Mexico will overturn the throne. There will be political confusion and every state will try to exploit it to its own advantage. There are many … hm, I don't want to call them spies, say representatives, who have to reconnoitre the terrain for their governments to know the suitable moment."

"And you are such a representative?" ventured Robert.

"Yes," nodded Danlola.

"For what government?"

"That, for the moment, is my secret. I have only informed you so far to show you that you can have a good future. If you have any news for me, you can reach me in the Hotel Hanover under the name of Captain Dans. But not for the next two hours as I have other business to attend to. Good bye. "Danlola finished his glass and left.

Robert inquired from the publican the way to the Hotel Hanover. He paid and left. He had two hours not to be surprised. He entered the guest room of the hotel and asked for a cup of tea. He noticed a peculiar smile on the face of the waitress and looked questioningly into her face. "Don't you know me, Lieutenant Brooks?"

He reflected for a moment and then remembered. "You are June Balmouth from Bradford. What are you doing here?"

"There are too many sisters and brothers in our home and I thought a job in London would be more profitable. The owner here is a distant relative of mine."

"That's good; I'll have to ask you for a favour."

"If it's in my power, I'll oblige."

"Firstly, I don't want anybody to know that I am an officer. Is a Captain Dans living here?"

"Yes, he has room number eleven."

"Does he have many visitors?"

"Not really. Only one man with a foreign accent once asked for him. He said that he would call again. Captain Dans is mostly away."

"Is number ten or twelve available?"

Number eleven is a corner room and he's paid for number ten as well, although he doesn't live in it."

"Is there a strong wall between the two rooms?"

"No, there is a connecting door, but it's locked?"

"Is there a possibility of hearing in number ten what is being said in number eleven?"

"Yes, if one is not talking too quietly." And with a smile she added: "You're after this Captain Dans, aren't you?"

"Yes, but it's secret."

"Oh, I'm discreet. I don't like this man. I like to do a favour to my dear Country man."

"May I have a look at number ten?"

"Sure."

"But without anybody noticing it?"

"Don't worry, none of the servants are there at the moment and I can get the keys." June left and soon brought the keys to number ten which she passed to him secretly. He opened the door. The room contained a washstand, a wardrobe, a bed a table and two chairs. He opened the wardrobe. It was empty. Its doors opened without a noise. He went down and the waitress asked? "Did you find it?"

"Yes," he nodded.

"You want to eavesdrop on this man?"

"That is my wish. Does he hand the keys in when he leaves?"

"No, he's very secretive and when the room is cleaned, he stays in it. If he leaves, he takes the keys with him without thinking that there is always a main key."

"Will you let me in when the Captain receives a visitor?"

"Yes, although he pays for number ten as well so that it should stay empty."

"That proves he's dealing with secrets that might be valuable for me to know." At this moment a new guest entered the room and sat down at a table. The waitress whispered that this was the man who had asked for the captain. She went over to him. He asked for Captain Dans.

When he was told that he wasn't here, he ordered a bottle of wine. The waitress returned to the Lieutenant who told her that he would like to go into number ten. He then paid and pretended to leave. But the waitress opened the room for him and locked up again. He went inside the wardrobe which he managed to close from the inside. Soon he heard somebody open the door to number ten. The voice of Danlola said:

"It's all right, nobody is there. We can go to my room."

The door was locked again and number eleven was opened. The sound they made when they took their chairs to the table enabled him to place himself against the connecting door. The first thing he heard was a reproach by the guest who told Danlola off for letting him wait in the guest room. "There are pictures of me about, if somebody recognises me, my whole mission is in jeopardy. People know that I've fought in Mexico, that I was recalled by the Emperor, that my brother is a tutor of the French crown prince and that I would only be given things of importance to handle. I have to negotiate with Russia, Austria and Italy; the foreign minister has instructed me to hand you this remittance, the contents of which contain deails of how the head of the Madrid policy should react. Here's the document. Read it and tell me if you find anything unclear."

"Thank you Excellency." There was a pause while Robert heard the rustle of paper, then the voice of Danlola: "The document is absolutely clear."

"Good," said the other voice. "The shortened version is: Napoleon has made this weakling Max a ruler of Mexico. North America is jealous and has asked France to withdraw troops and leave Max to his fate …"

"And Spain agrees to that …"

"Yes, she concerns herself as the rightful owner of this beautiful but neglected Country. Napoleon is prepared to agree if she would be prepared for a service in return."

"And what would that be?"

"Prussia wants to lord it over Germany – over Europe. It has to be humiliated. Napoleon wants revenge for Sodova. In case of this inevitable war, we must be sure that our back is covered. Herr von Bismarck is shrewd. He is going to ask Spain to occupy the borders. We, on the other hand, must let our army march only if the Pyrenees are free of enemies. We can only make war if Spain declares itself neutral.

England is not keen to let Napoleon grow too big either. Russia will provoke a rift between Germany and Poland. I have only to negotiate with Austria and Italy. You will accompany me to prove that France has nothing to fear from Spain."

"I am at your disposal; I have only to lock away this document."

Robert heard the sound of keys. "Are those documents safe in this little suitcase?"

"Certainly," maintained Danlola, "the keys of the room I am taking with me."

"All right, let's go."

Robert heard when they locked the room. He had to have possession of this document, but how? While he was thinking, the waitress came back. "They are both gone," she reported. "Did you hear anything?

"Yes. Is it possible to enter number eleven?"

"I have the main key; I hope the Captain will not surprise us."

"No fear. I won't be long and he'll be some time," answered Robert.

"Put the keys under the carpet when you go. I must leave now; new guests have arrived."

When June had left, he opened the door to number eleven. The room was furnished the same as number ten. There was a large suitcase by the wall. A much smaller one lay on top of it. He remembered having heard that the papers would be stored in the little case. He possessed a similar one and carried the key with him. These locks were often the same and he was lucky. The case contained papers only. The document he required was on top. It was all in French, with the seal of their foreign minister. Should he copy it on his note book? He decided to take the original with him as the original with its minister-seal was more powerful and effective. He locked the little case and the room door, left the key and some money under the carpet for the obliging waitress and made his way to the Minister of War, Ernest Gray.

He hoped the Minister would help him to arrest Danlola and throw some light on the whereabouts of his father, Dr. Stenton and the others. He was told that the Minister had gone to see the Queen. A short decision and he was on his way to the Palace. There it was made clear to him that an audience might only be had by application. "But I have reason to insist, Colonel, Sir."

"You are not even in uniform, Lieutenant."

"I had no time to put one on."

"There is time for that in any circumstance. By the way, the Queen is presently talking to the War Minister."

"It is him that I need to see. It is a most important affair that suffers no delay. It's about a spy and I am forced to put responsibility on your shoulders if you refuse to report me."

The Colonel in charge looked at the young man who spoke so compellingly. "You maintain it is important and cannot be put off?"

"That is so and every minute is costly."

"You want to put this matter to the Minister in the presence of the Queen?"

"Yes."

"When you say that, I am forced to report your plea. If, however, the matter is not of great importance, it will do your career no good. The responsibility is yours."

"Yes, Sir," replied Robert politely but-confidently.

The Colonel returned after a short while. On his wink Robert entered and faced the two most important people in the Country. He was eyed seriously by both and Robert waited until he was acknowledged. "Are you Lieutenant Brooks who is going to join the guards?" asked Her Majesty.

"I have been ordered to Her Majesty's cavalry."

"I have been informed of this order, but I find it bold for you to have entered it."

"I've been made to feel it , Your Majesty."

A quiet smile of regret went over the face of the Queen. "I trust you will fulfil your duty but why is it you appear here in such unsuitable attire?"

Robert handed the document to the Queen with a respectful bow. "Here, Your Majesty is my excuse."

She took the document from him and went to the window to read it. Her face expressed the greatest surprise. She passed the papers to the Minister and said: "This is a momentous communication."

The Minister, who had not moved, took the document and read it. His iron face did not show what impression the document had made. He looked at Robert. "Lieutenant, how did you get this document?"

By theft, your Excellency."

The Minister smiled. "It is possible I shall acquit you of this theft. Who was the former possessor of this document?"

"General Douai brought it to a person who is an American but also a spy for Spain."

"Where are they?"

"The spy lives in the Hotel Hanover. If Your Majesty and you Excellency will permit, I shall explain the events that brought me into possession of this document."

"Tell us," said the Queen with an eager expression on her face.

Robert started his report. When he had finished, the Queen went to him and shook his hand and said benevolently: "You have done us a great service, Lieutenant. For now you are dismissed as we have to take measures to catch this spy and the French General. I am happy to learn that you are in my guard regiment. You have introduced yourself well and can be assured that I am well disposed toward you, and that I will not let you out of my sight." The Queen passed her hand and Robert put it on his lips.

The Minister of War passed him his right hand. "Lieutenant," he said. "I like people who are prudent and energetically active. We shall meet again. For today I request complete discretion. No-one must know what has taken you to Her Majesty today. We realise now that the Frenchman wants a war. We can act accordingly and we have to thank you for it. That is of great value. We shall not forget you. Now go with God."

Robert left the palace. He was drunk with happiness. He had been treated with great distinction by two great people. He was no longer concerned anymore by his adversaries from the General to the last Lieutenant. At home he had been expected with impatience. "We expected you from the public house opposite," said the Count, "and now you arrive by cab. Where have you been?"

"You'll never guess that," laughed Robert. "Look at my suit. A schoolmaster dresses better and I've been to the Queen in this."

"With the Queen? Impossible," was the expression all round.

"With the Queen and the Minister of War."

"You're joking."

Helen searched his face. She knew him well. His sparkling eyes and his reddened cheeks told her that he was not joking. "It's true I can see it in his face," she said, while her beautiful eyes also lit up in genuine joy.

"In this outfit,?" called Don Manuel, "but what were you doing there?"

"I am not allowed to tell you, but I say I was dismissed with distinction. I'd managed to provide them with an unusual service. They both took my hand and promised to remember me."

"How nice! How beautiful!" rejoiced Helen.

"Where is Danlola now? asked Rosetta.

"Probably in prison by now," answered Robert.

But there he was mistaken. Danlola had returned and the first thing he did was look for the document. He opened the little case and jumped back, shocked. The document had disappeared. He rang the bell. The waitress had retrieved the key and found the money. "Was anybody here?" he asked.

"Nobody has asked for you."

"I mean if anybody was in this room?"

"No."

"Somebody must have been here, something has been stolen from me."

"A theft?" she asked and paled with shock. That must be a mistake. Lieutenant Brooks was no thief.

"You are in shock, you paled," called Danlola, "You have done it yourself. The document must be returned at once."

When she heard the word 'document' she knew that it must have been something unusual. "I?" she said, "you cannot treat me this way, I'll call the owner."

"That's right, the document has to be returned, whatever happens."

As she went downstairs, a number of policemen had entered. One, in plain clothes asked for the manager or owner of the establishment. She pointed to the kitchen. The official identified himself to the owner and asked whether a Captain Dans lived here.

"Room number eleven, one floor up," answered the owner.

"Please tell your staff not to talk about it." He went upstairs and knocked at number eleven.

"Finally," said the Captain, "are you the owner?"

"No."

"Who are you then? asked an astonished Danlola.

"I have the honour to belong to the police."

Danlola shocked but rallied fast. "Good, I have to report a theft."

"A theft?" smiled the official.

"Yes, an important document."

"You are mistaken. That document has not been stolen, it has been confiscated."

While Danlola was shocked at first, he was calm in the face of danger. He realised he was lost if they took him prisoner. He had to escape, but how? The staircase, he was sure, was occupied, the street, maybe not. It depended on getting close to the official without arousing suspicion. He opened the small case and showed it to the policeman. When he got nearer he said: "This has to be a mistake because …" Further he didn't go. He grabbed the official by the throat which stopped him breathing. His hands moved convulsively in the air, his limbs trembled; his arms sank and Danlola let him down slowly to the floor. He had lost consciousness..

"Ah, half saved. What is such a land rat against Captain Danlola," he mumbled.

He locked the little case and stepped to the window. The pavement was empty no police in sight. A cab had stopped nearby. The window was high, but the jump was not dangerous. He swung himself out of the window and on the pavement without being seen. He went to the cab and ordered: "To Oxford Circus, then I'll tell you where I want to get off."

It was important not to leave any tracks. He stopped the cab before he had reached the first given destination, paid the cab driver and went a few streets further. He hailed another cab and went to General Douai's address. "You, Captain," asked the General, "why are you here so soon?"

"To warn you, Excellency, you must run away immediately. We have been betrayed."

"Impossible."

"But unfortunately true. I narrowly escaped the police."

"Who has betrayed us?"

"I don't know."

"Where are the documents?"

"Confiscated."

The general paled. "We're lost if they catch us. You must have done something very stupid. You'll tell me on the way. Have you any money?"

"Yes, enough."

"So have I, my suitcase will be lost but I have enough cash to get over that." He put his wallet in his pocket, grabbed his coat and left. A cab carried the escapees away.---

Chapter 31

TWO DUELS

IT was evening of the same day. The officers' mess of the Queen's Guard Regiment was lit up. The whole regiment was present expecting the new recruit and wanted to show that they didn't want to have anything to do with him. The talk was also about Captain Dans who had frequented the officers' mess. They had heard that he was wanted by the police. "That's what you get if you let commoners into our circle. It's our duty to reject this newcomer," Edmonton said with a frown.

"There is a difference between a criminal and an honorary officer," ventured Lieutenant Pluton.

At this moment Colonel Winslow entered the mess and went straight to the table of the older officers. He was not a frequent guest, only to special occasions. He soon rose and asked for silence. Great expectations all around. "I bring you a special order for tomorrow evening. Please attend not on horseback but on foot. You can bring your lady with you." They all pricked up their ears. What did he mean? This was certainly unusual. "Yes," he laughed, "I have sixty invitations to a ball."

"A ball? Where, where?" The question came from everyone.

"The place you would least expect," Winslow continued.

"Who is the invitation from?"

"I bet ten months wages you won't guess it. I received the following letter just before I came here. I'll read it to you, here it is:

To Baron Winslow, Colonel of the queen's cavalry regiment.

*Colonel Winslow, Her Majesty the Queen has graciously consented to
allow me to use St. James' Palace as a venue for a ball that would take place
tomorrow evening. I have enclosed invitations for all your officers and I am
convinced to see everybody with their spouses and daughters as well as the
ladies of the unmarried officers.*

Yours sincerely,

Ernest Gray - Minster of War."

The Colonel looked at the audience and saw astonished faces. "What
can that mean?" asked Captain Winnington.

"My wife is of the opinion it could be a kind of award from above,"
ventured Colonel Winslow. "Who knows what's in the wind?"

"May I ask a question? asked Lieutenant Edmonton. "Will Lieutenant
Brooks receive an invitation?"

This curiosity was rather bold but the Colonel answered in a friendly
manner: "Why do you ask?"

"Because I would not attend if a commoner were there."

"You don't have to ask. We all have the same principles. Lieutenant
Brooks only starts tomorrow and will not get an invitation." He then
asked Captain Winnington to distribute the invitations. This was hardly
finished when the door opened and Robert entered. He went straight
to the Colonel Winslow's table, greeted him in the military manner
and said: "Lieutenant Brooks, Colonel Sir, I beg of you the kindness to
introduce me to my comrades."

The colonel, who had been playing a game of whist, turned slowly
round with his cards in his hand and pretended not to have understood.
"What do you want?"

"I allow myself the plea to be introduced. Colonel, Sir."

Winslow lifted his eyebrows, looked at Robert from head to toe and
said: "Over there is Captain Winnington, he may do it."

He thought that he had done enough but Robert asked: "Colonel
Sir, I have to make a comment."

"Well," said the Colonel turning his face, red with anger and
embarrassment. "Make it short."

"Brevity is my speciality. I did not come here because I wanted
to but at higher suggestion. I have found with most officers to whom
I have introduced myself an outrageous reception. I have to know
from this moment whether I shall be acknowledged by my comrades

or whether I have to fight my way through. Colonel Sir, I have been treated by you with disrespect that an officer must not allow even from his commandant. I have to ask you for an explanation."

The Colonel was a hot-tempered man, the worse for a few drinks. He jumped up and shouted at the young man: "Are you crazy? An explanation from me? If you must know, I have treated you insultingly on purpose"

"Thank you Sir. I will not bring this matter to a higher level but must ask you for satisfaction. Tomorrow morning I will send you my authorised agent." With this Robert turned on his heel, put his cap and sabre on the next hanger, took a newspaper and looked for a seat. The officers moved closer together. Nobody wanted him as a neighbour. Only Lieutenant Pluton offered a seat next to himself. Robert looked into the honest eyes of Pluton and accepted with thanks, "We have not been introduced but my name was mentioned. May I ask yours?"

Lieutenant Pluton introduced himself. When Edmonton called: "Let us continue our game of snooker." Pluton declined. "That's what I call leaving a glass of champagne for a glass of vinegar."

Robert pretended that the insulting remark was not meant for him and Pluton asked: "Do you play chess, dear Robert?"

"Among comrades, very often."

"Well, I am a comrade. Put down your paper and let's have a game. For honesty's sake, I have to tell you that I am classed here as invincible."

"I have to be equally honest. My teacher, Colonel Masterson, was a master of the game. He taught me so thoroughly that he no longer wins a game."

"Well, then, this is going to be interesting."

With this, Pluton had broken the ban. At the rear the card games started again. In front the billiard balls battered. After half an hour the chess game became so tense that the officers came to see the progress of the game. It was brilliantly won by Robert.

"I give you my respect," said Pluton. "This hasn't happened to me for a long time. If it is true that a good chess player makes a good strategist, then you will make a useful officer indeed."

Robert felt that Pluton had spoken these friendly words to win him some ground and answered: "You probably only tried my strength. The second game may turn out differently."

"You may be mistaken. By the way, you mentioned a Colonel Masterson. I think I know him. Coarse, gnarled and honest."

"That's him."

"I got to know him through my uncle, who is his banker."

"His banker's name is Walker, as much as I know."

"That's right, my aunt married a commoner. He is this banker Walker."

The others exchanged astonished glances. Pluton was related to the Colonel. Why did he reveal such family secrets?

Robert understood the intention which was to show him that even among aristocrats, not everything is as perfect as one would like people to think. The second game started and Robert won again. During the third game, attention was diverted by Edmonton who played a game of snooker with Winnington. "You are again fifteen points in advance; it must be true, lucky in love means unlucky at games."

"Ah, did you win the bet with Lieutenant Carrington?"

"The time is not up yet, but nobody doubts I am going to win the favours of a coachman's daughter. That any of us could do, but if our regiment is to be infiltrated by new elements, it will no longer be the case."

Robert lit a cigar and said: "Lieutenant Edmonton will lose that bet."

Nobody expected that Robert knew or would interfere in such matters. Everybody listened with astonishment and Edmonton quickly stepped to him and asked: "What do you mean, Robert Brooks.?

After a few calm puffs Robert replied: "Lieutenant Edmonton will lose that bet. He is only a braggart. I know this young lady and she's not a coachman's daughter. He entered their coach by force and was removed by a policeman."

All present stood up. This was going to be an evening everyone would remember and recount. Edmonton was ashen faced, whether with anger or at discovery nobody could tell. He stepped close to Robert and roared: You dare to tell me that and in this place."

"Why not; we are both at this place. It would be beneath me to take notice of such boasting. It happens that this lady is a friend of mine and I have to guard her reputation"

"Would you retract these words? At once," called an excited Edmonton.

"Retract the truth? Only a coward retracts truth."

Robert was the only one sitting now, smoking his cigar calmly. It was expected that Edmonton would teach this intruder a lesson.

"Do you know how one can force someone out of this uniform?"

"Every child knows that, one slaps him on the face."

"All right, will you retract your words, beg for forgiveness and promise to leave this regiment?"

Robert answered calmly: "I have come here on orders and not because I wanted to. As for the rest, ridiculous. I wouldn't fool around if I were you."

"Well, take this slap in the face." He threw himself unto Robert. Although he was fast, Robert was faster. He countered the dishonouring slap with his left arm and then lifted Edmonton high and threw him to the floor where he stayed unconscious. A military doctor stated nothing was broken and there was no inner injury. A few blue spots, was all he said.

Edmonton was carried onto the divan while Robert stood there as if the whole thing had nothing to do with him. Colonel Winslow thought that as the commander of this outfit he had to take matters in hand. "Lieutenant Brooks, I have noticed that you have laid your hands on Lieutenant Edmonton. I have to put you under arrest."

"All those present have witnessed that he offered to slap me. I could have slapped him but I did not do that."

"I am your superior and order you to stay in your room until I shall recall you."

The faces of those present cheered up considerably, but they still didn't know the new Lieutenant. "I am sorry, Colonel Winslow, tomorrow I would follow your orders but my service under you does not start until then. Your orders have no power over me. As for your wish for me to go into my room, I gladly follow that. Hitherto I have only frequented places where I was not offered slaps on my face I shall leave you now. Good night, gentlemen."

"This fellow is a real devil," said a major.

"Pah," snorted the Colonel, "we shall drive out his devilishness. Him, challenging me? Have you ever heard of such a thing?"

None of them noticed Lieutenant Pluton had also left the room. He caught up with Robert, grasped his arm and asked: "Lieutenant Brooks wait a moment. There was a conspiracy against you. Believe me I had no part of it."

"I believe you. You've proved it," answered Robert and passed his hand to Pluton. "Take my thanks. I must confess I expected difficulties but never such impertinence. I regret the happenings of this evening."

"You have defended yourself valiantly, almost too bravely. I am afraid you made yourself impossible."

"We'll see. I respect nobility, but the view of some that they are above other people is incorrect. A person's value is the value of his soul."

"You are right, although I also belong to the nobility. The colonel deserved your reprimand. Regarding Edmonton, do you really know these ladies?"

"Very well. They have told me what happened."

"How is it that Edmonton called her a daughter of a coachman?"

"My servant met Edmonton in a pub opposite where the ladies and I live with Count Miguel de Manresa. When he saw that he was being interrogated, he made Edmonton believe what was obviously not the case. Do you comprehend it now?"

"I understand everything except your strength. Are you equally experienced with weapons?"

"I fear no opponent."

"You'll have to use that. Edmonton will certainly challenge you. What do you intend to do about the colonel?"

"I will have to send him my second tomorrow."

"And who will that be?"

"I'm not clear about that yet. I don't wish to involve my people. They shouldn't know anything about my dissensions. I've no new acquaintances as yet."

"May I offer myself for this task?"

"You may be disliked for it by your comrades and superiors."

"I don't fear that. I am not serving for any carrier but out of pleasure. My wealth makes me independent. May I be your second? You have won my esteem. Let's be friends."

"I accept your friendship with all my heart. I have read in your eyes that you are a person I will value." They shook hands and Pluton asked:

"Would you accompany me for a glass of wine?"

"With pleasure" Robert did not suspect what role the previously mentioned banker would have in his life. When he reached home he found an unexpected guest with the Count. It was the Minister of War himself.

"Ah, there is our lieutenant," he smiled. "You are coming from the officers' mess?"

"Yes Excellency," reported Robert.

"Did you meet your colonel there?"

"He was present."

"Did you get an invitation?"

"I know of no invitation, Excellency."

"Ah, he wanted to exclude you but we'll surprise him. I have learned from the Count what difficulties you experienced and I've decided they should be proud to have Lieutenant Brooks amongst them."

"Excellency, I don't know ..."

"All right, all right," interrupted the minister, "I know your disposition, you don't have to assure me. The purpose of my visit has been fulfilled and I shall take my leave now." With this he said his good byes.

Robert learned about the invitations they received. He went to his room to get a good rest for the next day. He was hardly there when there was a knock at his door.

Expecting nobody at this late hour, it was a happy surprise when Helen entered upon his 'come in'.

"You?" he questioned, "come and sit down."

"Yes, I'll do that. I know a young lady should not visit a man at this hour but we are like siblings, aren't we?"

"Naturally," he said, to disperse her doubts, "does mother know you are here?"

"Of course she knows."

"And she gave you permission to come to me?"

"She even asked me to. There's something important I have to ask you."

He felt happy indeed. She came to him, trustingly, at such a late hour. He loved her with all his heart. He sat next to her and looked into her beautiful face. "Well, what do you want to ask me?"

"Give me your hand first. So. Do you know that we have always loved each other?"

He trembled at this question. An indescribable feeling gripped his heart.

He could only nod.

"And that we still love each other?"

"Yes," he gasped.

"I know, but do you think that I don't still like you as before? You know, if somebody loves someone, one knows everything. If one doesn't know, one suspects it. I can read your eyes. Do you believe that?"

Robert had to pull himself together to answer a straight "yes."

"Well, when you came from the officers' mess, your eyes were deep, transparent and deep down, troubled. I knew at once that you had suffered a bad welcome. A nasty dissension had ensued and you officers take quickly to weapons. Come, Robbie, look into my eyes." Helen put her hands on both his shoulders, drew him a bit closer. She looked in his eyes for a full minute and then dropped her hands. "Robbie, there will be a duel."

"Helen," he said shocked.

"Robbie, I can see it distinctly. Deep down there was something you wanted to hide. It looks like proud determination. Will you tell me the truth?"

"Always."

"Then tell me whether my supposition was right."

"Do you promise that you will tell no-one?"

"Naturally, we cannot betray each other."

The girl was charming in her childish simplicity. He forced himself to answer calmly:

"You've guessed it, Helen."

"Well then, a duel. Robbie, I felt it, I suspected it. Do you now believe that I love you?"

"It's my greatest happiness that I can believe that."

"Do you think this duel worries me?"

"It doesn't?"

"Not in the slightest. You know how to defeat an opponent. But mother is anxious. She knows these things can't be postponed and she has sent me to you."

Robert's eyes lit up when he heard of their trust. "Did you speak to anybody else about your premonition?"

"No, only to mother. The others would have tried to keep you from dealing with your enemies. You have to do that."

"Helen, you are a heroin," he called enchanted.

"May I ask who is your opponent?"

"There are two. Colonel Winslow and Lieutenant Edmonton." This was no boasting. It did not occur to him to oblige her to revenge herself on the man who had intruded on her.

"Two duels?" Helen was amazed. "Can you promise me only to punish but not to kill them?"

"Yes, I promise."

"I am glad and for thanks, you may kiss my hand again as you did before."

She held her hand toward him and smiled when he drew it to his lips. "That's how the knights' ladies did it. They also gave their knights a good luck charm. Will this do?" She unpinned from her blouse a bow of silken ribbon and passed it to him.

He pressed the bow to his lips. "I'll wear it next to my heart."

"Do that. I'll wear it again proudly."

"Does that mean I'll have to return it?"

"That's the custom, I believe."

"Then you'll have to redeem it."

"Redeem? How?"

"With a kiss."

"Have those ladies really done that? When I give you this ribbon as a present, then I don't have to redeem it?"

"No, then you don't."

"I have to think it over. Which do you prefer, dear Robbie?"

"I would like best to get the kiss and to keep the bow."

"You're going to outwit me! It isn't easy. I'll have to do some serious thinking about that to decide. For now, keep it. I'll tell you later what will happen."

She went and left a happy man. He again pressed the bow to his lips. It had a delicate scent. He loved Helen. He then sank on the sofa and thought of her a long time. His eyes closed without him noticing. Then he dreamt of her. ---

Next morning Robert had to go to his regiment. Eric Freeman, who was now his servant, saddled his horse. It was a splendid Andalusian black stallion, given to him by the Count as a present. As he rode into the roomy yard, most of the officers were present.

"The devil," called Captain Winnington. "Where did that son of a sailor get such a horse? His 'comrades' hardly acknowledged his greeting. Only Lieutenant Pluton said aloud: Good morning, Brooks, a fine stallion, have you got more of those in your stable?"

"It is my horse for ordinary services, the others I have to be easy on."

Colonel Winslow appeared. His face was dark; he could hardly conceal his anger. The adjutant rode toward him.

"Anything to report?" asked the chief.

"Only Lieutenant Brooks to enter the regiment."

"Lieutenant Brooks," ordered Winslow sharply.

Robert rode to him. He stopped still as if he and his horse were cast in iron. His superior inspected his attire, his riding gear and his horse. He would have loved to find something to criticise but could find nothing. "You are released from your duties until further notice."

Robert turned around and his horse jumped in a splendid bow out of the gate.

The drill took about two hours. The colonel had returned to his abode and was going to make himself comfortable when Pluton entered. "Ah, right that you came here, Lieutenant Pluton," said the chief sourly. "I have to remark on your behaviour yesterday that I do not understand. Why did you let this man sit next to you and even play chess with him?"

"Because I am of the opinion that it is impolite, especially of an officer, to treat a comrade given to us by the Minister of War, as if he were a black sheep."

"But you knew of our general agreement."

"I took no part in it."

"You even went away with him."

"Yes, I have found him a person I have to respect. We became friends."

"Ah," called Winslow angrily. Do you know you have made enemies with your comrades to associate yourself with a mangy sheep?"

"Lieutenant Brooks has won my respect and friendship. I have to beg you, to refrain from such comparisons in my presence. By the way, I have made this visit on his behalf."

"Not as a second?"

"Yes."

"Does he really dare to challenge me?"

"Yes, I, on his behalf, ask for satisfaction."

"This is careless of you. Do you realise that I am your superior?"

"Yes, as far as military service is concerned. In matters of honour we are all equal. My friend wants satisfaction and has asked me to come to an agreement with you."

Winslow walked agitatedly to and fro. He was in an unpleasant situation from which there was no way out. He asked: "Lieutenant Brooks cannot expect an apology from his superior. Go to Major Howard and arrange with him what you want.

Remember, satisfaction I give the uniform, not the person. By the way, the court of honour will have the last word." Pluton now went to Edmonton. "I have come to give you the address of Lieutenant Brooks."

"What for?"

"I think you will guess that. You will have to know it for making any communication."

"I don't think to need his address as you are probably his authorized agent."

"You are right; I am here on his behalf."

"That's enough. Winnington will be my second. What weapon does your so-called friend choose?"

"He leaves that choice to you."

Edmonton had a fierce look in his eyes. "Ah," he said, "does he feel so self-assured. I am the best fighter with the sabre in the regiment. If he is that stupid, let the weapon be the heavy sabre. The time you can arrange with Winnington. Have you anything more to say?"

"No, may I leave you now? I say my good bye with cool politeness"

Robert received the message with equanimity. "This honourable gentleman wants to kill me. He knows no mercy. It will be his look out if I practice leniency or not.

As for the colonel, he is a coward and will probably choose pistols and a large distance. When can I expect their decision?"

"Before nightfall."

"You will inform me?"

"Yes, before I attend the Ball given by the Minister of War. By the way, that's another trick they played on you. By right you should have received an invitation."

"Don't worry," smiled Robert, "I have a private invitation from the minister."

Pluton looked astonished. "You lucky fellow," he said, "you are favoured by the minister?"

"He was always well disposed toward me. Please don't tell anybody I'm coming. I'll enjoy the disappointment of my comrades who regard me as an unwelcome intruder. You can tell me the message at the ball when I can introduce you to the minister, the Count and the ladies."

"Heavens, what luck," said the Lieutenant, "By God, you are a riddle. I must confess it's no disadvantage to be your friend. Will you also introduce me to the lady of the unfortunate bet?"

"Yes, but let's part for now, as we have to prepare for the ball." ---

In course of the afternoon, the court of honour made their judgement. The members were all aristocrats and looked at Brooks as a mangy sheep, as Winslow had put it. They were influenced by him and their judgement was that, although Winslow had been abrupt toward Brooks, there was violation of respect on his part that would offset the situation and Brooks, therefore, had no right to ask for satisfaction. The colonel had no duty to give it. There would be no duel. Then came the remark that Lieutenant Brooks' behaviour was inconsidered and, therefore, unsuitable to gain the officers' friendly disposition. It should be suggested to him to let himself be transferred to another regiment, especially, as his views and social conditions were not in harmony with the Hussar regiment.

Pluton received the copy of this judgement. He saw that he was expected to remark on it. But he said nothing. He had the conviction that this matter was not finished. Winslow felt he was the victor. He thought that Robert would not dare to insist on entering his regiment. He went home with a feeling of satisfaction and put on his special uniform for the ball. His lady was ready and they went to the palace early, so as not to make the host of the feast wait.

The palace of St. James was festively decorated. The rooms were flooded with light. Busy servants were hurrying to and fro. At the entrance stood a court official to receive the numerous guests. According to principle the Lieutenants came first. The higher the rank the later was their arrival. They were received in the anteroom by an adjutant of the war-minister and escorted to their places. The last were the Brigade commanders and the Division General with their ladies.

In the big hall one could see the musicians. There was an air of expectation. People talked in an undertone. From the dining room one could hear the clinking of glasses and porcelain, promising the gourmet longed-for pleasures.

Finally the door was opened and the minister was announced. He entered with Rosetta de Manresa, presently Mrs. Stenton. Then came Don Miguel with Lady Margaret and the mother of Doctor Stenton. After them came Robert who had Helen at his arm.

The eyes of the gentlemen opened wide. Robert wore on his chest five distinguishing war medals. The eyes of the ladies were on the much decorated Lieutenant. The eyes of the men were on his lady.

All those present stood up. The minister went to the general to be introduced to his ladies, whereupon he introduced the names of those ladies who accompanied him. The appearance of Robert behind the minister made an enormous impression. Captain Winnington did not believe his eyes. "Do I see right," he mumbled to Lieutenant Carrington, "Isn't that Brooks?"

"By God, it is him, you are right," said Carrington, "How does that fellow get into the retinue of the minister?"

The amazement of Winnington increased when he saw the decorations on Robert's chest. "Four medals and a cross of merit, am I bewitched?"

"And on his arm the coachman's daughter. I think, Winnington, we were awfully teased."

"We shall see. The minister is introducing him to the General. What are they talking about? asked Carrington.

Pluton, who stood nearby, remarked smilingly: "He asked the general to introduce Lieutenant Brooks and the lady to the officers."

"That looks if the whole ball is meant as a satisfaction for this Lieutenant," called Winnington loudly.

"That's right," said Pluton. He is the minister's favourite and it is his way of reprimanding the officers."

The general stepped to the colonel. "Colonel Winslow, I have the honour to introduce Lieutenant Brooks and Miss Stenton. He is entering your regiment and I recommend him to your friendly care."

Winslow choked; he did not manage a single word. He only nodded obligingly. Brooks turned to the general: "Excellency," he said, "we have demanded already too much of you; please allow the colonel to introduce us to the gentlemen."

"A devil of a boy," growled Winnington, "now he forces Winslow who had declared him as not able to receive satisfaction to deny yesterday's behaviour and introduce him formally."

The general nodded friendly: "It would have been my pleasure to introduce you but if it is your wish, I shall pass this honour to the colonel."

Winslow had to bite the sour apple. On his wave, the officers of his regiment came closer and he was forced to name a long row of officers to the man he had insulted.

After finishing this task Robert thanked him coolly. He then went to Pluton and introduced Helen to him adding: "He is my friend. Would you introduce him to the minister?"

She passed her hand to Pluton and asked: "Do you dance, Lieutenant?"

"Passionately, gracious lady," he answered as his face reddened with joy.

"Robert will bring you my card. To his friend I shall grant the dance after him, but let us go now to the minister so that we can introduce you to the party givers."

They moved away and Winslow stood with his officers. He wiped the sweat off his forehead and confessed: "I think I'm going to faint, I'll have to sit down." He then went to his wife to seek consolation. The conversation was about Brooks and how he taught the regiment that he was not only a handsome man, but a man in the full meaning of that word. The ladies were enchanted and the gentlemen looked at him with other eyes. But it should even be better! The double doors opened and the announcement was heard: "Her Majesty the Queen!"

The minister stepped to the door to receive the gracious guest. She walked next to the minister and an adjutant who held a satin-covered flat box in his hand.

"I couldn't deny myself a few minutes on this occasion. Please introduce me to your guests."

Winnington could not be silent. "You can see the little box in the hands of the adjutant. That must be some kind of decoration for the minister."

The minister went toward the colonel who, in turn, came toward him. "Colonel Winslow, did you get my letter regarding Lieutenant Brooks?"

"I had the honour," the colonel answered.

"Did you read it?

"At once, as with everything from your Excellency."

"It is with astonishment that it had the opposite effect of what it was intended. Do you remember what I recommended?"

"Certainly."

"Nevertheless, I heard that Lieutenant Brooks was received with a general animosity. Many an aristocrat has his position despite having a hollow head. As head of the military it is rare to find someone of great use and it is therefore even more lamentable, when such men come across malicious difficulty." He turned away and left the colonel who stood absentminded a few moments on the spot before returning to his seat.

"He is morally and physically crushed for today," mumbled Winnington. "I wouldn't like to be in his skin. Lieutenant Brooks came to our calm like a bomb and the splinters are falling on our heads. Where is he now?"

"There, under the mirror," said an amazed Carrington, "he is talking to the minister."

"With the minister? By God it's true. I would give five months salary, if the minister would only nod to me. Heavens, even the Queen goes towards them. Those present looked with amazement at the young man on such good terms with those in high authority.

The Queen waved to the adjutant who began his announcement: "Ladies and gentlemen. By the very highest order, I have the honour to tell you that Her Majesty, in view of important services rendered during his brief period in the army, has bestowed Lieutenant Brooks with a Victorian cross. She graciously has also ordered me to hand to Lieutenant Brooks the decoration that goes with it and will proceed further in the near future."

He opened the satin box and fastened a medal to Robert's chest. The place was quiet as a church. What were the services that this man had made in so short a time? The Lieutenant was showered with good fortune. Queen Victoria then congratulated him. The minister and then everybody, except Winslow and Edmonton, followed.

After the Queen, the minister and the adjutant had left, the party goers let themselves go a little. The general buzz bore witness to the enthusiasm with which they talked about the event. The higher officers had already congratulated Robert and he stood alone for a moment when Helen approached. "Dear Robbie, what a pleasant surprise. Did you ever think of such favouritism?"

"Never. I am still amazed," he confessed. "I feel as if I'm in a dream."

"You have shamed your enemies." She pressed his hand and went back to her mother.

In the next room was the colonel with his adjutant Major Palms and Lieutenant Edmonton. The major said: "Gentlemen, after the events of this evening, it is impossible to adhere to the judgement of the Court of Honour. We would all be chased out. And you, Colonel Sir, would be the first. I shall call all the members of the court tomorrow morning. A pretext will be found to reverse the previous judgement."

"I think so as well," ventured Colonel Winslow. "I give you my word of honour, that I shall do my utmost to kill him."

"You leave that to me, Colonel," said Edmonton. I have challenged him with heavy swords. He cannot escape me. What do you say to the venue being the Park behind the brewery?"

"Very well, and the time?"

"I shall tell Pluton I accept the challenge," said Winslow.

"And I don't want to lose a minute splitting his skull. What do you say to four o'clock in the morning?"

"It is all right with me."

"I have an urgent plea," said Lieutenant Edmonton to Colonel Winslow. "You have a family and you are a father. I am not married and I ask you to let me go first."

In view of the fact that he had the higher rank, Winslow should not have accepted this arrangement. He thought of his family, the punishment that would follow and the possibility that there would be no fight at all, if Brooks were killed. He replied: "You are a decent man, Lieutenant. I shall not deny your plea. Major Palms, you should be present as an impartial witness. Captain Winnington, do you want to be my second?"

"With the greatest of pleasure," answered Winnington.

"Then go to Pluton at once and tell him I expect my opponent at four in the morning. I will bring pistols. We will be twenty paces apart and shoot until one of us is dead or unable to serve in the army. I'll also arrange for a physician."

"How will the shooting go?"

"On command, simultaneously."

"Your conditions are as strict as mine. Brooks will not leave the place alive."

Two seconds went to Pluton who was with Robert and Helen on a divan. "Lieutenant, we have to speak to you," they said.

"Let's go to the adjoining room," answered Robert. "The lady will excuse us for a few moments. The two Seconds informed Lieutenant Brooks of the conditions. He replied smilingly: "I can see that they mean to take my life. I am not all inexperienced as they seem to think, but I will not shut my ears to an apology. I am a man, not a hooligan."

The adjutant answered with an ambiguous smile: "As far as I know the other gentlemen, there would be no chance of their apology. They might think it cowardice."

"Speak to them anyway; what they might think is irrelevant. They'll get to know me better at the event. I shall be there at four o'clock punctually."

They parted with measured bows. ---

Chapter 32

EYE TO EYE

$\mathcal{T}$HE gentlemen who were participating in the duel did not wait until the ball was over. Robert was sitting in his room, reading a book when there was a knock at the door. Helen entered and bid him a good morning. "Did you sleep well?"

"Not at all."

"Did you make a will?" she joked.

He made a serious face and answered: "My dear Helen, a duel is even for the best a risky thing. If one is master of all weapons, one is still vulnerable. And if one stays alive, the thought that one has killed or even only wounded a person is depressing in any case."

"You are right, dear Robbie but I can't be worried about you; and what about your opponents? It depends on you to avoid all pangs of conscience. You know they want to kill you."

"But I won't kill them."

"I implore you not to exaggerate your leniency so as to put yourself in danger.

Edmonton is spoken of as a fence master and Winslow as a distinguished marksman. Not to worry, I feel superior to Both of them."

"And my ribbon, dear Robbie? That should be your talisman."

"I'll wear it on my heart. Did you think about asking for its return?" he smiled.

"That depends on whether I am satisfied with your behaviour against your enemies," she said. "It is three thirty now."

"I have to meet Pluton now, he is waiting for me."

"O Robbie, if you should be hit by a bullet," her eyes were tearful.

"Don't worry, dear Helen, I have to go now."

Once more she pressed his hand. "Go with God." Then she disappeared.

At the corner Pluton waited in a carriage drawn by two horses. "Coachman, let's be first at the venue." He had seen Winslow's and Edmonton's carriages turning in the same direction. At ten to four they arrived. They stopped at a place free of shrubs and trees. Soon the others arrived. The greeting was a silent nod. The servants were standing guard to ward off any disturbance. The physician prepared the bandages.

Pluton and Carrington searched the place and brought the weapons. The colonel and his adjutant came close to witness the battle. Major Palms, who was supposed to be impartial, had to try reconciliation and said: "Do the gentlemen permit me to speak?"

"You have my permission," said Robert.

"But not mine," called Edmonton, I have been greatly insulted; every trial of reconciliation is useless.

"I have nothing to add," said Robert. Please note that I was prepared to listen to Major Palms."

"Who ever is prepared to withdraw is a coward," declared Edmonton as he lifted his sabre from the ground. "Let us start."

Robert took his weapon as well. The battle would commence as soon as Major Palms gave the sign. The opponents stood eye to eye. Robert calm and serious. Edmonton with tightly pressed lips and trembling nostrils. It was a serious moment.

Major Palms lifted his hand. The sign that battle could commence. Edmonton immediately started powerful as if to beat down an elephant. Robert parried the Hercules blow with ease. With lightning speed he Countered from the side with such power as to hurl Edmonton's sabre from his hand. The seconds crossed their sabres between the opponents to stop Robert from attacking the now defenceless Edmonton. The physician picked up the sabre and returned it to him, who immediately pushed again toward Robert. The two heavy sabres clanked together. A loud cry was heard and Edmonton's sabre flew in a wide bow over the clearing. With horror the officers saw the severed hand still holding the handle of the weapon.

Robert lowered his sabre and asked the physician: "Would you please see whether one of us is unable to serve. This was the condition of my opponents."

"Edmonton stood with eyes not moving on one spot. From the lifted arm shot a thick stream of red blood. Then he staggered and his second stepped to him for support. The wounded man still didn't utter a word. He let the physician pull him down, looked at the stump were his hand has been and closed his eyes.

It took a long time to overcome the bleeding. One could hear the grinding of Edmonton's teeth. Was this because of pain or fury? His eyes were open now and threw a hateful glance at Robert.

"A cripple," he groaned, "a miserable cripple. Colonel, you must promise me to shoot him down."

"I promise," replied Winslow, overwhelmed by the sight of the wounded man. "I reject any plea for expiation."

"Good, that gives me strength again. Doctor, I have to see this fight, you mustn't deny me that."

The physician frowned in doubt. "With a wound like yours, any excitement is harmful, but I will allow you to stay. Actually you should go home immediately."

"That would be worse. No, I have to see this man fall. I shall gladly give up my hand and be a cripple. Don't let's wait."

Two swords marked the places of the opponents. The adjutant brought the pistols that the colonel had provided. Robert picked a pistol and asked: "As I am not used to these, may I make a trial shot?"

"Shoot," was the short answer of his opponent's second.

Over the face of the wounded man came a scornful smile. Robert loaded the pistol and looked around for a suitable aim. An apple tree stood nearby. He pointed to a visible fruit and said. Well, this apple must come down. He aimed a long time and pressed the trigger. One could hear many a 'hm' and clearing of throats as he missed the apple and hit a little twig about one metre away. "Thank God, he's a bad shot," thought Winslow.

"For heaven's sake, dear Robert, "said Pluton quietly to his friend. "If you don't shoot better, you'll be lost. The colonel gave his word of honour to Edmonton that he will kill you mercilessly."

"He may try," smiled Robert. "By the way, I found these pistols are excellent."

"How, what, you even make jokes? In spite of the excellence of the pistol you didn't hit your aim."

"On the contrary, I hit exactly the target I wanted to hit. I only mentioned the apple as pretence. I actually hit the twig I was aiming at."

"You are, by God, a terrible opponent. I wouldn't want to be an enemy of yours."

The time has come again for the major. "Gentlemen, I feel it to be my duty …"

"Silence, comrade," called Winslow. "I don't want to hear a word."

He had seen that Robert had failed to hit the apple by a metre. This confirmed his self-confidence.

"But I request the major to speak," said Robert. "One should not kill, if there are other ways for reconciliation. I declare myself satisfied if the colonel says sorry."

"Apologise? Only a madman would think of it. I have given my word of honour that one of us will fall here, let's start." Both were in their places and lifted their pistols, Robert aimed at the hand of the colonel and inclined his head slightly toward the major, to give the major's command to start greatest attention. It was necessary to anticipate by a miniscule second.

The major Counted: "One – two – three!"

The shots rang out.

"Heavens," called Winslow at the same time and stepped several paces backward. The pistol had dropped to the ground while the physician grasped his arm.

"Are you hit? asked the Second.

"Yes, in the hand," sighed the wounded man

The physician looked at Robert and declared: "Shattered, fully shattered. The bullet went through the hand into the wrist and into the arm."

"Can the hand be saved?" asked Winslow anxiously.

"No, impossible, it has to come off."

"Incapable to serve?" inquired Robert.

"Absolutely," answered the physician.

"I can leave my post then," declared Robert, threw the pistol to the ground and walked off.

"I am a cripple too, I too, do you hear, Edmonton?"

"I do, I do. This man has a bond with Satan. I hope he takes him to hell very soon."

"You are mistaken," said Pluton. "What you call Satan is an excellent usage of weapons. He is my friend and I must not listen to dishonourable talk. It was not he who spoke the insult. Nevertheless, he did not want blood. You intended to kill him. He only made you unable to serve, and that was another of your conditions. And now it has happened to you." After this reprimand he followed his friend.

There was sarcasm in the voice of Edmonton when he asked Winslow: "Colonel, Sir, I don't feel very well, may I ask for leave?"

"Go home," snarled his superior, "I am in the same condition and I wonder how this thing will develop with those in authority."

The doctor had finished the bandaging and the carriages rolled off. The clearing looked as if nothing special had happened here. At the corner where Robert awaited his friend to say his thanks and good bye. Pluton asked him what he was going to do.

"Are you voluntarily reporting yourself?"

"That is probably the best thing. At the moment I'm tired and I am going to have a rest."

"There is no question of rest for me. Service will keep me awake. I feel very disturbed. I'll see you later."

Pluton went off while Robert walked the short stretch home on foot. Nobody seemed to be awake when he entered his abode. He was hardly in his room when Helen rushed in. "You're not wounded," she rejoiced and sank for a moment, into his arms, while tears were in her eyes.

Robert told her briefly what has happened, and continued: "Actually I would have to report all this to the colonel. But, as he was a participant I, of course, cannot do it. I shall think about that after I've had a rest. For now, I thank God I've escaped death. It was also your talisman that guarded me."

"Ah, my ribbon. Yes, you were a valiant knight and have well defended the honour of your maiden."

"What will happen to the talisman? Do you want it back?"

Her face reddened. "That will be decided when you've had a rest. Such things have to be well thought over."

"Now you are teasing me," he smiled. "You promised me the decision now, depending on the outcome of the battle."

"Hm, that's possible. Is the decision really needed so soon?"

"Naturally," he laughed. "I have to know whether the talisman will be redeemed or not."

"With a kiss?"

"Yes, with a kiss."

There she stood, charming and lovely. The sunbeams surrounded the pretty girl. She put her hand on his arm and said: "You know, dear Robbie, I am very satisfied with you. You've risked your life for me and I shall redeem the talisman if it is all right with you."

He pulled the ribbon from his chest and passed it to her. "Here it is, Helen."

"And here's the kiss."

She put her hands on his shoulders, pursed her lips and gave him a kiss, delicately and carefully.

"Was that a kiss," he asked disappointedly.

"I think so," she laughed mischievously, "or was it something else?"

"It was a kiss – but one for an old aunt who has a long nose with a few warts on it."

"Did you kiss many old aunts, as you know it so well?"

"No, old aunts one doesn't like to kiss."

"Who else?"

"Beautiful young Helens."

"Go away; I have to punish you for that. Here, take the ribbon again."

He grasped at the bow and put it behind him on the table and said with an important expression: "That can't be done so quickly."

"How's that, dear Robbie?"

"The return of a talisman. In such important matters one must treat it justly."

"I'm always just. How did you mean it?"

"You've paid for it. If you return the talisman, my duty is to return the payment." Robert saw her heart was pounding. Her forehead and her temples were warm, her cheeks were hot. Suddenly she saw red and it became darker and darker. Couldn't she see or did she close her eyes? She didn't know. She only felt his arms around her shoulders. "Helen, dear Helen, look at me."

"No," she breathed almost inaudibly."

"Are you angry with me, my dear Helen?"

"O no, dear Robbie," she whispered.

"Then I shall cure the eyes you cannot open." She felt two warm lips. First on her on her right and the on her left eye. On her cheeks then on her mouth. Softly at first than harder and hotter. Helen felt dazed and couldn't think clearly. Should she defend herself? Oh no, she was caught and she couldn't. She heard his question. "Are you angry with me, my Helen?"

She answered from the depth of her heart, "No. Robbie," she whispered.

He took her tightly into his arms again until outside the shuffling steps of the housemaster were heard to start his daily routine. Robert had let go of her and she opened her eyes. He took her hands and said: "You see, dear Helen that was a kiss."

Her former being had returned and she asked him teasingly: "Not like an aunt?"

"Like an old one,"

"With a long nose."

"And with many warts on it."

Now they laughed heartily about the insinuation of an old aunt that Helen totally forgot the duel; and that she was the grandchild of a Count. Robert forgot that his father was a sailor. Helen turned back to the present. "I am going now," she said as if in apology.

"Good morning, dear Helen. I am going to sleep a little and I'll be dreaming of you."

He stood alone and happy in his room. "Oh, how I love her."

Helen went to her rooms. "What was that? What have I done? I must never tell mother about this, never."

Her maid came to her room and saw the unused bed. "You haven't slept at all? She asked.

"No, bring me my morning chocolate and I'll drive out afterwards," answered Helen. It was eight o'clock in the morning and not a time for visiting. "To the Minister of War," she ordered the coachman.

His Excellency was not available yet. She had to wait in the waiting room. The servant told him that there was a Miss Stenton who wanted to speak to him urgently. He knew the name and hurried to get dressed and see her. A lively dialogue ensued after which Miss Stenton left the waiting room. Her eyes were shining with the joy of an achieved success. The minister summoned Pluton for an immediate audience.

At home they were all surprised she had gone out so early. She thought it better to tell them everything.

Meanwhile Pluton had a shock. The summons could only be about the duel. How could the minister know about it so soon? He was led by a servant who apparently expected him, through several doors into a lady's room where the wife of the minister was sitting with a book in her hand. She nodded benevolently and offered him a seat.

He sat down and waited tensely for what would follow. The door to the adjoining room was ajar and a shadow of a man betrayed the situation. He understood that the minister had news of the duel and had reason to learn about it but not in the official way. As he had called Robert's second, Pluton suspected it was a special consideration.

"We wish to talk about the fact that you know Lieutenant Brooks," she began the conversation.

"I have the honour to be his friend," replied Pluton.

"Let me go straight to the point. The lieutenant had a duel this morning?"

"Indeed, I had no order to deny that."

"Who with?"

"With his colonel and Lieutenant Edmonton of his regiment."

"And the result of this?" searched the wife of the minister tensely.

"Brooks took both his opponents hands off to make them unable to serve. That was their minimal condition."

"My God, how terrible, please tell me."

Pluton reported the real conspiracy which had engulfed his friend as he entered the regiment, about Robert's manly behaviour and level-headed handling of the situation. He described the truth and did not let the slightest shadow fall on his friend.

"Thank you lieutenant. Your friend seems an excellent person. What is he doing to escape the consequences?"

"Escape? Excellence, he is not the man who would want to escape consequences of something that wasn't even his fault. I am convinced he will present himself to a relevant authority."

"Nevertheless, this matter is highly embarrassing. I ask you urgently not to mention that this was the subject of our conversation. Pluton noticed that the previously mentioned shadow had disappeared. She nodded good bye and he left with a deep bow. He had hardly closed the door when a servant begged him to enter his Excellency's room. He stepped into the office of the minister who apparently studied some files. The minister put these files away when he saw Pluton. "I have asked you to call on me for an unusual commission, Lieutenant Pluton," he began. "I have heard that you were present at a hunting enterprise this morning."

Pluton understood at once. The minister wanted the duel to be a hunting accident and assured him with an agreeing bow. "Yes, minister,"

"Unfortunately, I have learned that there were accidents where some people were hurt by being not careful with their weapons?"

"Unfortunately, Excellency. Not life threatening but, according to the physician, two men lost the ability to serve."

"This is deplorable. I have been told that it was the gentlemen's own fault. Has the news of this event spread already?"

"I am convinced of the opposite, Excellency."

"Then it is my wish that there should be complete silence about this. You will go immediately to the two gentlemen in question to indicate this to them strictly. The wounded will not want to leave their rooms and it is my order that they receive no visitors. They may regard this as a detention in their own rooms. I shall speak to Her Majesty about this and I expect you here again at eleven o'clock."

Pluton went to the colonel first. He was in his bed and the wife came to him red faced with anger. "Ah, Lieutenant Pluton, I have to tell you …"

"Please, gracious lady," he quickly interrupted, "this form of address I only permit to comrades or friends."

She paused for a few seconds and continued with a raised voice: "Lord Pluton, I have to tell you that it is disgraceful to batter my husband in this way."

"If you use the word disgraceful, I would say that it doesn't apply in this case. You are a lady and the wife and, therefore, unable to judge the matter impartially."

"I am judging this matter rightly. I am going to the general to have this man face justice."

"I am in the position to spare you this step. I am here by order of the Minister of War."

"Ah," she said, shocked.

The wounded colonel raised his head in surprise. "From his Excellency?" he asked, "what is this. I hear?"

"I have to bring you his order that nobody should mention this case to anybody. You should not leave your room and you should receive no visitors."

"Ah, so I am a prisoner?"

"That is what his Excellency means. He is well-disposed towards my friend and considers this as an accident during a hunting party. It is expected that through the influence of your despised opponent, you will be spared imprisonment. Good day, Colonel, Sir."

Edmonton received Pluton and his order with furious silence. After he had visited the physician he went to Brooks, who was still asleep. Don Miguel woke him up. Robert was astounded to learn that the minister knew already about the duel. Pluton said that he was surprised too. The Count told them what Helen had told him. Robert took Helen's hand and said with a smile of thanks: "You have already been busy for me. Do you realise how much you have dared?"

"I had to act because you preferred to sleep. Have I dared a lot? I'm not sure. The decision of the minister seemed to prove the opposite."

Pluton went to the war minister as arranged. "You are punctual, I like that. I know that your comrades are having their second breakfast now. About the hunting party; it began in the officers' mess and should end there. Go to Colonel Lord Marchfield now, take these letters to him then go to your friend and both of you join your fellow officers in the mess hall. I wish to tell you that I approve your behaviour in this matter."

Pluton delivered the letters and collected his friend to go to the officers' mess. There was an atmosphere of embarrassment when they entered. The reply to their greetings was neither polite nor insulting. They ordered a glass of wine each and took a newspaper. They were all present except Colonel Winslow and Lieutenant Edmonton. Everyone suspected but nobody asked a question.

Colonel Marchfield in full uniform with all his decorations, entered. Everyone was surprised to see this man from a different regiment. The captain and the major went to welcome him. "I thank you for the welcome you have extended to me. I am not here for the breakfast."

He took the letters from his briefcase and continued: "I am here by the order of the minister for war to give you the following information. I request your attention, gentlemen. Number one:"

Colonel Marchfield read the few lines. They contained the discharge of Colonel Winslow without pension.

Number two: "Lieutenant Edmonton is being discharged without pension."

This announcement created great stupefaction and excitement. "Number three:" The noise died down. "Captain Winnington to be transferred." The captain was greatly shocked, everybody wanted to console him but nobody dared. It was understood to be a satisfaction for Lieutenant Brooks. "Number four."

Not finished yet? What might there be now? The announcement came at once: "Colonel Marchfield to take over from Colonel Winslow. Number five: Lieutenant Pluton advances to Captain."

At the end Robert was advanced to Captain but was transferred to the diplomatic ordnance corps. This was a distinction for which one could envy ones best friend, let alone a man one has approached with hostility.

Pluton embraced his friend and whispered: "I attached myself to you because of my feeling for justice. Who would have thought that this would result in my advancement. Let us leave; you have had a brilliant satisfaction. I am going to ask my new commander for leave. I have to visit my uncle the banker."

"To your uncle? That means we'll go the same direction. I am asking for leave too."

There was great joy at home when he told them of his advancement and his transfer to the diplomatic corps. He then drove to the Minister of War. After Robert expressed his thanks the minister said: "You were warmly recommended and I have read your military reports and I am of the opinion that you should receive a commission abroad. I only hope you will refrain from hunting accidents and, for the moment, you have three weeks leave, after which we shall send you to Mexico on a special mission."

He spoke about the hunting accident in a jocular manner and continued: "For the moment I shall not introduce you to your new superiors. It is possible that we need you for a military mission with a diplomatic character. We need a man who has the courage of a hero, the astuteness of a detective and the cool bloodedness of age while looking inexperienced and not dangerous. You seem to be suitable. I have given you time to prepare yourself but I have to know your whereabouts as there is a possibility that I need you sooner."

"Excellency, I am too young to be sure that I shall be able to do all that is required of me but I shall do my best."

"Your modesty is an honour for you. Please remember me to the Count."

Robert left the minister even happier than before and decided to go to Bradford on Avon to tell his mother and Colonel Terence Masterson of the events and future assignment. ---

Chapter 33

THE SECRET OF THE WALL-CLOCK

$\mathcal{I}$T was the next morning. The two friends were sitting opposite each other in a train steaming toward their mutual aim. During the conversation Pluton offered Robert a cigarette. As he pulled off his glove, the morning sun fell on a ring.

"What a magnificent ring," remarked Robert, "surely an old piece inherited?"

"Indeed, but not from my own family. It was a present from my uncle."

"The banker you are visiting?"

"Yes, I was of service to him once and he gave me this ring. I would have preferred money, but he is too mean to part with any cash. This ring has probably cost him nothing. Do you want to have a look at it?"

"Yes, please."

Robert looked at it and remarked that it wasn't an English piece of work and it seemed quite old.

"I think it's Mexican by the looks of it, but how my uncle should come to possess anything from there is a riddle. My uncle possesses other things of foreign extraction too. He seemed anxious about these things and shows them to nobody. He has a workroom in his garden where I once surprised him. My appearance was a great shock to him. I had to laugh that apparently I had penetrated his secret."

"His secret?"

"Yes," said Pluton carelessly. "There was a wall-clock he had taken down and I saw a box in a hole in the wall where he seemed to hide these items. I saw a necklace hanging from the box which made me think that there was other jewellery there."

"How long ago was that?"

"Quite a few years. I don't think it does any harm that I have told you his secret," answered Pluton. Robert gave an appearance of indifference, but he suspected that these items might be connected with the lost Mexican treasures. He looked out of the window. "And if I had the desire to look at this jewellery?"

"Nonsense, why should you ask for that?"

"Dear friend, my father went to Mexico some years ago. He met his brother who was the owner of an old treasure. The way he got it I'll tell you another time."

"The devil, this gets interesting."

"The brothers were with a haciendero whose daughter was the bride of my uncle. During the war there, they became lost. Before they went away it had been decided by this uncle that one half of that treasure should be sent to my mother for my education. Benito Juarez, who was the chief judge at the time took it in hand, insured it and sent it to Bradford on Avon. He did not know my exact address and sent it care of Colonel Masterson who never received it."

"Where do you know all this from?"

"You have met Lady Castlepool who told me the day before yesterday about all this. Her father was present when the haciendero handed it to Juarez. He, her father, was subsequently taken prisoner by some bandits and only freed after three years. I never knew about it until two days ago, otherwise I would have made an investigation."

"A strange story, indeed. Perhaps my uncle got these things through others, perhaps they are not Mexican."

"Both these cases are possible but we have to convince ourselves."

"Certainly, you should get your possession and I want to know whether my uncle is a thief or an honest man."

"I thank you. You'll understand it is not my intention to insult you. It is my urgent wish to see these things."

"Well, you should see them. We'll ask my uncle to show these items to you. That is simple and open."

"Perhaps just as unwise. If he's guiltless, we have insulted him terribly. If he's guilty we achieve nothing."

"You may be right but what can we do?"

"Enter his garden-house without his knowledge."

"Good God, you mean burgle?"

"Breaking in, but not stealing anything. The items stay where they are."

"We'll see what we can do. Your possessions belong to you; in the other case I shall free my uncle from a grave suspicion. How shall we proceed?"

"You'll find an opportunity. We don't live very far. You'll inform me."

It was already the following day, when Pluton told Robert that his uncle is going on business to Manchester and will not return before midnight. "What will you do in case my uncle ..." Pluton paused. It was difficult for that honest officer to finish the sentence.

"Don't worry dear Pluton, it depends on the circumstances. You can be sure that, whatever the outcome, I shall have the greatest consideration for you. I haven't suffered because of this. I have had rich and high patrons. I'm not mad about wealth and the pleasures it might provide, but it is understandable that I cannot forego an heirloom and leave it in the wrong hands. By the way: I am your friend, you were my second during the duel and you now offer me the discovery of a possible fortune and I don't even know your first name."

Pluton laughed. There's no problem. My full name and title is: Lord Edward Pluton of Hammersmith! Just call me Ed. That will suffice."

There was no question about the welcome he received from his mother and Colonel Masterson. They were proud of his achievements. He didn't tell them of the possibility of recovering his father's parcel and its contents.

Ed and Robert rode to Bradford on Avon where Edward showed his friend the garden from the outside. As it was a corner house, the garden could be viewed from the side street. They arranged a time just after dark when they would meet again.

Robert went to a locksmith, who was also his school friend and asked his help. The man knew that Robert would not commit anything illegal and promised his aid. It was easy to get inside the garden, where

Pluton was already waiting. The garden-house had strong shutters to its windows. The door was of oak and had a metal strip across it with a hanging padlock. The locksmith found a suitable key in no time. In his leather bag he had several picklocks. It took two minutes and the second lock was open.

They closed the door behind them. Pluton lit a lamp and they found themselves in a small room containing garden furniture. A second door led to a room with a writing desk and several chairs and at the far end there was a wall-clock. Inside a hole they found a box they took out. While the locksmith tried to open its lock, Pluton found in a drawer several letters that were opened immediately,

Before they could read these letters they heard a call of amazement. The locksmith had opened the box and revealed it was full of sparkling diamonds, other stones and various pieces of jewellery, Mexican in origin. Robert was almost seized by the fever of which Buff-he had spoken to his uncle. "Such riches I did not expect," he confessed. He could understand that an otherwise honest man can become a criminal.

Pluton took a deep breath. "I'm sure you were right. My uncle couldn't possibly have bought a treasure like this. The value is several millions. Let's read the letters."

The first letter showed the signature of Benito Juarez. "The chief justice," Robert called out.

"Deception is no longer possible," said Pluton. "Read the letter."

"Do you understand Spanish?"

"No."

"I'll translate: "Bank Fielding & Walton in Bradford on Avon England ...""

"James Walton is my uncle," interrupted Pluton.

"I'm sending you this box with precious stones and other jewellery next to a list of its contents. It belongs to a boy whose father is a sailor and whose name is Brooks. He lives near Bradford on Avon on an estate that belongs to a Colonel Masterson. The father and uncle unfortunately were lost in Mexico. He, therefore, is the heir of these items. Be so good as to pass on this parcel if you find him. If you do not discover his whereabouts, I request you to give this box to your government authorities.

The other enclosed letter is to a Mrs. Stenton formerly Countess de Manresa who lives at the same address. Your outlay will be reimbursed by the receiver. I would further remark that I possess a copy of the contents of this box, which is insured.

Benito Juarez, Chief Justice, Mexico."

"There is no more doubt, my uncle is a thief," said Pluton whose face was pale as death. "After this description he must have found you. Read the second letter."

Robert glanced through the letter. "It is of a private nature, written by Lady Margaret Castlepool."

"It is all right. I know enough. These items belong to you. What are you going to do?" asked Pluton, depressed. "I'll put everything in its place. By tomorrow I'll know what to do. I'll go easy on your uncle. He should not know that my knowledge comes through you. There are some more papers. You don't mind if I peruse them?"

"Do what you like; I don't want to see any more."

Robert looked them all through and said that "except for the list of contents they are of no interest."

"I don't want the ring anymore, please take it."

"Let it be a present from me."

"No thank you, stolen goods burn on my finger."

"Then keep it for the moment. Your uncle should not notice that you suspect anything."

The locksmith locked the door again. Pluton said: "You know the way, allow that I leave you now, I have to be alone."

Robert crept to the wall and listened whether everything was clear when he heard two people who seemed to take pains to reach the little garden gate quietly. "Stop, someone is coming," whispered Robert. "Let's wait."

"Nobody can eavesdrop on us, I hope?"

The voice seemed familiar to Robert. "No, there's nobody here and they don't expect me until midnight," was the answer probably the banker's. Then they disappeared into the garden-house.

"You can go home now," whispered Robert to the locksmith. He himself waited for nearly an hour until the two came out again. He could hear nothing of their conversation while they were inside but he hoped they would repeat the important bits when saying good bye, which is quite usual with many people. He was right. Near the garden gate stood an elder shrub behind which he found a useful hiding place. The two came closer. At the gate they stood for a moment. Robert could have touched them with his hand. "The papers are really secure in there?" asked the voice that Robert now recognised as Danlola's.

"Don't worry, I have a good hiding place in there until a messenger collects it."

"Will you tell this man to go immediately to London which I had to leave in a hurry. There he will find a Russian envoy under the name of Albitroff as a dealer in furs. He carries his secret papers hidden in his hat. I am not sure which hotel, but he can find that from the foreign register."

"I'll do that as I don't think much of our government but are you sure they'll keep their promise to me?"

"Absolutely. They value your services and will treat you properly. I have to leave England as soon as possible. For now, good night."

"Good night."

With these words the banker unlocked the gate and Danlola left. Robert at first thought of jumping him, but that would alert the thief and he might remove the letters to another hiding place. He might also lose his jewellery box. By the time the banker had entered his house and Robert had climbed over the garden wall, Danlola had disappeared in the dark.

Robert went to the police and alerted them about Danlola. The official had received a 'wanted' description from London and was amazed when Robert told him that the wanted man had been in town. From there Robert went to the telegraph office. There he sent a telegram to the war minister, telling him to arrest a Russian spy under the name of Albitroff who had secret documents in his hat. The locksmith was well rewarded.

It was early in the morning when Robert went to see James Walton the banker. Pluton was with his uncle when a servant came into the room. "Mr. Walton, a military man wants to speak to you, here is his visiting card."

"Probably requesting a loan," said the banker. "These gentlemen usually need more than they earn. It's probably an aristocrat ..." He interrupted himself when he read the card. Red coloured his pale face, but he rallied fast. "I'm mistaken, it is a commoner. Someone called Captain Robert Brooks. Do you know him by any chance?"

Pluton was surprised his friend came so soon. "Yes, I know him, he is a friend of mine."

"In that case I'll grant him a loan. Anyway stay here, it will be a pleasure for you to greet a comrade. Bring him here." The last words were spoken to the servant, who brought in Robert.

"You are the banker James Walton?" Robert asked.

"That's me. What can I do for you?"

Robert had entered with a serious face but he cheered up when he saw his friend. "Ah, Edward Pluton, you here? I bid you a very good morning."

"I thank you," answered Pluton," I take it that you want to speak to my uncle privately. I'll withdraw. Please visit me afterwards in my room."

"There's no need. The captain will probably ask me for a loan that I shall give him, being your friend."

Pluton's forehead reddened with embarrassment as he replied: "My friend Captain Brooks has no need for a loan. It seems that I should withdraw rather for your sake than for his."

"What's the meaning of that? Now I insist that you stay. I have no need to be secretive in your presence."

Pluton looked questioningly at Brooks who said, with a slight lifting of his shoulders: "It makes no difference whether you are present or not. I came here with a small plea but not for a loan."

"Please speak," said the banker. A small plea did not sound like a request for handing over millions.

"May I take a seat?" Robert reminded the banker of a neglected politeness. Sitting down he continued: "I have come here to request the handing over of certain documents. Mr. Walton.

Pluton looked surprised and the banker shook his head in a superior manner. "You've come to the wrong place. I am neither a writer of documents nor a jurist.

"I know that," said Robert coolly. "As you misunderstand me, I am forced to be more precise. You had a visitor last night?"

"A visitor? No. I have been away."

"You had a visitor just before midnight and were handed some documents which you promised to hand over to a messenger who in turn was to pass them to a Russian fur dealer called Albitroff."

The banker grew pale and said: "Sir, what are you telling me?"

Pluton listened tensely. He expected his friend to ask for the jewels but not this development.

Walton stared at his visitor wide eyed. "Well, if you don't understand, I'll go now and I'll have to inform the police. I intended to make it easy for you as my friend's uncle. Do you understand that he will be unable to serve in the army with a traitor as a relative?"

"Ah, you are threatening me. I have nothing to fear."

"They will search."

"They won't find anything."

"They won't search only in the house."

"Where else?"

"In the garden-house behind the wall clock."

"Damn ..." The word stuck in his throat. He looked as if he'd been struck by a club."

"You see that I'm all-knowing. I have to deliver these documents to the minister of war. Will you give them to me voluntarily?"

"I know of no documents."

"Well, we'll find something else as well. A box of jewellery whose rightful owner stands before you."

Walton staggered. "I'm lost," he groaned.

"Not yet," said Robert. "If you return my goods I'll forgive you. About the other matter I'll think of a way out for the sake of my friend. It would spoil his career to have an uncle who committed high treason."

"High treason?" Pluton was amazed.

"Unfortunately, yes," answered Robert. "I'll go into the next room and you can speak to your uncle."

Without waiting for another word, Brooks went though the door into an anteroom where he sat down and waited. He heard voices. A long time passed until Pluton opened the door. It was obvious he had fought a hard battle. Walton sat shattered as if with fever. When Robert entered he said mechanically as if learned by heart: "Captain Brooks, a long time ago I received a parcel, but only today have I succeeded in finding the addressee. I shall give you the parcel undamaged."

"I thank you," said Robert simply.

After a pause during which Walton seemed to search for words, he continued: "A long time ago I have received some documents from a person unknown to me. I don't know their contents, but I know that a man called Albitroff should receive them. As you have assured me that their content is dangerous to me, I'm glad to pass them to you. Would you please come to the garden-house.?

"With pleasure, Mr. Walton."

The banker went ahead. The others followed. Inside the garden-house he gave Robert the key to the box. "Here, captain," he said.

Robert took the box and the documents. "Are they really that important?" asked Pluton.

"Tremendously important." Robert noticed that Walton had left and continued: "It's concerning a coalition against Prussia, and England is certainly interested that Napoleon doesn't grow too big for his boots."

"This unfortunate uncle of mine."

"Not unfortunate, but short-sighted and gullible. I am forced to hand in these documents, but I'll do my utmost to save him."

"Do it, Robert. He promised me he'll never do anything like that again."

They went back into the house. They went into Pluton's room, where Robert made the documents into a parcel when a servant called: "Captain Pluton, come to your uncle quickly."

"What does he want?"

"What he wants? Nothing, he wants nothing. I think he is - he is …"

"Well, what is he?"

"I think he's dead."

Pluton went and Robert stayed behind. After a while he returned. "You were right. He was short-sighted. His last action proves it. Whether it's his bad conscience or the loss of millions, I don't know. May God be merciful to his soul. ---

Chapter 34

A HARMLESS POACHER

WINTER had arrived and a fresh snow had come down. Hunters especially liked it because the trail of game was easily recognisable. It dawned but in spite of this early morning, a lonely human being came through the wood toward Bradford on Avon. It was a man of very unusual appearance. The bitter cold seemed to make no impression on him although he was not dressed for the winter. The blue trousers and his jacket, too tight for him, were torn on several places. On his head he wore a cap that had once probably a brim or shield. His jacket was open and displayed an unwashed shirt, open in front and showing a hairy chest. His shoes were of foreign make.

Around his long and meagre neck he wore an old large handkerchief. On his waist he wore a belt that had served many different purposes for a hundred years. Over his left shoulder there hung a leathern hose, whose purpose was a riddle for anybody but himself. On his back he had a large cloth filled with various items. The most unusual thing was his face. It was darkly tanned from sun and weather. His broad mouth had almost no lips. His eyes were small but sharp. His nose was monstrous, almost like a beak or a horn.

The stranger came to a bend in the road where he saw another little man walking. "Well, I calculate that this man knows the way to the Masterson Estate." He talked to himself. He had reached the other fellow who did not hear steps behind him because the snow subdued the sound. "Good morning, Sir, where does this road lead to?" he greeted the other fellow. The man turned around and was shocked when he saw this strange appearing fellow who looked like a tramp.

"Why don't you answer?" asked the stranger brusquely. It appeared it was better to be polite to this ill-clad rascal. "Good morning," he answered, "this road goes to Bradford-on-Avon via the estate of Colonel Masterson, where I'm going."

"That's where I'm aiming for. Do you live there?"

"No."

"What actually are you? The stranger asked with a searching glance.

"I'm a vet."

"Nice profession, I calculate. Animals are easier to cure than miserable mankind. Your business is on the estate?"

"Yes, there is a sick cow."

"Shoot it and you are rid of that nuisance."

The little fellow looked with shock at the taller one. "What are you thinking about? To shoot a cow?"

"Pah, I have shot hundreds."

The little one made a disbelieving face. "Don't brag."

"Pshtishshshsh," sounded as a thick beam of dark tobacco brew passed close to the face of the man, who withdrew shocked.

"Hell and damnation. Take care where you spit."

"I know exactly where I spit."

"Why don't you smoke or use snuff?"

"I have no taste for smoking and as for snuff I like my nose too much."

"I can see that you like your nose, but chewing tobacco is terribly unhealthy."

"Well, you, as a vet must understand that. Who does the sick cow belong to?"

"To a Mrs. Brooks, who lives in a house belonging to the estate of Colonel Masterson."

"Brooks? Hm. Is this lady a widow?"

"No, her husband was lost for many years but recently he has reappeared again in Mexico. By the way, why do you ask these questions?"

"That should be immaterial to you."

"Possibly, but you don't look the type to be connected to these people."

"No? Why not?"

The little one threw a disparaging look at the stranger. "You must agree that you look like a tramp."

"Pshtishshshsh," a thick jet of tobacco juice landed on his hat.

"Hell and damnation," said the angry little fellow, "you better take care with your spitting."

"Pah, tramps do this type of thing."

"But I will not tolerate that."

"That won't help you much if you continue to be coarse."

"Maybe I should touch you with kid gloves?" The little fellow was really angry. He pulled off his hat and held it toward the stranger.

"Wipe it off," said the stranger with indifference.

"Wipe it off? I? Wipe it off on the spot, otherwise you will get to know me. Wipe it off or ..." he lifted his stick threateningly.

"What – or?"

"Or you will get one over your face."

"Do it. Pshtishshshsh." Another jet landed on the jacket of the vet."

"I've had enough," called the irritated little doctor. He swung his arm back, ready to hit out but he did not succeed. The stranger tore the stick from his hand and threw it over the peak of the trees, grabbed the little fellow by his hips and shook him. Thereafter he sat him gently on the ground. "There you are," he said, "that is for calling me tramp. Now run away or I'll squeeze your whole science out of your body."

The vet breathed deeply. He wanted to reply, his eyes sparkled with fury but he thought it better to disappear. He vanished behind the trees.

"A little toad but courageous," the stranger smiled benignly. "I shall probably see him again on the Masterson estate. Hm, Bighorn a tramp. This damned civilisation calls a man a tramp if he doesn't wear a tail coat." He continued to walk on. The next moment he jumped behind a bush. He had heard a noise which, as a prairie hunter he knew too well. A splendid roebuck came out of the wood. "What luck my rifle is loaded." Without thinking he was not in the Wild West of America he took off his shoulders the thing that looked like an old leather hose, pulled the trigger and shot the animal.

He threw his canvas sack and rifle on the floor and started to gut the buck. He heard steps coming nearer but took no notice. The newcomer looked at the scene with astonishment. "What the hell are you doing?"

Bighorn turned his head. "Can't you see?"

"Yes, I can see, you have shot a roebuck."

"Should I have let it escape?"

"Man, you are mad."

"Mad? Pshtishshshsh."

"Bloody hell, do you think I'm a spittoon?"

"No, but an old ruffian. If calling me mad for shooting an animal is polite, I'll be hanged."

"Polite or not, you're going to hang."

"Ah, by whom?" grinned Bighorn.

"You'll know without me telling you. Don't you know that poaching will be punished?"

Bighorn opened his mouth so that one could count his teeth. "By God, I didn't think about that."

"I believe you, your type never thinks of punishment until you're caught. Who are you?"

"I? Hm, who are you?"

"I am Eric Freeman, in the service of the head forester and game keeper Colonel Masterson."

"But you're not in uniform."

"That's none of your business. You are arrested and will follow me."

"Not so fast. You're not wearing a uniform; I want proof that you are an official."

That was too much for the good Eric. "Hell and damnation," he called. "A rascal like this is asking me for proof. Your rifle is confiscated. Are you following willingly or not?"

"I don't have to do that"

"Then I'll help you." Eric grabbed the stranger's arm.

"Take your hands off me," called Bighorn with a commanding voice.

"Ah, you're wilful, I'll show you."

"Pshtishshshsh." A jet of brown tobacco juice hit Eric on the head.

"The devil; spitting as well You'll pay for that.

At that moment a voice came from one of the near trees. "He did that to me as well. Should I help you, dear Mr. Freeman?"

Eric turned around. "Ah, the vet. What are you doing here?"

The little man cam forward carefully. "I intended to go to Mrs Brooks, whose cow has gone sick. I met this fellow, we quarrelled and now I'll help you to arrest him."

"I don't really need anybody, but let's tie his hands."

Bighorn's mouth twitched strangely. "That would be really funny."

"How's that?" asked Eric, "I can't see anything funny."

"Oh yes. Isn't it funny if a poacher arrests a dealer in venison?"

"A dealer in venison? What do you mean by that?"

"I mean myself. I am a London dealer in venison and this little fellow is the actual poacher. For the last three years he delivered to me everything he had shot here in the woods."

The vet couldn't believe his ears when he heard these words. Eric made a baffled face. "Thunder and lightening," he called out, "is that true, doctor?"

Only now did language return to the speechless vet. "I a poacher?" he wailed with ten fingers high in the air as if swearing. I swear a thousand oaths that I've never even shot a mouse, let alone a roebuck."

"Oho, now he wants to deny it," smirked Bighorn. "Who does the old gun belong to?"

"Yes, to whom?" asked Eric, "to the doctor perhaps?"

"Sure! – And who shot the roebuck? Not I but this doctor. I only opened it up."

"Good God, is that possible?" exclaimed the little one. "Don't believe him, dear Mr. Freeman."

"I have to do my duty and take you prisoner as well."

The doctor jumped back, shocked. "For heaven's sake you are making fun of me, I'm as innocent as the sun in the sky."

"That will be a matter for the enquiry to decide."

"I'm tying you together now so that neither of you will escape."

"I'll put up with that," said Bighorn, I'm not the only guilty one.

After tying the doctor's left hand to Bighorn's right, Eric asked them to pick up the buck. Bighorn put his bundle over his shoulder and declared: "I've got mine."

"What have you got there?" asked Eric.

"Five rabbits the doctor has caught in a snare."

The poor doctor was speechless, but Eric made a grim face. "That makes matter worse for you. The big fellow carries the rabbits and the doctor shall carry the roebuck."

"But that's all a lie, a common lie. He caught the rabbits himself," the doctor finally managed to say.

Eric put the buck on the doctor's shoulders. "Holy Ignatius," wailed the doctor. Now I, totally innocent, must carry this heavy animal."

"The buck is not as heavy as all the others you have on your conscience."

"I'm going to poison you, once I get free."

"A poisoner on top of all that. The forester will be surprised at the people I'm going to bring him."

Colonel Masterson was in his workroom. He drank his morning tea and his mood was far from good. Eric entered and stood to attention. "What's new?" asked the sullen forester.

"I've caught two poachers."

"Two poachers? That's just right for me. I'll put them on a rack so that their legs will stretch from here to London. Where are they?"

"In the stables. They are tied up and two people are standing guard."

"Bring them here and call everybody to witness the procedure." Eric did as he was asked. When he reached the stables a servant had prepared a horse for the forester to ride out. "You can leave that for now," he told him, "and help me to call everybody into the boss' workroom."

As they crossed the yard, the American noticed the saddled horse and an amused smile twitched his lips for a few seconds. Eric led them upstairs and opened a door. Bighorn's glance fell on the lock. They entered and Eric pulled the door shut behind him. "Here they are," he reported to the colonel.

Everyone sat in a circle. Count Miguel and his household lived half a mile away in a villa built especially for them. The old fellow sat on his separate chair, like a Spanish inquisitor. "Unfetter them;" said

the colonel, "I've heard that criminals should not be bound in court."
A satisfied smile came over Bighorn's face. The vet was in a hurry to
protest his innocence before the trial had began.

"Silence," thundered the colonel, "it is I who speak here."

The little one shut up. The old one turned to Bighorn. "The other
one I know but who are you?"

"I'm a butcher who sells venison."

"What is your name?"

"Ramirez Danlola."

The old one jumped up. "Ramirez Danlola? Heavens, what Country
are you from?"

"I have come from Spain," fibbed Bighorn true to his role.

The forester looked at him. "Scoundrel, rascal, since when were you
a dealer in venison?"

"For only three years"

"What have you been before?"

"A sea captain."

"A pirate weren't you?"

"Yes, "answered Bighorn with complete calm.

"The devil will ride you, you paragon of evil. Ramirez Danlola, now
we finally have you. But how did you team up with this vet.?"

"He made the toxins for me if I wanted to poison someone."

The little one jumped into the air with horror. "By everything that
is holy, that's a complete lie. Not one word is true," he shouted.

"Silence, you poisoner," thundered Masterson. "Today is the day of
revenge. Today I am holding court. Today we shall unmask everybody
we couldn't unmask before. Ramirez Danlola, how many people have
you poisoned?"

"Two hundred and eighty-six."

The Colonel was shocked; he had a feeling of dread. "Satan, so
many? Why?"

"This animal doctor wanted it. I had to do it otherwise he would
have killed me."

"Jesus, Jesus," shouted the little one, "no-one can say that I have
poisoned him."

Bighorn shook his shoulders. "Naturally he denies it, but he was the
most bloodthirsty of all the pirates on my ship. I can prove it."

"Man, you're a monster. I've never been anything but a vet."

"Be quiet, I am dealing now with this Danlola. Robber, rascal, do you know a Carujo?"

"Yes," professed Bighorn.

"Ah, how did you get to know him?"

"Through this animal doctor. He is a brother-in-law of this Carujo."

"No, no, I don't know any Carujo. I've never heard this name."

"Silence or I throw you out," roared the colonel and turned again to Bighorn. "Did you do business with this Carujo?

"Quite often, the pirate ship belonged to him."

"This fellow at least has the courage to tell the truth. Do you know somebody called Stenton?"

"Yes."

"Did he once try to catch you?"

"Yes."

"What did you do then?"

"What I am doing now, I escaped. Good bye colonel." With these words he jumped to the door, closed it and turned the key. Three or four steps at a time he jumped down the steps into the yard. The next moment he untied the horse and galloped out of the estate. He met a man along the road and asked him for the villa Manresa. The man pointed in the direction behind him and said: "No more than five hundred metres in that direction."

This unforeseen course of events had surprised the gathering. Nobody thought to move. It was the colonel who pulled himself together and shouted: "After him! He's going to escape, fast, fast, after him!"

An old maid servant eventually opened the door. Everybody streamed out. A few got onto a horse, the others ran on foot. The vet was standing alone. "Now or never," he told himself and made his getaway, unseen. The sick cow had to recover by itself.

Bighorn meanwhile reached the Count's villa. They were all assembled for breakfast. The Count, Stenton's mother and sister, his daughter, his grandchild and Robert who had just arrived from his duties. Lady Margaret Castlepool had returned to her father in Mexico. It was Porido, the loyal servant, whom Bighorn encountered first. "Who are you and whom do you want to see?" he was asked.

"I want to speak to the inhabitants of this villa."

"I shall announce you, but you are actually not in the right attire to appear before the ladies and gentlemen,"

"Nonsense, I am always in the right attire." He pushed past Porido and stepped into the living room. The Count frowned. "You forced you way in here, who are you?"

"People call me Bighorn."

A smile crossed the Count's face. This ragged fellow with the oversized nose had chosen the right name. "Where do you come from and what do you want?"

"I've come from Mexico and bring you news – ah, here they come. I wouldn't have thought the Colonel would find me that fast." He looked out of the window and saw the pursuers arrive. "Did a man arrive here, in rags and a bundle on his back?"

"Yes," answered a zealous Porido.

"Where is he?"

"With the ladies and gentlemen in the living room."

"That's dangerous; I have to catch him before there is a calamity." Two moments later he tore open the door, saw the escapee and went for him without greeting the others. "Scoundrel, now I've got you I'll put you in irons."

"What, for heaven's sake, is the matter?" asked the Count. "Who is this man, dear Colonel?

"This man is the biggest criminal under the sun. He poisoned nearly three hundred people and, wait for it, his name is Ramirez Danlola."

"Danlola? questioned Robert. "The pirate? Oh no he is not, I know Danlola."

"He told us that was his name."

"That he is Danlola? Impossible."

"Ask him yourself."

"What is the connection? You say you are Danlola? Do you know this man?" asked Robert.

"I've heard of him."

"But what made you use his name?"

The American shrugged his shoulders and smiled. "Just a joke," he said.

"This joke could cost you dear. Around here we are not well inclined toward this name."

"I know that."

"Just the same," maintained the forester. "This scoundrel has five rabbits in his bundle."

"You're speaking in riddles," said the Count and turned to Bighorn. "Tell us again where you come from?"

"I come from Lord Castlepool." replied the American.

"From Mexico?" asked Rosetta tensely.

"Yes, directly, I haven't seen you before but according to description you are Mrs. Rosetta Stenton or Doña Rosetta de Manresa."

"Yes, I am."

"I have something for you." He pulled out a letter. "From Lord Castlepool," he continued. "I've been his scout and companion. We've experienced many events together and, if I may, I'll tell you about it."

"Should I first read the letter?" asked Rosetta.

"You may find that my story is even more explicit," ventured Bighorn and the Count agreed with him.

Bighorn talked about the miraculous rescue from the unknown island by Count Manuel de Manresa and ended with the sad news about their disappearance; about the searching by Lord Castlepool and by himself both ending in Santa Helena. Those present had heard part of the story from Lady Margaret, but when it came to the disappearance the mood changed dramatically. Rosetta sobbed quietly. Robert told them that he had to go to Mexico and would try his utmost to discover their whereabouts. "If they are still alive," he added thoughtfully.

"What is a scout?" asked the Colonel when Bighorn had finished.

"Every child knows that," replied Bighorn. "There are westmen with such a sense of direction that they never fail. They know every road, every river, every tree and shrub, they find their way in places where they have never been before. Such people are called scouts. Every caravan, every hunting party has to have one if they don't want to perish. Such a scout am I."

"My, my," said the Colonel, "so you know ever path in the American wilderness? You don't give the impression of such a man."

"Have I such a stupid face?" asked Bighorn.

"Very stupid."

"Pshtishshshsh." A jet of tobacco juice hit the Colonel on his chest.

"Scoundrel, how dare you to spit onto a forester of the Archduke and a Colonel. Do you think that you are the only one who can do that?" With these words he spat onto Bighorn's forehead.

The American wiped the unexpected saliva off his face with composure but also with disapproval. "Beginner," was his judgement. "How dare you to call a prairie hunter stupid. Do you think that a Colonel could measure up to an American scout? If you judge me the way I am dressed then you are stupid yourself."

"Masterson felt that this fellow was at least his equal in coarseness. He scratched behind his ears. "What about the roebuck and the five rabbits?"

"The roebuck I shot myself and the story about the rabbits was an invention."

"I want to know the reason you've deceived me?"

"No reason."

"Heavens, so you've made fun of me?"

"Yes," laughed Bighorn without malice.

"Fun, with me, do you hear that, with me! But what I like is that he didn't succeed and he'll go to prison."

Bighorn laughed. "To prison because of a roebuck? Nonsense."

"Nonsense you say? Don't you know our laws?"

"What do I care about your laws, I'm a free American."

"There you err tremendously. You are not a free American now, but a caught poacher and that's punishable with prison."

Bighorn made a doubtful face. "But we can shoot over there however much we want."

"That's over there but not here, do you understand?"

"I never thought of that. The buck stepped out of the woods and I shot it. If I must go to prison for that, I'll do a runner."

"Oh no you won't. How does it happen you escaped to here?"

"Because I am a delegate in matters of the family de Manresa."

"Why didn't you tell me that right away? Now I have to think what to do with you and the roebuck."

The others let them talk. The discussion was entertainment for them. They knew the forester would not report Bighorn to the authorities.

Don Miguel spoke again. "Tell us, please, what is your opinion of their disappearance?"

"As they were friends of Juarez, they are being kept prisoners as such."

"So there is hope that Don Manuel and my husband are still alive and that you might free them?" asked Rosetta.

"Yes, if we succeed in finding the trail. Juarez and Castlepool left no stone unturned, but in vain. They have sent me to tell you all about it."

Everybody looked gloomy, Rosetta cried quietly. Masterson cursed: "Oh, if I were young again, I would turn all Mexico upside down but, unfortunately, my bones don't allow that anymore."

"But mine are still young, dear godfather." called Robert.

"That's true but what have you to do with Mexico?"

Rosetta turned toward the two. "Ah, really, dear Robert, you are going to see Benito Juarez, the president of Mexico?"

"Yes, but I hope my task will leave me time to make the necessary searches."

The trapper viewed the captain with testing glances. "You want to go to Mexico? You'd better stay at home. The air over there is not very healthy; too many bullets are buzzing around."

"That's just what I like."

"But such a bullet may hurt, or worse," smiled Bighorn.

"I know that. Where are you going from here?"

"After I'll receive a reply here, I'll go straight back to Mexico."

"Do you want to travel with me?"

"With pleasure; I think I can be useful too over there. When do you intend to go?"

"It was arranged for tomorrow. Permit me a question. If an English minister wants honest information about the affairs of Mexico, would you provide that?"

"If he means to be honest with us."

"Do you doubt that?"

"Hm, one has to be careful, England is no friend of France and doesn't much care about the good Max in Mexico. But why do you ask?"

"Because I know a minister who would greatly appreciate it if you would tell him about Juarez and the conditions in Mexico."

"Where is he?"

"In London."

"Well, let's go there."

"You agree, I thank you but - hm. "With these words Robert gave a significant glance at the attire of the prairie hunter. "Your outer appearance is not suitable for such a visit."

"I have in my sack a genuine Mexican suit."

"In no case must you wear that. No-one must suspect you to be a Mexican. You must appear incognito."

"Incognito? Well, that sounds impressive. How should I start that?"

"Wear an ordinary suit. I'll get you one."

"Get me one? That means that you are paying for it? No sir. Bighorn is not the man for whom you have to buy a suit. A fellow who undertakes travelling from Mexico to Europe has enough money to pay for a jacket and a necktie."

"I had no intention of insulting you."

"I wouldn't advise you to. When do we go?"

"Tonight, with the last train."

"Together? No, I like to be independent. Tell me a place in London where we shall meet."

"That's up to you; how about meeting in the Hanover Hotel. The ladies and gentlemen will ask you questions, while I go to my room to prepare myself."

Robert went but he was hardly half an hour in his room when Masterson came in. "I only came to tell you that the American is leaving for London now. He'll come to me first in order to collect his gun, a real cudgel of a shooter. Actually, he ought to go to prison. I didn't know I had such a soft disposition." ---

Chapter 35

FUN IN READING

A FEW hours later Bighorn strolled slowly though the streets of Reading and studied the shops curiously. Finally he stopped in front of a house. He read the sign: "Old clothes and other items."

"I'll go in here," he growled to himself. As he opened the door the vendor looked at him with searching eyes. Bighorn's appearance did not promise much.

"What are your wishes?" asked the dealer.

"A suit."

"A suit? A whole suit?"

"Naturally," said the hunter. "A torn one I don't want."

"I don't sell torn suits, I am the best Tailor in town. May I ask where you come from?"

"That's none of your business."

"You're not asking for credit?"

"No, I'll pay right away." The man looked at Bighorn more attentively than before. "So you have enough money to pay for a whole suit consisting of a jacket, trousers and waistcoat?"

"You don't have to concern yourself about my purse."

"I only wanted to make sure."

"To make sure? Do you think that I am a tramp? The second hand dealer stretched his ten fingers into the air and stepped back. "What do you say? Did I speak a word that sounded like tramp? Be so kind as to look at yourself. What you're wearing is even too cold for summer."

"I've no time to go into such details. Are you going to show me a suit or not?"

"What kind of suit would you like?"

"Hm," said Bighorn thoughtfully, "I need something incognito."

"Incognito? I can offer you a tail coat that was very fashionable in Vienna at around the year eighteen-hundred and worn by a minister." The dealer brought a brown-red garment. It had cuffs, lapels and buttons, the size of plates.

"How much does this minister's outfit cost?"

"I can't possibly make it cheaper than seventeen shillings."

Bighorn was used to American prices, he handed the dealer eighteen shillings.

The dealer was surprised and said: "You've received this ministerial garment four shillings too cheap because you're buying a waistcoat and trousers as well."

"Yes but they must make me incognito as well."

"Perhaps sir will go as an artist?"

"Artist? Yes I'm made for that. How many types of artists are there?"

"First, there are the poets."

"No, thank you. They go hungry too often."

"Sculptor?"

"They hammer too much."

"Composers and musicians?"

"Hm, that sounds better. What kind of a waistcoat have I got to wear for this?"

"I'll bring you a green waist coat with blue flowers that will make you think you are a meadow of forget-me-nots. A pair of black-grey trousers in fashion at the time of Sebastian Bach, who composed many baskets full of notes."

"Bring me both, and a pair of boots too."

"Very well, I shall also bring you a hat as high and as wide as worn by the great Orpheus."

"Good, I'll buy the hat as well."

The hat was grotesque. Its brim was two foot wide and its height accordingly.

"If you go as a musician you will need some musical scores to show that you are a great composer."

"Well, get me some."

"And what about an instrument?"

"What have you to offer?"

"I have a violin and a trombone that overturned three walls of Jericho."

"Show me the trombone.

The dealer pulled the instrument from a heap of old iron. "Here it is."

"The devil," said Bighorn, "has this thing scars."

"How else could it be; I told you three walls of Jericho fell on it?"

"But there are also two holes."

"This is an advantage for the sound and the lungs. The air comes out from the holes instead of travelling all the way to the back."

"That's an advantage. What do I owe you?"

"It cost me twenty-five shillings so I will charge you twenty-two shillings."

Bighorn pulled out a bundle of pound notes, gave the dealer one pound note and two shilling pieces and stuffed the rest into his trouser pocket. The dealer followed his movements with keen glances. What carelessness to put so much money into trouser pockets. "Where can I change into this suit?"

"Right here, there is nobody else around." Bighorn proceeded to put on his acquired outfit. The dealer noticed that he did not take out the bundle of notes from his pocket and asked: "Should I clear your old things away?"

"You can buy the stuff."

"Buy? I cannot pay for these worthless things. How much do you want?"

"Two pounds or forty shillings, whichever you like."

"For heaven's sake, these things are worth nothing but I'll give you three shillings."

"Nothing doing, these garments are made of special wool to prevent a cold."

The dealer felt the paper notes from the outside of the pocket. "Five shillings is my limit."

"I have a train to catch and I have no time; forty shillings or I take the things."

There were at least twenty pound notes in that pocket and he is leaving town by train: a comeback would be unlikely. "I offer you ten shillings."

"Forty, no less."

"Thirty."

The dealer began to sweat. Under no circumstances did his greed allow the customer to take away his trousers. When Bighorn insisted on forty shillings, he gave in and paid back the amount he had just taken from this customer.

Bighorn had hardly left when the dealer's wife stepped out of the backroom. "I have heard about the deal, you must be crazy."

"Not at all, put your hand into the trouser pocket and you will find the reason why I have paid forty shillings. There should be at least twenty pounds in it."

The wife put her hand into the pocket and pulled out a number of newspaper cuttings."

"Impossible" The dealer was crestfallen. "I saw him put the money in this pocket, I have not taken my eyes off it and I thought I fooled him by selling him stuff that I thought not saleable and I had to throw away."

"It seems that you were the bigger fool."

Bighorn meanwhile laughed to himself. "He thought to fool me by monstrously overcharging me but he will learn that he has found his master."

His outrageous outfit was soon attracting the youth of this town. He noticed with glee the growing masses behind him. His retinue grew from street to street and soon made such a noise that the windows were opened.

"Oh George Washington. Do I cause a sensation here! Reading will remember Bighorn for a long time. It's a pity that I'm incognito."

His incognito did not last long. A policeman came around the corner, looked at the strange figure and the masses that followed him. He walked to the American and grabbed him by the arm.

"Hello, who are you?"

Bighorn stood still and looked at the man. "Pshtishshshsh!" the famous jet of tobacco juice went past his nose. "I? Who are you?"

"I represent the police of this town."

"Good, we are comrades. I am a hunter."

"Nonsense, do you know that you have to answer my question?"

"Did you not receive an answer?"

"Yes, but what kind of an answer. Where are you coming from?"

"From over there."

"From over there? What does that mean?

"That means I'm not from here."

"Man, if you don't answer properly, I'll have to arrest you. What's your name?"

"Bighorn."

The policeman became really angry. "If you want to tease me, it may cost you dearly. Where are you coming from?"

"From there." Bighorn pointed behind him.

"And where do you want to go?"

"There." He pointed straight on.

"That's too much. You are my prisoner."

"Not bad, what happens if I defend myself?"

"You get three years in prison."

"That makes thirteen. I should have got ten years only this morning."

"Ah, why?"

"That's none of your business."

"You are either mad or stupid."

"If one of us is crazy and the other is stupid, I'd rather be the mad one."

"I see I can't do anything with you here; follow me."

"Where to?"

"You'll find out. What have you in that sack?"

"My things for travelling."

"And in that hose?"

"My hunting rifle."

"Have you a licence?"

"Yes, I have."

"Who issued it?"

"Myself."

"Be prepared for another two years in prison for that."

"That makes fifteen in total."

"If that goes on, you'll have a nice long rest."

During this conversation they were followed by huge crowds and reached the police quarters. "This is the place where you'll learn the meaning of an arrest."

"I know that already."

"Ah, have you been arrested often?"

"That's none of your business."

"You're a ruffian; we'll shut your face. Step in here."

Besides several policemen, there were some people sitting there, apparently waiting for their affairs to be settled. The policeman asked him to sit down. Bighorn put his sack, trombone and rifle on the floor and sat on a chair meant for officials. "Stop, this chair is not a seat for people like you."

Bighorn shrugged his shoulders. "What do you mean by people like me?"

"People who belong on this bench."

"Well, in that case be so kind as to sit yourself on this bench. You seem to understand more of his type than of mine. I know best which place I belong to."

The other officials looked at Bighorn with amazement. A sergeant asked," a wilful fellow. What or who is he?"

"I don't know myself," said the policeman who brought him in.

"He walks about looking so strange. Is he mad?"

"I met him on the street where people ran after him in masses. He didn't want to show me papers of his identity, so I took him in."

"He will learn to talk here."

"I can do that already, old boy," said Bighorn. "Didn't think it to be so important on the street. I also haven't got the time."

"You will find the time here."

"Not much, I have to leave with the next train."

"That doesn't concern us. Where are you going?"

"Will you come with me?"

"With you? I don't think so."

"Then you don't have to know where I am going."

"Oho, you are the biggest ruffian I ever have come across. Here you'll learn politeness."

"Pshtishshshsh." Bighorn spat near his face. "Should I possibly learn that from you?" he asked. "You don't seem suitable."

"Hell and damnation," cursed the sergeant. "Get off that chair and on the bench where you belong."

Bighorn, made himself comfortable and crossed his legs. "Softly, softly, old boy. Anybody who sits on this chair will be honoured that I am sitting on it now."

"I'll give him a seat where he'll be comfortable without annoying or insulting other people. Come on, let' go into a prison cell."

"Into prison? I've no desire to go there."

"We're not asking, whether you desire it or not. Forward, let's go."

The policeman put his hands on Bighorn's arm. The prairie hunter shook him off, got up and said: "Listen to what I have to tell you. I did nothing wrong and I can dress the way I like. If people are stupid and run after me, I can't help that. I'll prove my identity if I am treated as a gentleman."

Bighorn's stand and words made an impression. The official looked at him strangely. "Gentleman?" he asked astonished. "Tell that to somebody else, we don't believe that." The dispute was held in a louder voice then usual at this post. The adjoining door was torn open and a man asked angrily: "What's going on here? Can't you handle this in a quieter fashion?"

The present policemen stood to attention. "Pardon us, sir; we've arrested someone who's obstinate in the highest degree."

The inspector viewed Bighorn. "The devil, what kind of fellow is that?"

"We don't know. He refuses to give any information."

"Why has he been arrested?"

"His curious appearance drew a lot of people. I asked him for an identity proof but he refused to tell me because – Hahaha – I did not treat him as a gentleman."

"Yes, and because he threatened me with prison," Bighorn joined in.

The inspector threw him a threatening glance. "You only talk when you are asked."

"I can't wait until someone asks me," returned Bighorn. "My time doesn't allow it, I have to catch the next train."

"Where to?"

"I see no reason to tell everybody."

"Ah, so I won't know it either?"

"If you have the necessary authority and you ask me politely, I won't refuse."

The inspector laughed. "What have you here in this leather hose?"

"My hunting rifle."

"A rifle? Have you a licence?"

"Yes."

"What have you in that sack?"

"Various things."

"That's not enough, I want to know details."

"That's not my business. Who wants to know what's in there, may look himself. Permit me a question: Is this the room where you intend to hold proceedings with me? I said I'm ready to give information, but not in the presence of all these people. It's no wonder I'm called wilful."

"Well, step in here."

The inspector withdrew into his room and gave the policeman a wink to bring Bighorn's sack and rifle as well. Bighorn walked into the room and noticed another man there who looked similar to the inspector. It was obvious that they were brothers.

His right hand was inside a glove and it was obvious that there was no living hand inside. The man was Lord Edmonton who had lost his hand at a duel with Robert Brooks. He examined Bighorn half amazed and half amused .

"Heavens, what kind of scarecrow is this?" he asked the inspector.

"He's a living puzzle, the solution of which we'll soon find out," answered the inspector. Then he turned to Bighorn: "To start with, tell me who you are?"

The hunter shrugged his shoulders. "First I must know whether you really are the man to whom I must give this information."

"Damn it, haven't you heard that I am the inspector?"

"Yes, but I don't believe it."

"That's funny. Why do you doubt it?"

"Because I believe that an inspector knows how to treat people politely."

"So you claim I was impolite to you?"

"I treat people the way they treat me. You have the choice."

The military looking gentleman stroked his moustache. "Damn fellow," he said. " He has a trombone; he probably is a beggar musician."

The inspector laughed." You're an artist and I'll treat you politely. I am Lord John Edmonton."

"Thank you," answered Bighorn coolly to these obviously mocking words."

"And you, sir?" asked the inspector.

"Before I'll answer that, I must know who this other gentleman is."

"This gentleman is my brother Lord Edmonton."

"Is he part of this police force?"

"No"

"So I'll be much obliged if you remove him."

The former lieutenant jumped off his chair. "What a cheek."

The inspector frowned and scolded Bighorn: "Don't go too far, who goes and who stays is my decision."

"Good, so I ask you to discharge me. I'm not being interrogated in the presence of a stranger."

"All right, I'll let you go but not into freedom. Into a cell where you'll have time to think differently."

"In that case I ask to speak to your superior. I want to know whether I can be put into prison because I don't want to be interrogated in the presence of an unauthorized person."

The former lieutenant cleared his throat and hissed: "Lock him up and give him the whip."

Bighorn lifted his hand and threatened: "One more word from you and you will get a slap in the face to make you feel your nose is an air balloon. If you think you can give orders because you're the brother of the man who should interrogate me, you're making a big mistake. I'm not to be intimidated by you or anyone."

The former lieutenant stepped back and looked to his brother. "What now? I hope you deal with this …"

"Stop!" interrupted the inspector. "No more words that put you in danger of contact with this – well, this man's fists. It's not the custom to interrogate somebody in the presence of others. I must ask you to withdraw for a few moments. I'll make it short."

"Ah, I should give in to this man?" asked the former lieutenant angrily.

His brother lifted his shoulders. "Official matters," he said.

"So you'll not be surprised if I withdraw completely. Our affairs we've discussed enough."

"I have nothing to add."

"Good bye then."

Without waiting for a reply he went out with head held high. This aristocrat could not understand that he had to yield to a vagabond. The inspector was grimly annoyed, but tried to hide his feelings. "Your rifle," he ordered.

"Here it is."

"The licence."

"Here." Bighorn pulled a piece of paper from his pocket and passed it to the official. It was in Bighorn's real name of Arthur Henderson.

"Open the sack," he ordered a policeman while returning the document. The first thing produced was a heavy purse with gold pieces. "Where did you get that money?"

"Earned," was the short declaration of the hunter.

"How? I have to know because this gold is not in harmony with your personality."

"Should my person for harmony's sake also be golden?"

"Don't be funny, it might cost you dearly. What else is in the sack?"

The policeman produced two revolvers and a large knife.

"Show it to me," he examined the knife and found some spots on it. "Is this blood?"

"Human blood."

"Did you kill a man with that?"

"Quite a few."

"Where?"

"In different places."

"Who were they?"

500

"I took no particular notice of that. The last one was an officer." Edmonton stared at the speaker. "Man, you are daring to confess all that to me? I shall have to put you in irons. Seek further," he ordered the policeman. He brought out a suit of the finest material, decorated with gold and silver cords. "What is that?"

"A suit."

"Where from?"

"Bought."

"This suit costs a lot of money. A musician doesn't have the money to buy such expensive disguise."

"First, only an ignorant person would call this a disguise. Second, who told you I'm a musician?"

"Your trombone."

"This trombone hasn't said a word yet. I bought it and this suit a half an hour ago."

"But man, how comes it that you decorated yourself with such conspicuous attire?"

"I like it and that's enough."

"I've seen your name is Arthur Henderson, but where are you from?"

"From New Orleans in the United States of America."

"What is your profession?"

"Usually a prairie hunter and scout. In time of war a captain in the army."

"The devil will believe that. Have you got proof or a passport?"

"Both, here." Bighorn pulled a leather bag from his sack and gave his pass to the official who studied it diligently. His face grew longer.

"Really a valid passport in the name of Captain Arthur Henderson who wants to go from New Orleans to Mexico."

"What about his personal characteristics?" chipped in the policeman.

"With this nose there can be no mistake. But are you coming to England instead of Mexico?"

"I've been in Mexico already."

"Can you prove that?"

"I think so. Did you ever hear about Lord Castlepool of Nottingham?"

501

"Yes, he's the English delegate bringing weapons to Juarez."

"You know Benito Juarez as well? Here are some documents from both of them."

The inspector read the documents twice in disbelieve. "Warm recommendation in two languages in the President's own handwriting." His face grew even longer. With visible embarrassment he continued: "You led me by the nose. Permit me, captain, to ask what brought you to England?"

"Family and political matters."

"Political matters? What can I understand by that?"

"Matters that I must not talk about."

"All right but may I ask where you are going from here?"

"To London."

"Ah, on a secret mission?"

"Possible. You can understand now that I could not talk in front of your brother."

"Certainly, and I beg your pardon."

The official was convinced now that Bighorn was who he had claimed to be. Those papers were genuine without a doubt. He told himself that a complaint by this odd man could cause inconvenience. "You have enough money to purchase a proper suit. Do you intend to keep that one?"

"I don't do anything wrong. Is there no freedom about the way one wishes to dress?"

"There is, as long as it does not cause public annoyance."

"Well, so I'll make use of this freedom. It provides entertainment." Bighorn left with two policemen in civilian clothes to prevent too many people running after him.---

Chapter 36

MISCHIEF ON RAILS

$\mathcal{B}$IGHORN wandered, followed by curious people, to the station. There he bought a first class ticket to London but he went to the third class waiting room. When the train was about to leave he entered the platform and was told to hurry up. There was only one first class carriage. As Bighorn boarded it a shout of: "Hell and damnation, where do you think you are?"

The one who called out these words was the only other occupant. No other than the former Lieutenant Lord Edmonton.

"None of your business, I calculate" growled Bighorn as he made himself comfortable.

The former officer was not satisfied. "Have you a first class ticket?"

"That's also none of your business," was the answer.

"It is my business. I want to know whether you have the right to be in this carriage."

"Be glad I don't ask you that. It is an honour for you if I condescend to travel with you."

"If you want to travel first class, you have to follow the usual custom; otherwise I'll get you thrown out of here."

"Ah, according to your behaviour you must have a fourth class ticket. If you want to challenge me, I'll put you out."

"Rascal," hissed the former lieutenant, "I should give you a slap in the face, you tramp."

"Oh, I can serve you with that kind of business. Here is a sample; I trust it's good quality." With lightning speed he gave Edmonton such a slap in the face that he hit the wall. "So," laughed the trapper, "that is for the rascal and the tramp. If you have any more such words, I'm prepared with the same answer."

Edmonton picked himself up. His cheeks were burning, his eyes full of fury and suffused with blood. He forgot that he could only use one arm and forced his way again onto Bighorn who was still sitting. Now he stood up and grabbed Edmonton with his left, pushed him into a corner and hit him with his right hand several times in the face. Then he dropped him on the seat. "Well," he said, "there seems to be great entertainment when one travels first class in England. I'm prepared to continue."

After these words he sat down with the greatest calm. Edmonton boiled with fury. Blood ran from his nose. He found no words. The locomotive gave a sign that they were reaching Maidenhead. He ran to the window and called: "Guard come here quickly," before the train had stopped.

The voice had something urgent and the official hurried to the department. "What do you want, sir?"

"Open up and call the chief guard and the stationmaster."

The man opened the door and Edmonton jumped out. The officials came in a hurry. "Gentlemen, I have to ask you for your help. First, here's my card, I am Lord Edmonton. I've been attacked."

"By whom?"

"This person." Edmonton pointed at Bighorn who sat comfortably and calmly on his seat.

"How did you get here?" asked the official.

"I entered," laughed Bighorn.

"Have you got a first class ticket?"

"Yes he has," confirmed the guard of that carriage.

"Lord Edmonton, may I ask what you mean by the word 'attack'?"

"He attacked and hit me."

"Is that true?" the stationmaster asked the American.

"Yes," nodded Bighorn with a friendly smile, "He called me a tramp and I gave him a slap in the face. Have you anything against that?"

The stationmaster ignored that question and asked Edmonton. "Did you use that expression?"

"I don't deny that. Look at this person; should I share the compartment with such rabble when I have paid for a first class ticket?"

"I cannot say anything against that, because ..."

"Oho," interrupted Bighorn, "have I not paid the same?"

"That may be so but ..."

"Do I walk about in ragged or torn attire?"

"Not exactly, but I think ..."

The engine driver, at that moment, gave a sign that the time was up.

"Gentlemen, I hear the train is ready to leave. I demand the removal of this impudent person."

"Impudent?" called Bighorn, "do you want another slap in the face?"

"Silence," ordered the stationmaster. "If you demand punishment, then I must ask you to break your journey and to give your evidence in a statement."

"I've no time for that; I have to be in London at a certain time."

"I'm sorry but I need your presence."

"I don't think this is necessary. I'm not going to sacrifice my time for that nuisance person. Arrest this fellow and send the file to London. My address is on this card."

"I am your servant sir." With these words he turned to Bighorn. "Get out you are arrested."

"But I have to be in London as well."

"Not my business."

"But the whole matter is his fault."

"Don't waste time with him," said Edmonton. I was present when he was arrested in Reading. He is a vagabond who has the cheek to go first class."

"Arrested before; get out now."

Before Bighorn got out he passed the former lieutenant who had entered the compartment again. He gave him another slap in the face to throw Edmonton on his seat. "That is payment for the vagabond; I am a man of honour and pay my debts promptly." He turned to the stationmaster and said: "If I am forced to get out I demand that this person come out as well."

"Shut your mouth, you have attacked this man."

"He admitted that he has insulted me."

"You don't belong in a first class department."

"To prove that might be quite difficult for you. I am prepared to show you my identity papers."

"There is time for that later. For now get out or I shall call more people to help."

"Good, but I have to tell you that your action will cost you dearly."

"Do you want to threaten me?"

"I am coming, but it's not so much a threat but a warning." Bighorn took his sack, his rifle and his trombone and followed the stationmaster. The train, meanwhile had left he station. Edmonton had a triumphant smile on his face. It was a minor station and there were not many personnel. The local policeman was called. Ho looked at the prisoner haughtily. "You have slapped Lord Edmonton in the face?"

"Yes," nodded the trapper, "because he insulted me."

"You are not allowed to hit him, you could have reported him."

"I've no time for that. He could have reported me if he thinks that I don't belong into the first class compartment."

"You seem to belong in the fourth class."

"Damn it, do you know what or who I am?"

"Have you any identity papers with you?"

"Naturally. I intended to show them to the stationmaster but he refused. He will have to pay for this." Bighorn showed all the documents seen by the police inspector in Reading. The present policeman started reading and his face grew longer. "Damn business that. Why do you wear this terrible suit and this tailcoat? Stationmaster, do you know who this man is? Firstly a prairie hunter and secondly an officer, namely a captain."

"Not possible!"

"Yes, really. This sir is an envoy of the president of Mexico and also has a recommendation from Lord Castlepool." They looked at each other, speechless.

The official paled. "Who would have thought it? It's the fault of your clothes that we misjudged you."

"Don't look for excuses, I offered to show you my identity papers. You refused. The entire fault is yours. What's going to happen now?"

"You're free to go."

"You didn't look at my papers but gave preference to this man's card that any swindler could produce. This may cost you dearly."

The stationmaster was in shock. "But sir, will you not be satisfied with my apology."

"Satisfied? As for me, I accept. I am easy going and have a good heart, but how others will take it I don't know."

"Others? May I ask who they are?"

"Actually no, but under the seal of official secret I shall entrust to you that I am going to the war minister."

The stationmaster stepped back. "To the minister of war? I hope you won't mention this affair."

"How else can I explain my delay?"

"My God, I am lost. Couldn't you go with the next train, captain?"

"No, that won't be in time."

"What a disaster! What can I do?"

"Nothing! Or do you think that because of your clumsiness I should take a special train?"

The anxious stationmaster breathed a sigh of relief. "A special train? That would be possible. That's the only solution to catch up on lost time."

"I'm prepared to accept this special train and I am even prepared to share the cost, providing that it will catch up with the other train."

"We've an engine here and a spare wagon. You can leave in ten minutes. There will be no problem to overtake the train, it's much slower. Now let me go to give the necessary orders and I shall send a telegram to the stations ahead to hold the train until you have passed it." With this he rushed out to make the necessary arrangements. Within minutes he returned and Bighorn asked him to write a note of the whole incident. The stationmaster asked him what he would do with the letter. Bighorn explained that this letter would serve as proof that I have not escaped from here, just in case Lord Edmonton creates further unpleasantness. The letter was written and Bighorn gave the policeman a good tip for having been troubled for nothing. Fifteen minutes later the special train rattled out of the station. ---

It was late afternoon when the train with Edmonton in it reached the next station. A new passenger entered the compartment. "Good afternoon," he greeted Edmonton.

"Hallo Colonel Winslow, good afternoon."

"Do you know me, sir? With who do I have the honour?"

Edmonton did not know what to think. "It's only two months since we met last. Do I really tell you my name? Have I changed that much?"

"Possibly," smiled Winslow. "Please tell me your name."

"I don't think that's necessary, here is my identity sign." With this he lifted his right arm with the artificial hand.

The former colonel stepped back. "Really, you are lieutenant Edmonton; did you look in the mirror lately?" Winslow pointed to a mirror and Edmonton went to it. He received a severe shock. "Heavens, I can't possibly be seen by anybody like this. Let me tell you what happened. But before that; tell me where you are going?"

"I've received a telegram from Captain Winnington. He tells me this rogue – you know who I mean - has been seen again in London. I was going on the way to revenge myself."

"I know you mean that commoner Robert Brooks. I had the identical telegram and I am also going there to seek revenge. When I think of those days; young, rich and a brilliant future, then came this damned rascal who will surely die this time. I have exercised with my left hand and I must say that I am even better now."

"The same here. I was going to be promoted but I haven't even a pension now and I must listen to my wife's reproaches. I also have exercised; this time I won't fail."

"Have you considered that we might have difficulties in finding seconds?" asked Edmonton wistfully.

Winslow was a little embarrassed. "Unfortunately, you are right," he sighed. "Those days damaged us in every respect. Our honour is not what it was."

"I don't give two-pence for it. What is honour? How is an officer's honour damaged if somebody touches him with a stick or slaps him in the face? Old wives' tales." Edmonton was angry. The American had hit him hard and his face was swollen. No wonder Winslow didn't recognise him.

"Hm, that sounds as if your swollen face is due to an assault?"

"Well, if it was the case, so what?"

"Who dared to give you such a slap?"

"A slap? Many more," laughed the former lieutenant but it was laughter of rage and fury."

"I'm amazed, I would have killed him. I hope you had him arrested?"

While Edmonton told him the story, the train stopped at a minor station where it stayed for an unusual length of time. Winslow put his head out of the window and asked a guard the reason for his delay. "A special train announced, we have to let it pass. Probably an important person has to be in London quickly." Not long after that the special train roared past. It consisted of the locomotive and just one carriage. Out of the window looked a man who examined the train stopped in the station.

"Heavens," said Winslow, "I've never seen a nose like that."

"It could not have been bigger than the one of the tramp who assaulted me this morning." Their train started moving again and, ten minutes later, stopped again at the next station. They heard a man asking if that was the train for London. "Yes, further back," replied the guard.

"Further back is the third class. I want first class."

"You? Show me your ticket."

"Here."

"Correct, get in here quickly, the train leaves right away." The official opened the door and the passenger got in.

"Good evening," he greeted politely. He received no answer. Edmonton could not speak – he was too amazed. Winslow did not answer because the new passenger was not a person he needed to answer. The stranger sat down and the train rolled on. "Satan," hissed Edmonton.

"Why? What's the matter?" asked Winslow.

Edmonton pointed to the stranger, who had made himself comfortable with his sack, rifle and trombone. "Colonel, do you know who this man is?"

Winslow answered equally quietly: "Yes, it's that man who passed us with the special train."

"That is the man – the vagabond who slapped me."

"I thought you told me he was arrested?"

"He must have escaped again."

"In a special train?"

"Who knows what happened, maybe he smuggled himself onto that train. We'll have him rearrested at the next station."

"Are you sure that's him?"

"With this nose and the trombone, how could I be mistaken?"

"We'll see."

The former colonel took on an imposing position, turned to Bighorn and asked: "Who are you?" He received no answer. "Do you hear me? I have asked who you are." Bighorn nodded friendly. "Who am I? A traveller."

"I know that. It's your name I want to know."

"Oh dear! I just haven't got it to hand."

"Don't talk nonsense; where are you coming from?"

"From Reading."

"Ah, you have been there with the police and have been later rearrested?"

"Unfortunately."

"How is it that you managed to get into this train again?"

"By means of a special train."

"Which you've smuggled yourself into. We'll see to it that you won't escape again, you vagabond."

"Vagabond? Listen, little man, if you repeat that word again you'll get an answer that you might not like."

"Is that a threat?"

"No, a warning."

Meanwhile Edmonton made a decision. He saw in Winslow an ally he could rely on. Together they could surely handle this stranger. "Please don't speak to this loutish creature. I'll give him to the police who know best what to do with these types."

510

Edmonton had not finished the last word when he received such a terrible slap in the face that he fell from his seat. The former colonel jumped from his seat and grabbed Bighorn. "Scoundrel, you'll pay for that."

"Hands off," demanded Bighorn, his eyes bright with anger.

"You want to order me? Take that." Winslow swung his arm back for a slap in the face but collapsed with a cry of pain. Bighorn had countered the attack und put his fist into the stomach of his foe, making him incapable to continue the battle. Edmonton could not help his ally. The last slap was of such a kind that he did not dare to risk another slap. Winslow crouched on his seat, whimpering.

"There you have it!" said Bighorn, "I'll teach you to be polite in future."

"Man; do you know what you have dared?" groaned the ex-colonel.

"Nothing. What could I have dared with you?"

"I'll have you arrested!"

"We'll soon see about that."

The engine, at this moment, gave sign that they had arrived at a station. When the train stopped, Bighorn opened the window and called the guard. "What are your orders?" he asked zealously.

"Quickly, call the stationmaster and the engine driver, I have been attacked."

Bighorn's body took the whole width of the window so that anything his co-travellers might say could not be heard.

"What is the matter? How can we help you?" asked the stationmaster from a distance.

"How long are you stopping here?"

"Only one minute - and that's almost gone."

"I won't keep you for long, I've been attacked twice in this carriage. Would you please arrest my two co-passengers. Here is my pass." Bighorn had it prepared. The stationmaster examined it in the light of a lantern and said: "I am at your disposal captain, who are these two people?"

"One pretends to be a lord, the other is his accomplice. Luckily I managed to render them harmless for the moment. May I get out?"

"Please do," said the stationmaster who then turned to the guard and asked him to bring help.

There were no police present, but following his request, several station workers appeared, enough to handle the two men. Winslow and Edmonton heard every word. Both were so confused over the unexpected action of Bighorn, that they were sitting speechless even when the guard opened the door to let the American out. The stationmaster put his head in the compartment and ordered, "Please step out here, quickly."

"That's not possible," said the former colonel. "We are ..."

"I know," interrupted the official. "Get out, get out."

"Damn," called Edmonton. Do you know that I am Lord Edmonton?"

The official put the light against his face and shrugging his shoulders said: "Very well, you look like a lord. Get out or should we use force?"

"Our luggage ..." protested the ex-colonel.

"We'll handle that. Out with it gentlemen. Both former officers followed the stationmaster. They were put into a secure room for the moment. Bighorn stayed with the guard who supervised the removal of the luggage. "Nice things," laughed one of the workers. "Really, an old trombone. Look at these dents and holes. It must be misery to listen to it."

"And here's a sack," ventured another. "That's the real proof that these fellows are rogues." The ex-officers only had hand-luggage. The stationmaster who had returned asked Bighorn to come to his office. The American now pulled out his other documents and showed them to the official, who read them and was duly impressed.

He handed them back and asked: "Captain, permit me a question, why don't you dress according to your station?"

Bighorn assumed a mysterious expression, put his hand to his mouth and whispered: "I am going incognito."

"Ah, you do not want to be recognised?"

"That's right. Therefore, the sack, the thing you would call a hose but is actually a rifle, for which I have a licence and the trombone, are mine."

"They are yours?"

"Yes, I'm travelling as a musician. I trust my incognito is not in danger with you."

"I have learned to be silent. Can I have your report now?"

"It started at Reading. As I entered the first class department, the younger of the two who pretends to be a lord started a quarrel with me. Actually, I think he is a French spy who is following me to prevent me going to the minister of war, to whom I am being sent as an envoy of President Juarez."

"We'll see to it that these French lose all desire for any more malice."

"I hope so. As I said, he started a quarrel and called me names. I gave him a few slaps in the face. At the next station the so called lord had me arrested. The stationmaster there did not have your penetrating mind. I was kept and the other one he released."

"What stupidity," said the flattered official. "It is obvious you are an influential man. "Carry on."

"The so called lord showed a visiting card he could have printed himself. He didn't even look at my credentials. When he eventually did and realised that I might miss my appointment because of his foolishness, he ordered a special train. I asked him to write a note as I expected to have more difficulties." The official read the letter and said: "This is of great value to me. My colleague tells me he was fooled by the false details given to him by the 'lord'. That fellow won't fool me. Please continue."

"The special train overtook the first train and I managed to board it again at the previous station. A second passenger was now in the first class compartment. They thought they could handle me now. The younger one received another slap in the face the other I made incapable of fighting on by giving him a punch in the stomach. Luckily we reached this station in time. Had they recovered they probably would have killed me."

"I'll soon settle them. The other one, was he French too?"

"No, I think he was Russian. You know the Russians have occupied their western borders recently. Who knows what this man's aim is?"

"We'll stop that. Do you mind if I interrogate them?"

"By all means."

"You'll be present. Please follow me."

The official led Bighorn into the room were the two prisoners were guarded by two station guards. When the stationmaster entered with

Bighorn, Edmonton flared up right away: "How dare you treat us as prisoners?"

"Silence," called the official, "you may only talk if I ask you a question."

Bighorn received a chair. The official then asked Winslow his name. The ex-colonel told him. "Have you any Identity documents?"

"Why? Should I carry a dozen passports if I am travelling a few stations to London?"

"Do you know Russia?"

"I've been there once. I have relations there. Why are you mentioning Russia?

"You'll know that better than I do. And now the other one. Your name, please?"

"I am Lieutenant Lord Edmonton."

"Have you any document to identify yourself?"

"Yes here." Edmonton reached into his pocket and produced a visiting card.

"Have you nothing else? This card is meaningless. Everybody can have them printed. Do you know France?"

"Very well, why?"

"You admit that you know France well. That's enough." He turned to Bighorn. "Captain Sir, should we tie them up?"

"Yes, do that, stationmaster," said Bighorn.

"What?" asked Edmonton, "he wants to be a captain? What kind of a captain, eh?"

An assistant had brought bonds. Edmonton looked questioningly at Winslow. "No use to defend yourself; these people will give us satisfaction shortly."

"A lord who is being slapped in the face cannot be very demanding; but I see that you both only have one hand?"

The official received no answer. Bighorn's face beamed; he said quickly: "I've just remembered. Two years ago, two spies were caught in Constantinople. One was a Russian pretending to be an English colonel, the other pretended to be an English lord and lieutenant. The sultan mitigated the death sentence but had their right hand cut off."

"Nonsense," shouted Winslow.

"Damn lie," bellowed Edmonton.

"Silence," ordered the stationmaster. "I know now who you are. Captain, do you wish to make a report here?"

"There's no need. The trial will be in London. The main thing is they should not be able to escape."

"We've made an important catch," said the official. Bighorn agreed and asked about the next train to London.

"In half an hour," he was told.

And so it was. Bighorn, in high spirits steamed to London while his opponents were thinking of revenge in a special vault prepared for such situations. ---

Chapter 37

BIGHORN MEETS THE MINISTER OF WAR

W HEN Bighorn reached Paddington Station he aroused no small
sensation although much less than in Reading. He took a cab and asked
the coachmen to drive to the Hotel Hanover. He smiled to himself when
he saw people glancing at him. He asked the receptionist if he could
have a room. The man gave him a searching glance and asked: "Have
you any identification?"

"Naturally."

"All right come on." With this he led the strange guest through the
hall into a yard where he opened a door. "In here," he said.

Bighorn stepped in and looked around. It was a dark, smoky vault.
At the window stood a shoe cleaning box. In the corner were tools. At
the walls he saw clothing ready to go to the cleaners. "Heavens, what
kind of a hole is this?"

"Servant's quarters."

"Did I ask for servant's quarters or a room?"

The receptionist smiled. "Are you used to something better?"

"Certainly," nodded Bighorn.

"You don't look like it."

"That may be; you don't think that I'm a gentleman but I am. With
you, unfortunately, it's the other way round."

The receptionist made a mocking bow. "If you wish for better you'll
have it. Come along." He led Bighorn to the best room in the hotel
and asked sarcastically, "Will that do?" He said it in the expectation

that the strangely dressed guest would decline, but had an answer he didn't expect: "Hm, it's a long way from elegance, but if you don't have anything better, this will do."

"The Count of Highfield lived here for the last two days."

"Surprising, I thought they're used to better places."

The receptionist intended to have some fun. What if that man couldn't pay? He named a high price for the room but received the answer. "I'm not interested in the price."

"Can I see your identification?"

"What's the hurry? Is this a cheap tavern or a proper hotel with a visitors' book?"

"All right, you can have the visitors' book."

"Bring it but tell me first whether a Captain Brooks has arrived."

June, the chambermaid, who had entered the room, said: "I know Captain Brooks."

"Did he live here?"

"No, I know him from Bradford-on-Avon, where I come from."

"I was there where I met him together with the Count of Manresa. We arranged to meet here."

"So he will come; should we reserve a room for him?"

"He didn't tell me to do so." Bighorn turned to the receptionist. "Didn't I ask you to bring the visitors' book?"

"At once, Sir," his tone was quite different now. "Do you wish for anything else?"

"A good breakfast."

The receptionist rushed away. Bighorn threw his sack, his rifle and the trombone onto the blue silken sofa and turned again to the chambermaid: "So you are from Bradford on Avon and don't know London very well?"

"Yes, but I've been in London some time now."

"Have you ever seen the War-Minister Ernest Gray?"

"Yes."

"Do you know where he lives and how to get there?"

"Yes."

"Describe the way."

The girl looked at him with amazement. "Do you really want to see him?"

"Yes, my child."

"Oh, that's difficult. You would first have to report at the ministry or some such place; I don't know it myself."

"Nonsense, I'll make short work of that." June then told him the way, when the receptionist arrived with the visitors' book. Bighorn wrote his real name and reminded the man about his breakfast. As he unpacked he was surprised by the waiter who brought breakfast. This man looked wide eyed when he saw the contents of the sack and the rifle. He hurried into the office to report to his boss who knew nothing about the new guest and was dismayed about when told the details.

"Why on earth did you give our best room to this person?" he asked the receptionist.

"I showed it to him to tease him but he took it," said the man.

"What is his entry in the visitors' book?"

"Captain Arthur Henderson from the United States."

"My God, not another swindler or spy like that Captain Dans we had before."

"He has the appearance of one. His nose is like an umbrella handle."

"What kind of a luggage?"

"Two revolvers, a large knife, a rifle and something that looks like an old trombone."

"An old trombone? I don't believe it. Was it made of brass?"

"That's difficult to say, it's darker almost like rust."

"Darker? Maybe cannon-metal?"

"Yes, that's possible."

"My God, who knows what kind of weapon that is? Maybe even a bomb?"

"We'd have to have a proper look."

"But how? This guest doesn't seem the man to allow it."

"Something must be done," said the receptionist, who felt that it was his fault. "I think he might plan an assassination."

The chambermaid added: "An assassination? Jesus Maria, he asked me for the address of the war minister."

The manager paled.

"Yes," added the maid, "when I told him that it would't be easy to see the minister, he said he'd make short work of it."

"There you are, there's no doubt he plans an assassination."

"I'll go to the police immediately," said the boss and rushed away.

Bighorn meanwhile finished his breakfast. "Should I wait? he asked himself. "Oho, Bighorn is the fellow who will speak to the minister without recommendation. With him I probably have to refrain from my follies. My things I leave here, but I'm curious to know what they'll say when such a strangely dressed man asks to see the minister."

"They'll probably want to know what else I have in my sack. I'll thwart their efforts by inserting my special screw inside the door lock." This he did and made his way without being seen by the staff who were all assembled in the main office to discuss the probable assassination of the war minister. They believed he was still engaged eating his breakfast. Little did they know the speed a hunter of the prairie swallows his meal. He followed the direction given to him by the chambermaid. The big-town people or even the younger boys had little inclination to run after someone who dressed conspicuously. When Bighorn saw the porter at the door, he walked toward him and asked in the friendliest manner. "Is this Ernest Gray's house?"

"Yes," confirmed the guard, looking at Bighorn with a smile.

"Is the master at home?"

"Master, who?"

"Well, the war minister."

"Do you mean His Excellency, Sir Ernest Gray the Minster of War?"

"Yes, I mean His Excellency, Sir Ernest Gray and also the War Minister himself."

"Yes, he is here."

"Well, that's all right then." Bighorn hurried past the porter who grabbed him by the arm.

"Stop, where are you going?"

"To him, of course."

"To His Excellency? That's not allowed."

"Why not?"

"Are you expected?"

"I don't think so."

"Then you must go the prescribed way."

"Prescribed way? What's that?"

"I must know for what purpose you want to see him. Is it a private matter, diplomatic or otherwise?"

"It's probably otherwise."

"Man," said the porter, now more serious, "if you think you're having fun with me, you're mistaken. If your purpose is otherwise, then you may go otherwise away."

"I calculate that you are right," the trapper nodded in a friendly manner. "I've no time to trouble you any more. Good day."

But instead of going away he went inside the building. "Stop," called the porter again. "I did not mean this way. You must not pass here."

"I'll prove otherwise." With these words, Bighorn lifted the man and put him aside.

He walked only five steps when the porter grabbed him again. "If you don't go willingly, I'll have to arrest you for trespassing."

"I'd like to see who'd manage that." Bighorn disentangled himself with ease and reached the steps before the guard caught up with him again. A hefty dispute would have ensued, but a lady appeared on the stairs. Her face showed condescending good will but her eyes were disapproving when she saw the men who were pushing each other. The porter let go of Bighorn and stood to attention. Bighorn used that moment and rushed up the stairs taking three steps at the time until he stood on the same step as the lady. He put his hand to his hat and greeted her: "Good morning, young lady. Could you please tell me in which room I might find His Excellency the War Minister?"

The 'young lady' looked at him and asked: "You want to speak with His Excellency? Who are you?"

"Hm, I can only tell that to the minister."

"You have an appointment?"

"No, young lady."

"Then, I am afraid that you have come here in vain."

The lady made an unusual impression on the prairie man and he refrained from answering in his usual uncouth manner. "It's not a private matter, but more I cannot tell you."

"Do you know anybody who could introduce you to the minister?"

"Yes, but he comes later and I don't want to wait for him."

"Who is this person?"

"He's a captain of the guard. His name is Robert Brooks."

The lady's face twitched. "I know him. He wants to come to London to introduce you to the minister?"

"Yes."

"In that case I shall introduce you, instead of the captain. Tell me who you are?"

"Not here, the porter might hear."

"Come then," smiled the lady and went ahead.

They reached an anteroom. "Can you tell me your name now?"

"I am a hunter in the Wild West and Captain Arthur Henderson of the United States army."

"So what you wear is the uniform of the United States army?"

"No. If you think that, you must have little understanding of the military. I am a peculiar fellow. I like to have fun."

"That is indeed a peculiar sport. If I should introduce you, I must know what you want to talk to His Excellency about. He has no secrets from me."

"Really? So you are a kind of trusted adjutant?"

"You might almost call it that."

"Then I shall dare to tell you, I come from Mexico."

The lady's face expressed great interest. "From Mexico? Did you fight there?"

"Certainly. To start with I was a scout to an Englishman who brought weapons and money to Juarez …"

"Lord Castlepool? Did you travel with him?"

"Up the Rio Grande, until we found Juarez."

"Did you speak to Juarez?" The lady listened with even more interest.

"Quite often: seen and spoken with him."

"What about his opponent, Maximilian?"

"Not good. His realm is shaky, his throne is shaky and his head is shaky too. As an American and supporter of Juarez, I don't care much for his throne. It's the head of this misguided man I am sorry for. Having told you that much, I might as well show you my papers."

Bighorn produced his documents and passed them to the lady, who read them quickly. She looked at him and said: "There are peculiar people over there …"

"Here as well," interrupted Bighorn.

"About that later. I'm going to introduce you now."

The minister made an astonished face. "Your Majesty here again? he said bowing deeply.

"Majesty? Called Bighorn, oh hell!"

The minister looked at him with an expression of horror.

"You needn't be shocked," said Her Majesty.

"I wouldn't dream of it," stressed the trapper, "but if this gentleman calls you Majesty then you must be the Queen of England?"

"Yes, I am she."

"Hey-day! What an ass I am. Bighorn, Bighorn, what kind of a fool must the lady think you are?"

"Who is Bighorn?" asked the minister.

"That's me. In the prairie everybody gets a nickname. I'm called Bighorn because of my nose. But Majesty, who is this gentleman?"

"It is Sir Ernest Gray, the Minister of War whom you came to see."

"Then, Your Majesty, please tell him who I am."

The Queen passed the documents to the Minister who read them quickly. The three went back into the minister's cabinet, where a lively discussion followed. ---

The first thing the hotel manager wanted to know when he came back from the police was, whether the suspect guest was still in his room. "Yes, he's still eating his breakfast," answered the waiter.

"He mustn't leave the house until the police are here. I'll go and wait near his door to make sure he doesn't leave." The police soon arrived. Inside and on the pavement were plain-clothe police. A cab waited at the corner to take the prisoner. The inspector went upstairs with two of his colleagues to arrest the suspect. "Is he still here?" he asked the manager."

"Yes, he didn't come out."

"You told me he'd spoken to the chambermaid. Would you please call her? I think she should go in first."

"But if he shoots her!"

"He won't do that. We'd be in greater danger. The girl has a reason to go there. She could tell us how she finds him." June, the maid, knocked at the door. When she received no reply she tried to open the door with her master-key, but found a device in the lock which stopped her from opening it with a key. "He must have gone out without being seen. We have to rush to the minister and hope to reach him before it's too late."

They had hardly gone when Bighorn returned. When he entered the hotel, several plain clothes police men were behind him. He thought they were ordinary guests. As he sat down, one of the detectives came to his table. He produced a metal disc and asked: "Excuse me, haven't we met before?"

"Get lost, I don' want your money. If you put your paw so near to my nose once more, I'll see it doesn't happen again."

"Ah, you don't know the disc, it is my identification that I am a policeman."

"You are police? Why tell me that?"

"Because I've a great interest in you. I have to ask you a few questions which you have to answer."

"You English are a peculiar people. Nobody is as keen to arrest people as you."

"Do you think so?"

"Hell, yes, very much so. This is the third time since yesterday I've been arrested."

"You were arrested twice yesterday and have escaped?"

"Completely."

"Well, you won't escape this time."

"I think I will!"

"Be so kind as to pass me your hands."

"What? You want to put fetters on me? Hell and damnation! What have I done to you boys, that you surround me like this?"

The other policemen had positioned themselves in a circle around Bighorn. "What have you done to us? Nothing. But you know best what you have done otherwise or intend to do. Where have you been?"

"I went for a walk."

"Where?"

"I'm a stranger here, I know no street-names."

"Have you perhaps visited the war-minister?"

"That is possible."

"You are a hard-necked sinner. Someone else's knees would tremble at the evidence that he has been seen through. You stay cool."

"Would you please tremble a little bit for me?"

"We'll stop your sarcasm. You've a kind of bomb in your possession – admit it."

The Westman looked amazed. "A kind of bomb?"

"Yes, made of brass or some other metal."

Bighorn suddenly understood. He wanted to laugh aloud but he forced himself to be serious. "I know nothing of that."

"Why did you lock your room?"

"Is that forbidden?"

"With a special screw so that no-one can enter?"

"I don't want anybody to rummage in my luggage."

"Please open up, I'd like to see your luggage."

"All right, but I must warn you, not everybody knows how to handle my weapons."

"Don't worry, we'll be careful. Now give us your hands."

"I'm in your power." Bighorn calmly let him put handcuffs on his wrists.

In spite of his handcuffs he managed to reach in his pocket and pulled out the keys for the patent screw and lock. The door opened, but the policeman urged others not to push forward. The prisoner should go first. I suspect dangerous devices and explosives to be inside. He would be the first one to be hit. Bighorn was slowly pushed into the room, the others followed. The police carefully took the rifle and asked: "What kind of a rifle is that?"

"A Kentucky-rifle."

"It doesn't look like a rifle, more like a cudgel."

"Yes, a policeman would not hit anything with that."

The official ignored the sarcasm, put down the rifle and took the knife. "What kind of a dagger is that?"

"Dagger? You don't seem to know the difference between a dagger and a Bowie-knife?"

"Ah, a Bowie-knife. Did you kill any people?"

"Yes."

"And here, these revolvers. Did you also kill people with them?"

"Certainly, they are good Belgian guns and hit wonderfully. But am I here to give you lessons in weaponry?"

"Patience! Now to the main item. What is that?" He pointed at the trombone.

"A bomb from hell."

"A bomb from hell? You admit that? Is it loaded?"

"Ready to explode."

"Ready to explode? Gentlemen, hold this man tightly. Prisoner, I ask you what is it loaded with?"

"With air."

"Ah, probably with exploding gases. Can we touch this thing without danger?"

"Yes," Bighorn answered with a serious face."

"How do we make it explode?"

"By simply blowing into it."

"Good, I'll touch it." He lifted the trombone to study the secret mechanism. Suddenly the thing came apart and fell on the floor. The man believed that it would explode andshrieked. He stood as if he expected to die. After the trombone fell there was an explosion, but different from that expected by the police. As he uttered the death-cry, Bighorn could no longer hold back. He burst into mighty laughter that seemed to shake the walls. The others now saw that it was a simple trombone joint. The official thundered at Bighorn: "Man, I think you are laughing at me!"

"Who else?" grinned Bighorn.

"I forbid you. Didn't you admit it is a thing from hell?"

"It is. Let somebody blow it for a long time."

"You said it was loaded."

"With air, isn't it true?"

"You said it would explode."

"If you blow into it. Will you quarrel with that?"

"You want to make a fool of me. Didn't you ask the maid the way to the minister of war?"

"Yes."

"And that you make short work of him?"

"No, I only said I shall make short work of people who prevent me from seeing him."

The policeman asked the chambermaid and she confirmed Bighorn's explanation.

"It's an excuse just the same. Try to see the minister the way you are dressed. You'd have no chance."

"A better chance than someone who thinks a trombone is an exploding mechanism. By the way I admit that I have already seen the minister."

"When?" asked the man mockingly.

"Shortly before I returned."

"They let you in?"

"Yes, Her Majesty herself introduced me."

"You are a madman!"

"No, he's not. He's telling the truth." Captain Robert Brooks stood in the doorway, behind him the police ordered to investigate the manager's accusation. The inspector stepped forward. "Take these hand-cuffs off at once." The order was obeyed immediately. He turned to Bighorn. "Sir, you have suffered great injustice. The fault lies with the manager of this establishment. I have orders from above to apologise and I'm prepared to give you satisfaction. What do you demand?"

"Good, I must have satisfaction. This man thought my trombone was something from hell. I demand that he takes it as a present to remind him of the day when he nearly saved the life of the minister of war."

Everybody laughed, including the one who received the present. "Do you want anything else?" asked the inspector.

"No, I'm satisfied. But now I wish to be alone again."

His wish was being obeyed and everybody, except Robert, withdrew. "Man, how could you walk about with such a masquerade?"

"That is part of my character," laughed Bighorn.

"But, seriously now. We should make our way to Mexico now. I suggest we start today."

"All right with me." ---

Chapter 38

IN DISGUISE

---

*A*T the old palace of the Count Miguel de Manresa y Cordoba ruled the false Count Aurelio and his parents: Rita and the Advocate Pablo Carujo. They had ruled for nearly fifteen years when a knock at the door disturbed their comfortable togetherness at a sumptuous evening meal at a cosy fire in the marble fireplace. A servant brought in some letters of which one from Mexico caught Pablo's eye. He opened it first and read the following lines:

> *Dear uncle!*
> *I'm writing this letter in a great hurry from the Hacienda del Alina. Something terrible has happened. Count Manuel is alive and in the company of all the people we thought dead. Stenton, Buff-he, the Brooks' brothers, Lady Margaret, Alva Wilson and Kaya. Danlola has betrayed us. They are now with Juarez. Father is not here but I've sent him a letter. If we don't succeed to render our enemies harmless — we are lost! With the greatest urgency,*
> *Your niece Josefa.*

His wife observed him as he almost fainted. He rallied fast and with determination he said: "Danlola is now in Barcelona. We both have to go to Mexico and put things right."

"Not you," said Rita. "Let Danlola and your brother do what's necessary."

"I can't entrust such an important job to anybody. It must be. I'm going first thing in the morning."

They could, of course, have no idea that the contents of this letter were long overtaken by other events. Not only the enemies of the Carujos but José Carujo and his daughter Josefa, were themselves in the power of the uncanny Dr. Hidalgo. Rita's hands sank down without strength. "They all live," she sighed, "we cannot enjoy the fruits of our work in peace. José's soft heartedness revenges itself.

"Leave your lament," said the exchanger of children. "That doesn't lead us anywhere, we have to act now. We knew that my brother José was going to put thumb-screws on us with his apparent mildness."

"Yes, he wanted to force Aurelio to marry his daughter. Aurelio didn't want to. I don't blame him but they never forgave us, although we left them in charge of the fortune of Count Manuel," wailed Rita.

"The same goes for Danlola, that rascal. When I think how cleverly we handled all this. The de Manresa's were completely left in the cold. Count Miguel could do nothing all these years.

It was almost evening of the next day when Carujo met his accomplice, the former pirate Ramirez Danlola living in a poor side-street under a false name. When he saw Carujo, he complained of boredom. "Don't worry about boredom," said Carujo, "I'm bringing you a task that'll keep you busy."

"What do you mean?"

"A journey to Mexico. You sold Don Manuel into slavery."

Danlola stared at Carujo; he was shocked. "Into slavery? What do you mean? Who told you that lie?"

"Don't deny it I know everything."

"Your brother must have talked."

"Do you say that my brother meant more to you than I did?"

"In Mexico, I had to go by what he said."

"Is that so? And what happened to Stenton and his companions?"

"They are dead."

"No, they have escaped from the island where you put them."

"You're dreaming."

"Unfortunately not. They are all alive and well in Mexico, where you and I will have to travel to make good your stupidity. Why did you let them live?"

"Because you didn't pay me enough. Rogues are not always honest. We're rogues; the thought that you might forget my favours and I would need some more money in the future, made me put them on an island."

"And now they are with Juarez."

Danlola walked to and fro several times; then he stopped in front of Carujo: "I think I've to go over and finish the job."

"You mean you want to kill them?"

"Yes."

"I've to think about that. I'm forced to be careful. I can only make a deal if I'm certain not to be cheated again."

"How much do you offer?"

"I offer nothing. The seller has to ask a price."

"The first time you gave me ten thousand duros, make it twenty now."

"No, five thousand at most. I'll come with you and I'll help."

"That's different. We've no time to lose. When is the next ship going?"

"I know that already," said Carujo. "There's no ship going to our destination. There is a steamer going to Rio de Janeiro. There we'll find a connection to Mexico."

"How do we get on board? There's a wanted poster out for me," said Danlola.

"I know that too. When you were spying in England, you were supposed to hand money to certain other people. You embezzled it."

"How do you know that?" asked Danlola amazed.

"I have my connections. We're going in disguise. I don't want Stenton and company to recognise me. You don't mind a false passport, do you?"

"I certainly don't. A false passport is an invention of the devil for the best of his family. I suppose you're able to fix that?"

"That and more. Do you know the French *colle de face?*"

"That's the famous paste whereby an old woman can turn herself into a young girl. It fills the deepest folds," answered Danlola "

"Yes, and for a man, a wig and beard to complete the outfit. I'm travelling as Aristo Derivante, authorized agent of Count Aurelio de Manresa to look at the Mexican estate of his late uncle."

"The authorization made out by yourself ..."

"I'll also need a secretary."

"That, obviously, will be me. A position I can be conceited about," said Danlola.

"Adios." They parted. "Damn thing," Danlola mumbled to himself. "Their return will harm the brothers Carujo more than me. Five thousand duros? I haven't said yes yet. This Pablo Carujo will bleed and José Carujo will pay. I'll seek a hidden corner on earth where I can enjoy my wealth in peace."

Their travel to Rio de Janeiro was uneventful. At the protected anchorage lay a good-looking steamer. A boat, rowed by four strong sailors and a fifth at its stern approached it. When they boarded the helmsman stepped to the captain and reported two men who have heard that we are going to Vera Cruz ..."

"And they want us to take them there." The captain finished the sentence. He walked to the two men and introduced himself. "I'm Thomas Wright, Captain of this ship.

"I'm Aristo Derivante fom Barcelona and this is my secretary," said one of the two men. "We've heard that you're going to Vera Cruz and want to ask you if you would be so kind as to let us come with you?"

The Captain's eyes examined the outward appearance of the two. They seemed to be gentlemen and he agreed. He said this was a private ship belonging to the Count Manuel de Manresa and didn't take passengers. He would make an exception in their case. He called a sailor: "Jenkins, please show these two gentlemen to the cabins at the front. Look after them. You are freed from other duties." He turned to the new passengers and invited them to have the evening meal with him. Jenkins took them to their cabins. "I'll bring water and washing utensils," he told them.

He was hardly gone, when Carujo asked: "What do you make of that? This ship belongs to Count Manuel de Manresa. How is that possible?"

"When we go to the captain later, we'd better be careful."

Jenkins returned with water and washing necessities.

"How long have you been in Rio?" asked Carujo.

"Only for three days," was the answer.

"Where are you coming from?"

"From Cap Hoorn."

"From Australia?"

530

"Actually yes, but now from Mexico."

"Have you taken a load there?"

"No, we unloaded passengers."

"We thought this ship takes no passengers."

"No ordinary passengers. It was the owner and his friends."

"Do you know the names of these friends?"

Jenkins hesitated. He looked at the two for a while without giving the required information.

"Why don't you answer?" enquired Carujo.

"Because I don't know any more."

"Everything else you knew so quickly."

"Señor, it depends very much on the enquirer whether one remembers or not." With these words he turned around and left.

Carujo looked at Danlola. "What was that? I bet he knew the answer but didn't say."

Danlola shrugged his shoulders. "It's your own fault. You were careless. You were too keen with your enquiries. One thing isn't clear to me. This ship belongs to Count Manuel. It costs a fortune. Where did he get the money from?"

"Not for his work as a slave. We'll find out." Carujo concluded.

The ship heaved anchor and went to sea with above average speed. The Captain stood on the bridge when Jenkins approached him. "What is it you want, my boy?" He asked in the affable manner he used with all his crew.

"The passengers…"

"What about them?"

"Terribly nosy."

"About what?"

"About the ship and the people we took to Guayamas."

"That doesn't matter."

"I found it conspicuous. One was questioning and the other stood there with his mouth open."

"If there's nothing else, send them to me and tell the cook that they are eating with me in my cabin." Jenkins was the type of person who couldn't put on an act. He therefore had an inborn feeling for falsity. He obeyed orders and told the passengers to go to the Captain for the evening meal. "Bring your papers along," he added.

When they arrived at the Captain's cabin he had already a glass of wine in front of him. "Welcome again, señores, let's deal with unwelcome formalities first. I take it you've your papers with you?"

Carujo passed him the documents. Wright read them and handed them back. "Actually, I should lock them away during the journey, but I think I don't need to be so particular today."

Carujo and Danlola answered with a bow before sitting down. The conversation developed slowly. Only after the meal did the Captain touch on the long expected subject: The matter of the Counts of Manresa. He told the interested passengers about Count Manuel's miraculous escape from Harare. About the no lesser miracle of the white slave girl Alva Wilson and the equally miraculous finding and liberation of Stenton and seven of his friends from an unknown island.

"No mean feat of yours to find this island." It was Danlola who made this remark.

"I might not have accomplished that feat, if not for Señor Stenton's calculation of the longitude and latitude of the island. And all without instruments. AlvaWilson remembered the figures. The good Captain was taken by the immense interest of his passengers and told them about the false Aurelio and Rudolfo who was brought up by robbers whose Captain gave him the best education. This was all so true and clear, that Carujo found it hard to suppress a hefty curse. Instead he said: "*Santa Madonna,* so is Rudolfo the genuine and Aurelio the false heir of the Count Miguel de Manresa."

"Yes, it can be proved. But now it's getting late. I hope this story will cost you no sleep. Good night, señores.

"Thank you for the meal and good night, Captain."

They had arrived in Guayamas. The passengers alighted and went straight to the agent Gonsalvo Verdillo whose abode was well known to Danlola. "What can I do, señores? they were asked.

"We would like to have some information about a certain Danlola."

"About who?"

"About Danlola the pirate."

The agent paled. He stared at the two strangers and said haltingly: "I don't understand you, señores."

"Oh, you understand me very well, you old rascal."

The agent was sweating. "Señores, I assure you that I don't know anybody with this name."

"You don't know your Captain? Is my disguise so good that you don't recognise me?" The agent's blood returned to his face. He joyfully stretched out his hands.

"Welcome, welcome, Captain. Your own mother wouldn't recognise you."

"This greasepaint must be excellent. A man who was with me for twelve years doesn't recognise me. Do you know this señor?" asked Danlola. Verdillo, in vain, searched Carujos features. He shook his head. "I've never seen this man."

"Quite often, in Barcelona."

"I can't remember."

"The ship-owner, Señor Carujo."

"Señor Carujo? Really? What a face. A masterpiece indeed," exclaimed the agent.

"Can you give us information about José Carujo or his daughter Josefa?"

"Unfortunately, no. The Señorita sent me a letter to be passed on to Señor Pablo Carujo. Did it arrive?"

"Yes," answered Carujo. "Two days before our departure."

"I've to report something else to you. Every day, for the last two weeks, a man calls here and asks whether there is any post from Señor Carujo from Spain has arrived. He had papers from Señor José Carujo telling me to hand him the expected letter. He comes punctually at …" The agent looked at his watch and added: "It is at this time."

"I'm curious," said Carujo.

Hardly had he said these words when there was a short but strong knock at the door. "Come in," called the agent, when a tall, sinewy figure entered. It was the stepbrother of Ramirez Danlola; Peter Danlola, the hunter. "May I ask whether any letter has arrived?" he requested politely.

Danlola, the pirate, clenched his fists. He had recognised his stepbrother immediately and asked with a slightly disguised voice: Señor, you'll wait in vain for this post. We have been sent by Señor Pablo Carujo to deal with his brother. As you were with him, do you know where he is?"

"He and his daughter are with Dr. Hidalgo in the monastery of Santa Helena. That's where I should deliver the letter."

"Before I ask you whether you are willing to lead us there, I'd like to know whether you're a supporter of Carujo?"

"I'm not interested in politics. My interest in Señor Carujo are his promises that he would let me find my stepbrother, for whom I've been searching for years."

"What do you want from him?"

"Only he will know that."

"It can't be anything good, as you're so reticent about it." Peter Danlola shrugged his shoulders. "Well," said the pirate, "if you'll be leading us there you'll meet him. He'll arrive there the same day as we do."

"Good, I'll take you there."

"But we've to go to Mexico first."

"I've no time for that."

"So you'll not find your stepbrother."

The hunter looked at them attentively. "I trust that you are playing an honest game. I'm coming with you to Mexico. When do we go?"

"As soon as possible." ---

Soon after Captain Wright's steamer, another ship arrived and threw its anchor a distance away from his yacht. He intended to go on land in spite of the feverish atmosphere of the town. When he was leaving the ship he passed Jenkins. Being in a good mood, he asked him: "Well, my boy, you've been mistaken about our passengers, haven't you?"

"No, Captain."

The surprised Captain asked: "No?"

"I was right. One was a seaman and both were swindlers. I can prove it."

"How?"

"Whoever goes under a false name is a swindler, isn't it?"

"Mostly, but in this case their passes were all right."

"That may be. But when they thought to be alone, they called each other by a different name."

"And you've heard them?"

"Several times and quite distinctly. This Señor Derivante was called by his secretary Señor Carujo and he called his secretary, Señor Danlola or Captain."

Wright drew back as if a fist had hit him. "Man, why didn't you report This immediately?"

"I did. But you forbade me to do it again, Captain."

"Damn." The Captain went to and fro several times. "Ah," he mumbled to himself, "I behaved like a schoolboy, I'll have to make that good – Jenkins." The so called rushed to him.

"Captain," he said while saluting with his hand to his cap. "Put on your good jacket. We're going on land. Would you recognise the two again?"

"From a distance of ten miles if there is no wall in between."

"Hurry, we've to find them again."

Jenkins was delighted to have the honour to go with the Captain. He left and came back within a few minutes. He had put on his best attire. Now they went several times through the streets of the town. The Captain became tired. For the second time they entered an inn where, the first time they looked out for their passengers. He steered toward the only free table, but drew back, almost horrified about the man at a neighbouring table. There was nothing unusual about his clothes but he had a gigantic nose that could give anyone a shock. This man noticed the stupefaction of the Captain and said with a smile: "Don't worry it doesn't do any harm."

Wright laughed. "So I can sit down without concern?"

"In God's name, yes. It isn't contagious either."

Next to the man whose nose caused momentary concern, sat a younger man of attractive outer appearance. Wright made a short bow and introduced himself:

"Captain Thomas Wright."

The young man reciprocated the bow. "Captain Robert Brooks.

His neighbour made a bow too. "Captain Bighorn."

Wright didn't know whether this was a joke. He looked at the younger man who asked with a polite smile: "Have we met before?"

"Hardly, but you look similar to a friend who has the same name as you."

Robert's face tensed. "Where does he come from?"

"From Bradford on Avon in England." Up to now the conversation was in Spanish. Joy as well as pain makes people revert to their mother-tongue. Robert jumped up and said in English. "My father. You know my father. What surprise.

"You're English? asked Wright in English.

"Yes, I am. Where did you see my father, where is he?"

"I don't know exactly but he's in the state of Mexico. I came here with my ship to take him and his comrades back home. But, for the moment, I've more important things to tell you. From Rio de Janeiro, I'd two criminals on board without knowing it. This young man here had suspicions which I, foolishly, disregarded. Only after they left the ship did I learn the names of these two. They were Carujo and Danlola."

Robert's face was full of joyous surprise. "They are here in Mexico? There is no time to waste. These rascals must be ours. You searched the whole town? The railway station as well?"

Captain Wright was embarrassed. "I never thought about the railway station." ---

Chapter 39

THE EMPTY COFFIN

CARUJO. Danlola and his stepbrother had arrived in Mexico City. Do we go straight to the cemetery?" asked Danlola.

"No, first we're going to an inn, then I must go to the palace of Manresa. It must be ownerless now."

"If the French haven't taken possession of it," ventured Danlola.

To his chagrin, Carujo found the palace under French administration. He was told that his papers from the owner, Count Aurelio de Manresa, were not sufficient and that he had to acquire the necessary permission in Paris. He was told about José Carujo's mishandling the finances but was not allowed to see the account books. Pablo Carujo returned to the inn without having reached his purpose, to take possession of the palace. "I thought you wouldn't succeed." Danlola remarked with some satisfaction. "Let's go to the cemetery now. We've to fill an empty coffin."

They went and soon found a grave with the right date. They also found a shed where the grave-diggers stored their tools. "We need somebody to keep watch." said Carujo.

"My gullible brother will do that, no doubt," answered Danlola. "He hates me and I'll tell him a fable that'll make him willing to assist us."

"I've an idea which won't need any shovels," said Carujo. "We take a nobleman from his tomb; he would have had similar attire and will suit our purpose."

Danlola succeeded with his fable in persuading his stepbrother to stand watch at the gate of the cemetery. "The sooner we finish here, the sooner we'll be able to go to Santa Helena to meet this Danlola."

"I can hardly wait until we're on our way again," said the hunter. For him, the sun went far too slowly in its course. But finally evening arrived and the three made their way to the cemetery. While Peter Danlola stood watch outside, the others went inside.

"Let's try the lock of Don Manuel's tomb first. It'll save us time later," suggested the pirate.

Carujo had prepared a number of keys which he tried out. "It's not locked," he almost shouted.

"Psst" shushed Danlola, "in your haste you haven't noticed that you unlocked it."

"I'd have noticed if the lock was moved by the pressure of my key. Let's listen."

There was no sound and they proceeded to go down the stairs. "Put on a light, it can't be seen from outside the tomb," said Danlola.

They reached the coffin without noticing anything suspicious. "I wish Don Manuel would be there or the devil, to find out whether your boast to ask him for a light is true."

"I'd do it," boasted Danlola again.

"I don't believe that. Not while you're wearing this disguise. With your natural face you could possibly do it. He knows that he'll get you anyway. In your disguise he'd have you by the neck."

"Do you think so?" laughed Danlola, and proceeded to open the lid without noticing that it was unusually light to push open.

The next moment both uttered a tremendous cry. They were in the greatest shock. Inside the coffin lay a figure with the most giant nose they'd ever seen. The eyes of the criminals threatened to fall out of their sockets. They stared anxiously into the face of the mysterious dead. ---

At the station, Robert Brooks, Bighorn and Captain Wright learned that within the last hour only three civilians had entered the train. By their description the captain recognised the two passengers. "The third person is not known to me," he stated.. "I've to send a messenger to Mexico and to the Hacienda del Alina," he continued, "to let Don Manuel have my reports. Will you permit me to join you?"

"With pleasure, providing that you're not a hindrance. Can you ride?"

"Quite well."

"Can Jenkins come as well?"

"Yes, indeed, he knows the two criminals well."

"I'll go on board to give the necessary instructions. The next train leaves in three hours. I'll return within two. We can meet here at the station tavern. Robert went to the stationmaster and asked him for the time of the next train to Mexico. He asked, although he already knew the answer. The official locked at his watch. "In two and a half hours. If you wish to go with it, I'm sorry to inform you that citizens and strangers are excluded."

"Allow me to introduce myself." Robert showed his papers which the official read. "I am your servant," he said with a deep bow. "How many seats do you need?"

"Four."

"You'll travel first class. In Mexico you'll need horses. I've some here. They belonged to French officers who returned home. They are good and cheap and they'll travel without any cost to you."

The deal was done and Robert reported all this to his comrades. "Thank God," said Bighorn. "Now I can hang my legs over a horse again. I was already in despair and intended to sit on my nose and ride off." Captain Wright and Jenkins returned an hour before departure. They were sitting together. He told them briefly about his meeting with Don Manuel and the liberation of Dr. Stenton and his seven comrades from the South Sea island. Robert knew this story already from Bighorn, who told them what happened after their return. In consternation Wright heard of their disappearance again.

"I hope to find their whereabouts – if they're still alive," said Robert. "Woe to the perpetrators when I settle with them."

"Perhaps we're on their trail already," comforted Bighorn. "I've my ideas. Where are Danlola and Carujo going? Most likely to their associates."

"That may be true. In any case we have to find the two. Then we'll learn where they're going."

Captain Wright, suddenly had other thoughts. "I mustn't leave my boys in this feverish atmosphere for such a long time."

"Then you must seek a healthier place, maybe the Bay of Bermeja."

"Good, I'll wait for you there, Jenkins will go with you. He'll be my messenger."

The parting was short but friendly. When the train started rolling, Wright waved his hat and shouted: "Find those crooks and beat their heads to pulp!"

"I know of two possibilities where we might find them," ventured Robert. "I'd be surprised if they don't make inquiries in the palace of Manresa."

"That's true. This wigwam we've to visit. And the second way?"

"They know that Don Manuel's coffin is empty."

"Of course, I know that, I've seen the dead one alive."

"Carujo and Danlola may well assume that we'll investigate the empty coffin. They'll fill it with a corpse."

"I'd credit these rascals with such a deed. Mister Diplomat, you're young but very astute. We've to beat them to it. There's no time to lose, let's hurry," said Bighorn.

They put up at the first inn. After a little rest, Robert went to the palace Manresa.

He presented his card and was politely asked to enter. "How can I serve you?" asked the official.

"I beg your pardon, the purpose that takes me here is a private inquiry. Was there a person here this morning who told you that he called on behalf of the Count of Manresa?"

"Indeed, he was here before noon. Has your inquiry a certain purpose, Monsieur?"

"Certainly, did he want to obtain information about your administration?"

"Oh, he wanted more. He wanted to take it out of my hands."

"That's what I thought. He called himself Aristo Derivante?"

"Yes."

"Are you aware of his whereabouts?"

"No."

"I'd very much like to know it. He's a smart swindler. It's possible that he's coming again, in which case I would ask you to have him arrested and inform the English embassy."

"Arrest him? Would you take the responsibility?"

"Completely. This Derivante is really Pablo Carujo, the brother of José Carujo, whom I assume you know."

"Ah, he's infamous enough."

"And his secretary is the equally infamous pirate Danlola. Both are disguised with greasepaint and their passports are faked."

"That's enough. Should he come here again, I'll have him arrested." Robert went to see the English ambassador and discussed his reasons for coming to Mexico, including the opening of the grave. The official advised him to take Mexican police with him. They'd serve as witnesses.

"Would they come?"

"I know the head of police. I'll give you a written recommendation."

Four policemen were hiding near the Manresa tomb. It was near midnight when Carujo and Danlola stepped into the vault and opened the coffin. The hardened criminals were horrified beyond believe to see such a creature. "What is that," cried Carujo."

"The devil," clamoured Danlola.

"Pshtsishshshsh." A well aimed, brown jet of tobacco juice squirted into their faces. Bighorn jumped out of the coffin and slapped them several times on their faces. With the speed of a prairie hunter he removed their weapons and threw them into a dark corner.

" Damn," called Carujo, "that's a man." When they thought Bighorn was alone, they were their old selves again.

"What are you doing here?" asked a furious Danlola.

"Arresting two major criminals."

The police, who had waited above, came down the steps. Carujo saw that resistance was impossible and let himself be handcuffed. Danlola defended himself, but superior force soon had him in handcuffs. Peter Danlola, who stood watch at the gate, heard loud voices and quickly understood that this Señor Derivante and his secretary were under arrest. "I've to free them somehow," he thought, "otherwise I'll never find my stepbrother." The group of police with their prisoners, Bighorn and Robert Brooks, went toward the town's prison, without noticing they were followed.

"Señor Carujo, your silence does not improve your position. I know all your misdeeds and do not need your confession."

Carujo broke his silence, looked contemptuously at the young man and said: "What would you know? Who are you?"

"I'm Robert Brooks, the son of the helmsman whom Danlola took to the island. Your game has ended here."---

Chapter 40

A PRAIRIE-MAN IN ACTION

MEANWHILE, the prairie-man Peter Danlola circled the prison building. When he saw one of the windows light up, he thought that would be where the prisoners were. He waited to see whether a second window lit up. It didn't. "At least I know they are together," he mumbled to himself. He then observed those who brought them in, leaving the prison. As he was scheming what he could do to free them he heard steps behind him. It was too dark to see who it was but when the man passed him, he noticed a French officer in uniform. "This man has about my build," he thought. "Forward, don't let this opportunity pass." He ran after the officer. "Monsieur, Monsieur," he called.

The man stopped. "What is it you want?"

"Are you Major Mangard de Vautier," asked the trapper, in order to be nearer.

"No, I don't know any officer with that name."

"Neither do I," laughed Peter. With these words he grabbed the Frenchman by his throat and knocked him unconscious with his gun. He lifted his victim on his shoulders and carried him to a lonely spot. He then took off his uniform, tied and gagged the man and left him on the ground.

Now in uniform, Peter went to the prison gate and pulled the bell.

"Who's there?" asked the guard.

"Envoy of the Governor. Open," he answered.

The key turned. Peter was let in. When the guard saw the uniform he greeted as regulated. "Is the inspector of this prison still awake?"

"No, Major," replied the guard. "He was woken a short while ago when two prisoners were brought in, but he went to sleep again.

"Who is in his place?"

"The key-holder."

Peter walked across the yard to the prison building and rung the bell. The French were the masters at present and all were obedient to their will. The key-holder opened the door. The hunter spoke with an air of authority: "I'm the envoy of the governor. Can you spare two men to guard two prisoners?"

"Yes."

"Bring them quickly, I haven't much time."

While the key-holder went to obey this order, the daring trapper observed the room. There were slates on the wall with the names of all the prisoners. Number 23 showed the name of Aristo Derivante and his secretario. On the writing desk were various papers, including receipts for prisoners. Quickly he put pen to paper and signed, without knowing the name of the governor, a receipt for two prisoners. He dried the ink, folded the paper just in time and put it in his pocket, before the key-holder returned with two guards.

"Here are the men," he reported.

"Do you have a master key?"

"I have it on me," the key-holder replied. "Follow me, let's go," commanded Peter Danlola. He stopped at number 23 and asked for the door to be opened. The key-holder did as asked. Peter took the light from his hands and pretended to look at the prisoners, but he held it up that the two could see his face. Carujo and Danlola recognised him right away but kept quiet.

"Tie their hands," he ordered. He then gave the receipt to the key-holder with the explanation that the prisoners were under suspicion to be agents for Juarez he would bring them back in two hours. "Forward, march." The prisoners followed his command. Accompanied by the two guards they were soon on the dark street.

"Do you hold them securely?" Peter asked the guards.

"Yes, we're leading them by their arms."

"I'd better check. Those straps sometimes give." Peter now pretended to check the straps but, unseen by the guards, he cut them through. "They seem all right," he told them. Only don't let go of their arms."

Three minutes later one of the guards cried out: "My prisoner has torn himself loose."

"After him," shouted Peter. "Hold on to your fellow," he called to the other before running after the first one. He'd hardly made a few steps when the other guard shouted:

"*Demonio!* Mine is running away too." He ran after his prisoner into the dark night. His steps had not rung out when the hunter turned around and walked back the way they had come from.

"I shouldn't be surprised if they escaped to here." He'd scarcely finished his sentence when two figures emerged from the dark.

"Here I'm again, Major" laughed one in an undertone.

"Me too," laughed the other. They were Carujo and Danlola.

"Where are the guards?"

"They've run into the night. I didn't run far, I just ducked down," said Carujo.

"I too," echoed Danlola. "How did you get that uniform?"

"I've knocked down a French officer. He's gagged and bound. I'll take his uniform back to him.

"All right, but we still have things to do before we go back to the guesthouse," said Carujo. "We're leaving town immediately," he told Danlola when they were beyond Peter's hearing.

"Without my stepbrother?"

"Yes, he'll think that we've things to do and will be waiting for us. We'll leave some luggage behind and he'll wait for days. By the time he follows us to Santa Helena, we'll be finished there," claimed Carujo confidently. ---

Bighorn was anxious. He didn't trust Mexican authority. Was the supervision in these prisons really enough? Yes, if one has a prisoner in the prairie or the jungle, one watches them oneself. Here, where bribery is rife, who can trust whom? He went to the prison to see for himself. He passed a dark spot where he heard a slight noise. He bent down and noticed a man who was tied up and gagged. Next to him he found a bundle of clothes. He took off the gag and asked: "Good friend, who are you?"

The man took a few deep breath and answered: "I'm a French officer. My name is Major Ruband."

"Why have you been undressed?"

"I don't know."

"Here are a pair of coarse long boots, old canvas trousers, an old jacket, a cotton scarf and a black hat that looks in the dark like a black cat."

"They're not my clothes. They belong to the man who's taken my uniform. He wore this hat. Please untie me."

Bighorn didn't listen to the man's plea. He rushed to the prison gate and pulled the bell. The guard asked: "Who's there?"

"Bighorn."

"I don't know you."

"Are the two prisoners, that were brought here two hours ago, still here?

"No, they were collected by a French Major, who took them to the governor."

"*Demonio!* Just as I thought. Those idiots let in a swindler, but me whom they have seen before …" he did not finish the sentence and ran back to the officer.

"Why don't you untie me?" pleaded the Major.

"On the contrary, I'll have to gag you again. Somebody is coming. Pretend you're still unconscious." Bighorn gagged the man again and withdrew, just in time as Peter Danlola returned. After putting on his clothes again, he took off the gag and left. Bighorn went to the prisoner, cut through his ties and followed Peter. He took off his boots so he could do that quietly. Peter went to his hotel. Bighorn went up and down and talked to himself: "I don't trust this situation. Carujo and Danlola might never come back here." Opposite the gate of a horse dealer opened and two riders came out.

At the gate stood a man.

"*Adios, señores,*" he greeted. "Have a nice journey."

"*Adios,*" answered one of the two. "You did good business tonight." They rode off, the man disappeared inside. Bighorn listened after them.

"By God," he mumbled, "the voice of the rider sounded like Danlola's. I can't trust this situation any longer." He went to the hotel and rang the bell. After the third time, a man with a sleepy, peevish face asked: "Who rings at this time of the night?"

"A stranger."

"I noticed that. What do you want?"

"I want to talk to you."

"Even that I've noticed but I've no time. Good night."

"My dear fellow, wait a minute. Do you know the value of a dollar?"

"Five times as much as a franc."

"I'll give you two dollars if you answer me one or two question."

That was a rare event for the man. He stared at the generous stranger: "Is that true? Well, give me the money first."

"No, first you must say whether you want to answer."

"Señor, I need my sleep badly, but for this money you can wake me any time, Yes, I'll answer."

"It isn't much I've to ask: Do you have many strangers here?"

"Not many – ten or eleven."

"Are there any three belonging together?"

"Three came together but one of them has a separate room. The two were a Señor Aristo Derivante and his secretario; the name of the third I don't know. He is simply dressed, almost like a poor vaquero or a hunter."

"Are they here?"

"I was not on duty this evening but I believe that two have gone out again a short while ago."

"I'd like to speak to this vaquero or hunter."

"If he's in and if you take the responsibility."

"He's in; tell him Don Velasquo d'Alentaro y Perfido de Rianza y Hallendi de Salvado wishes to speak to him." Bighorn said this name with pride in his voice that left no doubt about its nobility.

The employee went up some wooden stairs and knocked at Peter's room.

"Come in," said Peter, expecting one of his companions."

"Señor, there is a stranger downstairs. A man of nobility with a long name, impossible to remember. He wishes to speak to you."

The hunter shook his head. "Well, I'm curious, Let him come up."

Bighorn entered and closed the door behind him. They faced each other. "*Zounds,* Peter Danlola, I didn't expect you here."

"Hello, Bighorn, I didn't expect you here either."

"Peter Danlola," began Bighorn, "you've a good name in the prairie but, I know of someone with the same family name who is the biggest crook going."

"The *deuce!* You know him! I've been looking for this crook for many years.

Bighorn looked at him strangely. "Hm, do you say that you haven't found him yet?"

"Unfortunately, no."

"I'd have thought a hunter like you has eyes."

"I hope I have."

"But I doubt they've learned to see."

Peter's expression darkened. "Do you want to insult me?"

"No, but sit in your hammock and I'll take a chair." Bighorn bit into a large piece of chewing tobacco and started again. "I want to tell you, my friend, that you're either a great rascal or pitifully stupid."

Peter jumped out of his hammock drew his gun, stepped to Bighorn and asked: "Do you know how one answers to such an insult?"

Bighorn nodded calmly. "Yes, with a bullet if those words can't be proven."

"Let's hear your evidence, but watch your words."

"Your companions are a Señor Derivante and his secretario?"

"Yes, they are."

"You kept watch while they committed a crime."

"Yes, I did but there was no crime."

"You're convinced of that?"

"Yes, I can swear."

"I believe you. But it proves that you are no rascal but immensely stupid."

Peter wanted to flare up but Bighorn said quickly: "You knocked down an officer and freed those fellows?"

Peter was shocked. "How could you know that? It was a job I'm proud of and I trust you'll not betray me."

"I'm no traitor. About your achievement you won't be proud for long. Tell me, why are you looking for Ramirez Danlola?"

"The world knows that Bighorn is an honest and capable prairieman. I'd not let anyone else speak to me like that. Let me tell you that the pirate Danlola is my worst enemy. I've quite a reckoning to make with him."

"That's hilarious," laughed Bighorn. You are looking for a crook. We catch him and you free him." Bighorn now told the misled hunter the whole story and who his companions really were."

"My God, you can call me worse than stupid. I've saved this José Carujo and his daughter as well."

"You?" asked Bighorn surprised.

"Yes. Oh, all is clear now. Without me José Carujo would have been blind and his daughter would have been imprisoned."

"You've to tell me about it."

"I'll do that. You were right I was more than silly." Peter now told Bighorn the events when he first met José Carujo at the Rio Grande del Norte to the present day. Bighorn listened with great tension, then he said: "Now I'm glad I've met you, I now believe where to find those lost without trace."

"The two criminals are much nearer than you think," ventured Peter.

Bighorn smiled almost sympathetically. "Do you mean that Carujo and the pirate are in this hotel?"

"Yes, they are."

"Is there no end to your gullibility? Do you really believe they're still here?"

Peter was no longer sure of himself. "Let's go and find out." They took a light and went to their room. Bighorn was right, they weren't there. "They might still come,"

"They're not that stupid. Tomorrow morning the whole town will know the story of the false French officer and the escaped prisoners. They wouldn't wait. They're gone."

"And they left me here?"

"Why not? I'll prove it to you. Look on the floor. What do you see?"

"Hm, it looks like fresh soil."

"It's wet and soft. When did they leave this establishment?"

"Two hours before midnight."

"The soil would have been hard and dry by now. What we see here has come off their boots less than three quarters of an hour ago."

"They'll not succeed. They've gone to Santa Helena where we'll reach them."

"Listen to my advice," said Bighorn. "The police will find out very quickly that they lived here. If you'd be still here, you'd be in trouble."

"You're right. I'll leave at once – but where?"

"With me. Pay your bill. My presence is your excuse for leaving." Ten minutes later they'd gone. The horse dealer stood in front of his gate. Bighorn asked him if he had many horses for sale. "Only four left today. I just sold two to strangers from Queretaro. They left for Puebla."

Bighorn then asked for their description and was convinced, that they were Carujo and Danlola. He knew they would not go to Puebla. In a quick deal he bought the four horses and went to Robert. They decided to follow the escapees immediately. It was evening of the second day when they reached Santa Helena. While the others were looking for a guest house, Robert asked his way to the cloisters. ---

Chapter 41

SAVED

DR. Hidalgo had been away for a long time and Alfredo became worried. His uncle had promised to make him Count of Manresa. What if something had happened to the old man? As he was brooding whether to act by himself Carujo and Danlola rode though the gate. They asked for Dr. Hidalgo. Alfredo, told them the doctor was away and wouldn't be back for a few days or even weeks. When they asked for the whereabouts of señor José Carujo and señorita Josefa, Alfredo became suspicious and asked their names. Pablo Carujo saw no reason to keep his name a secret and told Alfredo that señor Carujo was his brother.

"What would my uncle do now?" Alfredo thought. "Here are two more in the know. I'll show my uncle I can act independently." "You can see your brother. My uncle gave shelter to him and his daughter. I'll have to get some keys and lead you to them." He left to get keys, but also some of his uncles poisoned powder with which he intended to make his guests unconscious.

He led them through the same passages as when they caught Dr. Stenton and companions unawares. He locked the first door of that gangway behind him and then walked in front of Carujo and Danlola, through the same door his uncle went when he disabled Stenton and his companions. He jumped through it, locked it, blew the knock-out powder through the keyhole and waited three minutes. Just as his uncle did. He then tied up their unconscious bodies and took them into the cell where José Carujo and his daughter were imprisoned He managed to put them in chains without using lights.

After he left, Josefa asked them who they were. She received no reply because the new prisoners had not yet regained consciousness. Alfredo was pleased with himself and expected his uncle's praise. He now went to prepare the prisoners's meagre rations of hard bread and water.---

Robert found the gate still open and went straight into the house. He met no-one and went further up the stairs. Through a slightly open door he saw Alfredo putting keys on a tray with food and drink. He instinctively stepped back and let Alfredo pass him by.

He followed Alfredo down another flight of stairs. Alfredo's light fell just in front of him. Robert was in the dark. Having taken off his shoes he managed to follow silently through rocky passages until they reached one with several doors.

Alfredo stopped before one of them. He pushed back two iron bolts, opened the lock with a key and entered. "Was there another passage or was this a prison cell?" Robert wondered. In the first case he must follow quickly, if the latter, he had to stay back. He listened. Ah, he heard voices. Without a sound he crept nearer. He dared to put his head a little forward and saw a square room at whose walls several prisoners were chained. Alfredo stood in the middle and put down his lantern. The light it gave was not enough to recognise the features of any prisoner.

"There is a way to save you," he heard Alfredo say.

"What is it?" asked a voice in the background.

"You know that Rudolfo is your real nephew and the present Count Aurelio is the son of Pablo Carujo?

"Yes."

"Well, I've two conditions and you will all be free."

"Let's hear them."

The old Count Manuel was speaking. Alfredo continued:

"First you declare Aurelio as a deceiver and have him and his relations punished."

"I agree to this."

"Second, Rudolfo has to renounce his claim and you recognise me as the child that had been exchanged."

552

An astonished silence followed

."Well, answer," ordered the Mexican.

"Ah," said the Count Manuel, "you want to be Count de Manresa?"

"Yes," answered Alfredo with impudent candour. Those are my conditions."

"I'll never agree to that."

"Then you'll stay in prison till your end. I'll call back here in half an hour. If you don't answer yes, you'll get neither food nor water until you die."

"God will save us."

"Don't speak to this scoundrel, Don Manuel." The deep voice of Dr. Stenton was heard from the other side of the cell.

"You call me a scoundrel?" asked Alfredo. "Here, have your reward." He stepped to the prisoner and lifted his arm to hit him. His arm was grabbed. Shocked he turned around and saw two angry eyes and a revolver pointing at him. The pallor of horror covered his face.

"Who are you? What do you want here?" he asked, stammering with fear.

"You'll hear that at once," answered Robert. "On your knees". Robert threw Alfredo to the ground. "Let's make sure we have you safe." He took his lasso and bound the arms of this willing tool of his uncle's vicious plans. Alfredo did not resist. Robert now took a deep breath. "Thank God I've succeeded. You're free!"

"Free?" they all called. "Señor, who are you?"

"You'll learn that soon. The most important thing now is to get out of this stench. Will you be able to walk?"

"Yes," said Stenton.

Robert managed to control his feelings for the moment and turned his attention to practical matters." How do I open your chains?"

"This man has the keys on him."

Robert emptied Alfredo's pockets, hurried from man to man and opened their chains. They all wanted to know who their saviour was. Tears of joy run over Robert's face: "Not yet. Tell me first if there are others to be freed?"

"No, we are all here," said Stenton who had the strength to remain calm."

They all left the cell. Robert pushed the bolts shutting Alfredo inside. He began the march through the passages. With every step the air improved. At the last cellar he put on the light to recognise the faces. Stenton took his hand and said: "Señor, we have air here, now tell us who you are."

"Yes, you should know it," said Robert, sobbing with excitement. But one of you should hear it first." With this he led one after the other bearded man to the light. When he stood before Captain Brooks he asked: "Will you have the strength to hear it all?"

"Yes," was the answer.

Robert put his arms around him and sobbed: "My dear, dear father." He pressed and kissed him. He was not aware that he spoke the last words in English. The seaman stayed silent. He stood semi-conscious in the arms of his son. All the others kept silent. Stenton rallied first. "Robbie, is it true? You are Robert Brooks?

"Yes, uncle Charles, it is me," answered Robert as he carefully lowered his father down and hurried into Stenton's open arms.

"I won't ask how you found us but, tell me: how are things in Bradford on Avon?"

"Everything is fine. They're all are alive and healthy."

The great man, who maintained most of his vigour and strength, sank to his knees and prayed:" God in heaven – saved for the second time. Should I ever forget this, disown me when the time comes and I ask for admission at the gates of heaven."

Another two arms embraced Robert. "Ah, uncle Anthony," he rejoiced. Now everybody wanted to embrace him.

"You've not come alone here." interrupted Stenton.

"In the cloister I'm alone but there are others with me in Santa Helena: Bighorn, Black Gerard and a hunter called Peter Danlola. The latter is searching for his step-brother, the pirate Danlola. But let's go upstairs. Who knows whether this Hidalgo has other accomplices. He took his father's right arm and proceeded to go upstairs. The others followed. At the end was Stenton with the light. He, who always thought of everything, had taken the keys and locked the doors behind him. One of the physicians on duty in the adjoining hospital was called. He was genuinely astonished to learn Dr. Hidalgo's secrets. He offered a special room, a bath, fresh laundry and a wonderful meal.

There was a knock at the gate. Robert's comrades, worried by his long absence, came to the cloister to find him. When he saw them all assembled, Bighorn had his mouth wide open. "There they are, all of them."

"Yes, we're all here," acknowledged Stenton joyfully. "We owe you infinite thanks for helping Robert to find us."

"Nonsense. But how the devil did this young man complete the task?"

"We'll speak about that later," said Robert. "Let's go and ask this nephew about Carujo."

"I feel all right now, I'm coming with you," said Stenton. Bighorn wanted to join them, but when he was told about the possibility of Hidalgo having accomplices and therefore being a possible danger to the ex-prisoners, he agreed to stay back. Black Gerard had no objection either. Peter Danlola thought that his stepbrother was still on the way to the cloister but wanted to see José.

"I'm innocent, I had to listen to my uncle," whimpered Alfredo.

"That's no excuse," said Stenton sharply. "I'll see whether you're making a true confession. Why did you and your uncle take us prisoner?"

"So that I should become Count de Manresa."

"Madness! Where is everything you have taken from us?"

"I only sold the horses. Everything else I still have."

"You'll return the stuff to us later. Where are José Carujo and his daughter?"

"They're in the same cell with his brother Pablo and Danlola the pirate."

"Man, I didn't expect to hear good news from you. Who took them prisoner?"

"I did, just before you were freed. I used the same method as my uncle used with you."

"You're now going to lead us to them."

"Yes, but this Señor has taken my keys."

"We have them, let's go." With these words he untied Alfredo's legs.

"Don' try to run away, I've locked the doors behind us."

Alfredo led Stenton, Robert and Peter to Carujo's and Danlola's cell. He unlocked the door but let Peter Danlola step in first. "Are you coming to let us out?" He heard the hoarse voice of José Carujo, who thought that Alfredo was alone."

"Let you out? You wretched rascal?" called Peter Danlola as he took the light from Stenton. This time I've got you and my dear brother. You won't escape me again."

Pablo Carujo stared at Peter Danlola. "How did you get here? Are you Hidalgo's helper now instead of Alfredo? Let us escape and I will pay you a million dollars."

"A million dollars? You worthless creature. Not a cent is your own. Everything will be taken from you, even your life."

"Why? I haven't done anything."

"You haven't done anything? Ask this one."

Stenton had stepped in. "Stenton!" Cried Pablo Carujo.

"He is free!" shrieked Josefa.

"The devil has betrayed us," cursed Ramirez Danlola.

"Yes, he betrayed you and God has begun his judgement. You will only leave here to be interrogated and punished."

"Pah" laughed Danlola scornfully, "who will force us to admit anything?"

"We don't need your confession, but you'll soon be talking."

Stenton and his companions left the prison and locked up again.

Chapter 42

IN ZACATECAS

$\mathcal{I}$T was afternoon when Stenton and Robert Brooks rode off after making their good byes. The day after next, they reached Zacatecas and Juarez. He was extraordinarily busy, but when he heard the names of his visitors, he greeted them with obvious joy.

"Is it really true, señor, that a great misfortune had befallen you?"

"It is true, señor," answered Stenton seriously. I and all my friends were in a desperate situation and have to thank this young man that we were saved. May I introduce Captain Robert Brooks from Queen Victoria's Diplomatic Services?

Robert bowed politely and Juarez nodded in a friendly manner. "Have I not heard this name before?"

"Certainly, replied Robert. Through your procurement, I've receive a box with precious items from the cave of the Mixtekas."

Juarez thought for a moment. "You're from Bradford on Avon? The son of Captain Brooks and the nephew of Old Surehand?"

"Yes I am."

"Welcome, but Doc Ironfist or Dr. Stenton, tell me how you were lost for the second time?"

Stenton told of his experiences. The face of the Zapotec took on a tense expression. Robert was silent as the desperate condition of Stenton and his companions was described.

"This Dr. Hidalgo is not unknown to me. For what purpose did he imprison you all and how did you escape?"

"These questions can better be answered by my young friend here," said Stenton and pointed to Robert.

"Tell me, please," asked Juarez.

Robert obeyed. He began with Bighorn's visit to Bradford on Avon and everything up to the present. The President's astonishment grew from second to second. Then his usually rigid features began to liven.

"What you are telling me, señor, is of great importance. There is a union, The Brotherhood, who want to topple me by forcing me to be the murderer of the Archduke of Austria. Dr. Hidalgo is now with Maximilian in Queretaro to tell him the lie that there are many places which have hoisted his flag. But I forget to be polite. Take a seat please."

Robert took this opportunity to pass a letter from England's War Minister to Juarez.

"Ah, that is an unusual recommendation."

"I needed this to offer you a second letter. Robert handed him a bigger letter. Juarez broke the seal and read it. His face expressed the greatest astonishment. *"Dios mio!* Such important documents of a great government! You're being recommended to tell me their wishes orally."

"Yes. They're concerned about what is going to happen to Emperor Max. My government is of the opinion that he can't hold his position."

"By what right do you call him Emperor?"

"He's been recognised by most governments."

"Pah! His game is up. I never knew a Max of Mexico, I only know a Max of Hapsburg who was misled by Napoleon to offer me *va banque.* The bank won. My answer to your question is that this señor can't hold on much longer. I'm not prepared to listen to anybody's wishes officially, only to a private exchange of ideas."

"And what do you think his fate will be?"

"If he leaves in time, he will get away with his life and the honour to have called himself Emperor of Mexico. Should he hesitate – he's lost."

"What do you understand by lost?"

"The government of Mexico will indict him."

Robert bowed politely. "And you'll be President?"

"Will be? Am I not now? Who has deposed me?"

"Napoleon and Max."

"You don't believe that. In a few weeks the whole of Mexico will be subject to me. I repeat, their game is over."

"You'll be judging Max? What will the judgement be?"

"Death by bullet."

"Will you not consider that a member of an Emperor's family cannot be shot so easily?"

"A thief, a murderer, a burglar will be punished. No matter who he is. Max signed his death certificate with his infamous decree of the 3rd of October, that anyone who helps me will be shot. I've lost two generals and thousands of Mexicans. The higher the man's intelligence, the harder the punishment."

"These are the principles of a strict judge, but not of the father of a nation who should let clemency prevail."

Juarez rose from his chair, walked to and fro several times before standing in front of Robert. "Young man, you have to tell me, it is the wish of your government to let clemency prevail?"

"You guessed right."

"I've only two things against Maximilian von Hapsburg. First, he trusted a man who himself became Emperor through blood and overthrow. Second, when the last Frenchman has left the country he, in inconceivable delusion, still hangs on."

"The other civilisations," Robert threw in.

"Leave out these civilisations. Once I counted the French among the civilized nations. But they raided my country like robbers or savages without a cause or reason. Did you count the drops of blood flowing during their occupation?"

Robert shook his head sorrowfully.

"These were no drops, but rivers. Is it injustice if I convict these wrongdoers? Every judge condemns a person for a single murder. What would the Austrians say if I were suddenly to lead an army into their country to prove I am a better ruler than the one they have."

He then went to his writing desk, started writing and handed the finished document to Robert. "Do not make use of this document lightly. I put great trust in you by giving you this. I'm giving my destiny into your hands. If the people find out that I helped Max to escape - ...

I'll say no more. It's the usurper's last chance of escape. Somehow, I think it will be in vain." ---

Chapter 43

A FATAL DECISION

EMPEROR Max had his headquarters in the cloister of La Cruz. He stood at the window and looked gloomily down into the gardens. In the middle of the room stood a squad man, equally gloomy. His features betrayed Red Indian descent. He was General Mejia, loyal to his Emperor to his death. After a pause, Max turned to him and asked: "And Puebla is lost too?"

"Irrevocably, Your Majesty."

"Yet I think that we could still take it back. We've fifteen thousand men at our disposal."

"We cannot spare a single man because Escobedo is threatening us."

"General Escobedo is in Zaratecas."

"Part of his battalion is already three days from here."

The Emperor turned quickly. "Ah, you fear Escobedo?"

Mejia didn't answer.

"Well?" asked Maximilian impatiently.

"I do not fear him," declared Mejia gloomily.

"But you're too gloomy."

"Not for me, but for my Emperor."

"But it is your doubt that stops us from taking Puebla back."

"Because I see no way to take it back."

"What prospects are there?"

"Unfortunately, we're surrounded, Majesty."

"Do you mean that we can no longer reach the coast?"

"No longer."

"With our troops in the capital we've altogether thirty thousand good men at our disposal. Should I decide to vacate Queretaro, our troops would surely bring me to Vera Cruz. You don't doubt that?"

"Unfortunately, yes."

"Why?" asked Max indignantly.

"Firstly, I don't trust our 'good troops', secondly, General Diaz has blocked our way."

"We're stronger ..."

"General Escobedo would immediately come to his help."

Max was no strategist. His views moved between high hopes and soon back to very low. "So it is your view that all is lost?"

"All," confirmed Mejia seriously.

The Emperor stroked his beard feverishly. His eyes rested reproachfully on his General. "You're definitely no courtier."

"I've never been that, Your Majesty. I'm a soldier and loyal to my Emperor. A truthful subject."

"General, I now want to confess, I wished I'd listened to you more often."

Mejia, with tears in his eyes seized the Emperors hand and said: "A thousand thanks for this word, Majesty. It compensates me for everything that I suffered."

"Yes, you're loyal and reliable. You believe that we'll have to go?"

"Go? Oh no we cannot do that. Where should we go?"

"Hm, I don't know."

"There is no way out. They will take Mexico City and Vera Cruz and then crush us."

"We'll fight."

"Fight and die."

"I don't like to hear that last word. I'm not afraid of death on the battlefield. They will not dare to lay their hands on the son of the House of Habsburg."

"They'll dare, Your Majesty."

"You think so? said Max almost threatening as he stood proudly erected. They wouldn't dare murdering an Emperor."

"The inhabitants of this country say, they don't know any Emperor."

"One would take vengeance."

"Who?"

"The powers."

"Were England and Spain capable of doing anything? They withdrew their troops at the first opportunity. Napoleon withdrew at the right time and left us to it."

"The voice of history," said Max with conviction.

"Perhaps this voice will condemn us."

"On the side of our murderers?"

"Allow Majesty to view this point without any passion. Juarez knows no Emperor. He regards the Archduke of Austria as an intruder who has spilt rivers of Mexican blood without any rights whatsoever."

"General, you're using strong expressions."

"These expressions describe the voices of the republicans. Besides I ask you to think of the decree of the 3rd October."

"Yes you warned me not to sign it. Don't mention it any more," called Max with a gesture of ill humour."

"There's only one way to avoid gruesome fate."

"What way have you in mind?"

"Flight!"

Flight? No, never."

"It's the only way."

"What will happen to my Generals? They'll be caught."

"That'll happen in any case."

"Who'll speak for them?"

"Any intercession will be useless."

"They would be lost, all of them – Marquez, Miramon…"

Mejia dared to interrupt the Emperor: "Does Majesty really trust himself to save Miramon through intercession?" He would be the first to be indicted."

"Anyway I can't agree to your plan to flee."

Mejia played his last trump. He knelt before Max, took his hands and pleaded: "I want to save my Emperor but I'm also thinking of Empress Carlotta. Maybe her spirits will come back to her when she sees the man she loves. Should her spirits hopelessly be disturbed when she hears that her beloved husband died the death of a criminal?"

The Emperor withdrew his hands from Mejia and put them to his deadly pale face. "Carlotta, oh Carlotta.." Max dropped his hands and said with tears steaming down his cheeks: "Mejia, you touched a side I cannot resist."

The loyal man jumped to his feet. "O my God, is it possible that you've steered my Emperor's heart?"

"Yes, He has steered it," countered Max. "My wife shall not remain with her mad condition, if I could possibly help her to regain her spirits. So you think rescue possible?"

"Yes, but only through flight."

"Do you mean secret flight?"

"No, for that I'm too proud too. Of course, not everybody has to know that Majesty has left the country. Allow me to call in a man who can help us."

"You've someone waiting? In any case the republicans will not let us through."

"Not if the have no orders to let us pass."

"Orders? By whom?"

"By Juarez."

"I'm astonished, call the man in."

Mejia called in Robert Brooks whose appearance made a favourable impression on the Emperor. "Who are you? He asked.

Robert bowed politely. "My name is Robert Brooks, I'm a Captain in Her Majesty, Queen Victoria's Diplomatic Service."

"How will you get us through the lines of the Republicans?"

"With this document." He passed the paper to the Emperor who read:

I hereby order to give every assistance to the bearer of this document and help himthrough the lines to reach his destination. Whoever acts against this order will be punished by death. Juarez.

"Extraordinary, this might work. He puts his life into your hands. We'll start tonight after dark."

"May I suggest Your Majesty wearing civilian clothing?" ventured Robert.

"An unfortunate necessity," smiled the Emperor while holding out his hand to Robert. "Until tonight then."

Robert saw himself as the rescuer of the Emperor; celebrated at home and elsewhere. He left a happy man but fate intervened. General Maramon turned up.

"More bad news?" asked the Emperor.

On the contrary, the news couldn't be better."

"Good news is rare nowadays. Let's hear it."

"Oh, Your Majesty will soon get used to the returning fortune and will continue to reign for the benefit of the country. Juarez will leave Zacatecas and Diaz the capital."

"That sounds impossible."

"They are forced to by people loyal to the Emperor. There is an uprising against Juarez and in our favour."

"An uprising against Juarez?"

"Yes, in many places. May I call in Dr. Hidalgo who brought this news, Majesty?"

"Yes. Of course, I'm really curious." Max's attitude altered peculiarly. Forgotten were the thoughts of retreat or flight. His eyes were shining, his pale cheeks became coloured. A benevolent look greeted the man who just entered."

"Your name is Dr. Hidalgo?"

"Indeed, Majesty," answered the old man, bowing deeply.

"Are you politically active?"

"No, I'm busy only with my patients."

"That's praiseworthy, what have you got to tell me?"

"About an uprising in Santa Helena, that's where I'm coming from, and here is the list of nine other places."

Max studied the list. "These are all places at the back of Juarez," he called. "Was this uprising considerable?"

"Yes, in Santa Helena it started with two hundred men in the morning then the population took part and by evening there were three thousand. The thought of an Emperor has taken deep roots and we cannot allow any republican enthusiast to tear them out again."

"The military results are invaluable," declared the Emperor beaming with delight. "Were the results of the other uprisings equal as in Santa Helena?"

"Certainly, the movement spreads like a wildfire. According to my calculation there are thirty thousand men at the back of Juarez, increasing from hour to hour."

"The republicans will have to turn north, thus giving us room for new movement.

"But," said the Emperor reflectively, "have you any proof?"

"I vouch for it with my head," answered Hidalgo demurely.

"It'll be evening soon, take Dr. Hidalgo to the best venta," said Max turning to the General."

"I'm begging my Emperor's pardon, but my patients need me," said Hidalgo anxious to get away.

"Then you've to go. We shall not forget you."

Hidalgo left with a bow. Happy to have acquitted himself well and dreaming of future rewards. Having an Emperor mislead and, with others, condemned to die, meant nothing to him.---

Again in Zacatecas where Juarez had dinner with Stenton. They discussed Robert's mission to save Maximilian, when a knock at the door interrupted the point Juarez was making. He doubted the success of this mission.

An officer came in and reported the capture of somebody who came through the Austrian lines from Queretaro. "Bring him in," ordered Juarez.

The man was brought in. Stenton stood against the wall and was not immediately seen by him.

"Who are you and what were you doing in Queretero?" asked Juarez.

"I'm a doctor visiting an ailing relation of mine."

"Interesting! A doctor without instruments. What is your name?"

"Porfirio Optera. My instruments I've left with my relative. I've others at home."

"I'll have to keep you for while. We'll take Queretaro tomorrow and we'll find out whether you tell the truth."

"But I've other patients expecting me," urged the doctor."

"And prisoners, Dr. Hidalgo," Stenton threw in.

Hidalgo became ashen faced; he turned around and saw Stenton whom he thought was in his cellars. He trembled, his mouth opened but he was unable to produce a sound. He staggered and was caught by Stenton who led him to a chair but had to hold him. It was obvious, Dr. Hidalgo was unable to hold himself upright. Nor was he able to speak.

"This man is of no use to us," said Dr. Stenton. "These are the symptoms of a stroke, either by the bursting of a blood-vessel in his brain or by a blood clot."

Juarez called one of the guards outside his door. "Take him to a hospital but watch him carefully," he ordered. ---

Chapter 44

AT THE DEVIL'S WELL

WHEN a letter from Stenton arrived, his relations were enraptured. They made it a day of celebration and thanksgiving. Meanwhile the spirits of the prisoners in Santa Helena were far from high. They did not have the greatness of soul of Dr. Stenton and his companions, who never lost faith during their fourteen years of exile or the imprisonment and inhuman treatment by Dr. Hidalgo. Pablo Carujo, Danlola and Alfredo were placed into a separate cell to José Carujo and his daughter Josefa.

"*Caramba!*" cursed Danlola, who was used to the free life at sea. The sticky air in prison and the constant darkness hit him most. "If this goes on," he said, "I'll go mad. I'd rather be before a judge. I can't take this life any longer. I'd give my soul to the devil, in which I don't believe in any case, if I could only once see the light of the sun and have the planks of a ship under me."

"I think you'll soon feel nothing under your feet when the hangman puts a rope round your neck." Alfredo was heard to say. "Oh, if I had my hands free, I wouldn't be here for long."

"Yes, if. This word has been invented by the devil. How would you get out of here with all these guards?"

"I haven't told you; there is another slipway out of this foxhole. It leads to a disused quarry. My uncle didn't enter it on any card, in case he might have to use it some day. But what is the use of this knowledge …"

Alfredo stopped talking because an outside bolt was pulled back. A man came in holding a lantern in one hand, a jug with water in the other and a loaf of bread under the arm.

Looking at him, Alfredo nearly called out in surprise, but he managed to control himself when he saw the man lifting his eyebrow to warn him. He then laid jug and bread between the prisoners with a meaningful look at the loaf. The next moment they were in the dark again.

"What was that?" asked Danlola. "It looked as if this fellow wanted to draw our attention to something. He wasn't the usual guard who brings the food. What's all this about?"

"Silence!" warned Alfredo. "Don't speak loudly; the guard outside the door could hear us. I know this man. He's one of the male nurses employed in this hospital. I once helped him out of a great difficulty. It's possible he wants to show his appreciation. I don't know how he managed to bring us our ration. He looked pointedly at the bread; let's see if there's something useful in it."

The prisoners were attached by chains which, in turn, were fastened on the wall so that they couldn't touch each other, but could reach the food. When Alfredo broke the bread in the middle, he couldn't see but felt the items that were baked inside the bread.

"A lighter of the kind used in the prairie," he whispered with suppressed excitement, and here I feel a piece of paper and a pencil."

The others listened hopeful and excited. "Make a light quickly," said Danlola.

What if the light can be seen outside?"

"Nonsense! Have you ever noticed any light from outside? By the same token our light can't be seen through that door. So, don't delay!"

Hidalgo's nephew did as told and soon the flicker of a weak flame was seen. By its light he saw the piece of paper with writing on it. He read:

"With great difficulties I managed to get permission to bring you food. Do you have a wish? Write it on this paper and put it into the jug."

"Valgame Dios!" called Alfredo, "we're saved."

"Not yet," said Danlola. "How will you get out of these chains? For that we'd need the necessary key."

"If that's all," said Alfredo. "In my uncle's room there is a second key in a little cabinet. I suspect that it is still in its place. If my man could get it, we'll be free."

"I suggest you start writing and put your wishes to paper," intervened Carujo eagerly.

Alfredo began writing. He described the little cabinet, the small key and asked for a knife. He then turned the flame off and hid the piece of paper on his body. If a guard had looked in at his moment, he would not suspect that the first step of their escape had been taken.

"What now?" whispered Carujo as the former darkness engulfed them again.

"We have to wait," answered Danlola. "What else can we do?"

"But how long?" asked Pablo stubbornly.

"At least three days."

"Three days," groaned Carujo. "Why that long? I believe I won't last three hours."

"You're a fool. You can tell yourself that before three days there is no chance."

"How's that?"

"Well, tomorrow, when our friend brings bread and water, he'll read the note. Another day will pass until we get the key and the knife. We can't leave there and then. We'll have to wait until the next day when the door opens again. We shall be rid of our chains and throw ourselves on the guard outside."

"What shall we do with him?"

"His life is forfeit, I'm afraid," answered Danlola. Our friend will be tied up. He won't mind otherwise it'll be too obvious who has helped us. But we're not that far yet."

"Unfortunately! There may be circumstances that will thwart our plans. What will happen if we succeed? Are we taking my brother and niece with us?"

"Hm," Danlola was thinking. "Do you have such longing for your relatives?"

"Actually – no. They don't deserve that we should take them with us."

"Our case in matters of the Manresa family is finished. We can warn your son, Aurelio, to liquidate and sell the two palaces before Juarez has completed his job. The money we'll split between Aurelio, you and I. We can live in luxury for a long time."

"You're forgetting a fourth," threw in Alfredo. "Should I go empty handed?"

"You'll be satisfied with us," answered Danlola. "If we succeed, we have to thank you, naturally and you'll get your part."

That sounded true and honest. Had Alfredo seen the sarcastic smile on Danlola's lips, he would have doubted his words. For the next few nights they couldn't sleep with excitement.

In the morning of the fourth day, the watchman who was to take over from the previous was horrified when he saw the guard on the floor, with blood all over him. A knife into his heart had ended his life. The prisoners had escaped. He opened the next door and found José Carujo and his daughter still in chains. They raged when they learned that the others had escaped without them.

Then he found the other guard bound and gagged. He freed him and reported the escape to Black Gerard. No sign could be found of how the prisoners' chains were unlocked. They could not have escaped without outside help. Gerard therefore ordered the arrest of the guard who had brought them food in the last few days.

The path of the escape would have remained a puzzle, but Gerard came up with an idea. He asked for a dog which could find the way the prisoners had taken. He was in luck. The local police had an English sniffer dog available. Fifteen minutes later the animal was brought to the cell of the escapees. The man, who kept the dog on a lead, held a bundle of straw under its nose.

The dog took up the scent and with its snout low on the ground, pulled his keeper along a corridor, up some steps and scratched on a wall. When this was examined, they found to their astonishment, a secret door. It took only minutes to find how it opened. It led into a lengthy passage and another door. Bright sunlight greeted them when they opened it.

The dog wanted to continue but Peter Danlola held the man and the animal back.

"The puzzle of their escape is solved. We can't lose any more time. They can't be too far yet and we've horses." He turned to the owner of the dog. "Would you let me have your dog? I'll pay you for it."

"Take it and I wish you good luck, but do you really want to go after them alone?"

"No," said Rudolfo, "I've too big a reckoning with these people. I'm coming with you and I hope you don't mind."

"So will I," said Black Gerard.

"And I," said Dinrallo. They made years of my life a hell.

"And I," said Don Manuel. I'll not have it said that..."

"Stop!" He was interrupted by several voices. "Your feelings are in all honour, Don Manuel. But isn't it important to watch over the other prisoners?"

Don Manuel and the helmsman George Brooks had to be satisfied with this decision. It has to be mentioned that Buff-he had left the group to join his wife, Kaya.

Within an hour, the four were on their way on excellent horses and provisions for eight days. At the head of that little group was the dog, his snout near the ground. The unseen track of the escapees led around the city in a wide bow. Against expectations, the dog suddenly turned sharply south. The pursuers believed the criminals would turn to a less populated area in the north.

"Señor, when do you think we'll catch up with them?" asked Rudolfo, turning to Peter Danlola.

"That depends whether and when the pursued will get horses. If they get them soon, we have to be prepared for a long ride. Don't forget they are an afternoon and a whole night ahead of us."

At noon they saw a lonely Rancho. The same moment the dog turned in its direction. It gave the ranch a wide berth and stopped where the ground was churned by the hoofs of horses. For a time it sniffed the air, then it wagged its tail and looked embarrassed. It was clear the escapees had mounted and the dog had lost the scent. Peter decided to look up the Ranchero. A vaquero received him with angry looks.

"*Buenos Dias.* Señor," he greeted politely. "May I ask whether three men had come by here yesterday?"

The eyes of the man became even angrier. "Do you possibly belong to them, Señor?"

"No, but we are looking for them. They are escaped prisoners and it looks as if they had come to this place."

The mistrust disappeared from the man's features. "If that is the case, I'll be pleased to give you the information you wanted. We saw nobody but we are missing three horses and three saddles."

"That's them, no doubt. Thanks for your information. *Adios, Señor.*"

"There's nothing to thank me for, but if you catch them, let them dangle from a high tree."

The examination showed that the tracks were from last night. They hadn't come much closer and it was expected that it won't be the case in the near future, because they would be riding during the night, when the pursuers wouldn't be able to see their tracks.

The four were convinced they would soon be able to catch up with the criminals. The escapees had no weapons, no food and no money. The acquisition of food would slow them down, that would give their pursuers a chance to catch up. It was dark when they stopped. There was plenty of grass for the stallions. Peter and Rudolfo went to see whether they could get some fresh horses. It would probably be the last opportunity to acquire some. ---

Four men rode on the Camino Real, the King's Way that led from Sayula over the Mountains. It was obvious they'd had a hard time. Their horses looked worn out and stumbled over the crevices and uncountable lava chunks on the way. There was no plant life whatsoever. The sun glowed with the heat of a baking oven; no wonder these men rode silent and sulky.

Even the dog which trotted behind the riders seemed upset. His tail was hanging down sadly, his eyes looked sleepy. The horses dragged their riders as if they were to stop at any moment.

"Our only consolation is that Danlola and companions are probably worse off than we are," said Rudolfo. "It's astounding that we're already ten days behind them and only have their tracks before us. Nothing else."

"Don't say that. According to the tracks they're only three hours ahead of us." said Black Gerard.

"Do you mean that we shall reach them by tonight?" Dinrallo asked hopefully.

"Yes, if nothing unforeseen comes in between."

"Then woe to them. Their end is inevitable." Peter ground his teeth.

The ride continued and their mood grew better. The sun rose higher and higher over the mountains, the road became bleaker. The area looked as if a volcano was going to erupt. After a while the mountains on both sides gave way to a substantial valley. In its midst was a small village whose few houses were built of lava blocks.

There was only one way through the village. The four travellers stopped in front of one of the buildings that differed only in that it had a sign outside on which, probably with boot polish, were written the words 'Hotel Dolores'. The Spanish word 'Dolores' was not only a woman's name but translated into 'pain'. The owner couldn't find a more suitable name to describe it.

This house was the saddest looking hotel the four had ever seen. When the owner heard the horses, he came out, clad only in a pair of trousers. He looked at the riders with suspicion.

"*Buenos Dias,* Señor," Peter greeted him. "Can we get something good between our teeth here?"

"If you are paying, why not?"

"There's no question that we're going to pay, but tell us whether three riders came past here?"

The distrust in the owner's face sharpened. "Do you perhaps belong to these three?"

"No, not that, but we've been on their tracks a long time. Why are you looking so suspicious? Have you had a bad experience with them?"

"To hell with them," said the innkeeper. "They treated me like a dog, threatening to hit me if I wouldn't give them something to eat quickly. When I asked them to pay afterwards, they just laughed and rode on."

"When was that?"

"Just over two hours ago."

"*Gracias á Dias!*" rejoiced Dinrallo, "we've finally got them.

"Not yet," countered Black Gerard. "Señor," he turned to the innkeeper, "what is the way like from here and up the mountains?"

"Bad, very bad! Up to the foot of the mountain in the west, it is passable. After that it will be dreadful. Lava blocks and deep crevices are everywhere. The worst is on top at the *'Fuente del Diablo.'*

"At the devil's well? What's that?"

"This whole area is volcanic. There hasn't been an eruption for a long time, but in many places hot wells are springing up and you could prepare your coffee with their water. The largest well is called *Fuente del Diablo,* a small basin fed from a subterranean source."

"What we want to know is the quickest way to get up there"

"There's only one way with horses and it was taken by the others. But I know a way on foot when you will be there before them. You can even eat something before going."

"If you can assure us that we'll be in time, we won't be so impolite as to refuse your invitation to eat."

"You can eat for half an hour and still be there an hour earlier than the others."

The hospitality was poor, quite in accordance with the name of the 'hotel'. While they were eating, they could look through the hole that served as an entrance. A dozen chickens were busy picking imaginary grains. They all had two metres of string tied on one foot. If the owner wanted to catch one, he only had to step on one of the strings. Just as they thought these chickens were the whole household, a naked youngster chased a large drove of turkeys into the stable, using a whip on which there were tied several of martens's skins. The marten is the turkey's most dangerous enemy. They were in terror even with the dead skins of their foe.

While they were eating, Peter asked the innkeeper whether he had heard any of the escapees' conversation and if they still feared to be followed. "I can serve you with an answer. One of them whom they called Danlola was asked by one of his companions, whether he thought if they were still pursued. He laughed and said any followers had long lost their trail and once they were over the mountains, all danger would be over."

"All right, said Gerard, "we've eaten and can pay and make a start. Don't let's waste any time."

The innkeeper took a donkey and joined the others who were already mounted. In an hour they were at the foot of he mountain. A short stretch into a gorge the innkeeper stopped. "If you climb up here for about two hours you have the Fuente del Diablo in front of you ... *Santa Madonna,*" he interrupted himself. Looking ahead on the path he saw someting on the ground. "It looks like a horse," he continued.

The short stretch was covered in no time. The riders stopped with a cry of horror. Next to the horse that lay there with a gaping cut in its throat was Alfredo in his blood – murdered. Gerard examined the ground. "It is clear, Señores, what had happened here. One of the horses couldn't get up after breaking its leg in one of the crevices. A quarrel ensued between two men. I wonder which one was the killer."

"I can help you there," offered the innkeeper. "There was only one knife between them and that belonged to the man they called Danlola."

They dismounted and began climbing. The horses they left to the innkeeper to look after. "This was Ramirez Danlola's last misdeed. I'm swearing that by all the devils in hell," said his stepbrother."

"I'm appalled by the heartlessness of these people," said Rudolfo. "After all it was Alfredo they have to thank for the secret exit. Now they've thanked him - in their fashion."

The innkeeper attended to the dead horse meanwhile. Four horses and his donkey carried it to his 'hotel'.

The two Spaniards, the American and Gerard and the dog, climbed the steep mountain. It wouldn't be possible for a horse to get up there that way. In less than two hours, they'd reached the 'devil's well'. They noticed they were in an area where subterranean powers were active. Various sources came roaring and hissing from crevices in the ground, to find their way downwards with black lava.

Dinrallo put his hand into these waters, only to withdraw it immediately with a cry of pain. The others laughed but couldn't resist trying it out for themselves. They soon stopped trying. The heat of the water was only bearable for the briefest moment.

"At leased seventy or even eighty degrees Celsius," ventured Peter. The others agreed.

Dinrallo was sent to a spot where he could observe the path from which the escapees were expected and from where he could overlook a longer stretch. The others stayed back at the *Fuente del Diablo* – The devil's well. All of them knew the place they would be hiding. There were lava blocks, some as big as houses. But they waited for a sign of Dinrallo and for the moment they sat together.

Rudolfo turned to Peter: "What shall we do with Carujo and your stepbrother when we've caught them? he asked.

"You tell me your opinion," answered Peter.

Rudolfo was pensively silent for a moment and then answered: "We should take them back to Santa Helena, from where they've escaped."

"To give them the opportunity to escape again and this time, maybe, for good?"

"We need their statement in evidence in the case of the Manresa family."

"Do you expect them to tell the truth? By the way, you still have José Carujo and his daughter. For my part, do what you like with Pablo Carujo, but Ramirez Danlola belongs to me."

The otherwise calm hunter was not recognisable. His cheeks were red and his features showed an uncanny determination. Rodolfo was spared an answer because Dinrallo returned with the news that he had sighted the escaped prisoners.

Gerard asked Rudolfo and Dinrallo to hide in a way that the escapees, if they turned back would confront them. Any shots should not be directed against their heads or their heart. He wanted them caught alive. He and Peter would confront them with the dog. Moments later, the Devil's Well was lonely and desolate as before.

The patience of those waiting was rewarded only after a lengthy time. Finally they heard voices and the expected ones appeared among the rock and lava wreckages.

Only those who knew them well, would recognise them. Their eyes lay deep in their sockets. The ten days of privation and hunger had left their traces on these, otherwise strong and healthy individuals. Near the well they decided to have a rest. Their dismounting was more a falling off their horses.

"*Aymé*, that was a stretch I'll not forget for a long time," sighed Carujo. You could have chosen an easier way."

"I thought I wouldn't get any thanks from you. An easier way maybe, but not a safer way."

"And now, do you think we're safe?"

"Completely! What is ahead of us, the way to the coast of Manzanillo, is child's play compared with what we have gone through. Leave it to me. I know my way around here and we'll soon be rid of financial worries. I have ways and means."

"If the case of Alfredo doesn't provide us with difficulties other than financial. Danlola, you're devilish quick with your knife."

"Pah! This story doesn't give me any worries. I believe people would thank us that I've saved them from the burden of judging and hanging him."

"But it was your horse that fell. He was within his rights to ask you to walk."

"I'm no fool. In such a position number one comes first. I've no bad conscience in that case."

"Just as well I know that. You'd do the same to me."

"Don't talk nonsense. We're talking about Alfredo. His fate was only accelerated, or would you be willing to share with him? You'd be the first one to find a suitable opportunity for him to disappear. But don't let's talk about these things, let's eat something."

"Horse meat! Brrr! I'd never believe I'd be forced to eat that."

"That's not the worst, but I assure you that it will not be for long. For this we need money. The next person we'll meet has to be our victim, if he looks as though he has money."

"I take it that this next person will be me?" Peter couldn't wait any longer. I the stepped forward with his gun in his arms.

Carujo and Danlola were deadly shocked by the unexpected sight of the hunter. But, while Carujo stared speechless at this sudden appearance, Danlola composed himself quickly. "The devil brought you here and now, go to the devil." The next second he had pulled his knife and jumped like a tiger upon his stepbrother. But he failed to reach him. The dog had followed his movements and threw itself on Danlola.

The weight and the force of this jump bore him to the ground. His knife had fallen out of his hand. Carujo did not resist when Rudolfo tied him. He was too shocked to offer resistance. With the dog's teeth at his neck, Danlola couldn't resist either. Once tied, they were dragged near the water where they were sat at some rocks. The victors and the dog were sitting around them. The dog kept its eyes on them, constantly,

"Now Señor Carujo," began Peter, after looking at his stepbrother with hate filled eyes. "You didn't expect to fall into our hands for a second time?"

Carujo kept silent. They both kept their eyes shut as if not to acknowledge their captors. "You want to play proud? Well, better for us, it will shorten the procedure. We're not taking you with us. There will be judgement on the spot by the laws of the prairie."

At this point, Danlola felt the cause to answer. "Don't imagine you'll be our judges, we're not in the prairie."

"But you're before a man of the prairie and will be judged accordingly."

"That doesn't interest us. We demand to answer to a proper court."

"If you want that so badly," said Peter, "why did you ran away from it.? that shows distinctly that you don't want to go before it. You have to be satisfied, to be judged by our standards."

"You've no right to do that."

"Are you really convinced about it, you who call yourself my stepbrother? countered Peter. "You have murdered my father, you lured away my bride, you have robbed me of my honour, my entire assets and inheritance. You somehow managed to put the blame for your misdeeds on me and didn't care that I was imprisoned for twelve years. And you dare to say that I've no right to judge you ? You're the biggest monster I ever knew, and as a monster you'll be treated."

Danlola listened to these accusations with secret anxiety. He knew he could not expect any mercy from his victim. His only possibility was delaying matters to win time. He therefore answered with forced laughter, apparently without worry: "You won't dare to do anything to me, Señor Rudolfo will not allow that."

He soon realised that he was mistaken. Rudolfo turned his face to him and said: "You're mistaken, Señor Danlola, if you think your life is of any importance to me. I've not the slightest intention to hinder any judgement against you."

"But if you take our lives, it will be impossible for you to prove that you're a Manresa. For this reason alone you have to let us live."

"You're mistaken. I don't need you for that. I've enough proof otherwise. In any case, José and Josefa Carujo are still at our disposal. You're lost, I'll do nothing to save you."

"Be cursed for all eternity," shouted the pirate, all composure lost ."Your farce is ended."

"This farce will become a drama for you," answered Peter. "Of what are you accusing this man who calls himself Ramirez Danlola? You can bring only crimes that concern you or your friends. We are not judging according to common civilian law."

"I accuse Danlola of trafficking in human beings and abduction."

"I do the same," added Dinrallo, "slave-trading myself and Don Manuel.

"Enough, Señores. What is the punishment for trafficking in human beings and abduction?"

"Death," came the answer as if from one mouth.

"And for multiple slave-trading?"

"Multiple death."

"Thank you, señores, you judged rightly. And now to Pablo Carujo. What are your accusations, Señor Rudolfo?"

"I accuse him of exchanging and foisting young children, attempted murder of my father and sister and robbery of money and possession. I also accuse him being an accomplice to piracy and all the other crimes of Danlola, many of which he himself caused."

"And you, Señor Dinrallo?"

"I accuse him of unlawful deprivation of my freedom and complicity in the crime of slave-trading and all the misery that Count Manuel and I had to endure during our years in slavery."

"And I repeat my previous question: What is the punishment in the law of the prairie for theft and robbery?"

"Death!"

"And robbery of several people?"

"Multiple death!.

Peter turned to the prisoners: "Your judgment has been pronounced: be ready to die."

Peter kept quiet. With an expression of satisfaction his eyes swept over the criminals, to see what impression the judgment made on them. Ramirez Danlola seemed not troubled. With clenched teeth and scorching eyes, he looked from one of his captors to the other. It was different with Pablo Carujo. He was gripped by indescribable anxiety and fear. He was ready to betray his best friend to save himself.

"Hurry up with these rascals," said Rudolfo. "We have to think about getting back before dark."

"Hurry? Was the suffering hurried that this man has caused me? Or were the fourteen years hurried that these devils have caused you and your friends to suffer? A bullet would be undeservedly merciful and I won't grant them that. What do you think of a hot bath?" Peter pointed at the seething waters.

"Excellent," said Dinrallo. That's what we'll do. We'll throw them into the Fuente del … "

He was interrupted by a long drawn out cry uttered by Carujo. With wide open eyes and blue lips he stared at his judges. Danlola had stronger nerves.

"Valgame Dios … God be with me," cried Carujo with terror in his voice. "Anything but not that. I implore you in the name of God, don't do that."

"Don't howl and whine. Leave God, which you don't believe in, anyway, out of this. Coming from you it sounds like blasphemy."

"Señores, if you do that, you're not human but devils."

"We are humans who are passing punishment on devils. Don't refer to our humanity, something you have never known in your life."

"I'm begging, yes I'm imploring you to be merciful just once. I swear that our paths will never cross. I know, Señor Rudolfo, you've a feeling heart and would not allow … "

"Silence, yellow-belly," interrupted Danlola who had listened with apparent indifference, as if the whole matter didn't concern him. "Don't you see that all your words are for nothing? That you only provide them with pleasure when you're begging and whining? Be a man and bear what can't be changed." He turned his back to show that he wouldn't say more.

Carujo started again. He begged and talked of a spark of humanity, He asked to be given a merciful bullet until Danlola interrupted again: "You miserable coward! Creep on your belly and lick their boots, you worthless creature. There is no way of dying good enough for you. That's what I think of you and now you know it, you coward."

For a moment Carujo forgot his fear. His face reddened. "You're telling me that, you scamp, you rascal, who caused all this misery. Now you can hear my opinion of you. By all the devils in hell, if there's one person I don't begrudge to be boiled in this hot soup. It's you Ramirez Danlola. You'd be a fine meal for Satan."

Danlola's face turned dark red. The veins on his forehead swelled. Extreme rage gripped him. He tugged at his fetters and suddenly managed to free his right hand. He grabbed Carujo, who was horrified and tried to pull back. Danlola's grip was like iron. "If I'm lost and have to go to the devil, at least you'll come with me."

Before the judges could intervene, Danlola pulled Carujo down the short slope into the seething waters; accompanied by the gruesome cries of Carujo and the hellish laughter of Danlola.

It was over.

There was silence for ten minutes among the four onlookers. They were as if in a trance. Then Gerard called them back to reality. It was time to go down the mountain. Rudolfo and Dinrallo took the horses and the longer route. In return for being given the horses, the innkeeper provided them with food for several days. It was early next morning when they were on their long way back. ---

Chapter 45

HAPPY END – FOR MOST

WITH the main culprits' end and with some imprisoned, the story could end here. The reader, I'm sure, would like to know what happened to the many other figures in this tale. I'll start with Benito Juarez. His army had taken Queretaro and with it Emperor Maximilian as prisoner. Juarez had now become President and the beguiled Archduke of Austria was shot with two of his main Generals.

Don Manuel claimed – and was given back, all his possessions, except, of course, those Carujo and his daughter had squandered. He travelled to England with the big group and intended to build himself a villa next to his brother Miguel.

He did not pursue his enemies. José Carujo was blind by now and walked the streets of Mexico City as a homeless beggar. His daughter Josefa ended in a mental home, still maintaining she was a Countess and the daughter of the president.

Rita Moreno, later the wife of Pablo Carujo, was given twenty years' imprisonment. She died after three years. Aurelio also ended his life in prison.

Bighorn roamed the prairie for a long time. So did Buff-he. The latter had two sons with Kaya which he brought up as warriors, but times were changing and they became successful businessmen. Dinrallo, well rewarded, went back to Manresa in Spain. Black Gerard, alias Gerald Mason, had settled in Guadelupe and father Rodrigo soon had someone else to complain about the weather to – a baby grandson.

The lure of the prairie had less effect on Old Surehand, alias Anthony Brooks. Although sometimes yearning for the life in the 'dark and bloody grounds', he settled down with Alva, her father Martin Wilson and Clarissa Moyes in the Hacienda del Alina. But not before joining his brother George Brooks, the Captain and helmsman on his journey to England. This was, of course, in the company of his wife Alva, Count Manuel, Dr. Charles Stenton, Rudolfo, now Count Aurelio de Manresa, Lady Margaret and Captain Robert Brooks.

The Duke Enrico de Zaragoza was not well, but his daughter Elena and son-in-law Max Masterson were present too. They went to Bradford on Avon as soon as they heard of Dr. Charles Stenton's regained freedom. They had arrived prior to the larger group. Even Lord Castlepool could not be stopped. He arrived two days later but still in time for the homecoming of the long lost.

Their arrival in Bradford on Avon caused a storm of jubilation, the extent of which was rarely seen anywhere. Everybody embraced everybody. The longest embrace took place between Stenton, his wife Condesa Rosetta and their beautiful daughter Helen, whom he saw for the first time in his life. Neither, of course, had she seen her father before. When he eventually let go, Helen turned round and saw Robbie patiently waiting his turn.

She flew at him and their long kiss was one of genuine love. Their engagement was announced later that day. The guests on their wedding day, three months later included the War-Minister. A congratulatory telegram came from Queen Victoria. Tears of joy ran unashamedly down the cheeks of Colonel Terence Masterson, Eric Freeman his valet, the loyal Porido and his wife Maria. They were, of course, included in the general embrace.

There followed a time of calm and deserved bliss. Under the care and guidance of Dr. Charles Stenton, Colonel Masterson reached the age of one hundred and three. They all reached a ripe old age.

Also by Henry Wermuth...

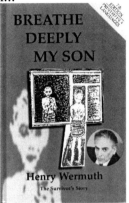

BREATHE
DEEPLY
MY SON

Henry Wermuth
The Survivor's Story

Henry Wermuth was born in Frankfurt a/M. Hs family was deported to Poland when he was fifteen. He survived one ghetto and nine concentration camps. In autumn 1942, during his stay in the first camp, he tried to derail Hitler's train. Hitler was to visit his troupes after their first major defeat in Stalingrad. The assassination attempt failed, but he received a medal from the Germans for trying. He is probably the only survivor who attempted to assassinate Hitler and the only survivor of his family.

Breathe deeply my son - breathe deeply and get it over with, was the advice given by his father before the Auschwitz gas-chambers. Fortunately both came through on that occasion: others were not so lucky. But Henry was a born survivor. Over and over again in these soul-searching memoirs he is faced with danger, dread and near-death; each time, miraculously he came through.

The difference between his account and others of the genre lies in his self-analysis, the detailed descriptions of the writer's feelings, hopes and fears and of his loss of faith for more than a quarter of a century in a seemingly uncaring God. There are also welcome elements of humour, for Henry Wermuth was a teenager like any other when the war came, and subject to all the usual preoccupations of adolescence despite the horrors of war.

To order, contact Henry at AHWermuth@aol.com.

Printed in the United Kingdom
by Lightning Source UK Ltd.
135255UK00002B/43-93/P